CORSAIR

AND

BUCCANEER

TIM SEVERIN, explorer, film-maker and lecturer, has
made many expeditions, from crossing the Atlantic in a
medieval leather boat to going out in search of Moby Dick
and Robinson Crusoe. He has written books all about them.
He has won the Thomas Cook Travel Book Award, the
Book of the Sea Award, a Christopher Prize, and the literary
medal of the Academie de la Marine. He made his historical
fiction debut with the hugely successful Viking series.

D1396050

Also by Tim Severin

TIM SEVERIN

✳

CORSAIR

AND

BUCCANEER

PAN BOOKS

Corsair first published 2007 by Macmillan
First published by Pan Books 2008
Buccaneer first published 2008 by Macmillan
First published by Pan Books 2009

This omnibus first published 2009 by Pan Books
an imprint of Pan Macmillan, a division of Macmillan Publishers Limited
Pan Macmillan, 20 New Wharf Road, London N1 9RR
Basingstoke and Oxford
Associated companies throughout the world
www.panmacmillan.com

ISBN 978-0-330-51764-5

Copyright © Tim Severin 2007, 2008

The right of Tim Severin to be identified as the
author of this work has been asserted by him in accordance
with the Copyright, Designs and Patents Act 1988.

All rights reserved. No part of this publication may be
reproduced, stored in or introduced into a retrieval system, or
transmitted, in any form, or by any means (electronic, mechanical,
photocopying, recording or otherwise) without the prior written
permission of the publisher. Any person who does any unauthorized
act in relation to this publication may be liable to criminal
prosecution and civil claims for damages.

3 5 7 9 8 6 4 2

A CIP catalogue record for this book is available from
the British Library.

Map artwork by Neil Gower

Typeset by SetSystems Ltd, Saffron Walden, Essex
Printed and bound by CPI Group (UK) Ltd, Croydon, CR0 4YY

This book is sold subject to the condition that it shall not,
by way of trade or otherwise, be lent, re-sold, hired out,
or otherwise circulated without the publisher's prior consent
in any form of binding or cover other than that in which
it is published and without a similar condition including this
condition being imposed on the subsequent purchaser.

CORSAIR

ONE

☾

THEY ARRIVED an hour before daybreak, forty men in two boats, cotton rags tied around the shafts to muffle the creak of the oars, and the rowers dipping their blades neatly into the sleek blackness of the sea. The boats were of local design, stolen from a fishing port a week earlier, and if a coast watcher had spotted their approach, the sentinel might have mistaken them for fishermen coming home early from the night's work. Certainly the raiders were confident that their mother ships had been invisible from the cliff tops for they had waited patiently over the horizon, hovering with sails lowered until they had the conditions they wanted: a calm sea and a thin veil of cloud to diffuse the starlight. There was no moon.

The oarsmen eased stroke as the two boats glided into the small cove. They heard the muted surge and backwash of small waves lapping the shingle, then quiet splashes as the bow men jumped out and held the boats steady while the raiders stepped knee-deep into the shallows. The water was warm for this time of year, yet it was far colder than the seas to which they were accustomed. Many of the raiders were barefoot, and as they began their march inland, the callused soles of their feet felt the change from smooth beach pebbles to tussocky grass, then the soft squelch of a boggy stream bed. A smell of rotting vegetable matter came up on the humid summer air. Ahead of them, a nesting marsh bird burst out of the reeds and flew away with a sudden clatter of wings.

Ten minutes of easy climbing along the stream bed brought them to the watershed. From a patch of level ground, they looked down the far slope at their goal. The village was less than half a mile away, a low cluster of dark roofs etched against the broad glimmer of the great bay which thrust far into the contorted and rocky coastline, providing a vast but empty anchorage. There was not a light to be seen, and still there were no warning shouts.

℃

THE RAIDERS descended the slope, moving faster now, and were at the outskirts of the village before the first dog barked. 'Who's there?' called a woman's voice from one of the turf-roofed cabins. She spoke in the soft fluid tones of the local speech. 'Go back to sleep, woman,' one of the raiders replied in her own language. There was a short pause as the men stopped and listened. The silence returned, except for the muted growling of the suspicious dog. The intruders moved forward quietly, spreading along the single main street.

At the very centre of the village, in one of the few stone-built houses, Hector Lynch opened his eyes. He lay in the pitch darkness, wondering what had woken him. On calm nights it was sometimes so silent that you could hear the distant boom of waves breaking on the rocks in the aftermath of a heavy swell as the Atlantic gnawed steadily at the granite coast. But this night there was something melancholy and stifling about the lack of sound. It was as if the village had been smothered in its sleep, and was dead. For almost as long as Hector could remember, he and his sister, Elizabeth, had been coming here each summer to study at the Franciscan friary on the island at the harbour mouth. Their mother insisted that he and Elizabeth, his junior by two years, learn Latin and the tenets of her own

Catholic faith from the Grey Friars. Her family were Spanish, shipowners from Galicia, and for generations they had engaged in the wine trade with this remote corner of south-west Ireland where she had met and married her husband. He was of minor Protestant gentry impoverished in the recent civil war and more interested that his children learn practical and domestic skills to help them prosper in the Protestant hierarchy which now ruled the land. The mixed ancestry of their children showed in the sallow skins, dark eyes and jet-black hair which Hector and Elizabeth had inherited from their mother – at fifteen the girl was on the cusp of becoming a real beauty – and in their fluency of languages. They used English when speaking to their father, Spanish with a Galician accent when alone with their mother, and Irish among their summer playmates from the poorer fishing families.

Hector turned on his side and tried to go back to sleep. He hoped that this was the last summer that he and Elizabeth would spend in this isolated backwater. In January their father had died, and after his funeral their mother had hinted to her in-laws that she was thinking of returning to Spain, taking her children with her. Hector had never visited Spain – indeed he had never been farther than the city of Cork – and he had a seventeen-year-old's longing to see more of the world. He nursed a secret and romantic belief that his own name, Lynch, was an omen because the Irish version, O'Loinsigh, meant 'seafarer' or 'wanderer'.

He was thinking about the possibility of a trip to Spain, and what it would be like, when he heard the first pistol shot.

It was the signal for the raiders to begin breaking down doors and wrenching open shutters. Now they made as much noise and racket as possible. They yelled and whooped, banged cudgels against doorposts, kicked over stacks of farm tools. In response every dog in the village began to bark furiously and somewhere a donkey brayed in panic. Inside the cabins the occupants were stupefied by the sudden din. Many slept on beds that were little more than piles of dried bracken covered with blankets on the beaten earth floor, and they were still getting to their feet groggily when the intruders burst in among them. Children clung to their mothers, babies began to wail, and the adults were disoriented and dazed as the raiders began to herd them out of doors. Those who resisted did so from confusion and weariness rather than a sense of defiance. A slap across the face or a well-aimed kick in the backside quickly changed their minds, and they stumbled out to join their neighbours in the street.

The first flush of dawn gave sufficient light for the raiders to make their selection. They spurned those who were bent with age and hard labour or obviously misshapen. A young man with a badly twisted leg was rejected, so too was a halfwit who stood helplessly, his head turning from side to side as he tried to understand the mayhem that surrounded him. Infants were also discarded. One raider casually pulled a baby of less than six months from the mother's arms, and handed the child to the nearest crone as if it was an unwanted parcel. The mother he pushed into the chosen group of able-bodied men, women and their children who had to appear at least five years old if they were to qualify.

But not everyone was caught. There was a flurry as a figure was spotted running away down the road that led inland. A shouted order, and the two raiders who had set off after the fugitive turned back to rejoin their companions. The running man was on his way to fetch help, to alert the local militia, but the invaders knew the village was too isolated for assistance to arrive in time. So they continued their selection with calm efficiency.

Hector scrambled out from his bed and was still pulling on his breeches when the door to his room slammed open. Someone in the passageway held up a lantern so that the light shone full on him. Behind the light he made out the shapes of three men who thrust their way into the room. He caught a brief glimpse of a mustached face as heavily muscled arms reached out towards him. He twisted to one side, trying to evade the grasping hands, but blundered into another man who had circled around behind him. Someone clasped him around his waist, and his nostrils were filled with the smell of sweat and some sort of exotic scent. Hector thrashed urgently from side to side, trying to break free. Then he jerked his head backward, as he'd done when tussling with friends in boyhood games, but viciously this time. He felt a satisfying thump as his skull struck his attacker full in the face. There was a grunt of pain, and the grip relaxed enough for him to twist free. He made a dash for the door, but one of the other men stepped across to block his escape. Once again he was held, this time with a stranglehold around his neck. Choking, he drove his elbow into his assailant's ribs, only to have a hand clamped over his mouth. He bit down fiercely. He heard someone swear, and a growled comment. He realised that the men trying to pin him down were unwilling to harm him, and this gave him hope. There was the bite of cord as someone tried to lash his wrists together, and again he foiled them, slipping his hand away from the loop. He made another dash for the door, only to be tripped this time and he fell sprawling, crashing painfully against the wall. As he tried to get back on his feet, he looked up and saw that the man with the lantern had been standing apart from the fray, holding up the light so that his companions could do their work. At last Hector could get a clear view of his attackers. They were swarthy-skinned and dressed in baggy pantaloons and workaday seamen's coats. The man with the lantern had a long cloth, patterned with red and white checks, wrapped several times around his head. Hector blinked in amazement. It was the first time that he had seen a turban.

A moment later a fourth man walked confidently through the doorway. He was dressed like the others, only more richly, with a brocaded waistcoat over his loose shirt, and his red and blue turban was even bulkier and made of fine cloth. He was a much older man, his white beard neatly trimmed, and he seemed unperturbed by the commotion. In his hand he held a pistol. For a moment Hector thought that he would be shot for resisting so fiercely. But the newcomer only walked across to where Hector was now half-kneeling and, neatly reversing the pistol, brought the butt down on the young man's head.

Just before the crash of pain and the black oblivion that followed, Hector heard the sound that was to haunt him for months to come: the frantic, repeated screams of his sister Elizabeth, calling for his help.

TWO

☾

THE HARSH RASP of timber against his cheek brought him back to his senses. He was propped against some sort of wooden wall, lying awkwardly, and his face had scraped against the planking as he slid downwards. A painful lump on his head throbbed, and his skin was cold and clammy. Worse, it felt as if he was spinning helplessly in a black void that constantly expanded and contracted with each beat of his heart. Nauseous, Hector kept his eyes closed and, from deep down in his stomach, he retched. He was miserably aware that the real world around him was swaying and lurching, while close beside his ear was the gurgle and swirl of moving water.

Hector had only ever been to sea in small fishing boats and when it was calm so he had never experienced the torment of acute seasickness. Thus it was several hours before he felt well enough to take stock of his surroundings. He was in the bowels of a ship. That much was clear. There was the fetid stench of bilge water, the discordant creaks and groans of wood on wood, and the sound of moving water as waves washed against the hull. The stomach-churning pitch and sway of the vessel was exaggerated by the fact that barely any light penetrated into the hold of the vessel. He presumed that it was day time but whether it was morning or afternoon, or how long he had been unconscious, he had no idea. Not since he had fallen out of a tree as a boy and landed on his head, had he felt so bruised and battered. He reached up tentatively to touch the lump on his scalp, only to find that his wrists were shackled with iron manacles from which a thick tarred rope led to a ring bolt set in a cross beam. He was tethered in place.

'That's to stop you making trouble or jumping overboard,' said a sly voice close by. Startled, Hector turned to see an old man crouched beside him. He was dirty and balding, and his face with its sunken cheeks and sickly blotched skin wore a pleased expression. Hector concluded that his observer was enjoying the sight of his sufferings. 'Where am I? How long have I been here?' he asked. The residue of vomit in his throat tasted sour. The man cackled and did not reply but scuttled away and laid himself down on the deck boards with exaggerated care, his face turned away from Hector.

Left without an answer Hector carried on taking stock of his surroundings. The hold was some five paces wide and ten paces long, and there was scarcely enough height for an ordinary-sized man to stand upright. In that airless space some thirty people were sitting despondently or slumped on the floorboards. A few had pulled old cargo sacks over themselves as blankets. Others were curled up with their heads buried in their arms. Hector recognised several villagers: the gangling figure of the carpenter and, seated just beside him, a brawny young labourer whom he had sometimes seen setting off from the village to cut peat on the hillside with his slean – a thin bladed spade – on his shoulder. Two men, clearly brothers, were the same fishermen who took it in turn to ferry visitors across to the island friary, and the older man with the gash on his jaw – where someone must have struck him with a club – was the cooper who made the barrels in which the villagers salted down their winter supply of pilchards. They were all still wearing the ragbag of clothes they had put on when they were snatched from their homes, and they looked broken and forlorn. There were also half a dozen children. One of them, perhaps six or seven years old, was whimpering with fear and exhaustion.

But the villagers were not the only occupants of the hold. There were several strangers. In addition to the bedraggled elderly lunatic who had accosted him, there was a small group of men who looked like seamen, and sitting by himself in one corner was a portly man wearing a wig. Judging by his expensive but soiled clothing, he must be a merchant or prosperous shopkeeper. How they all came to be thrown together in these strange and dismal surroundings was something that Hector could not comprehend.

Then, abruptly, he recalled his sister's despairing wail for help and, looking round the hold again, noted that there were no women in the group.

There was the thump of a hammer blow. It came from directly above, the sound magnified in the hollow space. Then a shaft of light struck down into the gloom. Hector squinted upward to where a hatch was being opened. A pair of bare feet and shins appeared as a sailor came down the ladder leading into the hold. The man was dressed in the same garb as those who had attacked him. A sailor's knife dangled from a lanyard around his neck, and he was swarthy and heavily bearded. He carried a large wicker basket which he set down on the floor. Without a word he climbed back up the ladder and closed the hatch. A moment later Hector heard the sound of wedges being driven home. Several of the men who looked like seafarers immediately made their way to the base of the ladder, and began to rummage in the basket.

Hector's tether had been left long enough for him to join them, and he found they were pulling out sheets of thin flat bread which they ripped to pieces and shared out amongst themselves. Beside the basket stood a small tub of water with a wooden scoop. Hector took a sip, spat to wash his mouth out, and then drank deeply. He broke off a piece of the bread and tasted it. It was slightly gritty but wholesome. In the basket were also small fruits which he recognised as a delicacy his mother had occasionally received from her family in Spain. He bit into one and spat out the stone, an olive. Picking out half a dozen of them and another chunk of bread, he retreated to his place by the hull and began to eat, feeling better with every mouthful. Now he realised that he was the only person who had been manacled and tethered. Everyone else in the hold was free to move about.

While his fellow captives fed, Hector picked steadily at the knot in the rope that bound him to the ring bolt. It was some sort of complicated seaman's knot but eventually he managed to work it loose. Holding the tether in a loop so it did not trip him, Hector moved across to talk to the villagers. He was feeling a little awkward. Though he had spent his summers among them, he did not know any of the older men very well. The difference in their backgrounds was too great; the son of a gentleman, however impoverished, had little in common with peasant labourers and fishermen. 'Has anyone seen my sister Elizabeth?' he asked, embarrassed to pose such a question when he knew that each one of the men must have his own immediate troubles. No one answered. He knelt beside the cooper, who had always seemed a sober and level-headed family man, and repeated his question. He noticed that the cooper had been crying. There were streaks where the tears had run down his face and mingled with blood that leaked from the gash in his chin. 'What happened? Where's my sister Elizabeth?' he repeated. The cooper seemed not to understand his question, for he only mumbled: 'God has made a second Taking. To Israel he promised a return from the captivity, yet we are twice punished and left in darkness.'

The man was a devout churchgoer, Hector recalled. Like all of the tradesmen, the cooper was a Protestant and regularly worshipped in the village chapel. It was the poorer sort – the fishermen and the landless peasants – who were Catholic, and they crossed to the island each Sunday to attend Mass with the friars. Hector, with his Protestant father and his Catholic mother, had never given much thought to this arrangement. He had little or no interest in religion, and veered as easily between one faith and the other as switching languages when speaking to his parents. He dimly remembered people talking about 'the Taking', but usually in hushed tones and he had never enquired further, believing it to be none of his business.

Deciding that he would have to take matters into his own hands if he was to find out what was happening, he rose to his feet and walked across to the ladder leading to the hatch. Climbing up, he started to beat rhythmically on the underside of the timber with his wrist fetters. Within moments he heard an angry shout and then the sound of running feet. Once again the hatch was opened, but only a crack, and for a brief instant he caught a glimpse of blue sky with white puffs of cloud before the end of a broad-bladed sword was thrust down to within a few inches of his face. He stood stock-still so as not to provoke the swordsman any further, then slowly tilted back his head so that he could look up and said carefully, first in English and then in Spanish, 'Please can I speak with the captain?' He was gazing past the blade and into the face of the same sailor who had brought the basket of bread. The sailor stared at him for a moment, then called out in a language Hector did not understand. Hector heard a murmured exchange and the hatch was opened wider and a second man, presumably a petty officer, was gesturing for him to climb up.

Clumsy in his manacles and with his tether still looped in his hand, Hector scrambled out of the hatch. After the stuffy darkness of the hold the world was full of light and sunshine, and he breathed deeply, glad to fill his lungs with fresh sea air and feel the breeze against his skin. He was standing on the deck of a fair-sized vessel, and though he was no sailor he could appreciate that the ship was making rapid progress over a sea of such vibrant blue that it almost hurt his eyes. When the vessel heeled slightly to a puff of wind he lost his balance and, recovering, glanced over the ship's side. There, a musket shot away, a second ship was running swiftly on a parallel course, keeping pace with them. From the tip of each of her two masts streamed out long pennants, blood-red in colour, and at her stern flew a large green flag decorated with three silver crescent moons. The petty officer, a short and muscular man, was balancing easily on the sloping deck and waiting for him to speak. 'Please,' Hector said, 'I wish to talk with your captain.' The man's dark brown eyes looked him over. Surprisingly the examination was not hostile, merely professional. Then, reaching forward to take hold of the young man's tether, he led him like a cow to its byre as he strolled towards the stern of the vessel. There, under an awning, Hector saw the same white-bearded man who had struck him down so expertly with the pistol butt. Hector judged him to be in his late fifties, perhaps older, yet he looked trim and fit, and radiated authority. He was comfortably seated on cushions, a dish of fruit lay beside him, and he was exploring his mouth with a silver toothpick. Gravely he watched Hector and his escort approach and listened to what the petty officer had to report. Then, laying aside the toothpick, he said, 'You have courage, young man. You put up a good fight, and now you do not fear what my men might do to you if you anger them.'

'If it pleases your honour . . .' began Hector, and then stopped abruptly. His mouth fell open. He had been about to ask what had happened to Elizabeth, and it had taken several seconds for him to realise that the ship captain had spoken in English. For a moment he thought he had misheard or was imagining. But no, the captain went on in English that was accurate, if a little hesitant, as though he was occasionally searching for the correct phrase. 'Tell me, what were you doing in the village?'

Hector was so astonished that he could barely get his own words out. 'I was a student with the friars on the island. With my sister. How is it . . . ?' he faltered.

'How is it that I speak your language?' the captain finished the question for him. 'Because I am originally from that village myself. Now I am called Hakim Reis, but once I was known as Tom Pierse. Though that is a long time ago now, more than fifty years. God has been kind to me.'

Hector's mind was in turmoil. He could not imagine how this exotic mariner with his foreign dress and outlandish manner could claim to have come from a poor village on Ireland's Atlantic coast. Yet the captain spoke English with the distinctive lilt of the region.

Hakim Reis saw his puzzlement.

'I was just seven years old when I was taken. So too were my mother and father, two brothers and my grandmother. I never saw them again after we were landed,' he said. 'At the time I thought it was the greatest tragedy. Now I know it was God's will and I thank him for it.' He reached down and took a fruit, chewed on it, and then placed the stone back in the dish.

'So I was curious to see what the place is like now. That is why I decided to pay a brief call, and what point would there be in a visit if I did not make a profit from it? I must admit that it is not as I remember, though of course I still knew the hidden landing place and how to approach without being seen. The village is smaller now, or maybe that is how it always seems when one revisits a childhood haunt. Everything has shrunk.'

By now Hector had recovered enough from his surprise to repeat the vital question that was preying on his mind.

'Please,' he tried again, 'I would like to know what has happened to my sister. Her name is Elizabeth.'

'Ah, the good-looking girl who was in the house where we found you. She clawed my men like a wild cat. Such ferocity must be a family trait. She came to no harm, and is safe.'

'Where is she now? Can I see her?'

Hakim Reis wiped his fingers on a napkin. 'No. That is not possible. We always keep the men and women apart. Your sister is aboard the other vessel.'

'When will I see her again?'

'That is in God's hands. We are homeward bound, but at sea one never knows.'

'Then where are you taking us?'

The captain looked mildly surprised. 'I would have thought you would have been informed. Did not the older villagers tell you? There must be some who remembered the last time it happened. But of course they are of a different generation, or perhaps those who were left behind chose to forget.'

'One of the men in the hold spoke to me of "the Taking",' Hector said.

'So that is what they call it. Not a bad name. It was Murat Reis who commanded at the time, a great captain, and his memory is still revered. Foreign-born like myself, a Flamand by origin. Mind you, he did not have my local knowledge and so he was obliged to use a Dungarvan man as his pilot to guide him in.'

Hector recalled that no villager ever mentioned the name of Dungarvan town without spitting, and also some talk of a Dungarvan man being hanged as a traitor. The foreign captain was growing nostalgic. 'When I was a boy I can remember my father forbidding my brothers and me from playing with the dirty children, as they called them. We were told that we would catch foul diseases if we did. He meant the Catholics, of course. In those days the village was remarkable for being home to so many Protestants. Tell me, is that still the case?'

'I believe so, sir. There is a new landlord now, and he has enlarged the chapel. He strongly favours those of the Protestant faith. The Catholics must go for Mass to the friars on the island, and they try to do so without attracting attention.'

'How little changes. The more I hear about the quarrels and rivalries between the Christians, the happier I am that I took the turban.' Noticing Hector's puzzlement, he added, 'Some call it "turning Turk".'

Hector still looked blank.

'I converted to the True Faith preached by the prophet Muhammad, may he be honoured and glorified. It was not such a difficult decision for someone whose memories of home were only of cold and damp, and a place where everyone had to work like a drudge to pay rent to a distant landlord. Of course I did not convert at once, but after serving the man who bought me. He was a kind master.'

At last Hector understood. Maybe the shock of his capture combined with the blow to his head and his fears for Elizabeth had obscured what was now obvious: Hakim Reis was a corsair. He must come from one of the pirate states of Barbary on the coast of North Africa whose ships plagued the Mediterranean and the Atlantic approaches. They intercepted and robbed ships and carried off their crews into slavery. From time to time they also made slave-taking shore raids. Hector wondered how he could have been so slow on the uptake. One evening, several years ago, his father had entertained a local celebrity, the vicar of nearby Mitchelstown, who was renowned for having been held as a slave of the corsairs. Eventually the vicar had been ransomed, and he was much in demand at dinner parties when he would recount his experiences. Hector had been allowed to stay and listen, and he recalled a tall, rather haggard man with a husky voice describing the conditions in the slave pens. Hector struggled to remember his name. There was a joke to it, someone had raised a laugh by referring to a fish being caught by the bay. That was it, the reverend's name was Devereux Spratt, and he was the captive of a foreign potentate called the Bey. Unfortunately the reverend had rather spoilt the pun by announcing primly that the jokester was confused in his geography of the Barbary states. The Bey was the title of the ruler of the state of Tunis, while he had been a prisoner of the ruler of Algiers whose title was Dey.

'I beg you in the name of your Muhammad,' Hector pleaded, 'that when we reach our destination, you will let me speak with my sister.'

'We will be at sea for at least another week.' Hakim Reis gave Hector a shrewd glance, and Hector noticed that the corsair's eyes were pale grey in contrast to the deep tan of his face. 'Will you give me your word that you will make no trouble during that time, now you know that there is a chance you can speak to her?' Hector nodded. 'Good, I will order those fetters to be removed. And do not look so glum. Maybe your life will be blessed, as mine was, and you will rise to command a fine ship. Besides, you will sell for a higher price if you have a happier face.' And to Hector's astonishment he held up the plate of fruit and said, 'Here, take a handful with you. They will remind you that life can be as sweet as you wish to make it.'

The captain spoke briefly to the petty officer, who produced a key and unlocked the manacles. Then he escorted Hector back to the hatchway and he gestured for Hector to go back down into the hold. Once again Hector heard the wedges hammered home.

He had expected his fellow captives to ask him what it was like up on deck. But most of them ignored his return. They were apathetic as though they had accepted their fate. Someone was muttering a prayer for salvation, repeating it over and over again. It was a depressing sound, and in the gloom he could not see who it was. The only person alert to his return was the elderly madman. As Hector settled himself back in his place, he crept up again and hissed, 'Is it to be Algiers or Tunis?'

'I don't know,' Hector answered, taken aback by the accuracy of the old man's question.

'As long as it's not Sallee,' muttered the old man, more to himself than to Hector. 'They say it's the worst place of all. Underground pens where you can drown in liquid shit, and chains so heavy that you can barely walk. They told me I was lucky to be in Algiers.'

'Who are "they" and what do you mean by "lucky"?' Hector asked, wondering what his fellow captive was babbling about.

He was answered with another shifty look. 'Trying to catch me out, are you? Well you won't this time,' the dotard wheezed, and suddenly grabbed at the young man's hand and demanded fiercely, 'What have you got there? Share! Share!' Hector had forgotten about the fruit he had been given. He supposed them to be olives, though they felt more sticky. The old man snatched one away, and thrust it into his mouth. He began to drool. 'Datoli, datoli,' he gloated. Hector tasted one. On his tongue it was the sweetest fruit he had ever known, as if saturated in honey, and there was a hard pip in the centre.

'Have you been in Algiers?' he asked, anxious to glean any information about their fate.

'Of course! Was I not there for five years and more? And then they doubted the tales I had to tell.'

Hector was growing ever more confused by the old man's rambling. 'It's not that I doubt you. Only I know nothing of these matters.'

'I swear to you that I was a beylik slave for all those five years, mostly in the quarries, but sometimes on the harbour wall. Yet I never renounced my faith, oh no, though others did. Even when they beat me, I resisted. What came later was more cruel.'

'What could be worse than slavery? And what's a beylik?'

The old man ignored the question. He was working himself into a frenzy. He grabbed Hector's arm and dug in with his bony fingers. 'After they bought me, they treated me like dung,' he hissed.

'You mean the Algiers people?'

'No. No. The canting hypocrites. After they paid my ransom, they thought I was their thing. They paraded me around, I and a dozen others. We were like monkeys to be stared at. Made us wear our old slave clothes, the red cap and the thin gown, even though it was shivering cold. They had us stand and call out from carts, shake our chains and tell our woes. That is, until they had enough of us. Then they turned us loose without a coin to our names. So I went back to sea, it is the only trade I know, and now I'm taken a second time.' He cackled maniacally and shuffled back to his corner, where he again went through the peculiar pantomime of laying himself down on the hard boards with exaggerated care, then turned his face away.

'Silly old fool. Don't believe a word of his gibberish. He's a charlatan.' The sour comment came from the stout man wearing the wig and the expensive but stained clothes who looked like a merchant. He must have overheard the old man's tale. 'There are plenty of tricksters who go about, claiming they were captives of the Moors and begging for alms. They're fakes.'

'But what did he mean by "paraded around"?' Hector found himself taking an instant dislike to the man.

'It's a technique the redemptorists use. They're the do-gooders who raise money to buy back the slaves from Barbary. After they bring them home, they trundle the wretches around the countryside, putting them on show so that the common people can see what sufferings they have endured, and this encourages them to part with their money to pay for more ransoms.' He gave a knowing look. 'But who's to say where most of the money goes? I am acquainted with a ransom broker myself, a City man who facilitates the meetings with the Jews that act as middle men for the Moors. My friend has done remarkably well, and that's why I tell myself that I won't stay long in Barbary. As soon as I can get word back to my friend, he'll make sure that I'm ransomed early. Then I'll get home to my wife and family.'

'And what happens otherwise?' Hector enquired, careful not to say 'to the rest of us'. The merchant's smug self-interest repelled him.

'Depends what's on offer. If you have money or influence, preferably both, then you won't stay long with the Moors. Those who have neither should be patient. Every nation that calls itself Christian tries to ransom back its citizens sooner or later, provided there are enough funds.'

'How is it that you are here yourself?'

'I'm Josiah Newland, a mercer from London. I was on my way to Ireland when I was taken. Someone in Cork was having money difficulties and obliged to sell off a shipment of linen cheaply. I thought to get there ahead of the competition. So I hired a fishing boat to take me there, but unfortunately it was intercepted by these faithless pirates and they carried off myself and the crew. Those are the crew members over there.' He pointed into the far corner, at the men who had earlier clustered around the basket of bread. 'As you can see, they stick together. They are not at all my type, nor are those base fellows.' He gestured towards the villagers in their miserable huddle. Clearly he thought that Hector was not of their company.

'We were all captured at the same time,' Hector replied, trying to keep his tone neutral. With every word Josiah Newland was revealing himself to be a selfish prig. 'There was a raid on our village.'

The merchant seemed taken aback, though not sympathetic. 'I didn't think that sort of thing happened any longer. There was a time when the corsairs were very bold. They infested our coasts until the King's ships began to patrol more actively. Nowadays those pirates confine their activities to capturing ships at sea, stealing their cargoes and carrying off their crews. Indeed I would not have undertaken my own coasting voyage if His Majesty had not concluded a treaty with the Barbary states. According to the newspapers the Turks promised not to molest English shipping. But then you can never trust the Turks, nor Moors for that matter, they are a treacherous lot. Or perhaps they thought the King of England would not trouble himself unduly about his Irish subjects, for he cares little for Papists.'

Hector did not reply. The mercer was only mimicking the attitude of the King and his ministers in London. To them

Ireland, though a part of the realm, was a troublesome place populated by awkward, difficult and potentially treasonable subjects, particularly if they were followers of the Church of Rome. Hector tried to imagine Newland's reaction if he was to tell him that the corsair captain who held him prisoner was an Irish turncoat who now sailed as a Muslim.

THREE

OVER THE NEXT several days Hector, who had an intelligent and enquiring nature, struck up a friendship with one of the seamen who had been captured with Newland. He was a Devon man by the name of Francis Dunton who seemed remarkably unruffled by their abduction. Hector made sure that whenever small groups of prisoners were allowed out of the ship's hold for exercise, he and Dunton were on deck at the same time.

'This ship we're on now,' he asked the sailor diffidently, 'is she anything like the vessels you've sailed yourself?'

Dunton turned to face the young man, and Hector was struck by the similarity between the Devon man and the corsair petty officer who had escorted him to see Hakim Reis. Both men had the same compact, muscular physique, an easy balance on the moving deck, and the same air of calm competence. Dunton's weather-beaten face was tanned to nearly the same colour as the corsair's swarthy complexion. 'No different,' Dunton answered in his slow, gentle accent. 'This here is a sailing ship like any other.'

'Would you be able to sail this ship as well as those who have her now?' Hector asked, impressed by his companion's self-assurance.

The sailor gave a derisive chuckle. 'Better. The man who cuns this ship, gripes her too much.'

'What is "gripes"?'

'Turns her head, her bow that is, too much towards the wind. That slows her down.'

'And to "cun" the ship?'

'That only means to steer her.'

'I wonder if I would ever be able to learn all the sea words, let alone how to manage such a vessel.'

'Seamanship comes natural to some,' answered the sailor in a matter-of-fact tone. 'Those who haven't the knack, can usually learn if they are given enough time. The rare ones are those who can tell a helmsman which way to cun his ship, or can decipher the stars and predict a sure landfall on a foreign shore where he has never been before. That's the man who his mates will want to sail with.'

'You mean a navigator?'

'Correct. Any fool can tell you that we've been heading south since we left the coast of Ireland, and a day ago I'd say we turned more eastward. You can tell that just by looking at the sun, and the fact that each night the air in the hold is getting hotter. I reckon we must have come at least four hundred miles and are close to Africa.'

Hector broached a subject that had been nagging at the back of his mind. 'As a boy I once heard a man speak about being taken as a captive by the corsairs. He told how their prisoners were made to work as slaves in galleys, working the oars. But I don't see any oars.'

'This ship is a sailing vessel, not a galley,' the sailor replied, 'nor even a galleass, which is a word for a ship that has both oars and a sail. A galley would be next to useless out here in the open ocean. Nigh on impossible to row in the waves, and the distances are too great. How would you feed a crew on a voyage of more than a few days? You must trust to the wind when you are far from land. No, this ship suits well enough for her purpose, which is pirating.'

'What about meeting another ship, is there a chance that someone might rescue us?'

'I'd expect we'll sight other ships all right, but whether we'll be rescued is another matter. For one thing, there's our companion over there.' Dunton nodded towards the corsair's sister ship still visible half a mile away. 'Two ships sailing in close company are best avoided in case they're hostile. They can gang up on a stranger. And should we get separated and must sail on our own, then who's to say that this is a corsair ship. If the crew take the trouble to cover those few guns, this vessel could as easy be a merchantman as a pirate. Pull down those pennants and that green flag and run up someone else's colours and she could be Dutch or French or a Brandenburger as much as Turk. That's why ships avoid one another when they meet at sea, just in case of trouble.'

℃

THE FOLLOWING AFTERNOON almost proved Dunton wrong. The captives were on deck taking their exercise when a distant sail was sighted from the masthead. Hector noticed Hakim Reis gazing intently in the direction of the approaching vessel before the prisoners were hustled back down into the hold and shut in. Dunton stayed on the lower rungs of the ladder, his head cocked to one side, listening. There was a squeal of ropes running through the wooden blocks. 'Hullo, they're bringing the topsails amain,' he commented. Soon afterwards there was a tramp of feet heading towards the stern. 'And there they go to peak the mizzen. They're heaving to.'

'What does that mean?' asked Hector in a whisper.

'They're stopping the ship, waiting for the other one to catch up,' Dunton explained as Hector felt the motion of the vessel change. Where before the ship had been sailing at a slant, now she was level and pitching up and down gently on the waves.

Dunton sat down against the side of the hold. 'No hurry, younker,' he said. 'It'll be some time before that other sail catches up with us, three or four hours at least.'

'Who do you think it is?'

'No idea,' answered the sailor. 'But my guess is that our captain is a foxy one. He'll pretend he is a friendly vessel, hang out some convenient flag, and wait for the visitor to come close enough, then close and board him. Take him by surprise.'

'Not fire at him?'

'A corsair doesn't use his cannon except in emergency. He doesn't want to damage his prey. Best lay board and board, and seize the other vessel with a rush of men.'

An air of excitement had also brought the other prisoners to life. Even the most depressed villager started to look hopeful of rescue. Newland, the cloth merchant, called enquiringly, 'Friend or foe, sailor?'

Dunton merely shrugged.

It must have been about three hours later – there was no way to mark the passage of time below deck – when suddenly an order was shouted on the deck above, and the prisoners heard the scamper of running feet. 'Hello,' said Dunton. 'Something's not what was expected.'

There were more shouts and then the chanting of a work song, its refrain urgent and forceful. 'They're setting sail again, and in a hurry,' commented the sailor. Within moments the prisoners could again hear the ripple of the waves along the flanks of the ship, and feel the vessel heel to the wind. A flat thud in the distance was followed by two more. 'Cannon!' announced Dunton. More cries on deck, and the answering bang of a cannon from directly above them. The vessel quivered with the recoil. 'God grant that we are not hit. If we sink, we'll never get out of here alive,' muttered Newland the mercer in sudden alarm. Hector glanced at the villagers. Their earlier hopes of being rescued had turned to dismay. Several were on their knees, hands clasped in silent prayer, eyes shut tight. 'What's going on?' he asked the Devon sailor. Dunton was still straining to hear the noises on deck. 'Wish I knew their language. No way of knowing. But my guess is that we're the chase.' Again Hector felt frustrated by his lack of sea lore.

'Does that mean we are in pursuit?'

'No, the chase is the vessel which is pursued.'

'God grant us salvation!' pleaded the cooper. 'Praise the Lord for his Mercy. He who watches over us! Let us pray together for our liberation.' He began to hum a psalm.

'Shut up!' snapped Dunton. 'I'm trying to hear what is going on.'

The cooper ignored him, and his co-religionists in the hold began a dirge which drowned out all but the distant occasional thud of the cannon fire which, as time passed, became fainter and more irregular until, finally, nothing more could be heard.

'Must have outrun them,' grunted Dunton, who had shifted to his favourite position beneath a crack in the deck planking where he could squint out at the sky. 'Or perhaps we lost them in the gathering darkness. It'll be full dark soon.'

The disappointed prisoners settled down for their rest, their stomachs empty, because for the first time in the voyage, no one had appeared at the hatch with their evening ration. 'Let us pray to God that our women and children are safe,' said the cooper, and Hector, who had naturally been silently wondering what might have happened to Elizabeth on the sister ship, found himself praying quietly for her survival as he tried to go to sleep, curled up against a bulkhead. He felt completely helpless as Hakim Reis's ship sailed on towards its unknown destination.

℃

BY NOON the next day the captives had still not been fed, and they were hungrily awaiting the arrival of their usual ration of bread and olives when there was another shattering crash of cannon fire. But this time it was not a single cannon. An entire battery of guns was shooting, and very close by. The ship's armament promptly answered, and the prisoners heard the thud of the gun carriages slamming down with the discharge. The sudden torrent of sound tipped the elderly madman over the edge of sanity. He leapt up from where he had been sleeping, and began to caper and shout nonsense. He hooted and bellowed, and nothing could restrain him. Again came the shocking crash of a battery, and an answering blast from the ship's guns. A strange smell wafted down – the acrid stink of gunpowder.

All at once the hatch was flung open, and not one but five sailors came hurrying down the ladder. But instead of bringing food, they began to shout and point excitedly, urging the captives to go up on deck. Dazed and uncomprehending, the prisoners shuffled forward. Those who stayed were pulled to their feet and thrust forward. Hector found himself following the grimy and naked feet of a villager as he climbed the ladder to the deck, and emerged to see a scene ahead of him never to be forgotten.

Off to one side, less than a hundred yards away, stood a formidable fortress constructed of massive stone blocks on a low and rocky islet. The sides of the fortress were a series of angled surfaces designed to deflect cannonballs. Its parapet bristled with cannon, and from a copper dome, which also served as a lighthouse, rose a tall flagpole from which floated a huge crimson flag. In the centre of the flag was the image of an arm, black on red, brandishing a broad-bladed sword like the weapons wielded by the sailors aboard Hakim Reis's vessel. As Hector watched, white smoke belched from the mouths of the fort's cannon, and a moment later he heard the echoing explosion. He flinched, waiting for the shock of cannonballs tearing into the fabric of the ship. But nothing came. Then he realised that the fort was firing a salute to greet the incoming vessel, even as Hakim Reis's men let off their own guns and gave a great cheer.

But what made him gape was the city which climbed the hill behind the fort. Blinding white in the midday sun, rank upon rank of tightly packed houses extended up the flank of a steep mountain to form a dense triangular mass. The flat roofs of the houses were topped with balconies, their walls pierced with rows of small arched windows. Here and there emerged a turquoise or gilded dome and the spikes of tall spires, and at the very apex of the triangle, far up the slope, was a sprawling complex which Hector took to be a citadel. To the left, outside the city wall and dominating the skyline, loomed another massive castle, its turrets decked out with flagpoles and banners. Orchards and gardens spread across the flanks of the mountains on both sides, and their show of greenery framed the dizzying spectacle of the corsairs' base.

The sound of cheering brought his attention back to the harbour. On the seaward side of the fortress a curtain wall had been built to protect an anchorage. This curtain wall, some thirty feet high and built along the crest of a reef, was also topped with battlements and cannon platforms. The rampart was lined with citizens who had come out to greet them. They were shouting and waving, and a small band of musicians – three drummers and a man with some sort of flute – had struck up a wild skirling tune. Those spectators who were nearest the musicians were clapping in time and a few of them were whirling and dancing with delight.

A shove on his shoulder from one of the crew pushed him into line so that he stood side by side with the other captives at the rail of the ship, facing across to the crowd of onlookers. Hector realised that he and the other prisoners were being put on show. They were the spoils of the corsair's cruise.

A few moments more and their ship was rounding the far end of the harbour wall, with the anchorage opening ahead of them. Moored in the middle of the roadstead were four sailing vessels similar to the one Hakim Reis commanded. But what caught his eye were the dozen vessels deep inside the harbour, their bows tied to the mole itself. Without being told, he knew what they were. Low and sleek and dangerous, they reminded him of the greyhounds his father and his friends had used to course hares in the countryside. He was about to ask Dunton if he was right in thinking they were corsair galleys, when the villager standing beside him said in anguished tones, 'Where's the other ship? The one with our womenfolk and the children?'

Shocked, Hector turned to look. Nowhere could he see the vessel that had accompanied them. She was gone.

FOUR

C

SAMUEL MARTIN, the English consul in Algiers, heard the salvoes of gunfire and walked to the window of his office. From long experience he knew the reason for the commotion. Squinting down into the harbour he recognised Hakim Reis's ship and sighed. The corsair's arrival meant there was work for him, and it was not a task he relished. By inclination and preference Martin was a trader. He would much rather have looked out of his window and seen merchant ships arriving and departing, laden with the honest merchandise from which he had hoped to make his living when he had first arrived in Algiers a decade ago. But it had not turned out that way. Legitimate trade between England and Algiers was on the increase but the Algerines much preferred to make their money by seizing captives for ransom or selling stolen goods, often back to their original owners. Hence the joyous reception being given by the populace to Hakim Reis and his ruffians down at the harbour.

Consul Martin, a small and active man, often wondered if the government in London had any inkling of the complications of being England's representative to a Barbary regency. For a start he never quite knew whom he should be dealing with. Officially the city ruler was the Pasha appointed by the Turkish Sultan in Istanbul. But the Sublime Porte was far away, and ultimately the Pasha was really nothing more than a figurehead. Effective power apparently lay with the Dey and his cabinet of advisers, the divan. But that too was a deception. The Dey was elected by the janissaries, the city's Turkish-born military elite. Known locally as the odjaks, the janissaries were professional warriors, but it was normal that they also followed a second occupation, usually as merchants or landlords. Certainly they devoted more energy to political intrigues than to soldiering. They made and unmade their Deys at an alarming rate, and their favoured method of getting rid of the current officeholder was by assassination. In Consul Martin's time three Deys had been killed, two by poison and one with the garrotte. The Consul was aware that the divan only paid him any attention when it suited them, but he nursed a hope that one day he would be able to influence the current Dey, an elderly odjak, directly through his favourite wife who was reputed to be an Englishwoman. She was a slave girl who had taken the old man's fancy and borne him two children. Unfortunately Martin had yet to meet the lady, and rumour had it that she was as avaricious and corrupt as anyone else in the palace.

The consul sighed again. Had the incoming vessel been a galley returning from a short cruise in the Mediterranean, the prisoners on board were likely to be French or Genoese, Greeks or Spaniards, and therefore not his concern. But Hakim Reis was known to range as far as the English Channel on his man-catching cruises. Recently Martin had helped negotiate a treaty between London and Algiers whereby the Algerines had promised not to molest English ships, or vessels sailing under English passes. But the consul was not sure that Hakim Reis would have honoured the pact. So it was best if His Majesty's consul established just who was on the corsair's roster of captives. And should any of his captives prove to be subjects of the King, then Martin's duty was to find out their identities and what price was expected for them. The best moment to do that was when the prisoners were first landed, before they were distributed among various owners or vanished into any one of the eight bagnios, the slave barracks.

Indoors, the consul liked to wear the loose cotton kaftans and slippers which the Moors of Algiers favoured, and he thought the dress very sensible in the heat. But in public he was expected to dress according to his rank and dignity. So now he called for his manservant, a Hampshire man awaiting the final instalment of an agreed ransom, and told him to lay out his street clothes – a three-piece suit of heavy cloth with a waistcoat and knee breeches, a starched linen shirt with a frilled front and ruffles at the wrist, and a cravat.

Half an hour later, sweating in this turnout, Martin descended to the street. His office and living quarters were in the coolest part of the building, the topmost of the three floors which served as the consulate as well as his residence and place of business. On the way downstairs he passed the rooms where his servants ate and slept, the dormitories occupied by several dozen captives whose ransoms were expected soon or who were part-paid, and finally on the ground floor the storerooms for the commodities he traded – mostly skins and ostrich feathers from the interior. His doorkeeper, a burly and necessary functionary who intercepted unwelcome callers at the house, pulled back the heavy nail-studded door. Martin adjusted his newly brushed periwig and, a little unsteady on the two-inch-high heels of his buckled shoes, he stepped out into the narrow street.

The noise and heat made a double blow. The consulate was situated halfway up the hill of Algiers, and its front door gave directly on to the main street which ran the length of the city, from the docks to the Kasbah at the upper end of the town. Never more than a few yards wide, with high flat-fronted houses on each side, the street was like a sultry ravine. Paved with worn stone slabs, it climbed so steeply that it had to be broken by occasional short flights of steps. The street also served as the main bazaar and emporium of the city, so walking along it meant stepping around stalls and dodging pavement vendors selling everything from vegetables to metalwork. Asses laden with panniers plodded up and down the slope, hawkers yelled, water carriers clattered tin cups against the brass flagons strapped to their backs. As the consul made his way slowly through the press of the crowd he wondered, not for the first time, whether he should retire and return to England. For years he had suffered the noise and heat of Algiers, and the roguery of its inhabitants. Yet he told himself once again that it was too soon to abandon the city. Property prices in England were rising so fast that he would not be able to afford the country estate on which he had set his heart.

On the quayside, Martin found the Dey's scribes already seated at the table where they would enter the new intake of captives in the city register. Martin knew the chief registrar slightly and bowed to him, a gesture of politeness which would do no harm as the Algerines, for all their villainy, valued good manners. The usual crowd of idlers had assembled to observe the landing of the prisoners and pass comments on their potential worth as slaves, while the first boatload of the captives had already been ferried ashore. Martin noted how bewildered and frightened the poor wretches looked as they gazed about them at the strange world into which they were being inducted. Glumly the consul concluded that the new arrivals were too fair-skinned to be Italians or Spanish, and he supposed they must be Dutch or English. The only prisoner taking an intelligent interest in his surroundings was a handsome, black-haired young man in his late teens. He was looking this way and that, apparently searching for someone. He seemed agitated. Beyond him was a short, pudgy man wearing a wig. He was standing slightly apart from his fellow captives and trying to look as though he was too superior to be in their company. Martin wondered if the man knew that his every action was telling his captors that he was worth a larger ransom.

The consul moved closer to the table. The registrar's assistant – a Greek slave who, to Martin's knowledge, spoke at least eight languages – was asking each prisoner the same questions: his name, age, place of origin, and profession. Martin found it difficult to hear their answers over the chatter of the onlookers until, all of a sudden, there was a respectful hush and they turned to look towards the harbour. The captain of the corsair ship was himself coming ashore. The consul was intrigued. To get such a close glimpse of Hakim Reis was unusual. Hakim operated from whichever base suited him so he might as easily have brought his captives to Tunis, Sallee or Tripoli to sell. He was welcome wherever he landed on the coast of Barbary for he was acknowledged to be the most successful corsair captain of them all.

Hakim Reis was dressed in an immaculate white gown edged with gold braid, and a scarlet turban decorated with a large ostrich feather. In his hand he held a light gold-headed ceremonial cane. He came up the landing steps with the brisk tread of a man half his age, though Martin knew the corsair must be at least in his late fifties. The consul watched as the corsair captain approached the registrar and stood beside the desk for a few moments. Martin guessed that he wanted to make his presence felt, so there was no false accounting. At that moment Martin heard someone calling out to him.

'You, sir, you there!' It was the portly man in the wig. He must have recognised the consul by his foreign dress. 'If you please. My name is Josiah Newland. I am a mercer, from London. I need to speak with the King of England's representative at once.'

'I am the English consul.'

'A fortunate encounter, then,' said Newland, puffing slightly in the heat and instantly adopting a self-important tone. 'Would you be so good as to send word by your most competent commission agent that Josiah Newland is taken and wishes to contact Mr Sewell of Change Alley in London, so that matters can be speedily resolved.'

'There is nothing I can do at this time, Mr Newland,' the

consul replied calmly. 'I am here merely as an observer. The Turks have a well-established routine which must be followed. Perhaps later, when the Dey has made his choice, I may be of assistance.'

'The Dey? What has he got to do with it?'

'The Dey, Mr Newland, is the ruler of Algiers and has the right to his penjic or portion. He takes every eighth slave, plus other benefits such as the bare hulls of all captured vessels. Tomorrow or perhaps the day afterwards when he has made his selection, I will see you again.'

'One moment . . .' the mercer was about to continue, but Martin's attention had again been distracted. The registrar's Greek slave wanted a word with him. 'Your honour,' began the slave, 'my master asks me to inform you that most of the captives are from Ireland, one or two are English. He wishes to know whether you will accept their charge.'

'Please tell your master that I will consider the matter, if he would be so good as to provide me with a list of names and other relevant details. I look forward to giving him my reply tomorrow.'

A burst of angry shouts and the sound of blows interrupted him. Farther along the quay, a gang of slaves had been manoeuvring a great block of quarry stone preparatory to fitting it into a gap in the causeway which led to the island fortress. The massive stone had been balanced on a crude sledge with the men harnessed to it like draught horses. The stone had slipped and toppled sideways, and the overseer had lost his temper. Now he was cursing and laying about him with a whip. As the slaves were still fastened to the sledge, they were unable to avoid the lash. They scrabbled and ducked, trying to avoid the blows. It was some minutes before the overseer had vented his anger, and in that time the majority of the men received a thorough thrashing. Martin had witnessed many scenes like it. The great mole at Algiers constantly needed repairs, and its maintenance was the responsibility of the Dey. There was a very good chance that those slaves who were unlucky enough to be taken in his penjic would be assigned to this dangerous and backbreaking chore.

Civilly Martin bowed again to the registrar and started walking back up the hill towards the consulate. He was already considering how best to arrange the fat mercer's ransom. That transaction should not be difficult. The man exuded the self-confidence of someone with access to ready funds, so a well-placed bribe would ensure that Newland was not sent to the bagnios. Instead he would be released into the consul's care for the three or four months that the ransom negotiations would take. The Irish captives were a different matter. If they were Protestants, he could assist them in some small way as he did with their fellow unfortunates who were English or Scots. He could provide them with pocket money which, spread in judicious bribes to their goalers, might ease their life in the bagnio. Later he would reclaim the sum from London.

But if the Irish were Papists, he would be throwing away his own cash. The tight-fisted bureaucrats in London would be sure to query his accounts, and he would never be reimbursed. Sourly he reflected that his own consular salary was three years in arrears. Still, he was in a better position than his colleague and sometime rival, the unfortunate consul for Spain. After four years he was still trying to negotiate the ransom of a Spanish nobleman being held prisoner in the most vile conditions. The captive was a Chevalier of the noble Order of the Knights of St John in Malta, whose ships were fighting an implacable holy war against the Muslims. The Barbary corsairs loathed the Knights, and the feeling was mutual. The Algerines wanted such a huge sum for the Chevalier that there was little prospect of him being released for several more years, if ever. In the meantime the Dey and his divan were stepping up the pressure on the Spanish consul. Recently the Spaniard and his local interpreter had been set upon in the street and beaten up. Now, for fear of their lives, they hardly dared leave their consulate.

Martin tripped on a loose paving stone. The mishap made him uncomfortably aware that his feet, in his fashionable high-heeled shoes, were beginning to swell in the heat. He found himself looking forward to the moment when he could change back into his kaftan and slippers. Setting aside any further thoughts about the corsair's captives, the consul concentrated on the steep climb back up the hill of Algiers.

FIVE

☾

HECTOR STUMBLED THROUGH the next few hours. Numbed by his sister's disappearance, he barely noticed what was happening as he was inscribed in the register, and he slept badly in the bleak holding cell where the captives were kept overnight. Again and again he wondered what might have happened to Elizabeth and how he might find out. But there was no opportunity to enquire. At first light he and the other prisoners were woken and, barefoot and still wearing the soiled clothes in which they had been captured, they were marched up the hill to the great building Hector had mistaken for the citadel. In fact it was the Kasbah, part fort, part palace. In a courtyard the men were mustered in three lines, and after a short wait the Dey's head steward appeared. He was accompanied by three men whom Hector later knew to be two overseers from the public slave barracks and a Jew who was an experienced slave broker. The trio walked up and down between the lines, occasionally stopping to consult with one another or examine a prisoner's physique. Hector felt like a beast in a cattle market when one of the overseers reached out to pinch his arm muscles, then prodded him in the ribs with the butt of a wooden baton. Finally, when the inspection was complete, the Jew in his black cap and black gown walked between the lines and tapped four men on the shoulder. Among them was the strapping young villager whom Hector had formerly seen going out to cut turf. As the four were led away by the guards, Hector heard the crazed grey beard standing beside him mutter under his breath, 'Beylik, poor bastards.'

The old man appeared to be in one of his more lucid moods, for he seemed to remember who Hector was, and announced his own name as Simeon. 'You noticed, didn't you?' he asked the young man. 'They took the strong ones. You were lucky not to be picked. Probably too skinny ... or too beautiful,' and he laughed coarsely to himself. 'This is Algiers, you know. They keep their pretty boys close to home, not sent off to work as public slaves.'

Hector was feeling light-headed in the heat. 'What's going to happen to us now?' he enquired.

'Off to the badestan, I expect,' explained Simeon.

The badestan proved to be an open square close to the Kasbah's main entrance. Here a large crowd of Algerines had already assembled, and before Hector could understand what was happening, an old man had taken him by his arm in a friendly way, and begun to lead him around the square. It was several steps before Hector realised that he was in the hands of an auctioneer. There was a shouted demand from an onlooker. The old man stopped, then pulled the shirt off Hector's shoulders so that the young man's naked torso was exposed. A few paces further and at another request called from the crowd, the old man produced a thin, whippy cane and, to Hector's shock, slashed it violently across his ankles. Hector leapt in pain. Even before he had landed, the auctioneer had repeated the blow from the other direction, so that Hector was forced to skip and turn in the air. Twice more during the circuit of the square, the cane was used and he was made to jump and spin. Then the auctioneer began to sing out what must have been his salesman's patter, for there were answering calls from the crowd, and Hector guessed that they were making their bids. The bidding reached its climax and the auctioneer was making what seemed to be his last appeal, when a dignified-looking Turk stepped out of the crowd and came across to where Hector was standing. The newcomer was clearly a man of substance. His purple velvet jacket was richly embroidered, and the silver handle of a fine dagger showed above the brocade sash around his waist. On his head was a tall felt hat with jewelled brooch pinned to it. The man said something quietly to the auctioneer who reached up and placed his wiry hand on Hector's jaw. Then he squeezed with a firm downward pull, and Hector involuntarily opened his mouth. The Turk peered into his mouth, seemed satisfied, and murmured something to the auctioneer who immediately led Hector back to his waiting companions.

'I told them my age already,' grumbled Hector to Simeon.

His complaint was met with a gleeful chuckle. 'It was not your age he wanted to know. But the state of your teeth.' The smirking grey beard opened his own mouth and pointed triumphantly at his own teeth. The few of them that remained were brown and rotten. 'Can't chew with them,' he crowed. 'I'd be no good at all. Even though I've done my time.'

'Where, old man?' asked Hector, growing tired of Simeon's vagueness.

The dotard snickered, 'You'll find out soon enough,' and would say no more.

Hector looked back at the well-dressed man who had bought him. The same purchaser was now interested in the sailor Dunton, and was again talking with the auctioneer even as the guards began shoving all the captives back into line. Those who had not been stripped to the waist now had their shirts or smocks removed. Then the auctioneer walked down the line, followed by an attendant holding a clay pot and a small brush. In front of each man the auctioneer stopped, checked a document he was holding, and then said something to the attendant who stepped forward. He dipped his brush into the pot and made marks on the man's chest in ochre paint. Looking down at the marks as they dried on his skin, Hector supposed they were numbers or letters, but whether they were the bid price or an identity number he did not know.

ℂ

CAPTAIN OF GALLEYS Turgut Reis had not intended to go to the badestan that morning, but his senior wife had hinted that he get out of the house so that she could have the servants do a more thorough job of cleaning his study. In her subtle way she let it be known that he was spending too much time poring over his musty books and charts, and he would be better off meeting up with his friends for cups of coffee and conversation over a pipe of tobacco. Indeed it was unusual for the Captain of Galleys to be in Algiers in the last week of July at all. Normally he would be at sea on a cruise. But this summer was out of the ordinary as well as stressful. A month earlier his galley, *Izzet Darya*, had sprung a bad leak. When hauled up for repairs, the shipwrights had discovered three or four areas of badly wormed planking that would have to be replaced. The Arsenal at Algiers was chronically short of timber as there were no forests in the neighbourhood, and the owner of the slipway had said he would be obliged to send away for baulks in suitable lengths, maybe as far away as Lebanon. 'Those Shaitan infidels from Malta are running amok,' he warned. 'In previous years I could get deliveries brought by neutral ships. But this year those fanatics have been plundering everything that sails. And even if I can find a freighter, the charges are already exorbitant.' And he had given Turgut a look which clearly told him that it was high time that the Captain of Galleys got himself a new galley, instead of trying to patch up the old one.

But Turgut was fond of *Izzet Darya* and did not want to abandon her. He admitted that the vessel was old-fashioned, hard to manoeuvre and over-ornate. But then he himself was a bit like his ship – old-fashioned and set in his ways. His friends always said that he was living in the past, and that he should keep up with the times. They would cite the case of Hakim Reis. Hakim, they pointed out, had shrewdly switched from a vessel propelled by oars to a sailing ship which had greater range and could stay at sea for weeks at a time. The benefits were obvious from the value of the prizes that Hakim Reis was bringing in, the recent batch of captives for example. But, thought Turgut, Hakim was also blessed with remarkable luck. He was always in the right place at the right time to snap up a prize, while he, Captain of Galleys, might loiter at the crucieri, as unbelievers called the areas where the sea lanes crossed, and not see a sail for days. No, Turgut assured himself, he preferred to stick with tradition, for tradition had elevated him to be Captain of Galleys. That appointment, with all its prestige as the acknowledged head of all the corsair captains of Algiers, was not in the gift of the Dey nor of the divan, nor indeed of the scheming odjaks of Algiers. The corsairs of Algiers had their own guild, the taifa, which came together to nominate a leader, but the Sultan himself had indicated whom they should choose. He had nominated Turgut Reis in recognition of the family's tradition of service in the Sultan's navy, for Turgut's father had commanded a war galley, and his most famous ancestor, his great-uncle Piri Reis, had been admiral of the entire Turkish fleet.

Turgut, when he had received the news, had been both proud and a little anxious. At the time he had been living in the imperial capital and he knew that both his wives would be reluctant to leave. But there was no question of declining the honour. The Sultan's wish was sacrosanct. So Turgut had rented out the family mansion on the shores of the Bosphorus, packed up his belongings, said goodbye to the other courtiers at court, and sailed for Barbary with his family and his entourage aboard the venerable *Izzet Darya*.

Of course they had found Algiers very provincial compared to the sophistication of Constantinople. But he and his family had done their best to adapt. He had deliberately skirted around the local politics and tried to set an example to the other captains, to remind them of the old ways. That is why he still dressed in the courtly style, with full pantaloons hanging low, a resplendent waistcoat and an overmantle, and the tall felt hat, decorated with a brooch that he had received personally from the hands of the Sultan of Sultans, Khan of Khans, Commander of the Faithful and Successor of the Prophet of the Lord of the Universe.

He had not intended to buy any slaves at the badestan until the young dark-haired man caught his eye. The youth had a look about him that said he might one day make an astute scrivano as the locals called their scribes, or, if he had been younger, perhaps even a kocek, though Turgut himself had never much time for clever dancing boys and their attractions. So it was on an impulse that he had bought the dark-haired one, and then, having made one purchase, it had seemed only natural to make a second. He bid for the second slave because the man was so obviously a sailor. Turgut could recognise a mariner of whatever nationality, be he Turk or Syrian, Arab or Russian, and Turgut felt he was able to justify his second purchase more easily. *Izzet Darya* was a rowing galley, but she also carried two enormous triangular sails and she needed capable sail handlers. Moreover, if he was very lucky, the new purchase might even possess shipwright's skills. That would be a bonus. Good timber was not the only shortage in the Arsenal of Algiers. More than half the workmen in the galley yards were foreigners, many of them slaves, and if the new purchase could cut, shape and fit timber, he would be a useful addition to the boatyard. Turgut would rent his slave out for a daily wage or have the cost of his labour deducted from the final bill for the repairs to *Izzet Darya*.

Having made his bids, Turgut followed the captives back to the courtyard of the Dey's palace. Now came the final haggling. It was an auction all over again. Each slave was set up on a block and the bid price, written on the man's chest, was called out. According to custom the Dey had the right to buy the man at that sum if the original bidder did not increase his offer. Turgut noted the frisson of interest among the spectators when a fat pale-skinned man was pushed up on the block. He was too soft and chubby to be a labourer, and the first price at the badestan was already substantial, 800 pieces of eight in the Spanish money or nearly 1,500 Algerian piastres. Turgut wondered if someone had secretly investigated the man's value. In the slave trade you had to know what you were doing, particularly if you thought you were buying someone worth a ransom. Then the bidding became hectic, both sides gambling on just how much money might be squeezed out of the infidel's family and friends. So a common technique when prisoners were first landed was to place among them informers who pretended to be in similar hardship. They befriended the new arrivals and, when they were at their most vulnerable, wormed out personal details – the amount of property they owned at home, the importance of their families, the influence they had with their governments. All was reported back and reflected in the price at the Dey's auction. On this occasion the fat man was clearly English for it was the English consul's dragoman who was defending the original bid, and when the Dey's agent increased the price only by 500 piastres before dropping out, Turgut suspected that the dragoman had already paid a bribe to the Dey to ensure that the fat man was placed in the consul's care.

Turgut had only a token tussle over the final price for the black-haired young man. The captive looked too slight to be much use as a common labourer and, besides, there was a glut of slaves in the city. So the eventual price of 200 piastres was reasonable enough, as was the fee of 250 pieces of eight which he had to pay for the sailor whose name, according to the auction roster, was Dunton. If the latter proved to be a shipwright then, according to Turgut's calculations, he would charge the shipyard 6 pieces of eight per month for his labour.

Turgut was leaving the Kasbah, well satisfied with his purchases, when he came face to face with someone he had been trying to avoid for the past few weeks – the khaznadji, the city treasurer. The encounter was unfortunate because Turgut was severely in arrears with his taxes on the value of the plunder that he had earned when his ship was seaworthy. Not that the Captain of Galleys believed the meeting was accidental, because the khaznadji was flanked by two odjaks wearing their regulation red sashes and yatagans, the ceremonial dagger. The odjaks, as Turgut was all too aware, would be formal witnesses to any conversation.

'I congratulate you, effendi,' murmured the tax collector after the usual compliments and civilities in the name of the Padishah. 'I understand that you have purchased two fine slaves. I wish you well of their employ.'

'I thank you,' answered Turgut. 'I shall put them to useful work in due course.'

'So your ship is to be ready soon?'

The khaznadji knew very well that *Izzet Darya* would be in dock for at least another month, and that as long as his vessel was out of commission, Turgut Reis had no income and a great many expenses, not least of them the mounting costs of the repairs. Being Captain of Galleys was a great honour, but unfortunately it did not carry a stipend. The plundering cruise, the corso, was the only way for him to make a living, just as it was for his crew. Turgut's petty officers and free oarsmen – about half the total – had long ago left to join other galleys. His slave oarsmen came from a contractor, and Turgut had been obliged to terminate the agreement prematurely. Unfortunately the disappointed slave contractor was also the khaznadji.

'Inshallah, my ship will be afloat before long,' Turgut replied smoothly, deciding it was better that he bought himself some time with a gesture of generosity, though he could ill afford one. 'Those two slaves, which you admire, perhaps you would do me the honour of accepting one of them on loan. That would give me pleasure.'

The khaznadji lifted his hand in a small graceful gesture,

acknowledging the gift. He had what he wanted, compensation for the cancelled hire contract. If the Captain of Galleys went bankrupt, which would surely happen if his antique galley was not repaired in time, the slave would automatically become his property.

Privately the khaznadji despised Turgut. He thought the man was an old fogey who considered himself superior to the Algerines and because the captain came from the Seraglio, the imperial court, he presumed that the young black-haired slave had been purchased for his sexual gratification. It would be amusing to humiliate the captain still further by exposing his handsome young man to abuse.

'You are too kind. I admire your generosity, and indeed it is a difficult choice. With your permission, I select the dark-haired one. But it would be improper to retain him for my household, so I shall place him to the benefit of the city. I will assign him to the beylik, to do public labour.'

He bowed and moved on, feeling that he had extracted the best possible outcome from the encounter.

ℂ

ON HIS WAY back home after the awkward meeting with the khaznadji, Turgut Reis knew what he would do to restore his normal good humour. His house was one of the privileges that came with his rank as Captain of Galleys. A four-storey mansion, it was positioned on almost the highest point of the city, with a magnificent view out over the harbour and the sea beyond. To take full advantage of the location, Turgut had caused a garden to be created on the flat roof. His servants had carried up hundreds of baskets of earth and laid out flower-beds. Sweet-smelling shrubs had been selected and planted, and a dozen trees rooted in large tubs to shade the spot where Turgut liked to sit cross-legged, gazing over the view and listening to the distant sounds of the city spread out below him. Now, reaching the roof garden, he called for his favourite carpet to be brought out. It was an Usak in the old-fashioned Anatolian style and made with the Turkish knot. In Turgut's opinion the more recent and popular Seraglio designs with their profusion of tulips and hyacinths and roses were much too showy, though he had to admit that the Persian knotting did give them a softer, more velvety surface. But only the Usak carpet with its pattern of repeated stars was the appropriate setting for his most prized possession – the Kitab-i Bahriye.

He waited patiently while his steward brought up the beautifully carved bookstand, and then the volume itself. Turgut looked down at the cover of the book and allowed himself a few moments of anticipation before he opened it and relished the treasures within. Of course, there were other versions of the Book of Sea Lore as the infidels called it. Indeed the Padishah himself owned the most lavishly illustrated copy in existence, a volume prepared specially for the Sultan of Sultans. But the copy lying before Turgut was unique. It was the original. Prepared 150 years ago by Turgut's forebear, the peerless Piri Reis, the book of maps and charts and its accompanying collection of sailing notes had been passed down in his family for six generations. It was the wellspring from which all other versions had been drawn.

Turgut leaned forward and opened the book at random. He knew every page by memory, yet he never failed to be awed by the vision of the man who had created it. 'God has not granted the possibility of displaying everyone of the afore-mentioned places such as harbours and waters around the shores of the Mediterranean, and the reefs and shoals in the water, in a single map,' he read. 'Therefore experts in this science have drawn up what they call a "chart" with a pair of compasses according to a scale of miles, and it is written directly on a parchment.'

Here was the genius of his ancestor, thought Turgut. The man who wrote those words was much more than the Sultan's High Admiral and a great war leader. He also had the curiosity and penetration to study and learn, and the generosity to donate his knowledge to others.

Gently Turgut untied the silk ribbons of an accompanying folder. It contained a very special map also prepared by Piri, a map of much greater ambition for it summarised what the admiral had been able to find out about the great western ocean beyond the straits which divide Spain and Ifriqya. This map depicted lands far, far out towards the setting sun, places which neither the High Admiral nor the Captain of Galleys had ever visited, but only knew by repute. Piri Reis had spent years sifting and collating information in the writings and log books of infidels as well as Moors in order to assemble this map, the first of its kind in the Padishah's Empire, copied and admired in many lands.

Turgut picked out a typical comment written in the admiral's neat hand, beside a sketch of a weird-looking beast on the west coast of Ifriqya. 'In this country it seems that there are white-haired monsters in this shape, and also six-horned oxen. The Portuguese infidels have written it in their maps.' Turgut sat back and considered. That sentence had been penned a century and a half earlier, yet already the infidels had been showing signs of surpassing the Faithful in their knowledge of the seas and how to navigate them. How had that come to pass? When he looked up into the night sky and searched for the stars that guide mariners at sea, they bore the names that the Faithful had given them, because it was the Moors who had first learned how to use them to find their way at night. Some said the Faithful were obliged to do this because they travelled on the haj across the vast expanses of the desert, and they needed the stars to guide them on their pilgrimage to the sacred places. So Allah in his infinite wisdom had placed the stars in the sky for this purpose. But now it was the infidels who were travelling farthest, and using these same stars to steer by. They were at the fore-front of knowledge. Infidels were designing and building the finest sea-going ships even in the dockyards of Algiers; infidel cartographers drew the best charts; and unbelievers had sailed all the way around the globe.

But Turgut Reis had a secret that he had never revealed to anyone: one day he would, in a splendid gesture, demonstrate that the Faithful still possessed the skills that Allah had bestowed on the followers of the Prophet and, at the same time, burnish his own family tradition. He, Turgut Reis, might never be able to circumnavigate the globe like an infidel, nor explore the farther fringes of the western ocean, but he had the means and the opportunity to expand the Book of Sea Lore that his ancestor had pioneered, and that was just as momentous. That is why, every time he went on the corso, he carried with him his notebooks and brushes, why he made notes of the harbours and anchorages, and drew sketches of the coastlines. The day would come, if Allah willed it, when he would organise all these notes and drawings, and produce a new edition of the Kitab-i Bahriye, updating it to show all the changes that had taken place in the Mediterranean since the days of the High Admiral. It would be his personal homage to the memory of his ancestor.

Belatedly he had come to realise the magnitude of the task ahead of him, and now he worried that its accomplishment was slipping from his grasp. Through God's will he lacked sons who might share in the great design, and with each passing year he felt the burden of his ancestry resting more heavily on his shoulders. In short, he needed a capable assistant to make sense of all his notes, organise his many sketches, and draw fair copies of his maps and charts. Perhaps, Turgut thought to himself, the young man he had bought that day might be just the amanuensis he needed. That, too, might be the gift of Allah.

Turgut bowed his head and closed his eyes. His lips moved in a silent prayer, as he beseeched the Most Merciful, the All-Merciful, that he would be granted a life long enough to fulfil that ambition, and that his eyesight would not fail prematurely.

Suddenly Turgut felt chilly. While he had been daydreaming, the sun had sunk behind the mountains, and the evening was growing cold. He clapped his hands to summon a servant and picked up the Kitab. Cradling it like his own child, he descended the stairs from the roof top, entered his library and replaced the volume in its box of cedar wood. Behind him the servant carried the precious ocean map in its folder, and then stood waiting until his master had laid it safely beneath a coverlet of dark green velvet. As Turgut took one last glance around his library to make sure that everything was in its proper place, he wondered if there was any way that he could retrieve the black-haired boy from the clutches of the khaznadji before the drudgery of being a beylik slave ruined him.

SIX

C

THE KHAZNADJI was quick to satisfy his grudge. A servant separated Hector from the other captives in the Dey's courtyard, and began to herd him briskly through the narrow city streets. When the bewildered young man asked where he was being taken, his escort only repeated, 'Bagnio! Bagnio!' and urged him to hurry. For a while Hector believed that he was being taken to a bath house to be washed, for he was filthy and dishevelled. But arriving before a grim-looking stone building he swiftly understood that his anticipation was completely misplaced. The building appeared to be a cross between a prison and a barracks, and the stench wafting out of its massive doors, which stood open, made him gag. It was a foul combination of human excrement, cooking smells, soot and unwashed bodies.

After a short delay a bored-looking guard took him in charge, then led him to a side room where a blacksmith fitted an iron ring around his right ankle, hammering down the rivet which held it shut. Next he was led to another anteroom where a barber roughly shaved his head, and then to a clothes store. Here the garments in which he had been captured were taken away and he was issued with a bundle containing a coarse blanket, a smock, and a curious item of dress which he at first took to be a woman's petticoat. Shaped like an open sack, it was

sewn across the base, leaving two slits through which he was
shown to put his legs so as to make a very baggy pair of
pantaloons. He was also given a pair of slippers and a red cap,
and another attendant recorded his name in a ledger. Finally he
was ushered down the length of a vaulted passageway and thrust
out into the open courtyard which formed the centre of the
great building. Here he was finally left to himself.

Hector looked around. He was in the largest building he had
ever known. The rectangular courtyard was at least fifty paces
by thirty, and open to the skies. On either side an arched
colonnade ran the full length of the building, its arches supporting a second-floor gallery. From dim recesses between the arches
came the sounds of drunken singing and loud voices quarrelling
and shouting. To his astonishment a Turkish soldier, undoubt-
edly the worse for drink, came reeling and staggering out of
the shadows and made his way to the gate. He weaved his way
past a number of sick or exhausted slaves lying on the ground
or sitting propped against the walls. Hector started to walk
hesitantly across the open courtyard, clutching his blanket and
wondering what he should do next, or where he should go. The
whole building seemed unnaturally empty, though it was clearly
designed to house at least a couple of thousand inmates. He
had walked no more than a few yards when he felt someone's
eyes on him. Looking up, he noticed a man leaning out over
the balcony from the upper floor, watching him closely. The
stranger was a man of middle age, round-headed and with his
dark hair cropped close. Half his body remained in shadow, but
it was evident that he was powerfully built. Hector paused, and
the stranger beckoned to him, then pointed to the corner of the
courtyard where a stairway led to the upper floor. Grateful for
some guidance, Hector made his way to the staircase and began
to climb.

He was met as he emerged on the upper floor and at closer
quarters he did not like what he saw. The man was dressed in
baggy pantaloons and a loose overmantle and wore the red cap

and iron anklet which, Hector now presumed, marked him as a fellow slave. But the man's smile was patently false. 'Benvenuto, benvenuto,' he said, indicating that Hector should follow him. He led Hector a short distance along the balcony, then turned to the right, and Hector found himself in what was evidently some sort of dormitory. Crudely made wooden bunk beds, four tiers high, were packed tightly together, with scarcely room to squeeze between them. There was no window and the only light came through the open doorway. With such little ventilation the room reeked of sweat. All the bunks were empty except for one which contained a lump under a blanket which Hector supposed was either someone asleep or dead.

'Venga, venga,' his guide squeezed his way between the bunks to the back of the room, and was again beckoning to him to follow. Hector saw that the corner of the dormitory had been curtained off by a length of cloth hung from a line. He stepped forward, and the man held aside the curtain so he could pass. As soon as Hector was inside the cubicle, the man dropped the curtain and, from behind, pinioned Hector's arms to his sides. He felt the man's unshaven cheek press against the back of his neck, and hot, fetid breath filled his nostrils. He dropped his blanket and tried to break free, but the stranger's grip was too powerful. 'Calma, calma,' the man was saying, as he wrestled Hector forward until his face was pressed against the wall of the cubicle. Hector felt the man's gut pressing against his back, as he was pinioned in position. A moment later his assailant was pawing at Hector's shirt with one hand, pulling upward, while the other hand was dragging downwards at his loose pantaloons which fell down towards his knees. His attacker was snorting with excitement and lust. Appalled, Hector realised that he was being raped. He thrashed from side to side, trying again to free himself, but it was useless. Every move was anticipated, and Hector was forced harder against the wall. The man was surging now, trying to force himself into Hector, and grunting with effort. Hector felt waves of revulsion.

Abruptly there was a choking grunt, and the pressure pushing him against the wall eased. 'Bastanza!' said a new voice sharply, and there was a gurgling sound. Hector pushed himself clear of the wall and turned to see his assailant clutching at his throat, his thick body arched back, and a third person in the cubicle, half hidden behind his would-be rapist. The newcomer was holding a leather belt which he had looped around the attacker's neck and was now using as a garrotte. 'Bastanza! Bestia!' the newcomer added, pulling the noose tighter so that the cord began to cut off the windpipe. Shaking with shock, Hector pulled up his pantaloons and staggered out of the cubicle, remembering only to scoop up his blanket from the floor.

He blundered past the ranks of bunk beds, and somehow managed to find his way out to the balcony. There he leaned against the balustrade, gasping for air. He felt defiled and frightened. Moments later he sensed someone emerge from the dormitory and stand beside him. 'Are you all right?' It was the voice of his rescuer, and the question was spoken in English. Hector raised his head to look into the face of the man who had saved him. His rescuer was about his own age yet resembled no other man he had seen in his life. His eyes were so dark brown as to appear almost black, and long, straight jet-black hair hung down to his shoulders, framing a narrow face with high cheekbones and a strong nose. His rescuer's skin, Hector was astonished to see, was the colour of peat.

'Malo umbre – a bad man, that one,' explained the newcomer. 'Best you stay out of his way. He's a kaporal and a friend of the aga di baston.'

'Thank you for what you did,' blurted Hector, still shocked.

The man shrugged. 'He cheated me last week. Took my money for a gileffo, and then did nothing. Now he's got a sore throat to remember me by.'

'I'm sorry but I don't understand.'

'A gileffo is what you pay when you want to have the day

off from work. It goes to a kaporal who then arranges with the scrivano that your name is not in the morning roll call.'

He saw that Hector was still too shaken to understand, so abandoned the explanation. 'I am called Dan,' he said, holding out his hand. As he shook hands, Hector noticed that his rescuer had a deep, lilting accent vaguely similar to the way the Devon sailor Dunton spoke.

'I'm Hector, Hector Lynch,' he explained. 'I come from Ireland.'

'I met some Irish when I was a small boy. With them I practised speaking English,' said Dan. 'They had run away from their masters and came to us. We sheltered them, the mesquins. Now I know what it was like for them to be slaves. They told us that they had been sold as punishment for making war in their own country, and sent far from their homes.'

It took Hector several moments to grasp that Dan was speaking about prisoners from Cromwell's campaign in Ireland. He remembered his father telling him how thousands of Irishmen had been shipped to the West Indies and sold off to work as slaves on the plantations. Some of them must have fled their masters.

'You are from the Caribbees?' he asked.

'From the Main, the Miskito coast,' replied Dan. 'My people are Miskito, and we have no love for the Spanish who would take our lands. My father, who is a great man among us, sent me on a mission to the King of the English. I was to request that the Miskito become his subjects and, in return, he would supply us with guns to fight off the Spanish. It was my bad fortune to be captured by the Spanish even before I left the Main, and they put me on a ship for Spain to show me off to the people. But their ship was taken by corsairs, and I have finished up here.'

'How long ago was that?'

'I've been here for six months now, and it was lucky for you that I was not at work today. I paid another gileffo to a more honest kaporal, and he arranged it. Here, let me carry your blanket. You need a proper place to put your things.'

Dan led Hector along the balcony, explaining that the bagnio was ruled by a senior Turk known as the guardian bashaw. Under him were his lieutenants, the assistant bashaws, and below them came the kaporals. 'Most of the kaporals are all right provided you pay them a few coins,' Dan stated. 'Not like Emilio who gave you trouble. He blackmails young men. Threatens to have them punished under false charges unless they agree to be his lovers. He and the aga di baston – that's the Turk in charge of beatings – have the same tastes. They both enjoy man love, and there are no women in the bagnio, only men.'

'But Emilio is not a Turkish name,' said Hector.

'The kaporals are not Turks. They are from other countries. Emilio is from some place in Italy, but there are also kaporals from France and Spain, from all over. They are rinigatos, men who have taken the turban, and now have an easier life. You'll find rinigatos everywhere. One has even become the guardian bashaw in another bagnio. A man like Emilio will never go back to Italy. He has too good a time here.'

They had reached another dormitory farther along the balcony. It was arranged in much the same way with tiers of closely packed bunks.

'All the bunks are already taken,' explained Dan, 'but there's enough room to sling a hammock in this space next to my bunk. Tomorrow I'll get hold of some cords and rope. We Miskito use hammocks when we go on hunting trips in the forest so it will be no trouble to make you one. For now you can borrow my straw mattress and sleep on the floor. I'll fix things up with the dormitory kaporal later.'

'I can't thank you enough,' said Hector. 'Everything around here seems so strange and brutal.'

Dan shrugged. 'In my country we are taught to work together when life is hard, and to share what we have. I would offer you some food, but I have nothing left over, and the next rations will not be issued until tomorrow.'

Hector realised that he had not eaten all day and was very hungry.

'The bagnio ration is not much,' Dan added. 'Just a hunk of black bread, and often that is mouldy. You want to stick close to whoever is your gang leader. He'll be given a bowl of vinegar with maybe a few drops of olive oil sprinkled in it. You can dip your bread into the bowl during the meal breaks.'

'Will you be there too?'

'No,' said Dan. 'I live in the bagnio because my master has not enough accommodation for his slaves. He pays a weekly fee to the guardian bashaw to house me. I work as a gardener. I look after my master's masseries outside the city wall, weeding, cultivating, harvesting, all that sort of thing. I go there each morning after roll call. That's where I'll be able to steal the cord for your hammock, from one of his work sheds.'

'So what will I be doing?'

Dan glanced down at Hector's ankle with its iron ring. 'You are a public slave, so you'll do whatever the scrivano assigns you to. It may be in the stone quarries or down at the harbour unloading boats. They'll tell you in the morning.'

'All these words you use, "scrivano", "masserie", and the others, they seem strange yet familiar. What do they mean?'

'That's our bagnio language. A scrivano is a scribe, and a masserie is a garden,' said Dan. 'You must learn the language fast if you are to get by in here. On the work gangs all the commands are given in that tongue – we call it lingua franca, though that seems odd because most of it is Spanish not French. Even the Turks use it when they are speaking with the Moors who don't understand Turkish. There are so many different peoples held in the bagnio, all with their own languages, that we must have a way of understanding one another.'

'My mother was from Spain,' said Hector, 'and she taught me and my sister to speak her language.'

'Then you are fortunate,' commented Dan. 'Some prisoners seem never to learn to speak the lingua franca – the moskovits, for example, who come from the northern lands. They are always apart, and I feel doubly sorry for them because there is never any chance that they will be free. No one in their own country sends money to pay for their release. Some other countries send priests with chests of coin to purchase the liberty of their countrymen. The French do that, and the Spanish also. But their priests often quarrel.'

'What about the English? Do they buy back their people?'

'I don't know for sure. There's a rumour that this will happen soon, when the King in London has enough money to spend on his subjects. If that happens I will continue my journey and bring greetings to the King of England from the Miskito.'

Hector could no longer hold back the question that had been tormenting him since he landed.

'Dan, you said that there are only men in the bagnio. What happens to women who are captured by the corsairs? Where do they go?'

The Miskito heard the anguish in Hector's voice.

'Why do you ask? Do you know a woman who was captured? Your wife, perhaps?'

'My sister, Elizabeth. She was taken at the same time as myself, but placed on another ship, and she did not arrive here in Algiers.'

'Is Elizabeth beautiful?'

'My sister's friends used to say that Elizabeth was bathed in May dew when she was a baby. Where I come from the young women go out at dawn on the first day of May to gather the morning dew and wash their faces with it. They believe the dew makes them beautiful for the coming year.'

'If she is as lovely as you say,' answered Dan, 'then you need have no fears about her safety. The Turks treat their women captives very differently from the men. They never expose the women in public, and they treat them with respect.

But they are still prisoners, and if they come from rich or powerful families, the Turks will demand a great ransom for their release.'

'And what if a woman does not have a rich family?' Hector asked quietly.

'Then a good-looking woman will find a place in her owner's household. Maybe she will be a servant or – and this has happened – she even marries her captor.' Dan paused. He was wondering how to explain gently that it was far more likely that Elizabeth would become her master's concubine when a sudden sound of catcalls and jeers came up from the courtyard. 'Come. The work gangs are returning. There's more to know if you are to survive in the bagnio.'

The two men returned to the balcony, and Hector looked down into the courtyard to see crowds of slaves pouring into the compound. All of them wore the red slave cap, and most looked gaunt and emaciated. One group was powdered with chalky dust which, Dan explained, showed that they had returned from a day working in the stone quarries. Others had streaks of dried mud on their arms and faces as they had been cleaning out the city sewers. A few slaves headed straight for the arcades, several climbed the stairways towards their dormitories but the majority loitered in the courtyard, gossiping or filling in time. Packs of cards and dice appeared as half a dozen gambling sessions began.

'Where do they get their money?' he asked Dan as a group of card players began tossing small coins into the centre of their circle. 'They don't get paid wages, do they?'

Dan laughed. 'No. They steal.' He pointed out a man whose face, even from that distance, looked badly mutilated. 'That one is the king of the thieves. He's a Sicilian. He was caught several times by the Turks, and thrashed. But it did not deter him. Finally the aga di baston lopped off his nose and ears as punishment. But that still had no effect. He simply can't leave off stealing. It's his nature, and now the Turks treat his thievery as a joke.'

More and more slaves were entering the courtyard, which was slowly filling up with men. Without warning a brawl broke out between two groups. There were shouts and curses. Punches were thrown, and two men were down on the ground, mauling one another.

'Remember what I said, about the moskovits,' observed Dan. 'They are the ones with the heavy beards and matted hair. The darker-skinned slaves they are fighting look like they are Spaniards. It's not enough that we are all slaves of the Muslims, but we have to quarrel among ourselves about who worships the Christ god properly. The Spaniards and Italians insult the Greeks, the Greeks spit on the moskovits, and all of them mock – what do you call it – the Puritana.'

'The Puritans. I know what you mean. The Puritana, as you call them, are those who enslaved the Irish you met at home,' commented Hector. 'In my country, too, there are bitter quarrels between those who call themselves Protestant and those who respect the Pope in Rome.'

Dan shook his head, perplexed. 'I have never been able to understand why the Christians manage to have so many quarrels and hatreds among themselves. We Miskito all believe in the same gods and spirits, whether they are of the sun or rain or hurricane or in the sea. Slavery to us is natural. We ourselves hunt slaves, taking them from the weaker tribes around us. But we make them slaves only to do our work and because it gives prestige to their owners, not because we hate their religion.'

The fighting in the courtyard had attracted the attention of the Turkish guards from the gate. They came running into the courtyard and began to break up the fight using whips and cudgels to separate the contestants. The Russians and their opponents drew apart, still looking sullen, but they offered no resistance to the intervention of the guards.

'Whatever happens,' advised Dan, 'whether you are kicked or whipped, or punched in the face by a Turk, you must never strike back. I could pull that unnatural beast Emilio off you because he is foreign-born. But if he had been a true Turk, my certain punishment would be death. Never hit or insult our Turkish masters, that is one rule which everyone respects. Even if the Turk is drunk.'

'But how can that be? I thought that the Mussulmen are forbidden to take alcohol.'

'I'll show you something,' answered Dan, and led him towards the stairway.

They descended to the courtyard and Hector followed the Miskito into one of the side rooms in the arcade. It was a tavern, and doing a thriving business. The place was crowded with slaves, drinking and carousing, the smoke from their clay pipes creating a thick fug that made Hector's eyes water.

'Where does he get the alcohol?' he whispered to Dan, nodding towards the landlord behind his counter at the back of the room. 'He buys it from the merchant ships who come to trade in Algiers, or from the corsair captains who capture it as part of their booty. Then he resells it, often to the Turks themselves because the city authorities turn a blind eye to their own people who come into the bagnio for a drink, provided they don't make an exhibition of themselves.'

Hector noticed a small group of Turks standing close to the counter who were obviously the worse for drink. 'Look behind them,' said Dan, lowering his voice. 'Those big men over there, they're paid by the landlord to keep an eye on the Turks. If any Turk gets drunk and it looks as if he will make trouble, one of those fellows will quietly escort him out of the bagnio. The landlord cannot afford a disturbance. If there is a fight, the guardian bashaw has the power to shut his tavern and order him to be beaten, even though the landlord is giving him a cut of the profits.'

'You mean to say that customers of the tavern can just walk in and out of the bagnio?'

'Yes, until an hour or so after dusk. That is when the gates are locked shut.' Dan cocked his head to one side. 'Listen, you hear that shouting? It's the beylik foreman. He's calling out what the jobs will be tomorrow. It's time we went back up to the dormitory. If it's your first day at work, you'll need all the rest you can get.'

As they climbed back up the staircase Hector asked why the slaves did not attempt to escape if the gates were left open.

'Where would they go?' Dan replied. 'If they run inland, the Moors of the countryside will catch them and bring them back to the city and receive a reward. If they get as far as the mountains, they will be eaten by wild animals. Should they reach the desert beyond the mountains they will get lost and die of thirst.'

'Couldn't they steal a ship?'

'The Turks have thought of that, too. When a galley comes into port after a corso, the first thing they do is order the galley slaves to dump all the oars overboard into the harbour. Then the oars are towed ashore and placed in a secure warehouse. A few slaves have managed to escape by swimming out to visiting merchant ships and stowing away. But the ship captains take good care to search their own vessels before they leave Algiers. If the Turks find an escaped slave aboard a visiting ship, they'll seize the vessel and put it up for sale. The captain and his crew are lucky if they are not enslaved as well.'

They had reached their dormitory, and Hector stretched out on the lumpy straw palliasse Dan had lent him. He lay there, listening to the sounds of the other slaves settling to their rest, the creaking of the bunks, the grumbles and mutterings, the coughs and spitting as men cleared quarry dust from their lungs and mouths, and the gradual chorus of snores. He felt the nagging, hard pressure of the iron ring around his ankle, and after everything he had learned that day he wondered if he would ever find out what had happened to Elizabeth.

SEVEN

©

'WAKE UP YOU DOGS! Rise you foul unbelievers! Wake and get to work!' Hoarse shouts from the courtyard of the bagnio roused Hector the next morning. The man in the lowest bunk close to him groaned. Then he farted loudly and deliberately so that Hector supposed it was his customary sardonic way of greeting the new day. Holding his breath, Hector got to his feet. 'Time to get going.' It was Dan's voice. The Miskito was already out of his bunk and folding his blanket. 'Get down to the courtyard and listen for your name in the roll call. Then follow what the others do. Try to stay in the background. I'll see you this evening.'

It was barely light, and Hector heard a thin wailing call, then another and another, the sound hanging in the air over the high walls of the bagnio as he descended the stairway to the courtyard. He had heard that cry five times a day since he had been landed at Algiers. It was the adhan, the Muslim call to prayer. At the foot of the stairway he almost tripped over an old man already down on his knees, touching his forehead to the ground. The iron ring around his ankle showed that he was a fellow slave and Hector presumed he was a convert to Islam. When the old man rose stiffly, Hector took the chance to enquire, 'The end of that call, the part which goes something

66

like as-saltu kairun min an-naum, what does that mean?' 'It means "prayer is better than sleep", the old man muttered grumpily, and shuffled off to join the throng of slaves gathering around the entrance to the passageway which led to the gates of the bagnio.

Hector followed and, peering over the heads of the crowd, saw the red-capped figure of a scrivano standing on a stone block, a paper in his hand. He was gabbling out names at a tremendous pace, speaking so fast that it was difficult to catch what he was saying though it was clear that he was directing the men to their day's tasks. Finally Hector heard his name called out, and managed to identify that he had been assigned to a gang of about fifty men forming up under the supervision of an overseer equipped with a short staff. Among them he recognised the Sicilian master thief with the chopped-off nose and ears. Hector looked carefully but he could see none of the men who had been taken prisoner with him in Ireland. He could only imagine they had all been placed in other bagnios. Mindful of Dan's advice, he mingled with his group, trying not to attract attention as they headed down the passageway towards the bagnio gates. No one spoke.

They walked for more than an hour. First through the city, then out of the landward gate and, after a long slow uphill trudge, to a place where the hill had been cut open in a long scar, the pale rock showing raw in the morning light. Only then did Hector understand that he had been assigned to quarry work. A scatter of tools lay where they had been abandoned the day before – sledgehammers, wedges, crowbars, shovels and coils of rope. All the equipment was battered and poorly maintained. Hector paused, wondering what was expected of him. Immediately the overseer was yelling at him, 'Aia! Subito!', and pointing towards a sledgehammer with a splintered handle. As the sun rose higher and the day grew hotter, he found himself working in partnership with a gaunt, silent Russian. Their task was to gouge a line of holes in the rock face, each hole about a yard from the previous one. They took it in turns, one man swinging the sledgehammer, the other holding a metal spike which served as the rock chisel. Very quickly Hector's arms and shoulders were aching from the weight of the hammer, and his hands were swollen and bruised from his grip on the spike though he took care to wrap his fingers in a rag. They had prepared four holes and were starting on a fifth when something changed. The nearby workmen had stopped work. The sounds of hammering and chipping had ceased, and suddenly the quarry was silent. Hector put aside the iron spike, stretched, and flexed his hand to ease the cramp. Abruptly the Russian said his first words in hours – 'Boum! Boum! Boum!' – flung aside the sledgehammer and took to his heels. Hector hesitated only for a moment, then started to follow. He had taken only a few strides when there was a deep, heavy explosion and the ground beneath his feet heaved. A blast of air pushed him forward and he fell face down, landing painfully on rubble. A moment later shards of rock and pebbles began to fall from the sky, pattering all around him. One or two struck him painfully on his back as he wrapped his arms around his head to protect himself.

Shaken and half deafened, he got to his feet. A wide section of the rock face close to where they had been working now lay tumbled down in great slabs at the foot of the cliff. The other slaves thought his narrow escape was a great joke, and were hooting and laughing. The Sicilian was making a weird braying and snorting sound as he guffawed, the air gushing out of his ruined nose. Hector understood that they had known about the impending blast, and deliberately chosen not to warn him. He smiled ruefully at them, rubbed his bruises and silently cursed them for their uncouth sense of humour. He blamed himself for failing to realise that the holes were for gunpowder charges that would split the rock. 'Subito! Subito!' the overseer was shouting again angrily and gesticulating that the slaves were to get back to their places. Hector turned and was about to pick up the sledgehammer when there was a second explosion, smaller this time and farther along the rock face. A cloud of dust spurted out, and several chunks of rock hurtled through the air. One fragment, the size of an orange, struck a man who had been walking forward to check the newly exposed rock face. There was a grunt of pain as the man staggered back, clutching his right arm.

This time there was no laughter. The other slaves looked on nervously. 'Subito! Subito!' bellowed the overseer. He rushed forward, this time striking the slaves with his goad, driving them back to work. Hector, still dizzy from the earlier blast, failed to move. The overseer caught sight of him and waved at him to go to the assistance of the stricken man. Hector went forward and put an arm around the victim, who was gritting his teeth with pain and cursing in English. 'Shit powder. Shitting cheap powder.' Hector helped him to where he could sit down on a coil of rope. The man bent forward in pain, still clutching his shoulder and swearing. He did not wear a slave's iron ring on his ankle, and was better dressed than the men from the bagnio.

'Is there anything I can do?' offered Hector. The man shook his head angrily.

'Should have known better than to trust that muck,' he said and kicked angrily at a nearby keg. Hector saw that it was marked with a triple x in red paint. 'Cheap bastards. Should learn to make their own powder,' continued the injured man.

'What happened?' asked Hector.

'Late blast,' came the short reply. 'Should have all gone off at once, but this powder is useless. The Turks must have bought it off some swindling trader who knew it was unfit.'

Hector supposed that the injured man was some sort of technician in charge of the blasting. The man kicked at the keg again, and it rolled on one side. It had the letters d, m, n scratched across the base.

'Those letters on the base. Maybe they are short for "damno"

– Latin for "condemned",' Hector volunteered. The technician looked at him.

'A smart-arse are you? But you're probably right. Here, go off and check the other kegs stored under that tarpaulin over there before this happens again.'

Hector did as he was told and came back to report that two out of the eight kegs stacked there also had the code scratched on them. The technician spat. 'I'll get the overseer to assign you as my assistant. I'm going to be useless with this damaged arm for the next few weeks, and the quarrying never stops.'

©

THAT EVENING Hector arrived in the bagnio so exhausted that he could barely put one foot in front of the other. He was also half-starved. As anticipated, the only meal of the day had been an issue of coarse bread, delivered mid-morning by two elderly slaves wheeling a barrow. To quench their thirst the slaves only had water from an open cask, filthy with a film of quarry dust floating on the surface. 'Here eat some of this,' offered Dan when they met up in a corner of the courtyard. He unwrapped a bundle and Hector saw that it contained a melon, some beans and several squashes. Hector accepted the offer gratefully.

'I usually manage to sneak away a few vegetables from my gardening at the end of the day,' said Dan. 'My master probably knows that this is happening, but he doesn't make a fuss. He appreciates it is as a cheap way of feeding his slaves to keep up their strength, and that we'll work better if we have a share in the crop. Anything extra that I don't eat myself, I sell in the bagnio.'

'Is that how you obtain the money for the gileffo?' asked Hector.

'Yes, everyone in the bagnio tries to have some sort of extra income. I sell my vegetables in the evening; others do odd jobs. In this place we have shoemakers, cutlers, barbers, tailors, all sorts. The lucky ones manage to get themselves jobs in the city, working for Turks or Moors, either full-time or on Friday, which is our day off. It's the ones who don't have a trade who suffer. They're work animals, nothing more.'

Hector told him about the accident at the quarry. 'The technician who was hurt, he was English yet he wasn't wearing a slave ring nor a red hat. How does that come about?'

'He'll be one of the skilled men to whom the Turks give their liberty in exchange for using their skills,' suggested Dan. 'Or he might be a volunteer, someone who's come to Algiers to find work. The Turks don't insist they convert, just so long as they do their jobs. Some of them have nice houses and even have their own servants. There's a master shipwright in the Arsenal, a Venetian, who is so much in demand that he's paid more by the Turks than when he worked at the Venice ship-yards.'

'The technician wants me to assist him until his arm has healed,' said Hector. 'He seems a decent fellow.'

'Then if I were you, I'd make myself as useful as possible to that powder man,' advised Dan without hesitation. 'It will mean that you have to spend less time swinging a sledgehammer or crawling through the sewers with the city work gang. Just make sure you learn the usanza.'

'What's that?' Hector asked. He bit hungrily into a piece of raw squash.

'It means custom or habit in the lingua franca. My own people the Miskito have something similar. Our elders who guide us – we call them the old men council – tell us how it was in the old days and they insist we follow the ancient customs.'

He broke off another piece of squash and handed it to Hector.

'It is the same here in the bagnio. The rules and regulations have built up over time and you learn them by watching others or following their example. If you break these rules, the Turks will tell you that it is against usanza and therefore a fantasia.

That means it is unacceptable conduct – and you will be punished. The system suits our masters. The Turks want everything to remain as it is, with them in control. So Jew must remain Jew, Moor must stay Moor, and there is no mixing between different peoples. The Turks go so far as to refuse to let any native-born Algerine become an odjak. Even the son of a Turk and a local woman is forbidden from joining the janissaries. To become an odjak you must either be a Turk from the homelands or a rinigato, a Christian who has converted.'

'I find it strange,' said Hector, 'that foreign slaves are given an opportunity denied to the local people.'

Dan shrugged. 'Many slaves do take the turban. It is said that there are only three ways of getting out of the bagnio: by ransom, by turning Turk, or by dying from the plague.'

EIGHT

ℂ

CONSUL MARTIN was finding mercer Newland a bore. He was beginning to wish that his dragoman had not been so adroit with his bribe to the Dey's office. The tubby English business-man had been released into consular care on the very same day as the slave sale, and for more than a month Consul Martin had been enduring Newland's tedious company while waiting to hear back from London about his ransom. The consul had given the cloth merchant a room in his house, and it was only common courtesy to invite him to dinner from time to time. Unfortunately the mercer had no interesting conversation to offer and held very entrenched opinions, so the invitations, which had originally been once or twice a week, had now lapsed. Consul Martin, however, made an exception when he finally got news that an official government delegation was on its way from London to Algiers to deal with the hostage question. Martin presumed that whoever was raising money in London for Newland's ransom would take the opportunity of sending the payment with the government delegation.

'One hopes that the delegation from London will have a fair wind for their voyage here, Mr Newland,' said the consul, rolling a small pellet of bread between his fingers. It was the last morsel of a flat loaf of particularly delicious local bread. When on his own, the consul adopted the Turkish style of eating, reclining on cushions on the floor. But when he had Christian guests, he kept a more normal service with table and chairs. However, he drew the line at serving hearty meals of roast meat and potatoes. He and his guest had just eaten a delicious lamb kebab and homous. 'The weather in the Mediterranean is very unpredictable. So there's no way of knowing exactly when the envoy will arrive.'

'Have the terms of my release been finally agreed, do you know?' asked the mercer bluntly.

'That I can't say. The envoy is on government business and his official duty is to arrange the ransom of ordinary English captives, not men of substance like yourself.' The consul watched Newland preen himself at the compliment. 'But it is to be expected that your own principal – I think you said it was Mr Sewell of Change Alley – will take advantage of this delegation to conclude the matter of your own release. If all goes well, you should be travelling back with the envoy himself.'

The mercer adopted his usual self-important tone. 'I hope that the negotiations over the ordinary captives, as you call them, will not delay matters.'

'That is difficult to predict. Unfortunately there is a history of the Algerines demanding high ransoms, and the envoy arriving with insufficient funds to meet them. Inevitably a period of offer and counter-offer follows until a final arrangement is agreed.'

'Could you not point out to the Dey and his bandits that I, and the others, should never have been taken prisoner in the first place; that our kidnap broke the terms of the treaty between our countries? You should insist.'

Inwardly the consul grimaced. The thought of insisting on anything with the Dey and the odjaks was counterproductive as well as dangerous. 'The Algerines enjoy bartering,' he commented blandly. 'They feel cheated if there are not some negotiations.'

'Then the bartering should be done by men who are used to

it, to men of affairs,' Newland asserted. 'We would get a better outcome.'

'I'm sure that the local intermediary who acted on your behalf, the Jew Yaakov, was very skilled in his negotiations,' reassured Martin.

'But the treaty, the treaty. The Algerines cannot be allowed to get away with ignoring their treaty obligations.'

The consul thought to himself that Newland, if he had not been so self-opinionated, should know by now that the Dey and the divan made and broke agreements as it suited them. He wondered if he should point out to Newland that many a merchant would vary or break a trade agreement if he could do so without being sued and it was to his advantage. Yet Newland was expecting the Algerines to behave differently when, in fact, their slave-taking was merely a matter of business. In the end the consul decided not to provoke the mercer.

'The fact is, Mr Newland, that when you and those unfortunate Irish were taken prisoner by the corsair Hakim Reis, the treaty was temporarily set aside. The Dey had announced in council that it was being suspended because too many ships were sailing under English passes to which they were not entitled, and that the English were abusing the terms of the treaty by selling their passes to foreign shipowners.'

'So that rascal Hakim Reis was within his rights to take us?'

'Technically, yes. The Dey and the divan had made their decision to abrogate the treaty some weeks earlier. They informed me that a state of war between our nations was being resumed, and I sent word to London to that effect. But there was no public announcement until the same week you were captured.'

'News travels quickly in this part of the world if that corsair scoundrel was so well informed.'

'Hakim Reis is an unusually successful and acute corsair, Mr Newland. He seems always alert to the most immediate opportunity. It was your misfortune to be in his path.'

'And how long did this state of war continue?' persisted Newland. The tone of his question indicated that he thought Martin was making excuses, and that he had failed to insist that the Dey met his obligations.

'For less than two months,' answered the consul, making an effort to keep even-tempered. 'Last week I was summoned to the Dey's palace and told that the treaty would be restored, on the orders of the Sublime Porte. That is an excuse the Dey uses often. He says one thing, then reverses his position, claiming that he has been overruled by the Sultan. But it does mean that the envoy from London will be warmly received and there is every likelihood that your own release is imminent.'

And not a moment too soon, he thought to himself.

℃

THE INJURED mining technician was the first to tell Hector about the rumour of a delegation from London. The two of them were at the quarry, weighing and mixing measures of gunpowder for a new set of blasting charges. The technician, Josias Buckley, seemed strangely unexcited by the news. 'Aren't you looking forward to going home?' Hector asked, puzzled.

'No, I won't be going home as you call it,' Buckley replied as he gently transferred another spoonful of the black powder from a barrel into a canvas pouch. 'I'll be staying here. This is where I've made my life.'

Hector looked at Buckley in astonishment. During his weeks as his assistant, he had grown to respect the man for his skill and the careful, patient way in which he had guided him in the art of handling explosives.

'What about your family? Won't they be missing you?' Hector asked. He was thinking back, as he so often did, to what might have happened to Elizabeth.

'I have no family left,' replied Buckley quietly. 'My wife and I never had children, and she was working at the mill when there was an accident. That was back at home in England, near two years ago now. She and a dozen others were blown to pieces. There was not even enough left of her to give her a proper burial, poor soul. Afterwards I decided I would seek my fortune here in Barbary. I imagined there would be a demand for gunpowder men like myself so I came here of my own free will. The beylik pays me a wage, and I share a house with others like myself, ordinary men who came here to find a new home. The Turks do not demand we change to their religion.'

They finished preparing the gunpowder and were carrying the mix over to the rock face where the work gangs had drilled out the holes ready to receive the charges. Hector noticed how the labourers moved away nervously as they approached. At the first of the holes, Buckley began to pour in the gunpowder. 'Two pounds' weight is about right,' he said to Hector. 'Make sure the powder is packed evenly. No lumps. Here pass me a length of fuse, will you?'

With the powder and fuse in place, he took a conical wooden plug from the sack which Hector had carried for him and, pressing it into the hole, began to tap it into place, the pointed end upward. The first time Hector had seen this done, he had dreaded an accident. But Buckley had reassured him that gunpowder would only ignite with a spark or fire, not from the blow of a hammer. 'Now, lad,' he said, once the plug was driven tight, 'fill the rest of the hole with earth and chippings and tamp everything down so that it is nice and snug. But not too tight so that the fuse chokes off and doesn't burn through.'

They moved on to the next hole in the rock to repeat the process, and Hector took his chance to ask, 'Where was the mill where you worked before?'

'In the county of Surrey where my family had lived for generations. Years ago we used to make up small quantities of gunpowder in our own house until the government regulations came in. Then the big mills took over, and the monopolists had their chance. The small family producers could not compete, so we went to work in the mill. Of course we got jobs straight away as we knew the trade so well. My father and grandfather and his father had all been petremen, as far back as anyone could remember.'

He saw Hector was looking bemused.

'Petremen,' he repeated, 'that's what they called the men who went round the country looking for saltpetre. They had authority to go into hen houses, barnyards, farm middens and take whatever scrapings they could find. Without saltpetre – and a lot of it – there's no gunpowder.'

'Sounds like Latin,' said Hector. 'Sal-petrae would mean "salt of stones", so how come you found it in a hen house?'

'There you go again. You're too smart for your own good, what with all that education,' answered Buckley, poking a wooden rod into the next drill hole to make sure that it was not clogged. 'You find saltpetre wherever stale piss or dung has had time to ripen. Don't ask me how. It's said that the best piss for saltpetre comes out of a drunken bishop.'

He chuckled. 'The petremen would gather up the ordure and carry it back to their homes where they could boil and strain and purify it. Slow work. It takes nearly a hundred pounds of scrapings to make a half pound of petre, and that's the main ingredient for gunpowder – seventy-five parts of petre to ten parts of brimstone and fifteen parts of charcoal, and you should use willow charcoal if you can get it.'

He laid the rod aside and reached out for the bag of tools and materials that Hector was carrying.

'Now everything's different. The gunpowder mills bring in their saltpetre from India. And there's no more grinding by hand, which used to take hours and hours. It's all done by machines. Big stamping machines. And of course the people who are employed don't have the old knowledge, and so accidents happen. A wild spark, and the whole lot goes up. So my wife dies, and both my cousins.'

He paused to cut off another length of fuse cord, and laid it carefully into the next hole before pouring in the correct measure of powder.

'When I first came here,' he went on, 'I had dreams of setting up my own gunpowder mill and supplying good powder to the Turks. In my family there was a story that in the days of Queen Bess we got our petre from Barbary and it was made into the cannon powder that stopped the Great Armada. So I thought I would find petre here in Algiers, and add brimstone from Sicily because everyone knows that you find yellow brimstone near volcanoes. But as it turned out, I never found the petre and the Sicilian brimstone was poor stuff, full of impurities. So I had to go round the local pigeon lofts, just like my great-grandfather, and collect up the droppings. In the end it wasn't worth it. I could make serpentine but not the corned powder that the Turks wanted for their cannon and muskets.'

'I don't know the difference,' Hector said deferentially. He felt that if he was to work safely with Buckley, he should learn everything that the technician was willing to tell him.

'There's a world of difference. Serpentine is what we made at home, basic gunpowder if you like. It's all right if you keep it dry and mix it well. But it's unreliable. It was a charge of serpentine, exploding late, which near cost me my right arm the other day. Corned powder is mill-made, and shaken through sieves so it is graded nice and regular. Small grains for muskets and pistols, larger grains for the big guns. There's no one making corned powder in all the lands of the Grand Turk, as far as I know. Certainly not here in Algiers. Anyone who managed to do so, would command his own price.'

'Talking about price,' Hector ventured, 'if it's true that there's someone coming from London to buy back captives, what sort of price will he be paying?'

Buckley gave the young man a sympathetic glance. 'Whatever his budget allows. And then only if he is an honest man.

There are a lot of sticky fingers when it comes to handling ransoms.'

ℂ

WORK AT THE quarry finished an hour before sunset, and as soon as he was free to do so, Hector hurried back to the bagnio, eager to find Dan. He was looking forward to telling him about the expected envoy from London and that they were soon to be ransomed. From his first day in the bagnio when Dan had rescued him from the lecherous kaporal, Hector had found himself increasingly grateful to his fellow captive. The Miskito had continued to share with him the vegetables he stole from his gardening, and had coached the young Irishman in the ways of the bagnio. Without that knowledge Hector doubted he would have survived.

Hector could not see his friend in the bagnio courtyard, so he went up to their dormitory to see if perhaps Dan had gone there. But without success. Wondering what had detained Dan, Hector was halfway back down the stairway when he noticed two Turkish guards enter the courtyard through the arched passage leading to the main gate. They were carrying a prisoner between them. Hector stopped short. The man hanging between the two guards was Dan, and his legs were trailing limply on the ground. Hector knew at once what had happened. He raced down the stair and across the courtyard, arriving just at the moment the two guards dropped their burden and Dan collapsed on the ground, face down. 'Dan!' he cried anxiously, 'try to get up on your knees, and put one arm over my shoulder. I'll lift you.'

Hearing Hector's voice, Dan raised his head and gave a grimace of pain. 'Usanza and fantasia,' he muttered. 'I forgot my own advice.' Then, his face contorted with the effort, the Miskito half-rose and clung to his friend so that Hector was able to assist him slowly and carefully up to the dormitory where he laid Dan gently on his bunk.

The normally phlegmatic Miskito groaned as he stretched out his legs.

'Was it bad?' asked Hector.

'Forty blows. But it could have been worse. Might have been fifty or more. The aga di baston was that pervert, Emilio's friend. He laid on specially hard for what I did to his crony.'

'How did it happen?'

'It was stupid of me. I was working in the masserie when a Turkish guard discovered a local woman hiding in the bushes nearby. I had seen her several times before, and knew she used to meet up with one of the other gardeners from time to time. He's a Spanish slave and sells stolen vegetables cheaply to her as she's a poor woman and has little money to spare. But the guard thought she was having a love affair with one of the gardeners, and began to beat her. I intervened as the Spaniard wasn't nearby. This made the guard think that I was the lover, and he began beating me too. The commotion brought other guards, and I was taken back down to the bagnio. They clamped my ankles in a wooden yoke which the two guards held up so my shoulders were on the ground and my feet in the air. Then the aga di baston laid on. I was lucky he was beating only the soles of my feet with his staff, for if he had hit me in the ribs I think he would have smashed them. Still, I'm probably luckier than the wretched woman. She'll be severely punished for consorting with a slave.'

'Lie still while I get some salve for your feet from that French prisoner who was an apothecary. He'll sell me some ointment,' said Hector. Dan winced as he reached inside his shirt and produced a purse dangling around his neck. 'Here take the money from this,' he offered. 'Don't let him cheat you.'

'What about tomorrow?' Hector was worried. 'It will be days before you can walk again, and you need rest.'

'Fix it with our friendly kaporal. Give him the remainder of the money. Make it a big enough gileffo so that I am excused work for the next week or so.'

'Leave it to me,' said Hector. 'At least I've some news to cheer you up. Someone's coming from London with money to purchase the release of all English slaves. Maybe when he hears that you were captured by the corsairs when you were on your way to London with a message for the King of England from the Miskito people, he will pay for your release as well so you can complete your mission.'

Dan grinned weakly. 'Your news, my friend, helps dull the pain more than any ointment. If I had to stay here, I don't think that I could face another dose of the bastinado.'

CONSUL MARTIN was a humane and sensitive man so normally he disliked visiting the bagnios. Quite apart from their stench and squalor, the slave barracks depressed him because they made him feel a fraud. His standing instructions from London were to be polite and friendly when meeting with his fellow countrymen held prisoner. But he was also told that he was to avoid being drawn into any discussions about possible release. If pressed, he was to discourage any speculation on the subject.

In the consul's opinion that turned him into a hypocrite.

So he was in an altogether more optimistic mood on the morning he accompanied Mr Abercrombie, the newly arrived English envoy, to interview the prisoners. At last there was a chance to redeem these unfortunate wretches, some of whom had been waiting five or six years for release back to their own country. Nor did the cheerless demeanour of the envoy – the 'commissioner' as he preferred to style himself – dampen the consul's good spirits.

Abercrombie was exactly the sort of person that Martin had expected. He had the manner of a long-serving bookkeeper, and the lugubrious expression on his narrow face was enhanced by a long upper lip and a voice that was lifeless and flat. The commissioner had arrived three days earlier aboard a 40-gun English warship now anchored in the harbour, and his present task was to visit the various bagnios where English prisoners were being held. There the envoy would audit the true value of each slave, for it had been agreed with the Dey that whoever owned the slave was to receive a ransom equal to the sum the slave had originally fetched at auction. Naturally the commissioner made it plain that he mistrusted the accuracy of the sums that the Dey's secretary had written down for him.

Abercrombie had also told the consul that he intended to check the identities of the captives on the Dey's list because it was not unknown for impostors to pretend to be dead or missing prisoners in the hopes of obtaining their freedom. In addition, Abercrombie saw it as his duty to make sure that the captives were in good health. It would be a waste of funds, he primly reminded Martin, to ransom an invalid who would then die on the way home.

The audit was well into its second day by the time that Martin and the commissioner, accompanied by their dragoman, arrived at the bagnio where Hector and Dan were being held. According to the official list there were no more than half a dozen English prisoners in the bagnio, and it was clear to Martin that Abercrombie was eager to finish up quickly. A lieutenant of janissaries met them at the gate. After apologising for the Guardian Pasha's absence, he informed his visitors that all the English prisoners were assembled and ready for their interviews. He then ushered them into the interview room where Martin found the vekil hardj, the Dey's under-treasurer, already waiting. With him was the Greek slave whom Martin remembered as the interpreter who assisted when new captives were landed in the port. Martin also noted that the interviews were to be held in the same room where new prisoners had their iron anklets fitted. A number of these chains and anklets had been left on display. Wryly he surmised that these manacles were a deliberate encouragement for the commissioner to pay generously for the prisoners' release.

The half-dozen cases were soon dealt with, and Abercrombie

was gathering up his documents and about to take his leave when the Greek, on a quiet suggestion from the vekil hardj, spoke up.

'Your Excellency, my master asks if you will be interviewing the other slaves today, or do you wish to return tomorrow?'

The commissioner kept his dour expression. Turning to Martin, he asked, 'What other prisoners? I hope this is not just an attempt to extract additional funds. We have already exceeded our budget as it is. According to the register, there are no other English captives in this slave barracks.'

Martin looked questioningly at the interpreter.

'The people landed by Hakim Reis,' the Greek murmured. 'Their status, you will recall, is undetermined.'

The commissioner was waiting for Martin to explain. 'What is all this about?' he enquired acidly.

'Hakim Reis is a well-known corsair,' began Martin.

'I know, I know,' interrupted Abercrombie. 'He was the man who took the mercer, Newland. His London agent has been pestering the ministry for weeks, and I have brought with me the first instalment of the money for his ransom. This matter need not detain us.'

'There were other prisoners taken by Hakim,' the consul explained. 'I put their names on a separate register and sent a copy to London.'

Abercrombie searched among his papers. 'I have no record of this,' he said peevishly.

'Should we not interview them while we are here?' suggested Martin.

'Very well. But let us not waste any more time.'

The Greek nodded to the guard waiting at the door, and he ushered in a man whom Martin instantly recognised. It was the intelligent-looking youth who had caught his attention on the dock. He was leaner and more tanned, but there was no mistaking his black hair and his alert expression.

'Your name?' snapped the commissioner, obviously impatient with the additional interview.

'Lynch, sir. Hector Lynch.'

'Your place of birth?'

'The county of Cork, sir.'

'That's in Ireland is it not?'

'Yes, sir.'

Abercrombie looked down at the paper on the table before him. 'I do not see your name on this inventory. Your parents and family? Have they made any attempt to contact the authorities in London?'

'My father is dead, sir. And my mother may not know what happened to me. She could have moved back to live with her own people.'

The commissioner raised his head and regarded the young man with mistrust. 'Her own people? Who are they?'

'Her family are from Spain.

'From Spain?' Suspicion had crept into the commissioner's voice. 'She is a Papist?'

'Yes, sir. My mother is of the Catholic faith, my father was Protestant.'

Abercrombie pursed his lips. It was obvious to Consul Martin that the English envoy was now hostile to the young man. His line of questioning soon confirmed his antagonism.

'Your deceased father, was he born in Ireland?'

'He was, sir.'

'And had his family lived there for several generations?'

'That is right.'

Commissioner Abercrombie gave a small dry cough. 'Then I regret, Mr Lynch, that your case falls outside my remit. The treaty between His Majesty's government and the authorities in Algiers regarding the redemption of prisoners, covers only those of His Majesty's subjects born or living in England, Scotland and Wales. There is no mention of Ireland in the text. It would therefore be improper of me to approve disbursement of funds outside the terms of my authority.'

Consul Martin saw a look of disbelief cross the young Irishman's face, followed by one of stubbornness. Lynch remained standing in front of the desk. The commissioner mistook his attitude for incomprehension.

'It means, Mr Lynch, that I am unable to authorise payment from the funds at my disposal in order to effect your release or that of others of his Majesty's Irish subjects. Doubtless that matter can be considered on my return to London. I shall draw attention to this omission, and it is to be hoped that the Council will amend the relevant clauses within the treaty. Until then the matter is out of my hands.'

Martin had been expecting the young Irishman to react with disappointment, even anger. But to his surprise the young man only glanced down at the Dey's list and asked, 'With your honour's permission, are there any women captives on your list?'

Irritably, the commissioner turned the sheet of paper face down and replied, 'That is none of your affair.'

'I ask because my sister, Elizabeth, was also taken captive at the same time as myself, and I have had no news of what has happened to her.'

Consul Martin, seeing that the commissioner was not going to answer the question, intervened. 'We have interviewed all the women prisoners currently in Algiers. There are only five of them, and all their ransom values have been agreed. There was no mention of any Elizabeth.' Only then did the consul see the light of hope fade from the young Irishman's eyes.

'That will be all, Mr Lynch. You may go,' said the commissioner curtly.

'I have a favour to ask,' said the young man. He was still standing his ground.

'You try my patience,' said Abercrombie. He was getting angry.

But the Irishman was not to be put off. 'There is a prisoner here in the bagnio who was taken by the Algerines while travelling to London with a message for the King. In all conscience, he should be considered for ransom. He is waiting outside.'

'This is as presumptuous as it is preposterous . . .' began Abercrombie, his voice sour with disbelief. And again the consul thought he should intervene.

'Where is he from, this message bearer?' he asked.

'From the Caribees, sir.'

Consul Martin glanced at the commissioner. Like everyone else engaged in commerce, he knew that the political influence of the West Indian merchants in London was very strong. Anything to do with the Caribees was a matter to be handled carefully. The commissioner clearly had the same reaction so Martin decided that it was best to be prudent. 'On your way out, please be so good as to tell this person to come in.'

As the young Irishman turned and walked towards the door, the consul found himself wondering if perhaps the authorities in London had been right all along, and that it was kinder never to encourage a prisoner's hopes, even for a moment. Martin tried to imagine how he himself would react if he had been repudiated so brusquely by the country he had expected to protect him. He very much doubted that he would have mustered the same dignity and self-restraint shown by the young man as he left the room. The consul hoped that the next interview would not turn out to be equally as shameful.

℃

HECTOR LOITERED in the bagnio courtyard as he waited for his friend to emerge from his interview. Deliberately he ignored the black disappointment of his own interrogation as he wondered how Dan was faring.

It was no more than five minutes before his friend reappeared, his expression unreadable. 'The man in the dark clothes did not believe me,' said Dan tonelessly. 'He asked to see a copy of my message for the King. I answered that the Miskito have no writing. We speak our messages, even the most important ones.'

'What did he say to that?' asked Hector.

'He told me that he needed proper evidence, something written on paper, that I was telling the truth. The man sitting beside him was more friendly. He said that he had heard of my people, the Miskito, and that they had helped the English. He even suggested to his companion that because the Miskito asked to be considered as subjects of the King, then my name might be added to the list of those who would be ransomed.'

'And the other man did not agree?'

'He answered that he would apply the same rules as he had followed in your case, and that, in addition, the treaty with Algiers only concerned English subjects taken from ships flying the English flag. I had already told him that the corsairs had taken me out of a Spanish ship, so it seems I could not be included on the ransom list.'

Hector looked down at the worn paving slabs of the courtyard. For the very first time in his captivity he despaired. He was crushed by the thought of spending year after year in the bagnio.

'I'm sorry, Dan,' he said. 'I'm really sorry. It seems that there is nothing we can do to get out of here. We'll stay until we rot. No one is going to lift a finger to help us.'

But to his surprise, Dan answered calmly, 'Then we ourselves will lift a finger.'

Hector looked at his friend in puzzlement. 'What do you mean?'

'I mean that we will turn Turk. It doesn't take much. All you have to do is raise a finger to the sky in the presence of two witnesses who are good Muslims, and acknowledge that Allah is the true God and Muhammad is his prophet. That's all there is to it . . . and of course you have to be cut.'

'Cut?'

'Yes, someone with a knife trims back the skin on your manhood, as a sign that you have converted.'

Despite himself, Hector looked queasy.

'Well, why not?' Dan went on. 'Once you have become a rinigato – become a Muslim – you have a much better chance of finding proper work that takes you out of the bagnio, and it is forbidden to send you to serve in the galleys. You may think that life is hard when working in the quarries, but it is nothing compared to being chained alongside three or four other prisoners and hauling on the handle of a 30-foot-long oar. It's late summer now, and soon all the galleys are coming back to harbour. But come the spring, every able-bodied man in the bagnio risks being sent to the oar benches.'

Hector thought for a moment. 'Is there no other way to get out of here? How about the gunpowder man? He's at liberty and he remains a Christian.'

Dan shook his head. 'No. The gunpowder man came to Algiers of his own free will. He can stay a Christian. It's not the same for us. That's the usanza.'

'Aren't you worried about becoming a Mussulman?'

Dan shrugged. 'As I told you, the Miskito believe in many gods and spirits. And so do the Turks, though they say there is only one God. My master who owns the masserie is a Mussulman but he still believes in what he calls djinns and efrit, the wicked spirits who might snatch him away or do him harm. So I can acknowledge Allah as the one God and still believe in the spirits whom my people have always respected.'

'Dan, it's easier for you to take this step than it is for me. My mother, if I ever see her again, will be heartbroken.'

'Maybe your mother would understand. Hector, listen to me. If you want to search for your sister, you have to get out of the bagnio. There's nothing you can do to find her or help her while you are confined here. If you become a rinigato, at least you can make enquiries among those who have taken the turban.

Maybe they have heard what happened to her. Besides, if you are worried about turning Turk, you can always wear a cross secretly. That's what some of the other rinigatos do, because they are afraid that their own God will ignore them after they die.'

'All right,' announced Hector. He had come to his decision. At times Dan seemed so much more level-headed, more confident than himself, even though there was little difference in their ages. 'I'll go through with this, but only if you do the same.'

'Of course,' said Dan. 'We are in this together.'

NINE

℃

TWO MEN STOOD in the late evening sunshine watching the English third-rate weigh anchor and then work clear of the Algiers mole.

Down by the harbour Consul Martin was feeling homesick, regretting that he had declined the invitation to accompany Abercrombie back to England. Martin had excused himself, saying that he had pressing commercial matters to attend to in Algiers, but the truth was that he did not relish spending the six-week voyage in close company with the glum commissioner and Newland the self-conceited mercer. The final details of Newland's ransom had been settled smoothly. Abercrombie had brought with him a down payment of ten per cent of the sum the Algerines demanded for the mercer's release. Newland's business associates in London had advanced the cash, and a professional ransom broker in Naples was standing surety for the rest. The balance was to be transferred when the cloth merchant reached home safely. The speed of this commercial transaction had underscored the cumbersome progress of the government redemption plan which had eventually allowed only three dozen English captives to depart. Not one of the Irish had been redeemed. The commissioner had made it clear, after the unsatisfactory interview with Hector Lynch, that he did not wish to encounter any more of the young man's countrymen. So Martin had given up trying to locate them in the bagnios.

No one would ever hear of these unfortunates again, the consul thought to himself as he turned to walk back up the hill to his residence, his despondency only tempered by relief that he was finally rid of the tiresome Newland.

The other figure watching the warship stand out to sea also felt mildly relieved. When Captain of Galleys Turgut Reis had heard that the English prisoners in Algiers were to be ransomed, he had bribed the Dey's secretary to remove the name of the English sailor-slave, Dunton, from his list. Dunton had proved to be a clever boat builder, and Turgut calculated that Dunton was worth much more than his purchase price if he continued to work in the Arsenal, particularly as the shipmaster there had finally found sufficiently lengthy timber to repair *Izzet Darya*. Turgut was all too aware that he had to have his galley ready for the start of the new cruising season in three months' time if he was to escape from his financial difficulties. Anything which speeded up her repairs was a priority, particularly the services of a skilled shipwright.

Looking down from his roof garden, Turgut was glad that his little stratagem had succeeded. He even took pen and paper to draw a rough sketch of the departing English third rate for future reference. It was quite possible that one day *Izzet Darya* might encounter the vessel during a corso, and previously the captain had found it difficult to tell whether the sailing ships of the unbelievers were fitted out for peace or war. To his eye they all had much the same lines and sail plans whether they were carrying rich cargoes or a broadside of cannon. How unlike his beloved *Izzet Darya*, he thought to himself. No one could mistake the galley's long, menacing hull for a plump trading vessel. *Izzet* was a platform for fighting men, not a tub filled with merchandise. He held up the completed sketch for the ink to dry in the faint breeze, and once again he reassured himself that he had been right not to switch to using a sailing vessel for the corso. There was something discreditable about the way those tall ships fought from a distance, gun to gun. Their opponents were no more than tiny figures in the distance. Far better to do battle honourably, hand to hand, and look your adversary in the eye. That was his personal usanza.

A discreet cough broke into the captain's thoughts. A servant had appeared on the roof garden, carrying a note. It had just been handed in, the man said, by a slave from the bagnio. Unfolding the paper, Turgut saw that the penmanship was neat and regular, the letters well formed as if prepared by a professional letter writer. Turgut's long experience in reading foreign charts meant that he was familiar with the crabbed script of the unbelievers, and he found no difficulty in deciphering the sentences written in the lingua franca. The author of the note stated that he wished to profess his belief in Allah and humbly asked the reis to give his consent to a ceremony of conversion. For a moment Turgut was puzzled. Then he recalled that a slave had to have his master's permission before adopting Islam. Turgut frowned. The note was unsigned. He wondered which of his slaves wanted to convert to the True Faith. Turgut presumed that the messenger had taken advantage of the rest period at sunset when the bagnio gates still stood open, and run up the hill to make the delivery. 'Where is the man who brought this?' he asked.

'He is waiting in the street,' the servant replied.

'Send him up,' he said. 'I'll hear what he has to say.'

A few moments later, the messenger appeared, and Turgut saw it was the young man whom he had loaned to the city treasurer.

'Who is responsible for this?' he asked, holding up the paper.

'I am, effendi. I wish to become a Mussulman.'

'And who wrote it for you?'

'No one, effendi. I wrote it myself.'

Turgut thought back to the day he had purchased the young man at auction. He remembered wondering even then whether the alert-looking young man might one day be a useful addition to his household, useful for his brains rather than his brawn. Had it not been for the malevolence of that greedy city treasurer he would have already found a more suitable use for this literate youngster. It occurred to Turgut that now he had a way to outwit the khaznadji. He would approve the young man's conversion, and then inform the treasurer that the young man would soon be a good Muslim and therefore should live in a household where the Faith was respected. That should shame the khaznadji into returning the slave to Turgut's custody.

'I am pleased that you have decided to say the shahadah. You have my consent,' Turgut said. 'You must remind me of your name so that I may inform the Guardian Pasha and arrange for the ceremony to take place here in this house. I will provide the witnesses.'

'My name is Hector Lynch, effendi.' Hector gave the reis a frank look. 'Would his excellency be so benevolent as to sponsor the same ceremony for my friend also? He too wishes to profess the Faith.'

Turgut was about to turn down the request when Hector went on, 'My friend has no fellow countrymen in the bagnio. He is a stranger from a distant land, far to the west across the ocean sea.'

Turgut stroked his beard, his curiosity aroused. An image from his ancestor's map came to mind – the chart of the western ocean, its far shore decorated with pictures of curious-looking animals and cryptic descriptions. Perhaps here was an opportunity to unravel some of these mysteries.

'I will talk with him. Return with him at this time tomorrow, and I will decide.'

©

THE FOLLOWING EVENING Hector brought Dan to the captain's mansion, both men wearing their cleanest clothes. After a short wait, they were shown up to Turgut's library. It was an airy, spacious room, its ceiling painted with interlocking geometrical patterns of red, green and black, cabinets and shelves lining the walls. They stood respectfully in front of the captain, who regarded them gravely.

'Peace be upon you,' he began.

'And upon you also be peace,' they chorused dutifully.

'Your companion tells me that you also wish to say the shahadah. Is that so?' the captain asked Dan.

'Your excellency, that is correct.'

'Have you told this to your master?'

'Not yet, sir.' Dan paused. 'If your excellency would be so generous as to buy me, the cost would be reasonable.'

'And why is that?'

'I was recently in trouble. But it was a mistake.'

'Whether you were in trouble justly or unjustly does not concern me. It is more important that you are useful to me,' said Turgut. He pointed to his bookstand. His ancestor's map of the western ocean was on display. 'Look there, and tell me if you see anything which you recognise.'

Dan stared at the map and, after a short interval, shook his head. 'No, your excellency. There is nothing. If it please your excellency, I do not know how to read.'

'You don't recognise any of those little pictures and drawings?'

Dan again shook his head, and Turgut was disappointed.

'Well at least you are honest. Can you think of any reason why I should buy you?' he asked.

Dan was at a loss, and there was an awkward silence until Hector spoke up.

'Effendi, my friend is highly skilled with ropes and ropework,' he said. 'He would be very useful in the Arsenal.'

Turgut turned his gaze on Hector, his brown eyes troubled. So even the slaves in the bagnio, he thought to himself, knew about his desperate need to get *Izzet Darya* ready for the corso. It was humiliating, yet he had to admire the quick wits of the young man.

'Very well,' he agreed. 'I shall discuss the matter with your master. If he quotes a satisfactory price, then I may decide on the purchase and you will be informed.'

As Dan and Hector hurried back down the hill to the bagnio, Dan asked, 'Your idea that I was a rope worker, and could help in the Arsenal. What made you think of it?'

'My first day in the bagnio,' said Hector. 'There was no spare bed in the dormitory and you offered to make me a hammock. You said that the Miskito made them when they went out on hunting trips, so it seemed logical that you could handle ropes, make knots and all that sort of thing.'

©

WITH THE GRUDGING agreement of the khaznadji, Hector was removed from beylik duties and reassigned to live and work in Turgut's household. He arrived there on a chilly winter morning, his meagre belongings wrapped in a blanket. The steward, himself a French slave, showed him to the room at the rear of the building which he would share with the other staff. 'You'll find the captain is a fair master,' the steward confided as they skirted the mansion's central courtyard with its trellises of flowers and vines and a large fountain splashing in the centre. 'He's a bit behind the times in his ideas as he's spent most of his time away in Constantinople in the Sultan's court. But if you serve him faithfully, he'll look after you well.'

'What about his family. Are they here?' asked Hector.

'Both his wives are,' said the Frenchman. 'But you won't see much of them. The reis keeps an old-fashioned establishment, and the women's quarters are separate. They occupy most of the second floor. You'll find a guard on duty at the door, so you're not likely to blunder in on them. As for children, the reis has none. It's his great regret. I'll introduce you to the other servants later, but right now you are due to start your first day's work. The captain is already with his books and charts. You're to help in his library.'

The reis glanced up from the parchment he was reading as Hector was shown in and, after greeting him courteously, waved towards an untidy pile of papers on a low table and said, 'Tell me what you make of them.'

Hector knew he was being set some sort of test. He began to sift carefully through the documents. Within moments he had identified them as pages torn from ships' logbooks. Most were in Spanish, but some were written in French or Italian, while others were in Dutch. A few were in languages he did not know but he could guess their content because shipmasters of every nationality seemed to be concerned with the same topics – wind, weather, landfalls, customs dues and lading. He said as much to Turgut, who seemed well satisfied with his answer.

'Good. Next I want you to check whether they contain any useful information, the sort of details that could be included in a map or written into a guidebook to instruct pilots.'

It took Hector the rest of the day to sort through the paperwork. He set aside those pages which were useless, and classified the remainder according to the areas they described. 'I've made a list of all the ports mentioned, and assigned a colour to each port,' he reported to Turgut. 'I've attached the appropriate coloured thread to every page where that port is mentioned.'

Turgut walked over to a large cedar wood chest in one corner of the room and lifted the lid. 'In here I keep the notes and observations which I have compiled during half a lifetime of voyaging. They are in no sort of order. I will want you to find a way of checking the information contained in them against the details in the ships' logs, and then work out which is more likely to be correct. To do that, you will first have to learn to read my writing, which is often untidy as it was done on shipboard, and the script is Ottoman.'

'I will do my best, effendi,' offered Hector. 'In the bagnio a Syrian Christian, who was taken prisoner in the Levant, showed me a little of the Arab way of writing. With practice, I should be able to carry out your wishes.'

'Excellent!' said Turgut, whose enthusiasm to update the Kitab-i Bahriye was increasing with every task he loaded on his new scrivano. 'I will arrange a tutor for you, a learned man of my acquaintance. He will give you some lessons in the formal elements of our calligraphy, and it would do no harm if you also began to acquire some Turkish from him as well. Lingua franca is all very well for basic communication, but there will be times when it is necessary to discuss the finer points of navigation and map preparation. This library is where you will work every day from now on, except Friday of course. I will give instructions to my steward that your midday meals are to be brought up here. That way you will not waste time.'

ℂ

IN THE DAYS that followed, Hector discovered he enjoyed the tasks set for him. He relished the challenge of deciphering faded or incomplete notes scribbled down by unknown shipmasters, then arranging the snippets of information into a coherent form which – the Captain told him – one day might take on the shape of a map or chart. He learned to read his master's writing, even though the captain had the disconcerting habit of using both the flamboyant diwani script of the court and more ordinary workaday lettering in the same sentence. Within a fortnight Hector also understood enough spoken Turkish to follow the captain as his master worried his way through the jumble of information accumulated in his archives over the years. At random Turgut would select a document from the chest and read it out, often hesitating as he tried to remember what exactly he had meant to record so many years ago. It was Hector's job to correlate that information with the material he had already extracted from the logbooks of the shipmasters. As the days passed and Hector showed more and more of his ability, Turgut Reis gradually slipped into the habit of treating him more like a talented nephew than a possession he had bought at auction.

☾

ONE MORNING Hector was alone in the captain's library, poring over the salt-stained pages of a Dutch sea captain's logbook, when his attention was distracted by a glint of light reflecting from a bright object on one of the cabinet shelves. Feeling in need of a break from his work, he strolled over to investigate. A shaft of sunlight was shining on a thin brass disc about as broad as the palm of his hand and inscribed with Arabic writing. There were four similar discs, one of which was cut away with a series of strangely shaped holes. It was obvious that the discs had been made to fit neatly into the face of a circular instrument made of heavy brass lying beside them on the shelf. He was standing in front of the cabinet wondering about the device, when Turgut Reis entered the room behind him and said, 'That was given to me by my father's father, peace be upon him. After you become a Muslim, you may one day be glad to own such an instrument yourself. Here, let me show you why.'

Picking up the instrument, Turgut brought it up to his eye. Hector saw that attached to the back of the device was a small brass bar with a peephole at each end. This bar could be turned on a pivot. 'You hold it like this,' said the captain, squinting through the peepholes as he moved the bar gently, 'and take a sight on the star you have selected. It is like taking aim with a musket. The alidade, which is the name we give this bar, measures for you the angle to the horizon.'

He turned the instrument over, and showed Hector the numerical tables inscribed on the back.

'If you have fitted the correct discs you can read off the time when the sun will rise and set wherever in the world you are, which stars and constellations will be in the night sky overhead, and the times they will rise and fall. That way you will know the qibla, the true direction of the kaaba in Mecca, and so you will be able to say your prayers in the right direction and at the right times.'

'A sailor on the ship that brought me to Algiers could tell which direction we were travelling and about how far we had come by looking at the night sky,' murmured Hector. 'He said there was much more to be learned from the stars.'

'He spoke the truth,' answered Turgut, 'and, by Allah's will, it is the people of the True Faith who enriched our understanding of the marvels of the firmament. Let me show you something else.'

He went to another cabinet and lifted out what looked like a round paper lantern, and rotated it carefully in his hands. 'See what is written on the surface.' On closer inspection, Hector saw that the lantern was made of parchment stretched on a fine mesh of copper wire. The surface bore dozens of pictures. He recognised a bear, the figures of several men, a creature which was part goat and part fish, another in the shape of a crab. It took a moment for him to realise that they were the signs of the zodiac and the constellations.

'It is a map of the heavens,' said the captain. 'I bought it many years ago from a merchant who was selling curios. The Sultan himself owns many such items – they are called celestial globes by those who study such things – and the Sultan's are far more substantial. One is an immense ball of pure marble carved to show the forty-eight constellations and more than one thousand and twenty-five stars. But this one, though humble, is important to me. Look closely.'

Hector examined the figures on the globe. Each picture was drawn to enclose a group of stars. But it seemed to him that the stars were so scattered and irregular that it took a great deal of imagination to see how they defined the figure. But the captain was speaking again, his voice animated.

'The salesman told me that one of the great scholars of the north – I believe he was a Dutchman – drew this star map more than a hundred years ago. It encompassed everything he knew about the heavens, all that he had learned from his reading and his years of study. The moment I saw it, I knew I had to buy it. Because I noted that when the Dutchman came to write down the names of the buruj, the constellations, he used the language and writing of the men whose wisdom he had acquired – the language of the holy Qur'an. See, here he has written Al Asad Buruj for the constellation shaped like a lion; and here is Al Akrab Buruj, the insect with a deadly sting in its curved tail.'

Now Hector understood his master's enthusiasm for the globe. It was true that instead of writing out the names of the constellations in Latin or his native tongue, the Dutch map maker of the stars had inscribed the names in Arabic. 'And here! And here . . . and here!' Turgut was pointing to the names of individual stars also marked on the globe. 'Note the names he has given them: Rigel, which means "the foot" in the language of true believers; Altair is "the flyer", and this star here, Alderbaran, signifies "the follower" because it appears to pursue that cluster of six stars in the constellation we call Ath-Thawr, the Bull.'

A memory stirred in Hector's mind . . . of a market day back in Ireland when his mother had taken him and his sister into a fortuneteller's booth. He had been no more than six or seven, but still remembered the shabby brown drape which served as a door. It had been spangled with stars and zodiacal signs.

'Using this star map and the brass instrument with the discs you showed me, can someone predict the future?' he asked.

Turgut hesitated before replying. 'The instrument and the globe, used together, can be used to calculate the position of the stars at the moment of a person's birth, and from that information it may be possible to foretell an individual's destiny. But great care is needed. The Prophet, peace be upon him, cautions us, "Behold what is in the heaven and earth! But revelations and warnings avail not folk who will not perceive."'

He replaced the globe carefully in the cabinet and, turning back towards Hector, added gravely, 'It is wiser to use these things for the true path of observance, even as the pilgrims of the haj rely on the stars to direct their paths across the trackless deserts and the seas.'

TEN

℃

'HE'S A VERY DECENT MAN,' Hector told Dan when the two friends next met at the bagnio on their Friday rest day. 'His steward told me that the captain never orders any of his servants to do any job that he would not be prepared to do himself. He said that Turks of the ruling class believe that the only people fit to rule, are those who have themselves served. The captain comes from one of the best families in Constantinople, yet he started off as a lad scrubbing slime off anchor cables as they were winched aboard the galleys. When he grew strong enough, he had to spend six months on the oar bench.'

'My master is reluctant to sell me to your captain, even if I want to turn Turk,' said Dan. 'Since my bastinadoing, I've been given only the most unpleasant tasks in the masserie. My master seeks to add to that punishment.'

Hector looked around the bagnio's grim courtyard and recalled his unpleasant experience with the lecherous kaporal. He had never seen his friend so glum.

'If only there was some way you too could help out in the library,' he said, 'then you too would be transferred to live in the captain's house.'

'A library job is not likely when I don't know how to read or write,' Dan pointed out. 'That page he wanted me to examine meant nothing. Just a lot of black lines and some pretty pictures poorly drawn. I could have done better myself.'

Hector looked at his friend questioningly. 'What do you mean, "done better"?'

'Those pictures of trees and fish were all very clumsy, and someone had tried to draw a bird you call a parrot. But it was not like any parrot I had ever seen. Wrong shape and the colours were all odd. That's why I told the captain that I couldn't recognise anything. Maybe I should have said there was a badly drawn parrot.'

'You mean you could have produced a better picture of it.'

'Yes.'

'Then show me,' said Hector, suddenly excited. He went to where one of the bagnio letter writers was squatting against the wall, waiting for clients. He paid for a sheet of paper and the loan of pen and ink and thrust them into Dan's hand. 'Draw me a parrot,' he demanded.

Dan looked dubiously at the materials. The pen was cut from a goose quill, and the nib was frayed and blunt. The paper was dirty and slightly crumpled. 'I wouldn't be much good with these,' he said.

'Why not?'

'I paint and draw on skin, not paper.'

'You mean on vellum made from sheepskin, like the monks who taught me in Ireland.'

'No. I make my pictures on human skin.'

For a moment Hector looked dismayed, thinking that his friend was about to reveal that the Miskito flayed human corpses to obtain their skins. But Dan's next words reassured him.

'I paint on living people. It is something that I learned as a youngster. There's a jungle tribe who live inland from the Miskito coast and go around half naked, with their skins painted with pictures of birds and trees and flowers. When I was a boy the Miskito council sent me to them as some sort of hostage, while one of their youths came to live in my family. Their women folk are the artists. They spend hour after hour painting coloured pictures on the skins of their men. They think it makes the men look handsome and attractive. If the work is cleverly done, the pictures seem to come alive because they move as the muscles ripple. Because I was a stranger from outside the tribe, they indulged me and showed me how to make the paints and brushes.'

'You had to make your own brushes?'

'It's not difficult. You cut a twig from a certain type of bush, chew the end until it is soft, and use that as the brush.'

'And what about the paints?'

'We mixed coloured earth or the powder of certain stones gathered in the river beds, and coloured sap from jungle plants. There was scarcely a colour that we couldn't create. Blues and reds were easy, yellow more difficult. For a special occasion like a feast or a wedding, the women would first paint their men with the pictures. Then they puffed grains of shiny sand over them while the paint was still wet, so that their men folk glittered.'

Hector looked at his friend in astonishment. 'Show me what you can do. Though we won't find any coloured earth or jungle plants in the bagnio.'

In response, Dan approached a huckster selling cooked meats from a brazier, and asked him for a small nub of charcoal. Returning to Hector, he took from him the sheet of paper and, laying it flat on the ground, smoothed it out. He made four or five swift strokes with the charcoal, and then held it up for Hector to see.

On the page was the unmistakable image of a seagull, swerving in mid flight.

'Will that do?' Dan asked.

Awestruck, Hector took the sheet of paper. 'Do! Even if I had all the time in the world, and the best materials, I could never have drawn something like that.'

'I'd prefer to be an artist than a gardener,' said Dan.

'Dan, if I can get you a supply of paper, and some pens of the sort we use here, do you think you can teach yourself how to draw and colour with them? You would have to learn how to make the sort of pictures you saw on that map, only better, much better.'

'Making pictures comes more easily when you do not know how to read or write,' the Miskito answered confidently.

Every Friday in the month that followed, Hector coached Dan in the art of illustrating maps and charts. He prepared a list of the subjects – mountains, ships, fish, wind roses – and made rough sketches to show Dan how they should look. Once, after much soul-searching, he stole a loose page from a disintegrating collection of charts held in the captain's library, and brought it to the bagnio to show his friend, replacing the page next day.

Finally, when he was satisfied that Dan had mastered the use of paper and ink, Hector was able to return from the bagnio to the captain's mansion carrying what he believed would be Dan's salvation.

ℂ

WHEN TURGUT entered his library the following morning, Hector was ready with his demonstration. 'With your permission, effendi,' he said, 'I would like to show you a drawing.'

Turgut looked at him enquiringly. 'A drawing? Something you have found among the logbooks?'

'No, effendi, it is this,' and Hector pulled from his sleeve a sheet of paper on which was Dan's most recent effort with pen and coloured ink. It was a picture of Algiers seen from the sea. All the salient features were there: the harbour mole and the lighthouse, the city walls, the Dey's castle on the summit and the gardens at either side.

Turgut recognised it at once. 'And you made this yourself?'

'No, effendi. It was drawn by the slave who is my friend. The one whose home is across the western ocean.'

Turgut was quick on the uptake. 'I take it that you are

suggesting he is qualified to help in the library, that his skill could be valuable in preparing a new version of the Kitab-i Bahriye.'

'That is so, your excellency.'

Turgut thought for a moment and then said quietly, 'Friendship has its obligations. I will increase my offer of his purchase price with his master. As soon as that is settled, your friend can begin work as a draughtsman and illustrator and come to live in this house. That also will be an auspicious time for both of you to celebrate your adoption of the True Faith. In the meantime you should be thinking about your new names.'

℃

'I HOPE THE ABDAL has a steady hand and a sharp razor,' said Dan on the morning that he and Hector were due to profess Islam. The two friends were at Turgut's mansion preparing for the ceremony the captain had called their sunnet. They had already paid a visit to one of Algiers' public bath houses and were putting on new white cotton gowns.

'Judging by the number of slaves from the bagnio who converted to Islam, the abdal must have plenty of practice in removing that piece of skin,' said Hector, trying to sound more confident than he was feeling. 'I'll be glad when it's over. It will put an end to all the jokes about being too sore to walk straight.'

'. . . or make love again,' added Dan.

'I wouldn't know,' confessed Hector. 'I've never been with a woman properly. Just had one or two encounters with village girls, but always brief and they never meant anything.'

'Then you've got something to look forward to, though you don't earn enough to visit the bordellos that the odjaks use. They aren't allowed to marry until they've reached senior rank and until then must live in men-only barracks. No wonder they appreciate good-looking young men.'

Hector ignored his friend's banter as he looked into a mirror to adjust his red slave cap which he had been told he should wear during the ceremony. 'Have you decided what you will be called in future?' he asked.

'I'll be Suleiman Miskita – Suleiman the Miskito. What about you?'

'The captain suggested that I become Hassan Irlanda – Hassan from Ireland. He's offered to act as my sponsor even though I really don't need one.'

'Turgut Reis has really taken a liking to you, hasn't he?'

'No more jokes, Dan,' said Hector seriously. 'I think it is because he doesn't have any family of his own.'

'Well then, let's not keep him waiting.'

Together the two friends made their way to the mansion's central courtyard where a small group of the other servants were waiting for them. Spread on the ground was a large carpet, on which stood jugs of flavoured drinks and trays of food – a first course of sheep's head and feet served with fried eggplant and cucumbers in yoghurt, followed by a sweet course of pears and apricots, grape paste and halva flavoured with almonds. Hector's tutor in calligraphy had already arrived and Hector caught a glimpse of the abdal, the specialist who would perform the circumcision, as he disappeared into a side room with his bag of surgical tools.

Moments later the captain himself appeared, resplendent in a dark red jacket over his embroidered shirt, full pantaloons, and a maroon turban with matching silk sash. With him were two of his friends, both elderly men with grave expressions and full white beards. They were to witness the act of profession. The captain was in an expansive mood. 'Peace be upon you,' he said genially to the assembled company. 'This is an important day for my household. Today you are my guests and I want you all to enjoy yourselves, so take your places and we will eat together.'

He seated himself at one end of the carpet and invited his two colleagues to sit beside him with the abdal next to them.

Dan and Hector were to be seated directly opposite. When his guests had eaten their fill and the trays had been cleared away, Turgut called for everyone's attention. 'My friends,' he said, 'the ceremony for the taking of the right path is always an occasion for celebration. When there is sunnet for the sons of the Sultan, the festivities last for fifteen days and nights. A thousand plates of rice and fifteen roast oxen are despatched daily to the people of the city, there are fireworks and parades, and the harbour is a mass of coloured lights attached to the masts of the assembled vessels. Today may seem very humble by comparison, but nevertheless it is equally a time of rejoicing, and the proper ritual must be observed.' Rising to his feet, the captain then beckoned to Dan to come forward. The Miskito stepped into the centre of the carpet and stood facing his master. Turgut asked him formally, 'Is it your wish to acknowledge the true Faith?'

'It is, effendi.'

'Then raise your finger, and pronounce the shahadah loudly and clearly so that all may hear.'

Obediently Dan did as he was told, and recited the words, 'There is no god but God and Muhammad is the Messenger of God.'

Turgut turned to his valet standing in the background, and nodded. The valet came forward with a pair of scissors. Removing Dan's red cap, he threw it on the ground and then deftly clipped away the Miskito's long hair leaving only a central top knot. Next the valet clapped his hands, and his assistant brought forward a length of tan-coloured muslin which the valet carefully wound around the Miskito's head as a turban. When the valet was satisfied, he stepped back and Turgut announced in a loud voice, 'From now on you will be known as Suleiman the Miskito. In the words of the holy Qur'an, "He who rejects false deities and believes in Allah has grasped a firm handhold which will never break."'

To murmurs of approval from the audience, the valet then escorted Dan away to the side room, even as the abdal quietly left his place and followed.

Next it was Hector's turn. Rising to his feet, he stepped into the centre of the carpet, and at the captain's prompting held up his index finger and repeated the words of the shahadah, as Dan had done. After his red cap had been removed and his head shaved, he too was given a turban, though this time it was a more expensive length of fine white cotton shot through with gold threads. Then, Turgut stepped forward and placed in his open palm a little container, the size and shape of a pill jar, fashioned of brass. As Turgut pressed a catch on the side, the lid sprang open revealing a little compass, its needle quivering gently. Engraved on the inner side of the open lid were lines of Arabic writing. 'Here are inscribed the names of the cities and countries of the known world,' said Turgut, 'and should you ever find yourself in such places, consult the needle to learn the qibla that you may worship towards the pillars of Islam.' Then, to everyone's surprise, he leaned forward and gave Hector a formal embrace. As he did so, he whispered in his ear, 'Don't be afraid. It happens at once, and is a wonderful thing as Allah has wished. Praise be to God.' Then he stepped back, as his valet led away Hector for his circumcision.

To his alarm Hector could not see Dan anywhere when he was ushered into the side room where the abdal stood waiting beside a low bed. The only other furniture in the room was a sturdy stool. 'Do not be afraid,' said the abdal. 'Your friend is recovering next door, and will soon rejoin the celebrations. The pain is quickly over. You may lie on the bed or be seated on the stool, whichever you prefer. Osman, the valet here, will remain to bear witness.'

'I prefer the stool,' said Hector, his voice unsteady.

'As did your friend. Pull up your gown, and sit down then, with your legs spread apart.'

Hector did as he was instructed, and the abdal reached

forward and took the young man's penis in one hand and gently teased forward the foreskin. Next, as Hector peered down anxiously, the abdal was holding in his free hand an instrument which Hector first thought was a set of dividers of the type he himself used when measuring distances across a map. But these dividers were made of wood, each limb flat-sided. Hector broke out in a cold sweat as he realised it was a clamp. Expertly the abdal closed the clamp upon the foreskin, nipping it tightly so that it could not retract. Hector shut his eyes and clenched his fists so that the nails dug deep into the palms of his hands. He sucked in air and held his breath, while hearing the soft mutter of a voice saying, 'Allâhu akbarre'. Then came an agonising spike of pain which made him gasp, and a shocking moment later the warm spurt of blood striking the inside of his thigh. Even as he quivered with the pain, he sensed the blessed pressure of some sort of poultice or bandage being pressed to his wounded manhood.

ELEVEN

☾

'GLORY OF THE SEA', *Izzet Darya* lay becalmed. The green
banner of Algiers with its spangles of silver and gold crescents
hung limp from its staff, and the sea around her hull had an oily
sheen. The passing of an occasional swell was so faint as to be
noticed only in the slight flexing of her monstrous main spar
made from three lengths of straight pine lashed together like a
great fishing rod. The spar and its furled sail weighed more than
four tons, and the Captain of Galleys had ordered them to be
lowered in order to ease the strain on the galley's single mast
with its enormous block and tackle. When a breeze did come, it
would take thirty strong men hauling in unison on the massive
six-inch halyard to raise the spar back aloft. Then the lightest
and most agile members of the crew would have to shin up and
let loose the bindings so that the single enormous sail fell open
and sent the galley slicing through the water. But for now there
was not a breath of wind. *Izzet Darya* was motionless, silent
except for the steady thump of her pumps and the gush and
trickle of bilge water falling back into the sea, for the galley's
elderly hull was incurably leaky, and only steady pumping kept
her light and manoeuvrable. Turgut Reis was resting his oarsmen because *Izzet Darya* was where he wanted her to be, lurking
at a cruciero, a crossroads of shipping lanes. Three leagues east

was the island of St Pierre where Turgut's men had recently taken on fresh water from a friendly population, and past this point came merchant traffic rounding Sardinia's southern cape on their paths between Marseilles, Leghorn, Sicily and the straits. So the corsair galley waited, as dangerous as an ageing pike poised in ambush among the reeds.

From his position on the aft deck Hector looked down the length of the venerable galley. In the flat light of dawn the vessel appeared even narrower and longer than usual. Her beam was only sixteen feet, less than a tenth of the distance to her bows where he could make out the squat black shape of her single bow chaser, an iron cannon pointing forward into the dense mist which blanked out the horizon. Earlier Turgut had confided to him that *Izzet* had once mounted three fine bow chasers of bronze made by skilled Hungarian gun founders, but he had been obliged to sell the more expensive guns to pay his dockyard bills and outfit his ship and get to sea. A single catwalk ran all the way down the spine of the galley. Here on most corsair ships the overseers patrolled, keeping an eye on the slaves and lashing them to their work if they shirked. But on *Izzet Darya* there was no need for such discipline because most of her oarsmen, now relaxing on the benches, were volunteers. In that matter, at least, Turgut had been fortunate. He had announced his impending departure for the corso in early March, and just two weeks later buba, the plague, had struck the city. To Algerines the plague was a commonplace, lurking unseen and occasionally emerging to decimate the closely packed population. But buba was a summer affliction and rarely felt so early. It had taken the city unawares. After several of the more important citizens had died, there had been a rush to escape the scourge. Scores of men had volunteered for *Izzet Darya*'s crew though Turgut was promising no wage, only a share in the plunder.

So now 160 men were packed aboard, not counting the squad of forty janissaries under their aga who were the ship's chief fighting force, and already the food rations were scrimped. Hector knew the precise details because he had come aboard as the captain's scrivano, charged with keeping track of how many sacks of grain and dried fruit, jars of oil and vinegar remained. *Izzet* had sailed from Algiers with supplies for less than a month at sea because this was all that Turgut could afford, and now, three weeks into the cruise, the men were grumbling about the meagre helpings of couscous, which was their staple diet. The last full meal they had enjoyed was after the marabout, the holy man, had led the prayers for success on the corso. Eight sheep had been ritually slaughtered when *Izzet*'s well-greased hull had been eased down the slipway, coloured bunting fluttering from her rigging. The blood and guts from the dead sheep were thrown into the sea as a sacrifice, but the flesh reserved for the crew's meal once the galley had made its ceremonial exit from Algiers harbour, the onlookers on the ramparts shouting their good wishes, and the crew saluting the tomb of Sidi Ketaka on the hill, without whose help no corsair crew could hope for success.

But their achievement had been indifferent despite the sacrifice. Off the coast of Majorca the galley had intercepted a dozen vessels, mostly small tartans and poleacres. Each time the galley had forced the stranger to heave to, then lowered a boat and sent across a team for the visita, the inspection to check the vessel's nationality and lading. Whenever the vessel proved to be Christian, it had been Hector's job to scrutinise the ship's papers while the anxious captain hovered beside him, pleading that he was an honest trader and carrying only protected goods. Several captains had produced passports issued under the terms of a treaty between their own government and the Dey in Algiers promising protection from seizure of vessel and cargo. Disappointingly, these claims had proved to be true, and Turgut had honoured the passes, allowing the captures to go free. Only two vessels had turned out to be genuine prizes, and even then their cargoes were wretched enough – bundles of firewood, bales of unworked goat hair, and some millet and cheese which had been added to *Izzet*'s dwindling stores. A minor consolation had been the discovery of some sacks of coffee beans, probably destined for some Moorish sheikh.

Hector stepped around the hooped canopy which sheltered the spot where Turgut and the aga of the janissaries spread their sleeping mats at nightfall. It still felt odd not to have the weight of his slave ring on his right ankle. The previous day Turgut had insisted that the ring be struck off. 'I am still your master, but now that you have adopted the Faith I have no wish to treat you as a chattel,' he had announced. 'From now on you should regard yourself as a member of my household, and a valued one at that. As the Prophet, peace be upon him, told us, "Your slaves are your brothers and Allah has put them under your command. So whoever has a brother under his command should feed him of what he eats and dress him of what he wears."'

Aboard the galley the captain was following the Prophet's advice. Like all his crew Turgut went barefoot and wore simple working clothes, a cotton gown or long shirt over a pair of drawers. Hector was grateful for the loose fit of the baggy garments because he was still conscious of his circumcision. His penis had healed during the two weeks' convalescence allowed after circumcision, but it was still inclined to occasional discomfort in the heat.

A sailor clambered up the companionway that led from the oar deck, and as he came level with Hector, there was something familiar about his face. A moment later Hector placed him. It was the English sailor Dunton with whom he had shared the hold on Hakim Reis's vessel. 'I had not expected to see you again,' he said.

Dunton checked in his stride and for an instant did not recognise the young Irishman. 'It's the lad from Ireland, isn't it,' he then exclaimed. 'You've changed. You look older and more grown up.' He glanced down at Hector's bare leg. 'Also it seems you've taken the turban.'

Belatedly Hector noted that Dunton was still wearing a slave ring on his ankle though he had discarded the red slave cap and, like everyone else, wore a nondescript cloth wrapped around his head. 'Yes, I converted,' Hector said simply.

'Can't say I blame you,' observed Dunton, not the least surprised. 'But how come you are on the aft deck with the officers? You've not become a garzon have you?'

'No, I'm the captain's scrivano,' said Hector. A garzon was lingua franca for the young men who sometimes shipped aboard as companions and bedmates for the officers and senior odjaks. 'I also help the captain in his chart-making.'

Dunton looked impressed. 'Always took you for a clever one,' he said. 'What's that you've got hanging round your neck?'

'It's my qibla finder,' said Hector. 'It shows me the direction in which to pray.'

'Mind if I have a look,' observed Dunton. He had opened the little case and saw the compass needle. 'Handy enough aboard a ship which turns every which way.'

'What about you? What have you been doing these past nine months?'

Dunton shrugged. 'Much the same as what I would have been doing at home if I had been stuck on shore for the entire winter,' he answered. 'I was put to work in the Arsenal, doing shipwright's work. I helped get this old tub back afloat. She's a right old-timer. Half her joints are shaky and she's long past her best days. Wouldn't wonder if this turns out to be her last voyage.'

He spat expertly over the side.

'I'm not sure I'd have joined her crew if I had been given the choice. But my master is the same captain, as you call him, and he was very keen to have me aboard because there's a shortage of good seamen. Plenty of volunteers to pull on an oar, but not many who know how to get the best out of a ship under sail. In all but name I'm the caravana, the foreman in charge of sail handling. Officially the caravana is a Turk, but he knows sod all about the job, and leaves it to me to organise the tasks. If this cruise goes well, I might even come back with a bit of cash to buy my freedom and then settle down in Algiers. I like the climate and the pay is very good if you've got shipwright's skills.

'But I thought that all the English prisoners had been ransomed last autumn and gone home?'

'Seems I was left off the list,' said Dunton. 'And we won't see another delegation from London for several years. I hear that the English consul died of the plague, and he's not been replaced as yet. So, my best hope is prize money from this corso. Then there'll be nothing to stop me from bringing my wife and children out to join me.'

'You mean you'll share in the plunder?'

'That's usanza. Even the humblest galley oarsman gets a cut of the prize money, and it doesn't matter if he is a slave. It's just a single share, and in theory he's meant to hand it over to his master. But if your master likes you, you get to keep it. By all accounts the captain is a decent old stick, and would let you hang on to what you earn if you serve him well.'

Dunton glanced up at the banner which was still hanging slack. 'I'd better get going. This mist won't last all day. I need to tighten those wooldings on the main spar while I have the chance. It's nice to get the chance to talk English for a change too.'

'So you haven't met my friend Dan? He speaks English.'

'No, who's he?'

Hector pointed to the foredeck where Dan was talking to one of the odjaks. 'That man there.'

'The foreign-looking one with dark skin? I took him to be an usif, a blackamoor slave. How come he's so friendly with the odjaks?'

'He's a musketeer,' Hector told him. 'He made quite an impression on them.'

℗

IT HAD HAPPENED on the afternoon before *Izzet Darya* set sail from Algiers. The captain had told Hector that he would take him aboard as his scrivano, but he had made it clear that there was no place for Dan aboard the galley. Naturally Hector asked the captain to change his mind, only to be reminded that an illiterate artist would just be an extra mouth to feed. So Hector had resigned himself to being parted from his friend when Dan arrived at the dockside on an errand for Turgut's steward. He had been told to bring Turgut's prayer mat and some extra clothes out to the anchored galley, and by chance had hitched a ride with a boatload of odjaks coming aboard with their bedrolls and weapons. As the odjaks climbed on to the galley, one of the janissaries had handed his musket to Dan to hold. Dan had taken the weapon and, glancing at the firing mechanism, commented that it was out of alignment. 'Are you armuriero, a gunsmith?' the janissary had asked. 'No, but I am a marksman, and this is a fine weapon,' Dan had answered. Flattered, the janissary had asked Dan if he would like to try out the musket for himself, and the two of them had gone to the galley's bow where Dan had loaded the musket and, under the watchful eye of the odjak, took aim at a mark, a dead cat floating in the water. He sank the carcass with his shot. The janissary had been so impressed that he had called on his fellow soldiers to watch another demonstration of Dan's marksmanship, and when he again hit his target – a clump of floating weed – they had applauded. By now the aga of the janissaries had strolled over to observe what was going on, and when Dan missed his third shot by only a narrow margin, the aga had enquired where he had learned to shoot so accurately. 'Among my people,' Dan had replied proudly. 'That's why we are called the Miskito. Outsiders believe that our name is taken from the flying insects which infest our coast, but that is wrong. The Spanish call us Miskito because we are the only native people in those lands who have learned how to use guns against them. So they call us the musket people.' 'If you are prepared to fight the infidel, then you should assist us,' was the aga's comment, 'we always need good marksmen, and those who can help repair our guns.' The aga's authority in matters of warfare was equal to the powers exercised by the captain himself, so Dan had found himself co-opted as an auxiliary with the odjaks, and – to Hector's delight – the Miskito had joined the corso.

NIMBLY Dunton swung himself up on the mainspar, straddled it, and began attending to a frayed rope binding when, abruptly, he raised his head and looked out into the mist. 'Hello!' he said softly, 'Something's coming our way.' Other crewmembers had heard the noise too, and there were calls for the pumping crew to cease work for a moment. In the silence that followed, a rhythmic heavy splash and groan could be heard. Quite where the noise came from was difficult to tell, but it was approaching. On the foredeck, the janissaries who had been smoking and talking put down their long pipes and took up their muskets, and quietly prepared the primings. Turgut, alerted by the sudden tension aboard, walked to the starboard rail and cocked his head to one side listening. 'Galleot or maybe brigantine under oars,' he said.

Dunton dropped down softly on the deck beside Hector. 'Friend or foe?' he murmured. 'The Religion doesn't normally operate in this area, though they've got eight large galleys in their fleet, about the same size as *Izzet*, which would give us a run for our money.'

'The Religion? Who are they?' whispered Hector.

'The Knights of the Order of St John of Jerusalem. A bunch of nobles who act like pirates when it suits them, and from the best families in Europe. Claim they are fighting for the Cross.

Hate Barbary corsairs. They operate out of Malta. One of their petty officers was a slave shipwright alongside me in the Arsenal.' Dunton stopped talking as the aga scowled at him, demanding silence as he also listened, trying to locate the direction of the approaching ship.

Several minutes passed, and it became clear that the unknown vessel was moving at a leisurely pace. The splashes of the oars were slow and unhurried, the sound increasing only gradually. *Izzet*'s own rowers settled in their places and dipped the blades of their thirty-foot-long sweeps quietly into the sea, awaiting orders. Some were looking expectantly towards Turgut on the stern deck, others half-turned, trying to peer out into the mist. Abruptly, through the mist, came a cry, 'Sieme! Sieme!' Dunton mouthed, 'Together! Together!' and made a rowing gesture. Moments later, a dark patch in the mist became the unmistakable shape of an oared vessel, and there was a startled shout, 'Aia! What ship?' '*Izzet Darya*! In the Name of Allah,' roared back Turgut. The advancing galley had stopped rowing, but her momentum carried her forward so that she could be clearly seen as a brigantine, an oared vessel about half the size of *Izzet Darya*. 'Merhaba, welcome! From what port?' called Turgut. 'From Djidjelli. Corsan!' The tension aboard *Izzet Darya* relaxed. 'Fellow corsairs from Barbary,' explained Dunton. 'Hunting the same patch of sea.'

Hector's knowledge of Turkish was good enough to follow the shouted conversation between Turgut and the captain of the newcomer. The brigantine had been on the corso for less than a week, and had managed to intercept three infidel vessels, two Spanish and the third French. None of the prizes were very valuable, but the captain of the French ship had curried favour with his captors by telling the corsairs that he had sighted a large merchantman, of unknown nationality, hull down on the horizon and apparently heading towards Leghorn. In pursuit of this potential prize the brigantine had ventured north hoping to intercept the vessel which would now be delayed by the calm. 'Have you seen any of those shaitans from Malta?' called Turgut.

'No, nothing. It's too early in the season for them. They like to lie in bed with their harlots,' came the reply.

'Will we join forces then?' enquired Turgut.

'D'accordo!' came back the reply. 'One hand makes nothing, two hands make a sound.'

Turgut smiled into his beard at the Turkish proverb as he called back, 'We wait until the mist lifts, then spread out but stay in sight of one another, and cruise northward.'

'Agreed! And may Allah go with us.'

'Our luck has changed!' said Turgut cheerfully, coming back across the deck. 'Let the storemen issue a double ration so we may eat our fill, and be ready for what fortune brings.' Dunton went forward to rejoin his shipmates and, as Dan took his meals with the odjaks, who had their own achtchi or camp cook, Hector found himself seated on the aft deck with the captain and his officers as they ate a simple meal of falafel and bread. From time to time the captain glanced across at the brigantine which lay hove-to half a musket shot away. He continued to be in a good mood.

'Allah has been kind to us,' he said to Hector. 'Having a second ship means we can sweep a wider swathe of sea in search of prizes. And should we find only small coasters, the brigantine is fast enough to catch them easily. It will save us from having to lower our ship's boats, and that means fewer visitas for you.'

'The brigantine comes from Djidjelli,' Hector observed. 'Already you have a drawing of their harbour in your files, but if you wish I could go across and interview their captain and update the information.'

'Maybe later,' answered Turgut. 'Less than four years ago I was in their port, not a good harbour, shallow and exposed but adequate if you want to take on supplies. The ruler of Djidjelli acknowledges the Dey as his overlord, and we leave him to his own devices. Just so that he does not interfere with our corsos.

The same is true of Bougie a short distance down the coast. Let us hope that his information about the rich merchant ship turns out to be correct.'

'Your excellency, if we do find and capture this ship how would we divide the spoils? The brigantine brought the news, so does her crew have first choice?'

'A shrewd question, and the answer is that together we return to Algiers, with our prize. In Algiers the division is made by a court of arbitration composed of senior reis who decide on matters of precedence, acts of valour in the fight and so forth.'

'And do they also decide who receives the prisoners as their reward?'

'Of course. Often the value of the prisoners exceeds the value of the captured hull.'

'And if we capture women, for example, where would they be held?'

Turgut looked at Hector searchingly. 'Do you have a special reason to ask that question, and is that why you volunteered to visit the brigantine?'

'Forgive me for asking, effendi. When I was taken by the corsair Hakim Reis, my sister was also captured. She was placed on one ship, while I was kept on another. Since that time I have not seen her. I wish to learn what might have happened to her, and where she is now.'

'Tell me the details, as best as you remember them.'

Hector recounted the story of his capture and when he finished his account, Turgut paused to take a sip of coffee before replying, 'I did not meet Hakim Reis after that venture when he raided Ireland. He was always lucky on the corso, quick to pick up prizes and welcome in any port to sell them. It would be normal for him to keep the women captives apart from their menfolk. I would do the same myself. The men are less likely to make trouble if they see their women could be punished. But I would have expected Hakim Reis and his escorting vessel to have entered their final harbour together and disposed of the booty in the same market place. That makes the final division of the profits easier as I have explained. I can only suppose that something happened to separate Hakim Reis from his raiding consort. You mentioned some sort of exchange of gunfire.'

'And where might the other ship have gone?' asked Hector. 'Could it have gone to Djidjelli or to Bougie? Is that where I should look for my sister?'

'If you volunteered to visit the brigantine in order to ask if anyone knew about her, then I'm afraid your enquiry would have been futile. Had the women captives been sold in Djidjelli, or Bougie for that matter, the news would have reached Algiers which is not so far away. No, I think your sister was taken farther afield.' Seeing the disappointment in Hector's face, he added, 'You must not be too hard on yourself. Consider your own captivity. You must admit, it has not turned out to be so disastrous. Here you are aboard a fine ship and one of Muhammad's people. Hakim Reis was right when he told you that, with luck, you could yourself rise to command. For all you know, your sister might be much happier than you fear.'

'It is difficult to think with such optimism, effendi. I still feel responsible for her well-being.'

'Hassan Irlanda,' said Turgut kindly. 'In Turkey we have a saying – "patience is the key to Paradise." We must all accept the fate that Allah decrees. Keep up your search for your sister, but pursue it in the knowledge that it may never reach a conclusion. Rest assured that your sister will have been treated well. She would have been classified as murtafa'at; that is, first class. Wherever your sister was brought ashore for sale, everything about her would have been recorded by the amina, the woman inspector who examined her. Even as a conscientious jeweller notes the qualities of a special gem, her good points, the nu'ut, and her defects, the uyub, will have been written down. Somewhere that record and description of your sister still survives. Find it and you will be on the trail of your sister. Or find someone who sailed with Hakim Reis on that corso or, better still, find Hakim Reis himself. Then ask why the vessels were separated and where the missing ship would have gone.'

Hector finished his meal in silence, turning over in his mind Turgut's advice and, still troubled, was on the point of asking again whether he could visit the brigantine to enquire if anyone had heard of Elizabeth, when there was an order for the oarsmen to stand to their sweeps. Dunton reappeared on the aft deck. 'The pilot must think the mist is due to lift soon,' he said as he checked the preventer ropes which secured the great spar. 'Or maybe he's worried how far we've drifted in the mist. Strange currents around here, according to the store keeper's assistant. He's a local man from Sardinia and used to fish these waters before he was captured by the Turks, and became a rinigato like yourself. Tells me that the current can be strong enough to set a ship ten or fifteen miles in a day.'

A series of calls and commands was heard along the catwalk as *Izzet Darya* slowly got under way, the same shouts repeated from the accompanying brigantine, whose sweeps also began to rise and fall ponderously as the two ships nosed their way forward. Occasionally Dunton looked up at the mast top where the captain's insignia, a long red and gold pennant, dangled listlessly. 'A sea fret like this normally lies close to the water, like a blanket,' he said to Hector. 'On a tall ship, you can send someone to the mast head as lookout, and often he'll be sitting up there in the bright sunshine with a blue sky above his head. Yet when he looks down past his feet, he can scarcely see the deck for the vapour. Ahha! There's a patch of blue now.'

Hector followed his gaze, and indeed the mist was thinning. A glimpse of blue sky had appeared, and on the aft deck around him the daylight seemed to be growing brighter. 'Shan't be long now before we are clear of this,' observed Dunton confidently. 'Then it'll be time for the brigantine to stand clear and take up her cruising station.'

But that manoeuvre was not needed. Half an hour later the two corsair vessels rowed their way out of the mist. In a few oar strokes they passed from the close damp haze and emerged into a bright open world with a sparkling calm sea of intense blue. Looking astern, Hector saw that the edge of the mist was like a sheer grey wall, yet scarcely higher than a ship's mast. A sudden exclamation from the galley's pilot made him swing round again.

'Alhamdullilah,' the pilot burst out, pointing ahead. There, no more than five miles away, was a ship. She was utterly becalmed. Hector had never seen a craft as large or ponderous. Like Hakim Reis's corsair ship which had raided Ireland, the vessel was an outright sailing vessel. Her three tall masts were rigged with great square sails which, at that moment, hung slack and empty and useless. Amidships her lowest point was twice the height of the low-slung galleys, and the stern of the vessel rose far above the sea in a series of decks that formed a wooden castle. Even at that distance it was possible to make out a massive ornamental lantern, twice the height of a man, which crowned the tall stern. The gilding on the lantern glinted in the sunlight.

'God's Blood!' muttered Dunton beside him. 'That's a royal ship, I wouldn't wonder. Can't make out her flags, but she could be Spanish or Dutch maybe. She'll be a tough nut to crack.'

A hurried council was already forming up on the stern deck of *Izzet Darya*. The captain, his chief officer, the pilot and the aga of the janissaries clustered in a group, and Hector could overhear snatches of their conversation. The pilot was urging caution, warning that the strange ship was too powerful to attack. The aga of the janissaries, stroking his mustache and striking an attitude, retorted that if the pilot could bring the galley close enough for his soldiers to board, his janissaries would soon clear the foreigner's decks. The galley's chief officer, a grizzled Turk, said nothing but waited patiently for the captain to speak, and all the while the oarsmen kept up their steady beat, moving the great galley forward.

Turgut Reis gazed thoughtfully at the sailing ship. This was not a vessel he had seen before, though it did have a certain similarity to the warship that had brought the English ransom agent to Algiers. He wished he had brought his sketch of that ship with him, even though this ship was much larger and, as yet, showed no flag. If only he had that sketch, it might help him decide whether the stranger was a warship or some rich merchant vessel. He looked again at the distant vessel. She was no more than four miles away now, and still helpless and becalmed. The captain thought about his ill luck on the corso so far, the debts that awaited him when he returned to Algiers, and that he had only a few days' supplies left before he would have to return to base. He thought, too, about the damage to his reputation if it was said that he had shirked a fight with a large infidel ship. He knew his pilot was a cautious man who would always advise care, just as he knew that the aga was certain to demand a direct attack and boast of the courage and the fighting spirit of his odjaks. The captain did not doubt that at close quarters the weight of numbers and the terrifying charge of the janissaries would win the day. But first he had to get *Izzet Darya* close enough to board the stranger.

'They're lowering their boats!' It was his chief officer who spoke, excitement in his voice. Turgut squinted into the distance. Yes, it was true. There was activity on the stranger's deck. They must have been shocked by the menacing sight of two corsair galleys emerging as if by magic from the mist, and heading towards them. Figures on deck were hurriedly lowering boats into the water, and a large boat which had been towed astern was being hauled closer so that oarsmen could scramble aboard. 'They're abandoning ship!' said a voice. Turgut wondered if this could be true. Often the crew of a vessel attacked by corsairs would leave their ship and flee for safety in their small boats. They would head for the nearest coast where they would run ashore and hide rather than be taken captive. But the Sardinian coast was too far for the small rowing boats to outrun the brigantine. 'No,' said another voice, 'they're trying to tow their ship out of trouble.' That was more likely. The ship's longboat and its tenders were moving to the bow of the becalmed stranger, and hawsers were being lowered to them. Maybe they were hoping to outpace their pursuit until darkness covered their escape.

The captain made up his mind. 'Allah concealed us from our enemy until the time was ripe! Now we attack!' he called out. Turning, he gestured to the accompanying brigantine that both ships were to advance at full speed and close with their prey from directly astern. Seeing this, the oarsmen in the waist of *Izzet Darya* began to cheer a rippling 'Ya Allah! Ya Allah! Ya Allah!' as they laid on their oars and began to increase the tempo of their stroke.

Hector felt the galley's motion increase beneath his bare feet, and looked to the bow platform where Dan was checking the muskets of the janissaries. Dan glanced up and waved. Beside him Dunton said quietly, 'Well here we go! The captain's not the sort of person to run away from a battle. Let's hope he's not about to catch a Tartar.'

'What do you mean?' asked Hector.

Dunton was staring intently at the sailing ship. 'Seems to me,' he said softly, 'that she could be built for war. That big stern castle and the heavy bulwarks on the bow are the marks of a fighting ship. Still, if the calm stays with us, it shouldn't matter too much. Right now, her main deck cannon – if she's got them – are nigh-on useless. If we attack from directly astern, they can't be brought to bear. She'll have only one or two stern chasers, so she's vulnerable.'

The words were scarcely out of his mouth when there was the sound of a cannon shot, and a puff of smoke from the ship's towering stern. A moment later, a cannonball skipped across the surface of the sea, sent up a trail of white splashes, then plunged into the sea, half a mile ahead of the approaching corsairs.

'Levarim! Levarim! Lay on your oars! Lay on your oars!' yelled the overseers on the catwalk. But there was little need for their exhortations. The oarsmen of *Izzet Darya* were already at full stretch, eager to close with their prey and earn the plunder they craved. Only in the bow, where there were three or four benches of slaves who had been placed aboard by their Algerine masters, was it necessary for the overseers to ply the courbash. 'Strongly! Strongly! My children,' Hector heard Turgut say under his breath, and he wondered if the captain had the same worry as Dunton that the aged galley was heading for a mistaken target.

Again the thud of a cannon, and the splash of a cannonball, this time closer to the galley. 'Good shooting,' commented Dunton. 'Those are not amateur gunners.'

'Why don't we fire back?' enquired Hector.

'No point,' came the reply. 'Our iron gun hasn't the range, and besides it will hamper the oarsmen if we have to load and train the weapon. We'll just have to take our medicine for the next few minutes. Run the gauntlet of those stern chasers until we are close enough to open fire ourselves. Better yet, get alongside and board her.'

©

'FORTSA! FORTSA! Row Hard! Row Hard!' the galley's overseers were cheering on their men, and *Izzet Darya* surged forward, steadily closing the gap.

A double thud as, one after the other, the two stern chasers of the sailing ship fired at the approaching corsairs. This time a cannonball threw up a burst of spray which drenched the portside oarsmen.

A closer explosion as *Izzet Darya*'s own gun answered. Hector felt the galley tremble beneath his feet. But the shot fell short.

'Watch out! She's coming round!' cried Dunton. Hector looked forward over the heads of the straining oarsmen. Where before the sailing ship had presented her tall stern to the galleys, now he could begin to see along her quarter as slowly she began to turn. Out to one side he saw her boats. Their crews were rowing frantically, the towlines taut. 'They're pulling her to bring her into position so she can use her main armament,' said Dunton. He sounded worried. *Izzet Darya*'s pilot had seen the danger, and called out to the helmsmen to try to stay directly astern of their prey.

Another twenty oar strokes, as 160 men in teams of five strained at each huge oar handle, and then their opponent began to open fire with her main deck guns. There was no broadside, just an irregular series of loud reports as each gunner found he could bring the advancing corsair vessels into his sights. Dunton was counting, 'five . . . six . . . seven.' He paused as the cannon shots ceased. 'Thank Christ for that!' he muttered. 'Seven, maybe eight cannon a side. She's an armed merchant-man. We should be able to cope with that.' His sigh of relief was cut short as another cannon fired, then another, and another. Looking ahead, Hector saw that the sailing ship was almost entirely obscured in a great cloud of gun smoke billowing around her. 'Oh shit!' blurted Dunton. 'Twenty guns a side, maybe more. She's a ship of war, a fourth-rate at least.'

There was a bellow of rage from the aga. The Turk was staring off to the side, at the accompanying corsair brigantine. One entire side of the brigantine's oars had stopped, the blades poised level with the sea. For a moment Hector thought that perhaps a cannonball had struck and damaged the ship. But then in a sudden moment of silence he distinctly heard the cry, 'Siya! Siya! Back! Back!' and the oars began to move again, but this time in reverse. Inexorably, the brigantine began to turn, swinging away from *Izzet Darya* in a tight arc, as the smaller ship altered course, away from the fight. 'Cowards! May you rot in hell!' The aga was brick red with anger, roaring and raging as the brigantine completed her turn. She was fleeing from the scene, abandoning the attack, and putting as much distance as possible between herself and the cannon fire. 'Seems they were counting cannon shots as well,' said Dunton bitterly.

Turgut Reis stepped forward to the rail that divided the stern deck from the lines of benches where his crew were still labouring their oars. Many of the rowers were beginning to show signs of exhaustion, others were wild-eyed with fear. 'My children!' he called out. 'We press on! Now there is all the more plunder for us. Allah will protect us! Soon we will be alongside. Fifty gold pieces to the first man who climbs aboard.'

There was a rattle of musket fire from the bow platform. Hector saw that the janissaries had begun shooting, aiming forward over the low breastwork that surrounded the bow platform. He wondered whether their target was really within range or whether the odjaks were firing their muskets to vent their frustration. He could not see Dan.

Suddenly there was an appalling crash and the galley quivered from stem to stern. A cannonball had struck the vessel, but for a moment Hector could not identify any damage. Then he saw the gaping hole on the port side, where the shot had torn away the outrigger support for the forward oars. He heard screams of pain and fear, then remembered that this was where the slave oarsmen had been placed, chained to the oar benches. *Izzet Darya*'s iron cannon fired, and a neat round hole suddenly appeared in one of the stranger's limp sails.

'They're firing too high, stupid bastards,' said Dunton. 'We can't take much more of this. We've got to get closer.'

Another crash, and this time the cannonball cut a bloody path through the rowers on the starboard oar benches. The rhythm of the oar strokes faltered. Hector felt the galley slow down. 'Avanti! Avanti! Forward! Forward!' yelled the overseers, and this time they were lashing even the volunteer oarsmen. Hector could detect that the crew was very close to panic. 'Ya Allah! Ya Allah! Ya Allah!' The rowers tried to take up the cadence of their work again, but the galley was partially crippled. Hector was reminded of a many-legged insect which struggles onward even when a third of its legs has been torn away. He looked forward, trying to see what was happening to Dan, and could not see his friend. Astonishingly, he saw that the janissaries were utterly unperturbed. He witnessed one of the odjaks set down his musket, calmly relight his long pipe, then pick up the musket again before taking aim.

'Bloody hell!' Dunton gasped, dismay in his voice. Hector looked round, trying to see what had alarmed the sailor. The enemy ship was less than a couple of hundred yards away now, every detail clearly visible. In a few moments *Izzet Darya* could close the gap, and then her boarding party would get in action. Soon the fight must be over.

Then he knew what had unnerved Dunton. The long pennant which hung from the stranger's masthead was stirring. Hector could make out its colours, red and white. And the gun smoke which had shrouded the tall hull was drifting clear in wisps. The calm had ended, and a light breeze had sprung up. Even as he watched, Hector saw the great sails begin to flap and lift as they filled with the wind, and slowly the sailing ship began to move through the water. Even as the crippled corsair galley desperately tried to close the gap, the great ship began inexorably to slide out of reach.

'Fortsa! Fortsa!' The overseers were in a frenzy, demanding a final effort from the oarsmen. But the oarsmen were nearly collapsing. Hector, his nostrils filled with the smell of gunpowder, heard their sobs of exhaustion and effort. Several of the men were merely going through the motions of rowing, trying to keep time with their comrades. Here and there Hector saw a rower give up the effort, and slump to the deck.

Another crash, and this time a cannonball smashed a bloody track through the oar benches, body parts flying into the air. The fervour and discipline of the oarsmen began to disintegrate, as more and more of them realised that their efforts were useless.

Izzet Darya could not catch the sailing vessel. Several teams of oarsmen stopped rowing, releasing their grip on the oars and sitting down on the benches, their bare chests heaving as they gasped for breath. The motion of the corsair galley slowed to a crawl as their prey steadily drew farther and farther away.

Dunton was shouting at one of the Turkish petty officers. Hector guessed the Turk was the caravana in charge of sail handling. 'Leva! Leva!' Dunton was bawling, waving his arms frantically. 'Hoist sail! Hoist sail!' But there was no response. The Turk seemed at a loss, unable to act. It was the captain himself who responded. Moving to a position where the oarsmen could see him clearly, he called out, 'Well done, my children! You have given of your best. Now is the time to make best use of the wind that comes also from Allah. We will become falcons!' He had raised his right arm in a gesture of encouragement when, shockingly, he was struck by a hail of metal. One moment he was standing on the aft deck, and the next instant his body had been flung backward and he was just a lifeless heap on the deck, his white gown like a rumpled shroud. Nor had his officers escaped unscathed. The pilot was clutching at his face, blood seeping between his fingers, and the aga was staring down, numbed, at a mangled foot. 'Oh Lord be our Protector!' groaned Dunton. 'Perrier guns. They're going to finish us off.'

Hector tore his gaze away from the sight of the dead reis and looked towards the big sailing ship. The crew were brailing up the sails, slowing their vessel now that she was at a safe distance from the crippled galley and could manoeuvre. Even as he watched he saw activity on the high stern deck. Men were clustering around the light swivel cannon mounted along the rail, the perrier guns which could send hails of small shot and sweep a deck clear of men.

'Leva! Leva!' Again Dunton was roaring and gesticulating. He leapt up on to the main spar and frantically began unlacing the sail ties. Farther forward, the braver and more experienced sailors on the crew were hastily uncoiling the main halyard where it had been stowed, and laying it out along the catwalk.

Those overseers still on their feet began to push and shove men into position where they could begin to raise the sail. A tall, thin Algerine with a wild look in his eye began to chant a work song, and incredibly some sense of order and discipline returned as perhaps a score of those not wounded began to haul on the great rope and the massive mainyard slowly began to rise.

The spar was dangling some ten feet in the air when there came another crash of cannon, the loudest yet. This time it was not the irregular thump and report of individual guns, but the ragged roar of a broadside. At point blank range the warship's gunners could not miss. The broadside struck the stationary galley amidships, and broke her back. Men and oars were flung into the water. The bow and stern both tilted upward as the mid section of the venerable hull began to sink under water. The sea rushed in on the benches and Hector heard the desperate screams of the slave rowers still chained to their benches and unable to escape. The stern deck slanted under his feet, and sick at heart he watched Turgut's corpse slip down and come to rest against the rail, itself already half under water.

Shocked and dazed, he grasped at a splintered post. Then, as the stern section began to roll over, he was washed into the sea.

As he came back to the surface, he realised that something had changed. The sounds of firing had nearly stopped, though the air was still thick with gun smoke. He coughed and choked. Something nudged against his shoulder, and he clutched at it blindly. He found he was grasping the canopy from the galley's stern deck. Air had been trapped within the cloth so that it had risen to the surface, and was bobbing, half submerged. Steadying himself with one hand on the makeshift raft, Hector looked around.

The captain's bloody death had distracted him from thinking about Dan's fate, but now he scanned the mess of flotsam and wreckage, trying to spot his friend. The bow section of the galley was almost gone below the surface, and he saw only the heads of a few strangers nearby. Dan had disappeared. Closer to hand he glimpsed a face that was familiar. Thirty yards away was Dunton. He was clinging to a small piece of floating wood which was insufficient to keep him afloat. Every few seconds Dunton would submerge, coming back to the surface with panic in his face. 'Here! Here! Swim over here!' Hector called out. Dunton heard him, and twisted round to face him. Again he half-disappeared and was spitting water as he came back to the surface. 'I can't!' he gasped. 'I cannot swim!'

Hector had learned to swim during his summers on the Irish coast and now he slid into the water and struck out for the English sailor. 'Here, hang on to me,' he gasped as he reached Dunton. 'I'll tow you back.'

Dunton was floundering desperately. 'It won't work. That slave ring on my ankle pulls me down.'

'Come on!' snarled Hector. 'Hold on round my neck. You can do it!'

With a sudden lunge Dunton abandoned the sinking flotsam and grabbed on to his rescuer. Hector clenched his teeth and began to swim, trying to regain the raft. The effort was enormous. However hard he swam, he was making little headway. Dunton was a dead weight on his back, pulling him down. Hector took great mouthfuls of air and knew that his strength would soon ebb away. He swallowed a mouthful of seawater, gagged, and for a moment he thought that he too would drown. Squeezing his eyelids shut to clear his eyes of the salt water he looked ahead, trying to judge how far he had come. He was still not halfway to the makeshift raft. 'I said you could not make it,' whispered Dunton behind his ear, and then – miraculously – the sailor's grip relaxed and Hector found himself swimming free. He glanced over his shoulder and had a last glimpse of Dunton as he slipped under the water.

Even without the English sailor on his back, Hector was at his last gasp when finally he reached out and touched the floating canopy. Pulling himself up on its slippery wet surface, he lay there panting. Dimly he was aware of other survivors from the disaster who approached the raft. Once or twice he felt the canopy shift beneath him as they too heaved themselves on to its surface. He lay with his eyes closed, utterly spent and still in shock from seeing the captain meet his death. The captain had bought him in the same way as a farmer buys a promising colt at auction, yet Hector could only remember Turgut's kindness, his compassion, and the words of encouragement when his protégé had faced his sunset – 'Don't be afraid. It happens at once, and is a wonderful thing as Allah has wished. Praise be to God.' Hector hoped that the same was true for the manner of Turgut's death.

Abruptly a hand was seizing the collar of his loose shirt, and he found himself dragged off the canopy, then hauled bruisingly over the edge of a small boat, and dumped into its bilges. A voice said in English, 'We've got another of the bastards.' Someone knelt on him painfully and tied his wrists behind his back. A short while later he was pulled to his feet and then half lifted and half thrown up the side of a ship where he found himself on a steady, dry deck. Swaying with exhaustion, he kept his eyes down and watched the salt water trickle out of his clothes and make a wavering line across the planks. He felt wretched.

'Ti! Moristo? Mauro? Turco?' a voice was asking aggressively. Someone was trying to establish his nationality, speaking in rusty lingua franca and standing so close that he could smell the interrogator's foul breath. But Hector felt too tired to answer. 'He's not wearing an ankle ring. Must have been one of the crew,' claimed another voice gruffly. Someone was fingering the qibla still hanging from its thong around his neck. 'Look at this,' said the first voice. 'He's an Allah worshipper all right. Saw this when I was in the bagnio at Tunis.'

Hector raised his head and found himself looking into the hostile face of a common sailor. A jagged scar running from the corner of his mouth to his right ear gave him a brutish look. Behind him stood a short, badly shaved man wearing a wig and dressed in clothing which had once been of fine quality but was now shabby and stained with grease spots. Hector took him to be a ship's officer.

'My name is Hector Lynch,' he said, addressing the officer. 'I am from Ireland.'

'A Papist turned Mussulman, that's droll!' mocked the officer. 'A bucket that has dipped twice into the sink of iniquity.'

'My father was a Protestant,' began Hector wearily, but his reply was cut short by the officer's retort. 'You're a renegade and turncoat, whatever stripe of faith you were before. To be serving with Barbary pirates means you deserve to hang. But as you are worth more alive than dead, you will be kept in chains until we reach port. Then you will wish you had gone to the bottom of the sea along with your thieving friends.'

Hector was about to ask the ship's destination when the sound of a hammer on iron distracted him. A little distance behind the officer, the ship's blacksmith was striking off the ankle ring of a starved-looking galley slave who must have been rescued from the wreck of *Izzet Darya*. Standing next in line, awaiting his turn and dressed only in a loincloth, was Dan. The Miskito, Hector recalled, had been wearing his slave ring when he had joined the corso, and Turgut Reis had not ordered it to be removed. Clearly the warship's crew had mistaken Dan for a slave they had liberated from the corsairs. Deliberately Hector forced himself to look away. Any sign that he knew Dan would betray his friend.

'Take the renegade and put him with his fellow blackguards!' ordered the officer, and Hector found himself pushed across the deck to join a group of bedraggled survivors from the galley; among them were several odjaks. As he stood waiting to be led away to the prison hold, Hector heard a cheer go up. The starved-looking man had been freed from his slave ring, and several of the warship's crew were gathering round to slap him on the back and congratulate him on his liberty. As Hector watched, Dan stepped forward impassively and placed his foot on the blacksmith's anvil. A few sharp blows and the blacksmith had knocked out the rivets from the ring, and again a cheer went up. But this time, the congratulations were cut short as the starved-looking man suddenly turned and, snatching at Dan's loincloth, whipped it away so that the Miskito stood naked. Pointing at Dan's circumcised penis, his accuser screamed, 'Rinigato! Rinigato!' and gave a vindictive whoop of triumph.

TWELVE

C

CHEVALIER ADRIEN CHABRILLAN, Knight Grand Cross of the Order of St Stephen, was thoroughly satisfied with his day's purchase. Through his agent, Jedediah Crespino of the well-known Tuscan banking family, he had just acquired thirty prime slaves for galley service. The slaves had appeared on the Livorno market unexpectedly and Jedediah had snapped them up. An English warship, the *Portland*, had sunk a large Algerine corsair off Sardinia, and pulled a number of her crew from the water. Naturally the *Portland*'s captain wanted to profit from his victory so he had landed his captives at what was the biggest slave market in the Christian Mediterranean, with the possible exception of Malta. Tall and aristocratic, Chevalier Chabrillan was a familiar figure in Livorno. Always immaculately dressed in the red uniform of the Order, he had a reputation as something of a dandy. Indeed observers had been known to remark that such a renowned galley captain had no need to take so much trouble with his appearance, always powdering his cheeks and parading the latest fashion in periwigs and buckled shoes. His celebrity as a warrior for the Faith, they said, was already suffi-cient to make him stand out. Chabrillan, they agreed, was a true heir to the days when the Duke of Florence had been able to send two dozen galleys under the flag of St Stephen to confound the Turk. And when the Grand Magistry had announced that it could no longer afford to equip and man such a large fleet, the Chevalier had offered to meet the costs of keeping his own vessel in commission, and had obtained permission to cruise in company with the vessels of the Order of St John of Malta. So his frequent appearances in Livorno were usually to buy and sell slaves or to negotiate the disposal of prizes.

Livorno was ideal for such transactions. Declared a free port by the Duke of Tuscany less than a decade earlier, it was now a thieves' kitchen on a grand scale. On the waterfront and in the counting houses it was quietly acknowledged that the transactions of men like Chabrillan were best not investigated too closely. Ostensibly the galleys of the Orders were licensed only to cruise the sea in search of vessels belonging to 'our enemies of our Holy Catholic Faith', as Grand Master Cotoner in Valletta put it. Such vessels could be seized and sold, together with their crews and cargoes. And should a Christian ship be found to be carrying Muslim-owned goods, then the Order's captain could impound only the goods but must release the vessel. Often, however, both goods and ship were confiscated, and on occasion the Christian crew themselves were held for ransom or even sold as slaves.

In such delicate traffic Livorno relied on its Jewish population. There were nearly three thousand of them, and they had been granted exceptional privileges. Here a Jew could own property, wear a sword at any hour, employ Christian servants and did not have to wear the Jewish badge. They also operated a complex network of commerce with their co-religionists in Tunis, Malta and Algiers. It was for this reason that Chevalier Chabrillan valued his connection with Jedediah Crespino so highly.

℗

'ONE HUNDRED SCUDI a head, a most satisfactory price if I may say so, though the English captain did insist that he was paid at once and in silver,' observed the Jewish banker. He and Chabrillan had met in the Crespino's private apartments at the end of the day's business. Jedediah lived in great style even though his office was only a minor outpost of the Crespino mercantile empire. He ran his business from a building overlooking the docks, and the first-floor room in which the two men now sat was sumptuously furnished with heavy brocades, fine furniture, rich rugs and a brilliant display of coral ornaments — a sign of the commerce in trinkets and religious artefacts which had been the mainstay of the Crespino fortune in the early days. 'Will you be selling on the slaves or keeping them for yourself?' the banker continued.

Chabrillan turned back from the window where he had been admiring the fine bronze statue put up on the waterfront to honour the memory of Grand Duke Ferdinand. It was most appropriate, he had been thinking, that the Duke's statue was supported by the figures of four Turkish slaves in chains. 'No, I want this batch shipped to Marseilles,' he said. The Jew nodded appreciatively. 'Ah yes, I hear that King Louis plans to expand his galley fleet.'

'He intends to develop the most powerful naval force in the Mediterranean, and his royal Galley Corps needs oarsmen wherever they can be got. The French are running out of convicts to put to the benches, and I have been commissioned to act as their purchasing agent for foreign slaves. My budget is impressive.'

Crespino regarded the tall aristocrat with interest. He wondered why Chabrillan, who was known for his piety and his fierce hatred of the Muslims, should now seek to serve the Sun King, Louis XIV of France, whose antipathy to the Turks was not so consistent. The answer was not long in coming.

'I have accepted a captaincy in Louis's Galley Corps which was offered to me. I will devote most of my time to it. I believe the Corps will soon become an essential ally in the Everlasting War.'

The Everlasting War, the Jew thought to himself, was madness. A mutual destruction pact between the Christians and the Muslims, it had been going on for centuries, and if men like Chabrillan had anything to do with it, would go on forever. Meanwhile, of course, the Crespinos in Livorno, the Cohens in Algiers, and his particular acquaintance Lazzaro dell'Arbori in Malta did very well out of arranging ransoms, negotiating prisoner exchanges, disposing of plunder, bartering slaves, and a host of discreet commercial transactions.

'Are you not afraid that Louis and his galleys might become so powerful that one day they will surpass the Order of St John in the Mediterranean?'

Chabrillan shrugged. 'Most of the Knights of St John are themselves French. They serve the Order and the Pope, but they retain allegiance also to France.'

'A fine balancing act.'

'No less than yours.'

The Jew inclined his head. 'If you wish, I can also arrange the delivery of the slaves to the royal galley base at Marseilles.'

'Yes. Please do that. I need the men there as soon as possible. In Marseilles they will be assessed and distributed among the French galleys so it would be helpful if you could provide me with their individual details, ahead of time, so that I can pre-select the best ones and have them added to the crew of my own vessel when it joins Louis's fleet.'

'Then I will arrange for the slaves to be forwarded to Marseilles in two lots. If you can arrange for the selected slaves to be identified, they will be sent – after some delay – in a second consignment. By the time they arrive in Marseilles someone will be ready to allocate them to your ship.'

'One more thing,' the Chevalier added. 'When you are preparing the paperwork, you might value the slaves at one hundred and thirty scudi per head. The French will pay the extra money without question, and I would be obliged if you would forward the surplus to Malta for the benefit of the Order of St John. Grand Master Cotoner needs all the available funds so he can proceed with his improvements to the fortifications of Valletta. Once that work has been completed, La Religion shall have the finest harbour in the Mediterranean.'

So this was what the Christians meant when they spoke about robbing Peter to pay Paul, the Jewish banker thought. Chabrillan was living up to his reputation as a fanatic who stopped at nothing to prosecute the Eternal War. Little wonder that he was known as 'the Lion of La Religion' and his galley, *St Gerassimus*, flew Chabrillan's personal banner, which displayed the Five Wounds of Christ. The Jew had heard extravagant stories about Chabrillan: that he had accomplished more caravans, as the marauding cruises against the Infidel were called, than any Knight whether of St John or St Stephen, and that he had played a heroic part in the valiant defence of Crete against the Turk. There, it was said, he had been taken prisoner by the Muslims and tortured. Perhaps this accounted for his hatred of Muslims.

In all his experience Jedediah Crespino had never encountered a man so fiercely zealous for his faith.

©

'I'M AMAZED that you did not sink and drown,' Hector said to Dan. 'That iron ring around your ankle should have pulled you under.'

Dan laughed. 'Every Miskito has to be a strong swimmer. The Miskito coast is a place of swamps and backwaters. In the rainy season the rivers flood and everything is submerged. So we build our houses on stilts and sometimes we must swim to reach the places where we keep our boats. And when we go to the sea for fishing we think nothing of it if our canoes, which are no more than hollow logs, capsize and tip us into the water. Every Miskito child learns how to turn the canoe the right way up, then climb aboard and bale it out. So when the galley sank it was easy for me to reach the nearest piece of floating timber and scramble up on it. I was there only a short time before the sailors from the warship came in their small boat and collected me.'

'I'm sorry that you were identified as a renegade, Dan. I feel responsible because I encouraged you to become a Muslim.'

'Hector. If you think back, it was me who first suggested that we take the turban. Now, as a result, we find ourselves both back in a situation which seems much like the one we sought to escape. Perhaps together we can again find a way out of it.'

Hector found it difficult to share his friend's optimism this time. The two of them were shackled hand and foot, then attached to a length of iron chain linking them to a third captive, a taciturn and luxuriantly mustached odjak from *Izzet Darya*. The janissary's name, Hector had learned, was Irgun. Well over six feet tall and big-boned, he rarely smiled and had an unshakeable calm manner. Standing nearby were four more odjaks, all prisoners taken from the sea by *Portland*, and similarly chained together in a group. They were waiting at the head of a gangplank and about to disembark from the merchant ship that had brought them from Livorno. 'That's Marseilles up ahead,' a sailor had said to Hector as the ship made her landfall. 'Richest port in all of France. Full of whorehouses and taverns. Not that you'll enjoy them. You're the King's property now.'

Hector had no idea what the sailor was talking about, for they had caught only a brief glimpse of the man who had paid for them, a Jewish commission agent who had come aboard the English warship in Livorno and spent some hours closeted with the captain in his cabin. The next morning they had been taken ashore and placed in a noxious cell where they were then held for three weeks, being fed on scraps, before being shipped out again.

Gazing about him, Hector could see evidence of Marseilles's prosperity. On two sides the basin was overlooked by fine buildings, five or six stories high and roofed with slate. Part warehouses, part offices, their tall fronts glowed yellow in the afternoon sun. To the west, behind him, two powerful forts guarded the entrance to the harbour whose waters were furrowed by an armada of wherries, skiffs, palangriers, tartans and lighters, being rowed or sailed about their errands. At the foot of the gangplank, the wharf was bustling with activity. Dockers were piling up bales and crates, rolling huge barrels and man-handling enormous brown earthenware storage jars, cursing and cajoling as they loaded the goods on to donkeys and ox carts. Stray dogs ran here and there. Porters staggered past, bent-kneed under the burdens hoisted on their shoulder poles; and, ignoring the chaos, little gatherings of merchants and store clerks, traders and dealers were busy gossiping or bargaining with one another. 'Allez! Allez!' a shout came from behind him. A grey-haired man in a leather waistcoat had come aboard clutching some papers, and was now ordering the prisoners to go ashore.

It was awkward to negotiate the slope of the gangplank without snagging their chains, but, once on land, Hector and his companions shuffled in the direction the man in the waistcoat indicated – towards an enormous building which dominated the south-eastern corner of the waterfront. Its walls were painted blue and decorated with yellow motifs which Hector recognised as the fleur-de-lis, the symbol of the French king. Another huge yellow fleur-de-lis surmounted the great dome which rose from the interior of the building. Smells of pitch and tar, of raw timber and hot metal, and the sounds of hammering and sawing told Hector that they were approaching a vast Arsenal and shipyard.

'Allez! Allez!' Their drover was shouting at them to go around the building and approach it on the landward side. As they turned the corner, Hector saw ahead a sight he would never forget. Coming down the busy street which led from the heart of the city was a column of about fifty men. They were dirty and dishevelled, with long matted hair and unkempt beards.

Most were dressed in rags, and some wore broken boots or clogs while the rest were barefoot. They moved slowly as if exhausted. All of them wore metal collars, and from each collar a light chain joined each man to a central heavier chain, so that the entire column was linked together as a single unit which made a mournful clanking sound as it limped forward. At the head of the column rode an overseer mounted on a bay horse, and on each side were more mounted men, clearly guards, equipped with bullwhips. Three or four carts brought up the rear of the column and – to Hector's astonishment – several desperate-looking women were keeping pace, occasionally darting into the column to speak to one or other of the chained gang.

'Halte-là!' The leather waistcoat shouted at Hector and his companions to stand where they were and allow the column to pass in front of them. As Hector and Dan looked on, a double gate in the Arsenal's yellow outer wall swung open to receive the long, sad file. Led by the mounted officer, the column began to be swallowed up, though the women were prevented from entering. Uniformed sentries blocked them from going any further. The women beseeched and begged, but the soldiers firmly held their muskets crosswise as a barrier, holding them back. One tearful woman fell to the ground, keening in anguish.

'Allez! Allez!' The leather waistcoat was bawling urgently at his charges to move forward and enter the Arsenal before the gates were shut and barred. Once inside they found themselves in a large open parade ground where the prisoners of the column were standing meekly. Guards were removing the iron neck collars, and then dividing the prisoners into small batches. As each batch formed up, it was escorted to what looked like the main administration building and taken inside. Several minutes would pass, and then a guard appeared and shepherded away another batch of prisoners. Eventually all the prisoners had been removed, and the square was empty except for Hector, Dan and the odjaks. Their escort in the leather waistcoat had walked away, ignoring them. Moments later a guard came to the open door and beckoned to Hector, Dan and Irgun.

They were directed into a large whitewashed room where bent over a table was some sort of official dressed in an ill-fitting black coat with tarnished silver buttons. His pen was poised over a ledger. 'Nom?' he enquired curtly, without even raising his head which, Hector observed, was flecked with specks of dandruff. Clearly the official was a receiving clerk and had mistaken them for another batch of prisoners from the column. Grateful to the friars who had taught him French Hector replied, 'Lynch, Hector.'

The clerk scratched down the information in the ledger. 'The crime of which you are condemned?'

'No crime,' said Hector.

Angrily, the clerk looked up and saw the three prisoners from *Izzet Darya* standing in front of him. 'Where are you from?' he demanded. 'You are not with the chain.'

'We are from the galley *Izzet Darya*.'

At the mention of the galley, Hector thought he saw a glimmer of recognition in the official's eyes. 'And your name?' he asked Dan. The Miskito understood what was wanted, and answered simply 'Dan'. Again the pen scratched across the surface of the ledger. Next it was the turn of the odjak but he did not answer, and stood silent and staring down at his interrogator from his great height. 'He does not comprehend,' Hector intervened.

'Then you tell me what he is called.'

'His name is Irgun.'

'Any documents to confirm your identities?' the clerk said irritably.

'No.'

'Then I shall put you all down as Turks. That will be all,' and he began to fill in a column he had left blank in the ledger.

'Guards! Uncouple that big Turk and put him with his fellows where he belongs. Take the other two away, take off the linking chain, and keep them separate from the rest. Tomorrow they will be assigned to their duties. And if there are any more Turks outside, you can conduct them to their cells without bothering me with the details.'

The guards led Hector and Dan down a long corridor, across a courtyard, and through a series of doors which were unlocked and then relocked, and finally left them in a cell some twenty feet by twenty feet. It was unfurnished except for a layer of damp straw, two benches and a bucket that was evidently being used as a latrine. Stretched out on one of the benches was a tough-looking man with close-cropped dark hair who sat up as the cell door slammed behind them and regarded them with distaste.

'How come they put you in with me?' He spoke French with a strong accent. At some time his nose had been badly broken.

'What's that?'

'You're Turks.'

'No. I'm from Ireland, and Dan here is from the Caribees.'

The broken-nose man hawked and spat in the straw. 'Then how come he's wearing a leg ring? Anyhow Turks, Moors, slaves – doesn't matter which. They all mean the same thing if you're condemned to the oar. And if you're Irish, how come you're here?'

'We were in the bagnio in Algiers, and converted. Now we're treated as renegades.'

'You're lucky they didn't hang you the instant they caught you. That's King Louis's usual way of dealing with renegades. They must be in too much need of oarsmen to give you the long drop.'

'Who are they?'

'The King's Galley Corps. I've been here before, and that's

why they're keeping me apart from the others. To stop me tipping them off about what's to come and how they can dodge the worst.'

'What others?'

The man nodded towards a small barred window, set high in the wall. Hector stepped up on the bench, took a grip on the bars and hauled himself up so he could look out. He was staring down into a large hall, as bare and bleak as his own cell. Seated or lying on its straw were the crowd of disconsolate prisoners who had just arrived with the chain column.

'I was with that lot on the stroll from Paris,' explained the fellow prisoner disdainfully as Hector lowered himself back down. 'Took us nearly a month, and more than half a dozen died on the way. The argousins . . .' Seeing that Hector did not know who he meant, he explained, 'The argousins are the convict-warders. They weren't any worse than usual, but that thieving bastard of a comite who was in charge had done the usual corrupt deal with the victuallers. We were served half rations, and nearly starved.'

'If you're not a slave, what are you here for?'

The man laughed without mirth, and turned his face to one side, exposing his cheek. 'See here.' Beneath the grime Hector could just make out the letters GAL marked in the skin. 'Know what that means?'

'I can guess,' Hector answered.

'That's how I was branded three years ago. I was a galerien, a convict galley oarsman. But I was too slippery for them, and managed to get myself a pardon. Paid a clever lawyer to say that there had been a case of mistaken identity and there were plenty of other vagabonds and rogues called Jacques Bourdon – and they had taken up the wrong one. But it took him so long to get my case heard that I had already been marked for galley service by the time my pardon came through. And the lawyer had cost me all the money I had, so I had to go back to my old trade when I returned to Paris. That was the only way to stay alive.'

'Your old trade?'

Jacques Bourdon shot out his right hand, and for a moment Hector thought the convict was going to hit him. But Bourdon only raised his thumb. Burned into the soft flesh between thumb and forefinger was the letter V. 'Don't often see someone with two brands, do you?' he boasted. 'That one stands for voleur. I'm a thief, and a good one too. Started by nicking things when I was a youngster, and didn't get properly caught until I was in my teens when I stole a pair of candlesticks from a church. That's how I got my first brand. But I wouldn't do anything so obvious as church robbing now. I pick pockets and locks. It's less risky, and I wouldn't have been caught the second time if a jealous rat had not informed on me.'

'What about all those others?' asked Hector. 'What have they done that they find themselves here?'

'I didn't bother to ask. But you can be sure that they're the usual riff-raff. There'll be swindlers and murderers and thieves like me. Some won't have paid their debts, and others have committed perjury. Probably some smugglers, too. Rascals caught moving contraband tobacco or avoiding the salt tax. Then there are the deserters from the army. Like you, they're lucky not to have been hung or shot. And naturally every last one of them will swear that they are innocent of the crimes for which they have been found guilty and sent here. A few might even be telling the truth.'

Hector was silent. It seemed to him that this prison was the sink of injustice. Then he said, 'But surely, if you were able to get a pardon, the innocent ones could do the same.'

The pickpocket regarded him sardonically. 'Yes, if they have enough money hidden away or someone on the outside who can help. But once inside here, the chances of getting out are almost nil. Deserters and renegades like yourself are condemned for life, and even if by some miracle their cases come up for review, the Galley Corps has often lost track of its own oarsmen and can't locate them.'

Hector recalled the clerk who had just written down their details in the ledger. 'But surely it's all recorded in the official files.'

Bourdon laughed outright. 'The clerks couldn't care less whether their book entries are correct. Half the time they know they are being told lies, and so they scribble down what pleases them. If a man gives a false name, that's accepted. And if he lies about the reason why he is sent to the galleys, then that's all right too. And if the entrant stays silent before the clerk, or he's too frightened and confused to answer why he's been condemned, or he doesn't even know the charge against him, do you know what the clerks write down then? They note down that he has been condemned to the galleys and add "without saying why". Goodbye to any hope of redemption.'

'I find that difficult to believe.' Hector's spirits were sinking even further. 'Everyone knows why they are here, or at least has some idea of the reason?'

'Listen to me, Irishman,' said the pickpocket, seizing Hector by the arm. 'There were people who walked with me all the way from Paris who had not the least inkling why they were in chains. Maybe an unknown enemy had reported them to the authorities. All it takes is an accusation planted in the right quarters and accompanied by a juicy bribe. Then there's a show trial at which you have to prove your innocence when you are already presumed to be guilty. And heaven help you if you are a Protestant and you are answering to a Catholic judge. Being a Protestant is getting dangerous in France.'

THIRTEEN

NEXT MORNING Hector awoke from a fitful sleep to hear his name being shouted aloud. A guard was banging on the open cell door and calling out that he and Dan were to make themselves ready for an interview with the commissaire of the Arsenal. As he got to his feet, Hector was surprised to hear Bourdon call out impudently, 'What about me?' In answer, the guard opened the door, walked across the room and struck him hard across the mouth. Undeterred, the pickpocket asked, 'So who's the commissaire now? Another of Brodart's friends?' The guard scowled as he turned on his heel and the pickpocket called out to his retreating back, 'Whoever it is, tell him that Jacques Bourdon's a man with whom he can do a little business!'

'What did you do that for?' Hector asked. 'It only made him angry.'

The pickpocket shot Hector a quizzical glance. 'I don't suppose you even know who Brodart is,' he said.

Hector shook his head.

'Jean Brodart is our lord and master. He's Intendant of Galleys and chief administrator of the Galley Corps, appointed by Minister Colbert himself. He's also one of the most corrupt men in the kingdom. Brodart and his cronies are skimming every livre that King Louis pays out for his precious Galley Corps. They're up to every trick, whether putting non-existent workers on the payroll, demanding kickbacks from suppliers, selling off surplus stores, writing up fraudulent bills of lading. Believe me, compared to the Intendant and his gang, the swindlers and fraudsters on the chain were innocent lambs. Wait and see, my message will get through. Brodart's underlings can't resist even the smallest crumb.'

When the guard returned half an hour later it was to escort Hector and Dan back to the administration building and up a staircase to the first floor until they arrived before a door guarded by a sentry in a blue uniform with white crossbelts. Their escort knocked, and they were shown into a large room lit by tall windows which gave a view across the city.

'I understand you are latecomers with the consignment from Livorno,' began the commissaire, who had been standing looking out towards the distant roof tops. Commissaire Batiste was a pear-shaped man, badly shaved, and with several expensive rings glittering on his puffy fingers. 'I have a note here saying that you are to be assigned to the galley *St Gerassimus*. That is very irregular, particularly because the *St Gerassimus* has not yet joined the fleet, though she is expected shortly. Do you have any idea why you are singled out for special treatment?'

'No, sir,' Hector answered. 'No one has told us anything.'

'The Arsenal is going to need every able-bodied man that can be found so I have decided that you will be held here pending the arrival of the *St Gerassimus*, and put to work. Later her captain can explain matters more fully.' He scribbled something on a piece of paper and, turning towards the guard, said, 'They are to be enrolled under premier comite Gasnier. Go and find Gasnier, wherever he is, and deliver them in person, and get his signature on this paper as a receipt. And tell the comite that he's to train them to be productive.'

They returned to the ground floor and, escorted by the guard, began to make their way through the Arsenal, searching for the comite. The place was an immense, sprawling maze of warehouses, magazines, depots and armouries, so their quest took them first to an iron foundry where anchors and chains and metal fittings were being forged, then to a vast draughty shed where sails were spread on the floor or hung from beams to be cut and sewn. Next was a ropewalk in which teams of men were twisting huge ropes and cables, then several wood-working galleries where mast makers and carpenters were shaving and straightening spars and oars, and finally a melting shop where half-naked labourers toiled over the huge pots that bubbled with boiling pitch and tar. Finally they reached a series of long, low, barn-like structures. The smell of rotting seaweed and the sight of ships' masts protruding over the perimeter wall told Hector that this side of the Arsenal bordered directly on the harbour. Their escort took them through a side door and, all at once, they were looking down on the skeleton of a galley which lay in dry dock. Two dozen men armed with mallets were swarming over the vessel, busily knocking her to pieces. 'Comite Gasnier!' the guard called out over the din of the hammers. A paunchy bald man, dressed in scuffed work clothes, was standing at the edge of the dry dock, supervising the work. He waited for a moment, to satisfy himself about some detail, then came over to speak to them.

'New recruits for you, comite,' said the escort respectfully. 'The commissaire says that you are to make something useful out of them.'

Gasnier looked at Hector and Dan thoughtfully. Hector had the impression of a solid, sensible man. The comite's calm gaze took in their manacles. 'Right then, leave them with me,' he answered, then turned back to his duties, leaving the two prisoners standing where they were.

It was almost another hour before Gasnier paid them a second glance when, after shouting something to an underling who seemed to be his foreman, he came over to the two prisoners and announced, 'I don't want to know what you did to get yourselves here, only what you can do for me in the future. First let me say that if you behave yourselves, I'll treat you fair. But if you give any trouble, you'll discover what a hard man I can be. This is the moment for you to tell me what you think you are good at. Speak up!'

Hector stumbled over his words as he answered. 'I was a clerk on a galley for a few weeks,' he said. 'And my friend here was with the musketeers.'

'A musketeer, eh?' The comite looked at Dan. 'He doesn't speak French, does he?'

'No, sir.'

'Well, that's no harm. He doesn't need to speak the language if he's got clever hands. Can he mend guns?'

'I believe so, sir.'

'What about you? A clerk, you say.'

'Yes sir. I was responsible for keeping track of stores.'

'Any good at it?'

'My master seemed satisfied.'

'Well if you're going to be a storekeeper here, you need to keep an extra sharp lookout. All sorts of things go missing. See that galley down there?' the comite nodded towards the dry dock where the men were keeping up an incessant thumping and banging with their mallets. 'Notice anything unusual?'

Hector stared down at the workers. The men were busily breaking down the galley, carrying away the timbers and setting them on one side in neat piles. Most of the workers were wearing what seemed to be a prison uniform of a parti-coloured jacket of dark red and brown worn over heavy canvas trousers. The legs of the trousers were also in different colours, one brown and one buff. All of the men wore bonnet-like caps, but some were dark blue and others were scarlet. He guessed that these marked a different status between the prisoners, and was about to comment when he noticed something else. The planks, frames and beams that were being stacked up were freshly cut.

The workers were taking to bits a galley that had never been put to sea. He said as much to the comite.

'That's right,' confirmed Gasnier. 'That's what they're doing,' but he did not explain further. He only beckoned to an assistant and instructed him to take Dan to the armoury and leave him there in charge of the chief armourer for assessment as a gunsmith. Then, addressing Hector again, he said, 'You report to the head storekeeper. He'll tell you what to do. You'll find him in the main depot over by the sail loft.'

℃

THAT EVENING Hector and Dan met when work at the Arsenal finished for the day and they were shown to their dormitory.

'I never imagined there were so many muskets in all the world,' Dan told his friend. 'There are ten thousand of them stored in the Arsenal – four galleries lined with rack after rack of guns, and they all have to be checked and cleaned and repaired as necessary. I'm to be one of forty gunsmiths employed in that task.'

'Will you be able to manage?' Hector asked.

The Miskito nodded confidently. 'I passed my test. The head armourer handed me a musket and used sign language to ask me what was wrong with it. I pointed to a dangerous crack in the barrel which would burst one day, and I mimed the sort of injury the explosion would do to the man who fired it. He would lose an eye or be scarred for life.'

Dan stretched luxuriously, extending his arms above his head.

'As soon as I passed my test, an armourer removed my wrist and ankle chains and only left the ankle ring in place. He told me that I will be handling gunpowder from time to time, and the less metal I have about me, the less chance there is of a spark setting off an explosion.'

'Wish the head storekeeper would do the same for me,'

commented Hector. 'Wrist fetters are a real handicap when it comes to handling a pen.'

He was about to continue when a voice behind him said, 'I told you that the commissaire would snap up the least crumb.' Hector turned to see Jacques Bourdon standing in the doorway, a smug look on his branded face. 'It only goes to prove the old saying that appetite comes with eating,' the pickpocket added as he sauntered into the room.

'You mean you managed to bribe the commissaire?'

'It didn't take much, just two small silver coins.'

'And where did you get the money?'

'And wouldn't I have been stupid not to make a few advance arrangements when I heard I was to be taken south from Paris with the chain? I sent my lass on ahead to Marseilles with the cash from my last robbery. I couldn't hide it on me because I knew those swine of argousins would strip and rob us on the way down here. So she was waiting at the Arsenal gate for one last embrace and it was the sweetest kiss she ever gave me. A mouthful of silver.'

The pickpocket sat down on a bench. 'It seems I've also managed to get myself assigned to that missing galley of yours. What's her name? *St Gerassimus*, though who was Gerassimus, or what he did to deserve his sainthood, I've no idea. But the rumour is that the galley's to receive the pick of the new Turkish slaves in from Livorno, and that's good news. Turks make the best oarsmen, as anyone in the Galley Corps will tell you, and if your fate is to be a galley oarsman there's no better place on the bench than alongside a great big strapping Turk. Which reminds me,' the pickpocket nodded towards Dan, 'you said your friend here isn't a Turk, then why's he wearing that ring, and no chains?'

'He's working in the armoury,' Hector explained. 'It's to avoid accidents.'

Bourdon appeared unconvinced. 'Tell him not to get any

fancy ideas about running away, now that his legs are free. He looks enough of a foreigner, with that long ugly face and brown skin, to be mistaken for a Turk.

Thinking back, Hector recalled that few of the men he had seen dismantling the galley had been wearing chains.

'That's how you'll recognise the Turks among the other galley men,' Bourdon continued, 'Turks don't wear leg chains or even wrist fetters when on shore.' He leaned back against the wall, clearly pleased to be showing off his superior knowledge. 'They only wear an ankle ring. The authorities know that the Turks will very seldom try to escape, because where would they go? They would find it very hard to get aboard any ship to take them home, and here in France who would take them in? So there's no point in keeping them chained up, except on a galley at sea for fear they mutiny and take over the vessel. And even a mutiny is unlikely. The funny thing about the Turks is that they'll settle down to whatever job is given them. They'll work as hard on a Christian galley as on one of their own religion, and often you'll get better treatment from the Turk on the galley bench beside you than from your Christian neighbour at your other elbow.'

'Surely a Turk will try to escape if an easy opportunity presents itself,' said Hector doubtfully.

'If that happens, the good people of Marseilles enjoy a spot of fun,' answered Bourdon. 'There's a fat reward to anyone who brings him in to the authorities, so the local folk organise search groups and pass the word to be on the lookout for a foreign-looking cove. When they locate their quarry, they chase him, just like running down a hare or stag.'

'And when they catch him?'

'They bring him back to the argousin-major, and collect their reward.'

'And the Turk?'

'He doesn't run away a second time. His ears and nose are

cut off, and from that moment onward he is kept chained to the bench, and not allowed to go ashore.'

ℂ

HECTOR HAD BEEN only a fortnight in his job as a storekeeper's assistant when he came to appreciate the truth of Bourdon's claim that the management of the Arsenal was riddled with graft. He was standing at the iron-bound gates of the powder magazine, making a tally of the gunpowder kegs arriving from an inbound galley, when he noted something strange. There was a strict rule in the Galley Corps that whenever a vessel returned to port she sent ahead her ship's boat loaded with all her kegs of powder. These were placed in the Arsenal's thick-walled powder magazine for safe storage because some years earlier a fully armed galley had blown up in harbour, either by accident or sabotage, and there had been heavy loss of life. Hector had issued gunpowder to the same galley just two days previously, and now he observed that while the number of barrels he received back was the same as had been given out, several of the markings on the kegs were different. Since his days in the stone quarry of Algiers he had made a habit of noting down the different markings on the kegs, and when he checked with the head storekeeper his suspicions deepened. 'Our gunpowder comes from all over France,' the storekeeper told him blandly. 'It depends on the contractors. They're all small producers because there are no large gunpowder factories, and naturally each maker has his own marks. Just write down the number of barrels returned, and leave the list with me.'

When Hector mentioned the incident to Bourdon that evening, the pickpocket rolled his eyes in mock surprise. 'What do you expect? The commissaire who organises the purchases of supplies for the Corps will have lined his own pocket when he placed the original powder contracts, and naturally the head storekeeper takes a cut when the materials are delivered into store. So he looks the other way when the captains and quarter-masters on the galleys have a bite at the same cherry.'

'But how do they do it?' asked Hector.

The pickpocket shrugged. 'I have no idea, but you can be sure that if there's a way of turning a quiet profit, someone will have found it. My guess is that the galley captains are selling the better quality powder to the Marseilles merchants, and replacing it with low-grade, cheaper material. But it's not your job to say anything. You don't exist as far as France is concerned. You are a non-person. Even if you reported your suspicions to someone like comite Gasnier who has the reputa-tion of being incorruptible, and he brought the matter before the authorities, you could not serve as a witness. Once you've been committed to the oar, you are legally a dead man. If I were you, I'd try to work out how the fraud is being done, and then keep that knowledge to yourself until you can use it to your own advantage. But be very careful! The people who run this place take good care that King Louis stays so besotted with his precious Galley Corps that he doesn't ask awkward ques-tions. They wouldn't look kindly upon anyone who might upset their cosy schemes.'

©

JUST HOW FAR the Intendant and his staff would go to impress the King became clear when the head storekeeper summoned Hector to his office the very next afternoon.

'I am selecting you for special duty. The Intendant has informed every department that next Thursday the Arsenal is to demonstrate its skill and efficiency in the Royal Presence by building, launching and equipping a new war galley in just thirty-six hours.'

Hector was too astonished to reply.

'Of course it's nothing more than a stunt,' the storekeeper sniffed. 'But that's what Intendant Brodart has ordered us to do, so we have to put up with it. The Intendant boasted to the King and to the minister that the Arsenal is capable of such a feat. Premier comite Gasnier has known about it for weeks. Now it's official.'

'With respect, sir, do you think it can be done?' Hector asked carefully. 'I thought that a galley took at least a year to build, maybe twice as long. And the timbers have to be kept until they are seasoned, and that takes at least a couple of years.'

The head storekeeper regarded the young Irishman suspiciously. 'Who told you that?' he asked.

Too late Hector realised that much of the timber he had seen in the Arsenal was green, although according to the official records it had been kept in store for years. The head storekeeper, he concluded, was well aware of the fraud.

'I don't know,' he said vaguely. 'Maybe that's something that the boat builders do at home and I picked it up there.'

'The royal Galley Corps uses only the finest hand-picked timber,' his superior said quietly, and with a slight edge of menace in his voice continued, 'Anyhow we will not be issuing timber for this new galley from stores. Everything has been prepared, as you would have noticed if you had kept your wits about you.'

The remark reminded Hector of comite Gasnier's comment when he had first seen him at the dry dock.

'You mean the new galley which will be built in the presence of the King, has been built before?'

'You have sharp eyes,' admitted the storekeeper. 'Gasnier's dry dock gangs have been practising for weeks. Pulling apart a galley, then putting her back together again. Not the whole vessel, of course, just the more awkward sections. This time it will be the real thing, and I'm loaning you to Gasnier as a tallyman. Your task will be to keep track of the materials, ensuring a smooth flow. The royal demonstration is scheduled to start at dawn next Thursday and the galley must be ready to put to sea, fully armed and crewed, by noon on Friday.'

©

AS IT TURNED OUT, the King, who was known for his capricious decisions, cancelled his visit to the Arsenal at the last moment. But Intendant Brodart decided that the demonstration would go ahead, knowing that reports of its outcome would reach the court. Long before daylight on the appointed day Hector reported for duty at the dry dock. There he found some five hundred carpenters assembling on the edge of the dry dock, which was empty except for the 160-foot keel of the galley lying ready on its chocks. In the flickering light of banks of torches the carpenters were being divided into squads of fifty, each led by a senior shipwright and a foreman. Nearby were marshalled two companies of nailers, and behind them again a hundred caulkers were preparing their caulking irons and pots of tallow and tar. Each man was already wearing a cap whose colour told him on which particular section of the vessel he would work. Hector's responsibility was to a gang of porters, forty men, standing by to carry the ready-cut timbers from stacks on each side of the dry dock. He was to make sure they picked up the right pieces in the correct order, and took them to the proper sector the moment they were needed.

'Listen to me, men,' bellowed comite Gasnier. He was using a speaking trumpet and standing on a scaffolding where he could look down on the entire dry dock and direct the progress of the building. 'You're doing a job that you've done over and over again in the past. So just follow the orders you get from your foremen and supervisors and think about nothing else.' He paused while an assistant repeated his words in Turkish. Looking around, Hector realised that at least every fourth man in the building teams was a Turk. Among them he thought he recognised the hulking figure of Irgun, the odjak from *Izzet*

Darya. 'It is vital not to get in one another's way,' Gasnier went on. 'Do your job as fast as possible, step back and let the next man get on with his work. Above all, there will be no talking or shouting. You are to work in silence and use hand signals. Anyone caught talking will receive ten lashes. Only supervisors and master shipwrights may speak, and then only in a quiet voice. All other instructions will be given by whistles, and there will be a drum beat every hour, on the hour, so that you can keep track of time. Now stand by for the signal to begin.'

The start whistle blew. The porters seized the first dozen frames and carried them at a run down the ladders into the dry dock. The shipwrights hoisted them into position and began to peg them into place. By the time the first frames were secure, the porters were already arriving with the next frames in the sequence. Hector had to admit that the skill and discipline of the workforce was astonishing. In less than half an hour every frame was fitted in its proper place, a task that would normally have taken fifteen days to complete. Then, without pausing, the carpenters turned to the task of laying in the deck beams and then the planks, bending and clinching the timber so adroitly that by noon the entire hull was finished, and the carpenters were kneeling on the upper parts, urgently pegging down the deck boards. Below them the teams of caulkers were hammering oakum into the seams. By then, the cacophony of hammering and sawing had risen to such a deafening crescendo that Gasnier's rule against talking was unnecessary, for no one could have heard themselves speak. Only at dusk, when most of the wood-working was done, did the noise begin to subside as the carpenters withdrew, leaving the painters and carvers and gilders to add their decorative touches by the light of torches. By midnight the caulkers had begun to check their work, pumping water into the hull, then looking for leaks and plugging them before draining out the vessel, and applying a final underwater coat of tar. Even as the master caulker reported to Gasnier that the hull was watertight, his workmen were scrambling out of the dry dock to avoid the rising water, for the sluice gates had been opened and the dock was flooding. A priest came aboard to bless the vessel and was still saying his prayers as the galley was warped out into the harbour and alongside the quay.

By now Hector's job was done, and no one paid him any attention as he stood, bleary-eyed and exhausted, watching the riggers step the masts and spars. 'Just short of nine o'clock,' said someone in the crowd beside him, as Dan's colleagues from the armoury manhandled on to the fore deck the galley's main armament, a 36-pound cannon and two smaller artillery pieces. The Arsenal's porters were in a human chain, loading and stowing the galley's ballast, munitions, oars and sea-going gear. There came the tramp of feet and the clank and rattle of iron. Along the quay marched five companies of galley men, fifty men in each company, all in new multi-coloured prison garb and their chains newly blackened. Reaching the galley, they halted. Their argousins blew a short blast on their whistles, and the oarsmen turned and ran up the gangplanks where they dispersed to their benches and then quietly sat while the argousins chained them to their seats.

Now, for the first time in thirty-six hours, Hector saw Gasnier relax and give a quiet smile of approval. The galley's captain and officers, resplendent in their best uniforms, went aboard, and a lad unfurled the standard of the royal Galley Corps, the golden fleur-de-lis on a red field. A trumpet sounded, and the galley pushed off from the quayside. More blasts from the argousins' whistles and the oarsmen laid in place their 38-feet-long sweeps, rose to their feet, and stood ready, hands on the oar grips. A drum began to beat and the oarsmen took up a steady deep-throated chant as the great oars began to move to the rhythm, dipping into the dirty harbour water, propelling the galley away from the dock. 'Brodart promised His Majesty that the galley would be ready for sea trials before noon on the second day,' said the same voice, 'and he's kept his word.'

Hector raised his arm to shade his eyes as he watched the

newborn galley heading towards the harbour entrance. It was a beautiful sunlit morning, with scarcely a breath of wind, and another galley was inward-bound, entering between the guardian forts. As the two galleys passed, they saluted one another, dipping their ensigns as they passed. Hector saw that the arriving galley flew a flag whose badge was a red fork-tailed cross on a white field. 'St Stephen's Cross,' said the longshoreman. 'That must be our new recruit. That's the *St Gerassimus*.'

FOURTEEN

C

'WELCOME, CHEVALIER, your visit to the Arsenal is indeed an honour.' Commissaire Batiste had a fulsome greeting for Adrien Chabrillan as the Knight of St Stephen was shown into his office. 'Intendant Brodart asks me to present his sincere apologies that he cannot be here in person. He has had to leave on an urgent matter – an audience with His Majesty.' The commissaire looked pleased with himself. 'We launched a new galley yesterday, after building her in less than thirty-six hours, a most prodigious feat, don't you agree? His Majesty wishes to hear the details from the Intendant himself.'

'I saw the new galley,' commented Chabrillan dryly. He suspected that Brodart, far from going to answer the King's questions, was headed to court to make sure that as many people as possible knew about the successful demonstration.

'Remarkable, truly remarkable,' the commissaire added immodestly. He crossed to a table where a scale model of the galley was on prominent display. 'One of our galeriens, a jeweller who got a little too free with his clients' possessions, took more than eighteen months to produce this model. Yet our Arsenal craftsmen managed to build the full-sized vessel, 185 feet long and 22 feet beam at the waterline, in little more than a day. And no skimping on the materials either, finest Provençal oak for the knees and planks. Tough stuff to work. An exceptional achievement.'

He looked at his visitor, expecting a gesture of approval, and was unprepared for Chabrillan's chilly response. 'A galley is only as good as her crew, and I've come to you for more men. *St Gerassimus* had a brush with a Turkish brigantine on the way here. Nothing conclusive as the Turk fled, but I lost five banks of oarsmen from a lucky shot, and my galley was already under-strength. A tenth of my regular oarsmen were bonnevoles, volunteers, and they are accustomed to work for plunder not pay. Many of them have chosen not to enter the service of the King. I trust you will be able to make up the shortfall.'

'These extra oarsmen you seek, would they be in addition to the Turks and demi-Turks who arrived from Livorno six weeks ago and are waiting to join your vessel?'

Chabrillan looked down his nose at the commissaire, not bothering to conceal his disdain. 'Of course. Though I have no idea what you mean by a demi-Turk.'

'A private joke of mine. A circumcised renegade,' the commissaire explained. 'There are two of them in the Livorno batch, a young Irishman who has proved useful as a storekeeper, and his foreign companion works as a gunsmith. They have received no training for the oar and may not be as strong as the Turks. But perhaps they would be adequate.'

'If they are renegades then all the more reason that they serve aboard my vessel,' Chabrillan replied. 'On the *St Gerassimus* we pride ourselves on the number of backsliders who have been made to see the error of their ways. I understand that you received a chain from Bordeaux recently.'

The Chevalier was altogether too nosy, the commissaire thought, as he regarded the tall, dandified figure before him. Chabrillan had been ashore for only a few hours, yet already he had been making enquiries about the facilities available to him now that *St Gerassimus* was part of the royal Galley Corps. The commissaire disliked meddlesome galley captains. They were a distraction from the serious day-to-day business of profiteering from the operations of the Arsenal. Batiste was from a mercantile background and held his lucrative post because he was a first cousin to Intendant Brodart, and he mistrusted those commanders who were aristocrats and put on airs.

'Yes, yes. A chain did arrive, about eighty felons, mostly tax evaders and vagrants. Several may not be suitable material for the oar . . .' he began, but Chabrillan cut him short. 'I'll be the judge of that. When can I inspect them?'

The commissaire hesitated. It was nearly noon, and he was looking forward to a leisurely lunch with a trio of echevins, aldermen of Marseilles. They were finalising a plan to acquire a parcel of land adjacent to the Arsenal, so that next year the King could be informed that the galley base needed more space and, after a suitable interval, that a site had been found which was good value. The transaction ought to net a fourfold profit for the syndicate. 'Regretfully, I have pressing duties for the rest of the day, but if you would be willing to inspect the prisoners in the company of the receiving clerk, that can be arranged at your convenience.'

'Without delay, if you please,' retorted Chabrillan.

The commissaire summoned an aide and ordered him to escort Chabrillan to the holding cells where the convicts of the chain from Bordeaux were waiting their assessment.

'And while the Chevalier is examining the convicts,' the commissaire added, 'you are to arrange for the Turks from Livorno and the two renegades to be made ready for galley service and delivered to the *St Gerassimus*, also that pickpocket, what's his name – Bourdain or something like that.' Turning to Chabrillan, he enquired, 'Who should my man ask for at the quayside? He will need a receipt.'

'He can deliver the oarsmen to my premier comite, Piecourt. He has full authority in these matters. Piecourt will also see to the necessary training of the men while I am away. As soon as

I have selected the extra men I need, I set out for my estates in Savoy. In the meantime *St Gerassimus* needs maintenance work and I trust you will have this done promptly now that you have told me how fast your workmen can perform. When I return, I expect to find my vessel fully seaworthy again and her complement properly trained.'

'The Arsenal will make every endeavour to meet your requirements, Chevalier,' the commissaire assured his guest, though inwardly Batiste was already scheming how he could rid himself of the troublesome Chevalier. On his desk was an instruction from the Minister of the Marine. It ordered the Galley Corps to conduct trials to establish whether a new artillery invention, an exploding shell, was suitable for use at sea. He decided to recommend to his superior, Intendant Brodart, that the most suitable vessel for the test was *St Gerassimus*. The sea trials would keep the Chevalier of St Stephen busy, and if they went disastrously wrong might even blow him to smithereens.

Chabrillan stalked out of the commissaire's office with the merest hint of a polite farewell, then made his way to where the receiving clerk was already waiting, his black coat hastily brushed in an attempt to smarten his appearance.

Chabrillan nodded at the clerk as he strode into the large gloomy hall where the chain prisoners were being held. 'Have the prisoners paraded in a line,' he ordered crisply. Slowly the newly arrived convicts shuffled into position, urged on by casual blows and curses from their goalers.

'Now have them strip.'

Awkwardly, for many of them were hampered by their fetters, the prisoners removed their tattered and lice-ridden clothing, and dropped the garments to the stone floor.

'Over against the opposite wall,' Chabrillan commanded. The prisoners, trying to conceal their nakedness with their hands, shuffled across the room and stood, shivering, to face their examiner. Chabrillan walked along the line, looking into their faces and glancing at their bodies. 'This one, and him, and this one,' he announced, selecting the strongest and fittest, until he had picked out a dozen men. 'Make a note of their names, have them dressed properly and sent to my ship,' he instructed the receiving clerk, 'and now let me see your ledgers.'

Meekly the clerk brought the Chevalier to his office, and showed him the list of names he had entered for the newly arrived chain. Chabrillan ran his eye down the columns, picking out those he had selected. He found he had chosen three army deserters, a poacher, a perjurer, and two sturdy beggars.

'What about these?' He pointed out the entries for five men against whose names the clerk had written, 'without saying why'.

'Just as it says, sir. They were unable to tell me why they had been sent to the galleys.'

Chabrillan fixed the clerk with a questioning stare. 'So why do you think they were condemned to the oar?'

The clerk shifted uneasily. 'It's hard to say, sir,' he answered after a short pause. 'My guess is that they are Protestants, those who call themselves the Reformed. They have made problems for those of the Apostolic and Roman faith.'

'Excellent. The Reformed make reliable oarsmen. They are serious and honest men compared to the usual felons and rogues who are condemned to the oar. I shall be glad to have them aboard,' and without another word, Adrien Chabrillan left.

'Hector, did you find out anything more about where your sister might be?' asked Dan as he wriggled his shoulders inside the red and black woollen prison jacket he had just received from the Arsenal stores. Clothes issued to prisoners came in just two sizes, small and large, and the Miskito's jacket was too tight on him. It was a warm afternoon in early summer and the two friends, together with Bourdon the pickpocket and a dozen Turks taken captive from the *Izzet Darya*, were being led along the Marseilles quay by an elderly warder whose relaxed manner indicated that he did not believe they would try to escape.

'I asked everyone I could for information about where the Barbary corsairs land and sell their captives, but I didn't learn anything more than I already knew. She could have been landed in any one of half a dozen ports,' Hector answered. He too was uncomfortable in his new clothes. In Algiers he had grown used to loose-fitting Moorish clothing and, working in the Arsenal, he and Dan had continued to wear the garments they had been wearing when captured. Now his legs felt constrained by the stiff canvas trousers issued by the Arsenal stores. The trousers fastened with buttons down the outer seams so that they could be put on over leg chains while his other new garments – two long shirts, two smocks in addition to a jacket, and a heavy hooded cloak of ox wool – could all be put on over his head. He had also been issued with a stout leather belt, which was there not just to hold up his trousers. It was fitted with a heavy metal hook over which he could loop his leg chain while he was at work so that leg irons did not hamper him. 'I wrote a letter to an old friend of my father's, a clergyman in Ireland who had been a prisoner of the Moors. I asked him if he had heard anything. But when I tried to send the letter, I was told that prisoners in the Arsenal were forbidden from communicating with the outside world. I had enclosed a note for my mother in case she is still living in Ireland, though I suspect she has moved back to Spain to live with her own people. Maybe she has heard directly from my sister. It's impossible to know. Life as a convict galerien in the Arsenal is as cut off from the outside world as being a slave in the Algiers bagnio.'

'Maybe that will change now that we're being transferred to a galley,' Dan tried to cheer up his friend.

'I doubt it. Look over there,' Hector nodded towards the far side of the docks. 'Aren't those the masts and spars of galleys? At least ten, I would say. All neatly lined up side by side.'

'Which one's ours?'

'Can't tell from this distance. But I heard that she's hired to the royal Galley Corps by her commander who's a Knight of one of the Orders. It's being said that he is a fire-eater and his premier comite is a cold-hearted tyrant.'

'Maybe someone aboard her can give you the information you're looking for,' Dan responded. As usual he was quick to point out the best possible outcome. 'Don't the Knights take their galley slaves and convicts from wherever they can get them?'

'That's true. I've not given up hope of tracing Elizabeth. The thought of finding her helps to keep me going. I sometimes wonder why you never get discouraged.'

Dan gave his companion a steady look. 'I have often thought about my homeland and the mission I was given by my people, but when that sour-faced man from London came to Algiers to ransom the English prisoners and he refused to help me, I realised the world is a much larger and more complicated place than the Miskito imagine. Now I'm resigned to the fact that I am unlikely ever to deliver the council's message to the King of England. Yet I feel that my travels may turn out to be for my people's benefit. Something tells me that I will surely get back home. When I do, I intend to bring something worthwhile with me.'

The prisoners had turned the corner of the harbour basin, and were approaching what looked like a busy pedlars' market. The wharf was covered with open-sided stands and booths which served as shops and stalls. As the convicts threaded their way between the booths, Hector saw men repairing shoes and doing metalwork, butchers and barbers, tailors, a man making hats, and stallholders selling every conceivable item from haberdashery to pots and pans. For some odd reason nearly every stall had dozens of pairs of knitted socks for sale, which hung up like strings of onions. Looking more closely, Hector realised that every one of the stall holders was a galerien.

'Same old junk,' Bourdon spoke up. 'I wouldn't be surprised

if some of those goods were on sale when I was last here.' The pickpocket was staring hard into the face of a man standing by a barrow on which lay a strange mixture of items – a pair of scissors, several fine handkerchiefs, some carved buttons, a snuff box, and various small articles which Hector could not immediately identify. 'Some of the vendors are no different either.'

Hector saw the stallholder's right eyelid flicker very slightly as he winked at Bourdon.

'Who is he?' he whispered to Bourdon.

'A thief like myself,' came back the quiet reply. 'I would say that he also fences stolen goods on the side, though it looks as if trade is a bit thin at the moment.'

'But how . . .' began Hector. They had paused while the Arsenal warder stopped to examine some lace on sale in one of the stalls.

'These baraques?' said Bourdon. 'They're run by the comites of the galleys. The port officials rent the stalls to the comites from the galleys, and the comites then put their galeriens into the booths to staff them. If the galerien has a useful skill, a carpenter or lacemaker for instance, he conducts his trade from the baraque, and the townsfolk come there for his services. Any money he earns is handed over to the comite. If he's lucky, the comite may let him keep a bit of it for himself. But if the galerien doesn't have a trade, then he has to learn to make himself useful in some other ways. That's why you see so many knitted socks. The comites hand out wool and knitting needles to their most useless galeriens, and they have to take up knitting. Naturally the comites claim that by keeping the galeriens busy in port they are less likely to make trouble. But of course the main reason is that the comites earn a nice living from their charges.'

He gave Hector a nudge. 'Look. Over there. That's someone who's either so clumsy or so stubborn that he cannot earn his comite any money, at least not yet.' Hector saw a man dressed in a galerien's parti-coloured uniform. He was wearing leg irons and cradling a cannonball in his arms. 'His premier comite will make him carry that cannonball around until he learns something that'll earn a bit of money,' Bourdon explained.

Their easy-going guard had finished at the lacemaker's stall and was strolling towards the far end of the quay. There he turned aside and pushed his way between two booths to bring his charges before what Hector thought for a fleeting moment was a fairground tent of blue and white striped canvas. It took a second glance to establish that the tent was a great canopy which covered the full length of a 26-bench war galley of the first class.

A halberdier stood on sentry duty at the foot of the gangplank. Dressed entirely in scarlet and white, from the red stocking cap on his head to his spotless red breeches with a contrasting white belt and coat lapels, he came smartly to attention, and bawled out at the top of his voice – 'Pass the word for the premier comite!' From somewhere inside the huge tent the call was repeated, and Hector heard the summons passing down the length of the galley. Then came a pause filled with the incessant background noise of the shoppers at the baraques, the mewling of the gulls, and the distant shouts of watermen. Finally, after a delay of about five minutes while Hector and the other prisoners waited patiently on the quay, a man appeared at the head of the gangplank and stood there, quietly surveying them. Dangling from a cord around his neck was a silver whistle which glinted in the sun.

Hector was taken by surprise. He had expected a rough brute of a man, violent and coarse. But the man who now stood looking them over had the appearance of a mild-mannered shopkeeper. He was of medium height and dressed in sober dark clothing. He would have passed unnoticed on the street except for his skin, which was uncommonly pale, and the fact that his close-cropped hair was a light sand colour. He did not wear a wig. 'That will be all, warder. You may leave the prisoners with me and return to your work,' the comite spoke quietly, barely raising his voice, yet every word carried clearly. His duty done, the elderly guard strolled off. But the comite made no move. He stayed at the head of the gangplank, gazing down on the prisoners, judging them. 'You are joining the galley *St Gerassimus*, and from now on you belong to her,' he announced. 'My name is Piecourt, and I am the premier comite, so you also belong to me. Serve the vessel well and you will become proud of her. Serve her badly, and you will regret the day you were born.' He spoke in French with an Italian accent. Then, to Hector's surprise, he repeated his warning, this time in fluent Turkish. Hector felt the odjaks around him stir uneasily. A moment later, Piecourt was repeating his caution a third time, using lingua franca. Aware of the impression he had made, the premier comite of the *St Gerassimus* reached for the silver whistle hanging around his neck and held it up for them to see. 'From now on the only language that matters to you is the language of this whistle, because this whistle is my voice. Everything you do will be controlled by it. You will soon be like dogs, the best-trained dogs. Obedient dogs are fed and cared for; disobedient dogs are whipped. Remember that.'

Without turning, Piecourt called back over his shoulder – 'Rowing master Yakup! New recruits for the oar. Introduce them to their benches.'

This time the creature who emerged from beneath the canvas awning was what Hector had anticipated, a broad-set, squat, dark-skinned man with a shaven head, enormously developed shoulder muscles, naked to the waist and wearing a pair of loose drawers. Also he sported a luxuriant mustache. Branded on his forehead was an eight-pointed cross. Hector deduced that *St Gerassimus*'s rowing master was a Christianised Turk, a renegade who had scarred on himself the symbol of the Knights.

'Get in line, tallest to the rear!' Yakup demanded, padding barefoot down the gangplank. Bourdon hesitated for a moment and opened his mouth to speak. Immediately the rowing master casually cuffed the pickpocket on the side of the head. The blow seemed lightweight, but the Frenchman gave a gasp and nearly fell. 'You heard what the comite said, no chattering.' Confused as to what they were meant to do, the prisoners milled around until they were in some sort of order. Hector, smaller than most of the prisoners, found himself near the head of the little column which followed the rowing master up the gangplank and on to the *St Gerassimus*.

His first impression was that the galley was identical to Turgut Reis's *Izzet Darya*, but then he realised that *St Gerassimus* was less ornate, more workmanlike. The blue and white canopy was held above head level on posts and under it three or four dozen of her crew were hard at work. Some were scrubbing and cleaning the woodwork, others were industriously splicing and mending ropes, and one squad had formed a human chain to empty one of the vessel's stores, handing up boxes and bales through a hatch and stacking them neatly amidships. Hector followed the rowing master almost halfway up the central gangway, heading towards the galley's bows, before he identified what was unusual. There were upwards of sixty men aboard, yet there was no sound of human voices. The men were working in total silence. Whenever one of them looked up from his chores to glance at the new arrivals, he took only the quickest glance before hurriedly looking back down again at his work. The quiet aboard *St Gerassimus* was eerie.

Yakup came level with the last half-dozen oar benches, halted, and turned to face the prisoners. As they advanced towards him in single file along the narrow gangway, the rowing master pointed to one side or the other, indicating to which bench each prisoner should go. Hector stepped down from the gangway to his bench and, looking back, saw that his new overseer was distributing the prisoners in balanced groups, so that each rowing bench had at a mix of large and small oarsmen, old and young. The last man assigned to each bench was an odjak. 'Tomorrow you begin to learn. Now you clean,' grunted the rowing master. He pulled up the plank which covered the gangway. Beneath was a cavity which served as a locker. From it Yakup extracted a long-handled deck brush and an iron scraper which he tossed to the prisoners. 'Clean!' Hector noticed the padded leather covering on the bench where he stood was stained. It appeared to be dried blood. The bulwark next to him was newly patched. Someone had made a temporary repair where, by the look of it, a cannonball or a hail of grapeshot had damaged the vessel.

'Pretend to be busy!' hissed Bourdon out of the side of his mouth. The pickpocket had been assigned to a place on the bench beside Hector. 'This is worse than I thought.'

'What do you mean?' whispered Hector, keeping his head down so that the rowing master could not see his lips move.

'This is a ship of fanatics,' answered Bourdon. 'No booze, no rest, plenty of lash.'

For the rest of the afternoon Hector and the other prisoners worked in silence, scrubbing and cleaning the area around the benches they had been assigned. When they finished, they replaced the brushes, scrapers and swabs into the locker under the gangway, and stowed their spare clothing in the same space. Yakup, who had been hovering on the gangway, suddenly jumped down among them. Bending down he picked up a length of heavy chain lying under the oar bench. One end of the chain was fastened to a beam, and now he threaded the loose end through the leg irons of each man, tethering them to their place. Finally he secured the end to a metal hoop with a heavy padlock. They were chained in place. Pointing to the central gangway he said '*Coursier!*' Next he slapped the padded seat of the oar bench with his hand and growled '*Banc, banc trois!*' Placing his foot on a removable board raised about a foot off the deck, he declared '*Banquette!*' Using this board as a step, he braced his other foot on a wooden bar attached to the oar bench in front, which he called the '*contre pedagne*'. He mimicked rising up with both hands extended as if holding an oar, then falling back with all his weight. 'Vogue! Tomorrow vogue!'

The sound of singing interrupted the demonstration. Hector turned to see a column of galeriens shuffling along the gangway. All of them wore leg irons, and the chains between their ankles were looped and held up on their large metal belt hooks. They were singing a hymn as they advanced, and they must have been the galley's regular oarsmen for they made their way straight to their allocated benches and sat down, five men to a bench. The leader of each group then leaned down and picked up the deck chain by their feet, passed it through their ankle fetters and meekly held up the loose end so that an argousin could come forward and attach a padlock. Only then did the galerians end their hymn, and wait silently.

A whistle sounded. At the far end of the galley, a figure appeared on the stern deck. It was Piecourt again. 'A galerien has uttered execrable blasphemies against the Virgin Mary and all the saints in Paradise,' he said. His soft voice contained a tone of menace which Hector found unsettling. Piecourt descended the short ladder down from the stern deck, and walked along the gangway until he was about a third of the way down the vessel. Turning towards the port side he ordered, 'Quarterol, strip. Vogue avant administer punishment. Black bastinado.' Hector watched as the fourth man along the nearest oar bench stood up and began to peel off his shirt. The man's hands were shaking. An argousin released the padlock on the bench chain so that the half-naked galerien could clamber up on the gangway. There he lay down, face to the deck. His arms and legs were seized and held firm by the oarsmen on the nearest benches so that he was stretched out, spreadeagle across the walkway. Slowly the largest oarsman from his bench climbed up and stood over his prostrate companion. Piecourt handed him a length of tarred rope. Then Piecourt stepped back and waited. The man hefted the rope in his hands. Hector could see that the rope flexed but did not curl. The dried tar, he concluded, must make it almost as stiff as a wooden stave. 'Strike!' ordered Piecourt. The oarsman took an upward swing with the rope and brought it down on the victim's back with all his strength. From where he sat Hector could see the red slash where the blow had cut the flesh. 'Strike again!' snapped Piecourt, expressionless. Only after twenty strokes and the victim appeared to have fainted, did the premier comite stop the punishment. 'Send for the barber surgeon. Vinegar and salt. Then put him in the cable locker till he heals.'

'Doesn't want the poor bastard to get gangrene and die,' muttered Bourdon. 'They never waste a trained oarsman.'

Hector had been feeling sick to his stomach. 'Does that happen often?' he enquired quietly.

'Depends on the premier comite,' Bourdon told him. 'Don't let it put you off your food. That should be next.'

Another whistle sounded, and this time it signalled the distribution of the evening meal. A small kitchen had been set up on the port side, where the eighteenth bench had been removed. There three galeriens were tending a large cauldron of soup. This broth was now ladled into small buckets and carried along the coursier by trusted galeriens, who slopped the broth into wooden bowls held up by the chained prisoners. Another trusty followed, handing out fist-sized loaves of bread. When the food arrived at Bench Three where Hector waited, he noticed that the big odjak seated nearest to the gangway received a larger portion. Beside him Bourdon whispered, 'Don't complain. The vogue avant always gets a larger helping than the others. It's to keep up his strength. You'll not begrudge it, I can promise you that. The vogue avant is the key man on the rowing team.' The pickpocket bit into his bread. 'At least the food's good aboard this ship. Something to be thankful for.'

Hector looked doubtfully into the wooden bowl he had been handed. It contained a small portion of oily bean soup. It smelled fermented. 'It can be worse than this?' he enquired. Bourdon nodded, his mouth full. 'Bastard contractors provide the Galley Corps with rotten provisions, and the comites serve short measure on the daily rations because they want their galeriens to spend any money they earn in buying extra stores and grog from the comite's shop. This meal is full measure and decent grub.'

Hector's guts churned at the smell of the soup, and he realised he needed to relieve himself. 'How do I get to a latrine?' he demanded.

'Over there,' Bourdon nodded towards the outer rail of the galley. 'Stick your arse over the side and let go.'

Miserably Hector crawled over his companions as each man on his oar bench shifted so that he could slide his leg chain along the central tether until he had enough slack to reach the edge of the galley. Life in the bagnios of Algiers had never been as vile and degrading as this, he thought, as he defecated over the side of the galley.

He was crawling back into his place in the middle of the bench, when there was another call on the whistle, followed by a subdued muttering among the galeriens. It must have been the signal that gave them permission to talk among themselves. Immediately Bourdon leaned forward, tapped the galerien in front of him on the shoulder, and asked where he came from. When the man replied 'Paris', the two of them began to speak together, keeping their voices low and talking so rapidly in city slang that Hector was barely able to follow their conversation though it was obvious that Bourdon was asking questions. Only when the pickpocket eventually sat back straight on the bench beside him was he able to enquire, 'What did you find out?'

Bourdon looked thoughtful. 'That man's a forcat, a convict. Says he ran away to sea as a youngster, got into various scrapes and finished up on a merchant ship sailing out of Lebanon. He signed on thinking that the owner of the vessel was a Christian Greek but when the ship was intercepted by a Maltese galley of the Order of St John and searched, it turned out that the real owner was a Turk and they were carrying cargo for an Egyptian Pasha. He was taken off the merchant ship, brought back to Malta as a prisoner and tried in the Order's court. The judges found him guilty as a traitor to his country and to his faith, and condemned him to the oar for life. They even put a slave price on him to reward the crew who had captured him. Apparently the owner of *St Gerassimus* bought him – paid for him right on the courtroom steps – and he's been on the galley for the past three years. He doesn't expect ever to get off it unless by death or illness.'

'So he's as badly off as we are,' commented Hector.

Bourdon still looked pensive. 'And that's what puzzles me. He says that nearly all the oarsmen on the *St Gerassimus* are renegades captured or bought from many different countries, plus a number of Turks. Hardly anyone is serving out a set number of years at the oar. They are all lifers, and the last of the volunteer oarsmen left the galley at Malta. He thinks that the galley's owner wants a permanent crew so that the *St Gerassimus* becomes the crack galley in the fleet. Our friend claims that the galley is already the best-managed and best-disciplined vessel in the Mediterranean. It seems odd, but he was almost proud of being aboard.'

The comite's whistle shrilled yet again, and the galerien who had been talking with Bourdon called, 'Five-minute warning. Better get yourselves ready for the night. Take a leak and spread out your cloaks. The nights can be chilly. No more talking as soon as the lights are out.'

Looking down the galley, Hector saw some oarsmen were assembling small platforms perched on short poles about three feet high. Moments later they had erected little canopies over the platforms so that there were half a dozen smaller tents within the great awning. 'What are those for?' he asked. 'That's where the comites and the senior argousins sleep,' answered the galerien. 'Floating above our heads like in the clouds. Those oarsmen beneath their beds have the "reserved seats". They wait as servants on the comites, and eat scraps from their food.'

'What about us? Where do we sleep?' Hector wondered looking around.

'Just where you sit,' came the answer. 'Take it in turns to stretch out on the banc, or down on the deck. There won't be room for all five of you, so a couple of you will have to sleep kneeling, with your head on the bench.'

'There doesn't seem enough room.'

'It's luxury now,' the galerien assured him. 'Just wait until you have to share your bench with the handle of your oar.'

Belatedly Hector realised that he had not yet seen any oars on the *St Gerassimus*. He was wondering where they might be when the whistle blew again and a total silence fell on the galley.

©

NEXT MORNING he discovered what had happened to the galley's sweeps. After a meagre breakfast of water and bread the crew of the galley were marched off the *St Gerassimus* and along the quay to where two small vessels were lying. They were galliots, half-sized galleys used by the Corps as training ships. Neatly laid out on their benches were long oars with scarlet and white blades and shafts. Hector recognised the livery of the *St Gerassimus*. 'Crew to divide,' bellowed the rowing master who had accompanied them. 'Benches one to twelve on the first galliot; benches thirteen to twenty-six in the second vessel.' Hector and his companions found their way to the forward benches and were shackled in place when Yakup, armed with a bullwhip, appeared on the gangway above them. 'You with the GAL on your cheek,' he said, pointing at Bourdon, 'show them what to do.' Bourdon gripped the wooden handgrip pegged to the side of the massive oar shaft which was thick as a man's thigh. He placed his right foot on the edge of the bench in front of him. 'Now take a stroke!' Bourdon struggled to push the loom of the sweep away from him, rose up as if climbing a stair, then fell back with all his weight, tugging on the handgrip. The huge oar did not stir. 'Again!' ordered the rowing master. He flicked the bullwhip's lash across Bourdon's shoulders. The pickpocket gritted his teeth and repeated his effort, still the oar did not budge. 'Now you!' barked the rowing master, pointing at Hector. Hector took hold of the adjacent handgrips and copied Bourdon's movements. Very slightly the oar handle moved. 'And you!' This time it was Dan who joined the effort, and ponderously the massive sweep began to shift. 'And you!' The fourth man on the oar bench added his weight, but it was only when the burly odjak, seated farthest inboard, helped the other oarsmen that the heavy sweep began to rise and fall in a ponderous movement. 'Enough!' barked the rowing master, turning his attention to the next bench of novice oarsmen. As soon as Yakup was out of earshot, Bourdon hissed, 'Once the galley starts moving, watch out for the oar handle behind us. It'll knock our brains out. Here we go!'

The rowing master had finished his instructions and now gave a signal to a comite standing on the poop deck. The comite brought a whistle to his lips and gave a single blast. Every one of the oarsmen swayed forward, still seated on his bench, arms extended, pushing the oar handles in a low arc ahead of them. The whistle sounded again, and the oarsmen stood up all together, raising their hands so that the blades of the oars dipped into the sea. A fourth blast, and the oarsmen flung themselves backward, dragging the blades through the water as they fell back on the leather-padded benches. Scarcely had they regained their seats than the whistle was signalling them to repeat the movement, and a drummer alongside the comite struck the first beat of a slow steady tempo as the galliot gathered way.

'Get the rhythm, get the rhythm,' grunted Bourdon beside Hector. 'It's not strength which matters, it's the rhythm.' He gave a gasp as the rowing master's whip slashed across his shoulders. 'No talking,' came the harsh command.

The training galley lumbered forward, heading towards the harbour mouth, and Hector could see the other galliot keeping pace. Then they had passed the guardian forts, and all at once were in choppy water. It became difficult to control the massive sweep as the galliot began to roll in the waves. Seawater splashed across Hector's feet making him aware of how low the vessel lay in the water. On the oar directly behind him the inexperienced crew lost their balance. He heard a yell. Something made him duck, and the heavy handle of the loose sweep passed over his head, its oarsmen having lost their grip. The next moment the blade had tangled with its neighbour, and the massive handle swung back through a short arc and he heard a crunch as it struck an oarsman on the chest, cracking his ribs.

A burst of swearing, and the rowing master was running down the coursier towards them, his face twisted in anger, as the galliot faltered. 'Row, you dogs! Row!' he shouted, hitting out with his whip while the unfortunates on the oar handle tried to get back on their feet and bring their sweep back into action. Their injured companion lay crumpled under the bench. In one swift movement the rowing master jumped from the gangway and kicked the injured man under the rowing bench like a bundle of rags where he would not impede his fellows. A moment later he was back up on the coursier shouting at the crew to increase the pace.

For the next three weeks, Hector, Dan and the other new recruits to *St Gerassimus* learned their trade at the oar. It was a cruel apprenticeship. They rowed until their backs and shoulders ached. Their hands blistered, and when the blisters burst, the skin peeled away leaving the flesh raw and bleeding. The soles of their naked feet were bruised by the constant pressure against the banquette and bench in front of them. Night after night they came back to the *St Gerassimus* to eat the same unpalatable ration of bean soup and bread, and then fell into an exhausted sleep, only to be roused at dawn by the comite's insistent whistle. However, as the days passed, their muscles strengthened and grew accustomed to the strain; thick calluses developed on their hands and the soles of their feet, and they achieved the knack of setting an even rhythm and obeying the steady pounding of the drum. Before long they could recognise each call on the comite's whistle, so that they stopped and started, increased or lowered the speed of their strokes, or reversed direction of their blades as fluently as if they were a single machine. And with the improvement in their skill, Hector found that he and his companions on bench three were developing a conceit. At first it was a matter of winning races against their colleagues in the other training galliot. Then, after the Arsenal dockyard workers had finished their repairs on St Gerassimus and the galley could put to sea, it became a demonstration of their superiority over the other galleys in the fleet.

They never saw their captain. In his absence Piecourt ran the galley, adjusting the performance of St Gerassimus with a care that reminded Hector of a harpist he had once seen tuning his instrument. Piecourt and the rowing master shifted oarsmen from one bench to another, varying their weights and strength until they had achieved the best performance. Hector, Dan and Bourdon were regulars on the third bench, with the big odjak Irgun as their vogue avant, but it took some time to find the best quinterol, the fifth oarsman who sat farthest outboard. Then, one day, Piecourt put beside them a man whose nose and ears had been crudely sliced away. When Hector quietly asked the newcomer his name, there was no reply only a snuffling sound through the cratered nostrils. When Hector repeated the question, the unhappy man turned his ravaged face towards him and opened his mouth. The tongue was missing, torn out. Even Bourdon, the hardened pickpocket, was shocked.

The mute leaned forward and with his fingernail slowly scratched some signs on the oar handle, then sat back.

Hector stared at the marks. They meant nothing to him at first, but then the memory came back to him of lessons with the monks in Ireland. They had taught him the rudiments of Greek, and the letters made by the mute were Greek. They spelled out 'Karp'.

'Your name is Karp?'

The mute nodded. Then cupping a hand on each side of his

head, he stared straight at Hector. 'You can hear, but you cannot speak?'

Again the nod, and Karp sketched out a cross in the Greek style, the four arms of equal length.

'You are a Christian? Then why are you here?'

Laboriously Karp tried to explain but Hector could only piece together occasional scraps of his story. Karp's homeland was somewhere to the east and ruled by the Turks, but how he came to be a slave on the *St Gerassimus* was not clear. Nor could Hector unravel the reason for Karp's mutilation. He could only presume that it was punishment for trying to escape or, perhaps like the Sicilian thief in the bagnio of Algiers, he was an inveterate criminal.

At dusk when the comite's whistle blew and Hector knelt down and placed his head on the rowing bench to begin his rest, he fell asleep listening to Karp's breath rushing in and out of the wreckage of his face.

℃

CHEVALIER ADRIEN CHABRILLAN returned to his ship for the Festival of the Galleys. Piecourt had prepared for the great day with his usual meticulous attention. The great blue and white awning had been taken down and stowed, and the crew had washed and scrubbed the deck planking until it gleamed. The dockyard's painters and gilders had been busy, primping and beautifying the galley's carved decorations. The sailmakers had sewn and fitted new canopies and tilts for the poop deck, using roll after roll of velvet and brocade and given the added touch of gold fringes. The spars and rigging of *St Gerassimus* were hung with bright flags and banners, some showing the fleur-de-lis of France but many more with the cross of St Stephen. The halberdiers of the guard were in their best uniforms.

The Chevalier came aboard at noon with his guests, a cluster of well-born gentlemen, several wealthy merchants and their ladies, and all were dressed splendidly for the great occasion.

They paused to admire the wonderful spectacle of the fleet: galley after galley neatly moored, flags and pennants rippling in the light breeze, their gaily painted oars fixed at an upward angle so they seemed like the wings of birds. Then they sat down to a splendid meal at tables arranged on the poop deck and covered with white linen. All the while, there was no sight nor sound of a single oarsman aboard the galley. *St Gerassimus*'s benches stretched away empty, leather padding gleaming with polish, as the Chevalier's guests savoured their way through the seven courses of their repast. Only when they were toying with dessert – served with a sweet wine from Savoy – did Piecourt, who had been standing in the background, step forward and blow a single long blast on his whistle.

Hector, Dan and two hundred other galeriens had spent the past four hours crouched in the narrow space between the benches. Piecourt had promised thirty lashes of the black bastinado to any man who spoilt his surprise for the captain's guests. Hearing the whistle, Dan and his companions took a deep breath and, as one man, exclaimed 'Hau!' At the same time they stretched up their right arms, fingers extended, in the air. The Chevalier's guests startled by the sound which seemed to come from the belly of the vessel, looked up to see a forest of fingers appear above the benches. 'Hau!' repeated the hidden oarsmen as they extended their left arms, and the number of fingers suddenly doubled. 'Hau! Hau!' and they raised first one arm and then the other. 'Hau!' This time the galeriens lay down on the deck boards and waved their right legs above the benches, then their left. The guests looked on, amazed. Now the oarsmen sat up. All together, they suddenly raised their heads above the galley benches. Each man was wearing his red prison cap issued by the Arsenal, so that the effect was as if a field had suddenly sprouted a sea of red flowers. So it went on. More than two hundred oarsmen performed the routines that Piecourt had made them rehearse for days, standing up, sitting down, taking off their shirts, opening their mouths, coughing in unison, bowing to their audience, removing their caps, putting them on again, until finally they all stood, half naked and facing their audience. Then they gave the chamade, rattling their chains in a sustained clattering roar until Piecourt gave a final sharp blast on his whistle and every galerien abruptly stopped, dropped his arms to his side, and stood silently to attention, staring straight ahead.

The distinguished guests broke into spontaneous applause.

FIFTEEN

C

A MILE FROM WHERE *St Gerassimus* floated on an indigo blue sea, the first slopes of the Barbary mountains rose behind the close-packed buildings of a small Moorish town where a river drained from a cleft in the mountains. In front of the town a dozen or so feluccas and caiques lay at anchor in the roadstead, their decks deserted. The foreshore too was empty except for the rowing boats abandoned by the sailors who had fled their vessels the moment that *St Gerassimus* had appeared over the horizon. The arrival of the galley had taken them by surprise. In the past the town's walls had proved stout enough to resist all but a prolonged attack, and the place was too insignificant to reward a major assault by any enemy. So the attention of a first-class war galley caused some puzzlement among the citizens though there was no great concern as they watched the new-comer hover quietly in front of the town, her oars occasionally moving as she maintained her station. The more observant of the townsfolk did, however, note something a little unusual about their visitor. The galley was not floating level. She was down by the bow.

On board *St Gerassimus*, premier comite Piecourt too was anxious – but for other reasons. The morning after the Festival of Galleys the Chevalier had summoned Piecourt and the sous comites to tell them that the galley was to put to sea within the week. During the banquet Commissaire Batiste had informed the Chevalier that the galley was to proceed to the Barbary coast, there to test the newest artillery weapon in the Corps Arsenal. The order came from Minister Colbert himself, and was to be obeyed with all despatch. Details of the armament were kept secret, and it was not until Piecourt saw the monstrous device floated out to his galley on a pontoon that he feared the result. The weapon was grotesque: a short, black cannon that reminded him of a gargantuan beer pot sitting on a heavy wooden sledge. What this monstrosity weighed he had no idea, but it had required a triple tackle to hoist the gun on to his galley's foredeck, the rambade. As the monster was lowered into position he distinctly felt the galley tilt forward. He had removed the ship's other guns, and shifted ballast further aft. He had also ordered the galley's main anchor, normally kept in the bows, to be stowed below deck nearer the stern. Yet even when this was done, *St Gerassimus* still felt unwieldy, and the squat black mass on her foredeck appeared to him like an ugly wart.

But worse was to come. On the morning *St Gerassimus* left Marseilles harbour, she hove to outside the pier head so that the Arsenal's gunpowder barge could come alongside to offload the test ammunition for the cannon – a hundred hollow cast iron globes filled with explosive and half as many kegs of a fine-grade gunpowder as propellant. The gunpowder was stowed in the galley's magazine but the bombs, as the technician who accompanied the shipment called the heavy spherical projectiles, had to be kept separate. Some were already primed and fused and coated in sticky tar. Apparently they were to be sprinkled with gunpowder immediately before they were inserted into the gun's gaping mouth. In theory the gun then shot the bomb high in the air, the tar-and-gunpowder coating ignited and, as the bomb blazed through the sky, the weapon lit its own fuse. When the device dropped into the target, it cleared any defences and smashed through any obstacle before exploding with massive damage. What happened if the fuse caught fire too soon and the bomb burst prematurely inside the cannon did not bear thinking about. *St Gerassimus*'s mission was to test the reliability of the weapon.

'Do you think the gun will work with the new bombs?' Hector had asked Dan as they sat in the warm sunshine, chained to their oar bench and waiting for orders as the galley drifted on the glassy calm.

'I don't know,' answered the Miskito. 'I heard about it when I was in the armoury in the Arsenal, but never saw it for myself. The gun was kept in the artillery park.'

'Yet the technician recognised you when he came aboard.'

'He visited the gunsmiths a couple of times while I was working with them, to ask if we could improve one of the new designs of fuse. It's a plunger which is screwed into the bomb casing. When the bomb lands on target, the plunger is meant to drive inwards, striking sparks from a flint and igniting the powder inside the bomb, just like a musket. He didn't know much about boats as far as I could tell. He's more a technical man.'

'You would have thought they would have picked someone with better sea legs. He was seasick all the way here from Marseilles,' said Hector. He looked over his shoulder for at least the twentieth time, to gaze at the coast of Africa.

'Apparently a galley makes an ideal platform for his mortar – that's his name for the launching gun – because the weapon is so heavy and awkward to move about on land,' Dan continued. 'But a ship can take the gun wherever it is wanted, and a galley can aim the mortar accurately by manoeuvring so that the gun is exactly at the right range and angle to throw its bombs on target—'

His explanation was cut short by Piecourt's voice. 'You there! Get up on the rambade! The gunner wants you.' The premier comite was on the coursier, pointing at Dan. 'Secure your oar, and take your companions with you.' He bent down to unlock the padlock to the bench chain and allow the men to slip clear, but when Karp and the vogue avant Irgun made as if to move, Piecourt raised his whip threateningly. 'Stay where you are!' he ordered.

Dan led Hector and Bourdon on to the wooden platform of the rambade. The technician was fussing over the mortar. It sat on its massive sled, pegged and chained to the deck. Nearby a large tray held several bombs, a tub of fuse cord, and a number of fuses to be tested. At a safe distance, lashed against the rail, were some small kegs of gunpowder.

'The first job is to check the bombs and their contents,' said the technician, a small worried-looking man with badly bitten fingernails. It seemed he was also to act as gunner. 'Any of you know about gunpowder?'

Bourdon gave a sardonic laugh. 'Only how to make this mark,' he said, pointing at the letters GAL branded on his cheek. 'That's how they make the brand permanent. They rub in gunpowder as soon as the hot iron is lifted.'

'I've worked in a quarry,' Hector interjected. 'I'll show him.'

'Good. The gunpowder must be kept separate at all times. Even empty barrels can contain fine particles which may explode,' warned the gunner, then turned towards Dan. 'I need you to make sure that the correct charge is loaded into the mortar's chamber, and that the firing fuse is properly inserted in the bomb, and in working order. You'll find all the tools you need in that canvas bag over there.'

As Dan prepared the mortar, Hector and Bourdon checked over the bombs. They removed each bomb's wooden plug, mixed and poured in more gunpowder through a funnel, made sure the powder settled evenly in the hollow sphere, and finally tamped home the plug again. It reminded Hector of the days when he was setting blasting powder into the rocks of the Algiers quarry. Careful to observe the gunner's safety instructions they returned the empty barrels to their place against the rail. The sailors and the galley's gun crew normally stationed on the rambade had made themselves scarce. Even Piecourt was standing far enough away to avoid the worst effects of an accident.

'I'm ready to try a ranging shot,' called out the technician. 'Line up the vessel, if you please. The bow must point straight at the target.'

Piecourt squinted ahead at the town, then blew a series of calls on his whistle. Obediently the oarsmen dipped their blades into the sea, the starboard side pulling ahead, while their companions backed water. The galley slowly swivelled. A sharp blast on the whistle and the oarsmen maintained the galley in position. Glancing astern, Hector saw that the officers of *St Gerassimus* had all gathered on the poop deck. They were too distant for him to recognise individuals and he wondered which was the captain, the celebrated Chevalier who was said to be such an implacable adversary of the Muslims. Even when Chabrillan had hosted his celebration of the Festival of Galleys, the galeriens had been forbidden to look directly at the Chevalier and his guests. To do so, the oarsmen had been warned, would be treated as insolence and punished with the lash.

His thoughts were interrupted by a deep coughing thud, a large cloud of dense black smoke, and the galley shuddering along her entire length. Beneath his feet Hector felt the bow of the galley suddenly dip into the sea as the massive recoil of the mortar thrust downward. A ripple spread out from her hull as if a giant rock had been dropped into the water.

The bomb could be seen high in the air, a black spot trailing smoke and flame as it raced upwards, hurtling towards the shore. Then it arched over and dropped back towards earth, only to splash harmlessly into the shallows, a hundred yards short of the town wall. There was no explosion.

'Bring the vessel in closer, please,' asked the gunner.

Again Piecourt's whistle blew. The galeriens took a dozen strokes, then paused. The galley glided nearer to the thin line of surf.

Another bomb was loaded, and this time when it was fired, the projectile landed halfway up the beach and there was a muffled explosion.

'Closer yet, please,' asked the gunner. 'Bring the galley nearer to the target area.'

'There may be shallows here,' Piecourt warned. 'I'll not risk the ship. If we come much closer, it may bring us in range of the town's own cannon. They could have a few great guns, and be holding fire, so as not to waste powder. Just one shot could do us a lot of damage.'

'I cannot increase the angle of the mortar,' complained the artilleryman. 'It's already set at forty-five degrees for maximum range. I can only add to the propelling charge, and that might burst the barrel.' He gave Dan a worried look. 'Get your friend from the quarry to help you measure accurately. We don't want any mistakes.'

All through the afternoon Dan, Hector and Bourdon worked on the rambade. They checked and primed the bombs, loaded them into the gun's maw, cleaned out the mortar's chamber after each shot and cleared the touch hole, helped the artilleryman to recharge the mortar and set the fuse, then to fire the weapon once the oarsmen had placed the galley in position. Bomb after bomb was sent towards the town, sometimes dropping short, occasionally veering off course and falling wide. One detonated in mid-air with a premature explosion that sent fragments of the metal casing pattering into the sea, an accident that drew a frightened intake of breath from the artilleryman. With practice, they learned just how much powder was needed to propel the bombs to reach their target, and just how much coating of powder was needed so that the missiles exploded on impact. The plunger fuses were soon abandoned for they usually failed to work. By the time the sun was setting, every bomb they fired was landing on target, and they could see the dust spurt up when they hit.

But there was no apparent effect on the town. The place

remained silent and still. No one emerged from the gates, nor was anyone seen on the battlements. No one fled into the hills. No fires broke out. It was as if the place was abandoned and uninhabited. Only a thickening of the dust haze above the buildings hinted at the destruction that must have taken place. By the time the light faded nearly all the bombs in the ammunition store had been fired away, and there was a tone of disappointment in the gunner's voice as he called a halt to his bombardment.

Piecourt ordered the oarsmen to row a safer distance offshore and there the *St Gerassimus* dropped anchor.

Black with powder smoke and half deaf, Hector and his two companions returned to their oar bench and were shackled in place. 'We did more damage to the galley than the town, I think,' said Hector quietly.

'What do you mean?' asked Dan.

'The rambade shuddered badly every time the mortar fired. It was worse after we increased the charge in the mortar's chamber. The deck planks started to lift. By evening the beams under them also were loose. When Bourdon and I went aft to fetch more powder from the magazine, the water in the bilge was rising faster than usual. I'm surprised that no one else noticed.'

'Perhaps they did and they kept their mouths shut. The officers were all too far away, and the rest of the petty officers are too frightened of Piecourt to interfere. He seemed to enjoy bombarding the town. He's someone who relishes other people's discomfort even if it's only at a distance. I doubt that the townsfolk enjoyed their day.'

'I wouldn't be surprised if the galley was being shaken to pieces,' said Hector. 'I've seen a galley built and know how fragile the joints are. Once the main fastenings give way, there's little to stop the vessel falling apart.'

'What would you say are our chances of surviving in that town,' muttered Bourdon. He was shaking his head from side to side, still trying to clear his hearing, and staring towards the distant land.

'I expect they would hang us from the walls after the damage we've been inflicting.'

'Not if they knew we had been forced to our work.'

'And how would you get there?'

'I'd go for a swim right now if it wasn't so far,' said Bourdon with a wink and shook his sleeve. One of the gunner's work tools dropped into his hand. It was the thin spike used for cleaning out the touch hole of the mortar. 'Never seen a better picklock. I lifted it from his tool bag when he was packing up, and he'll not miss it until the morning. I could have us loose in no time at all.' He folded his fingers over the implement, and when he opened his hand again, the tool had disappeared as if by magic. 'Told you I was a good pickpocket,' he said, a confident grin on his branded face.

Piecourt's whistle blew the signal for the galeriens to take their rest, but Hector found it difficult to go to sleep. He lay there, thinking whether it would be madness to take up Bourdon's suggestion of an escape and – as always – whether he would ever be able to track down Elizabeth. He shifted uncomfortably on the wooden deck and looked up at the sky and noted that the stars had vanished. The heavens had clouded over. From time to time he heard the tread of Piecourt or one of the sous comites walking the coursier as they carried out their night patrol, and he heard the call of the sailor on watch on the rambade, reporting all was well. As the hours passed, Hector became aware of a gradual change in the motion of the anchored galley as she tugged at her cable. St Gerassimus was beginning to pitch and roll. The noise of the waves increased. Pressing his ear against the deck planking Hector was sure that the sound of the bilge water swirling back and forth was louder. He sensed a general discomfort spreading among the galeriens as they slept or dozed all around him. Little by little he became aware of men waking up, and he heard the sound of retching as those with weak stomachs began to succumb to seasickness. He sat up and listened. The voice of the wind was definitely louder. A large swell passed under the galley and made her lurch. He heard raised voices. They came from the foredeck, and almost immediately there was the sound of Piecourt's whistle. It was the order to man the sweeps. He struggled to his feet and sat down on the bench, his ankle chain tugging painfully. Fumbling in the darkness, he joined his companions in freeing the handle of the great sweep from its lashings, and sat ready to take a stroke. It would not be easy. Now *St Gerassimus* was rolling heavily in the waves, and with each minute the motion of the galley was growing wilder. Piecourt's whistle sounded again. Hector and the other oarsmen took a long steady stroke, then another, and tried to set a rhythm. There were shouts from the foredeck, and he heard the command for the rambade crew to hoist anchor. In reply there were yells and curses, and a surge of water passed across his naked feet. He detected a note of alarm, even panic.

The galley was definitely in some sort of trouble. Hector tried to make sense of the sailors' shouts. Farther aft a sous comite was shouting. He was ordering three benches of galeriens to set aside their oars and man the pumps. The anchor must have been raised, for he felt the galley slew sideways, and there was a sudden tremor as she fell aslant the waves. Hector and his bench mates nearly lost their footing as the galley canted over so far that they were unable to reach the water with their blades, but rowed in the air. A moment later the galley had tilted in the opposite direction, and their blades were buried so deep it was impossible to work them. The chaos increased. In the darkness men missed their strokes, slipped and fell. Piecourt's insistent whistle cut through the darkness, again and again, but it was useless. Rowing was impossible.

The wind strengthened further. It was keening in the rigging, a thin, nagging screech. *St Gerassimus* rolled helplessly. Someone shouted out an order to hoist sail, but was immediately countermanded by another voice which said that this was too dangerous, that the main spar would tear the mast out of its step. Sailors ran aimlessly up and down the coursier, until a petty officer roared angrily at them.

Gradually the sky grew lighter, bringing a cold, grey dawn and a vista of angry waves racing down from the north. The galley was in real distress. Designed for calm waters, she was unable to hold up against the force of the sea. She was drifting helplessly, no longer controlled by her crew. Hector looked downwind. The galley was perhaps two miles away from land, though he did not recognise the coast. The gale must have driven her sideways during darkness. He saw a bleak expanse of bare mountain, a narrow beach, and the sea thrashing into foam on a coral shelf that reached out from the shore towards them.

'Let go the bow anchor again!' bellowed Piecourt. 'And bring the main anchor up on deck and made ready. Fetch up the main cable!'

A seaman on the rambade leaned out over the sea, knife in hand, and cut free the lashings which held the smaller bow anchor in place so that it plunged into the sea. Half a dozen of his mates ran back along the coursier and opened the hatch leading to the aft hold where the main anchor had been stowed. Two more men squeezed down into the cable locker in the bows where the galley's main hawser was kept only to reappear a moment later, wild-eyed with fear. 'She's sprung her bow planks,' their leader shouted. 'She's taking water fast!' Hardly had the words been uttered than the men who had gone aft also re-emerged on deck. 'There's four feet of water in the bilge,' someone cried. 'We'll never be able to get the main anchor up.'

Piecourt reacted coolly. 'Get back down in the cable locker,' he snapped. 'Find that main cable and bring it up.' The frightened sailors obeyed, and returned, dragging the end of the six-inch main hawser. 'Now fasten it to that bitch of a mortar, and fasten it well,' the comite told them, 'and bring levers and a sledgehammer.' His men did as they were ordered, and soon the mortar was trussed up in a nest of rope. 'Now break the gun free! Smash the bolts and planks if need be,' urged Piecourt, 'then dump the cannon overboard!' Working in grim silence the men attacked the fastenings that held the mortar in place. It took them nearly twenty minutes to loosen the gun so that they could take advantage of a sudden tilting of the deck and slide the monstrous cannon and its carriage overboard. It disappeared into the sea with a hollow, plunging sound that could be heard even over the roar of the gale. The hawser ran out, then slowed as the mortar struck the sea bed. The sailors secured the hawser, and the galley felt the drag of the monstrous cannon so she slowly turned her bow towards the waves and hung there, no longer drifting helplessly down on to the coast.

Hector had to admire Piecourt's composure. The premier comite eased himself into the cable locker to see the extent of the leak for himself, then calmly made his way along the coursier to the poop deck where Hector saw him confer with the ship's officers. Next, Piecourt beckoned to the foredeck crew who also went aft and began to unship the galley's rowing boats from their cradles above the oar benches. The galley heaved and wallowed but eventually the two boats were hoisted out and lowered into the water where they rose and fell, bumping wildly against the galley's side. It was when the sailors and several of the warders, the argousins, climbed into the boats, and were joined by the artillery man and the officers from the poop deck, that Hector realised they were abandoning ship.

The other galeriens realised it too. A low moan arose from the oar benches interspersed with angry shouts. Piecourt spoke quietly to the remaining warders who loaded their muskets and stood to face the oar benches. The two boats, filled with men, pushed off and began to pull for the shore. Their course was downwind, and within minutes the men were scrambling out of the boats and splashing up on land while the oarsmen turned and began to row back out to the galley. Their return trip was slower, and by the time they reached the *St Gerassimus*, the water which had been around Hector's ankles was now up to his knees. Whatever injury the galley had suffered, she was sinking fast

The boats made two more trips to the beach and soon there was no one left on the poop deck except Piecourt, the rowing master and half a dozen armed argousins. Just before mid-morning the galley was awash, the sea lapping the tops of the oar benches, and the galeriens were frantic. They swore and pleaded, raged and wept, tugged at their chains. Piecourt gazed at them pale-eyed and utterly implacable. 'May you rot in hell,' one of the oarsmen shouted. 'No,' called the premier comite. It was the first word he had spoken directly to the benches. 'It is you, you infidels and heretics, who will suffer torments. I shall not even think of you.' He lifted from his belt the ring of the heavy keys for the padlocks on the oar benches, held it up for all to see, and deliberately tossed it into the waves. Then he turned, stepped into the boat and gestured at his men to row for shore.

Spray from a wave crest wetted the back of Hector's neck. In front of him was a piteous sight – the heads and naked torsos of two hundred galeriens glistening above the waves as they stood on their benches and tried to escape the rising water. Flotsam, odd lengths of timber, a galerien's cloak half filled with air so it floated, all drifted past him. Beside him, Bourdon blurted, 'I dared not move while those swine argousins were watching. I'd have been shot. Let me have some slack on that chain so I can try to get at the padlock.' Irgun, the big Turk, reached sideways, seized the padlock where it was attached to the coursier and held it steady. The galley was so low in the water now that every wave submerged the padlock, and sea water gushed out of the keyhole as it reappeared. Bourdon lay prone across his companions and began to feel inside the padlock with the tip of the spike. He choked as a wave crest filled his mouth, then closed his eyes as if asleep as he concentrated on feeling for the levers within the lock. Twice the spike slipped out, and once the point stabbed into Irgun's fist. The big Turk did not flinch. Finally Bourdon withdrew the tool, bent the thin tip at a right angle, then plunged it deeper and gave it a twist. The padlock popped open.

'Well done!' blurted Hector, the pressure on his ankle chain suddenly relieved. He took a deep breath and bent forward, head underwater. He groped for the heavy bench chain, pulling it clear of his leg irons. To his right he felt Karp do the same. Coughing and spluttering all five men scrambled up on to the coursier whose top was already being lapped by the waves. 'Help us!' screamed an oarsman from a neighbouring bench. Bourdon turned and handed him the spike. 'You'll have to help yourself,' he shouted back. 'There's too little time.'

Hector looked around him. Amidships the galley was entirely underwater. Only the poop deck and the rambade were above the waves. The rambade was only a few paces away. Hitching up his leg chain to his belt hook, he shuffled on to it.

'What do we do now?' asked Bourdon, looking at the distant shore. 'It's too far to swim. Our leg irons will drag us down. They'll be the death of us.'

'Not if you do as I show you.' It was Dan who spoke. He crossed to where the empty gunpowder kegs were still lashed in place. Selecting a barrel, he unbuckled his heavy galerien belt, wrapped it around the keg, and cinched it tight. 'Hold the barrel in your arms, sideways like this, and jump overboard. When you're in the water, make sure you get the centre link of your leg chain on to the belt's hook. Then push down with both feet. It'll be like riding in stirrups. The barrel should take your weight. Don't try to swim, just concentrate on staying upright, clutching the barrel, and the wind and waves will carry you ashore.'

With that, he jumped into the sea, holding the barrel against his chest.

Hector watched his friend come back to the surface, the keg in his arms dipping this way and that, spinning and turning in the water so that one moment Dan was on the surface, the next he was beneath the sea. But soon Dan had found his balance and could be seen leaning forward across the keg, with his face far enough out of the water so that he could breathe. The barrel gyrated slowly as it drifted towards the shore. 'Come on. Hurry!' he shouted back at his companions, and one after another they leaped into the sea.

©

IRGUN DID NOT reach the shore. Perhaps he was too heavy to be supported by an empty keg or it filled with water and sank, or he failed to secure his leg chain on the belt hook. But Hector, Bourdon and Karp drifted into the shallows where Dan was waiting to assist them on to land. 'What made you think of that?' asked Hector. He was shaking with exhaustion as he sat down on the beach to rest. 'Our canoes at home,' said the Miskito. 'I told you how we turn them the right way up after they capsize. But it's not always possible. So if the wind and waves are right, a sensible fisherman just hangs on and waits until he is blown ashore. That's if the sharks don't take him.'

'I've never seen a shark. If there are any in this region, they'll soon be feasting on those poor wretches,' said Hector. He was looking back towards the galley. All that was now visible of the *St Gerassimus* was a section of the outrigger which had once supported her great sweeps and the blades of several oars pointing to the sky like enormous spines. The galley must have capsized while he and the others were coming ashore. That way, he thought to himself, the galeriens chained on board would have drowned more quickly than if the vessel had settled on an even keel. He had scarcely known any of them, yet a sense of great weariness and gloom oppressed him.

A touch on his arm abruptly brought him back to his surroundings. Karp was pointing up the beach and making an alarmed snuffling sound. A man was walking towards them. For a moment Hector thought he might be another survivor from the wreck, because he was wearing what looked like a galerien's long hooded cloak. But the stranger's garment was loose and grey, not brown. Then he saw other men, similarly dressed, cautiously making their way down the rocky hillside behind the beach.

'Greetings,' Hector called out, getting to his feet and forcing a weary smile. He spoke first in lingua franca, then in Turkish, but received no answer.

The group of strangers, about a dozen men, came closer, and stopped a few yards away. They were Moorish-looking but with paler skins. Most kept up the hoods of their cloaks, but those who did not, had shaven heads except for a long lock of hair which hung down the back of their scalps. They wore thin fillets of leather across their foreheads. Only a few carried old-fashioned muskets. They stared at Hector and his companions.

'Greetings,' he tried again. 'Can you help us, please?'

One of the strangers said something to his companions in a language Hector did not understand.

Then, to Hector's surprise, Dan intervened. He spoke slowly and haltingly, choosing his words carefully. The man who seemed to be the leader of the group replied and the two of them exchanged a few sentences.

'Who are they?' Hector asked his friend. 'And what is that language you are speaking?'

'They call themselves amazigh, "the free people", Dan replied. 'Several of the gardeners who worked with me in the gardens of Algiers spoke the same language, or something very similar. I can't understand everything they say, but they are from a village in the hills. Apparently they saw the galley in difficulties and came down to the beach to investigate if there was anything to salvage. They were frightened of the armed men who came ashore earlier in the boats so they kept out of sight.'

'That must have been Piecourt with the ship's officers and the other sailors.'

'Apparently they went off along the beach, and turned

inland. The amazigh said that they won't get far. Their clan chief lives in that direction and they'll fall into his hands.'

'So what about us?'

'They've recognised that we are slaves from the galley, and I've told them that you and I are Muslims. If they're like my workmates at the masseries, they're also followers of the Prophet.'

'What about Bourdon and Karp?'

'I didn't say anything about them. The amazigh seem friendly enough. They're taking us to their village. Once we're there, they'll get the village blacksmith to remove our leg irons.'

The climb through the foothills was almost more than the four castaways could manage. The land rose steeply, one rocky slope succeeding another, the narrow footpath twisting and turning its way along dried-up watercourses and then up screes of fallen rock. Occasionally they passed clumps of pine trees, and beside the track Hector noted plants he remembered from his days in Algiers – wild lavender, purple thyme and white rock roses. Eventually, when the sea was far below them, their guides led them into a small settlement made up of single-storey houses, their walls of unmortared stones. In the centre of the village a mountain spring had been diverted through wooden pipes to splash into a stone trough placed in the shade of a venerable cedar tree. Here the village blacksmith knocked out the rivets that closed the ankle rings on the visitors' legs, demanding no payment except that he keep the metal for himself, and the village headman asked Dan to go with him the following day to meet with the clan's council of elders. They would decide what was to be done with the castaways. In the meantime they were his guests.

Dan and the headman left long before daybreak, and Hector and Karp waited all morning for his return, seated in the village square and watching Bourdon entertain the village children with sleight of hand, making pigeon eggs and other small objects appear and disappear. Trying to remember what he had learned from Turgut Reis's maps and charts, Hector broke off a twig and was drawing in the dust so that he could work out where *St Gerassimus* had sunk. He had made a rough outline of the Mediterranean when, unexpectedly, Karp took the twig from his hand and scratched a mark to the north of Constantinople, then pointed to his chest

'Is that where you come from, Karp?' Hector asked. His companion nodded, then clumsily drew some letters in the dust. Hector managed to puzzle them out.

'You are a Bulgar?' he asked. Again Karp nodded, and held out his hands, the wrists close together. 'You were taken prisoner?' Again the nod. 'Where was that?' Karp looked down at the map in the dust and, hesitantly, placed his finger at its eastern end. 'In the Holy Land?' This time Karp shook his head, and drew some more letters in the dust. They read 'Kan—'. Hector stopped him. 'You were taken prisoner at Kandia?'

Turgut Reis had told him all about the siege and fall of Kandia. It was a famous victory for the Turks. As a galley commander Turgut had witnessed the final capitulation of the city to the forces of the Sultan. It had taken the Turks fourteen years of siege to bring Kandia to its knees, and they had allowed the defenders, Venetians and their allies, to leave after handing over the keys of the city.

'But the Christians were given free passage out of the city, were they not?' Hector commented. In response, Karp opened his mouth, pointed to the mangled root of his missing tongue, and made an angry gurgling noise as he shook his head.

'The Turks tore out your tongue?' Now Karp was really agitated. He shook his head furiously from side to side. 'If it was not the Turks, then who did that you?' asked Hector gently. He hoped to calm the Bulgar. To his astonishment, Karp got to his feet, drew a cross in the dust, and deliberately stamped down on it.

The sound of distant musket shots prevented further questions.

There was a flurry of consternation in the village. The women and children rushed inside their houses to hide. The menfolk grabbed up their guns and ran to take up position to cover the approaches to the village. But when the volley of musket shots was repeated, it must have been some sort of announcement because the men relaxed and began to gather in the square, looking expectantly towards the path that led up from the coast. After a little while Hector was relieved to see Dan appear. He was accompanied by the headman and a distinguished-looking elder whom Hector guessed must be the clan chief. But what caught Hector's attention was the armed escort following on their heels – a dozen fierce-looking Negroes carrying spears and muskets. With them was a white man dressed in a long gown of red satin decorated with lines of pink silk ribbons tied in bows. His rapier hung from a wide baldrick of red brocade, and he was wearing a wide-brimmed hat embellished with a white ostrich plume.

This flamboyant apparition strode towards Hector and his companions and announced formally, 'In the name of the Emperor, I summon you to attend on His Majesty, Moulay Ismail.' To Hector's stupefaction this command was delivered in Spanish.

©

'HIS NAME IS Luis Diaz and he's an officer in the army of the Sultan of Morocco,' explained Dan some time later when the two friends had a chance to talk together privately. 'The amazigh are tributaries of the Sultan, and Diaz and the soldiers were on a tax-collecting mission among them when he heard about the wreck of the galley. He wanted to interview the survivors about the bombs dropped on the town. He showed up while the amazigh council of elders were still discussing what to do with the other survivors from the *St Gerassimus* whom they had picked up.'

'News travels fast,' observed Hector.

'The mortar bombardment was a sensation. Everyone's talking about a wonder weapon.'

'And did Diaz learn anything?'

'Piecourt is in charge of the survivors, and is claiming to know nothing about the mortar. He said that the *St Gerassimus*'s commander and all the ship's senior officers had taken the two small boats in order to go along the coast and try to reach a friendly port to fetch help, and the bomb technician had gone with him. There was not enough room in the boats to carry all the survivors so the premier comite had been left in charge of the land party.'

'I wonder where the boats were heading.'

'Piecourt didn't say. He and the rowing master were there with a dozen sailors and several petty officers, some of whom I didn't recognise. They weren't at all pleased to see Diaz. They had already asked me if I could persuade the amazigh to send word to Algiers, to the Jewish ransom brokers there, about their plight. Piecourt even offered me a reward if I could arrange this.'

'Well, all that's changed now. I have the impression that the amazigh will do whatever the Sultan or Emperor, however he styles himself, wants.'

'No doubt about it. They made no objection when Diaz told them that he was taking charge of survivors from the galley. He said they were his prisoners from now on, and he would be sending them to the imperial capital at Meknes to be questioned.'

'And does that include us?'

'I expect we will be better treated. The amazigh informed Diaz that we had been slaves aboard the galley. Apparently convicted criminals and runaway slaves from other countries are given their freedom once they reach the Emperor's territory, provided they can make themselves useful.' Dan hesitated. 'Hector, there's something else you should know, though you may not like what you hear.'

'What's that?' asked Hector.

'The Emperor accepts tax from the amazigh not just in cash but in kind. If the amazigh cannot pay in cash or goods, they sometimes offer their young women for the Sultan's harem. They pick out the girls with the palest complexions. The Sultan has a special liking for women with fair skins. He also buys them from the corsairs. In Meknes you may be able to trace what has happened to your sister.'

SIXTEEN

C

'I PICKED UP the hat and gown from the rubble of one of the forts outside Tangier, though the feather was sadly mangled,' said Luis Diaz, preening himself in his colourful costume. 'One of the English officers must have dropped them when the garrison ran back inside the main defences after blowing up the fort. I was with the Emperor's siege army at the time. Moulay is determined to capture Tangier from the King of England and add it to his dominions.'

'This Emperor Moulay, what's he like?' asked Hector. In the two weeks he had been in the Spaniard's company, Luis had proved to be an amiable escort, friendly and always ready to talk as they travelled into the interior on their way to Meknes, the imperial capital. Until now Hector had tactfully avoided asking how the Spaniard came to be serving a foreign emperor in Barbary.

'Moulay Ismail is shrewd and utterly ruthless,' answered Diaz frankly. 'He's the most unpredictable and dangerous man you would ever wish to meet, a despot who treats everyone as his personal slave. Oh yes, and he loves animals.' He gave Hector a mischievous glance. 'It's just that some of his animals expect to be fed. Last time I was in the palace, Moulay was watching the senior comptroller of his treasury trying to avoid several hungry lions. Moulay suspected the comptroller of false accounting so he had the man lowered into the lion pit in the palace menagerie. The Emperor was sitting up on the edge of the lion pit, looking down as the animals stalked their prey, and he was enjoying every minute of the show. The wretched financier ran around for a good ten minutes, whimpering and pleading for his life, before the lions finally pounced.'

'Was the man genuinely guilty?'

Diaz shrugged. 'Who knows. The Emperor didn't care, and he had other things to think about. The lions were still excited. One of them leaped up and tried to pull the Emperor off the wall. If Moulay hadn't been wearing a mail shirt as he always does, he would have been dragged down into the pit as well. But the lion's claws didn't get a grip.'

'Why on earth do you serve a man like that?'

The Spaniard grimaced. 'I've not much choice. An unfortunate matter of a death at Ceuta where I was serving as a soldier. Someone was killed in a brawl over a woman. I thought it best to leave the city and offer my services elsewhere. Besides, I'm in good company. Men from almost every nation serve Moulay – two of his doctors are French; his field artillery is operated by Hollanders and Italians; there's a clever gardener from England who does the royal parks, and so many Spanish are enlisted in his cavalry or as musketeers that we have formed a mess of our own. You'll meet some of them when we reach Meknes which should be tomorrow, or perhaps the next day, if this cursed mud and rain doesn't slow us down too much.'

Hector and his companions were riding mules commandeered from the amazigh, while Ruis was mounted on a handsome cavalry horse of a breed native to the region. Somewhere far behind them Piecourt and the group of captives from the galley were on foot, herded along by the black soldiers. Hector did not feel sorry for the premier comite and his people though it had been cold and wet for most of the journey.

Luis Diaz swerved his horse to avoid a particularly treach-erous-looking puddle. 'When we get to Meknes, I'll bring you to see the Emperor. He'll reward me if I've done the right thing in fetching you to his presence. But if you anger him and he gets irritated, I'll suffer. So listen carefully to what I have to say. First of all, take note of what Moulay is wearing. If he is wearing green, that's all right because that's his holy colour and Moulay prides himself on being a direct descendant of the Prophet and a good Mussulman. He always has a copy of the Qur'an carried in front of him, prays five times a day, observes the month of fasting, all that sort of thing. So if his clothes are green, he's likely to be in a good mood.'

The Spaniard adjusted his plumed hat to a more rakish angle before continuing.

'But if Moulay is wearing yellow, be very, very careful in what you say. That's his killing colour. On the days he dresses in yellow, he tends to have people executed or mutilated. Of course I'll try to avoid your meeting him on a yellow day, but it may be too late by the time we get an appointment. But whatever colour he is wearing, you must always treat him with the greatest deference. Fall down on your face before him, answer his questions honestly and clearly, and above all, don't go so near to him that you touch him. The last time that happened, the unfortunate man had his arm instantly sliced off with a scimitar by one of the Black Guards. And watch out for changes in the emperor's complexion. Though his skin is tawny, you can tell his mood by the reddish tinge that spreads right across his face when he is getting angry. If that happens, stand clear. Something terrible is going to happen.'

Hector decided this was the moment to ask the question that had been troubling him ever since Dan had told him about the Emperor's harem. 'Are there any women in the palace?' he asked. 'And is there any way of making contact with them?'

Diaz gave a yelp of sarcastic laughter. 'You are looking to get yourself treated with something nastier than being thrown to the lions, like being stretched out on a rack and sawn in two parts, from the crutch upwards. That was the fate of the last person who meddled with the Emperor's women. Of course there are women in the palace. Moulay's harem is the largest in the known world, several hundred women according to rumour, and he considers himself a great stallion. He rarely lies with the same woman twice. One of the French doctors told me that in the space of three months no less than forty sons were born to Moulay in the harem. The palace grounds swarm with his children, and a pestilential pack of brats they are. Completely out of control as no one can lay a hand on them.'

Though shaken, Hector persisted. 'Is it true that he prefers light-skinned women?'

Again, the sarcastic bark of laughter. 'The Light of the Earth, as he is called, prefers virgins of whatever colour. But he's not choosy. If someone's wife takes his fancy, then he'll make the necessary arrangements, for he pretends he follows the Qur'an in all things . . .'

Seeing Hector had not understood, the Spaniard went on, 'The Qur'an forbids adultery, so the Emperor makes sure that the woman becomes a widow.'

'The man sounds like an ogre.'

'Oh, he certainly is,' answered the officer blithely, and spurred his mount forward.

©

MEKNES CAME IN SIGHT the following afternoon, and the travellers paused to take in the view. The city was built on a spur of land overlooking the river Fakran, which flowed across their path on its way towards the Atlantic. The valley floor was intensively cultivated, the greenery of the fields and orchards rising up the slope to lap against the suburbs of the imperial capital. The nearest houses were unexceptional, low buildings in the natural colours of the mud and clay from which they were built, their roofs of tile or thatch. Behind them stood the city proper, a great number of more substantial houses huddled together in a dense mass with the domes and spires of mosques rising above the congestion. There was no sign of a city rampart. Instead, to the left from where the travellers stood, a great boundary wall reached to encompass what was almost a second city. This wall, painted white, was four stories high and seemed to go on for ever, curving away out of sight. Hector judged that it was perhaps three miles long, and beyond it he glimpsed the tops of pavilions and towers, turrets clad in shining green tiles, the domes of mosques, some of them gilded, and a series of edifices in blue and white whose functions he could not guess. Clearly the whole enormous conglomeration was some sort of gigantic, sprawling palace. Beside him Bourdon let out an exclamation. 'That place makes even King Louis seem restrained!' Luis Diaz looked across at him enquiringly, and the pickpocket added, 'I mean the King's new palace at Versailles. His builders had just made a start on it when I was last in Paris, so I went to have a look. It was vast, yet it was nothing compared to this. What manner of king could command such an undertaking?'

'Not a king, but an emperor,' corrected the Spaniard, 'and the work never ends. Moulay wants his palace to extend from here to the sea, that's more than eighty miles.'

'He's mad!' muttered Bourdon.

'Perhaps so. But that's no consolation to the poor wretches who are building it. Squads of men are perpetually working on the wall. They are either heightening it or lengthening it, or painting it, or repairing it because sections of it are always cracking and crumbling or falling down. And inside the enclosure it is even worse. The Emperor is forever ordering some new building or other. Then he tears down one after only six months or wants it changed. It is mayhem. But come, you will see for yourself,' and he rode forward down the hill.

Hector could not keep his eyes off the palace enclosure as he rode forward. Perhaps this was where his sister was to be found, he wondered. As he approached, he began to hear a curious sound. At first it was only the barking of dogs. He had never heard such a cacophony of howling and baying in all his life. It was as if the entire city was populated by the animals. Noticing his puzzlement Luis Diaz commented, 'You'll get used to that din. The city is plagued by dogs, most of them are strays and curs. They run in packs and eat the rubbish. Yet no one seems to do anything about it. Maybe because the Emperor is fond of animals, and the citizens fear his anger if they cull them.'

'It's not just the barking of the dogs,' Hector answered, 'it's that other sound, the thumping in the background.'

'Like I said, the building work is constant in Meknes, and nearly everything is made out of hardened clay. What you are hearing is the sound of that clay being pounded into position. Look over there, and you'll see what I mean.'

They were passing along the face of the palace wall, close enough to see the work in progress. At the foot of the wall a gang of about forty men was standing over great wooden troughs and using shovels and heavy bars to mix what looked like a thick pinkish-yellow dough. Other men were then carrying buckets and baskets of the stuff up crude ladders propped against the wall. Reaching the top of the wall they tipped the mixture out in front of a third team standing on the summit. These men were creating the strange thumping noise by pounding down on the mix in unison, using great wooden mallets to beat it into shape between heavy wooden planks and adding to the height of the rampart. The scene reminded Hector of a colony of ants working to fortify their nest. Looking more closely, he noted that all the labourers were white men. They were dressed in ragged clothes, bare-headed and without shoes. They seemed half-starved and desperate. He realised they were slaves.

Diaz led them into the city itself, guiding them along narrow lanes ankle-deep in mud. A number of the passers-by wore the grey hooded cloaks of the amazigh, but the majority were Moors or Arabs in brightly coloured jackets sewn with decorative buttons and wearing red caps. Their loose linen drawers reached down to mid calf, leaving their feet bare, a sensible arrangement given the condition of the muddy streets, though some of the wealthier ones teetered along on thick-soled cork slippers trying to steer clear of the muck. Against the damp and chill, most were swathed in a fine white blanket wrapped around the body, leaving only the right arm bare. They showed little interest in Hector and his friends, and even Karp with his damaged face attracted scarcely a second glance, which left Hector wondering if such mutilation was perhaps another of the imperial punishments.

'This is where I live,' announced Diaz as they reached an unprepossessing building that looked more like a cattle byre than a dwelling and, after tying up their mounts, pushed open the door. Inside, the place was no more attractive, a large room poorly furnished with a couple of tables and some plain chairs and benches. Several doors apparently led off to bedchambers, and there must have been a kitchen somewhere to the rear as Hector could smell cooking. He also noticed that the roof leaked in one corner.

'It's not much, I know,' said Diaz, 'but this is what the Emperor assigned to his Spanish officers. We were told to evict the Jew who owns the place here and, believe it or not, the Jew now has to pay rent to Moulay for letting us live here. I know it makes no sense. But you'll find that is the rule here in Meknes. Everything is back to front.'

A trio of white men, dressed in vaguely military costume, were sitting at one of the tables, playing cards and drinking from earthenware mugs. 'Let me introduce you to my fellow officers,' said Diaz. 'This is Roberto, Carlos and Lopez. Like myself, they are all cavalrymen. A couple of musketeers from Castille are also billeted here, but right now they are away on campaign. The Emperor has an army in the south, putting down a local rebellion among the mountain people, and they've been sent to help out. You can use their room until they return.'

He clapped his hands and shouted out for food to be brought. Somewhere to the rear of the building a voice answered him.

Over a meal of grey, stringy boiled mutton and couscous Diaz explained to his countrymen that he had brought the castaways to Meknes after hearing about the great mortar. 'A wise decision,' said the man called Roberto as he idly shuffled the pack of cards. 'If Moulay had learned about the gun, and that you were nearby and failed to act, he'd have had you tossed.' He turned towards the visitors. 'Being tossed, for your information, does not mean being thrown out of the imperial army. It means just what it says. Being thrown up in the air, and you'll be lucky to escape with your life when it is done by the Black Guard. They are very skilled at it. The Emperor gives the nod, and those devils step forward and grab you, one at each limb. Then they fling you up in the air, and stand back. It's a fine art and they have it to perfection. They calculate how you will fly up in the air, how far you go, and whether you turn or spin.' He gave a sardonic chuckle. 'A bit like judging the way the bomb flies out from that big gun Luis just told us about. When you get tossed, the Black Guard stand back and let you crash back on the ground. They can arrange it so you fall on your face, or your back, or your side. Whatever they choose. It is up to them whether you are stunned or merely bruised, or break a leg or an arm. Then if the Emperor commands, they'll do it several times so you are suitably battered. Or if he wants you dead, they can make sure that you land on your head at just the right angle to break your neck. It helps, of course, when they do this over a marble floor.' He began to deal out the cards to his companions. 'For a moment when you first came in,' he added, looking at Dan, 'I thought you might be a member of the Black Guard, and that gave me a fright, I must admit.'

'Those tax collectors with you were they Black Guardsmen?' Bourdon asked Diaz.

'Not exactly, though one day they might become that,' he answered. 'Blacks are the backbone of the Emperor's army. Some are recruited from the tribes. But the majority are bred to the service. They are the sons of soldiers who have served previous rulers, and are brought up to a military life. They are trained to be tough, live in special camps, exercise in fighting with sword and spear, and are shown how to handle a musket.'

Here one of the Spaniards interrupted. 'Not that they use guns very much. The weapons they are given are shoddy rubbish, and likely to blow up in your face. And the powder is no better. Half the time it doesn't explode. The Emperor's infantry often finish up using their muskets as clubs. Still, don't let me interrupt our friend's yarn.'

Diaz waved his hand dismissively. 'You may have noticed that my escort of tax collectors was lightly dressed even though we were in the mountains. That's part of their training. They are issued only with a thin cotton shift and no footwear, not even a turban. After five years' instruction they are considered to be fit for duty. Later, if they distinguish themselves in battle, they may advance to the elite company which protects the Emperor's person. Then they're Black Guards, and utterly loyal to Moulay. He has them drilled like mastiffs, vicious and ready to attack anyone.' He stretched his legs to ease his riding muscles. 'But enough of that. It's time to return my horse to the imperial stables, and we might as well drop off the mules there too. You'll see for yourself that Moulay's cavalry get better equipment than his foot soldiers.'

Remounted, Diaz took Hector and his companions back through the muddy city streets to a great gateway in the outer wall of the royal enclosure. Its enormous doors of worked bronze stood open and, as they passed under the archway, Luis said, 'We buried a wolf's head here last year when this gate was used for the first time. The Emperor killed the wolf – it was from his menagerie – with a scimitar. Then he told us to bury the head in the centre of the gateway, while he himself interred the body outside in the main road. I suppose it's meant to bring good luck.' He turned his horse to the left as soon as they were inside the gate, explaining that it was wiser to avoid the centre of the palace compound. 'You never know where you might run into Moulay,' he warned. 'He roams the palace with his escort, poking and prying into every corner. If he comes upon a work gang putting up a building, he's been known to take off his outer robes, strip down to his shirt and seize a shovel, then work alongside them in some sort of frenzy. Equally, if he is in a bad mood and thinks someone is slacking, he'll send in the Black Guard with cudgels and have the labourers thrashed on the spot.'

They rode for some distance when, at the far side of the compound, they entered on a broad, well-made roadway carried on a series of arches across a shallow valley. 'I always feel a little more relaxed when I reach this point,' admitted Diaz. 'There's less chance of meeting Moulay out here. The only time he's likely to come this way is if he's taken it into his head to go on an outing with some of his harem. He has them put up on mules and donkeys, and he rides at the head of the procession like some sort of peacock. His eunuch guards fan out ahead to clear away any onlookers, using whips and swords. But everyone who has any sense has already made himself scarce. Should you be unlucky enough to be trapped with nowhere to run, the best course is to bolt behind a bush and fall flat, with your face to the ground and hoping you are not noticed.'

The Spaniard gestured towards the ground beneath his horse's hooves. 'Moulay boasts that his horses regularly walk over the heads of his Christian captives. There are twenty-four arches to this causeway, and all but the central one have been closed off to make a row of cells. That's where his Christian prisoners are lodged. We are actually riding over the slave pens.'

'Dan and I have spent time in the bagnios of Algiers,' Hector told him. 'So we know what it's like to be a slave.'

'So how did you get out? Did you convert?'

'Yes, we both turned Turk. It seemed the only escape.'

Luis nodded his understanding. 'Not much different from my deserting my post in Ceuta, and joining the Emperor's army. The trouble is that there's little chance of going back. I doubt I would be accepted again into the service of Spain and so I had better make the rest of my life here, or perhaps I will find my way out to the Americas where my history would not be discovered, and even if it was, no one would pay much attention.' He pointed ahead to a series of long, low buildings arranged in parallel lines. 'There are the imperial stables now. To a cavalryman they rate as the eighth wonder of the world.'

In the next hour Hector understood the Spaniard's enthusiasm. The stables of the royal palace were awe-inspiring. There were three miles of barn-like buildings, and an army of ostlers and grooms was hard at work, cleaning and watering, sweeping up the horses' droppings, and trundling barrow loads of manure out to the gently steaming middens. 'There are never less than a thousand horses stabled here, with one groom for every five animals so the place is kept spotlessly clean,' Diaz announced. He was relishing his self-appointed task as a guide and clearly was someone who was prepared to talk for hours about horses and their care. They were his passion. 'Note the drains of running water which run the length of each stable so the horse piss is carried away. You will notice also that there are no mangers. The local custom is to feed the horses with chopped hay and sweet herbs strewn on the ground, and use nose bags for their barley. Those outhouses over there are filled with enough fodder for at least six months.'

He marched to the end of one stable block and threw open the door to a vast harness room where saddles and bridles hung in neat lines. A little farther on was an armoury with rack after rack of sabres and muskets which reminded Dan of what he had seen at the Marseilles Arsenal. But the Spaniard saved his greatest surprise to the last. He led his companions to a smaller stable, set apart from the others, and more substantially built. Nodding to an attendant, he led Hector and his friends inside where they found themselves looking at two dozen horses kept in open stalls. The animals turned their heads to gaze at the men, and one of them whickered softly. 'Look under them,' said Diaz. Peering in, Hector saw that each animal, instead of standing on sawdust or straw, was standing on a fine Turkish carpet. 'These horses are revered,' explained Diaz. 'They eat only hand-sifted grain and fresh green stuff. No one but the Emperor himself may ride them, and he does that very rarely. Instead they are led at the head of parades, all decked out in rich trappings of silk and brocade, wearing harnesses made of tooled leather inlaid with precious stones, silver and gold thread woven into their manes and tails. An attendant, preferably a Christian slave, follows close behind to catch their droppings in a bucket, while another groom immediately lifts up their tails to wipe them.'

'Why all this for a bunch of ageing nags?' demanded Bourdon sceptically.

'Because these horses have made the journey to Mecca,' answered Diaz, 'and don't scoff. If you are ever in real trouble with the Emperor, your best chance is to throw yourself between the feet of a sacred horse when the Emperor rides by, and claim the Emperor's benevolence. That way you at least stand a chance of having your request granted.'

©

IT WAS ANOTHER two days before a palace messenger showed up at the Spaniards' billet with a summons. Diaz was ordered to appear before the Emperor with the survivors from the galley and they were to explain the workings of the great cannon. 'I told you that Moulay is keen to capture Tangier,' the Spaniard said gleefully to Hector and the others as they hurried towards the palace. 'Normally one has to wait weeks for an audience with Moulay.'

'But none of us – Dan, Bourdon, Karp nor I – know much about the mortar,' Hector objected. 'All we did was prepare the bombs, load them, and clean the weapon.'

'But you must have noted the shape and size of the gun, the thickness of its barrel, the design of its chamber, the way the bombs were prepared. Put all those details together and there should be enough information for Moulay's master gun founder to make a copy. And if he is able to make a replica, we will all be richly rewarded.'

Despite Diaz's confidence, Hector was full of misgivings as the Spaniard led them through the wolf's-head gate. The weather had improved, and it was a warm, bright morning. They walked along a series of avenues in the palace grounds. Now and then Diaz had to stop to get his bearings, apologising that so much building work had been done since his last audience with Moulay five months earlier that he was in danger of losing his way. 'The messenger said that we were to meet the Emperor by the place where he keeps his cats,' he explained.

'You mean at the lion pit? That doesn't sound very encouraging,' commented Bourdon dryly.

'No, no, his cats. The Emperor is very fond of cats. There are more than forty of them, all sorts of colours and types, from tabbies to pure white. The Emperor collects cats. He is sent the most remarkable ones from all over his kingdom, and also from foreign countries. He has cats with eyes of different colours, long-furred cats, cats that love to swim, cats with no tails. He keeps them in a special enclosure and they are trained to come to him when he calls.'

They passed through a bewildering array of pavilions, arcades and courtyards, many of them embellished with marble fountains and reflecting pools. They skirted around a sunken garden planted with cypress trees and surrounded by balustrades of jasper, and then made a detour around a handsome colonnaded building which Diaz warned was the residence of two of the Emperor's principal wives. Everywhere was a profusion of inlay work, cut-stone tracery and delicate stucco, and when Diaz risked taking a short cut down a long corridor leading through a reception hall, Hector marvelled at the painted plaster ceiling overhead and the thousands of small tiles, red and green and white, which had been laid to make a chequerwork pavement. Very occasionally he glimpsed a servant who quickly darted away out of sight, so this entire, remarkable assemblage of buildings and open spaces gave the impression of being deserted.

Finally they came upon a small group of courtiers standing beside yet another sunken garden. It was crossed by a causeway covered with trellised vines so that it formed a long leafy tunnel. Judging by the nervous expressions on the faces of the courtiers, who were all dressed in rich Moorish costume, they too were awaiting the arrival of the Emperor. Hector glanced into the netted enclosure behind them, and saw it was home to a variety of cats who were sunning themselves, sleeping or prowling the perimeter of their cage.

The largest and most magnificent of the cats, a spotted creature the size of a small leopard, alerted them to the approach of the Emperor. Long before the humans could detect anything unusual, the animal suddenly sat up and gazed with its huge, yellow eyes down the leafy tunnel. Then the big cat yawned luxuriously, curving its pink tongue, rose to its feet and padded over towards the edge of the enclosure where it sat down again and gazed fixedly towards the causeway. The cluster of courtiers stirred with apprehension, adjusting their robes, shifting from one foot to another, making small coughing sounds as they cleared their throats.

'Here he comes now,' Diaz whispered in Hector's ear. 'Get ready to fall down flat on your face.' Hector waited, standing long enough to see a bizarre cortège approaching down the trellised causeway. It was led by two immensely tall black soldiers in white gowns and holding muskets. Behind them came half a dozen veiled women wearing a harness over their flowing garments. The traces of their harness led back to a wickerwork chariot on four wheels which they were pulling along at a slow walk. On each side of the chariot marched more members of the Black Guard, and to the rear a footman was holding a yellow and green umbrella over a man riding in the chariot. The latter was wearing a huge white turban, at least a yard in circumference, and even at that distance there was the flash of the jewelled brooch pinned to the cloth. Hector obediently prostrated himself in the dust after he had noted thankfully that the Emperor, for it had to be Moulay riding in the chariot, was wearing green.

'Bono! Bono!' a deep voice said some moments later, and he sensed that the chariot had stopped and the Emperor had got out and was speaking over the backs of the courtiers. Still no one on the ground stirred. 'Allah ibarak fi amrik sidi! God bless thy Power!' the courtiers around him chorused, their faces still pressed to the dust. 'You may rise,' announced the Emperor, and Hector heard the courtiers getting to their feet. As he followed their example, he looked out of the corner of his eye and noted that all the Moors were standing meekly, still staring at the ground. Only when the formal ritual of blessing and response in the name of the Prophet had been completed did they raise their eyes and look upon the potentate they addressed as Light of the Earth.

Moulay Ismail was thinner than Hector had expected. He was a man of medium height with a very black skin. His face, beneath the huge turban, was gaunt, and he had a pronounced hook nose which contrasted with a full-lipped and sensuous mouth. His beard jutted forward and had been dyed light ginger, as had his bushy eyebrows. His dark eyes were expressionless as he surveyed his submissive courtiers, and the Black Guards of his escort watched them suspiciously. The umbrella holder had moved forward so he was now standing directly behind the Emperor and twirling the umbrella constantly. The women had retreated demurely into the background. 'Admiral!' Moulay demanded sharply. 'Where are the men who can tell me about the ship gun?' He spoke in Arabic, and Hector understood the gist of the question. One of the courtiers, a distinguished-looking Moor in a dark brown robe trimmed with black and silver braid, gestured towards Diaz and his companions, then bowed deeply. Moulay said something which Hector did not catch, and then the courtier, whom Hector took to be the commander of Moulay's navy, began to translate in heavily accented Spanish.

'His Majesty the Light and Sun of the Earth wishes to know about the big gun carried on a foreign vessel. We hear reports that a city has no defence against such a weapon.'

Hector felt a nudge. Diaz, standing beside him, wanted him to answer. Hector swallowed hard, and then took the risk he had been calculating from the moment he had seen the Emperor. He replied in Turkish, speaking directly to the Emperor.

'Your Majesty, the gun is called a mortar. It fires shells called bombs filled with gunpowder that explode on reaching the target. They travel up into the air from the gun and drop from the sky.'

Moulay turned his head to look directly at him, and the black eyes were like coals. Hector felt a shiver of anxiety, but kept his gaze fixed on the great jewel in the Emperor's turban.

'Where did you learn to speak Turkish so well?' Moulay asked.

'In Algiers, Your Majesty.'

'And what country are you from?'

'From a country called Ireland, Your Majesty.'

For a moment Moulay paused, as if considering a rebuke. Then he said curtly, 'You have told me nothing that I do not know already.'

'The principle of the gun has been known for many years, Your Majesty,' Hector went on. 'But only now is it possible to make bombs which are so destructive.'

'Are they strong enough to knock down city walls?' asked Moulay.

'I believe so, Your Majesty. If they strike at the right point.'

'Good, then I want to have such guns and bombs, many of them, in my army. That must be arranged.' The Emperor obviously considered the subject closed because he turned his attention towards one of the courtiers.

'But Your Majesty . . .' began Hector when he felt another nudge in his back, much more urgent this time.

It was too late, Moulay had swivelled back to face him, and Hector saw a faint red flush beginning to spread in the Emperor's cheeks. It was clear that Moulay was not accustomed to being interrupted.

'What is it!' he enquired sharply.

'There are others from the ship who may know more about the gun,' Hector ventured. 'Those who were in charge of the vessel. They are now your prisoners.'

Moulay looked towards his Admiral, and raised his eyebrows questioningly. 'That is correct, Your Magnificence,' the courtier confirmed smoothly. 'They will arrive here soon, a party of petty officers and sailors. They are on foot.'

An amused smile twisted the sensuous mouth.

'I take it that you were a slave on the galley,' Moulay said, addressing Hector again. 'So I appoint you to be the examiner of these infidels. You will interrogate them about the gun and its bombs, and pass on that information to my gunfounder. And when you have done that, you can help my Jews assess the amount of ransom we will demand from the King of France for the return of the captives. I am told that the ship flew the flag of France.'

'I have a favour to ask, Your Majesty.' For a second time Hector interrupted the Emperor, and he heard a low moan of dismay from Diaz beside him. He also detected two small white patches beginning to appear beside the Emperor's nostrils. They too, he had been warned, was a sign that the Emperor was losing his temper. But he pressed on, 'I beseech Your Majesty to help me in finding my sister. She was taken by corsairs and must be somewhere in Barbary. Her name is Elizabeth . . .'

Around him Hector felt the courtiers draw back in alarm as if to distance themselves from such insulting disrespect to their overlord. Two of the Black Guards, sensing the fraught atmosphere, moved forward threateningly. Unexpectedly, Moulay laughed. It was a laugh of incredulity tinged with cruelty. 'You expect me to help you find your sister? What a creature she must be! Lovelier than a houri in Paradise, and her brother among the most impudent of men.' Moulay paused to make a strange clucking sound. 'Why should I care about a stranger's sister when I have eighty-three brothers and half-brothers and I cannot even count the number of my own sisters. However, you are a brave man. If you deliver a wall-destroying gun to me, a kale-kob, this will be your reward: I will order the release of your sister should you find she is a captive in my realm. I will do this in honour of Allah's Apostle, peace be upon him, for he released the sister of his mortal enemy Aidiy ibn Hatim, when she was his captive. And by this act he won the allegiance of Aidiy ibn Hatim who thereafter became his treasured companion.' Again the Emperor made the strange clucking sound, and this time Hector, who had fallen silent, realised that Moulay was summoning one of his cats. There was a scrabbling sound as a magnificent white cat, with a bushy tail and a coat like fluffed silk, clambered up the sides of its enclosure and leaped to the ground. Tail straight in the air, the animal ran across the ground and leaped up into Moulay's arms who began to cradle and pet it as he repeated, 'Remember! I want a kale-kob, a castle smasher!'

SEVENTEEN

'I THOUGHT YOU WERE going to get your neck broken,'
grumbled Diaz as he hurried Hector and the others away.
'Moulay is not usually so forbearing. He's like those cats of his.
You never know what he is thinking and which way he will
jump. He'll toy with a victim for hours before pouncing. Then
it's all over in a moment.'

They were returning through the palace compound by a
route that took them towards an area of large, square buildings
with the appearance of storehouses and depositories. 'I think
you were saved by the fact that you come from Ireland. I dare
say Moulay's met very few people from that country, and when
you appeared in front of him to answer about this miraculous
new gun and said you were Irish, he must have thought that
fate had taken a hand. His master gun founder is an Irishman.
He's been casting cannon or repairing Moulay's artillery for
years, and he's very popular with those of us who like to
celebrate now and then, because he's allowed to keep large
stocks of alcohol. He claims it's an essential ingredient for his
craft. Ah! There he is, the small man in the leather apron just
coming out of the foundry.'

Hector saw a stooped, white-haired figure emerge from the
nearest of the buildings, wipe his face with a cloth, then stand

in the open, fanning himself. His clothes were soaked with sweat.

'Greetings Sean,' called Diaz. 'I've got some helpers for you. By order of the Emperor himself.'

The gun founder looked at them placidly. Hector judged him to be about sixty years old. Beneath his shock of white hair he had clear grey eyes in a face permanently discoloured with ingrained grime, and his hands and bare forearms were marked with dozens of small burns and scars. The gun founder coughed to clear his throat, spat carefully and wiped his face again before replying.

'Help's always welcome,' he said, looking Hector and his companions over. Hector noted that his voice, like all his movements, was calm and unhurried. His Spanish was slow and deliberate. 'What are they meant to do?'

'Explain to you about some sort of new artillery the Emperor wants copied,' said Diaz cheerfully. 'This is Hector. He's a countryman of yours.'

'Is he indeed?' responded the old man and, addressing Hector, said, 'I'm Sean Allen from Meath though it's a long time since I was there. And yourself?'

'Hector Lynch from Cork County, and these are my friends: Dan is from the Caribees, Jacques Bourdon from Paris, and Karp is a Bulgar, though he's a mute.'

The gun founder shot Karp an amused glance and said, 'He's a silent bugger, so?' No one understood the quip and he added, 'Buggers or bugres, that's what you call someone who's awkward. It's on account of so many Bulgars being trouble-makers. Something to do with their religion. They are said to be extreme heretics. Not that I care.'

He paused to wipe his brow again.

'I saw enough bigotry back home when I was at the siege of Limerick with Cromwell's son-in-law, Ireton. I minded and mended his cannon for him, and what he did to those who led the resistance sickened me and I left poor unhappy Ireland.

Since then I've served the Sultan in Istanbul, the Bey of Tunis, and now the Emperor of Morocco. They all need guns and will employ those who have the knowledge to make them. Now tell me about this artillery I'm supposed to copy. What's so special about it?'

'I don't know the technical details,' Hector answered, 'but it's a short, fat gun which shot flaming bombs in the air and they fell into a town and exploded.'

'Nothing new there,' said the gun founder, now mopping the back of his neck with the cloth. 'Mortars have been used for years. Ireton had four of them when we besieged Limerick, and a Hungarian built a truly enormous one for the Grand Turk when he besieged Constantinople and that was two centuries ago. I saw his great mortar on display in the city. It was so big that it shot stone cannonballs that weighed five hundred pounds. Mind you, it must have taken the stonemasons a month of Sundays to chip and shape each cannonball so it fitted right. Not exactly a rapid rate of fire.'

'The gun we saw used ready-made hollow shells of metal fitted with different sorts of fuses. Some worked, others didn't. The gun was mounted on a galley, and that's why we are here. It shook the galley to pieces.' Hector stopped talking, conscious that he had said something which had caught the gun founder's attention.

'A mortar carried on a ship. That's different altogether,' Allen said thoughtfully. 'Some clown failed to compensate for the recoil. It would need a different sort of carriage from the usual one for land guns, something that would allow the downward thrust to be converted to a sideways motion. I heard that a Dutchman – Coehorn I think is his name – has come up with an improved mortar, perhaps that is what was being used on board that ship.' He was half talking to himself, imagining the practical problems of his new commission from the Emperor, and Diaz had to interrupt him. 'Sean, I've got to get back to my own billet. I'll leave your new helpers with you. I presume you can find space for the extra members of your team.'

'Yes, of course,' said the gun founder absent-mindedly, 'I'll see that they are looked after.'

Allen turned towards the building behind him, and pulled open the door. His visitors quailed at the blast of heat though the gun founder seemed to be oblivious to the temperature as he led Hector and the others inside. 'This is the foundry itself,' he explained, as they stepped around a mass of glowing metal in a pit. 'We had a pour a few hours ago and are waiting for the metal to cool down. It's nothing special, just a small brass culverin. The Emperor likes to boast that he has a full-sized gun foundry, but in fact we haven't the facilities to make anything much bigger than this. Most of our work is repairing damaged cannon or casting round shot and grape for his field artillery. A ten-pound ball is heavy enough to knock down the mud walls of the forts that the tribes build for themselves in the interior. But a true siege cannon, like the weapon you are talking about, is another matter altogether.'

He had reached the far end of the foundry, and passing through a double door and then across the narrow lane he brought his visitors into an even larger building. It was an arms depot. Here were rack upon rack of sabres and muskets, trays of pistols, bundles of pikes and an array of blunderbusses. Clusters of bandoliers hung on pegs, and disposed here and there on the floor were heaps of body armour, corselets, greaves, and helmets of many different styles and in varying condition. 'The Emperor hates to have any war material thrown away,' confided the gun founder. 'Half of this stuff is so antiquated as to be useless, like that arquebus over there. But when Moulay comes on an inspection he'll suddenly ask to see some piece of equipment which he remembers from months earlier, and there's all hell to pay if it can't be produced immediately. You there!' He called out to a lad who was replacing an old-fashioned

Spanish helmet in a chest. 'Don't put it in like that. Wrap it first in paper so it keeps its gleam.' Hector noted that the gun founder had spoken in English. 'Does everyone in the foundry use English?' he asked. 'I should hope so,' answered the Irishman. 'I've got a score of youngsters working here for me, and every one of them is English. It's another quirk of Moulay's. Every time his people capture an English youngster, the lad is assigned to work with me in the Arsenal. My guess is that Moulay thinks the English make the best gun founders and gun-smiths.'

'And do they?' Hector enquired.

'Depends who you speak to. The French gun foundries at Liège are among the most advanced in the world, and the Spaniards would claim that they make the finest musket locks. The Italians write well about the theory of gunnery; while the Dutch are great innovators. And from what I witnessed in the Grand Seignor's foundry outside Istanbul, I can assure you that the Turkish topcus as they call their gun founders are no slouches.'

They entered a room, clearly Allen's office, which was partitioned off from the rest of the armoury. Looking around, Hector noticed a shelf of books and pamphlets on the art of gun founding and the manufacture of powder and rockets. Sean Allen carefully closed the door of the study behind them, opened a cupboard and took out a large green glass flask and several glasses. 'One of the privileges of my post,' he explained, as he removed the stopper from the flask and began to pour. 'It's a blessing that the making of incendiaries can require spirits of alcohol. Take the repair of spoilt gunpowder, its restoration as you might call it. We get a great quantity of bad gunpowder brought to us. Either it got wet while on campaign with the Emperor's army, or maybe it was captured out of some foreign ship and we find that it got damp from lying in a ship's hold for too long. The Emperor is very pleased to receive such tribute, but unless the gunpowder is repaired it is useless. So what do we do?'

The gun founder took a gulp from his glass, walked over to the bookshelf, and took down a volume. It was written in Latin and entitled *The Great Art of Artillery*. Clearly Allen was an educated man.

'It's all written up here,' continued the gunsmith. 'We make up an elixir of two parts brandy with one measure each of white wine vinegar and purified saltpetre, and add half measures of oils of sulphur and samphire. Then we sprinkle the elixir over the damaged powder and put it out in the sun to dry. When the powder is completely dried out we package it again in barrels, and place it in dry store. Then it's as good as new.' He closed the book with a snap and took another mouthful of his drink. 'Of course there's always brandy left over, and it's amazing what a thirst a man works up when he is in the heat of a gun foundry.'

Noticing that Hector had barely touched his glass of brandy he went on, 'Drink up! Surely you're not an abstainer. That would be a disappointment, what with your coming from the old country.'

'No,' replied Hector, 'Dan and I did profess Islam when we were slaves in Algiers but that was under duress. And anyhow we saw plenty of Turks who came to drink in the bagnio's taverns. Neither of us care much for religion.'

'Very understandable. Half the captives here in Morocco take up Islam just to make life more bearable. It's mostly the fanatics who refuse.' The gun founder produced paper and pen from his desk. 'Now, give me a description of the mortar that you saw on the galley.'

'Maybe it will be easier if Dan draws a picture of it for you,' suggested Hector. 'He's good with pen and ink.'

'All right, then,' answered Allen, handing the pen to the Miskito and he watched as Dan quickly sketched out the mortar and its sledge. 'Ah! I see the fault. The gun carriage was wrong. If it had been designed so that the mortar rolled back when it was fired, and was not pinned in place, it would not have shattered the foredeck. Perhaps a rocker or a curved slope to absorb the recoil would have done the trick.' Taking back the pen from Dan, he quickly drew an improved gun carriage. 'That's one problem likely solved,' he said, 'but that's not what the Emperor wants. He's after those exploding bombs, and as noisy and spectacular as possible. Can you tell me anything about them?'

'They were about twelve inches in diameter and a perfect globe,' answered Hector, 'except for the hole where they were filled and fused. At that point there was a collar like the neck of your brandy flask though much shorter. The globes were already packed with gunpowder when they were loaded on the galley, but if one of them needed topping up, we poured in more gunpowder through the hole, then plugged it with one of the fuses.' He went on to describe the different fuses that were tested, and finally added, 'The bombs had small handles on each side of the fuse so when Karp and I were loading them into the mortar, we could get a grip to lift them. Each bomb must have weighed maybe forty pounds.'

Allen looked pensive. 'I imagine the hollow globes were cast, and not made from wrought iron. Cast iron bursts with more destructive power, throwing smaller shards of metal and doing more damage. But the thickness of the wall of the globe has to be just right, and the gunpowder inside calculated nicely, as well as being of the highest quality.' He sighed, 'And that is going to be my main problem here. Getting hold of the right powder to make the bombs. As I said, much of the stuff we hold in stock here is repaired powder, and that would never do.'

'I worked in a quarry once, in Algiers,' ventured Hector, 'and I remember how the ordinary corned powder was unreliable. The powder we used on the galley to top up the bombs, as well as for the charges inside the mortar, was fine-grained and very black.'

'Would you recognise it again if you saw it?' asked Allen.

'I think so.'

'Then come with me,' said the gun founder. 'You others can stay here and pour yourselves some more drinks. We won't be long.'

Allen took Hector to a low, squat, windowless building, half sunk in the ground and made with immensely thick walls of stone. Unlocking a heavy wooden door, he led the young Irishman inside the gunpowder magazine. It was two-thirds empty, with perhaps a hundred barrels and kegs of gunpowder set out on the earth floor.

Allen crossed to the farthest corner where a single small keg stood by itself. Tipping it on its side, he rolled it nearer to the daylight from the open door, and removed the plug. He poured a small quantity of its gunpowder into the palm of his hand and held it out for Hector to see. 'Is that the sort of stuff you used on the galley's mortar?' he asked.

Hector looked at the little heap of black grains. 'Yes, or something very like it.'

'Thought so. That's French powder. Best-quality pistol powder, hard to find,' he grunted. He replaced the bung, rolled the keg back into its place, and ushered Hector out of the magazine. As Allen carefully locked the door behind him, Hector asked, 'Will you be able to get more of that powder? Enough for the bombs?'

'We can't make that quality here and my supplier is, you might say, irregular,' Allen replied. He gave a hiccup, and Hector realised that the gun founder was slightly tipsy. 'He's a corsair who calls in at Sallee. Mostly he operates in the Atlantic, off the Spanish coast or as far north as the Channel. Sallee is convenient for him whenever he has interesting goods to sell. He's a countryman of ours who took the turban as you did, though rather more seriously. Name of Hakim Reis.'

Hector felt his spine tingle.

'Hakim Reis.' he repeated. 'He's the corsair who took me captive.'

'Don't hold that against him. Man-catching is a good slice of his profession, and he's a decent enough sort.'

Hector tried to keep his voice steady. 'Will there be any chance of meeting him?'

Allen gave him a shrewd look. 'Not thinking of taking revenge, are you? I wouldn't recommend it.'

'No, no. I just wanted to ask him some questions. When do you think Hakim Reis will next be here?'

'Impossible to say. He comes and goes as it suits him. He might show up next week, next month or perhaps never again if he's been sunk at sea or died of the plague. But one thing about him is that if war is declared, he seems to be early on the scene, and the first to come into port with the spoils.'

Hector thought furiously as he tried to find another thread that might lead him to locating Hakim Reis. 'That powder he sells to the Emperor. Where does he get it?'

'I'd say he has good contacts on the Spanish coast. There are plenty of small bays and inlets where you can meet up with people willing to sell war material to the highest bidder, and never mind where the guns and powder finish up.'

'But you said that was French-made gunpowder. How would he obtain that?'

'Gunpowder's a valuable commodity. It could have changed hands several times, passed from smuggler to smuggler until it reaches someone like Hakim Reis who has a ready market for it.'

'And you have no idea who any of these smugglers might be, and whether they know where to find him?'

The gun founder looked at Hector searchingly. 'Why so keen to meet Hakim Reis?'

'He may be able to help me locate a member of my family –

my sister. She was also taken captive, and I've heard nothing of her since. I promised myself I would find her.'

Allen pondered for a moment, and when he spoke his tone was sympathetic. 'I wish I could help you. I've known Hakim since the early days when he used to come in with shoddy muskets to sell. I did ask him on one occasion whether he could get me a further delivery of best powder, and he said he'd consult with someone he called Tisonne, or maybe he said Tison, I can't remember exactly. But he never mentioned the name again, and I've never heard of it, not in these parts anyhow. And if Tisonne or Tison is a professional smuggler, it could be his cover name, not his real one. Then he'll be even more difficult to locate than Hakim himself.'

Hector and the gun founder had arrived back in the armoury where they found Dan examining a musket from the display. 'What do you think of it?' asked Allen.

'This is exactly the sort of gun we have at home among my people. I hadn't expected to find one here. The weapon must be at least fifty years old. It still uses the old-fashioned matchlock,' observed the Miskito.

'Indeed it does. Have you worked with guns?'

'Back home, and for a brief period in the workshops of King Louis's Galley Corps in Marseilles.'

The gun founder gave a grunt of satisfaction. 'You've just talked yourself into a job. Rather than helping me concoct exploding bombs, it will be more use if you could supervise these English lads here in the armoury. Show them how to repair the older weapons. Your French friend and the silent bugger can help you. Meanwhile Hector can assist me in providing Moulay with his castle smasher.'

'Perhaps I could start by interviewing the other survivors from the galley,' suggested Hector. 'They should reach Meknes in the next few days, and I could ask them for more information. They might cooperate if they think it will help obtain their early release. Moulay has already appointed me as the go-between to arrange their ransom.'

'That's just the sort of quirky idea that would entertain the Emperor,' Allen agreed. 'Our friend Diaz will be able to tell us when the prisoners from the galley arrive and where they will be held. He stops by here most evenings as he and his cronies are fond of my brandy.'

℃

IN THE END it was several more days before Diaz reported that comite Piecourt and the other captives from the *St Gerassimus* had arrived in Meknes. They had been added to the palace labour force, and were being held in the cells built into the arches under the causeway leading to the royal stables. The following evening when all slaves would have returned from their work, Hector set off to find his former masters. Walking along the line of twenty-four arches, he caught sight of the unmistakable figure of Yakup, the rowing master. The renegade Turk was squatting against one of the stone pillars supporting the roadway above. He was stripped to the waist and had tilted his head back against the stonework. The distinctive fork-tailed cross branded on his forehead was clearly visible. As Hector approached, two men emerged from the archway, deep in conversation. One was a tall, ascetic-looking figure and Hector did not recognise him. The other had a pale skin and close-cropped sandy hair. It was Piecourt. Both were dressed in the loose tunic and cotton pantaloons worn by slaves. 'Good evening, comite, I would like a word with you,' said Hector quietly. Startled, Piecourt broke off his conversation and swung round towards him. As he did so, the slanting rays of the evening sun fell square on his companion's face and Hector saw that his otherwise handsome features were marred by a scattering of small dark blue spots spread across his right cheek from just below his eye to the jaw line. 'Who are you?' asked Piecourt. A moment later the light of recognition dawned in his eyes. 'You are from the galley, aren't you? Middle oarsman, bench three, port side.'

'That's correct, comite,' said Hector. 'But I am now in the employment of the gun founder to His Majesty Moulay Ismail.'

Piecourt's mouth twisted in a sardonic smile. 'Come to think of it, we've already met your bench companion, the brown man. He interviewed us when we were first captured. So more than one of my dogs have survived. What do you want?'

'I need to interview the technician who looked after the mortar on *St Gerassimus*, also her captain and anyone else who can provide information about the gun.'

Piecourt was expressionless. 'Then you will be disappointed. The technician and the captain are not here. After the galley foundered, the captain took the two ship's boats and headed west along the coast, to seek help. The technician went with him.'

'Is there anyone who could provide me with any information about the gun? It would help your case. The Emperor is disposed to look kindly on anyone who is cooperative.'

'That is not enough reason for me or anyone else to help the infidel. On the contrary, you would be doing yourself a great favour, if you would send word to Algiers, to Iphrahim Cohen the Jewish ransom broker. Once he learns that we are being held here, he will arrange our release. As I already told your brown friend, you could earn yourself a handsome reward. Later you and your friends from bench three might even receive a royal pardon from His Majesty King Louis. I have friends who can arrange such things.'

'It is too late for that, Piecourt. Moulay Ismail has already given orders for your ransom. I am to advise and consult with his own ransom broker, here in Meknes.'

The comite still seemed unperturbed. 'We are not worth very much. There are only myself and the sous comites and a number of common sailors. The officers left in the boats. I repeat: the sooner you get word to Algiers, the more you will benefit.'

There was something about Piecourt's manner which made Hector suspicious. The comite was hiding something.

'I'll take a moment to look around your cell,' he said.

Piecourt shrugged. 'You don't need my permission.'

Stepping inside the cell, Hector was immediately brought back to his days in the Algiers bagnio. The far end of the archway had been blocked off with a wall of bricks, and the near entrance could be closed at night with double doors. The result was a narrow, high room where the only light and air came in through two small windows high up in the far wall. Looking about him, Hector was impressed with the cleanliness of the cell. The occupants were keeping it swept and there was no sign of rubbish. Everything was neatly in its place. It was evident that discipline among the occupants was very good. For their sleeping arrangements the Frenchmen had rigged up a series of bunks from lengths of timber and matting. Due to the height of the cell, these bunks extended upwards for four tiers, and the topmost could only be reached by climbing a ladder. Several of the beds were now occupied by men relaxing after their day's work, while a group of another half a dozen were playing cards on a home-made table placed on the ground between the tiers. Among the card players were two sous comites who had been subordinate to Piecourt, and a sail handler who had worked on the rambade. They glanced at Hector incuriously before returning to their game. It occurred to him that the ship's officers and freemen had known no more about galeriens toiling in the waist of the vessel than the latter had known about the occupants of the poop deck. And Piecourt had been right, there was no sign of the technician who could have answered questions about the mortar and its bombs.

As he left the cell, Hector saw that Piecourt had now deliberately placed himself so he could ignore his visitor. He was seated next to the rowing master and also leaning back against the pillar of the arch. The two of them had their eyes closed as they basked in the sun waiting for the time when the prisoners had to return to their cells and be locked in for the night. Their colleague with the speckled cheek was nowhere to be seen.

Walking back through the gathering darkness, Hector was troubled. There was something he had failed to notice during his visit to the prisoners. Piecourt had been too cool, too composed. It was almost as if, by his nonchalant indifference, he was trying to distract Hector's attention.

He voiced his disquiet to Dan the following day. They were in the armoury where the Miskito was carefully examining the long barrel of an old-fashioned musket. At a work bench nearby Jacques Bourdon was dismantling the weapon's obsolete firing mechanism. 'Piecourt's hiding something,' said Hector, 'or at least he was not telling me the truth.'

'Hardly surprising,' Dan replied. 'In the bagnio, if you remember, it was wise to say as little as possible to strangers or anyone in authority in case you got yourself or a friend into trouble.'

'But this was more than that. Piecourt deliberately discouraged any conversation with me. I have a suspicion that he knows one of the prisoners can supply information about the mortar but didn't want me to identify who the man is.'

'And you are sure the technician wasn't there?'

'Definitely. I had a good look round and couldn't see him anywhere, though I did recognise one of the men who normally worked on the rambade.'

'I doubt that the sailor would know very much,' said Dan. He was holding the musket barrel up to the light so he could squint down inside the barrel. 'If you remember, the regular rambade crew was terrified that the mortar would burst, or a bomb explode while still on deck. So they kept well clear when the gun was being tested.' He picked up a small file and scraped at a rust mark on the musket barrel, then put the musket barrel on one side, and called out to Bourdon, 'No need to fix that lock, Jacques. This gun's so rotten that it would blow up the face of the man who used it. Get one of the lads to give it a polish and put it back in the rack so it looks good on display if Moulay comes round on an inspection. But make sure that it doesn't get issued for active service. I'm condemning it.'

'That's one of the guns I got from Hakim Reis, back in the old days,' commented Allen. The gun founder had just come out of his office on his way to the foundry where the new brass culverin was being chipped out of its mould. 'Those muskets were made specially for the export market. Shoddy, cheap stuff.' Turning to Hector, he asked whether he had come back with any more information about the galley mortar. When Hector admitted that he suspected the French comite of the *St Gerassimus* was holding something back, Allen suggested a new approach. 'Why don't you go to speak with Joseph Maimaran, Moulay's ransom agent? He's very clever. See if he can devise a way of putting some pressure on the comite to make him talk. I know Joseph quite well as I obtain all my brandy and spirits from the Jews because they have the monopoly on distillation. I'll send one of the English lads with you, and he'll bring you to Maimaran's house. It's in the Jewish quarter, of course, so you'll need to explain your business to the guards at the gate.'

℃

THE MELLAH, the Jewish quarter, lay deep within a maze of narrow streets to the rear of the palace compound, and the young lad who guided Hector took gruesome delight in explaining that its name meant 'the place of salt' because Jewish butchers were obliged to pickle the heads of traitors before the heads were nailed up on the city gates. The youth also managed to get himself lost, and it was only by following a stranger dressed in a Jew's black skull cap and cloak who was walking bare foot – the boy explained that the Jews had to go shoeless by Moulay's order – that they finally came to the gateway in the wall enclosing the Jewish enclave. Here Hector and his guide were allowed to pass after handing over a small bribe.

Joseph Maimaran's house lay at the end of a narrow alley and had a modest unpainted door set so deep in the surrounding wall that it was easily overlooked. The humble appearance of the building was as unassuming as its owner who greeted his visitor warily. Maimaran was at least sixty years old, and possessed one of the saddest faces Hector had ever seen. There were deep shadows under his doleful eyes, and the small mouth beneath the prominent nose was permanently downturned and despondent. Hector had to remind himself that Joseph Maimaran, according to Allen, was one of the richest men in Morocco. His wealth had helped bring Moulay to power and he was acknowledged leader of the Jewish community. This meant he had to tread a delicate path. Often, when Moulay needed money, Maimaran was expected to extract it from his fellow Jews, and he could not ask for the return of any loan to the Emperor. If he did so, he risked suffering at the hands of the Black Guard.

'I've come about the prisoners from the French galley *St Gerassimus*,' Hector began carefully. 'The Emperor gave instructions that I was to assist you in setting the amount of their ransom.'

'So I believe,' answered Maimaran, who made it his business to stay closely informed about the Emperor's latest whim.

'He also wants to acquire a siege gun similar to one on the galley, and for that I need information from the prisoners.'

'And have you had any success?'

'Not yet. I was wondering whether it would be possible to reduce the amount of their ransom if they cooperated in the matter of the gun.'

'It is a proposition fraught with risk,' commented the Jew. As he observed the young Irishman in front of him, Maimaran wondered if the young man knew just how angry and violent

Moulay would be if he learned that he had been denied a full ransom.

'Sean Allen thought you might be able to suggest another way forward.'

Maimaran pretended to give the matter some thought. But he had already decided he would prevaricate. He spread out his hands in a gesture of helplessness. 'At this stage I don't know what to propose. I know too little about the case. It would be helpful to have some more information about the French prisoners, any details that would help me calculate their ransom.'

Hector looked disappointed. 'Would there be any advantage in getting in touch with other ransom brokers? The leader of the prisoners is a man called Piecourt. He has twice asked that someone send word of their capture to Algiers. Apparently there is someone there – an Iphrahim Cohen – who can arrange their speedy release.'

This time Maimaran's hesitation was genuine. Hector's suggestion was a surprise. Of course, Maimaran knew that the leading ransom brokers in Algiers were the Cohen family. He had dealt with them in the past, though in matters of trade, not as ransom brokers. Again the Jew was cautious. 'Did this man Piecourt give any reason why this Iphrahim Cohen should be told?'

'No. He only asked that someone contact him.'

'An interesting idea . . .' It was odd, Maimaran reflected, that a comite of the French Galley Corps should know the identities of the leading ransom agents in Algiers. 'Again, it seems that we need to be better informed about the Frenchmen. One of my assistants will visit them. He will assess their ransom value – he is an expert in these matters – and report back to me. In the meantime I suggest you also try to learn more about them. You said that is the Emperor's wish: that you act as the go-between.'

With that remark, Maimaran shifted the responsibility back to Hector and brought the interview to an end.

ⓒ

Luis Diaz was waiting in Sean Allen's office when Hector got back there, and the grin on the Spaniard's face contrasted with the gun founder's tone of exasperation. 'One moment the Emperor wants a castle smasher,' Allen was saying, 'and the next instant he sends word that there's to be a fantasia. That means we'll have to waste some of our small stock of pistol powder so there will be even less for bomb experiments.'

Hector was startled. 'Is the Emperor going to have someone blown from the mouth of a cannon?'

Diaz laughed aloud. 'Whatever makes you think that?'

'In the bagnio of Algiers our Turkish guards accused us of a fantasia if we did or said something insolent or disobedient.'

'This is a different sort of fantasia, thank god,' the gun founder reassured him. 'One which delights our horse-mad friend here. It involves a lot of over-excited cavalrymen charging around on their horses and firing guns in the air. It's spectacular and very profligate as it uses up a great deal of gunpowder. It is aptly known as Laab al-Barud or Powder Play.'

Luis Diaz's grin only broadened. 'Sean, don't be so grumpy. Our young friend deserves a day out from this smoky hellhole. I'll take him and his companions along to see the show. In the meantime you might be so good as to issue me with half a keg of good pistol powder so I can bring it to the royal stables without further delay. The fantasia is scheduled for today, after the evening prayer. There's no time to waste in gossiping.'

Diaz's good humour continued as he left the Arsenal with Hector and his companions, closely followed by a servant leading a mule loaded with the precious powder. 'A fantasia is really something special. You'll never have seen anything like it before. Two or three hundred first-class riders mounted on some of the very best horseflesh in the world.'

They came to the causeway where it crossed over the prison cells, and Diaz advised them to wait there: 'This is the best place to see the show. It'll take at least a couple of hours for the riders to get ready, so you can spend the time catching up with your former shipmates from the galley. As it's Sunday, they'll be having the day off. But leave someone up here to keep yourself a good spot as it'll soon get crowded.'

Leaving Dan to hold their place, Hector went down into the shallow gully with Karp and Bourdon and headed towards the arch where the crew of *St Gerassimus* were lodged. He was intent on cross-examining Piecourt, but as they reached the Frenchman's cell, a surly-looking inmate told him that the comite was absent, and so too was the rowing master. Nor would anyone tell him where they had gone. Hector was left with the impression that the crew members of the *St Gerassimus* had been told to be as unresponsive and obstructive as possible if he returned with any questions. Only when Bourdon met up with some of his countrymen who failed to recognise him was the pickpocket able to learn that the comite and the rowing master were at mass. 'Apparently there's a clandestine chapel in the last archway. It's been set up secretly by two Franciscan priests who came to Meknes to negotiate some prisoner releases. Moulay has been keeping the priests waiting for months, quibbling about the size of the ransom. In the meantime they conduct secret masses for the faithful. The comite and a couple of the other men from the galley are there now.'

'Karp, would you mind coming with me into the chapel and having a look round?' Hector asked. 'I have a feeling that it might be dangerous for me to go in there by myself. Jacques, perhaps you can stay outside and keep watch. Warn us if you think that we might get ourselves trapped inside.'

The three men made their way to the furthest archway. It was much smaller than the others, and had been closed off with a wooden doorway. Quietly Hector pushed the door open and slipped inside with Karp at his heels.

It took a moment for their eyes to adjust to the almost total dark. A service was in progress. The chapel was tiny, so cramped that it could hold no more than a score of worshippers. All of them were crushed together and on their knees as they faced a portable altar set up against the far wall. In front of the altar a priest was also kneeling, his hands clasped in prayer. There was no window to the tiny room, and the only light came from a single candle placed on the altar which illuminated a cross made from woven straw pinned against the far wall. In the dense gloom Hector could not identify the individual figures of the worshippers. They all appeared to be dressed in slaves' clothing though he thought he recognised the broad shoulders of the rowing master. Deep in their prayers, none of the congregation turned their heads as they murmured their responses to their priest's invocation.

As unobtrusively as possible, Hector sank down to his knees. Beside him he felt Karp do the same. The chapel was so crowded that he found it difficult to avoid the bare feet of the man directly ahead of him. Hector kept his head bent forward, wondering at the intense devotion of the worshippers. The chapel was airless and the smell of the close-packed bodies filled his nostrils. He admired the courage of the priest who would risk holding such a mass, and the ardent devotion of his flock.

Slowly he became aware that Karp beside him was beginning to shake. At first it was a slight quivering, but then it became a pronounced movement, an uncontrollable tremor that shook the man's body. For a moment Hector wondered if Karp was about to have a fit. When he glanced sideways he saw that the Bulgar's eyes were wide open. He was staring in horror at the ground in front of him, as if witnessing something terrible. Hector tried to make out what was frightening his companion. In the half-light all he could see were the feet of the man kneeling directly in front of Karp. Looking closely he saw that on the sole of each foot was a brand. Someone had burned the sign of the cross deep into the flesh, leaving a hard scar.

Fearful that Karp would draw attention to their presence, Hector reached out and grasped the Bulgar's arm reassuringly. Karp turned his anguished face towards him, and Hector gestured that they should leave. Quietly rising to his feet and still keeping his hold on Karp, Hector eased open the chapel door and the two men stepped outside into the daylight. Looking into Karp's face, Hector saw that the Bulgar had tears in his eyes. He was still shaking.

'What is it, Karp? What's the matter?' Hector asked gently. The Bulgar was making incoherent strangled sounds, though whether they were from terror or rage it was difficult to say. Something warned Hector that it would be wiser if he and the Bulgar were not seen near the chapel.

'We had better move away,' Hector went on. 'It's safer.'

Bourdon joined them and the Bulgar began to calm down, but his chest was still heaving and he was making unhappy guttural sounds. Suddenly he leaned down and pulled off the sandal he was wearing. Holding up his foot, he sketched the sign of the cross on the sole, then pointed into his ruined mouth and made a fierce gurgling sound. 'The man with the branded foot is something to do with your tongue being torn out, is that it?' Hector asked. Karp nodded vehemently. Squatting down he drew in the dust the outline of a ship, a galley. Next he marked a flag with a cross and, pointing down towards the ground, uttered a deep anguished roar. 'He's from the galley? From our galley?' Karp nodded. 'Karp, we'll sit down quietly when we get back to the foundry. There Dan can help us with pen and paper and you can tell us precisely what it is that you want us to know.'

At this point there was a shout. It was Dan leaning over the edge of the causeway and beckoning to them. 'Come on up,' he called, 'the fantasia is about to start. Hurry!' Hector, Bourdon and Karp made their way up to the crest of the causeway to find that a crowd of spectators had assembled. Most were courtiers from Moulay's entourage, but there were also a number of foreigners, including the three Spanish cavalrymen they had last seen at Diaz's billet. Everyone was jostling together and looking towards the royal stables. Hector placed himself near the edge of the crowd where he could look down and also watch the entrance to the secret chapel. Soon he saw figures appear. The Mass must have finished, and the celebrants were leaving. They emerged in twos and threes, and hurried away quietly. Hector guessed that the priest must have instructed them to remain as inconspicuous as possible. He saw the rowing master, his squat figure unmistakable even though he was in the deep shadow cast by the setting sun. Close behind the rowing master came Piecourt. Once again he was accompanied by the same tall figure of the man he had been with when Hector had visited the cell. Then, finally, he saw the figure of the priest holding to his chest a box which must be the folding altar.

Behind him there was an excited murmur and Hector turned to see that the crowd was now gazing intently down the broad road which led towards the royal stables. In the distance was movement, a low cloud of dust. He strained his eyes and the dust cloud resolved itself into a line of horsemen advancing across a broad front towards the causeway at a slow walk. As the riders drew closer, he began to distinguish that they were all dressed in white robes which flowed and billowed around them. Soon he heard the low rumble of many hooves, hundreds of them, and he realised that there were many more horsemen behind the first squadron. Rank after rank of riders were coming forward. Suddenly, as if on a single command, the front troop of horses passed straight from a walk into a full gallop. They were heading directly towards the spectators as if determined to ride them down. Their riders began to whoop and yell, standing in their stirrups and waving muskets. Some were throwing their weapons up in the air and catching them as they continued their headlong rush. Hector felt his heart pounding as the ground trembled under the hooves of their charge. The horsemen were much closer now. He could see the magnificent accoutrements of their mounts – deep saddles covered with brocade, bridles and reins of tooled leather stamped with gold, velvet saddle blankets edged with silver and gold fringes and tassels, broad breast bands worked with filigree. He heard the cries of the riders urging their animals to gallop even faster. Involuntarily he flinched back expecting the onrushing horsemen to crash into the crowd. Suddenly one of the riders, an older man riding to one side, gave a signal. As one, the front rank of the horsemen swung their muskets forward, holding them two-handed across their bodies so the muzzles pointed over their horses' ears and fired their guns. There was a single, ear-splitting salvo, and the air was filled with puffs of smoke torn through by the arcing sparks of the burning wads. In the same instant, the front rank of riders had reined their horses to a halt, so that the horses heaved back on their haunches only yards from the onlookers. A touch on the reins, and the animals spun on the same spot and went tearing away, with the robes of the riders flapping out behind them and their exultant cries ringing in the ears of the crowd.

Again and again, troop after troop, the riders charged down in the fantasia, fired their guns, wheeled around, and raced away only to regroup and charge down again. As Hector got over his surprise, he began to recognise the pattern in their movements. There were ten squadrons of riders, each performing their manoeuvres at the full gallop, perhaps a thousand horses in total. Each squadron was distinguished by its own particular feature – the colour of the bridles, the size and colour of their horses. One squadron in particular was more magnificent than all the rest. It was composed mostly of horses that were the palest cream in colour. Their tails and manes had been allowed to grow almost to the ground so that they streamed out spectacularly as they galloped, and their discipline was perfect. In that pale squadron three horses stood out. Two were jet black and the third was a handsome pale grey covered with black spots. Each time this squadron charged forward, these three horses were always a few paces ahead of the rest, and they were controlled by a single horseman. The animals were superbly schooled for they stayed close together at a full gallop and allowed their rider to leap from saddle to saddle, occasionally throwing up his musket and catching it again. And it was always this same rider who, as he came careering up to the crowd in advance of his squadron, was the one who gave the command to fire the guns. On the third occasion that this squadron, now like ghostly riders in the near-darkness, completed the fantasia, their leader came to a halt so close to Hector that flecks of foam from his horse's mouth – it was the speckled grey – flew out and landed on his face. At that moment Hector recognised the rider was Moulay Ismail.

EIGHTEEN

☾

JOSEPH MAIMARAN'S hooded eyes regarded Hector with the same caution shown on the young man's previous visit to his house only twenty-four hours earlier.

'I am sorry to disturb you again,' Hector began awkwardly, still standing at the half-open door, 'but there have been important developments since we last spoke. They concern the French prisoners.'

Maimaran could see that his visitor was agitated. Hector had arrived alone in the Mellah and his manner was hesitant, yet eager. Without a word he led the young man along a narrow corridor to the plainly furnished back room where he normally discussed business with his commercial clients. Waving Hector towards a chair, he sat down at a small table, folded his hands and asked, 'Have you been able to learn more about that great gun?'

'No. Sean Allen thinks that it will be very difficult, if not impossible, to satisfy the Emperor's request.'

'That is disappointing. His Majesty, as you must be aware, expects a prompt and successful response to all his demands. If you fail to supply him with a great gun, then perhaps you should make sure that Moulay receives a considerable sum for the ransom of the prisoners. It could save you and your friends from the unpleasant consequences which often result from Moulay's displeasure.'

'That's why I came to talk to you again.' Hector's careful tone put Maimaran on his guard. He waited for Hector to continue. 'It's about the prisoners themselves. Do you know very much about them?'

'Only what my assistant reported. He interviewed them this morning. He tells me that they are of the middle or lower rank, and none of them are likely to have rich families who would pay large sums for their release. So we will have to apply to their master, the Galley Corps of France, for their redemption. My assessment is that the French will offer a prisoner exchange – captive Muslim oarsmen for the Frenchmen – rather than any cash. Unfortunately, in the past the French have bartered one Muslim oarsman for every four of their nationals in these circumstances. They say that our rowers are three or four times more durable than their own nationals.'

Hector took a deep breath before stating, 'One of the prisoners is a fraud. I believe that Moulay Ismail can obtain a very great ransom for him.'

Maimaran felt a sense of disappointment. He had been curious about the Irishman's suppressed excitement. Now he feared he was about to hear an all too familiar story. Maimaran had been arranging prisoner ransoms for many years and was thoroughly experienced in the twists and turns of the process. Of course the captives lied. They had good reason to fake their identities and pretend that they were not who they seemed to be. Those who came from poor backgrounds tried to get better treatment from their captors by claiming they had wealthy families who could pay for their release. Others who came from rich families pleaded poverty so that their ransoms would be set cheaply. Very occasionally a master even changed places with a loyal servant. The master was then allowed to return home in the role of a negotiator to arrange a ransom for his 'master'. But on getting to his own land, he revealed the deception knowing that the captors would release the servant as being of little value. But these ruses were so well known to men like Maimaran that they seldom worked any longer.

Hector sensed the Jew's scepticism. 'Please hear me out. If the Emperor discovers that a captive of such high value has slipped through his fingers, both of us will suffer.'

Maimaran bridled at the warning. Such implied threats often came from those who sought to profit from his disadvantaged status as a Jew.

'What do you think is the real value of our French prisoners?' he enquired, smoothing his black robe, then placing both hands palm down on the table in front of him.

Hector chose his words carefully. 'Have you heard of a man known as "The Lion of La Religion"?'

'Naturally. His reputation has reached us though he operates, if I recall, in the farther end of the Mediterranean.'

'What do you know of him?'

'That he is a Knight of Malta and a most virulent and implacable enemy of Islam. He is perhaps the most notorious of all the knights of the Order of St John. He has become a figure of hatred for the followers of Muhammad. They both fear and loathe him.'

'I believe he is now here in Meknes and held captive among the French prisoners from the galley.' Hector made the statement with as much certainty as he could muster.

'That, if I may say so, is hardly likely,' Maimaran replied. There was an edge of sarcasm in his voice. He was losing patience with his visitor. 'If the Order of St John knew that a leading member of their order was in the Emperor's custody, the grand council would already have opened negotiations with His Majesty for the knight's redemption.'

'That would be true if the Lion of La Religion were a knight of the Order of St John. But he is not. He belongs to the Order of St Stephen. The two orders are easily confused. They share the same symbol, the forked cross. I gather that the Order of St Stephen has almost abandoned the crusading zeal.'

'And now you tell me that this knight was aboard the French galley? That seems even more difficult to believe.' Maimaran remained incredulous.

'My informant is someone who knows the knight well, and has served under him.'

'And why has this informant not come forward before?'

'Until yesterday he was unaware that the Chevalier, as he is known, was among the prisoners.'

'And is he so sure that he is the right man that he can persuade others to believe him?' When Hector hesitated in his reply, Maimaran sensed that he had touched on a weakness in the young man's argument so he pressed his point. 'Your witness would have to give clear evidence about this so-called Chevalier's identity.'

Hector looked directly at Maimaran. 'That would be difficult,' he admitted. 'My witness is a mute. He lacks a tongue.'

Despite his usual self-restraint, Maimaran gave a derisive sniff. 'So your chief witness is dumb! How can you expect anyone to believe such a wild fiction.'

'There is evidence which supports his claim,' said Hector. He had expected that it would be difficult to convince Maimaran, and he knew his only hope of persuading him was to engage his curiosity. 'When your assistant visited the prisoners this morning, was he able to learn the name of the Frenchmen's galley?'

'Of course. Without knowing the vessel's identity, we could not begin to open negotiations with the French.'

'And that name?'

Maimaran failed to see what was the point of Hector's question. 'Surely you know yourself,' he said irritably. 'Were you not an oarsman on her crew?'

'Yes I was,' answered Hector. 'But it is important that these details come from an independent source.'

Maimaran sighed. 'The galley was named *St Gerassimus*. I thought it an unusual name when my assistant told me. But then I know little of these maritime traditions, except that the Christians often give saint's names to their ships, believing them to bring divine protection.'

'Are you familiar with the story of St Gerassimus?'

'I have not the least idea of who he was or what he did.'

'Then perhaps you will have heard of the story of Androcles and the Lion.'

'The fables of Aesop are known to me.'

'The tale of St Gerassimus is very similar. He was a Christian monk living in the desert. One day he removed a thorn from the paw of a lion, and thereafter the lion came to live with the saint, and protected him from his adversaries. Whenever anyone threatened St Gerassimus, his lion attacked his aggressors. You might say that the lion with the wounded paw became the saint's protector.'

'And now you are telling me that the Lion of La Religion is another St Gerassimus?'

'No. St Gerassimus represents the Faith, and the Chevalier sees himself as the Lion fighting to protect it.'

'And how would he have arrived at that strange vision of himself?'

'The Chevalier carries injuries on both feet. The injuries, now healed, were inflicted on him by the Muslims. According to my informant, the Chevalier was captured by Muslims early during his career. He was already known as a cruel and ruthless enemy of Islam, so they tortured him before releasing him in a prisoner exchange. Before letting him go, his captors branded the sign of the cross on the sole of each foot. It was their form of revenge for the Chevalier's fanaticism. They humiliated him by making sure that for the rest of his life, with each step that he took, he would tread on the symbol of his faith.'

Maimaran's mouth twisted in a grimace of distaste. 'And you

learned all this from your mute informant? He seems remarkably well informed.'

'He was there when the knight was tortured. He saw it for himself.'

'And why did he not suffer the same fate?'

'The Muslims took pity on him because already his tongue had been torn out.'

'And why was that?'

'He tried to explain to me but it was difficult to follow the details. But I did learn that it was the Chevalier who had ordered his mutilation.'

There was a long silence while Maimaran considered Hector's tale. The young man's claim seemed altogether too fanciful. 'Can anyone else testify to the supposed identity of this prisoner?'

Hector shook his head. 'I pulled an oar on the galley *St Gerassimus* but I never saw the Chevalier close enough to identify him now. As commander he joined the vessel shortly before we left harbour, and throughout the short voyage he stayed in his cabin or on the stern deck with the other officers. All but a handful of the other oarsmen are dead. They drowned, chained to their benches when the galley sank. Only the men on my oar bench got ashore, and one of those, a big Turk, never made it.'

'What about the other French prisoners, would they testify?'

'From what I have seen they are highly disciplined and loyal to the Chevalier. They would lie to protect him.'

'Is there anything else which makes you think this mute is telling the truth?'

Hector shook his head. 'The only other thing I can think of is the banner flown on our galley. It was the private flag of her commander. It showed the Five Wounds of Christ. Maybe that, too, referred to the injuries that the Chevalier had suffered at the hands of his enemies.'

Maimaran half-closed his eyes, and for a moment Hector thought that the elderly Jew was about to fall asleep. But the ransom broker was pondering his best course of action. If he went to Moulay with a tale that proved to be false, the Emperor was sure to fall into one of his murderous rages. Yet the young man seemed to be speaking in earnest, and there might yet be some slight substance to his extraordinary claim about the identity of one of the French prisoners. Maimaran opened his eyes and looked down at his hands. 'So what do you suggest?'

'We set a trap to unmask the Chevalier. The leader of the Frenchmen, a man named Piecourt, has twice asked for word of their capture to be sent to Jewish ransom brokers in Algiers. He tried to get a friend of mine to send this message soon after the Frenchmen were taken by the amazigh, and then yesterday Piecourt made exactly the same request to me. He mentioned the name Iphrahim Cohen. It seems that Cohen in Algiers would know who the prisoners are, and would be prepared to obtain their release.'

'And how do you set this trap?'

'The Frenchmen receive a note from Iphrahim Cohen, a note apparently smuggled in from Algiers. In the note Cohen writes that he has heard about the Chevalier's capture and has made arrangements for the Chevalier to regain his freedom before his identity is known. The note will contain details of an escape plan, the time and place.'

'And why would the Chevalier – if he is indeed in disguise among the prisoners – trust the note and not suspect a forgery?'

'Because the note will contain certain details known only to the Chevalier and the Cohens. I can supply those details.'

Maimaran reached up to readjust his black cap more comfortably before commenting quietly, 'For someone who has never met the Chevalier face to face, you seem very sure of what is in his mind.'

'If the trap fails, I will accept full responsibility for whatever goes wrong. There will be no mention of the Cohens or a forged letter. I will confess that I was paid by the Frenchmen to arrange their escape. But if the plan works, the Chevalier will have confirmed his identity.'

'I take it that you are proposing that I connive at the flight of one of his majesty's prisoners by helping forge this letter and then delivering it as if it came through the Jewish community?'

'Yes. It is the only way. Everything must be done properly. The French must not suspect anything, until they fall into the trap.'

Maimaran weighed up the young man's suggestion, then enquired, 'You realise, don't you, that even if your plan succeeds, you are asking me to compromise my relationship with my fellow Jews in Algiers? If word of this scheme gets out, the Cohens will regard me as someone who forges their correspondence for my own purposes.'

Hector's answer was sure and steady. 'The Emperor promised me that he would arrange the release of a member of my family if I served him well. If I deliver into his hands the Lion of La Religion, I will have sacrificed a Christian who is a hero to many of his own people. I will be doing this for the sake of my captured sister.'

Maimaran already knew of Hector's audacious request to Moulay Ismail for help in finding his captive sister. The young man's reckless bravado had been court gossip for several weeks. There was something about the strength and sincerity of Hector's resolve which made the old man say, 'Very well. I will prepare that forged letter if you supply the necessary details that make it seem authentic, and I will make sure that it reaches this man Piecourt. But if your scheme goes wrong, I will deny all knowledge of it . . .'

'I cannot thank you enough,' Hector began, but Maimaran held up a hand to stop him. 'Naturally I also expect some recompense for my cooperation. If the Chevalier is not a myth but a real person and is taken into custody, then I want you to give up any interest you may have in the negotiations for his full ransom which, as you say, should be very, very substantial. I alone will conduct those negotiations, and take the appropriate commission.'

'You have my word on it,' Hector assured him. 'All I want is to track down my sister and obtain her release.'

©

AT MIDNIGHT immediately before the next new moon Hector found himself crouching with Dan at the foot of the rampart around the palace compound. He was breathing through his mouth and with shallow breaths. The ditch which ran along the outer face of the wall was used as a rubbish dump and the stench was appalling. The rotting carcasses of dead animals lay half-buried among pieces of broken pottery, discarded rags and all manner of unidentified nastiness. To make matters worse, the ditch was also a lavatory for the slave workers who by day had been repairing the wall above him. Hector feared that he had just rested his bare hand on a soft smear of recent human excrement. The advantage, he reminded himself, was that the ditch was so foul that it was avoided by the guards who occasionally patrolled the perimeter of the palace. Forty yards to his left Karp and Bourdon were also hidden. Diaz and his Spanish cavalry friend Roberto lay in wait in the opposite direction.

'We don't know exactly where Piecourt and the others will attempt to cross, so we need to cover as broad a section of the wall as possible,' he had told his companions that morning. 'I expect they will use the ladders which I saw in their cell to scale the inner face of the wall. Once on top of the wall, they will be able to dangle a rope on the far side and descend. The most likely place is where they themselves have been working during the day on their slave shift. They were repairing a section where the baked earth facing is crumbled away, and here the damaged wall offers a series of footholds. Once they are safely down, they only have to get across the ditch at the foot of the wall and then make their way to one of the villages in the valley. They will be expecting to meet a guide who will take them across country to the coast where a ship will be waiting to pick them up.'

'What makes you think that they will attempt their escape this evening?' Diaz had asked.

'Because there is no moon, and because tomorrow is the feast day of one of the local marabouts or holy men so the Muslim guards will be preparing their celebrations.'

'What happens if a whole gang of prisoners swarms down the ropes? There are not enough of us to deal with all of them.' It was Diaz's cavalry friend Roberto who spoke. He was checking over the pair of pistols that Hector had provided, weapons Hector had borrowed from the Arsenal without consulting Sean Allen.

'There should be only three men, perhaps four,' Hector had reassured the Spaniard. 'In the letter they have received, they have been told that the guide refuses to take more than three men at a time because a large group would be too noticeable as it made its way across country.'

'Let's hope the Frenchmen heed that advice,' the Spaniard had grunted. 'I don't fancy facing a whole lot of them with just a pistol in my hand and no back-up.'

'Try not to harm any of them,' Hector had reminded him. 'We want to take them alive.'

As the hours of darkness had dragged past, Hector was becoming aware of a flaw in his plan. He had failed to take into account the incessant howling and barking of the city's population of dogs. As one pack of dogs fell silent, another group started up, filling the night with their clamour of useless noise and evoking a counter chorus which slowly faded away, only for some lone animal to howl plaintively and start the whole process over again. The racket made it impossible to hear the sounds of anyone who might be scrambling down the wall across the ditch from him, and the face of the wall was so obscured in the gloom that his eyes played tricks on him. Several times he had imagined a shadowy movement, only to be disappointed when, after a long interval, all remained dark and still.

Beside him Dan seemed impervious to the long wait. The Miskito was squatting on his heels, not moving. Hector, by contrast, was obliged to shift his legs from one position to another whenever he felt the first warning twinge of cramp. And as the wait grew longer, Hector grew more and more fretful. He had expected something to have happened by now. He wondered if Piecourt and the others had become suspicious of the note they had received, or if they had decided it would be better to wait for the Franciscans to arrange their ransom. He looked up at the stars, trying to calculate how long he and his companions had been lying in ambush. It was a clear night with only a few shreds of high thin clouds, and he could easily identify the constellations he had studied on the star globe in Turgut Reis's library. It seemed so long ago that he and Dan had been held in the Algiers bagnio and discussed the possibility of their own escape. Now he was trying to prevent the escape of others. Everything seemed to have assumed a different shape. Back in Algiers he had told himself that he must survive the bagnio so that he would be free to track down his sister Elizabeth. Yet he had always known such an ambition was a fantasy. Now, however, he found that he was allowing himself to believe genuinely that he might locate her. He struggled to justify the reason for this new hope. Partly it was because he knew from Sean Allen that Hakim Reis's ship might put into port one day, and he would have the chance to interview her captain. Yet there was something else which was making him more optimistic: he sensed that at last he was gaining control of his own fate, albeit slowly, and that he was no longer at the mercy of others.

A light touch on his hand interrupted his thoughts. It was

Dan. The Miskito had not moved for so long that Hector had almost forgotten his presence. Now Dan was pointing upward. Hector looked towards the top of the rampart. For a second he glimpsed a shape, the outline of a man's head, dark against the starry sky. The town dogs had renewed their howling, so he could hear nothing except their uproar. He kept absolutely still, gazing up towards the parapet. Time passed, and he wondered if he had been mistaken. Then Dan tapped him again on the hand twice, then once more. A moment later Hector could make out two heads against the sky and, almost immediately the head and shoulders of a third man who was leaning out, looking downwards cautiously. Hector felt for the loaded pistol that he had placed beside him, slid his fingers around the butt of the weapon, and waited.

There was a faint sound, so close now that he heard it over the distant crying of the dogs, a gentle slap. Hector guessed that it must be the sound of a rope's end knocking against the wall as it dropped from above. He strained his eyes, trying to see the rope, but the outer face of the wall was in shadow from the starlight and he could see nothing. Looking upward he again detected movement, and this time he was certain. There was the dark outline of someone clambering out over the edge of the wall. The man, whoever it was, was starting his descent. Hector calculated that he would reach the ground about ten yards to the right of where he and Dan lay in wait. Still he did not move.

The figure passed into shadow and disappeared. Hector found that he was gripping the butt of the pistol so tightly that his fingers were numb. Gently he relaxed his grip. He no longer smelled the stench of the ditch. All his senses were concentrated on trying to gauge just how far down the rope the man had come, and to identify the spot where he would touch the ground. No more than half a minute later he heard a noise which he supposed was the sound of someone setting his feet carefully on the edge of the ditch. The base of the wall was so deep in shadow that Hector imagined, rather than saw, the dark shape of a man now standing and waiting there.

A scrabbling sound, and Hector realised that he had missed the start of the descent of a second man. He was already halfway down the rope and descending more swiftly than the first. The second man reached the ground even as Hector was coming to realise that he might have miscalculated badly, and had placed Diaz and his Spanish friend too far away to have noticed what was happening. He feared that they were too distant to help once the trap was sprung. Momentarily Hector dithered, his mind whirling. He did not know if he should act as soon as the next man reached the ground – he was now halfway down the wall – or wait to see if there were other escapees, more than the original three. He feared that if he delayed too long, those who were already on the ground would cross the ditch and escape into the darkness. And if they included the Chevalier, he might never be recaptured.

Hector came to a decision. He rose to his feet and called out, 'Stand where you are or you will be shot.' Hastily he climbed up the slope of the ditch, and ran to the point where he faced directly across to the three men. Dan was at his heels. The three fugitives remained in the deep black shadow at the foot of the wall and it was impossible to make them out distinctly. He hoped that there was enough starlight for them to see that he and Dan both held pistols.

There was silence from across the ditch.

'Now come across towards me, one by one,' Hector ordered.

The first shadow moved, stepped out into the starlight. Immediately Hector knew it was Yakup, the rowing master. The man's squat shape was unmistakable as he made his way down into the ditch, slipping slightly, then squelched his way across and clambered up until he stood in front of the young Irishman. Yakup exuded such a sense of raw physical power that a prickle of fear ran up Hector's spine, and he retreated a pace. 'Come no closer! Step over there and lie face down on the ground,' he ordered, motioning with his pistol. He heard movement over to his right, thankfully Diaz and the Spanish cavalryman were coming to his aid.

'And the next,' Hector called out. 'Move slowly. No tricks.'

A second dark figure detached itself from the shadows and began to make its way across the ditch. When the man climbed up level with him, Hector saw what he had expected: it was the tall stranger, the man with the speckled cheek, whom he had twice seen in Piecourt's company. 'Stand still, just where you are,' he commanded again. Then, speaking over his shoulder to Diaz who had joined them, he added, 'Keep your eye on this one and don't hesitate to shoot.'

He was certain that the third man in the shadow was Piecourt himself. There was a note of triumph in his voice as he called out, 'Now, comite, it's your turn,' and he watched as the third of the escapees made his way across the ditch and stood obediently in front of his captors. Hector felt the tension ebbing. His ambush had succeeded just as he had planned.

Piecourt was peering into his face and speaking. 'So my dogs have betrayed me,' he said. He must have recognised Dan and Bourdon as well, for he murmured, 'Bench three. I always suspected that you were trouble. What will you do with us now?'

'Hand you over to the guards,' said Hector.

'And then?'

'Tomorrow someone will decide your punishment for attempting to escape.' The words were hardly out of his mouth when he was roughly brushed aside. Someone had run up behind him and shoved him out of the way. His foot slipped on the edge of the ditch and for a moment he was off balance, sliding sideways. He half-turned and saw Karp. The expression on Karp's face in the half-light was frightening. His mouth was a dark hole from which emerged a yowling scream. For a ghastly moment Hector was reminded of a stray dog howling at the moon, though the sound that Karp made was more piteous. The Bulgar was moving with shocking speed. His hands reached out. A moment later he had seized the tall stranger by the throat. The force of the lunge knocked the man off his feet and he fell backward, Karp on top of him. In appalled astonishment Hector, Dan and the others stood gaping as the two men writhed on the ground while Karp tried to throttle his victim. Piecourt was the first to recover his senses. He lashed out at Hector, who was still off balance so that Hector fell back on one knee. Whirling round, Piecourt swung an arm at Dan standing guard with his pistol, and forced the Miskito to duck. Then Piecourt took to his heels, running directly away from the wall and heading towards the distant village. Dan straightened up, coolly raised his pistol and called out. 'Stop or I shoot!' When Piecourt failed to respond, Dan pulled the trigger. There was a bright flash, a spurt of red and yellow sparks, followed by the flat explosion of the shot. Thirty yards away the fleeing shadow tumbled forward.

Neither the pistol shot nor Bourdon's whoop of delight had any effect on Karp. He had succeeded in pinning his victim on his back, and was kneeling on his victim's chest with his hands still around the stranger's throat. His frenzied yelling had given way to low, fierce growls as he tried to kill his opponent with his bare hands. 'Karp! Karp! Leave him alone! Let him be!' Hector bellowed in Karp's ear. But the Bulgar was oblivious to Hector's shouts. He bore down with his full weight and was shaking his victim's head from side to side. Hector seized Karp by the shoulder and tried to restrain him. 'No, Karp! No!' he yelled. But it was useless. Karp was in a red mist of rage. In desperation Hector threw an arm round Karp and tried to drag him back, using all his strength. But Karp was berserk. 'Help me, Dan. Help me get Karp under control,' Hector gasped, and with Dan's assistance he wrestled the Bulgar away from his opponent who now lay choking and groaning on the ground.

'Control yourself Karp,' Hector begged. The Bulgar was

sobbing in distress. He was sucking in great gasps of air through his mangled mouth. Tears of rage were streaming down his cheeks, and he was still trembling. 'Everything's under control, Karp,' Hector reassured him. 'You will have your revenge.' Karp gave a gurgling choking sound, and turned his face away. To Hector's utter amazement, the Bulgar dropped to his knees and began to pray. He was weeping uncontrollably.

Hector helped the stranger up. The man was still in a state of shock, appalled by the naked ferocity of the assault. He was unsteady on his feet, coughing and wheezing as he massaged his bruised throat. 'Remember what you did to Karp, Chevalier. You could not have expected less,' Hector said. The stranger did not answer at once, but waited until he had regained his self-control. Then he raised his head and, looking straight at Hector, snapped, 'I should have strung up the villain when I had the chance. But such a death was too gentle for him.'

Dimly Hector became aware of Diaz's voice. The Spaniard was cursing steadily and fluently. 'He got clean away, the bastard,' Diaz was lamenting. He was rubbing his elbow. The rowing master was nowhere to be seen. 'We thought the pair of us had him under control, but the man has the strength of a bull. He took advantage of the commotion and jumped up off the ground and knocked both pistols out of my hands. When I tried to grab him, he twisted out of my grip as if I was a child. Then he dealt Roberto such a clout on the head that he was dizzy for minutes. By the time I recovered my guns, the brute had bolted. It was too late to take a shot at him and, besides, you had your hands full over here with Karp and his friend. I thought it better to come and help you secure the one bird that we had in the hand. There was no need to worry about that fellow Dan picked off. From the way he fell, I'd say he won't get up again.'

'Let's get away from here,' said Hector, suddenly feeling very weary. 'We've got the prisoner we were looking for, and the guard will arrive any minute. They must have heard Dan's shot and all the commotion. We can leave them to find Piecourt whether he's dead or only wounded. He never lifted a hand to help us, so now we'll repay him the compliment. Tomorrow I'll find out just what our captive is worth.'

℃

'TEN THOUSAND louis d'or, that's the ransom that I will be demanding for the Chevalier. I congratulate you,' said Maimaran. The Jew had sent word for Hector to meet him in the imperial treasury, and Hector was astounded by the contrast with the Jew's humble home. Maimaran was waiting for him in a reception chamber whose barbaric opulence was hidden deep in the palace compound. Sunlight poured in through the fine fretwork of arched windows and threw patterns across a tessellated floor of white, blue and red. The walls were hung with arrays of sabres, shields and muskets inlaid with gold and mother of pearl. Several iron chests, bolted and padlocked, stood against one wall. 'His true identity is Adrien Chabrillan, Knight Commander of the Order of St Stephen of Tuscany. He also holds various lesser titles of nobility and rank including the honorary rank of captain in the Galley Corps of France. As you rightly surmised, he is also known as the Lion of La Religion. The Emperor is away for a few days so I have not yet informed him of his captive's identity, but I know that he will be very pleased. It will enhance his reputation as a champion of Islam as well as make a very significant contribution to his treasury.' Maimaran nodded towards the iron-bound chests. 'The Emperor always needs money. His expenses are voracious, and his revenues unpredictable. The ransom of Chevalier Chabrillan will ensure a steady stream of income for quite some time.'

'I had no idea that the Chevalier could be worth so much.'

Maimaran gave a tight smile. 'His Majesty leaves it to me to act as the unofficial comptroller of his finances, and to maintain a balance between income and expenditure. The sum of ten thousand louis d'or is so enormous that it will take several years to raise. Doubtless Chevalier Chabrillan has friends and family who will advance what they can, and their contributions can be added to the sale of the more valuable possessions that he either inherited or accumulated over years of cruising against the Muslims. But that preliminary effort will raise no more than a down payment and will have to be followed by annual payments – perhaps for as much as another ten years. His supporters and family might even have to borrow additional funds from financiers, such as the Cohens in Algiers.' There was a hint of satisfaction to his voice as he added, 'If the Cohens charge their usual ten per cent interest, it will lessen any resentment should they ever discover that their name was used to trap the Chevalier.'

'And what will happen to him while all this ransom is being collected?'

'As long as the payments keep arriving, he will be kept closely confined and well treated. No one wants to see him perish. But should the flow of payments cease or slow to a trickle, then his conditions of imprisonment will worsen, and he will be given the opportunity to inform his family of his suffering. That should help loosen the purse strings once again.'

'And what about the other men who tried to escape with him? Do you know what happened to them?'

Maimaran glanced meaningfully at one of the muskets displayed on the wall. 'Your companion, the one with the dark skin, is an excellent shot. The man he brought down with his pistol died this morning. The pistol ball broke his spine.'

'And what about the other one? There was a third man who ran away. Has he been caught?'

'Not yet, as far as I know. But he won't get far. He is on his own and in a strange country. The commander of the palace guard has sent word to all the surrounding villages that a watch is to be kept for him. The commander wants him caught before the Emperor returns to Meknes, because it will look bad for him if a slave has been allowed to escape.' Maimaran broke off for a moment as he reached out to readjust a pile of ledgers on an elegant table inlaid with mother of pearl. 'But I did not ask you to come here to talk about the fate of the runaways. You told me earlier that you were trying to trace your sister who, you believe, might be captive in Morocco, and for this reason you wished to render a great service to the Emperor. Now that you have succeeded in the first part of that ambition, I was wondering what you planned to do next, and if there is any way in which I might help. You've made my task as comptroller of royal finances much easier, and I feel that I am in your debt.'

Hector looked around the strange disorder of valuables on display. There were enormous ostrich feather fans, heaps of costly rugs, beautifully worked saddles, an intricate-looking clock lying on its back on the floor, several looking glasses in gilded frames, a leopard skin. He guessed they were items of tribute rendered to the Emperor or seized by Moulay from his hapless subjects, and he remembered that Sean Allen had mentioned how Hakim Reis occasionally brought gunpowder as tribute to the Emperor.

'Do you know a ship captain by the name of Hakim Reis?' he asked.

'Another seafarer with piratical habits,' commented Maimaran softly. 'You seem to have a broad knowledge of such people.'

'I was wondering if you knew how I could contact him.'

To his disappointment, the comptroller replied, 'I've never met him myself. He usually stays with his ship down on the coast, at Sallee, and is tactful enough to send his Majesty some little curiosity by way of a gift. You see that clock over there, not the one on the floor, but on that far table. That is one of his presents which he sent to Meknes. It was made in London, and taken out of an English merchant ship that Hakim and his fellow corsairs waylaid off the coast of Spain. Naturally I keep a record of all such gifts. His Majesty has a habit of suddenly enquiring what happened to particular items. He has a remarkable memory.'

'Sean Allen said the same about the weapons he has to preserve in the armoury, even if they are so old that they are useless. He told me that he gets them also from Hakim Reis who in turn is supplied by someone called Tisonne or Tison. Do those names mean anything to you?'

There was a pause, and Hector's hopes rose very slightly as Maimaran said slowly, 'A name like that is vaguely familiar. I seem to remember hearing it in relation to the emperor's finances, but I cannot remember exactly where. However . . .' Then he reached towards his pile of ledgers and selecting a volume began to turn the pages, before he continued, 'This should tell me.'

Hector watched the old man fastidiously read down the columns until Maimaran gave a little satisfied grunt and said, 'I thought so. Here it is. A substantial payment in the name of Tison. The money was paid two years ago.'

'Was it for weapons? For gunpowder?' Hector asked eagerly. 'Sean Allen said that Hakim Reis obtained these materials from Tison or Tisonne. Does the ledger give any details who he is or where he might be found?'

'I'm sorry to disappoint you, young man,' said Maimaran, looking up from the page, 'but this entry is nothing to do with guns or smuggling. It relates to a horse, and if you want to find out more about it you need to go to the royal stables.'

NINETEEN

Ⓒ

'A HORSE!' Diaz wiped his mouth with the back of his hand as he set down his drink. Hector had waited for the Spanish cavalryman's next visit to Sean Allen's office to ask his help in solving the mystery of the entry for Tison in Maimaran's account books. 'I wonder what the old Jew was referring to. I can't think what he meant.'

'You've never heard of Tison or Tisonne yourself?' Hector enquired.

'Yes, of course. Every Spaniard has,' Diaz replied cheerfully and, reaching down, picked up his sword and slapped it on the table. 'This is a *tison*, though in Castile we pronounce it *tizon*. It's a word for a sword, and celebrates one of the most famous weapons in our history. Our greatest hero, El Cid, possessed two swords; one was called Tizon, the other Colada. Every schoolboy is made to learn the poem of El Cid by heart. Even now I can still remember the line,' and he flung out an arm dramatically as he recited. 'Well worth a thousand golden marks was the great sword Tizon.'

'What did El Cid do with his sword?'

Diaz looked at Hector in astonishment. 'You don't know the story of El Cid?'

'No.'

'Six hundred years ago he helped drive back the Moors and used Tizon and Colada to do the job. According to legend, each sword was half as long again as the span of a man's arms, and its blade so broad and heavy that only El Cid could wield it in battle.'

'Then it seems strange to find a "tizon" in the stables of a devout Muslim prince. You would have thought it more likely that the great sword was kept here in the armoury or on display somewhere in Moulay's palace. Only yesterday Maimaran showed me various trophies that Moulay has put on show to celebrate his victories over the Christians.'

Diaz grimaced. 'Probably looted them from Spanish towns he captured in the north. Still, the only way to solve the puzzle is by going to the stables themselves. If Sean can spare you, we can set out right now. Just as soon as I finish this drink.'

℃

DOZENS OF GROOMS and ostlers were busy bedding down the horses for the night when Diaz and Hector arrived at the stables. The air was heavy with pungent stable smells, squads of slaves were spreading fresh straw and carrying buckets of water to replenish drinking troughs, and Hector could hear the stamping of hooves and the snuffling of the animals as they waited hopefully for an evening feed. Diaz led him straight to meet the stable master, a small wizened Moor who must have been at least seventy years old and walked with a heavy limp which was the result, according to Diaz, of a riding accident. 'Haddu is from one of the desert tribes who are great horse handlers and breeders. He has been here since the first day Moulay began building his stables. Recently Moulay wanted to make him a kaid, a nobleman, as a reward for his services. But Haddu refused. He told the Emperor that he didn't want to be a kaid. Moulay was about to get very angry at being snubbed – you could see his eyes going red – but then Haddu added that he preferred horses to men and, as you know, Moulay

likes his cats better than his servants, so he merely laughed and
turned away.'

Unfortunately for Hector and Diaz, the stable master found
it difficult to understand exactly what his visitors wanted. Hector
and Diaz took it in turns to try to explain, but they had no
success. Haddu looked from one to the other, increasingly
puzzled. 'Tison? Tizon? Tisonne?' Hector repeated, trying every
pronunciation he could think of. 'The Emperor's treasurer told
me that he found the word Tison written in his ledgers, and it
was something to do with a horse.'

'I know nothing about any Tison,' said the stable master,
'but everything to do with the royal horses will be found in the
section of the stables reserved for the Emperor's animals. If we
look there, perhaps you will discover your answer.'

The three men walked across to the imperial stable block
that Hector remembered from his previous visit. There Haddu
led them between the long lines of open stalls. The animals
peered at them curiously, their ears pricked forward, heads
turning to follow the progress of their visitors. Haddu stopped
often to stroke a nose or scratch between a horse's ears. He
knew the name and breeding of every animal, and all the while
he delivered a running commentary about the creature's history
and character. This horse came from the amazigh, the next was
a present from the Caliph in Egypt, another was very elderly
and stiff in the joints now but had been to Mecca and was
sacred. Eventually they came to the last section of the stalls
which, Haddu explained, was where the Emperor's own riding
animals were stabled. These horses were kept exercised and fit,
ready for Moulay to ride in procession and state occasions.
Hector and Diaz looked at each one and complimented the
stable master on the good condition of the animals. It was when
they had reached the very last animal in the line that Diaz
stopped dead, and then slapped his forehead and gave a cry of
triumph. 'What an idiot I am,' he exclaimed. 'This is what

Maimaran must have meant.' Turning to the stable master, he asked, 'How long have you had this horse here?'

'Some two years. It is a most unusual animal, one of the Emperor's particular favourites. He would have had to pay a great deal of money for it because such horses occur very infrequently. This one has proved not only beautiful but easy to train. It is truly a gem.'

Diaz looked across at Hector. 'All that talk of El Cid's great sword distracted me. The clerk who wrote up that ledger Maimaran showed you didn't know very much about horses. He put down "tison" when, more correctly, he should have written "tiznado". The two words are both to do with the ashes or embers in a fire. Do you remember that evening when we watched the fantasia? Moulay himself was riding the three lead horses in the main squadron. He put on a great display, and I remember one of my colleagues, another cavalryman, spoke admiringly of the tiznado. I didn't know what he was talking about, and he explained that it was a word used in the Spanish colonies to describe a horse of a particular colour. This is just such a horse, a rarity, come and see for yourself.'

Hector went up to the stall. He found himself face to face with a handsome stallion who looked back at him, head held high, an intelligent gleam in its eye. The creature was strongly built with a powerful chest and a short back, clean legs and neat small hooves. Every line of its body told of speed and stamina. But what was truly eye-catching was the creature's coat. It had been brushed until it shone. The background colour was a pale grey, and scattered over it were dozens and dozens of small black spots. It was the horse that Moulay Ismail had been riding at the fantasia.

©

'I COULD HAVE saved you the trip,' commented Bourdon when they got back to Sean Allen's office in the Armoury and reported on their visit to the stables. 'A spotted horse is called a tisonne in French. I know that because I once worked at an inn on the outskirts of Paris. I was only a youngster and the lowest of the low, so I was given the job of cleaning out the grates and fireplaces. Sometimes I had to climb halfway up the chimneys to get them swept. One of the local aristocrats, a vicomte, had a dog of that same speckled colour which had been trained to run along beside his carriage when he went driving out from the chateau. It was just showing off because the dog was a real eye-catcher with its black and white coat. Sometimes the vicomte stopped at the inn to take refreshment, and I remember one of the other inn servants took a great liking to the dog. He would pet the animal and feed it titbits. He had his own name for it. He called it Tisonne, and said his master really should have a tisonne horse to match. For a joke he sometimes even called me a tisonne saying that I had the white and pasty skin of a city dweller and was covered with specks of smut and soot from the fire.'

At that moment the door to the gun founder's office swung open and Diaz's friend Roberto burst into the room. There was a triumphant expression on his face. 'They got him!' he exulted. 'They got that apelike bruiser who escaped us. I just heard.'

'Yakup, the rowing master, may he rot in hell,' said Bourdon after Hector translated the Spaniard's announcement. 'Let's have a celebration. But speak slowly so that Hector can tell me the details as you go along.'

Roberto sat down on the bench and launched into his tale with relish. 'Apparently he managed to hide himself away in the countryside until by chance he was glimpsed by some locals when he came into a village to steal food. He beat up one of the villagers very badly, almost killed him. But he got himself lost and started wandering in circles. As luck would have it, he blundered into the path of Moulay Ismail's cavalcade as it was returning to the city. The Black Guards managed to overpower him and bring him before Moulay. It seems that the Emperor was in a foul mood. When the prisoner was brought before him, he flew into an even more vile temper. Moulay was so enraged by the sign of the cross on the rowing master's forehead that he ordered the Black Guard to toss the rowing master into the bottom of a nearby ravine, and if he tried to scramble out, they were to push him back with their spears. Moulay then turned to his son, that brat Ahmad who is called "the golden one", and told him that he needed to improve his shooting skills and that it was time he tried out his new muskets.'

'I know all about those,' interjected the gun founder. 'I adapted a pair of guns specially for the lad. He's only about ten years old though tall and lanky for his age. Dan here trimmed down the stocks to size, and fitted the latest locks.'

'Dan did a good job because the guns never misfired. Young Ahmad stood on the edge of the ravine and took one pot shot after another at the rowing master as he scrambled among the rocks and bushes trying to dodge. You could hear the bullets skipping off the rocks. Moulay himself stood watching, shouting advice and encouragement. When one of the Black Guards whose job was to reload the muskets was too slow, Moulay whipped out his sword and chopped off the man's fingers. Eventually young Ahmad succeeded in knocking over the rowing master with a lucky shot, but his target managed to get back on his feet. It took another three musket balls to bring him down for good. Moulay then gave orders that the corpse was to be flayed, and the skin nailed up on the city gates to discourage other runaways.'

'A fitting end for the bastard,' observed Bourdon. 'Let's drink to the eternal damnation of all rowing masters. When they arrive in Hell, may they be chained to red-hot oar handles, lashed with whips made from bulls' pizzles pickled in brine, and suffer from swollen piles whenever they fall back on the rowing bench.'

Hector noticed that Karp had been listening, his eyes flicking from one speaker to the next. With Piecourt and the rowing master both dead, the Chevalier seemed to have got off lightly, and Hector recalled the Chabrillan's sour remark that hanging would have been too gentle a death for the Bulgar. 'Karp, there are some questions I have to ask the Chevalier,' he said. 'I'm going to try to get permission to visit him in his cell. Do you want to come along?'

Karp gave a gagging sound and shook his head vehemently. Hector thought it strange that he looked not angry, but ashamed.

©

CHEVALIER ADRIEN CHABRILLAN'S prison was close to the imperial menagerie. Hector could hear the coughing roars of the lions and a strange high-pitched whooping which he took to be the call of some exotic bird as he approached. The low featureless building looked from the outside like a servants' dormitory, and the sprawling imperial compound was such a maze of pavilions, mosques, guardhouses, stores, walkways and courtyards that, without the help of a guide provided by Joseph Maimaran, Hector would never have arrived at the Chevalier's cell on the ground floor. Only when he went inside and was brought to a heavy wooden door guarded by a suspicious goaler did Hector appreciate that Chevalier Chabrillan was, in effect, hidden away from the rest of the world.

The guard unlocked the door with a heavy iron key, and stood back to allow Hector to enter the cell alone. The room was simply furnished with a mattress on a low bed frame, a wooden table and two chairs, and a chamber pot. A blanket lay neatly folded on the mattress, and the only light entered through a small, barred window high up in the wall opposite the door. Hector noted that the wall itself was two feet thick. The room reminded him of a monk's cell, an impression strengthened by the fact that its lone occupant was kneeling in prayer, facing a simple wooden cross nailed to the wall.

The turnkey closed the door behind Hector, but the kneeling figure did not stir. The man was dressed in a loose cotton gown, and once again Hector found himself staring in fascination at the cross-shaped scars on the soles of his naked feet. Finally, after several minutes, the prisoner rose and turned to face his visitor. For the first time Hector saw the Chevalier close up in daylight and he was taken aback by the contemptuous stare. 'I gave orders that I would receive visitors only if they were here to discuss the conditions of my incarceration,' said Chabrillan. 'If I am not mistaken, you are an associate of that tongueless heretic. You will be disappointed if you came here to gloat. I have nothing to discuss with you.'

'I want only a few moments of your time,' said Hector civilly, marvelling at the unshakeable self-confidence of the Chevalier. He did not harbour any hatred for the man, now that he knew Chabrillan was very likely to be held prisoner for many years. 'I did not come to take pleasure from seeing your captivity. I only hope to understand why this has come about.'

'I would have thought that was obvious,' Chabrillan snapped. 'The schismatic wanted revenge. But it will make no difference in the eyes of God. I may remain here for many years, but he will spend all eternity in the fires of Hell.'

'He seemed so harmless until—' Hector began, but he was cut off in mid sentence by a snort of disdain.

'Harmless! That viper! He is no more harmless than the Satan whose path he follows, and whose poison he was injecting into others until I had his tongue removed.'

'But Karp could never have been a threat to someone as powerful and well connected as yourself.'

Chabrillan regarded Hector scornfully. 'What do you know about these things?' Belatedly Hector realised that he had come with the intention of questioning Chabrillan, but was already deferring to the aristocrat's arrogance. He resolved to stand his ground.

'Karp told me that you had his tongue torn out when you were both in Kandia.'

'Told? How could he have told you anything? He lacks

the means to do so.' This time there was a note of cruelty in Chabrillan's tone.

'He did so by dumb show. He also drew a map and tried to make me understand that you have the sign of the cross marked on the soles of your feet. At the time it made no sense.'

'And did he also tell you that he is a traitor to Christendom, a festering contagion eating away at the True Faith?'

Abruptly Chabrillan turned away. For several moments there was silence as if he was considering whether to put an end to the interview. Then he swung round to face his visitor, and in a flinty voice said, 'Kandia was where we took our stand against the Turk. There were thousands of us who believed that it was our sacred duty to hold the bastion. The rest of the island had already fallen, but the city itself held out month after month, year after year. Venice sent us supplies and reinforcements, and her fleet kept the sea-lanes open. I and other knights came with our galleys to try to stiffen the resistance shortly before the end. Doubtless that was when Karp wormed his way in. He was among the volunteers who arrived from all over Europe to assist us.'

'Karp is from the Bulgar lands ruled by the Turks. He would have risked his life to get to Kandia,' agreed Hector. He had intended to encourage the flow of the Chevalier's narrative but his remark only brought an angry retort.

'And that should have made me beware! He is no more a Christian than that blackamoor who guards my cell door. His homeland is a wellspring of heresy. From there the pestilence oozes and threatens to infect all.'

'I don't follow your meaning,' Hector muttered.

Chabrillan's lip curled. 'How would you understand? Am I right in guessing that you have taken the turban and your manhood has been trimmed?'

'I did convert when I was in the bagnio of Algiers,' Hector acknowledged, 'but only in the hope that it would ease my captivity. My faith has lapsed since then, both in the teachings of Muhammad and in the religion I was taught as a child by monks. They were good men who knew their gospel.'

'What would those monks say if they knew you had lifted a forefinger and pronounced that there is no God but Allah, and that Muhammad is his prophet,' Chabrillan sneered. 'In that benighted corner perhaps your monks have not yet heard the serpent's hiss, those who preach that Satan is the creator and ruler of the visible world. They deny the Holy Cross and refuse to worship the Virgin Mary and the Saints. That is what Karp and his foul companions do. They claim that the Romish Church is not the Church of Jesus Christ but a Harlot, while only they themselves hold to the truth.'

'But if men like Karp came to fight at Kandia alongside you, what mattered was their hatred of the Turk.'

'Karp did not come to Kandia to fight. He came to convert. He persuaded others in our garrison that atonement and redemption were meaningless, that the sacrament of unction was to be spurned because it is reserved for the rich, that every good layman is himself a priest. His blasphemy was endless.'

Hector felt he was getting nowhere. The Chevalier was clearly a fanatic, but that did not seem sufficient reason for him to have mutilated Karp, a fellow Christian, in the midst of a gruelling and prolonged siege. 'What reason did you give when you ordered Karp's tongue to be removed?' he asked.

'I needed no authority. Karp had attached himself to my troops in the guise of a cook, and he was under my command. It was enough that he was preaching disobedience, not only to Mother Church but to military authority and to natural order. He would have my men lay down their arms and renounce all violence. They were to call themselves "dear to God", and trust to prayer. That was sedition. So I stopped his mouth. I made an example of him so that others should take warning.'

'And how did he come to lose his nose and ears as well?'

Chabrillan gave a shrug as if Hector's question was

superfluous. 'When Kandia fell, the Turks allowed us to leave unmolested. I took Karp with me as a slave, intending to keep him as an oarsman on my galley. I felt that his punishment was not yet served out. Later he tried to run away. He lost his ears and nose for that. My comite carried out the sentence.'

'Piecourt is dead,' said Hector flatly.

'Then he will have his just reward,' replied Chabrillan. 'He always followed the true doctrine of the Christ, of the Gospel, and the Apostles.'

'And the scars on your feet? How did you suffer them?'

'In Christ's service,' answered the Chevalier grimly. Deliberately and rudely, he looked at the wall over Hector's head. 'The Venetians had agreed secretly that I alone of all the defenders of Kandia was to be handed over to the Turks. The infidels wished to take revenge for an earlier incident in my struggle against them. They mistook Karp for my personal slave and arranged that he dress my wounds after they had finished with me.'

'Is that when you first met Hakim Reis?'

Hector's question had a remarkable effect. Chabrillan dropped his gaze and stared hard at Hector. The Chevalier's supercilious manner had been replaced by a long, calculating appraisal of his visitor. After a lengthy pause he said softly, 'I thought that it was the Cohens in Algiers who had betrayed me.'

'The Cohens had nothing to do with it. They probably do not even know that you were taken prisoner from the *St Gerassimus* or where you are now.'

'Then who wrote that letter promising our escape?'

'It was prepared here in Meknes.'

Chabrillan's eyes searched Hector's face. Hector could tell that the Chevalier was struggling to work out the events of the past few days. 'Then Karp was the mischief-maker. But I don't remember that he ever laid eyes on Hakim Reis. And it is strange that he knew Hakim is expected soon in Sallee. From

Kandia onwards Karp has been nothing more than a mute beast, pulling an oar.'

'It was not Karp who prepared the letter,' Hector assured him. 'He recognised you by the scars on your feet, and identified you as the Lion of La Religion, but nothing more. As for Hakim Reis, no one knows when he will next visit Sallee.'

'Yet the message said that Hakim Reis would be waiting to pick me up.'

Hector decided that this was his moment to press forward. The Chevalier was off guard and might be shocked into a confession. He watched for his reaction as he said, 'I needed to confirm that you had dealt with Hakim Reis in the past and that you would expect him to connive at your escape. I had to be sure of my evidence.'

Chabrillan did not move a muscle. His eyes never left Hector's face as he asked, 'And what evidence was that?'

'First, the gunpowder in the magazine. It is a special pistol powder, impossible to manufacture in Barbary. It was not damaged or damp as if it had been captured at sea. The powder was in a keg, in perfect condition, fresh from the makers. I had seen similar kegs aboard the *St Gerassimus*. The gun founder Sean Allen said that the gunpowder had come from Hakim Reis, who in turn may have got it from a smuggler called Tisonne. That was when I first heard the name. Later a friend of mine, working in Moulay's armoury, came across some shoddy muskets made for the export market. Again the gun founder said that he had obtained the weapons from Hakim Reis.' Hector waited for several seconds before adding, 'I presume you got those marks on your cheek when a faulty musket barrel exploded in your face. Were you giving a demonstration of the weapon, and did Hakim accept the shipment?'

For a moment Hector thought he had broken through Chabrillan's calm detachment. The Chevalier moved a hand as if to touch the scatter of blue specks on his cheek, but then changed his mind.

'I shared an oar bench with a man with exactly that colour of mark on his cheek,' Hector added. 'He is marked with the letters GAL for galerien. He had told me that when the brand was first scorched into his flesh, it was made permanent by rubbing gunpowder in the fresh burn.'

'You seem to have an abundance of low-life friends,' Chabrillan remarked witheringly.

'Someone else said that to me recently,' Hector acknowledged, but then moved on. 'It was not until I learned that tisonne is a word for a horse with a spotted skin that I made the connection. My guess is that Hakim Reis gave you that cover name, and that you enjoyed the coincidence that tizon is also the name for a weapon which the heroic El Cid wielded against Muslims.'

'You have a very vivid imagination,' said Chabrillan. It was evident that he had regained his composure fully. 'Why should it matter to you that I am this Tisonne. I am held in this cell because I am a knight of the Order of St Stephen of Tuscany, not because weapons and gunpowder reached Meknes.'

'I will come to that in a moment,' Hector answered him. 'But there is something else which must come first, something more important than arms smuggling.'

'Please continue.' Chabrillan's voice dripped with sarcasm.

'Hakim Reis has the reputation of a lucky man. He always seems to be at the right place and at the right time. His galley intercepts merchant shipping with uncanny accuracy, and he is first on the scene when a peace treaty breaks down and a Barbary state reverts to piracy. It is as if someone highly placed in the councils of his victims is supplying him with vital information. I believe that informant was you.'

'And why should I do that?'

'That is what I did not understand until you told me why you had Karp's tongue removed: you nurse a violent hatred for those who you see as enemies of your Church, whoever they are, whether Muslims or dissenters. You would damage them in whatever way you can.'

Hector could feel Chabrillan's arrogance returning. It was like a physical force radiating from the aristocrat, his absolute certainty that his cause was correct, and that his breeding and privilege placed him above others.

'As a turncoat you would not understand,' Chabrillan said, his voice contemptuous. 'Christendom will prevail. But first it must cure itself of the heresies within. That is where the real and present danger lies. Schismatics and agnostics gnaw at the heart of Mother Church. Men like Karp must be rooted out. Nations who would question the authority of Rome must be put to flight. Only then should we turn our full attention to the Eternal War.'

'And is that why you allied yourself with Hakim Reis?' Hector spoke quietly. He knew now that Chabrillan's self-belief was his weakness.

'Consider where Hakim Reis operates – in the Atlantic, where he encounters ships from the trading nations of the north, from protestant nations. His activities and the attacks of corsairs like him weaken these nations and distract them from rivalry with the Holy Mother Church. The arms and gunpowder he brings to. Moulay are used to drive the English from Tangier. A share of the money he receives, from the slaves and cargoes he captures and the arms he provides, goes to good purpose. Through me it has built galleys for La Religion, strengthened fortifications, and holds back the Turk.'

'Then why did you join the Galley Corps of France?'

Chabrillan gave a cynical smile. 'Did you not notice how many of the Reformed, as they like to call themselves, sat alongside you on the benches of *St Gerassimus*? Increasingly France condemns them to the oar. One day, I predict, King Louis will recognise the Reformed openly for the pestilence they are, and then the galleys of France will join in our crusade, rowed by unbelievers.'

'What about the innocent victims of your alliance with Hakim?' Hector asked. This was the moment he had waited for.

'Eighteen months ago Hakim Reis with two ships raided a small and undefended village on the coast of Ireland. He carried off slaves, both men and women. The villagers were taken by surprise because the authorities believed there was a peace treaty between Barbary and the English king. They did not know that the treaty had been torn up. Yet Hakim knew, and he profited from his knowledge. If Tisonne was his source – and you are Tisonne – then you are responsible for both Catholics and Protestants having been sold into slavery.'

'I care not for the Catholics of Ireland,' snapped Chabrillan. 'They failed us. When Ireland fell to the protestant English, she no longer sent her noblemen to Malta despite the requests of the Grand Master. Yet at home they continued to enjoy the Order's lands and estates. Your countrymen were too craven.' He looked at Hector with a sudden flash of understanding. 'Hakim Reis matters to you because you were taken in that raid?'

'Yes, I was a victim, along with my sister. She was carried away aboard another ship. I have not seen her since.'

A vindictive smile appeared on Chabrillan's face. 'Your sister?' he said slowly.

'Yes.'

The Chevalier considered for a short while before he declared, 'I had not intended to admit that I am Tisonne, but now I shall do so for the satisfaction it gives me when I address a weak renegade. Yes, I did work together with Hakim Reis. I supplied him intelligence and I provided him with weapons and gunpowder sold corruptly by the administrators of the Galley Arsenal and by other venal merchants. In return, whenever Hakim Reis sold prize goods, he paid me a share through the Cohens in Algiers, and in turn they placed credit for me with the Crespinos in Livorno. No one could trace the money, not even the Jews. Sometimes I met with Hakim at an arranged rendezvous at sea when I handed over guns and powder, and he provided me with his captives for me to sell in Valletta or Livorno.'

Chabrillan's manner was utterly self-assured. It occurred to

Hector that the Chevalier was pleased to have an audience to whom he could explain himself.

'For all his faults, Hakim Reis had scruples. Unlike you he believed sincerely that he should help his fellow Muslims. He would exchange his Christian captives for Muslims which I had taken. Hakim would then set his people free, and many of them went on to serve as crew aboard his ship. The men and women I received, if they were protestant, I sold in Valletta or Livorno, or kept them at the oar. I remember his raid on Ireland and you are right: I had sent him word that the treaty with England was soon to be repudiated. He took advantage, as I had expected. We had agreed to meet at sea afterward – to conduct our usual exchange of prisoners. But our rendezvous was disturbed. A foreign warship appeared and Hakim Reis wisely fled. He made for safe harbour. There he sold his captives – yourself included.'

'What of the other vessel? When Hakim raided Ireland, he came with two ships. What happened to the second vessel? Where did it go?' Hector was finding it impossible to keep the tension out of his voice.

'Some time later Hakim Reis sent me my share of the sale of the prisoners from that vessel. They were women. His colleague had got an excellent price for them. I was delighted by the sum. Your sister was no doubt among the wares.' He paused, coughed to clear his throat. A spiteful gleam had appeared in his eyes. 'Do you wish to know more?'

Hector's mouth was dry, and though he already knew the answer, he murmured, 'Of course.'

'Your sister and the other women from the Irish raid were landed in Sallee. If she was young and desirable, she would have been sold into Moulay's harem.' Chabrillan dropped his voice and spoke slowly and distinctly, relishing every word as he added, 'The thought that your sister is likely confined not so far from this cell is my consolation for the harm that you have done me. You would do well to reflect that once Moulay breeds on a woman, he casts her off like a used brood mare.'

TWENTY

Ⓒ

HECTOR'S MOOD OF appalled dismay stayed with him all the way back to the armoury. His meeting with Chabrillan had shocked him into acknowledging that he had avoided facing the reality of what might have happened to Elizabeth. Chabrillan's malice had brought him face to face with the sordid possibilities.

Once again, it took Dan's calm advice to produce a glimpse of hope. 'You don't know for sure that Elizabeth is in Moulay's harem. She could have been sold to one of the kaids in Sallee and kept in his household. And don't forget that Moulay promised to set your sister free if he got his castle smasher from us. We could yet think up another way of pleasing him.'

Sean Allen was more cautious. 'Moulay may not honour that promise if it turns out that Hector's sister is in his own harem. The Emperor is not known for being open-handed with his possessions.' But the gun founder realised that he had been tactless, and quickly added, 'Hector, your best course is to try to find out whether Elizabeth really is in Meknes, and that's going to be difficult enough. The imperial harem is jealously protected. Every one of Moulay's wives is accompanied at all times by a eunuch guard as well as a serving woman who reports back to Lala Zidana.'

'Who's Lala Zidana?' Dan asked, for Hector was still sunk in dejected silence.

'Moulay's first wife and his most important one,' the gun founder answered, 'though the Lord knows why. She's an enormous woman, black as night and big as a hippo according to report. Moulay bought her for sixty ducats when she was a domestic slave and she seems to have established some sort of hold over him. There are rumours that she practises witchcraft. Certainly she rules the harem, and she keeps Moulay sweet by supplying him with the choicest girls. That nasty young pup Ahmad for whom we adapted the guns, is Zidana's son. His mother wants him to be Moulay's heir and she always keeps the lad in the forefront so that he is under Moulay's eye. That's her real influence: as long as Ahmad is the Emperor's favourite, the mother has direct contact with the throne.'

'Then we should use her to find our way into the harem,' suggested Dan. He earned a look of astonishment from the gun founder by asking, 'Could you arrange for me to meet young Ahmad? You could send word that his two new muskets need to be checked over to see if they require adjustment or have new flints fitted. You could flatter the youngster by saying that you had heard of his brilliant marksmanship when he shot down the rowing master.'

Sean Allen shook his head in wonder. 'Dan, you should be a full-time courtier. You're devious enough. I'll do as you suggest, although I don't have the slightest idea of what you have in mind.'

©

ONLY A FEW DAYS later Dan casually announced to his friends that he had been commanded by Lala Zidana to call on her. The cries of astonishment which greeted this announcement were followed immediately by questions as to how he had achieved his invitation. 'It wasn't difficult,' he said with a knowing grin. 'I went to Ahmad's quarters to work on the two muskets, just as Sean had arranged. Naturally the lad keeps the muskets close by him. They are his latest toys. He's very proud of what he did to the rowing master and boasts about it constantly, and likes to show off the guns. For sheer cruelty he really is his father's son. Sometimes he loads the guns and fires out of the window at passers-by. Luckily no one has been killed yet. When I arrived, he even grumbled that the guns no longer shoot straight, and complained that I should have come sooner to mend them.'

'But how did you turn that into an invitation to meet Zidana?' Diaz demanded.

'There were several serving women hovering in the background in Ahmad's rooms. I guessed that they were part of his mother's household and keeping an eye on the youngster. Of course they were curious about what I was doing. They came over to look at the guns and I showed them the inlay work. It's very ornate, you'll remember, with lots of curls and curves done in mother of pearl, and there's scroll work picked out in gold. I pretended that I had set the inlays myself and then, as if to prove it, I showed them this,' and he slid back the sleeve of his shirt. On his forearm was an intricate pattern of leaves and flowers, painted in reddish brown and indigo, with here and there a touch of yellow. Dan glanced across at Hector. 'My friend, maybe you've forgotten that I know how to do skin painting. At one time you were clever enough to put it to good use, and get me appointed to help colour Turgut Reis's maps. This time I've been able to assist you.'

He slid his sleeve back down so the skin paintings disappeared before continuing, 'Women who have little to do, love to primp and paint themselves. They'll spend hours at it, and run after anything that's new. Can you imagine the boredom in Moulay's harem – dozens, if not hundreds, of women all cooped up together. One thing I was certain of when I left young Ahmad's rooms was that those same servant women would carry word back to their mistress that there was someone newly arrived in Meknes who could beautify a woman's skin. It's taken less than twenty-four hours for my summons from Zidana to arrive. Hector can accompany me as my helper. When we meet the hippo, maybe I can put her into a good enough mood so that she'll let Hector try to seek out his sister. From what Sean has said, I'll have a broad enough surface for my paints.'

©

FIRST WIFE Zidana proved as daunting as her reputation. When Dan and Hector were ushered into her presence, she was sprawled on a vast yellow satin couch fringed with tassels and heaped with cushions. Nearby was a clutter of low tables, stools, more cushions, and several large trays laden with bowls of fruit and sweetmeats. Behind the couch stood two elderly eunuchs, and half a dozen female attendants busied themselves in various corners of the room. The female attendants, Hector noted, wore veils or kept a fold of cloth across their faces, but their hands and arms were bare and decorated with intricate dyed patterns. Zidana herself wore no veil. She had slightly bulging eyes in a broad, pudgy and heavy-set face, and her massive bulk was swathed in layer upon layer of a shimmery green gauze-like material. On her head she wore a strange cap made of flexible sheets of gold and silver which had been cut through so that they resembled lace. The fringes of this headgear swung and tinkled as she heaved herself into a more comfortable sitting position and regarded her visitors. Her bare feet, which now touched the thick carpet, were surprisingly small and delicate. Hector thought that her eyes glittered dangerously.

'Which of you paints?' she asked in a harsh voice. She spoke Turkish with a strong accent.

Dan inclined his head politely. Zidana focused her attention on him and demanded, 'What country do you come from?'

'From across the western ocean. My people are called Miskito.'

Zidana frowned. 'Why is your skin dark? You look like the southern people from near the desert.'

'All my people are this colour. It is said that some of our ancestors came from Ifriqya and they mixed with the native peoples whose skin is the colour of copper. So our skin is halfway between the two.'

'Do your women guard their skin against the sun?' The question was blunt.

'No.'

Zidana turned towards one of her serving women and said, 'You! Come over here. Show him your hands.'

The woman did as she was ordered, and Zidana demanded of Dan, 'Can you do better?'

Dan looked at the patterns drawn on the servant's skin and murmured, 'They are well drawn but could be more striking and colourful.'

Zidana waved the servant aside and heaved her bulk closer to the edge of the couch. She extended her right arm and pulled back the silk sleeve. The arm was very fat. 'Could you make good colours on my skin?'

'I believe so.'

'Then proceed.'

'First I must tell you that what I will paint is not permanent,' Dan said. 'The colours will last only a few days.'

'That is not important. If I like your work, I will summon you again when the colours fade. You can paint them again or make different pictures for me. You will paint no one else.' It was clear that Zidana was used to giving orders.

Dan opened the cloth satchel he had given Hector to carry, and took out several small clay pots and jars. Hector knew that his friend had found the necessary ingredients for his skin paints in the Meknes marketplace which sold all manner of brightly coloured spices and powders. He had mixed them with coloured minerals that Sean Allen used in his foundry work.

Carefully licking the end of a brush, Dan dipped it into one of the jars, advanced on the plump arm and began to draw on it carefully. Zidana looked on in critical fascination.

'My assistant here,' said Dan casually as if making light conversation, 'believes he has a sister among the Emperor's women. He has not seen her in a long time and, with your permission, would like to speak with her.' He had drawn the outline of a flower on the pudgy arm, and was beginning to colour in the first of the petals.

'What is the name of his sister?' Zidana was so intrigued with the pictures appearing on her skin, that she hardly seemed to listen for the answer.

'His sister is called Elizabeth, but she may have another name here.'

Zidana withdrew her fat arm and held it up in the air, turning it this way and that to admire the first pictures that Dan had drawn. The images gleamed brightly, the paints still wet. Abruptly Zidana called across to one of the eunuchs. She spoke rapidly in a dialect that Hector could not understand, and the man beckoned to him to follow. Leaving Dan to continue with his drawing and painting, Hector followed his guide through a door concealed behind a heavy velvet curtain, and down several empty corridors until he was brought into a plain unfurnished room with bare walls. The room had two windows, both screened with a fine lattice of stucco. The window facing him was already blank, shuttered from the far side. His escort crossed to the open window where the sunlight entered the room and closed its shutters. 'Stay here,' he said and left the room, leaving Hector in near-darkness.

Hector did not know how long he would have to wait. His heart was pounding in his ears, and the dense gloom and stifling airlessness of the room made him feel adrift from the real world. As the minutes dragged past, he slowly became aware that the shutter facing him had swung open. He heard a soft footfall behind him and he sensed that the eunuch had returned. A moment later he felt a hand guide him forward so that he stood with his face close to the lattice of the window in front of him. His eyes had grown used to the dim light, yet he could see nothing except the pattern of the stucco a few inches away. He shifted sideways, trying to squint through the gaps. As far as he could make out, the room on the far side was similar to the one where he now stood. It, too, was in darkness except for a small glimmer of light seeping under a door to one side. He could just distinguish a dark figure standing in the middle of the floor.

'Elizabeth?' he blurted out. 'Is that you?' His mouth was dry with excitement and anticipation, and the fear of imminent disappointment.

There was no reply. 'Elizabeth. It's me, Hector.' What he had thought was a single figure, was in fact two people standing close together. One of them moved aside, and the shadowy outline came a little closer.

'Elizabeth,' he repeated. 'If it's you, please say something.'

There was a long silence and he could hear the wheezing breath of the eunuch standing somewhere behind him. Again the figure moved slightly. Hector's nostrils detected a slight musky perfume. He did not remember his sister ever smelling that way.

Finally, a woman's voice, barely audible, said, 'Are you well?'

Fighting down his anxiety Hector tried desperately to remember his sister's voice. It had been so long since he had seen her that he had forgotten what her voice sounded like.

'It's me, Hector,' he said again. 'Is that really you, Elizabeth?'

The answer was so soft that he had to strain to hear. 'Yes.'

Hector sagged against the latticework, his head pressed against the stucco. He felt dizzy.

'Are you keeping well?' he asked, trying to keep his voice gentle though his head was in a whirl.

'I am . . .' there was a pause. 'I am healthy.'

Hector swallowed hard. Suddenly his throat was unnaturally tight. He wanted to speak in a normal voice but somehow it seemed that if he did, it would break the spell and destroy his fragile link with his sister.

'How long have you been here?' he croaked.

But he was answered with a question. 'What happened to you? And the others?'

'We were sold as slaves in Algiers. I don't know what happened to the others afterwards, but I worked for a Turkish sea captain for a time, then was aboard a French galley. Now I'm here in Meknes.'

'Are you still a slave?'

'No. I'm not. I'm here with friends, and one day we may be allowed to leave. I want to take you with us, to bring you away.'

There was a long silence as the dark figure stood silent. Then Elizabeth's voice said,

'That's not possible.'

'Yes, it is,' said Hector fiercely. He was feeling better now, more sure of himself. 'The Emperor has promised to give you your freedom if I and my friends serve him well.'

Elizabeth seemed not to grasp the importance of what he had just said. She ignored his answer and instead enquired, 'Have you news of our mother?'

'I have heard nothing from home, nothing at all since we were taken. I'm hoping that she went back to Spain to live with her own people. You and I will go to find her as soon as you are released.'

Again, a long pause followed by a low whisper, 'I told you, Hector. That's not possible.'

'Elizabeth, listen to me,' Hector pleaded. 'I'm sure that I can get you set free. My friends will help me. We can get Moulay to agree. You must not give up hope.'

'You don't understand. That is not how it can be. Please don't ask again.'

'But what of our mother? You want to see her again, don't you?'

'Of course.'

Hector could tell that his sister was very close to tears. He could hear the tremor in her voice. But he knew that he had to insist.

'Please, Elizabeth, please. You must not give up hope. You will not be here forever.'

He heard a stifled sob, and then Elizabeth's voice said, 'It is not so bad here. We look after one another. I've learned to speak languages, and we try to keep ourselves busy. Our servants look after us so there's no drudgery. We gossip and amuse ourselves.'

'Elizabeth, I made myself a promise long ago, when I was first a slave in Algiers. I told myself that I would find you and bring you home.'

When Elizabeth spoke next, her voice was firm, and her response came like a blow. 'Hector, please go away.'

Hector felt his stomach turn hollow. For a moment he could not believe his sister's words. He was stunned at the rebuff.

'Are you frightened of Zidana?' he hissed, angry now. He was exasperated by his sister's obstinacy, and had to struggle to keep his voice level. 'Please don't be fearful of that old harridan. She can be got round. I can arrange that Moulay remembers who you are, that he treats you as special.'

There was a sudden note of alarm in Elizabeth's immediate reply. 'No, don't do that, Hector, I beg you. Don't do anything to attract Zidana's attention to me. She is dangerous. She is jealous of anything that may threaten her own position or her son as the Emperor's favourite. Zidana will destroy anyone who could be a rival to Ahmad. I told you, the women and mothers in the harem all gossip. They scheme and they plot. It's how they pass the time. No one is safe.'

'But you need not be involved . . .' Hector began, and then the meaning of her words sank in. 'Elizabeth,' he said slowly, 'are you telling me that you have a child?'

Her silence gave him his answer. He felt mortified, but he had to know.

'Is it a boy? And the father is Moulay?'

'I have called him Mihail. It sounds almost the same whether spoken here or back at home. He has our mother's eyes.'

'You could take Mihail with you when you leave,' Hector beseeched in desperation.

'You know that is not true. Moulay would not permit it, and what sort of life would the boy have, the son of a concubine from Barbary.'

'Then let Mihail grow up here. He's also the son of an emperor and can make his own way.'

'I cannot abandon him. I know what happens to Moulay's offspring. If they are not his favourites, they must fend for themselves. They have no one to help them except their mothers. I am not alone, there's an Englishwoman here who has had a son by Moulay, and several Spanish women. We have promised to help one another and our children, as best we can.'

'What am I to tell our mother?' Hector asked, his voice a hoarse whisper.

'Tell her nothing. Don't even tell her that you found me. Say that I have disappeared.'

Hector pressed his head against the surface of the lattice, the stucco hard against his forehead, feeling the pain. He felt completely empty, striving for words that would change his sister's mind. But he knew that it was useless. She had reached her decision much earlier, and nothing would change that. He gave a small groan of anguish.

'Hector, please try to understand,' his sister begged him. She had stepped closer to the grille now so that her words were very clear. 'I love my Mihail. He is my life now. I will watch over him, raise him as best I can. Moulay will not touch me again. He rarely returns to any of his women. I can forget him but I cannot forget my child. Through Mihail I will find happiness.'

Hector was drained of all emotion. He was numb, at a loss what he should do.

Elizabeth must have sensed his despair for she said gently, 'Hector, I did not mean to hurt you. I had never expected to see you again, and I am grateful that you did manage to find me. That was truly noble of you, and I'm desperately sorry that it has come to nothing. I know that it is a difficult thing to ask, but it would be best if you did not think of me again, except to recall your memories of our childhood together. I am a woman now, and a mother. My life has taken me down one path, and your future will be very different. I know that when you've had time to think about all this, you will be able to come to terms with our separate lives.'

Hector's eyes filled with tears. A great sadness was tearing at his inside. He leaned forward in the near-darkness, his eyes squeezed tight shut to hold back the tears, and reached up to cling to the lattice to stop himself from sliding down the wall, his legs weak. He reached with his fingers through the lattice and gripped tightly, feeling the pain as the sharp corners of the stone cut into his flesh. He was whirling in a misery of black despair. Out of that pit of desperation, he felt – or perhaps he thought he felt – a light touch on the fingers of his right hand where they gripped the lattice. It was as if someone on the far side had stroked them gently. But when he lifted his head and opened his eyes, the tears wet on his cheeks, he saw that there was no one standing in the far room.

TWENTY-ONE

WITH THE BACK OF his hand Hector brushed the moisture from his cheek. The gesture reminded him of his parting from Elizabeth. She had urged him to forget her, yet the pain of her rejection was ever present. For several days after his meeting with her he had considered returning to Ireland to find out what might have happened to his mother, to learn whether she had stayed there or gone, as he had suspected, back to her own people in Galicia. But in the end he abandoned the idea, as he felt too bruised to embark on another search. And, he asked himself, what was he to tell his mother when he found her? He was unsure that he would be able to sustain the deception that Elizabeth wanted, to tell their mother the lie that he had never found his sister. He decided that if he was to find his mother, it would only be when there was something positive to say, something to make her proud, something that he had achieved. He was very concious that, at eighteen years of age, with his father dead and his only sister vanished into a Barbary harem, he was left to make his own life. Now, a month later, they were not tears which were running down his face. They were beads of sweat.

The day was as hot as he had ever known, hotter even than when he was working in the quarry at Algiers. He turned to look back at his companions. Dan, Bourdon and Karp were riding in single file behind him, Karp leading their packhorse on a halter. They had all wanted to take the chance of leaving Meknes. Dan, always level-headed, had made the initial suggestion. Perhaps his friend had wanted to jolt him out of his despondency by pointing out that staying so close to Elizabeth was only adding to his distress. There was no future in lingering in Meknes, Dan had said. There was nothing Hector could do to save his sister, and the day would come when Moulay demanded to see his castle smasher, and when it failed to materialise, Moulay's disappointment would have dangerous consequences. Better to slip away quietly, the Miskito had advised, provided that Sean Allen did not suffer as a result. The gun founder had assured him that there was no need to worry on that score because the Emperor always valued a man who would make and mend his cannon. Go south, Allen had urged, for that will give you several days' start on any pursuit. Moulay's people will search for you as soon as it is known that you have left without his permission, and they will presume you are heading west or north, directly for the coast. No one will imagine that you've gone towards the Great Desert. Then the gun founder had insisted that they accept his gifts of money and weapons – the latest muskets, pistols and powder – because their flight would surely lead them into wild lands.

Hector glanced up at the sun. It was well past the zenith but still blazing down, its heat reflecting from the rocky ground. He could feel his horse tiring beneath him. From time to time the exhausted animal tripped on a loose rock, the stone clattering away down the slope of the barren hillside across which the little column was moving. He reached inside his shirt for the qibla that he had bought in the market at Meknes. No one had thought it strange that a renegade should want to buy a little prayer compass. He checked the direction they were travelling in, for the land was featureless, a succession of rocky slopes with scrubby vegetation and dry water courses. From the outset the little group had avoided main roads. For the past week since leaving Meknes they had travelled by compass, using tracks and byways wherever possible, skirting around the towns and cities, visiting villages only to obtain fodder for the animals and some basic supplies for themselves. Diaz's cavalry friend Roberto had provided the essential directions. He had campaigned with the imperial army in this region, and Hector had written down the Spaniard's recollection of the towns, passes and days marched with the army, then transferred it all to a rough sketch which summarised the terrain. He hoped that the Spaniard's memory had been accurate. He dreaded wandering in a circle, like the dead rowing master, and perhaps stumbling on a detachment of Moulay's troops. But the others, riding behind, had confidence in him, insisting that he should be their leader. 'You're best qualified,' Bourdon had assured him. 'You're thoughtful as well as educated. It's more than just making a map of our route. You are good at making plans, and at taking everything into consideration. That's what a leader's for.' Hector had tried to dissuade the others, but they were adamant. They had resolved on trying to reach Negritia, the Land of the Blacks. From there they would find a ship far beyond the reach of Moulay Ismail.

Hector had fallen in with their plans because, in truth, he was uncertain where his own future lay. He had only his friendship to sustain him, his friendship with Bourdon and Karp, but above all with Dan. So when the three of them spoke of trying to reach the coast beyond Negritia, he had drawn a map, recalling details from the great map of Piri Reis. He had marked as many of the countries as he could remember and added the conjectured course of a substantial river curving through the interior. This river was reputed to join in one direction to the Nile of Egypt, he told his companions, while in the other direction it was known to empty into the sea at a place where the ships of many trading nations came to do business with the natives, carrying away gold, spices, elephants' teeth and slaves. 'Where do those ships return?' Bourdon had asked. 'From wherever they came – from England, France, Portugal, Spain, Brandenburg. We could take passage aboard them. You could go home to France,' Hector had replied. 'Do any of them sail onwards?' the pickpocket had asked, his finger tracing a course directly out into the ocean. 'That would take them towards the Americas,' Hector answered, and his words had decided their mutual fate. With a grimace Bourdon had touched his galerien's brand and murmured he would never be welcome back in France. Dan announced that he too would prefer to head westward and return to his own people. Finally Hector had looked across at Karp, who had been staring at the map and listening to their discussion. Karp had nodded his agreement without being asked. And so the decision was made.

Hector wiped his face again. He hoped that the ridge ahead of them would be the final one before they came in sight of Oued Noun. That was the name of the oasis which lay on the edge of the desert, according to Roberto. It was the last place where they would see real houses built of brick and stone. Everything beyond was nomad territory where people sheltered under tents. 'Whatever you do, don't try to cross the Great Desert on your own,' the Spaniard had warned. 'You wouldn't stand a chance. You have to know the exact direction and distance of each waterhole, and whether you will find water at that particular season and in that year. Sometimes the waterholes fail. If they do, then you perish. Your best chance is to join a coffle, a caravan, which is properly equipped and has a reliable guide. Just hope you find one when you reach Oued Noun.'

Cresting the ridge, Hector found that the land sloped away as a barren, stony, dun-coloured plain dotted with clumps of thorn bushes and an occasional acacia tree. Among the thorn bushes were the ungainly shapes of camels, at least a hundred of them, foraging on the prickly vegetation. Even as he reined in his horse to take in the view, there was a startled shout. A small boy, evidently a camel herd, had been dozing in the shade of an acacia. He sprang to his feet and went running away towards the low roofs of a small settlement in the distance to carry a warning.

Taking care to stay in view they rode forward. At the outskirts of the cluster of flat-roofed mud-brick houses, they dismounted and walked, leading their horses. A reception committee of about a dozen men, traders by the look of them, was already waiting. They were heavily armed and unfriendly looking. Hector noted more armed men lurking in the alleyways behind them. 'Salaam aleikom,' he called out, and when he had received the stock response, he added, 'If you are going south, we would like to join you.'

'Where are your trade goods?' demanded the group's spokesman suspiciously. He was dressed in a faded red burnous, and eyeing the solitary packhorse and the array of weapons that Hector and his companions carried.

'We have none. We ask only to accompany you,' Hector replied politely.

'And for what reason? We have prepared our coffle these past three months, fattened our camels, and shared our expenses. All our arrangements are made. We have no place for extra travellers.'

'We would be willing to pay our share of any expenses,' Hector offered. 'We ask only to be able to ride with you.'

'On those horses?' The spokesman gave a sarcastic laugh.

Hector was about to ask whether the coffle would accept an additional payment when there was a stir among the merchants. Several reached hurriedly for their muskets. Out of the corner of his eye Hector detected a movement. He turned to see that Dan had brought his musket to his shoulder, and for a moment he thought the Miskito was about to shoot down the man in the red burnous. Then he saw that Dan was aiming high and to the left. He pulled the trigger. There was a report of the gun, a puff of black smoke, and a vulture which had settled on a nearby roof was thrown bodily backward by the force of the bullet, and fluttered untidily to the ground.

'Tell them,' said Dan quietly, 'that we can protect the coffle from the desert marauders.'

There was a shocked silence from the merchants. Hector repeated Dan's offer, and they conferred in low voices until their spokesman announced reluctantly, 'Very well. You may join us, but on condition that you place yourselves wherever you may best protect the coffle, both by day and by night. As for the camels you will need, we have none to spare. You must arrange that with our guide. You will find him over there, by the village well.'

©

'Assheads! I don't trust them for a moment. They'd sell their own grandmothers, given half a chance,' Bourdon muttered angrily as he and the others led their horses in the direction of a herd of camels clustering around a watering trough. Amid the camel dung and smells and the continual bawling, groaning and grunting of the animals, a black slave was hauling a leather bucket up from the well. Hector asked where he might find the coffle's guide, and the slave nodded towards a nearby thorn bush. Spread across its branches was a tattered scrap of cloth. In front a young man sat cross-legged on the dusty ground. He was bent forward, braiding a new girth to a camel saddle.

As Hector approached, he saw that the young man could not have been more than sixteen years old. He was barefoot and dressed only in a long and ragged gown. His unkempt black hair was so long and stiff and wiry so that it stood out from his head in a great bush. 'Are you the guide for the coffle?' Hector asked uncertainly. He spoke in simple Arabic, and the youth raised his head to reveal a cheerfully intelligent face and a ready smile. 'No, that's my grandfather. I am only his assistant. My name is Ibrahim.' Without turning round he called out something in a language that Hector did not recognise. In answer something stirred in the patch of shade under the thorn bush. What Hector had taken to be a bundle of rags proved to be a very old man, who climbed very slowly to his feet and came forward. Great age had so shrunk his frame that he could not have been little more than four feet tall, and he walked with the aid of a stick. Most astonishingly of all, when he came close enough for Hector to look into the lined and weather-beaten face, he saw that both the old man's eyes were filmed over with a milky glaze. The guide was stone blind.

Hector was about to speak up when, to his surprise, Dan greeted the old man politely. The response was a cluck of pleasure, and for several moments the two men talked together. Then Dan turned to his friend and said, 'He also is amazigh. He speaks the same language I learned when working in the gardens of Algiers. His accent is difficult but I have been able to explain that we will be joining the coffle as guards.'

'What was his answer?'

'He says that he is pleased. We will be acting as an armed escort. There has been much difficulty this year with a people he calls the Tooarick. They live by banditry. He knows we have good muskets for he heard my musket shot. He says it was the sound of a good weapon.'

'And can he provide camels?'

'He offers to trade our horses for camels. They can be left behind here, and he has cousins who will come to collect them later. In exchange he will provide us with camels from Talifat – apparently they are famous for their stamina – and supply saddles and teach us how to ride them. Also he will arrange that we have proper clothing for the desert. We must wear loose cotton gowns and cover our heads with cloths to keep off the sun. He says it would also be wise to leave behind our boots and shoes, and wear sandals.'

'I'm not giving up my boots,' interrupted Bourdon. 'Everyone knows that the desert is full of poisonous insects and serpents. I don't want to get bitten or stung.'

Hector hesitated. 'Ask him if we can't keep our horses. We might need them again on the far side of the desert.'

Dan translated his request to the old man and relayed his reply. 'He agrees that a horse is capable of crossing the desert, but only if accompanied by a camel carrying water. That means six water skins for every horse, plus another camel to carry dried grass, grain and blocks of dried dates as horse feed. Even so, the horse will die if it goes lame, or if the camel falls sick. He recommends we take only camels.'

'Tell him that we will follow his advice.'

©

A WEEK LATER, with Oued Noun far behind them, Hector was regretting that he had accepted the old man's counsel. Riding a camel was uncomfortable. The creature's loose-limbed gait meant that he spent most of each day swaying back and forth awkwardly in an lurching rhythm. If he dismounted to walk beside the animal, he had to beware of the creature's foul breath and moody temperament. Before leaving the village Ibrahim, the guide's grandson, had shown them how to make the camels kneel, how to hobble them loosely so they could graze when there was any vegetation, and to tie them more closely by the knee when they camped for the night. 'Place your trust in Allah, but tie up your camel,' the young man had joked. But Hector still found the camels to be fractious and awkward to control. He would much have preferred to be mounted on a horse as he tried to ride at the flanks and rear of the coffle in case there was an attack from the mysterious Tooarick of whom the merchants were so fearful. He had expected the caravan to march as a long single column. Instead it advanced on a broad front, walking slowly across the bleak, flat landscape, each merchant and his slaves and servants attending to their own band of camels. Out in front rode Abdullah, the old guide, accompanied by his grandson. Each night when the caravan halted at a waterhole, Hector and the others would join the two amazigh at their campfire. The merchants completely ignored them.

'My horse could have come this far without any difficulty,'

Hector confided to Ibrahim one evening. It had been natural to strike up a friendship with the cheerful and enthusiastic young man. 'Each night we have arrived at a waterhole where the animals could drink. My arms are aching from trying to steer my camel in the right direction.'

'There's a saying that "the camel driver has his plans – and the camel has his",' was the light-hearted reply, 'and this is only the early stage of our crossing. Later we will find water only every three days, or less often. And there are places where the surface of the desert is dangerous. The ground seems firm and hard, but it is only a thin crust. It gives way suddenly. A horse would break its leg in the hole, but a camel is more flexible. It can be pulled out with ropes, and continue on the journey.' The young man tossed another dry branch from a thorn bush on to the fire and watched the sparks fly up into the night air. 'Besides, my grandfather tells me that tomorrow we will have the irifi, the desert wind. He predicts that it will only last a few hours but it will make life difficult for our beasts. You should warn your companions that they will need their sheshs, their turbans.'

The sky dawned an ominous reddish grey. The caravan had barely begun its march when the first puffs of a gentle breeze began to lift the dust and sand into little spirals that skittered and twisted across the ground before collapsing and disappearing. By mid-morning the wind had increased until sand particles were blowing painfully into the men's faces, making them sneeze and their eyes water. They were obliged to dismount from their camels, wrap cloths about their heads, and plod onward, heads bent low. Beside them the camels walked on, their nostrils narrowed and their eyes half-closed behind their long eyelashes. Until evening the irifi swirled around them, rising in strength to a full gale. Visibility fell to less than twenty paces, and the coffle huddled in a dense mass, fearful of losing touch with one another. A horse in such hostile conditions, Hector reflected, would have refused to advance and turned to stand miserably with its tail against the scouring wind.

'Now I know why Abdullah doesn't need good eyesight to lead the caravan,' Hector commented to Ibrahim as they rested by the campfire. 'I could scarcely raise my head against the sand blast. When I did, it was impossible to see anything.'

'It could have been much worse. The irifi sometimes blows for five or six days, and much more strongly. Entire caravans have been known to perish, unable to move forward or backward until buried by the sand. That was what happened to my father. He was leading a coffle which the wind destroyed. We never found his body. I expect he is lying somewhere beneath the surface of the desert, a dried corpse along with his camels and the merchants he was guiding. Sometimes, years later, the wind blows away the sand again. So maybe he will be found, and we can give him a proper burial.'

Picking up two metal bowls, Ibrahim rose to his feet and said, 'You and Dan can give me a hand. In less than a week we begin the most difficult stage of our journey. There will be no water for ten days and not a blade of grass nor a single leaf for our camels to eat. There's an old jmel among our beasts which will not survive the ordeal. It is better we put it to good use now.'

He led the way to where the camels were hobbled. Singling out the animal he wanted, he led it a little distance away. There he made the beast kneel, and showed Dan how to pull the halter so that the camel turned its head to one side, stretching its neck in a curve. While Hector held the bowl beneath the artery, Ibrahim expertly cut the animal's neck so that the blood splashed into the receptacle. 'Put the bowl on the embers of the campfire,' he told Hector. 'In a few minutes the blood will thicken to a good soup. Dan and I will start to deal with the carcass. Tonight we feast on the entrails. Tomorrow we'll begin to dry the meat in the sun, and we'll save the hide for when it's needed.' He slid his knife blade into the dead camel's gut, exposing a globular paunch which he carefully cut open. Inside was a thick green gruel, foul smelling with lumps. Taking the second bowl he scooped out the contents. 'This too can be cooked for our supper,' he said. 'It has already been eaten by the jmel. But we can enjoy it too. In the desert nothing goes to waste.'

A week later the camel hide was put to use when Bourdon reluctantly agreed to abandon his battered footwear despite his fear of snakes and biting insects. By then his boots had been cut to shreds on flinty gravel. Ibrahim expertly cut double-soled sandals for him using the skin of the dead jmel whose meat already hung in strips from their pack saddles, drying in the sun. They were now in the most difficult sector of the desert crossing, a desiccated brown expanse of sand and rocky outcrops which, in the simmering heat haze, could be mistaken for the roofs of distant towns. At its worst the heat was so intense that the coffle had to travel by night. The men spent the days sheltering from the sun under strips of cloth or in the shadow of piles of camel packs. The sand became so hot that it was painful to stand barefoot, and their precious water skins daily grew more flabby as their contents dwindled through evaporation. Finally, when it seemed that the ordeal would never end, Abdullah declared that they had passed the halfway mark. Hector, who had long since given up using the qibla to trace the direction of travel, was amazed by the blind man's certainty.

'How can your grandfather be so sure?' he asked Ibrahim. 'I have not the least idea how far we have travelled.'

'My grandfather has crossed the desert at least thirty times,' Ibrahim answered proudly. 'In his head he keeps a count of the days and hours on this journey, even the number of paces. He listens to the sounds of the desert, and he says that every part has its own feeling which tells him where he is. When in doubt, he smells the sand.'

Hector had indeed noticed how, from time to time, the old guide took up a fistful of sand and held it to his face. Now he was too tactful to question Ibrahim's assertion. Bourdon, however, was more dubious. He quietly scooped up some sand and wrapped it in a cloth. The following day he placed the sample in the old guide's hand and asked Ibrahim to enquire from his grandfather how many days were left until the coffle reached the next watering place. The old man sniffed the sample and, with an angry outburst, flung it down in disgust. 'What did he say?' Bourdon asked. Ibrahim looked hurt as he translated, 'My grandfather says that he is being taken for a fool. Either that, or the caravan has gone in a circle and we are back where we were yesterday.'

Bourdon was crestfallen. 'Please apologise to him from me. I meant no harm. All my life I have lived among rogues and charlatans so I always suspect some sort of cheat.'

Yet even Hector had reason to doubt the old man when the caravan crossed a low range of rocky hills and Ibrahim rode up to him to say that his grandfather had announced that they should be in sight of the longed-for watering hole. Hector strained his eyes, but could see nothing. The desert stretched out as usual, bare, monotonous, and utterly devoid of life. There was not even the false glimmer of a distant mirage which so often duped him into thinking that a lake lay ahead. Suddenly his camel lurched off at a trot, and within a dozen strides was plunging along at a mad gallop. All around, the other camels were similarly stampeding. They surged forward in a roaring, incoherent mass. Ahead, Ibrahim was goading his camel even faster, kicking up a cloud of dust. After some three miles of this mad careering gallop, Ibrahim drew to a halt, jumped down and began to scrabble at the ground, peeling back a cover made of camel and goatskins. Beneath the cover the ground was a water soak which had been protected from the sun. Ibrahim and the camel drivers dug troughs which filled with a few inches of water, and the thirsty camels shoved and jostled, biting and kicking one another as they fought to suck up the water that they craved. Ibrahim's face beneath his great bush of hair broke into a broad grin. 'My grandfather has succeeded again,' he exulted. 'The worst is over.'

When the camels had slaked their thirst, he asked Dan,

Hector and the others to go on ahead with him. 'There's a second, better, waterhole about an hour away. I will show you how we can harvest the desert's bounty. It's time to celebrate with a feast.'

'Please, no more camel's intestines,' groaned Bourdon.

'No. This time we'll have roast ostrich.'

Sure enough, as they approached the next waterhole, a flock of about twenty ostrich ran off. The giant birds paced away across the desert, their wings outspread. Hector had come across ostriches in the Emperor's menagerie. But this was the first time he had seen the birds in the wild.

'We'll never get close enough to shoot them. They run as fast as a galloping horse,' he said to Ibrahim.

'That's not how we'll do it,' the young man replied. 'This waterhole is where the birds prefer to drink. All we have to do is dig some holes in the sand where you and the others can lie hidden with your muskets. The birds are suspicious of camels so I'll take them back to the coffle, and bring the caravan here at dusk. Good hunting!'

The ambush was easier than Hector had anticipated. He and his three companions prepared their hiding places. Less than an hour after Ibrahim had ridden away, the flock of ostriches came walking back across the desert, unaware of any danger. The hidden musketeers waited until the great birds made easy targets. Their first volley brought down three ostriches. When the flock foolishly came back a second time, they killed another four. That evening the entire caravan fed better than it had done for many weeks, and Hector fell asleep on a patch of soft sand. He was gorged on roast ostrich meat.

A cry of pain awoke him. He sat up, feeling slightly groggy, and looked around. His eyes had to adjust to the half-darkness. It was still several hours before dawn but the moon had risen and was shedding enough light to see that the camp was in uproar. Dan was already on his feet, a pistol in his hand. Their camels, which had been hobbled kneeling, were straining at their bonds as they tried to rise to their feet. They were roaring and moaning in fright. In the distance there were shouts of alarm. Suddenly a figure flitted between Hector and the last embers of the campfire. For a heart-stopping moment he thought it was a djinn, one of the spectres which Ibrahim had spoken about, evil spirits which wander the desert in the form of men or animals or dust devils. This one had assumed the shape of a human. It was pale grey from head to foot, gaunt and stark naked. It held a spear in each hand, and the hair on its head was long and filthy. As the figure glanced towards him, the creature's eyes glittered for a moment in the moonlight. It took Hector a few seconds to realise that what he was looking at was a desert thief.

The attack was over before anyone could react. Ibrahim lit a brand from the fire and went to check their losses. Two camel saddles were missing, and several strips of dried camel meat. One of their animals was bleeding from a deep gash where a thief had stabbed it in the shoulder with his spear. 'The bandit probably hoped to cripple the creature so we had to leave it behind,' he commented glumly. He called out for his grandfather to come to look, and when there was no reply, went to where the old man had lain down to sleep beside a thorn bush. He found him sitting, dazed from a blow to the head. With his acute hearing Abdullah had been the first to detect the presence of the thieves as they crept into camp, and had tried to intercept them. They had struck him down without mercy. 'They must have been watching the waterhole, waiting for a coffle to show up,' said the old man after he had recovered enough to speak, and various merchants arrived with similar tales of thefts and losses. 'This time we were lucky. They were only sneak thieves. If there had been more of them, we might have been murdered as we slept.'

'Will they attack again?' demanded the merchant's spokes-man angrily. He was wearing the same faded red burnous as the day Hector first saw him, and was in a foul mood. He had lost several packs of trade goods.

'They are Tooarick of the Labdessah tribe. They live by plunder,' answered the guide. 'It is best that the caravan moves on tomorrow before the word gets out that we are here, and the Labdessah summon their fellows.'

The spokesman rounded on Hector. 'You are meant to be our guards! Instead you were snoring by the fire.' He was spitting with rage. 'When we march, you will be sure to protect us. Otherwise it will be the worse for you!'

'There is no point in quarrelling,' the old man intervened. 'Save your strength for the journey. Now that the Tooarick have found us, they will not give up. They will follow us like jackals.'

His prediction was painfully accurate. The coffle moved on the next morning but the thieves struck again during the following night. Hector and his companions stayed on guard with their muskets but failed again to detect the intruders and did not fire a shot. The Labdessah were expert thieves. Stripped naked, their bodies smeared with ashes, they crept their way into the encampment and made off with more trade goods. They cut the hobbles of a dozen camels and drove them off into the darkness. A merchant who tried to stop them was stabbed in the stomach and died four hours later. The merchants swore and raged. They shouted at Hector and his companions, and blamed Abdullah for their troubles. But there was no remedy. On the third night the caravan was robbed yet again, and however urgently the travellers marched onward, they knew they were failing to shake off their tormentors. They embarked on a sand sea where a succession of tall dunes extended in every direction like waves on the surface of an ocean. If they looked behind them from the summits of the taller dunes, they could see in the far distance a Labdessah outrider mounted on his camel. He was tracking them, waiting for them to make camp so that his fellows could plan their next attack.

Hector grew more and more frustrated. 'We can't go on like this,' he confessed to Ibrahim on the fourth day of their ordeal.

The young man, who normally rode beside his grandfather in advance, had dropped back to join the rear guard. 'The caravan is being bled to death.'

Ibrahim shook his head. 'My grandfather tells me that it is impossible to shake off the Labdessah once they have attached themselves to a coffle. They are like the parasites that feed on the camels. Once they fasten on to their victim they do not let go.'

'Then I suggest we give the Labdessah a nasty surprise.'

Ibrahim cocked his head on one side as he looked at Hector with sudden interest. 'You have a plan?'

'The Tooarick don't yet know that we have good muskets,' Hector said.

Ibrahim thought for a moment before replying. 'Not unless they witnessed you shooting the ostriches. Otherwise you have not yet used your guns in their presence. The Labdessah have always attacked in the dark, and they are armed with spears or knives.'

'Then I propose we deal with them as we dealt with the ostriches. When we come to a suitable place – a dip between the sand dunes where we are out of sight of the pursuit – Dan, Jacques, Karp and I will get down off our camels and prepare an ambush. We will scrape out shallow holes where we can lie in wait with our muskets. You ride on, taking our camels with you, and rejoin the coffle. With luck the Labdessah will blunder straight into the trap, and we will give them a bloody nose. Later you can come back and collect us.'

Ibrahim's face lit up. 'We could set the ambush right now, over the next sand ridge. I'll tell my grandfather about it later. But please be careful. The thieves have the eyes of falcons and would immediately notice anything unusual. We must work quickly.'

The next hollow between the dunes proved an ideal site for the ambush. There was a patch of soft level sand on which grew a few withered bushes, no more than two feet high. Here Hector and his companions slid down from their camels and hastily scraped out shallow trenches for themselves. Placing their muskets before them, they lay down, and Ibrahim quickly threw sand over them to cover them. Then he remounted and led the camels off in the direction of the marching caravan. 'I'll be back before nightfall,' he called. 'In the name of Allah, shoot straight!'

Hector lay on his belly, feeling the heat of the sand spreading up through his thin cotton garments. To his right, about twenty paces away, Karp was similarly buried. Away to his left lay Bourdon and Dan. Each man had picked a location where a low leafless bush gave additional cover but did not interfere with his sight line. They lay in a shallow arc, facing the way they had come. Before them the dune sloped upward quite steeply, then came to a crest some fifty yards away. That was were they expected the Labdessah to show.

Gently Hector checked that the lock of his musket was in working order. Unwinding the end of his head cloth, he draped it loosely around the delicate mechanism to protect it from the sand. Then he lowered his face down to the sand, blew gently to clear a few loose grains from his nose and mouth, and closed his eyes. He settled down to wait.

After some time he became aware of a tickling sensation on his forehead. A small creature was burrowing up through the sand towards his face. He raised his head slightly to ease the pressure on the sand and give the creature an easier passage. The tickling became more of a scratching. He lifted his head higher still, allowing an inch or so of free space, and felt a slight rasping sensation just below his hairline. The creature was almost clear. He opened his eyes to see what it was. Less than an inch away stood a scorpion as long as his middle finger, and as fat. The insect must have detected the flicker of his eyelid, for suddenly it stopped and raised its sting, curling its body ready to strike. Hector held his breath. The green sea-pale transparency of the scorpion's shiny body was the colour of the tiny crabs which had crawled across the rock pools when he was a boy. Its armoured body was like a miniature lobster, only curled in reverse. He was almost cross-eyed with the strain of keeping the deadly creature in focus, yet holding completely still. The muscles of his neck complained as he arched his head even farther backwards. Ibrahim had warned them of the Saharan scorpion. The sting would kill a dog within six or seven minutes. A man would die in as many hours, from convulsions.

For what seemed like an age the black tip of the venom sting wavered in his face. Then the scorpion relaxed. The body slowly uncurled, and the insect crawled off on its crooked legs.

The next time he raised his head, Hector was shocked to see two camel riders had already started down the slope of the sand dune before him. They were Labdessah. Both men were swathed in loose blue garments, and their heads and faces were wrapped in folds of black cloth leaving only a narrow slit for their eyes. They were halfway down the slope, the feet of their camels plunging into the soft sand, when another half-dozen Tooarick appeared on the skyline behind them. Hector reached forward gently. His arm was numb where he had been lying on it, and he could feel a tingling as the blood began to flow again. Very gently he peeled aside the cloth protecting the musket lock. He took slow deep breaths. His eyes never left the two Labdessah as they rode closer.

A single low bush stood in isolation some thirty paces in front of him. It had been agreed with the others that this bush would mark the point where they would spring their ambush. The two cameleers were only a few paces away from it now. He raised his musket and took aim at the leading rider. The target came level with the bush, and he fired even as he heard the sound of Bourdon's musket to his left, and then a shot from Dan. Through the small cloud of black smoke Hector saw the lead rider crash from his saddle, hitting the ground so heavily that Hector knew he must be dead. The second man lurched sideways. He managed to stay on his camel, which gave a great swerve and began a panic-stricken run across the face of the sand dune. Farther up the dune were sudden shouts of dismay and alarm. The six Labdessah wrenched their camels around, and applied their goads as they forced their beasts into an urgent retreat. Within moments they had fled over the crest of the dune, closely followed by their wounded colleague and the runaway camel of his dead companion.

Bourdon gave a whoop of triumph. 'That should have stopped them in their tracks,' he exulted as he sprang up from his hiding place, and began to reload his musket. Hector and Dan waited for Karp to join them before they approached the downed Labdessah. The man had been killed outright. He lay on his back, one leg bent under him, an arm flung out.

'Did you get a good look at the ones who got away?' Hector asked Dan.

'Yes,' the Miskito replied. 'I'd say they learned their lesson. Only two of them were carrying muskets, and both weapons were obsolete and near useless. They know now that we can bite back.'

'Let's hope they leave the caravan alone in future,' Bourdon intervened. He was still jubilant. 'Maybe those bastard merchants in the coffle will treat us with a little more respect now they know what we can do.'

'We should not wait down here,' said Hector. 'If the Labdessah decide to come back, we're dangerously exposed. We'd better climb back to the crest of the dune. From there we can keep a lookout, and wait for Ibrahim.'

Feet sinking deep in the loose sand, they scrambled to the top of the dune. There was no shade anywhere, and the sun beat down on them out of a clear sky as they sat and waited for Ibrahim to bring their camels. The hours passed, and they became more and more thirsty. From time to time Jacques, the most impatient, stood up and scanned the horizon. There was no sign of the Labdessah, nor of Ibrahim. There was not a living creature in view except the distant black speck of a circling bird of prey. Finally, as the sun began to set, the

Frenchman voiced what all of them had been thinking. 'What do you think is delaying Ibrahim? He should have been here long before now. The coffle will have moved on so far that it will be impossible for us to catch up with it on foot.'

Hector rose and shook the sand from his clothing. 'Wait here and keep a good lookout. I'm going down to check the body of the Labdessah. Maybe he had some food on him, and a waterskin.'

But when he reached the corpse, he found that the man had carried only a dagger strapped to his forearm, and a small leather purse on a cord around his neck. The purse contained a handful of worn copper coins. Nearby lay two spears which had fallen to the ground when he was shot. His food and waterskin must have been on his camel, which had bolted. The effort of plodding back up the dune made Hector realise just how weak and thirsty he had become. He felt slightly dizzy by the time he rejoined the others, and was glad to drop down on the sand and rest. 'Nothing,' he reported. 'We'll have to spend the night here, and hope that Ibrahim shows up in the morning. It's sensible to stay where he knows to find us.'

After sunset the temperature began to fall rapidly. The four men shivered in their light clothing, huddling together trying to share their warmth. They took it in turns to keep watch, though none of them slept for more than a few moments. They heard scuffling noises from below, and guessed that a sort of scavenger was investigating the corpse of the Labdessah. Fearful that the dead man's companions might return, they jumped at shadows. Bourdon caught a glimpse of a flitting movement in the darkness. He raised his musket and was about to take a shot when the shadow revealed itself as a tiny fox-like animal with huge ears which gazed at them for a second, then turned and vanished.

Hector was on watch when the red-orange glow of another fiery sunrise began to light up the horizon. Below him was a remarkable sight. A blanket of white mist, no more than a few feet deep, had silently occupied the sand valley in the night. He marvelled that the vapour could form in such an arid land, and licked his cracked lips at the thought of the moisture, so close yet unobtainable. His gaze travelled down the length of the valley and there, some distance away, were the heads and shoulders of five men coming towards him. They must have been on camels for they swayed back and forth with the characteristic movement of their mounts. Yet the animals themselves were invisible, submerged within the layer of white mist. Briefly he was reminded of the day when Turgut Reis's galley had glided through the sea fret of Sardinia, and the sailor Dunton had told him that the lookouts at the masthead could be in clear sunshine above the fog. Now, even as he watched, the mist began to ebb. It shrank down, thinner and thinner, and the corpse of the dead Labdessah appeared like a dark rock when the tide receded. Hector came to his senses. He had been so cold that his thoughts were sluggish. He nudged Dan with his foot. 'Riders,' he said softly. 'Coming our way. Stay low. I'll let you know what's happening.'

As he watched, the camel riders continued their approach. They were in single file, with one man some distance in front. Presumably he was their scout. Something about the way they rode told Hector that they were keeping a watchful lookout. 'Slide back over the edge of the dune, and keep out of sight,' he warned the others. 'They look like Labdessah, five of them. Maybe they've not seen us and will ride by.' All five riders were dressed in the loose blue garments of Tooarick, and the black cloths wrapped around their heads gave them a sinister appearance. The only difference among them that Hector could see was that their leader rode a particularly fine-looking camel. Its bridle and trappings were hung with red and blue decorations.

'They'll be within musket range very soon,' he said softly. 'Get your guns ready. I'll give the word if we need to fire on them. They're still in single file. Karp, you take the second man in line. Jacques, the third. Dan, your target is the same as mine. The leader.'

'Why let them pass?' hissed Bourdon. 'They'll be carrying water, and without water we will die out here.'

'Let's wait and see,' Hector answered.

The main group of riders had halted. They were still out of musket range. Only their leader had continued forward. He was heading directly for the corpse of the Labdessah, clearly visible among the last wisps of mist. When he reached the corpse, he reined in his camel and looked down. Then he dismounted and walked across to the body. Leaning over, he began to search through the dead man's clothes. He was plundering the corpse. Turning about, he tied a hobble to his camel, hitched up the hem of his gown with one hand, and began to climb the dune. He was heading straight for where Hector lay.

'What's going on?' It was Bourdon. He had crawled up beside Hector and was peering down. When he saw the advancing Tooarick he pushed forward his musket, cocked the weapon, and began to take aim. 'Don't shoot,' warned Hector. 'He knows we are here. He wants something.' He had noticed that the man had left his musket strapped to his camel.

Thirty paces below them the man stopped. Reaching up, he unwound the black cloth which covered his lower face and called out to them. 'Peace be with you. I am Sidi Hasem of the Wadelim.'

'Greetings,' Hector called back. 'We are travellers.'

'You killed this dog of a Labdessah?'

'We did.'

'Then I welcome you. The enemy of my enemy is my friend.'

Hector rose to his feet.

'What are you doing? He's Tooarick!' blurted Jacques anxiously.

'Keep me covered. He wants to talk. He's our best chance of getting food and water.'

Hector slithered down the slope until he was a few paces from the stranger. The man who called himself Sidi Hasem had a sharp, narrow face. His skin was the dark olive of the desert dwellers, and Hector guessed he was about forty years old. His eyes were deep-set, almost black, and they regarded the Irishman calmly.

'You are from the coffle that passed this way two days ago?' he asked.

'Yes. We are waiting for our friends to come back to collect us.'

'Let me show you something,' said the Tooarick. 'Your companions up there can come down if they want. They will not be harmed. Or they can stay where they are, if they wish. We know that you can defend yourselves.' He glanced meaning-fully at the musket that Hector carried. 'It will be easier if you left that here. We need to travel only a short distance and will be back very quickly.'

Sidi Hasem's self-assurance was persuasive. Hector found himself trusting the man. Turning towards Dan and the others, he shouted to them that he would be back shortly. Then he followed the Tooarick to where his camel was kneeeling. The camel saddle, Hector noted, was different from the plain pack-saddles he had ridden with the coffle. It had two elegant horns which curved upward like the wings of a butterfly. Hasem unhobbled the animal and gestured for Hector to climb up behind the saddle and hold on. The Tooarick then settled himself in his seat and prodded the camel with his goad so that it rose to its feet with a great belch. A moment later Hector found himself clinging on tightly as the animal moved off at a rapid trot.

Hector could see little beyond Hasem's blue-clad back as he guided his beast in the direction that the coffle had gone. There was a smell of camel and human sweat, and the occasional bubbling complaint of the animal as it was urged to climb the steep slopes of one dune after another. His owner remained silent. After about four miles the Tooarick slowed his camel to a walk, and Hector, peering over his shoulder, knew that no words were necessary. Even from a distance he could recognise Ibrahim's great shock of wiry hair.

A short distance ahead was an area of flat ground where the gravel showed through the layer of sand. Here a few stunted thorn bushes had taken root. Lying among the bushes was a body.

Hasem brought his camel to a halt. Dismounting, he led Hector to where the young man lay face down. The killers had stripped him bare. Blood had crusted black where there was a spear wound in his back. 'Is this the man you were expecting?' asked Hasem. 'Yes,' answered Hector. He felt sick to the stomach that his plan for the ambush had provoked such a disaster. 'We came across the body by accident when we were tracking the Labdessah,' said the Tooarick. 'They caught him, and then will have taken his camels.'

'What should we do now?' asked Hector. There was a lump in his throat, and he was at a loss.

'We bury him. Then we leave without delay.' He saw that Hector was dazed.

'Later you can grieve. Allah has relieved your friend of his burden.'

TWENTY-TWO

C

'SIDI HASEM says that his group are already dangerously far out of their own territory. They were on a tribal raid and must withdraw before the Labdessah learn they are here,' Hector informed his friends after he had rejoined them and told them of Ibrahim's murder.

'Can they help us rejoin the coffle?' asked Bourdon. He was looking hopefully at the Tooaricks' camels.

Hector shook his head.

'We'll never catch up. The caravan's three days ahead of us. Old Abdullah won't know what has happened, and the merchants certainly won't turn back. They will presume that we were all killed by the Tooarick. That will make them travel away from us even faster, to save their own skins.'

'So what do you suggest?'

'Sidi Hasem is the denim, the leader of the raid,' Hector answered. 'He offered to carry us back to the Wadelim camp.'

'And what do we do when we get there?'

'He knows about the great river where the foreign men come with their ships. Every year the Wadelim send someone to a native market near the river to trade ostrich feathers and tree gum for blue cloth. This man could bring us there if we gave him a suitable present. Hasem didn't mention the price or whom he had in mind as our guide, but I suspect he means he himself would take us if we gave him one of our muskets.'

'Sounds like a bargain to me.' Bourdon had experienced more than enough of the desert.

'Saying that, Hasem and his men are carrying only enough water for themselves. With four more men, double-mounted on the camels, he warns it will not be comfortable as we have to travel fast.'

'Can't be much worse than what we've endured on the galleys,' Bourdon declared confidently.

He was much less complacent six hours later when the Wadelim made a brief halt to roast strips of dried meat over a tiny campfire made from pellets of camel dung. The Frenchman lay on the ground, complaining bitterly that a camel's bony rump had worn holes in the skin of his thighs and buttocks. The Wadelim had ridden at a fast trot, and Hector and his companions had clung on as best they could, using makeshift stirrups the desert people had fashioned for them from strips of cloth. But it had been an agonising experience, splay-legged, jolted on the camel's spine and rattled against the wood and leather backrest of the Tooarick saddle.

'Ask them what we will do when the water runs out,' Bourdon asked with a groan. Hector relayed the answer with a mischievous grin. 'Sidi Hasem says that when we are really thirsty, we drink camel's urine.'

Fortunately the water ration held up long enough for the party to reach the Wadelim camp three painful days later. As they rode to the cluster of skin and wool tents hidden in a fold in the ground, Hasem warned Hector and his companions not to be seen staring at the flocks of long-legged goats grazing among the rocks and scrub nearby. The Wadelim believed that strangers brought the evil eye.

'We don't have to stay for long,' Hector reassured Karp when the clan's children ran away screaming from poor Karp with his ravaged face. They were convinced that he was a yenun, one of the grotesque evil spirits who emerged from the desert in human form to harm them.

'Something has been puzzling me ever since we ambushed the Labdessah,' Hector continued. 'I never heard your gun go off, even though you were close by. And afterwards you did not need to reload. You never fired a shot at the camel rider, even though he was a mortal enemy. Yet when we hunted the ostrich, you hit your mark every time.'

Karp looked back at him. His face was strained.

Hector went on, 'You have no need to worry, Karp. I also remembered the time we trapped Chabrillan, the man who had caused you so much pain and grief. You attacked him under the city wall and nearly strangled him. Yet afterwards you cried. Was it because you were ashamed of your violence?'

Karp nodded. Now his expression was one of release. It was as though he was being relieved of a burden.

'You don't believe in violence, do you? It is part of your religion, something that you believe in profoundly. That is what you preached in Kandia when you joined Chabrillan's men when they fought the Turks. That is why you suffered all that time on the galley, and you never tried to expose the Chevalier. You did not want revenge. You believe in peace and forgiveness.'

Tears had filled Karp's eyes.

Hector felt a surge of admiration. 'Karp,' he said, 'you are a good man. It is my duty to tell the others that we cannot expect you to help us if we must fight our way to get clear of Moulay Ismail. But as long as I lead our little band, you will continue to be one of us.'

Sidi Hasem was so eager to earn his payment of a musket that the travellers stayed only long enough for him to assemble a consignment of trade goods. Then he led them southward, at a more sedate pace this time and with one man to a camel. They crossed a dreary flat countryside where the sun had baked the reddish brown soil as hard as marble. At night they camped under the sky or they stayed with other small groups of nomads friendly to the Wadelim who greeted them with bowls of zrig, camel milk mixed with water. Gradually the countryside became less austere. There were low hills and the occasional dry riverbed where, by digging in the gravel, they found a seep of water for their camels. Later they came across small wells. The shafts were dug so deep that they had to climb down wooden ladders to clear away a surface layer of blown dust and camel dung before they could fill their leather buckets. Finally they began to arrive at settlements, no more than a dozen or so mud huts which marked the outer fringes of the desert. Instead of zrig, they were given bowls of porridge made from millet. They had reached the land of cultivators. There, at a village known to Hasem, they left behind their camels and rode forward on donkeys, always heading towards the great river which now had a name. The local people called it the Wadnil.

The countryside continued to grow more luxuriant. They began to pass fields of grain guarded by old men and small boys who chased away flocks of thieving birds. There was pasture and woodland and herds of cattle. The people changed too. They were many more, living in village after village of round straw-thatched huts, and their appearance was very different from the sinewy, olive-skinned desert people. They were taller, loose-limbed and wore their wiry hair piled up on the top of their head in the shape of a pointed cap. Instead of flowing loose robes, the common folk dressed in no more than a small loincloth, and their women went bare-breasted, often with a baby slung on their back – a sight Hector had never seen before. As the travellers came closer to the river, more and more of the people they encountered were a deep midnight black, and their skins glistened for they loved to wash, then oil their bodies.

On the twentieth day of their journey their guide claimed his payment. 'Tomorrow,' he told them, 'we reach the market where I will sell the ostrich feathers and gum. You continue south, and by mid afternoon you will arrive on the banks of the river you have been seeking. But you must hurry. The local people say that soon the Wadnil will shrink within its banks. Then the river traffic ceases. They also tell me that there is a foreign ship anchored, even now, in the river.'

'That's good news,' said Hector. 'I had thought we would have to go down to the coast to find a foreign ship.'

'The local people also tell me that there are powerful merchants who resent the presence of this vessel. They see it as a trespasser, a danger to their trade. I think you know who I mean.'

'Are you talking about traders from Moulay Ismail's kingdom?'

'Yes. To them this territory is their own. They come here to take away the elephants' teeth, the gold, the slaves. They are like jealous hunters who believe that all the animals in a forest belong to them.'

'It's strange to think of merchants as hunters.'

Hasem frowned. 'The merchants, as you call them, bully the people into handing over their possessions, and if they resist, they hurt them. If they want them as slaves, they simply seize them and carry them away. I am told that is what their lord Moulay Ismail does to them. So they do it to others.'

Suddenly Hector felt despondent. After so many days' travel he had thought that he had heard the last of Moulay. Now, it seemed, the Emperor's malign influence extended even to the banks of the great river.

The Tooarick was watching him closely. 'There is more to tell you.'

'What is that?'

'The ship anchored in the river is a small vessel and has been in the same place for nearly two weeks. My informants don't know why it does not leave, because soon the falling river level will trap the vessel. No one comes ashore seeking to trade. It just stays there. Perhaps you can join the ship. I think that is good news.'

'And there is bad news as well?'

'The local people also say that the traders from the north have heard about the ship. They are sending some people to drive it away, or maybe to capture it and seize its cargo. My advice is that you hurry. Try to reach the ship before they do.'

The following morning, after thanking Sidi Hasem and leaving him with Karp's musket and most of their remaining stock of gunpowder, Hector and his three companions set out on foot. The road towards the river was well trodden, and they found themselves walking between thick, green plantations of palm trees and banana plants. The air was hot and oppressive so they were amazed at the costume of a local chieftain who was proceeding to the river ahead of them. The man was wearing what looked like a nightshirt of thick, stiff, striped cotton laced at the neck and extending to his ankles. He had a heavy felt cap, and his voluminous robe was hung with dozens of pieces of red coral, clusters of small seashells, amulets and charms which clattered and jangled with each step. The costume was so stifling and cumbersome that the chieftain was obliged to march along very slowly, accompanied by his squad of sword-bearing body-guards. Hector decided it would be prudent to turn aside and use a footpath through the trees which after a little distance brought him and his companions out on a bluff overlooking the river itself.

The Wadnil was more than a quarter of a mile wide, its turbid brown flood moving steadily towards their right. On its surface floated large branches and the occasional fallen tree, its great bulk circling slowly in the current. It was obvious that the river level was already dropping. Mud banks were beginning to show in the centre of the river, and nearer at hand the shoreline was a broad expanse of rich, black mud, already cracking in the sun. A few canoes were drawn up on the bank, stranded by the receding water.

Lying at anchor in the middle of the river was a small ship. To Hector's eye she was not much larger than the fishing boats he had known in his childhood. She had a single mast, from which flew a plain red flag, and a neglected air. A ship's boat was attached by a rope to her stern. Her deck appeared deserted.

'What do you make of her?' he asked Dan.

The Miskito squinted against the glare of the sunlight. 'She looks like the trading sloops that come to the Miskito Coast. At a guess I'd say she has a crew of no more than half a dozen. They must have had hard work getting her up here against the current.' He dropped his gaze towards the riverbank below them. 'Look who's here!' he said softly. 'We should keep out of sight.'

The chieftain and his bodyguard had reached the landing place where the road came to the riverbank. With him was a Moor who wore a faded red burnous. He was the same man who had been spokesman for the coffle.

'I wonder where the others are?' Hector said.

'There, about thirty paces farther along the foreshore,' said Dan who had the sharpest eyes. 'You see that big, grey tree trunk lying stranded? Men are crouched behind it. They've got muskets with them. I'd say that they're the rest of the merchants from the caravan.'

There were shouts from below them. The group standing on the landing place was calling and waving towards the anchored boat. The chief was trying to attract the attention of whoever was on board.

'The landing place is in easy range of the hidden guns,' said Dan. 'Whoever comes ashore from that boat, the minute they set foot on land, they'll be shot down. The Moors can then use the ship's boat to row out and capture the vessel.'

Hector glanced up and down the shoreline. 'We must warn whoever is on the ship. This may be our only chance of getting downriver.'

'We could fire a musket,' suggested Bourdon. 'That would warn them.'

'No. It would also alert the Moors. They would not treat us

kindly for interfering. Besides, if the crew of the vessel know they are in danger, they will raise anchor and sail away.'

'Then what are we to do?'

'We must get out to the vessel ourselves. Dan, what are our chances of using one of those canoes to reach the ship?' Hector pointed to the canoes drawn up on the bank.

The Miskito looked at the craft, then said, 'They're dugouts, hollowed from a single log. Even the smallest will be too heavy to be shifted by the four of us. We'll have to think of something else, and quickly. Someone on the boat is getting ready to come ashore.'

A figure had appeared on the deck of the anchored vessel. He was hauling in the ship's boat. A second man was getting ready to assist him. In a few moments they would be starting out for the shore.

'We'll have to risk the musketeers,' Hector said. 'They are on the far side of the landing place from us, and may not be good shots. We wait until the ship's boat is halfway across, then we leave our hiding place and run down to the shoreline. We'll have the slope in our favour so we should be able to move fast, and we'll have the element of surprise to help us. We should have covered most of the distance before the Moors even notice us. So we keep silent, just run like the devil.'

'And what then?' asked Bourdon.

'We run right into the water, heading for the boat. We get to the boat before it's in range of the musketeers, scramble aboard, and have the crew take us out to the ship.'

'You've forgotten one thing,' said Jacques quietly. 'Neither Karp nor I can swim well. This time we don't have empty barrels to float us.'

'I hadn't forgotten,' said Hector. 'If you look closely, you will see that the foreshore slopes very gently. Almost certainly it stays shallow for a long way out, far enough for you to wade out to the rowboat. It's our only chance. We must reach the boat before it falls into the trap.'

He looked around at his companions. 'No point in keeping your muskets now. Get rid of them. Strip off any clothing that may hinder you as you run. When I give the word, make a dash for it. As you run, spread out. That will make us a harder target for the musketeers. If anyone trips and falls, he must look after himself as best he can. The musketeers are bound to get off at least one shot, probably two. Any more will depend on how quickly they reload.'

He laid his own musket on the ground and unbuckled the belt that held his powder horn and stock of bullets. He removed his heavy sandals. Young Ibrahim had made them and he had planned to keep them as a memento of the young man. But running in bare feet was more important now. He pulled over his head the long loose shirt that he had worn in the desert. Now he was wearing only a pair of loose cotton drawers. The others followed his example, and when they were ready, he waved them forward. They crouched on the edge of the bluff, watching the ship's boat moving closer. There were two men in her. They were rowing steadily, taking a slanting course to counteract the pull of the river current. They were nearly halfway to the shore.

'Get ready!' said Hector quietly. 'See you aboard . . . let's go!'

He stood up and launched himself over the edge of the bank. The face of the bluff fell away in a steep slope, part sand, part gravel. The surface was loose and crumbly, and he felt his bare feet slipping and slithering. He plunged onward, concentrating on keeping his balance. It was impossible to control his speed. The angle of the slope made him set one foot after the other just to keep himself upright. He could hear the sound of his companions as they too pelted down the hill. Belatedly he realised that he should have told them to swerve a little from side to side as they ran, to put the musketeers off their mark. But there was no sound of a shot. As yet they had not been seen.

He was almost at the bottom of the slope when he heard the

shouts. Hector took another dozen strides before the explosion of the first musket shot. A moment later, there came the sound of a volley. He thought there was the sound of a musket ball whizzing past, but his breath was coming in great gasps so he could not be sure. He glanced around to see if anyone had been hit. To his shock he realised that he was the slowest runner of the four. Dan was several yards ahead of him to his left, and Bourdon was close behind him. Karp was level with him, a little distance away and running steadily.

Now they were on the level ground of the shoreline itself. The hardened mud of the beach was beneath the soles of his feet. It was easier to run without the fear of tripping or losing balance. The baked river mud stretched out before him, and he found himself wondering at the regular surface of plate-like cracks. He ran on.

He glanced to his left towards the rowing boat. The two men in it had heard the shots, and turned to see what was happening. They were resting on their oars. The boat had come to a standstill. In a few moments the current would catch it and it would begin to drift downstream. Hector hoped that the current would not take it out of reach.

His legs were tiring now and he could feel the air harsh in his throat. He forced himself to concentrate on taking steady strides. Soon he would be at the water's edge, and then in the shallows.

Without warning his right foot broke through the crusted mud. In a shocking plunge his right leg dropped straight down into the slime beneath. It was as if he had stepped into thin air. He was thrown forward and sideways and slammed face down, the breath knocked out of him. As he fell, he felt an agonising pain in his ankle. He twisted to one side, desperately trying to free his leg, grimacing at the fierce, lancing pain, and he remembered what the coffle's blind guide had said: a camel was uninjured when its foot broke through a crusted salt pan, but a horse would break its leg.

He looked up to see what had happened to his companions. Both Dan and Bourdon had turned back. They had seen him collapse. Now, to his mingled dismay and relief, they were hurrying towards him.

'Here, let me get you back on your feet,' offered Dan. He bent down and seized him by an arm. A moment later the Frenchman was on his other side, and had grasped him around the waist. Together they began to tug him clear. 'Leave me,' Hector gasped. His leg was buried up to mid thigh. 'Run for yourselves. I'll be able to manage.'

They ignored him.

'Here, put an arm over my shoulder,' Dan ordered. Working with Jacques, he wrenched Hector bodily upward. The trapped leg came out of the mud like a rotten tooth from its socket.

Several more muskets shots. Hector was amazed that no one had been hit. He tried to put his right foot on the ground, and gasped in agony. He almost fell again. Together his two friends began to carry him towards the water's edge, Hector's right leg trailing uselessly behind him.

'I said, leave me! I'll manage.' He spoke through clenched teeth.

Again they ignored him.

'Leave me, please!' he insisted fiercely. 'Three of us together make an easy target.'

Now he became aware of Karp. The Bulgar also had abandoned his headlong dash for the river, and had come to join them. He was hovering nearby, anxious to assist. Another musket shot rang out. It could not be long before one of them was struck down.

'Karp! Run on,' Hector pleaded. 'Get to the boat. There's nothing you can do.'

To his astonishment, Karp raised his hand in some sort of salute. Then he turned and began to run. But he did not run towards the shore. He ran directly towards the red-robed Moor still waiting at the landing place. As he ran he let out a great raw screech and began to flail his arms. He was like a madman, half-naked and howling with rage. There was a single musket shot, then a brief lull in the firing as the hidden musketeers decided what they should do.

In that pause Dan and Bourdon reached the shallows, with Hector hanging between them. The rowing boat was forty yards away, still motionless. As Hector felt the splash of water, he turned his head to see what was happening to Karp. The Bulgar was less than twenty paces from the man in the red burnous. Several of the other Moors had jumped up from behind the tree trunk and were running forward. The chieftain's bodyguards had panicked at the terrifying sight. They were fleeing. Karp screeched again, a long piercing howl which could be heard clearly, and bounded forward like a wild beast. The remaining musketeers had gathered their wits and took him as their target. There came a ragged volley. Karp was impossible to miss. Several musket balls must have struck him for he sank down on one knee.

As Bourdon and Dan lifted Hector farther into the river, the boldest of the Moors ran forward, sword in hand. Hector had a last glimpse of Karp as the scimitar swung up in the air and came slicing down towards the Bulgar's head.

Hector turned back towards the rowing boat. It was much closer. The two oarsmen were blacks. 'Help us!' Hector shouted.

His companions dragged him to where the water was up to their chests. Bourdon the non-swimmer could go no farther.

There was a peculiar whirring noise, closely matched by a gunshot. Hector realised that he was hearing the sound of a musket ball skipping off the water. The musketeers had turned their attention back to the fugitives now they had dealt with Karp. The range was too great for accuracy, but they were taking random shots, hoping to make a lucky hit. For a moment Hector felt like ducking out of sight beneath the surface of the river, but he knew it was futile. The gunmen would simply wait until he reappeared, then shoot. It was better to try to swim out of range. But he could not abandon Bourdon. Despite the excruciating pain in his leg, he and Dan would have to pull the Frenchman along with them as they swam.

Hector clenched his teeth. Every time he moved his injured leg, he felt a stab of pain from his ankle. Bourdon was reluctant to move out of his depth. 'Come on, Jacques,' Hector snapped angrily. 'Dan and I will hold you up. Trust us.' The Frenchman took a deep breath and floundered forward. He had the clumsy movements of a man who had never learned to swim properly. Hector reached out to hold his head out of water, and he was aware that Dan was supporting Jacques on the other side.

They made little progress. Bourdon was too frightened to relax. His frantic struggles only hindered them. Another musket ball struck the water just beside them – Hector saw the splash – and then went whirring onward.

Suddenly he felt Bourdon begin to sink. For a second he thought that the Frenchman had been hit. Then he knew that Dan had let go. Dan was swimming away.

Hector felt a brief surge of anger and disappointment. He had never expected Dan to abandon them. Then he looked up and saw that Dan was swimming strongly out into the river. He was heading towards the ship's boat. It had stopped. One rower had dropped his oar in fright. The other rower was shouting at him.

Dan reached the rowboat. He gripped the gunwale and in one smooth wriggling movement had hauled himself aboard. He pushed the frightened oarsman aside and took his place. He barked an order at the man beside him, and began to spin the little craft. The musket fire from the beach had slackened. Hector wondered if perhaps the Moors were running out of powder and bullets. He concentrated on keeping Bourdon's head above water until Dan had brought the little rowing boat close enough for him to grab on. He let go of Bourdon, who seized the boat so desperately that he nearly capsized it. With Hector pushing from below and Dan hauling him up, they hoisted Jacques into the boat, and a moment later the Frenchman was flopping on the floor boards like a landed fish. Then Hector pulled himself aboard.

The boat was over-loaded and sluggish in the water. Looking back towards the shore, Hector thought he could make out Karp's body lying on the strand. There was the puff of smoke from a musket, but the bullet flew wide. A group of Moors was clustering around one of the dugout canoes. With the help of some blacks, they were beginning to shift it down the beach. Dan had been right. The dugout was an awkward burden, and they were making slow progress. There was still time to reach the anchored vessel.

Bourdon had recovered from his fright. He began to search for something to help the oarsmen. There was a wooden paddle lying half hidden in the bottom of the boat. The Frenchman tugged out the paddle and began to take great scoops at the water. The speed of the little boat increased. They were almost out of musket range.

Moments later they had reached the anchored vessel. Her side was low enough for them to scramble aboard without difficulty. On deck there were the usual heaps of rope, some sacks, wooden buckets. But no sign of life.

A musket shot, and this time the musket ball slapped into the side of the ship. The Moors had succeeded in launching their dugout, and it was now being paddled out from the beach. There was a single marksman in the bow. He had fired the shot. There must have been a dozen men in the leading dugout, and a second canoe was being launched.

Dan sprang into action. He ran forward to the bow, and began to throw off the coils of the anchor line. But the knots had jammed. He turned towards one of the two black men who had come aboard with them, and mimed a cutting gesture. The negro understood him at once. He groped under a piece of sacking. A moment later he produced a long-bladed knife and running up to the bows began to saw through the anchor line. The first strands sprang up as they were severed. The river current was so strong that the anchor line was taut as an iron bar. Half a dozen more strokes of the blade, and the anchor cable parted. Hector felt the vessel fall back as the current took hold of her.

'Come on,' Dan was standing at the foot of the mast beckoning. He had a rope in his hand. 'Here haul on this! Jacques, you help him.' Hector limped over and took the rope. Dan and the two blacks had begun to unfasten the bands which held the sail along the boom. Then he and Bourdon heaved on their rope and the upper spar rose, the sail opening beneath it. The blacks and Dan joined them and added their weight. There was no one at the helm so the boat was spinning slowly in the current. The riverbank was sliding past and above their heads the sail flapped three or four times. The gap between the vessel and the pursuing dugout was widening. 'Almost there now,' called Dan. 'Make fast!'

The vessel began to gather pace. Looking aft, Hector saw the paddlers in the dugout had given up the chase. They were turning back to shore.

☾

'THERE WAS MUCH sickness on the ship,' said a deep, husky voice. Hector swung round in surprise. The speaker was one of the blacks who had rescued them. The man noted his astonishment. 'My name is Benjamin. I speak French and Portuguese also as I work with the foreign ships on the coast. When you ran down the hill, I thought you are runaway slaves so I wanted to help. I too was a slave once. Now I have been given my freedom. The foreign sailors call me a Laptot.'

'We were slaves too, at one time.'

Now it was Benjamin's turn to be taken aback. 'Your dark-skinned friend here was a slave, that I understand. But I have never met white slaves before.'

'We have reason to be grateful to you. Thank you for picking us up.'

Benjamin regarded him hopefully. 'You are a ship's captain?'

'No. The most I've ever been is a captain's secretary, or a galley slave. I've never been in charge of any ship.'

'This ship needs a captain. The old one is dead, and so are the first and second mates. All died from the sickness. That is why we were anchored. We did not know what to do. Maybe it is your turn to help us.'

Benjamin went on to explain that he and his companion, another Laptot, had been hired when the sloop called at the Residence of St Louis, the French trading station at the river mouth. The two of them had helped bring the vessel upriver until, two weeks into their journey, a fever had broken out aboard. The hard-driving captain had refused to turn back. He insisted on proceeding until finally the crew were so short-handed that they had been forced to anchor and wait for the sickness to abate. But the fever had raged all the more fiercely. One by one the foreign crew had died until only the two Laptots were left alive. Unable to handle the vessel by themselves, they had been marooned.

'What about the cargo?' Hector asked.

'We have touched nothing,' Benjamin answered. 'I will show you.'

Hector hobbled behind him as the Laptot led the way to a hatch, opened it, and disappeared below. As Hector's eyes got accustomed to the gloom in the hold, he had a vivid recollection of the interior of the ship in which he had been carried away by Hakim Reis. But what he saw now was different. Along each side of the hull were built rows of shelves as if in a trading post. On them were stacked what looked like trade goods. There were bundles of chintz cloth, axe heads, knives, and iron agricultural tools, trays of brass medals. But many of the shelves were bare. They also seemed unnecessarily wide and the gap between them was barely eighteen inches.

'Our captain had planned to go far upriver where there had been a native war. He was sure he would fill the shelves. He had already laid in stocks of food and water for the captives.'

Hector realised that he was looking at the interior of a slave ship. The wooden shelves were where the slaves would lie during the long passage to the Americas.

'Where did the captain keep his papers?'

Benjamin showed him into a small cabin in the stern of the vessel. A quick search of the dead captain's documents revealed that the vessel was the *L'Arc-de-Ciel* from La Rochelle. There were maps and charts of the west coast of Africa, of the mid-Atlantic, and the Caribees. There was no doubt that *L'Arc-de-Ciel* was a slaver.

Benjamin and Hector returned on deck. It was growing dark. Soon there would be the short tropical dusk, then night-fall. 'Should we anchor for the night?' Hector asked Dan. The Miskito seemed confident in his ship handling.

Dan shook his head. 'Our remaining anchor is not heavy enough to hold us in this current. With a little moonlight we should be able to avoid the mudbanks. We had best keep going.'

Hector turned to the Laptot. 'How far to the mouth of the river? When we get to St Louis, we can put you and your companion ashore. But we cannot visit the place there ourselves. One of us,' he nodded towards Bourdon, 'is a rowing slave who has run away. His former masters were French and would seize him.'

Benjamin looked doubtful. 'What will happen to the ship?'

'I don't know,' said Hector. 'My friends and I are hoping to go to the Americas.'

Bourdon spoke up. 'Then why don't we try to sail this boat all the way?'

Hector looked at Dan. 'Is that possible?'

Dan thought for a long time before replying. 'It could be,' he said cautiously. 'We'll need good weather. And our greatest difficulty is that we are so few aboard. Jacques, Hector and myself – that's not enough to manage the ship.'

'Then take us with you,' said Benjamin suddenly. Hector

blinked in surprise. Benjamin spoke urgently to his companion in their own language, then turned back to face the others.

'If we return to St Louis, the governor will want to know what has happened to the ship. We will be accused of failing in our duty to the captain, or even of killing him and the foreign crew. We may be hung and certainly we will lose our freedom and be sold again as slaves.'

'Can't you go ashore somewhere else, not at the Residence?'

Again Benjamin shook his head. 'We are Laptots. We were brought to St Louis as slaves, and our own homelands are far away. The local people would not accept us. Besides, without us you will never cross the bar.'

'What do you mean?'

'There are many sandbanks and mud shoals where the river runs into the sea. Ships can come in and out when the river is in flood, but now it is almost too late. This is the season when the sea breaks heavily on the bar, and it is very dangerous. It needs local knowledge to find a way through the obstacles and a travado to help us.'

'A travado?'

'A great gale of wind from the north-east, from the desert. The wind blows opposite to the sea, and drives back the waves. Also the ship is pressed forward and crosses the bar quickly.'

'Then we must all hope for a travado.'

Benjamin appeared to hesitate, then asked, 'Once we are out to sea, who will show us the way, who will navigate the ship? You said you were not a ship's captain, but now you are sounding like one.'

Hector found himself saying nervously, 'I've never navigated a ship before. But I think I can learn.'

©

WITH THE RIVER CURRENT sweeping her along, *L'Arc-de-Ciel* took less than a week to reach the bar at St Louis. Hector spent much of the time studying the dead captain's sea charts and trying to understand his navigation instruments. The main item was a mystifying device as long as his arm and carefully stored in a cherrywood box. Its open frame supported two wooden arcs engraved with degrees of angle. Three small vanes were attached to each of the arcs, and he found he could slide the vanes back and forth. One of them was fitted with a lens. Puzzled, he took the instrument on deck and tried to use it. But it defied logic. He held the instrument up to his eye and tried looking through the lens. Then he slid the vanes to different positions. The angles they recorded made no sense. He turned the device around, and tried looking through it the other way. Still nothing worked. Bourdon strolled over to see what he was doing, and commented that he had seen an architect using something similar when he had visited the building work at Versailles. 'It's for measuring angles,' he commented. 'I know that already,' snapped Hector, increasingly frustrated. 'If I could use it to find the angle of the sun or of the north star, then it would be better than the astrolabe I learned to use among the Turks. There's a book of tables among the captain's possessions which gives the height of the sun or the star at different locations at different times of the year. With that knowledge I might even be able to take us to the Caribees.'

The Frenchman tactfully withdrew, leaving Hector to wrestle with his problem. Unexpectedly Benjamin provided the solution. He had seen the captain of a visiting ship use a similar gadget. Benjamin had thought the captain was touched in the head, for he had held the instrument to his eye in broad daylight and when facing out to the open sea. There was nothing on the horizon to look at. 'You must be wrong, I'm sure he was measuring the angle of the sun,' Hector growled. He was really irritated now.

'No,' the Laptot insisted. 'He was looking out to sea. The sun was behind him.'

To save his dignity, Hector waited until Benjamin had walked away before, still doubtful, he turned his back to the sun, peered through the lens, and fiddled with the vanes. By chance he saw the shadow of a vane pass into vision and across a graded arc. He lifted the instrument until it was level with the horizon and adjusted the vanes again. He placed the vane's shadow steadily on the arc, then brought the instrument down and took the reading. It was in the range of numbers in the captain's book of tables. He had discovered how to bring the ship to her destination.

They stopped only once on the river voyage, a brief halt at a friendly village to take fresh supplies and top up their water barrels. Then they dropped downriver until they began to feel the rise and fall of the tide, and Benjamin warned that the Residence of St Louis lay just ahead. 'We must stay close to the left-hand shore. The guns of the Residence do not reach that far. A few ships will be anchored in the roadstead, maybe a man of war also, but we can slip past them if the wind favours us.' He pointed to the north. A small dark cloud could be seen, far in the distance. 'I think we are lucky with the weather.'

As the day wore on, banks of thick, dark cloud formed on the horizon and began to coalesce into a solid black mass. From the underbelly of the clouds flickered distant flashes of lightning. Along the river there was an atmosphere of foreboding. The breeze dropped away and was replaced by an oppressive calm. The air seemed to thicken and become slightly opaque. It was difficult to breathe. The sloop glided on, her sails slack, carried only by the current. Hector listened carefully. There was a faint roaring sound far away. 'What's that noise?' he asked Benjamin. 'That's the sound of the waves breaking on the bar. Let us hope that the travado reaches us before we are in the overfalls, and that the ship survives the wind.'

Half an hour later the storm broke. There was a tremendous thunderclap and a great gust of wind swept across the river, driving spray from the surface. The squall struck the sloop like a fist. With a loud clap of canvas, the mainsail bellied out, and the sloop heeled over. Hector heard the groan of the stays under the sudden strain. *L'Arc-de-Ciel* surged forward as Dan and Benjamin struggled to control her helm.

A peal of thunder close at hand, and suddenly the horizon was blotted out by torrential rain which reduced visibility to a few paces. Hector's clothes were saturated in an instant. He remembered the long parched days in the desert and tilted back his head in sheer delight. He opened his mouth and let the rain pour in. When he swallowed, he could taste the faint grains of dust which the travado had brought from the interior. Benjamin appeared at his side, gripping him by the elbow. 'Go help Dan at the helm,' he shouted. 'I will show which way to steer.'

When Hector reached the wheel, Benjamin was already standing in the bow, peering into the murk. He raised his arm and pointed away to starboard. Obediently they steered to his instructions. Now the rain was hissing down, ochre rain on a brown river, and it was impossible to tell where the air and water met. More thunder, a massive growl which seemed to shake the sloop. A tremendous crack of lightning split the gloom.

Moments later the sloop was bucking and lurching as she was caught in the overfalls. Out of the murk raced a continuous onslaught of breaking waves. A lightning flash close at hand lit their foaming crests and turned them blinding white. *L'Arc-de-Ciel* surged on, the wind driving her forward. Benjamin gestured again, urgently this time, and Dan and Hector spun the wheel to bring the ship on her new course. There was no pattern to the waves breaking on the bar. They came from different directions, now smashing into her bow so she was tossed backwards, now heaving up along her sides so that she slewed sideways.

They never glimpsed St Louis. For two hours they battled with the overfalls, trusting to Benjamin's directions, ploughing onward until they were sure that the turbulence was easing.

Then the little ship ceased her wild gyrations and, though she still pitched and rolled uncomfortably, there was no mistaking that she was sailing on smoother water.

By nightfall the rain had ceased. The sky was still overcast so it was impossible to tell when the sun set, but the wind had eased to a moderate breeze and the air felt washed and clean. Benjamin came back from his lookout in the bow, and announced that they had cleared the bar and passed through the anchorage as well. They were in open water. Hector went down to the cabin and brought up the ship's compass and set it down beside the helm. 'Steer west,' he said to Dan. 'Tomorrow I will check the charts and set course for the Americas.' He looked up at the sky. As swiftly as it had arrived, the travado had swept onward and out to sea. The first stars were showing through rents in the clouds. He thought he recognised the constellation of Orion. Now he would use its stars to find his way across the ocean. He gave a slight shiver of apprehension. There was so much to learn, and it was so easy to make mistakes. He thought back to Ibrahim, his corpse lying on the sand and the crusted blood of the wounds where the Labdessah had speared him to death, because he had followed Hector's plan to ambush the Tooarick. And he recalled his last glimpse of Karp, the glint of the scimitar as it descended in a killing stroke. Poor mutilated Karp had believed in peace and forgiveness to the end, refusing to resort to violence even as he found a way to save his friends. Despondently Hector wondered if Dan and Jacques had been wise to place their trust in him. Too often he seemed to bring death and suffering upon his comrades.

His sense of gloom deepened as he allowed himself to recall his final meeting with Elizabeth, only to find that the details of that heart-rending encounter were already blurred. It seemed that the ordeal of the long trek across the desert had not only separated him from her physically, but was part of a great void that was growing wider and wider. In a moment of unhappy clarity he knew that, although he might return one day to trace what had happened to his mother, he would never see or hear from Elizabeth again.

Then he heard someone singing under his breath. It was Bourdon somewhere in the shadows. Hector could not distinguish the words of the song but it sounded like a Paris street ballad. Clearly Jacques was in good spirits and looking forward to reaching the Americas. At the helm there was a slight movement as Dan adjusted the wheel to hold the little sloop on her westward course. The Miskito appeared untroubled by the violent and sudden changes of fortune of recent days. Hector found himself taking comfort from his friend's composure. 'What's it like there, out in the Caribbees?' he asked quietly. There followed such a long silence that Hector thought Dan had not heard his question. Then the Miskito's voice answered, 'There are places more beautiful than anything you could dream, sea as clear as glass, sand so fine and white that it looks and feels like flour, wreaths of mist hanging over jungle-covered hills.' There was another long pause. 'The people who live there are no different from those we have already known. Some are honest. Others are rogues and cheats. A number are men who have known hardship and are seeking a fresh beginning. They are like ourselves. When you have brought us across the ocean and I have visited my people, maybe we should try to join them.'

HISTORICAL NOTE

In 1631 a particularly brazen Barbary corsair was operating from Sallee on the Atlantic coast of Morocco. A sea captain from Flanders, he had 'turned Turk' and taken the name Murat Reis. That year, with two ships, he made a surprise raid on the Irish coastal village of Baltimore and successfully kidnapped almost the entire population: 107 men, women and children. He then took them back to North Africa to sell. A French missionary priest working in Algiers saw several of Murat's Irish victims put up for auction. After that, very little more was heard of them.

Slavery in various guises was flourishing on all sides of the Mediterranean throughout the seventeenth century. The Regencies of Tunis, Algiers and Tripoli were infamous in the Christian world as places where the unfortunate captives were either set to work or held for ransom. Yet there were also thriving slave markets in Malta and Livorno where Muslims – and sometimes non-Muslim as well – were bought and sold. The Knights of St John of Malta were at the forefront of the trade in much the same way that the corsair guilds in the Regencies, the taifas, were the chief providers of human merchandise in North Africa. By the same token, it was virtual slavery to be condemned to the oar in France's Royal Galley fleet, one of Louis XIV's pet projects. On the Sun King's galleys, French convicts sat alongside Turkish prisoners of war as well as Iroquois Indians captured in North America. The Turks could hope to be freed in a prisoner exchange, but many of the French galeriens died in chains while the unfortunate Indians mostly perished from fevers and malnutrition.

The turbulence of politics in the Mediterranean encouraged this state of affairs to continue. Against the general background of the

Eternal War between Cross and Crescent, the various European nations were competing with one another for commercial and territorial advantage. France was suspicious of Spain; the Spaniards mistrusted the Portuguese; the English, Dutch and other Protestant nations jostled with one another even as they warily dealt with the Catholic powers. Everyone was nervous of the Turkish Sultan in Constantinople. Amid such disarray the Barbary corsairs thrived. A shipping list for the period between 1677 and 1680 (roughly the time of Hector's and Dan's fictional adventures) shows that the Algerines captured no less than 160 British ships. This would have provided approximately 8,000 British captives for the slave pens of that Regency.

This was also a time when the nature of naval warfare in the Mediterranean was altering. Oared vessels, the preferred warships since the days of ancient Greece, were obsolete. Too expensive to build, their huge crews were too costly to maintain, and their hulls and rig insufficiently seaworthy. Above all, they could not carry the numbers of heavy cannon which gave their rivals, the sailing ships, such devastating firepower. Nevertheless the flamboyant galley with its colourful pennants and massed ranks of half-naked oarsmen remained a potent symbol, much loved by contemporary painters and illustrators, many of them Dutch. They often depicted imaginary battle scenes between galleys and sailing ships. These same artists also found the Barbary city states, particularly Algiers, to be a worthy subject, basing their images on the reports of the embassies to the Regencies as well as the harrowing tales told by returned captives. There were many such memoirs by the 'white slaves' from Barbary though, by contrast, hardly any of the galley slaves of Christendom wrote about their experiences. An exception is the account written by a Frenchman, Jean Marteilhe, a Protestant condemned to the oar in 1701. He joined his first galley at Dunkirk on the Channel coast and describes the extraordinary pantomime – hiding under the oar benches, kicking their legs in the air, holding up their hands, coughing, bowing, and so forth – which he and his shipmates had to perform for the amusement of their captain's guests on board.

Unlikely though they may seem, several of the characters mentioned in the preceding pages were real: the reverend Devereux

Spratt, Rector of Mitchelstown in North Cork, had been a slave in Algiers. Samuel Martin was the English consul in Algiers between the years 1673 and 1679, while Jean Baptiste Brodart, the Intendant of the Royal Galley base at Marseilles, was renowned for his venality. Joseph Maimaran, a Moroccan Jew, acted as chief financial adviser to the megalomaniac Emperor Moulay Ismail and served for many years as virtually his first minister as well as chief money lender. Unwisely Maimaran asked for repayment of a loan, and paid for his lese-majesty with his life. He was knocked down and trampled to death in the street by a loose horse belonging to a member of the Black Guard. The death looked like an accident but contemporary opinion held it was an assassination ordered by Moulay. The Emperor himself ruled until 1727, dying in his eighty-first year, and he did have an Irish gun founder who was overfond of the bottle. What happened to his monstrous favourite wife, Zidana, is not known. Famously, Moulay is reputed to have sired 888 children – 548 sons and 340 daughters – during his lifetime.

BUCCANEER

In 1679 the Caribbean was a dangerous and lawless sea. Jamaica, Hispaniola and the arc of islands known as the 'Caribees' were variously claimed by rival nations – notably France and England. The opposite shore, the 'Main' or continental coast, was jealously guarded by Spain as the vulnerable frontier of her vast land empire in the Americas. Smuggling was rife. For years the island governments had made up for a lack of men and ships by deploying irregular local forces, which operated as little more than licensed brigands. They had acquired a taste for plunder, and – though officially the region was now at peace – these soldiers and sailors of fortune were prepared to attack any easy and lucrative target.

ONE

HECTOR LYNCH leaned back and braced himself against the sloop's mast. It was hard to hold the little telescope steady against the rhythmic rolling of the Caribbean swells, and the image in the lens was blurred and wavering. He was trying to identify the flag at the stern of a vessel which had appeared on the horizon at first light, and was now some three miles to windward. But the wind was blowing the stranger's flag sideways, directly towards him, so that it was difficult to see against the bright sunshine sparkling off the waves on a late-December morning. Hector thought he saw a flicker of blue and white and some sort of cross, but he could not be sure.

'What do you make of her?' he asked Dan, offering the spyglass to his companion. He had first met Dan on the Barbary coast two years earlier when both had been incarcerated in the slave barracks of Algiers, and Hector had developed a profound respect for Dan's common sense. The two men were much the same age – Hector was a few months short of his twentieth birthday – and they had formed a close friendship.

'No way of telling,' said Dan, ignoring the telescope. A Miskito Indian from the coast of Central America he, like many of his countrymen, had remarkably keen eyesight. 'She has the legs of us. She could be French or English, or maybe from the English colonies to the north. We're too far from the Main for her to be a Spaniard. Perhaps Benjamin can say.'

Hector turned to the third member of their small crew. Benjamin was a Laptot, a freed black slave who had worked in the ports of the West African coast before volunteering to join their vessel for the voyage across the Atlantic and into the Caribbean.

'Any suggestions?' he asked.

Benjamin only shook his head. Hector was unsure what to do. His companions had chosen him to command their little vessel, but this was his first major ocean voyage. Two months ago they had acquired their ship when they had found her stranded halfway up a West African river, her captain and officers dead of fever, and manned only by Benjamin and another Laptot. According to the ship's papers she was the *L'Arc-de-Ciel*, registered in La Rochelle, and the broad empty shelves lining her hold indicated that she was a small slave ship which had not yet taken on her human cargo.

Hector wiped the telescope's lens with a strip of clean cotton rag torn from his shirt, and was about to take another look at the stranger's flag, when there was the sound of a cannon shot. The noise carried clearly downwind, and he saw a black puff of gun smoke from the sloop's deck.

'That's to attract our attention. They want to talk with us,' said Benjamin.

Hector stared again at the sloop. It was obvious that she was closing rapidly, and he could see some sort of activity on her stern deck. A small group of men had clustered there.

'We should show them a flag,' Benjamin suggested.

Hector hurried down to the dead captain's cabin. He knew there was a canvas bag tucked away discreetly in a locker behind the bunk. Pulling open the bag, he tipped out its contents on the cabin floor. There were some items of dirty linen and, beneath them, several large rectangles of coloured cloth.

One had a red cross stitched on a white ground, which he recognised as the flag worn by the English ships that had occasionally visited the little Irish fishing port where he had spent his summers as a child. Another was a blue flag with a white cross. In the centre of the cross was a shield bearing three golden fleurs-de-lys. That flag too he recognised. It had flown on the merchant ships of France when he and Dan had been prisoner-oarsmen at the royal galley base in Marseilles. The third flag he did not know. It also displayed a red cross on a white background, but this time the arms of the cross ran diagonally to each corner of the flag, and the edges of the arms of the cross were deliberately ragged. They looked like branches cut from a shrub after the shoots had been trimmed away. It seemed that the deceased captain of *L'Arc-de-Ciel* had been prepared to fly whichever nation's flag suited the occasion.

Hector returned on deck, all three flags under his arm in an untidy bundle. 'Well, which one is it to be?' he asked. Again he glanced across at the unknown vessel. In the short interval he had been below decks it had come much closer. Well within cannon shot.

'Why not try King Louis's rag,' proposed Jacques Bourdon. In his mid-thirties Jacques was an ex-galerien, a thief condemned to the oar for life by a French court and who had 'GAL' branded on his cheek to prove it. He, together with the second Laptot, made up their five-man crew. 'That way, our colours will agree with our ship's papers,' he added, shading his eyes to scrutinise the approaching sloop. 'Besides . . . if you look there, she's flying the French flag as well.'

Hector and his companions waited for the stranger to come closer. They could see someone at her rail waving his arms. He was pointing at their sails and gesturing that they should be lowered. Too late, Hector felt a prickle of suspicion.

'Dan,' he asked quietly, 'any chance that we can get away from her?'

'No chance at all,' Dan answered without hesitation. 'She's a ketch and carries more sail than us. Best heave to and see what they want.'

A moment later Bourdon was helping the two Laptots loose the sheets and lower the sails so that *L'Arc-de-Ciel* gradually slowed to a halt, and lay gently rocking on the sea.

The approaching ketch altered course to come alongside. There were eight cannon on her single deck. Then, without warning, the little group on her stern deck parted to reveal someone hauling briskly on a halyard. A ball of cloth was being pulled aloft. A puff of wind caught it and the folds of cloth shook out, revealing a new flag. It carried no marks, but was a plain red sheet.

Jacques Bourdon swore. 'Shit! The jolie rouge. We should have guessed.'

Startled, Hector looked at him. 'The jolie rouge,' Bourdon grunted. 'The flag of the flibustiers, how do you call them – privateers? It's their mark. I shared a Paris prison cell with one of them once, and a right stinking bastard he was. Smelled worse than the rest of us gaolbirds all put together. When I complained, he told me that in the Caribees he had once gone two years without a proper wash. Claimed to have dressed in a suit of untreated cattle skins.'

'You mean he was a buccaneer,' Dan corrected him. The Miskito seemed unworried by the sight of the red flag.

'Are they dangerous?' Hector wanted to know.

'Depends what sort of mood they're in,' replied Dan quietly. 'They'll be interested in our cargo, if there's anything they can steal and sell. They'll not harm us if we cooperate.'

There was a clatter and slap of canvas as the strangers' vessel came up into the wind. Her helmsman must have carried out the manoeuvre many times and was obviously an expert for he deftly laid the ketch alongside the smaller *L'Arc-de-Ciel*. Hector counted at least forty men aboard, an uncouth assembly of all ages and shapes, most of them heavily bearded and deeply tanned. Many were bare-chested and wore only loose cotton drawers. But others had chosen a ragbag of clothes that ranged from soiled lawn shirts and canvas breeches to seaman's smocks and broadcloth coats with wide skirts and braided cuffs. A few, like Jacques's former cell mate, were dressed in jerkins and leggings of untanned cattle skin. Those who were not bare-headed displayed an equally wide range of hats. There were brightly coloured head cloths, sailor's bonnets, tricornes, leather skull caps, and broad-brimmed hats of a vaguely military style. One man was even sporting a fur hat despite the blazing heat. A few hefted long muskets which, Hector was relieved to observe, were not being pointed at *L'Arc-de-Ciel*, nor were the deck guns manned. Dan had been right: the buccaneers were not unduly aggressive towards a ship's crew that obeyed their instructions. For the present the mob of ill-assorted strangers were doing no more than lining the rail of their vessel and looking appraisingly at *L'Arc-de-Ciel*.

The slightest thump as the hulls of the two vessels touched, and a moment later half a dozen of the buccaneers dropped down on *L'Arc-de-Ciel*'s deck. Two of them carried wide-mouthed blunderbusses. The last man to come aboard seemed to be their leader. Of middle age, he was short and plump, his close-cropped reddish hair turning grey, and he was dressed more formally than the others in buff-coloured breeches and stockings, with a purple waistcoat worn over a grubby white shirt. Unlike his fellows who preferred knives and cutlasses, he had a rapier hanging from a shabby baldrick. He was also the only boarder wearing shoes. The heels clumped on the wooden deck as he strode purposefully to where Dan and Hector were standing. 'Summon your captain,' he announced. 'Tell him that Captain John Coxon wishes to speak with him.'

Closer up, Captain Coxon's face, which at first sight had seemed chubby and genial, had a hard set to it. He bit off his words when he spoke and the corners of his mouth turned down, producing a slight sneer. Hector judged that Captain Coxon was not a man to be trifled with.

'I am acting as the captain,' he replied.

Coxon glanced at the young man in surprise. 'What happened to your predecessor?' he demanded bluntly.

'I believe he died of fever.'

'When and where was that?'

'About three months ago, maybe more. On the river Wadnil, in West Africa.'

'I know where the Wadnil is,' Coxon snapped irritably. 'Have you any proof, and who brought this ship across? Who's your navigator?'

'I did the navigating,' Hector answered quietly.

Again the look of surprise, followed by a disbelieving twist of the mouth.

'I need to see your ship's papers.'

'They're in the captain's cabin.'

Coxon nodded to one of his men who promptly disappeared below deck. As he waited, the captain slipped his hand inside his shirt front and scratched at his chest. He seemed to be suffering from some sort of skin irritation. Hector noticed several angry red blotches on the buccaneer captain's neck, just above the shirt collar. Coxon gazed around at *L'Arc-de-Ciel* and her depleted crew. 'Is this all your men?' he demanded. 'What happened to the others?'

'There are no others,' Hector replied. 'We had to sail shorthanded, just the five of us. It was enough. The weather was kind.'

Coxon's man came out from the cabin door. He was holding a sheaf of documents and the roll of charts that Hector had found aboard when he, Dan and Bourdon had first set foot on *L'Arc-de-Ciel*. Coxon took the papers and stood silently for a few moments as he read through them while absent-mindedly scratching the back of his neck. Abruptly he looked up at

Hector, then thrust one of the charts towards him. 'If you're a navigator, then tell me where we are.'

Hector looked down at the chart. It was poorly drawn, and its scale was inadequate. The entire Caribbean was shown on a single sheet and there were several gaps or smudges on the surrounding coastline. He placed his finger about two-thirds across the parchment, and said, 'About here. At noon yesterday I calculated our latitude by backstaff, but I am unsure of our westing. Twelve days ago we saw a high island to the north of us, which I took to be one of the windward Caribees. Since then we could have run perhaps a thousand miles.'

Coxon stared at him bleakly. 'And why would you want to go due west?'

'To try to reach the Miskito coast. That is where we are headed. Dan here is from that country, and wishes to get home.'

The buccaneer captain, after a brief glance towards Dan, looked thoughtful. 'What about your cargo?'

'There is no cargo. We came aboard the ship before she had loaded.'

Coxon gave another jerk of his head, and two of his crew opened up a hatch and clambered down into the hold. Moments later, they reappeared and one of them said 'Nothing. She's empty.'

Hector sensed the captain's disappointment. Coxon's mood was changing. He was becoming annoyed. Abruptly he took a step towards Jacques Bourdon who was loitering near the mast. 'You there with the brand on your cheek!' Coxon snapped. 'You've been in the King's galleys, haven't you? What was your crime?'

'Being caught,' Jacques replied sourly.

'You're French, aren't you?' A ghost of a smile passed across Coxon's face.

'From Paris.'

Coxon turned back towards Hector and Dan. He still had the sheaf of papers in his hand.

'I'm seizing this ship,' he announced. 'On suspicion that the vessel has been stolen from her rightful owners, and that the crew has murdered her captain and officers.'

'That's absurd,' Hector burst out. 'The captain and his officers were all dead by the time we came aboard.'

'You have nothing to prove it. No certificate of death, no documents for transfer of ownership.' It was evident that Coxon was grimly satisfied with himself.

'How could we have obtained such papers?' Hector was getting more angry by the minute. 'The bodies would have been put overboard to try to stop the contagion, and there were no authorities to go to. As I said, the vessel was halfway up an African river, and there were only native chiefs in the region.'

'Then you should have stopped at the first trading post on the coast, sought out the authorities, and registered the events,' countered Coxon. 'Instead you set sail directly across to the Caribbees. It is my duty to regularise the matter.'

'You have no authority to take this ship,' Hector insisted.

Coxon treated him to a thin smile. 'Yes I do. I have the authority of the Governor of Petit Guave, whose commission I carry on behalf of the kingdom of France. This vessel is French. There is a branded convict aboard, a subject of the French king. The ship's papers are not in order, and there is no proof of how the captain died. He could have been killed, and the cargo sold off.'

'So what do you intend to do?' Hector asked, choking down his anger. He should have realised that from the start Coxon had been trying to find an excuse to seize the vessel. Coxon and his men were nothing more than licensed sea brigands.

'This vessel and those found on her will be taken to Petit Guave by a prize crew. There the vessel will be sold and you and your crew will be tried for murder and piracy. If found guilty the court will decide your punishment.'

Unexpectedly, Dan spoke up, his voice grave. 'If you or

your court mistreat us, you will have to answer to my people. My father is one of the old men council of the Miskito.'

Dan's words seemed to have carried some weight because Coxon paused for a moment before replying. 'If it is true that your father is of the Miskito council then the court will take that into account. The authorities in Petit Guave would not wish to anger the Miskito. As for the rest of you, you will stand trial.'

Coxon again slipped his hand inside his shirt front and scratched at his chest. Hector wondered if the itching was what made the man so irritable. 'I need to know your name,' the buccaneer said to Hector.

'My name is Hector Lynch.' The hand stopped scratching. Then Coxon said slowly, 'Any relation to Sir Thomas Lynch?'

There was a wariness in the man's tone. His question hung in the air. Hector had no idea who Sir Thomas Lynch was, but clearly he was someone well known to Coxon. Hector also had the distinct impression that Sir Thomas Lynch was a person whom the captain respected, perhaps even feared. Alert to the subtle change in the buccaneer's manner, Hector seized the opportunity.

'Sir Thomas Lynch is my uncle,' he said unblushingly. Then, to increase the effect of the lie, he added, 'It was why I agreed with my companions that we sail for the Caribbean without delay. After we had brought Dan to the Miskito coast, I intended to find Sir Thomas.'

For an alarming moment Hector thought that he had gone too far, that he should have kept the lie simple. Coxon was staring at him with narrowed eyes. 'Sir Thomas is not in the Caribees at this time. His estates are being managed by his family. You didn't know?'

Hector recovered himself. 'I was in Africa for some months and out of touch. I received little news from home.'

Coxon pursed his lips as he thought over Hector's statement.

Whatever Sir Thomas Lynch meant to the buccaneer, the young man could see that it was enough to make their captor reconsider his plans.

'Then I will make sure that you are united with your family,' the buccaneer said at last. 'Your companions will stay aboard this ship while she is taken to Petit Guave, and I will send a note to the authorities there that they are associates of Sir Thomas's nephew. It may stand in their favour. Meanwhile you can accompany me to Jamaica – I was already on my way there.'

Hector's mind raced as he searched Coxon's statement for clues as to the identity of his supposed uncle. Sir Thomas Lynch had estates on Jamaica, therefore he must be a man of substance. It was reasonable to guess that he was a wealthy planter, a man who had friends in government. The opulence and political power of the West Indian plantation owners was well known. Yet at the same time Hector sensed something disquieting in Coxon's manner. There was a hint that whatever the buccaneer captain was proposing was not entirely to Hector's advantage.

Belatedly it occurred to Hector that he should put in a good word for the Laptots who had proved their worth on the trans-Atlantic voyage.

'If anyone is to be put on trial in Petit Guave, captain,' he told Coxon, 'it should not be either Benjamin here, nor his companion. They stayed with the ship even when their previous captain had died of fever. They are loyal men.'

Coxon had resumed his scratching. He was raking the back of his neck with his nails. 'Mr Lynch, you need have no worries on that score,' he said. 'They will never be put on trial.'

'What will happen to them?'

Coxon brought his hand away from his collar, inspected the fingernails for traces of whatever had been causing the irritation, and wriggled his shoulder slightly to relieve the pressure of the shirt on his skin.

'As soon as they are brought to Petit Guave, they will be sold. You say they are loyal. That should make them excellent slaves.'

He looked straight at Hector as if to challenge the young man into raising an objection. 'I believe your uncle employs more than sixty Africans on his own Jamaican plantations. I am sure he would approve.'

At a loss for words, Hector could only stare back, trying to gauge the buccaneer's temper. What he saw discouraged hope. Captain Coxon's eyes reminded him of a reptile. They protruded slightly and the expression in them was utterly pitiless. Despite the balmy sunshine, Hector felt a chill seeping deep within him. He was not to allow himself to be deceived by the pleasantness of his surroundings, with the warm tropical breeze ruffling the brilliant sea, and the soft murmuring sound as the two ships were gently moving against one another, hull to hull. He and his companions had arrived where self-interest was sustained by cruelty and violence.

TWO

COXON'S tatterdemalion company wasted little time in securing their prize. Within half an hour *L'Arc-de-Ciel* had been cast off and was bound for Petit Guave. Hector was left on the deck of the buccaneers' ketch wondering if he would ever see Dan, Jacques and the others again. As he watched the little sloop grow smaller in the distance, Hector was uncomfortably aware of Coxon standing not ten feet away and observing him closely.

'Your shipmates should reach Petit Guave in less than three days from now,' the buccaneer captain observed. 'If the authorities there believe their story, they'll have nothing to worry about. If not . . .' He gave a mirthless laugh.

Hector knew that Coxon was goading him, trying to get a reaction.

'Unusual, isn't it . . .' the captain went on and there was a hint of malice in his voice, 'that Sir Thomas Lynch's nephew should associate himself with a branded convict? How does that come about?'

'We were both shipwrecked on the Barbary coast, and had to team up if we were to save ourselves and get clear,' explained Hector. He tried to make his answer sound casual and unconcerned, though he was wracking his brains to think how he could learn more about his supposed relative, Sir Thomas

Lynch, without arousing Coxon's suspicion. Should the buccaneer discover he had been hoodwinked, any hope of reuniting with his friends would be lost. It was best to turn the questioning back on his captor.

'You say you are bound for Jamaica. How long before we get there?'

Coxon was not to be put off. 'You know nothing of the island? Didn't your uncle speak of it?'

'I saw little of him when I was growing up. He was away much of the time, tending to his estate' – that at least was a safe guess.

'And where did your spend you childhood?' Coxon was probing again.

Fortunately the interrogation was interrupted by a shout from one of the lookouts at the masthead. He had seen another sail on the horizon. Immediately, Coxon broke off his questioning and began bawling orders at his crew to set more sail and take up the chase.

*

AMID ALL the activity Hector sauntered over to the freshwater butt placed at the foot of the mainmast. It was only a few hours to sunset yet the day was still uncomfortably hot, and a pretence of thirst was an opportunity to move out of Coxon's earshot.

'What's Jamaica like?' he asked a sailor who was drinking from the wooden dipper.

'Not what it was,' replied the man. He was a rough-looking individual. The hand which held the pannikin lacked the top joints of three fingers, and his nose had been badly broken and set crooked. He smelled of stale sweat. 'Used to be a grog shop at every corner, and harlots on parade in every street. They'd stroll up and down in their petticoats and red caps, as bold as you like, ready for all kinds of fun. And no questions asked about where you got your silver.' The man belched, wiped the back of his hand across his mouth, and handed Hector the dipper. 'That changed when our Henry got his knighthood. Things went quiet, but it's all still there if you know what to look for, and hold your tongue afterwards.' He gave Hector a sly look. 'I reckon that even though he's Sir Henry now, he still looks after his own. His sort will never be satisfied, however much he's got.'

Another titled Jamaican, and a rich one, Hector thought to himself. He wondered who this Sir Henry might be, and if he had any dealings with his 'uncle'. He took a sip from the pannikin.

'Wouldn't mind getting a taste of those harlots myself,' he observed, hoping to strike a comradely note. 'We were more than six weeks at sea from Africa.'

'No whoring this cruise,' answered the sailor. 'Port Royal is where the strumpets wag their tails, and the captain stays clear of that port unless he's invited in. Nowadays he carries a Frenchy's commission.'

'From Petit Guave?'

'The deputy governor there gives them out already signed and the names left blank. You fill in what you want and then go a-hunting, just as long as you let him have a tenth of any takings. Used to be much the same in Jamaica until that bastard Lynch started interfering.'

Before Hector could ask what he meant, he heard Coxon's steps on the deck behind him, and the captain's voice snapped.

'Enough of that! You're speaking to Governor Lynch's nephew. He'll not wish to hear your opinions!'

The sailor glared at Hector. 'Nephew to Lynch, are you! If I'd known, I'd have pissed in the dipper before you drank from it,' and with that he turned and stalked away.

＊

HECTOR BROODED on the sailor's information throughout the two days and nights it took to reach Jamaica. The pursuit of the distant sail had been abandoned when it became clear that there was no hope of catching the prey. Each night the young man bedded down on a coil of rope near the sloop's bows, and by day he was left alone. Any buccaneer who came his way either ignored him or gave him a black look so he presumed that his alleged relationship to Lynch had become common knowledge. Coxon paid him no attention. When dawn broke on the third morning he was feeling stiff and tired and concerned for his own fate as he got to his feet and looked out over the bowsprit towards their landfall.

Straight ahead, Jamaica rose from the sea, high and rugged, the first rays of the sun striking patterns of vivid green and dark shadow across the folds and spurs of a mountain range which reared up a few miles inland. The ketch was heading into a sheltered bay where the land sloped down more gently to a beach of grey sand. There was no sign of a harbour though beyond the strand was a cluster of pale dots which Hector presumed were the roofs of huts or small houses. Otherwise the place was deserted. There was not even a fishing boat to be seen. Captain Coxon had made a discreet arrival.

Within moments of her anchor splashing into water so clear that the rippled sand of the sea floor could be seen four fathoms down, Coxon and Hector were being rowed ashore in the ship's cockboat. 'I'll be back in less than two days,' the buccaneer captain told the boat crew as they hauled up on the beach. 'No one to stray out of sight of the ship. Stay close at hand and be ready to set sail as soon as I return.' He turned to Hector. 'You come with me. It's a four-hour walk. And you can make yourself useful.' He removed the heavy coat he was wearing, and handed it to the younger man to carry. Hector was surprised to see the curls of a wig sticking out of one of its pockets. Underneath his coat Coxon was wearing an embroidered linen shirt with a ruffled front and lace at the cuffs. His stockings and breeches were clean and brushed and of fine quality, and he had changed into a new pair of shoes with silver buckles. Hector wondered at the reason for such elegant clothes.

'Where are we going?' he asked.

'To Llanrumney,' was the brusque reply.

Not daring to ask an explanation, Hector followed the buccaneer captain as he set off. After so many days at sea since leaving Africa, the ground tilted and swayed beneath the young man's feet, and until he found his land legs it was difficult to keep up with Coxon's brisk pace. At the back of the beach they skirted around a small hamlet of five or six wooden huts thatched with plantain leaves and occupied by families of blacks, usually a woman with several children. There were no menfolk to be seen and no one paid them a second glance. They came upon the start of a footpath which led inland, and very soon the hollow, open sounds of the sea had been replaced by the buzzing and chirping of the insects and birds in the dense vegetation on either side of the trail. The air was hot and humid, and in less than a mile Coxon's fine shirt was sticking to his back with sweat. At first the track kept to the bank of a small river but then it branched off to the left where the river was joined by a tributary stream, and here Hector saw his first native birds, a small flock of bright green parrots with yellow beaks which flew away with quick wing beats, chattering and scolding the intruders.

Coxon stopped to take a rest. 'When was the last time you saw your uncle?' he asked.

Hector thought quickly. 'Not since I was a boy. Sir Thomas is my father's oldest brother. My father, Stephen Lynch, died when I was sixteen and afterwards my mother moved away and kept in touch only with an occasional letter.' At least part of that statement was true, he thought to himself. Hector's father, of minor Anglo-Irish gentry, had died while Hector was in his teens, and his mother, originally from Galicia in Spain, could well have returned to her own people.

He did not know what had happened to her since he had been locked away on the Barbary coast. But one thing was sure: his father had never referred to anyone called Sir Thomas Lynch, and he was certain that Sir Thomas was nothing whatever to do with his family.

'Rumour has it that Sir Thomas is seeking to be reappointed as governor. Do you know anything about that?' said Coxon. He had begun scratching again, this time at his waistband.

'I haven't heard. I've been away from home too long to keep up with family news,' Hector reminded him.

'Well, even if he was already back on the island you wouldn't find him at Llanrumney . . .' – again the strange name. 'He and Sir Henry never saw eye to eye on anything.'

Hector seized his opportunity to learn more. 'Sir Henry . . . ? Whom do you mean?'

Coxon gave him a sharp glance. There was mistrust in his look. 'You've not heard of Sir Henry Morgan?'

Hector did not answer.

'I was with him when he captured Panama in seventy-one. We needed nearly two hundred mules to carry away what we took,' Coxon said. He sounded boastful. 'Panama silver bought him Llanrumney, though he fell out with your uncle who accused him of false accounting of the spoils. Had him sent as a prisoner for trial in England, but the old fox had powerful friends in London, and he's back here now as lieutenant governor.'

The buccaneer captain stooped down and removed a shoe. There was a patch of blood on the heel of his stocking. A blister must have burst.

'So it will be in your best interests to be discreet until we know his mood and what is our own situation,' he added darkly.

It was another several hours of hot and weary walking before Coxon announced that they were almost at their destination. By then the captain was limping badly, and they were making frequent stops so that he could attend to his oozing blisters. A journey he had predicted would last four hours had taken nearly six, and it was almost nightfall before they finally emerged from a patch of woodland and into an area of cultivation. The native vegetation had been cleared back here and, in its place, field after field had been laid out and thickly sewn with tall green plants like giant stalks of grass. It was Hector's first sight of a sugar plantation.

'There's Llanrumney,' said Coxon, nodding towards a substantial one-storey building situated on the far slope so that it looked out over the cane fields. Off to one side were various large sheds and outbuildings which Hector took to be workshops for the estate. 'Named it after his home place in Wales.'

They found their way along a cart track cut through the cane fields, seeing no one until they were close to the house. Coxon seemed cautious, almost furtive, as though he wished to conceal his arrival. Eventually a white man, apparently a servant for he was dressed in a simple livery of a red jacket and white pantaloons, stopped them. He looked at them doubtfully, the buccaneer captain in his sweat-stained garments, Hector barefoot and wearing the same loose cotton shirt and trousers he had worn aboard ship. 'Do you have invitations?' he asked.

'Tell your master that Captain John Coxon wishes to speak with him privately,' the buccaneer told him curtly.

'Privately will not be possible,' answered the servant, hesitantly. 'Today's his day for Christmas entertainment.'

'I have come a long way to see your master,' snapped Coxon. 'I'm an acquaintance of long standing. I need no invitation.'

The servant quailed before the testy edge to his visitor's voice. 'Sir Henry's guests have already arrived and they are in the main reception room. If you would wish to refresh yourself before meeting them, please follow me.'

Hector had been standing with the captain's coat over his arm. It was evident that he was thought to be some sort of attendant and was not included in the invitation into the house. 'I'll be introducing my companion to Sir Henry,' Coxon announced firmly.

The servant's glance took in Hector's workaday costume. 'Then if you'll allow, I'll have him given something more suitable to wear. Sir Henry's gathering includes many of the most important men on the island, and their ladies.'

They followed the man to a side entrance of the main building. Tethered in front of its long sheltered porch were a dozen or more horses, and off to one side stood a couple of light, two-wheeled open carriages.

The servant showed Coxon into a side room, telling him that water and towels would be brought. Then he led Hector to the rear of the building and into the servants' quarters.

'I took you for an indentured man like myself,' he apologised.

'What's that?'

The servant, evidently an under-steward, had opened a cupboard and was sorting through some clothing. He found a pair of breeches and turned to face Hector.

'Indentured?' he said, sounding surprised. 'It means pledged to serve your master in return for the cost of your passage out from England and your upkeep while you're here.'

'For how long?'

'I signed for ten years, and still have seven years left. Here, try these breeches on. They are about the right size.'

As Hector pulled on the garment, the under-steward managed to find a short waistcoat and a clean lawn shirt with a frilled neck and wristbands. 'Here, put these on too,' he said, 'and this broad leather belt. It'll hide any gaps. And here's a pair of shoes that should fit, and stockings too.' He stood back and looked Hector over. 'Not bad,' he commented.

'Whom do these clothes belong to?' Hector asked.

'A young fellow came out here from England a couple of years back. Was intending to become an overseer, but he caught a flux and died.' The servant gathered up Hector's old clothes and tossed them into a corner. 'Forgot to ask your name,' he said.

'Lynch, Hector Lynch.'

'No relation to Sir Thomas are you?'

Hector decided it was wiser to be vague. 'Not as far as I am aware.'

'Just as well. Sir Henry can't abide Sir Thomas ... or his family for that matter.'

Hector saw his chance to learn more. 'Does Sir Thomas have a large family?'

'Big enough. Most of them live down near Port Royal. That's where they have their other properties.' He paused, and his next words came as a shock. 'But this being so near Christmas, Sir Henry has invited a few of them this evening. They came by carriage, a full day's journey. And one of them is quite a beauty.'

Hector could think of no escape as he was led back to where Coxon was waiting. The buccaneer captain had cleaned himself up and put on his wig. He looked more of a gentleman and less of a brigand. Taking Hector by the elbow, he led him aside and whispered harshly. 'Once we step into that room, you are to hold your tongue until I've found out Sir Henry's temper.'

The under-steward brought them before a pair of tall double doors. A buzz of conversation could be heard coming from the other side, and the strains of music, a couple of violins and a virginal by the sounds. As the servant was about to pull open both doors, Coxon stopped him. 'I can manage that myself,' he said. The buccaneer captain eased open one door and quietly stepped inside, pulling Hector behind him.

The room was thronged with guests. They were mostly men, but there was also a scattering of women, many using fans to lessen the stifling atmosphere. Scores of candles were adding to the lingering heat of the day, and although the windows stood open, the room was uncomfortably warm. Hector, who had seen the lavishly decorated salons of wealthy Barbary merchants, was surprised by how plainly this reception room was furnished. Although it was some thirty paces long, its plaster walls were bare except for one or two indifferent paintings, and there were no carpets to cover the hardwood floor. The room had a raw, unfinished look as though the owner, having constructed it, had no further interest in making it comfortable or attractive. Then he saw the sideboard. It must have been forty feet in length. It was covered from end to end with refreshments for the guests. There were heaps of oranges, pomegranates, limes, grapes and several varieties of luscious-looking fruit unknown to Hector, as well as massed arrangements of coloured jellies and sugar cakes, rank upon rank of wine bottles, and several large basins of some sort of punch. But it was not the array of exotic food which caught his eye. Every one of the platters, salvers and bowls holding the food and drink, as well as the ladles, tongs and serving implements beside them, appeared to be of solid silver, and if they were not of silver, they were made of gold. It was a breathtakingly vulgar display of bullion.

No one in the gossiping throng had noticed their entrance. Hector felt Coxon's hand on his elbow. 'Stay here until I come to fetch you, and remember what I said ... not a word to anyone until I have spoken with Sir Henry.' Hector watched the captain make his way discreetly through the assembly of guests. He was heading towards a group of men in the centre of the gathering. They were standing talking to one another, and it was evident from the space that had been left clear around them, the richness of their dress and their self-confident manner that they were the host and his chief guests. Among them was a tall, thin man with a sallow, almost sickly complexion, dressed in a plum-coloured velvet gown with gold trimming and a full-bottomed wig. He was talking to a fat, red-faced colleague in vaguely military attire who had several decorations pinned to his chest and wore a broad sash of blue silk. All the men in the group were holding glasses, and from their manner Hector guessed they had been drinking heavily. As he watched, Coxon reached the little group and, sidling round until he was next to the taller man, whispered something in his ear. His listener turned and, on seeing Coxon, an expression of irritation crossed his face. He was either annoyed at being interrupted or angered by the sight of Coxon. But the buccaneer stood his ground, and was explaining something, speaking rapidly, making some sort of point. When he stopped, the tall man nodded, turned and looked in Hector's direction. It was clear that whatever Coxon had been saying, it concerned Hector.

Coxon pushed his way back to where Hector waited. The buccaneer was flushed and excited, perspiring heavily under his wig, the sore patches on his neck prominent against the paler skin. 'Sir Henry will see you,' he said. 'Look smart now and follow me.' He turned and began to lead Hector into the centre of the room.

By now the little exchange had attracted the attention of several guests. Curious glances followed the newcomers' progress, and a path opened up for them as they walked forward. Hector felt himself light-headed as well as awkward in his borrowed clothes. With chilling certainty he knew that his deception was about to be exposed.

By the time the two men had reached the centre of the room, the babble of conversation was lessening. A hush had spread among the nearest spectators. The late arrival of two unfamiliar faces must have been some sort of diversion, for people were craning their necks to see what was happening. Coxon came to a halt before the taller man, bowed, and announced with a flourish:

'Sir Henry, allow me to introduce to you a young man that I took from a merchant ship recently. The vessel was stolen from its rightful owners and was in the hands of the thieves.

This is the young man's first visit to our island, but he comes with excellent connections. May I introduce Hector Lynch, nephew to our esteemed former governor Sir Thomas Lynch who, no doubt, will be in your debt for the rescue.'

The tall man in the plum-coloured coat turned to face Hector, who found himself looking into the pale eyes of Sir Henry Morgan, lieutenant governor of Jamaica.

'Lynch, did you say?' Sir Henry's voice was surprisingly thin and high pitched. He spoke with a slight slur, and Hector realised that the lieutenant governor was tipsy. He also looked very unhealthy. The whites of his eyes had a yellowish tinge, and though he must have been in his late forties, he did not carry his years well. Everything about him was gaunt – his face, shoulders and legs, yet his belly was bloated and jutted out unnaturally, straining the lower buttons of his coat. Hector wondered if Morgan was suffering from some sort of dropsy, or perhaps the effects of regular heavy drinking. But the eyes that looked him over were bright with intelligence, and speculative.

'Byndloss, did you hear that?' Morgan was speaking to his military-looking colleague, evidently a drinking companion to judge by the familiar tone. 'This young fellow is Sir Thomas's nephew. We must make him welcome to Llanrumney.'

'Didn't know Sir Thomas had any more nephews,' grunted Byndloss rudely. He too was drunk. His complexion was on its way to matching his red uniform jacket. Hector sensed a stir of unease from Coxon beside him.

'A junior branch of the family,' the buccaneer captain explained swiftly. His tone was obsequious. 'His father, Stephen, is the youngest of Sir Thomas's brothers.'

'Then how come he's not been out to visit us before? Some Lynches must think themselves too grand for us?' observed Byndloss petulantly. He took another drink from his glass, spilling a few drops down his chin.

'Don't be so prickly,' Sir Henry Morgan chided his friend.

'This is the Christmas season, a time to put aside our differences, and of course for families to get together.' Turning to Hector, who had still not said a word, he added in that high voice, 'Your family will be delighted by your arrival. I am pleased that it should have taken place under my roof.' From his greater height he looked out over his guests, and called out, 'Robert Lynch, where are you? Come and meet your cousin Hector!'

Hector could only stand helplessly, paralysed by the certain knowledge that his deception was about to be exposed in public.

There was a stir at the back of the gathering and a young man shouldered his way forward through the crowd of onlookers. Hector saw that Robert Lynch was about his own age, a round-headed, pleasant-looking fellow dressed fashionably in a brocade vest tied with a buckled girdle. His freckles and round grey-blue eyes gave him a remarkably boyish look.

'My cousin Hector, did you say?' Robert Lynch sounded eager, yet puzzled.

He stepped into the circle surrounding his host, and looked closely at Hector. He seemed baffled.

'Yes, yes. Your uncle Stephen's son . . . he landed unexpectedly just this morning, with Captain Coxon.' Morgan answered, and turning to Hector asked, 'Where did you say you are from?'

For the first time at that gathering, Hector spoke. His false identity was about to be exposed, and he knew he could no longer maintain the deception. 'There's a misunderstanding . . .' he croaked. His throat was dry from nerves.

Morgan checked, his eyes narrowed and he was about to speak, when Robert Lynch announced in astonishment, 'But I don't have an uncle. Two aunts, yes, but no Uncle Stephen. No one ever said anything about a cousin Hector.'

For a long, unpleasant moment, Sir Henry Morgan said nothing. He stared at Hector, then switched his gaze to Coxon, who was rooted to the spot. Hector and all those in earshot tensed, awaiting an outburst of rage. Instead Morgan let loose a sudden, ringing neigh of laughter. 'Captain Coxon, you've been taken in! You've swallowed the gudgeon, every last morsel. Sir Thomas's nephew indeed!' Beside him, Byndloss let out a guffaw and, waving his glass, added, 'Are you sure that he's not Sir Thomas's son and heir?'

A wave of sycophantic laughter washed around them as the crowd of onlookers joined in the mirth.

Coxon flushed crimson with embarrassment. He clenched his hands by his side and swung to glare straight at Hector. For an instant the young man thought that the buccaneer, his face working with anger, was about to strike him, but Coxon only snarled, 'You will regret this, you little swine!' and turned on his heel. Then he stalked out of the room, followed by the hoots of laughter, and someone calling out over the heads of the crowd, 'He's *Sir* Hector, you know.'

Like a good host, Morgan turned back to his friends who were still smirking at Coxon's humiliation, and they took up their former conversation. Pointedly, Hector was ignored. Awkwardly he stood there in his borrowed clothes, uncertain what he should do next. He feared to follow Coxon in case the buccaneer captain might be waiting for him outside the door.

While he stood there hesitating, a sharp rap on his elbow made him jump, and a female voice said playfully, 'I would very much like to meet my new cousin.' He turned to find himself looking into the mischievous smile of a young woman in a light evening cloak of turquoise satin. She was a couple of inches shorter than himself, and no more than seventeen years old. Yet the shape of her body was accentuated by a tight bodice whose low neckline was only partially covered by a lace-trimmed gorget to reveal the curves of full womanhood. Involuntarily Hector found himself reflecting that women ripened in the Jamaican climate as early and seductively as the island's exotic fruit. Her dark brown hair was arranged so that it tumbled down to her shoulders, but she had left a fringe of curls to frame the wide-set blue eyes which now regarded him with such amusement. In her hand was the fan which she had used to attract his attention. 'I am Susanna Lynch, Robert's sister,' she told him in a light, attractive voice. 'It's not often that a relation appears from nowhere.'

Hector found himself blushing. 'I'm sorry,' he began, 'I meant no disrespect. Lynch truly is my family name. The deception was forced upon me to protect myself and my friends . . .'

She interrupted him with a quick grimace. 'I don't doubt it. Captain Coxon has a reputation as a ruthless man, always eager to advance himself. In him you have made a dangerous enemy. Someone you had best avoid in future.'

'I know almost nothing about him,' Hector confessed.

'He's a ruffian. He used to consort with Henry Morgan in the days when harrying the Spanish was permitted. But that's against government policy now, largely thanks to the efforts of our "uncle".' Here she smiled teasingly. 'Men like Coxon still hang around on the fringes, waiting to snap up anything that has been overlooked. There are plenty who would help him.'

'I gather that sometimes includes Sir Henry.'

She gave him a sharp glance. 'You are quick on the uptake. I heard Morgan say that you only landed this morning in Jamaica, yet you've already sniffed out a few truths.'

'Someone told me that Sir Henry Morgan's preferences still incline towards his former buccaneering friends.'

'Indeed they do,' Susanna said casually. Hector had to admire the young woman's self-confidence, for she did not bother to drop her voice. 'Henry Morgan is still as gold-hungry as ever. But he is now on the governing council and a very powerful man. He's someone else you should be wary of.'

With every moment Hector found himself appreciating much more than Susanna Lynch's self-confidence. The way she stood before him, with her eyes boldly seeking his, left no doubt that she was deliberately calling for his attention. She was a very alluring young lady, and knew it. With a pang, Hector realised that he had never before had an opportunity to engage closely with a young woman so obviously on display. He realised that he was succumbing to her good looks and, without wishing to, falling under the spell of her provocation.

'Then I'm at a loss as to what I should do next,' he admitted. 'I feel stranded. I don't know anyone in Jamaica.'

She gave him a calculating look, though there was softness in it. 'No one at all?'

'My friends were despatched to the French colony at Petit Guave, and I need to try to join them.'

'One thing is for certain. You should get away from Llanrumney as soon as possible. You'll get no sympathy in this place.' She thought for a moment, then treated him to a quick smile which made his heart race. 'Tomorrow Robert and I return home – we live on the opposite side of the island, near Spanish Town, not far from Port Royal. You can travel with us, and from there continue to Port Royal itself. That's the best place to find news of your friends, or even a ship that will take you to rejoin them.'

THREE

THAT NIGHT Hector found it almost impossible to get to sleep. The friendly under-steward arranged a cot for him in the servants' quarters, but keen yearnings for Susanna Lynch kept the young man awake for several hours, and when he opened his eyes soon after dawn, her image was the first thing in his mind. Dressing hurriedly, he went to find someone who might be able to tell him where she could be found. To his delight the under-steward told him that the carriage belonging to Susanna Lynch was already prepared. She and her brother Robert were to set out for home shortly, and word had been sent that Hector was to travel with them.

'Will they breakfast with Sir Henry first?' he asked, impatient for his first sight of Susanna that day. The indentured man gave a world-weary laugh.

'Sir Henry and his cronies were up drinking until well past midnight. My master will not be out of his bed much before noon.'

'What about Captain Coxon? Where's he?' Hector asked. He had a sudden, vivid recollection of the furious expression on the buccaneer's face as he had left the party.

'Disappeared last night, after you made such a fool of him. I suppose he went back to his ship with his tail between his legs.' The servant grinned. 'He's an arrogant blackguard. Likes to let everyone know what a hard man he is. Can't say I would want to be in your shoes if he ever gets his hands on you.'

'Someone else said much the same to me last night,' admitted Hector, 'and talking about shoes, shouldn't I be returning these borrowed clothes to you?'

'You can keep them.'

'Won't your master find out?'

'I doubt it. The rum has been rotting his brain for a long time now. When he was campaigning against the Spaniards some years back, he and his friends blew themselves up. They were sitting carousing in the wardroom of a King's ship, and some drunken fool dropped his lighted pipe into a scatter of loose gunpowder on the floor. The explosion split the vessel into matchwood. Sir Henry was only saved because he was sitting at the far side of the table.'

Thanking the man for his kindness, Hector made his way outside to find that one of the carriages he had seen the previous evening was already standing before the front door of the main house. 'Is this the Lynches' carriage?' he asked the driver who, by the look of him, was another indentured servant. But before the man could answer, Susanna and her brother stepped out on the porch. Suddenly Hector felt his stomach go hollow. Susanna had chosen to wear a loose gown of fine cotton, dark pink, with short sleeves. It was open at the front to reveal a bodice laced with ribbon, and her grey skirt was looped up at one side to show a matching satin petticoat. Her hair was held back by a ribbon embroidered with roses. She looked ravishing.

Her brother greeted Hector cheerfully. 'You caused quite a stir yesterday evening! I'm told that the fellow you discomforted is an utter scoundrel, and well deserved to be put in his place. Always creeping about and trying to ingratiate himself. My sister tells me that your family name really is Lynch.'

'It's a happy coincidence which I was obliged to turn in my favour.'

'Well, no harm done. Susanna tells me that you will travel with us, so I've arranged an extra horse for you.'

To his chagrin Hector saw that a groom had appeared from behind the house, leading two saddle horses. But Susanna came to his rescue. 'Robert, you are not to deprive me of Mr Lynch's company. It will make the journey pass more agreeably if he joins me in the carriage, at least for the first few hours.'

'As you please, Susanna. His horse can be attached to the carriage until needed,' answered her brother meekly, and Hector could see that Robert usually gave way to his sister. Susanna Lynch climbed into the carriage and took her seat. 'Come, sit beside me, Hector. After all, we are cousins,' she said invitingly, and gave a throaty chuckle which sent Hector's mind reeling.

The road was very bad, little more than a dirt track which, after passing a neighbouring plantation, climbed inland by a series of tight curves on to a spur ridge covered with dense forest. On either side grew immense trees, mostly mahogany and cedar, smothered with rope-like lianas and other climbing plants. Some showed the pale flowers of convolvuli, others hung from the branches in shaggy grey beards. Here and there was the bright crimson or yellow blossom of an orchid. A profusion of ferns and canes sprouted between the massive tree trunks, forming impenetrable thickets of greenery above which hovered butterflies of extraordinary shapes and colours, dark blue, lemon yellow and black. In the background was the constant chatter and calls of unseen birds, ranging from a flute-like whistle to the harsh cawing of crows. All this Hector barely noticed. For him the first few hours of the journey passed in a daze. He was acutely aware of the nearness of Susanna, her warmth and softness, and the jolting of the carriage which occasionally brought her knee in contact with his, a contact which, if he was not mistaken, she occasionally allowed to linger. Her brother rode on ahead so they were left alone to their conversation, ignored by the driver seated on the box in front of them.

In this heady atmosphere Hector found himself pouring out his life story, telling his companion about his days in Barbary, the time he had spent as a prisoner of the Turks, his escape, and how he came to be aboard *L'Arc-de-Ciel*.

It was as they crossed the watershed and began to descend the farther slope and the forest began to thin out in more open woodland that he finally thought to ask her, 'Why did Captain Coxon bring me to Llanrumney?'

Susanna replied without hesitation. 'Knowing Coxon's reputation, I would say that he was trying to curry favour with Henry Morgan. As you already know, Sir Henry is at odds with my uncle who is expected to return here for a second term as governor. Morgan is always looking for ways to gain advantage over Sir Thomas, whom he sees as his rival. The fact that a nephew of Sir Thomas was found aboard a stolen ship could have been useful in his power struggle. Coxon would have been keen to deliver you into Henry Morgan's hands so that it could be shown that the Lynch family stooped to robbery on the high seas.'

'But Coxon had no proof of that,' Hector objected.

'If the French at Petit Guave decide that your friends stole *L'Arc-de-Ciel*, then you too would be guilty of piracy, and Morgan could have you hanged. That would be a neat twist and give Morgan a great deal of satisfaction because it was Sir Thomas who brought in the death penalty for buccaneering. He said it was little better than piracy. Then again, perhaps Morgan would have you thrown in prison and held, to be used as a pawn when Sir Thomas returns.'

Hector shook his head in bewilderment. 'But it is Coxon who acts the pirate, not me.'

Susanna gave a snort of derision. 'The truth is of no consequence. What matters is the way the wind is blowing, who has the most power on this island, the most influence back in London, or the most money to lay out in bribes.'

She broke off her explanation as her brother Robert

appeared alongside the carriage and reined in his horse. He was looking worried. 'Listen!' he said, 'I think I hear noises in the woods, somewhere over to the left.'

Moments later came the sound of a gunshot, followed by whoops and shouts, and then the baying of dogs. The carriage driver hastily reached under his seat and produced a blunderbuss even as Robert pulled a pistol out of his saddlebag and began to load it. 'Hector,' he said urgently, 'I think you had better get up on your horse in case we have to defend ourselves. There's a sword in my luggage. I trust you know how to use it.'

'What's the trouble?' Hector asked as he began to search for the weapon.

'No one lives in these woods,' came the reply. 'I fear we might have run into a roving gang of maroons.'

'Who are they?'

'Runaway slaves.'

Hector paused as the shouts came again, very much louder and closer. Now there was also the noise of bodies crashing through the undergrowth. Unsheathing the sword that he found, Hector unfastened his horse from the carriage and swung up into the saddle. The disturbance seemed to be coming from behind the carriage, and he turned his horse to face back down the track. A minute later several black shapes burst out of the undergrowth and raced across the path before vanishing into the thickets on the opposite side. They were pigs, wild ones, led by a massive boar, its jaws flecked with foam. The boar smashed a gap through the undergrowth, and behind him scampered at least a dozen piglets, small dark hairy creatures, which disappeared equally suddenly from view. Then came an interval when the track was empty until, equally abruptly, a human figure sprang out onto the path. He was a tall, black man with long matted hair down to his shoulders. Barefoot and naked to the waist, his only garment was a pair of tattered loose pantaloons. In one hand he held a hunting spear, and there was a heavy cutlass hanging from a strap over his shoulder.

He was some thirty yards away. He checked his stride and turned to face Hector. For a moment he paused, seeing the young man, sword in hand, the carriage behind him with its driver and the seated woman, a second rider armed with a pistol. There was no fear, only calculation in the black man's expression. Behind him half a dozen hunting dogs appeared on the track, running nose down and following the scent of the wild pigs. They also crossed the path and disappeared on the far side. But the black man stayed where he was, eyeing the travellers. Hector felt a cold spike of fear as a second, then a third black man appeared from the bushes. They too were armed. One of them held a musket. All three stood still, sizing up the travellers. Hector tightened his grip on the sword, the hilt now slippery with his sweat. Beneath him the horse, alarmed by the dogs and the wild-looking strangers, began to fidget nervously. Hector feared that the animal might rear up. If he was thrown to the ground, the hunters might take their chance to attack. He was also very conscious of Susanna in the carriage just behind him. She must be looking back, seeing the danger and aware that only he stood between her and the runaway slaves. For what seemed like an age, both sides regarded one another in total silence. Then a sudden burst of barking deep within the undergrowth broke the tension. The hunting dogs must have cornered their prey because the sound rose to an excited crescendo. The nearest black man turned and, raising his spear, waved his comrades onward towards the sound of the hunting pack. As suddenly as they had arrived, all three hunters vanished into the undergrowth.

Hector found himself in a cold sweat of relief as he looked back at Susanna. She was slightly pale but otherwise remarkably calm. Her brother seemed to be the more shocked. 'I never thought there were maroons in this area,' he said, and he sounded contrite. 'If I had known, I would have arranged an escort, or made sure we had travelled in greater company for safety. They were hunting well outside their usual territory.'

'Those men looked savage,' Hector commented.

'That's how they got their name,' Robert explained. 'The Spaniards called them *cimarron*, meaning wild or untamed. The first maroons were slaves whom the Spanish left behind on the island when the English took Jamaica from Spain. Now the maroons have gone native. They've established themselves in the roughest parts of the country, in areas too difficult for them to be rooted out.'

'Mr Lynch was telling me that his best friend is also a native, a Miskito,' Susanna intervened.

'Oh, the Miskito are very different,' her brother replied. 'They are good allies to the English and the French, or so I'm told. Besides, they are not found in Jamaica. They live on the mainland, and they hate the Spanish.'

'Mr Lynch's mother is Spanish,' warned Susanna.

'I'm sorry,' Robert replied, blushing. 'Nothing I say seems to strike the right note.'

'I've never heard of the maroons before,' Hector hastened to assure him. 'They seem to live in much the same way as the first buccaneers . . . by hunting wild animals.'

'That's true,' said Robert. 'Indeed my uncle told me that the buccaneers are named after the boucans, the racks on which they grill the flesh of the beasts they kill. It's a French word, the same which the Spanish call a barbacoa or barbecue.'

'I'm sure Mr Lynch finds all this fascinating,' said his sister. 'But don't you think we should be getting on our way. If we stand here talking long enough, the maroons may return and find us here.'

'Yes, yes. Of course,' her brother replied. And then to Hector's chagrin he added, 'Just in case we do encounter any further trouble, perhaps it would be best if he kept my sword for the moment and stayed on horseback.'

❋

THE LITTLE GROUP travelled on and as if to make up for his lapse of judgement, Robert made a point of riding beside Hector. He chatted with the young Irishman in his friendly manner, explaining to him the more interesting features of the countryside as gradually the land began to slope downward and became more open until eventually they were riding through open savannah. He pointed out wild cattle grazing among the low bushes, and spoke enthusiastically about the fertility of the soil. 'What you do is purchase one hundred acres of prime Jamaican land and invest just four hundred pounds in half a dozen slaves and spades and tools. You have your slaves clear the ground, then plant and cultivate cocoa, and in the fourth year the crop will give you back your original investment. After that, if you are shrewd and your slaves have also set cassava and maize and built their own huts, you have no further expenses. Year after year your cocoa will bring in four hundred pounds back and maybe more. Everything is pure profit.'

But Hector could think only about Susanna riding in the carriage so close to him, and he found it difficult to pay attention to her brother and his business talk. He forced himself not to glance around to look at her, for fear of seeming foolishly besotted. Luckily Robert did not seem to notice his listener's preoccupation and prattled on until, from behind, Susanna called out.

'Robert, do stop talking about money and point out that bird to Mr Lynch. There, over to your left beside the bush with orange flowers. He will not have seen anything like it before.'

Indeed, at first sight, Hector thought that Susanna was mistaken. A large brown and grey butterfly was feeding on the blossoms, moving from one flower to the next. Then Hector saw that it was not a butterfly but a tiny bird, just over an inch long, which was hovering in position, its wings a blur. Turning aside he rode closer, and the bird suddenly rose from the bush and came towards him. For several seconds the tiny creature hovered close beside his head, and he distinctly heard the sound of its wings, a delicate hur! hur! hur!

'Your first hummingbird, Mr Lynch!' called out Susanna.

'It is indeed a remarkable creature. It makes a sound like a miniature spinning wheel,' Hector agreed, able at last to turn and look directly at her.

'You have the soul of an artist, Mr Lynch,' she said, with a smile of delight which made him dizzy. 'Wait until you've seen its cousin. The one they call a streamer. It flies in the same way and has two long velvet black tail feathers which dangle in the air, and you can hear them fluttering. When the sunlight strikes its breast, the feathers flash emerald, then olive or deepest black as the creature turns.'

Hector was tongue-tied. He wanted desperately to say something gallant to this divine creature, to continue the conversation, but he could find no words. The way he looked at her, though, could have left no doubt about the way he felt.

It was some hours later, as the sun was nearing the horizon, that he heard a sound he recognised. It was a long-drawn-out call like a distant trumpet and he had heard it before, on the coast of Africa, and knew it to be someone blowing a call on a conch shell. 'Are we so close to the sea?' he asked Robert.

'No,' the young man replied. 'It's one of our farm workers calling in the hogs. They feed by day in the savannah, but come back to the sty at night when they hear that call. They are unexpectedly intelligent animals. That sound also means that this is where we turn off for Spanish Town.'

He reached out to offer Hector a handshake of farewell.

'The road to Port Royal is straight ahead. It's no more than a couple of hours' walk to the ferry. If you hurry, you should be able to get there while it is still daylight. I wish you well.'

With sudden dismay, Hector realised that his journey beside Susanna was at an end. Crestfallen, he swung himself out of the saddle of his borrowed horse, and handed the reins to Robert.

'Thank you for allowing me to accompany you this far,' he said.

'No, it is I who have to thank you,' Robert replied. 'Your presence helped deter the maroons from attacking us. If we had been fewer, we might have become their prey.'

Walking stiffly across to the carriage, Hector stood beside its door and looked up into Susanna's blue eyes. Once again, he did not know what to say. He did not dare to take her hand, and she did not offer it. Instead she gave him a demure smile, less coquettish now, more serious. 'Goodbye, Hector,' she said. 'I hope you find your friends and, after that, perhaps your path will lead you back to Jamaica so we will meet again. I feel there is more that we have in common than just our names.' With that the carriage moved away, leaving Hector standing in the red dirt road, and hoping fervently he had been more than a day's amusement for the first girl he had ever fallen in love with.

FOUR

PORT ROYAL had more taverns than Hector imagined possible in such a small area. He counted eighteen of them in the ten minutes it took him to walk from one end of the town to the other. They ranged from The Feathers, a grimy-looking alehouse close by the fish market, to the new-built Three Mariners where he turned back, realising that he had reached the town limits. Retracing his steps along the main waterfront, Thames Street, he found himself skirting around stove-in barrels, broken handcarts, discarded sacking, and several drunks lying snoring in the rubbish or slumped against the doors of the warehouses which lined one side of the street. The wharves across the road were built on pilings because Port Royal perched on the tip of a sand spit and land was very scarce. Every berth was occupied. Vessels were loading cargoes of tobacco, hides and skins, indigo and ebony, and above all sugar whose earthy, sickly sweet smell Hector was beginning to recognise. Whenever he met a longshoreman or a half-sober sailor he asked if any of the vessels might be bound for Petit Guave, but he was always disappointed. Often his request was ignored, or the hurried reply was accompanied by an oath. It seemed that Port Royal was a place where most inhabitants were too busy making money or spending it in debauchery for them to give a civil response.

The town was also astonishingly expensive. He had arrived there at dawn on the morning after saying goodbye to Susanna and her brother, and the ferryman had demanded six pence to bring him from the mainland. It was no more than a two-mile trip across the anchorage, and Hector had been obliged to spend half the night on the beach until the night breeze was favourable. He had no money for the fare so he had sold his coat to the ferryman for a few coins. Now, looking for something to eat for his breakfast, Hector turned into one of the taverns – it was the Cat and Fiddle – and was taken aback by the price of a meal. 'Just a drink of water will suffice,' he said.

'You can have beer, Madeira wine, punch, brandy, or rap,' the man replied.

'What's rap?'

'Good strong drink made from molasses,' came the reply, and when he insisted that water was enough, he was advised to stick with beer. 'Nobody drinks water here,' observed the potman. 'The local water gives you the gripes. The only drinkable stuff has to be brought in barrels from the mainland so you'll still have to pay: a penny a jug.'

Hungry and thirsty, Hector abandoned the tavern and went back out into the street where a frowzy strumpet flaunted herself from an upper window and beckoned to him. When he shook his head, she spat over the balcony. It was not ten in the morning yet, but the day was already hot and sticky, and he had not the least idea what he should do, or where he should stay. He had resolved to remain in Port Royal until he could find passage to catch up with Dan and Jacques, but first he had to find some sort of employment and a roof above his head.

He cut through a narrow laneway and emerged on the high street. The close-packed houses were substantial, brick built and two or three stories high. Most had shops or offices on the ground floor, and living accommodation above them. Shoulder to shoulder with alehouses and brothels were the premises of tradesmen – cordwainers with their shop windows full of shoes, tailors displaying rolls of cloth, two or three furniture makers, a hatter and a pipemaker as well as three gunsmiths. Their businesses seemed to be flourishing. He passed a vegetable market at the central crossroads and reached the end of the street. Here the early-morning meat market was already closing down because the slabs of hog flesh and beef on display would soon begin to stink. Large, black flies were settling on the blood-encrusted tables, and he was puzzled to see two men lugging between them what looked like a heavy shallow cauldron. On closer inspection it turned out to be an unsold turtle, upside down and still alive. Curious to see what they would do with it, he watched them carry the animal to a short ramp leading down to the water's edge. There they placed it in a fenced holding pen half in and half out of the water, a turtle crawl where the creature could drag itself into the shallows, to await the next day's sales.

At the end of the high street, he was close back where he had started, for he recognised the bulk of the fort which guarded the anchorage. Turning left, he entered a thoroughfare that looked more respectable, though the roadway was still nothing more than an expanse of hard packed sand. He noted the door plaques of several doctors, then a goldsmith's shop, securely shuttered. Next to an apothecary's hung a trade sign which raised his hope: it depicted a pair of mapmaker's compasses and a pencil stub. The proprietor's name was written underneath in black letters on a scroll: Robert Snead.

Hector pushed open the door and stepped inside.

He found himself in a low-ceilinged room, furnished sparsely with a large table, half a dozen plain wooden chairs and a desk. In the light of an open window an older man was seated at the desk. He was wearing a shabby wig and a rumpled gown of brown linen. His head was bent over his work as he scratched away with a quill pen. On hearing his visitor enter, he looked up and Hector saw that the man had thick spectacles balanced on a nose that showed a drunkard's broken veins.

'Can I help you?' the man asked. He removed the spectacles and rubbed a hand across his eyes. They were bloodshot.

'I would like to speak with Mr Snead,' Hector said.

'I am Robert Snead. Are you looking for a design or practical advice?' The man's near-sighted gaze took in Hector's clothing which, now that he had sold his jacket, was not as respectable as it had seemed earlier.

'I hope to find employment, sir,' Hector answered. 'My name is Hector Lynch. I have worked with maps and charts, and have a fair hand.'

Robert Snead looked uneasy. 'I am an architect and surveyor, not a mapmaker.' He shifted uncomfortably in his chair. 'Anyone who makes maps and charts, or sells them, needs to have a licence.'

'I did not know,' Hector apologised. 'I saw the sign outside and thought it was for a mapmaker.'

'We use many of the same tools of trade,' Snead admitted. He gave Hector a shrewd glance. 'Is it true that you can work with charts?'

'Yes, sir. I have worked with coastal maps, harbour plans, and the like.' Hector thought it politic not to mention that his work had been for a Turkish admiral in Barbary.

Snead thought for a moment. Then, sliding a sheet of paper and a pen across the desk towards him, he said, 'Show me what you can do. Draw me an anchorage protected by a reef, showing the depths and marking the best place where a vessel might lie.'

Hector did as he was asked, and after Snead had inspected the little drawing, he rose from his chair and said cautiously, 'Well ... there may be something for you to do after all, for a few days at least. If you will follow me.' He led Hector up a flight of stairs at the back of his shop and brought him into the room directly above. Its balcony looked out over the street. Here too was a broad table, apparently used for entertaining as it was set with pewter plates and mugs and there were several chairs and a bench beside it. Snead pushed aside the tableware to leave a clear space, and crossing to a chest standing in one corner lifted the lid and took out several sheets of parchment. He laid them on the table and began to leaf through them. 'These are for the conveyancing lawyers and landowners,' the architect explained. The top sheets were surveyor's plans of what seemed to be plantations, and it was evident that an important part of the architect's job was to make drawings that established the boundaries of newly cleared estates. These sheets Snead laid aside until he came to what was obviously a sea chart concealed among the other papers. The chart was in some detail for it extended across two sheets of parchment. Snead took just one of the pages and spread it out on the table. 'Can you make a fair copy of that?' he asked, peering over his spectacles, and carefully turning the second sheet face down.

Hector glanced down at the map. It was a navigation chart. It showed a length of coastline, various off-shore islands and a number of landmarks which would be useful to anyone navigating along the coast. He had no idea what coast it displayed.

'Yes,' he replied. 'That should not be difficult.'

'How long would it take you?'

'Two days, perhaps less.'

'Then you've got yourself ten days' work if the first copy is to my satisfaction. I'll want five copies made and I'll pay two pounds for each, plus a bonus if they are ready by next Wednesday.' He paused, and gave Hector a sly look. 'But you don't leave this house, and you don't speak to anyone about the work. I'll arrange for my housekeeper to prepare your meals, and you can sleep in a spare room in the garret. Do you understand?'

'Yes, of course,' said Hector. He was scarcely able to believe his good fortune. On his first morning in Port Royal he had found both employment and accommodation. With the pay he could resume his search for a ship that would take him to Petit Guave.

'Good,' said Snead, 'then you can begin work as soon as you have gone to collect your things.'

'I have nothing to collect,' Hector admitted.

Snead looked him up and down, a gleam of understanding in his eyes.

'Runaway, are you? Well, that's no concern of mine,' he said with obvious satisfaction, 'but if you breathe a word to anyone about your work, I'll see to it that your master learns exactly where you are to be found.' He nodded towards the pile of surveys. 'Most of the big landowners and the wealthy merchants come to seek my services, and I can soon find out who is missing an indentured man.'

*

BEFORE THE DAY was out, Hector had discovered that Snead was not as fierce as he at first made out. The architect had scarcely left the young man to his work in the upper room when he came back up the stairs and announced that he was closing his shop and would be back in half an hour. If Hector needed additional supplies of paper, pens and ink, he would find them in the downstairs office. A moment later the young man heard the front door close, and glancing out of the window he saw Snead walking off down the street, then turn into a nearby alehouse. When Snead came back rather more than an hour later, Hector concluded that his employer was drunk. He heard him knock over a chair as he fumbled his way back to his desk. By then Hector had identified the region shown by the chart he was copying.

It was a map of the Caribbean shores of Central America. He remembered the general outline of the coast from the smaller scale chart that he had used aboard *L'Arc-de-Ciel*. Now he was being asked to copy out a larger and much more accurate version which covered the northern half of that coast. He guessed that the second sheet, the one that Snead had hidden from him, showed the southern portion. Clearly someone had recently sailed along the coast and made numerous observations. The sheet in front of him was covered with handwritten notes to help a navigator recognise his landfall, then track his progress, avoiding reefs and other outlying dangers, select from a number of different harbours and anchorages, and find watering places. Whoever had written these notes had not ventured more than a few miles inland because the interior of the countryside was left blank.

The map seemed harmless and it was puzzling that Snead was being so secretive about it. Hector supposed that even if the architect was caught dealing in maps without a licence, he would receive only a minor penalty. Yet more mysterious was the fact that he needed five copies.

As Hector began work, Susanna's image kept appearing in his thoughts. He saw her walking in the garden of her father's plantation house, or as he had last seen her, seated in a carriage and smiling at him gravely. From time to time he put aside his drawing materials and gazed sightlessly out of the window, dreaming of what it must be like to hold her in his arms. Once or twice he even dared to wonder whether she too was thinking about him.

His reverie was broken by the sound of Snead's footsteps on the stair. With a start Hector realised that it was late in the day. When the architect entered the room, he glanced over the part-finished copy that Hector had been working on, and appeared to be satisfied with what he saw, for he sat down heavily on the bench at the end of the table and announced that it was time for Hector to stop work. 'So you say your name is Lynch,' he observed, picking up the quill pen that Hector had been using. 'Not a convincing nom de plume.' He waved the feather in the air, smirking owlishly at his pun. 'I would have thought you could have come up with something more original.'

Hector realised that Snead was convinced that he was sheltering a fugitive indentured man, also that the architect was very tipsy. He smelled the rum on his new employer's breath.

'Lynch is my real name, sir,' Hector protested.

Snead seemed not to hear him. He gave a drunken hiccup and stared at Hector. 'You can't be a Lynch. You don't look like one.'

Hector saw his opportunity. 'You know the Lynches, sir?' he asked.

'Who doesn't? Richest family on the island. I've done surveys for three of their plantations. They must own at least thirty thousand acres.'

'Have you met Robert Lynch or his sister?' Hector was desperate to glean a few more details about Susanna.

'Young Robert? He came to the office a few times when I was doing drawings for their new townhouse here in Port Royal. And a very elegant structure it is, if I do say so myself,' Snead hiccuped.

'And what about his sister?'

'You mean Susanna? I think that's her name. Quite a catch, that one. I doubt there's anyone on the island who would be a match for her. She'll probably find her husband in London next time she goes there. Pretty girl but said to be headstrong.'

Snead swivelled round on the bench to face the door. Raising his voice, he shouted for food to be brought. A voice answered from somewhere deep within the house, and a little while later an elderly woman, whom Hector presumed to be Snead's housekeeper, appeared with a tray of food which she placed on the table.

'Come on. You share this with me,' said the architect, waving to a seat near him as he began to ladle soup into his mouth. Hector came to the conclusion that the architect was a lonely man and eager for company.

*

IT WAS MID-MORNING on the following day that Hector received an unwelcome jolt of recognition. He had slept the night in a small room on the topmost floor of Snead's premises, and next morning with the tropical sunlight flooding his work table from the open window, he had made good progress with copying the first chart. He was at the stage when he had drawn the coastline and all its islands and reefs, and begun to write in their names, consulting the handwritten notes from the original. He was labelling the anchorages and harbours when he saw that one of the anchorages was marked 'Captain Coxon's Hole'. He checked the handwritten notes again, and there was no mistake. A small natural harbour on one of the islands had been named after the buccaneer. Hector could see that it made an ideal refuge. The island lay far enough off the mainland to be rarely visited, and the anchorage was very discreet. It was concealed behind a reef, and protected by a low ridge of hills. So when Snead came to check on his employee's progress just before his noontime visit to the tavern, Hector casually asked how Coxon's Hole had got its name. The reaction he received was a surprise.

'It's named after a friend of mine,' Snead announced and he sounded proud of the association. 'He used to have a house here in Port Royal. Knows that coast as well as anyone. Discovered that anchorage and been using it on and off ever since.'

Hector puzzled over the architect's answer all that afternoon, and when Snead was in a particularly good mood at supper, he asked the architect when he had last seen his friend. 'Not for the past couple of years but – who knows – he could turn up at any time.'

Hector noted how Snead had cast a quick glance towards the finished chart still lying on the end of the table. Alarmed, Hector risked a further question.

'Is Captain Coxon a good customer then?'

His enquiry was met with a suspicious stare. Then Snead must have decided that he could trust his new assistant. Rising from his chair he took the second page of the chart from the chest and laid it beside the one that Hector had just completed. As Hector had suspected, the two maps covered almost the entire Caribbean coast of Central America. Waving his hand over the maps, Snead exclaimed, 'There you have it! The key to the South Sea!' Then he sat back down heavily in his usual place and picked up his tankard.

'The South Sea?' Hector asked. 'But that's on the far side of the isthmus. Is that not another word for the Pacific?'

'You misunderstand me,' Snead declared, waving at the map again. 'Here we have the gateway. The riches lie beyond. We are opening the way for our clients.'

'And will we also provide them with charts of the South Sea?' Hector enquired.

Snead looked at him in drunken astonishment.

'Charts of the South Sea!' he exclaimed. 'You speak of Golconda and the Valley of Diamonds! If I had such charts, either I could command a king's ransom or both of us would find ourselves victims of a Spanish stiletto.'

'For what reason?'

'How else do the Spaniards sail up and down the coast of Peru, and safely bring back the silver from their mines and the other products of their possessions in South America, if they did not have such maps? But they are state secrets. Men would murder for them. That is why men talk of the South Sea Adventure.'

Abruptly the architect must have realised that he had said too much for he quickly swept up both charts, rose to his feet and walked unsteadily across the room to put them back in the chest. Then, mumbling a farewell, he set out for his evening's drinking in the tavern.

*

NEXT MORNING Snead had still not appeared in his shop when Hector heard a knock on the door to the street. Opening it, he found a middle-aged, weather-beaten man dressed in a sea captain's coat that looked the worse for wear. 'I wish to speak with Robert Snead,' the visitor asked.

'I'm afraid he is not available,' Hector said. 'Perhaps I can help.'

The man stepped inside, and closed the door behind him. He looked carefully at Hector, then said, 'I've come for a chart.'

'I'm afraid that Mr Snead is an architect . . .' Hector began, but his response was brushed aside.

'I know all about that,' the man replied, 'but I've bought maps from him before. The name is Gutteridge, Captain Gutteridge.'

'Then perhaps you will wait here, and I will consult Mr Snead,' Hector answered. Leaving Gutteridge in the shop he hurried up to the architect's bedchamber. He found Snead still in bed, huddled under a quilt and dressed in his nightclothes. He was looking liverish and the room stank of liquor.

'There's a Captain Gutteridge in the shop,' Hector began. 'He's come for a map. I told him that you do not deal with maps. But he says he's bought them from you before.'

Snead gave a groan. 'And never paid me for them either,' he said sourly. 'Go back down, and tell Captain Gutteridge that he won't get any more charts until he's settled his account.'

On his way back to the shop, Hector found that the captain had followed him up the stairs and was now standing in the room where Hector worked, looking down at the chart being copied.

'That . . .' said Gutteridge, tapping the chart with a blunt forefinger, 'will do me very well.'

'I'm afraid it is not for sale. It's a special order.'

'I suppose it must be for that lot who are assembling off Negril.'

'I have no idea. They are for Mr Snead's private clients.'

Gutteridge noticed the stain of ink on Hector's fingers. 'Are you his draughtsman?' he asked, and when Hector nodded, he gave the young man a sideways look and said, 'How about letting me have a copy, on the side. I'd make it worth your while.'

'That's not possible, I'm afraid. And Mr Snead asked that you settle your account.'

Gutteridge shrugged. He seemed unperturbed. 'Then I'll do without. A pity. I wish you good day.' He descended the stairs but on reaching the ground floor, he turned and made one last appeal to Hector. 'If you change your mind,' he said, 'you'll find my ship, the *Jamaica Merchant*, at the quay at Thames Street. She'll be there for three days at most, then I sail for Campeachy to load logwood.'

Hector hesitated for a moment before asking, 'By any chance will you be calling at Petit Guave on your way?'

Gutteridge fingered the lapel of his shabby coat. 'I'm thinking of it. French brandy is popular with the Bay Men.' Then he walked across the shop and let himself out into the street.

The moment Gutteridge left, Hector hurried back to his work table. He still had two more charts to prepare and it was only three days before they must be ready. If he could finish them in time and get his pay from Snead, he might be able to purchase a passage aboard the *Jamaica Merchant* and find his way to Petit Guave to rejoin Jacques and Dan. Glancing out of the window as he picked up his pen, he watched Gutteridge walking away down the street. As the sea captain passed the door to Snead's favourite tavern Hector saw a figure which he recognised. Loitering on the doorstep of the grog shop was the sailor he had met on Coxon's ship, the man with the broken nose and missing fingers.

'I'll want you to be on hand next Wednesday when my clients come to collect their charts,' said Snead who had finally

49

come into the room behind him. The architect was unshaven and pale. 'There may be last minute changes to be made. I trust you will have all five copies ready.'

'Yes, of course,' said Hector. He tried to sound confident, but it was on the tip of his tongue to ask if Captain Coxon was one of the clients and likely to collect his chart in person. He was fearful of meeting the buccaneer again. If he and Coxon came face to face, it could only turn out badly. Coxon was certain to take revenge for his humiliation, and at least one of his men was in town to help him do so. Hector imagined he would be lucky if he escaped with nothing more than a severe beating, but it could be much worse. From the little he had seen of Port Royal, it was a lawless seaport where corpses were regularly found floating in the harbour.

*

WHEN WEDNESDAY came, Hector was in an agony of anticipation. By ten o'clock in the morning he had completed the fifth copy of the chart, though the ink was still wet and he had to go down to Snead's desk to take a pouncet box of sand to sprinkle over the parchment. 'When will your clients arrive?' he asked the architect.

'We gather in the tavern this evening,' Snead told him. 'As soon as everyone is present, I will bring them across to inspect the work.'

The architect had dressed more carefully than usual and was shaved though he had nicked his chin with the razor in several places, and there were flecks of dried blood on his neckcloth. Hector wondered how much longer the architect would be able to do his own drawings now that his hand shook so badly. If the evening passed off well and Coxon did not appear, perhaps it was the moment to ask for permanent employment as a draughtsman. If Snead took him on permanently, it would mean that he could stay on in Port Royal and perhaps meet Susanna again. Increasingly Hector was aware that his attraction to the young woman was in conflict with his loyalty towards Dan, Jacques and his former shipmates. He could still accept Gutteridge's offer and sail for Petit Guave and there rejoin his friends. But he would have to hurry. The *Jamaica Merchant* was due to sail next day. Unable to make up his mind what he should do, he told himself that the events of the evening would decide the matter for him.

At sunset just before Snead left for his meeting in the tavern, he told Hector to prepare the upper room. He was to have all five copies of the chart set out on the table for inspection, and make sure that wine and grog were to hand. Then he was to go up to his own room in the garret and be ready if Snead called him. If summoned, he was not to speak to anyone, and he was to forget the faces of those in the room. Hector, still hoping that his fears of meeting Coxon were unfounded, made sure everything was ready but instead of withdrawing to the garret he stationed himself at the upper window. From there he could at least see who would be coming to collect the charts, and if necessary he could make his escape.

The street outside was as busy as usual in the cool of the evening. Clumps of drunken sailors stumbled and lurched from one alehouse and grog shop to the next, working whores paraded enticingly or disappeared up sidestreets and into doorways with their customers, several gaunt beggars importuned for alms, and – just once – a small patrol of militiamen straggled past, their uniforms ill-fitting and shabby. It was ten o'clock before he saw the door of the tavern open, the light spilling out, and a group of half a dozen men emerge. He recognised Snead at once, for the architect's walk was familiar. There was enough of a moon to cast shadows, and as the little group began to walk towards the shop they passed into a pool of darkness. A few moments later Snead's clients were at the door. Hector stood very still, listening. He had left the window open, and the sounds of the visitors came up to him clearly. He heard Snead, tipsy as usual, fumbling at the lock. The architect was apologising to his guests.

'Hurry up, man,' said a voice. 'I don't wish to be kept standing in the street for all to see.'

Hector knew Coxon's voice at once. The buccaneer's harsh bullying tone was unmistakable. The door opened, and Hector heard the men walk towards the stairs. Footsteps sounded on the boards.

Hector quietly tiptoed across to the table, gathered up one set of the charts, folded it in a neat square, and stuffed it into his shirt front. Stepping out onto the balcony, he swung a leg over the rail, and climbed over until he could let himself hang, his arms at full stretch. Then he let go. He had expected to land on the hard packed sand of the street. But as he dropped, his feet touched something soft, there was a grunt of surprise, and Hector sprawled sideways. As he struck the ground, he realised that he had not seen the man who was standing in the shadow of the doorway. Someone had been left as a lookout, and he was as startled as Hector.

Hector sprang to his feet as the stranger recovered and with a grunt of anger reached out to grab him. The young man ducked and twisted to one side, and sprinted away up the street. He expected to hear the sounds of running feet behind him as the lookout gave chase. But there was nothing. Hector could only imagine that the sentinel had gone inside to report on the incident and ask instructions. Hector forced himself to slow down to a walk. Earlier that afternoon he had consulted a town plan that Snead had made for the town commissioners. The drawing showed the haphazard pattern of Port Royal's roads and alleyways, and Hector had picked out a discreet route that would bring him to the quayside on Thames Street. There he would search for the *Jamaica Merchant* and offer his services to Captain Gutteridge. But he had not calculated on colliding with

one of Coxon's men. He was certain that the lookout was from
the buccaneer's crew, most likely the man with the broken nose.

Hector shivered slightly as he tried to anticipate how the
buccaneers would hunt him. Port Royal was such a small place
that, without shelter, he would soon be found. He wondered
just how many of the citizens, besides Snead, were friends with
Captain Coxon and would be pleased to join the pursuit. If
Snead were to mention that his assistant had been speaking with
Captain Gutteridge earlier, the buccaneer would quickly guess
where his quarry was heading. The young man was uncomfortably aware that, if he was to escape Coxon, he would have to
move very quickly but also in an unexpected direction.

Making up his mind, Hector walked rapidly in the direction
of Thames Street and turned up a narrow alleyway, Sea Lane,
which brought him out on the waterfront. Away to his right
stretched the line of ships tied to the wharves, their masts and
spars and rigging making a black tracery against the night sky.
His difficulty was that he did not know which of the vessels
was the *Jamaica Merchant*. The most likely candidate was a
small sloop almost at the farthest end of the wharf. But there
was no one he could ask for information, and he did not want
to draw attention to himself by rousing a night watchman and
asking for directions.

For several moments he stood motionless, wondering what
he should do. He had paused in the shelter of a warehouse
doorway, and as he looked along the quay, two men appeared
not fifty yards from him. They ran out from a laneway and
turned to look in his direction. Hector shrank back farther into
the shadow and when he peered out again, he saw that the men
had decided to go in the opposite direction. They were proceeding briskly along the waterfront, looking into every side road,
clearly searching for someone. At the farthest end of the quay,
they halted. They appeared to confer together, and then one
of them walked away and out of sight. His companion stayed

where he was. There was enough moonlight to show that the figure had seated himself on a pile of lumber at a position where he could scan the waterfront.

Hector tried to think of a way of getting past the lookout. He toyed with the idea of mingling with a gang of sailors returning to their ship, but then rejected the scheme. There was no guarantee that such a group would show up or welcome him in their company. Nor that they would be returning to the *Jamaica Merchant*. Or he could wait until Coxon's watchman – there was little doubt that the lookout was one of Coxon's crew – grew inattentive or was withdrawn from his post. But that might not happen and Hector was still faced with the problem of identifying the *Jamaica Merchant*.

Then he remembered the turtle crawl.

He slipped quietly out of the warehouse doorway and darted back into Sea Lane. Keeping to the shadows he retraced his steps until he reached the high street. There he turned to his right until he came to the empty stalls and tables of the meat market. It would be another two or three hours before the butchers and meat sellers arrived to prepare their booths. Finding his way to the ramp, Hector climbed over the low palisaded fence which surrounded the turtle pen. Removing his shoes and stockings, he walked barefoot down the slope until he felt the sea water on his feet. Treading carefully, he continued forward down the slope. He was in the shallows now, the water up to his knees. He put each foot down gently and slowly, anxious not to make any splashes. Suddenly his foot touched a hard round surface, which moved sluggishly to one side. He had trodden on a resting turtle. Cautiously he pushed forward with his leg until he found a gap between the animal and its neighbour. There must have been at least a dozen large turtles lying in the shallows, close-packed like flat boulders. Most of the creatures ignored him, but one of them rose up with a swirling surge that almost knocked him off his feet. Then he had reached the far end of the turtle pen, where the water was now up to mid-thigh. Floating, half submerged at the far end of the turtle pen was a small dugout canoe. He had noticed it on his previous visit, and supposed that the turtle men used it to bring their catch closer to the ramp, loading the captive turtles on the canoe rather than dragging them through the water.

Carefully Hector lifted one end of the canoe and placed it on the fence. Here the wooden palings projected less than two or three inches above the water. Slowly Hector eased the little canoe out over the fence, sliding it carefully across the obstruction. As soon as the canoe was on the seaward side, Hector clambered over the fence, and hauled himself aboard, straddling the dugout. He paused for a moment to check that the charts in his shirt were still dry, and then he lay back and pulled his legs inboard. The canoe was very small, barely longer than his own body and it fitted him like a narrow coffin. But that suited his plan.

He lay face up, the bilge water soaking into the back of his clothes. Dipping his hands into the warm water of the harbour on either side of his little vessel, he began to paddle gently. Barely moving, the dugout drifted forward, and Hector gently steered it towards the town quays.

He kept close to the shore where the looming bulk of the fort threw a dark shadow. Only someone standing right at the edge of the parapet and looking directly downward would have seen him. There was no warning shout, and as soon as he reached the wharves themselves, he pushed himself in amongst the wooden piles, sliding the little dugout into the space beneath the decking. Twice he thought that his progress was blocked by a cross brace, but he managed to find a way around. The fetid air under the quay stank of ordure, and he heard the rustle and squeak of rats. As he progressed, Hector counted the number of ships' hulls he passed. The first one was obviously a ship of war, probably the frigate on the Jamaica station, for he heard the stamp and call of a sentry answering the officer of the watch. Then there were two more hulls, large merchant ships, too substantial to belong to Gutteridge who had said the *Jamaica Merchant* was his own vessel and Gutteridge was not a wealthy man. Hector eased past the next five hulls until he came to the last in line, the modest vessel he suspected being the *Jamaica Merchant*. The stem post was worn and chewed, and there was a patched area where the hull had been poorly mended.

Gently Hector eased the little canoe from under the wharf and around the rudder of the sloop. He could hear the gentle slap of wavelets against the timber. With one hand he fended off the hull as he paddled forward until he had brought the canoe to the farther side of the sloop, away from the dock. He sat up carefully and placed a hand in a scupper hole. Silently he blessed the fact that the little sloop was so small that it lay low in the water. Then, taking a deep breath, he stood up in the bottom of the canoe, feeling it tilt alarmingly beneath him. He reached up with his right hand and laid hold of the capping rail. Then he pulled himself aboard. As his foot left the canoe, he gave a gentle kick and it floated away out of sight. With luck it would not be found until much later, and such a worthless craft might not even be worth reporting.

There was no one on deck as he began to worm his way cautiously aft. If the little sloop was anything like *L'Arc-de-Ciel* this was where he would find the captain's cabin. He still had no idea whether he was aboard the *Jamaica Merchant* or another vessel but now there was no turning back. When he came to the cabin door, he crouched down. Judging that it was another three or four hours until daybreak, he did not wish to alarm whoever was asleep inside. So he waited.

As the time passed, he became aware of soft snoring from within the cabin. That was reassuring. Sometimes a ship captain would choose to spend his nights ashore rather than on his vessel, but Hector had an idea that Captain Gutteridge, if he did not pay his bills, was not welcome in the local boarding houses. The young man squeezed himself more tightly into a corner behind a pile of sacks, hoping that he was not discovered by a sailor before he had a chance to speak with the captain.

The sky began to lighten, and he heard the sounds of the port awakening. There was the cry of gulls, the hawking and spitting of a longshoreman arriving for work, the mutter of voices as dockers began to assemble. He felt, rather than saw, Coxon's watcher still on the quay, not ten yards away, still scanning the length of the wharves, waiting for him.

The snores behind the cabin door changed in pitch. They stopped, then started again, and Hector heard the sleeper turn over in his bunk. He was nearly awake. Softly Hector tapped on the door. The snores continued. The young man tapped again, and this time the snoring ceased altogether. A short while later he heard the sound of bare feet as someone came to the door, paused, and opened it cautiously. In the half light Hector was relieved to see that it was indeed Captain Gutteridge. He held a cudgel in his hand.

'May I come in? I have your chart,' Hector said, speaking in scarcely above a whisper.

Gutteridge looked down at him, and there was a flash of recognition in his eyes. He drew back the door, and Hector slipped inside. The captain closed the door behind him.

Inside the small cabin it was stuffy and airless. It smelled of unwashed clothes, and Gutteridge himself was dishevelled.

'Here, I have your chart for you,' Hector repeated, bringing out the charts from his shirt. 'But Mr Snead will not be pleased.'

Gutteridge reached for the folded sheets, opened them, and gave the maps a quick glance. He looked up, a look of satisfaction on his face. 'Serve the greedy sot right,' he said. 'What do you want in return? We never agreed a price.'

'Mr Snead has men searching for me.'

Gutteridge gave him a penetrating look. 'Mr Snead . . . or Mr Snead's friends?' he said grimly. 'The word's out that there's an assembly off Negril. Several hard cases are recruiting for some sort of mischief. One of my own men ran off yesterday to volunteer.'

'So you'll be needing a replacement,' said Hector.

'Yes, but I wouldn't want to make enemies of that lot.'

'No one need know. You could conceal me aboard until your ship sails. Then I can make myself useful until we reach Petit Guave. That would be a fair price for the map.'

Gutteridge nodded. 'All right. We have a bargain.' He reached down and pulled at a trap door in the cabin floor. 'This leads down to the aft hold. You can stay down there.' He reached for an earthenware jug standing on the floor beside his bunk. 'Take this water with you. It'll be enough until I can get you some food later in the day.'

Hector sat down on the edge of the open hatch, his legs dangling into the dark space below. He looked up at Gutteridge. 'And when do you expect to reach Petit Guave?' he asked.

Gutteridge avoided his eyes and did not answer.

'You said you were stopping there, to take on brandy,' Hector reminded him.

Gutteridge was shamefaced. 'No, I did not say that. I said only that I was thinking of stopping there on the way to Campeachy.'

'But I have friends in Petit Guave . . . a Miskito and a Frenchman. This is why I want to join you.'

Gutteridge continued to look evasive. 'Maybe on the return trip . . .' he said lamely. 'And if we bring back a good load of logwood, I'll cut you in for five per cent of the profit.'

He gave Hector a gentle push with his foot, and the young man dropped down into the darkness, suddenly aware that he was unlikely to see either Susanna or Dan and his friends until his voyage to Campeachy was over.

FIVE

'CHRISTMAS,' said Captain Gutteridge cheerfully, 'is the best season to take up logwood.' He was leaning over the rail as his vessel edged slowly along a low swampy coast. Beyond the swamp a cloudless sky came down to the horizon in a pale harshness that made Hector's eyes ache. The land was so flat that all he could see was the endless dark green barrier of mangroves on their tangled mud-coloured roots and the feathery top of an occasional palm tree. It had taken less than ten days to sail from Port Royal to the Campeachey coast, and Gutteridge was in good humour. 'You'll be back in Jamaica before you know it,' he was saying. With Hector's stolen chart in hand, he was carefully tracking their progress. 'Logwood fetches a hundred pounds a ton on the London market, and with your share of the profit you can begin to make your fortune.'

Everyone in the Caribees, Hector thought to himself, was ready with advice on how to make vast great riches. Earlier it had been Robert Lynch, now it was the threadbare captain of a worn-out trading sloop. He no longer resented Gutteridge for his dishonesty over the mythical trip to Petit Guave. It was three weeks since Hector had last seen Dan, Jacques and the two Laptots, and he had accepted that whatever had happened to them in the French colony it was too late for him to make a difference. As for his yearning to see Susanna again, perhaps the captain was right. The niece of Sir Thomas Lynch would be more impressed with a rich suitor than a penniless admirer. Maybe a lucrative trip to the Campeachy coast would be his first step on the road to making a fortune.

He turned his attention back to the shoreline. 'The logwood cutters call themselves Bay Men and they live scattered all along the coast,' Gutteridge told him. 'Maybe five or six of them live together in a shared camp. They could be anywhere, so we cruise quietly along the shore until they spot us and make a signal. Then we drop anchor and they'll come out to trade. They'll exchange their stock of logwood for the goods we bring. Our profit is rarely less than five hundred per cent.'

'How do we know what they want?'

The captain smiled. 'They always want the same thing.'

'But wouldn't they get a better price if they brought their logwood to Jamaica themselves?'

'They can't. Too many of them are wanted by the authorities. They'd be arrested the moment they set foot ashore. Many of them are ex-buccaneers who failed to come in and surrender when there was an amnesty. The rest are knaves and ruffians. They like the independent life, though I can't say I envy them.'

Now Gutteridge was staring fixedly at a stretch of mangrove. 'Is that smoke?' he asked. 'Or are my eyes playing tricks?'

Hector looked carefully. A light grey haze was rising from the greenery. It might be smoke or a patch of late-morning mist that had not yet cleared. 'They hide themselves like fugitives. Surely the authorities would not send ships here to arrest them,' he said.

'It's the Spanish they are afraid of,' Gutteridge explained. 'The Spaniards claim all of Campeachy as their territory and regard the Bay Men as trespassers who steal the timber. If the

Spanish patrols catch the loggers, they are carried off to the cities where they are thrown into prison or auctioned off as slaves.'

He was shading his eyes with his hands and staring long and hard. He gave a grunt of satisfaction. 'Yes, that's smoke all right. We stop here.'

He despatched Hector with a sailor into the ship's hold with orders to bring up a barrel of rum. Stooping under the deck beams, Hector noted that the cargo space was three-quarters empty. In one corner were stacked a few rolls of cloth. Elsewhere were several cases of hammers, axes, cutlasses, wedges, crowbars. Against a bulkhead several more chests contained blocks of refined sugar. But the bulk of the sloop's cargo was three dozen barrels and casks of varying sizes, ranging from a little eighteen-gallon rundlet to a massive puncheon. He checked their contents. Perhaps a quarter of them were kegs of gunpowder, the rest held rum, great quantities of it. With the help of his companion, Hector rolled a rum barrel to the companionway, and rigged a block and tackle to raise the cask on deck. There a rough table had already been made by laying planks across yet more barrels, and was set with loaves of ship's bread, ham and salted beef.

'Here they come now in that pirogue,' said Gutteridge, looking towards the shore. A large dugout canoe was already halfway out to the ship, paddled by three men. It was difficult to see much of the men because all were wearing hats with extravagantly broad, drooping brims which completely shaded their faces.

The captain himself went to the ship's rail, ready to hand his visitors up on deck. 'Greetings, my friends, greetings! Welcome to my ship!' he called out jovially. Hector could see that the newcomers were heavily armed. Each man had his musket, and there were pistols tucked in their belts. One of them paused his stroke for a moment, waved his paddle in the air, and let out a great whoop of elation.

Moments later their canoe was alongside, and the three logwood cutters were climbing over the rail. Gutteridge was slapping them on the back and gesturing towards the table of food and the keg of rum. Hector had never seen such uncouth characters. Their tangled hair hung down to their shoulders, and their beards were matted and unwashed. Every garment was filthy and reeking of sweat. Two of them had facial wounds – one had a scar that ran from his ear down the side of his neck, and another was lacking an eye. The third man in the group seemed to be their leader and was a colossus. He stood nearly six and a half feet, with heavily muscled shoulders and arms, and the knuckles on his enormous hands were callused. His face looked as if it had been struck a dozen times for there was a tracery of fine scars across his forehead and cheeks, and his nose had been flattened by a cruel blow. All three men carried themselves with a swaggering menace as they set foot on deck and looked around. Most striking of all was the colour of their skin. Their hands and faces were a strange dark red as though they had been roasted on a spit or were suffering from some strange disfiguring disease.

To Hector's astonishment, Gutteridge continued as if he was greeting long-lost bosom friends. 'Come! Be seated! You are most welcome. This is the festive season!' He was ushering the new arrivals to the empty kegs which served as seats beside the rough table, and already had begun to pour neat rum into pewter mugs which he handed to his guests. With barely a word said between them, the loggers swilled down their first drinks and held out their tankards for more. The giant reached out for a loaf of bread. He tore it in half, and then began softening it by splashing rum on the crust. He crammed the soggy mass into his mouth.

'Hector!' called the captain. 'Take the top off that barrel. We must not stint our guests.'

As Hector was prising open the barrel, a musket shot rang out just behind him, and he almost dropped the chisel. He turned to find one of the logwood cutters had loosed off a shot into the air. 'Bravo!' cried Gutteridge, not in the least taken aback. He poured the man another drink, and then took a swig from his own tankard. 'Here's to Kill-devil! There's plenty more where it came from.' Then he ordered the ship's cannon, a miserable little six-pounder, to be loaded and primed. With a theatrical gesture, he brought a lighted match to the touch hole, and the resulting explosion caused a flock of pelicans to flap up from the mangrove swamps and fly away in fear.

The headlong carousal lasted all afternoon, and by sunset the three logwood cutters were incapable of getting to their feet. One had fallen from his seat and was sprawled on deck, and the others were head down on the table, snoring. Gutteridge himself was little better. He tried to make his way to his cabin, but staggered so drunkenly that Hector feared his captain would blunder over the ship's side. He put an arm round Gutteridge's shoulders, and steered him back to his cabin where the man toppled face down onto his bunk.

Next morning, to Hector's awe, the Bay Men were calling for more rum to wash down their breakfast. They had iron constitutions because they seemed no worse for their debauch, and to all appearances were ready to carry on drinking for the rest of the day. Gutteridge was looking bilious as he appeared shakily from his cabin and finally managed to steer the conversation around to the question of trade. Did the Bay Men have any stocks of logwood ready for sale? He was told that the three men cut their timber individually, but pooled production. They were willing to exchange their timber for barrels of rum and additional supplies, but would need a few days to bring all their logs to a central stockpile close to a landing place.

'Hector,' said Gutteridge, 'perhaps you would oblige me by going ashore with our friends. They can show you how much logwood they have ready, and how much more is yet to be got together. Then we can calculate a fair price. Meanwhile I'll take the sloop farther up the coast and locate other suppliers.

I should be gone two or three days, at most a week. When I return we will commence loading.'

Hector was eager to go ashore and see the countryside, but before he clambered down into the pirogue, Gutteridge found an excuse to take him aside and speak to him privately. 'Be certain to put some mark on the existing stocks, something to show that we have a claim to it,' he said. 'The Bay Men can be fickle. With you on hand, they will not sell to the next ship that turns up. But I also want you to check on the logs they have on offer. There's something I must show you.'

He led Hector to a cubbyhole beneath the poop deck, and pulled out a billet of wood about three feet long. The timber was close-grained and the darkest red, almost black. 'This is what cost me the profits of my last voyage,' the captain said, handing the sample to Hector to inspect. 'That's logwood. Some people call it bloodwood because if you chop it into shavings and steep it in water, the stew looks like blood. Dyers add it in their vats for colouring cloth. They pay a handsome price, but only for the best quality. What do you make of it?'

Hector hefted the billet in his hands. It was very heavy and seemed flawless. It gave off a very faint odour, like the smell of violets. 'Here, let me show you,' said Gutteridge, taking it back from him. He struck the length of timber fiercely against a bulkhead, and the end section of the billet flew off. The exposed interior was hollow, rotted through. The cavity had been packed with dirt as a makeweight. 'More than half my last cargo was like that,' Gutteridge said. 'Useless, though I had paid top price. The loggers had already sold all their good stock, and they then spent weeks preparing the dross. They had covered the ends of all the rotten billets with plugs of decent wood, disguising the rubbish. It was cleverly done, and I was taken in. That's how I lost my capital.'

Shortly afterwards Hector rode thoughtfully ashore in the pirogue with the three Bay Men. By an unspoken agreement it seemed that he was assigned to accompany the giant whose name was Jezreel. But beyond that he knew nothing. Jezreel only grunted, 'Get a hat and bring some cloth' and had then fallen silent. Hector presumed that their solitary life made the Bay Men taciturn. None of them had said a word of thanks when Gutteridge handed each of them a sack stuffed with provisions and several bottles of rum to take back ashore.

His companions steered the pirogue into a gap in the mangroves, and a little way inside beached the vessel on a patch of hard sand. From there a narrow path threaded its way through a dreary wasteland of swamp. Within a few paces Hector felt a fierce stab of pain on the back of his neck as if a hot ember had landed on his skin. It was a biting insect and he slapped it away. Seconds later there were three or four more stings as he was attacked by swarms of mosquitoes. He squirmed in discomfort, for the insects were gorging on every exposed part of his body, even biting through his clothing. He stooped and splashed water from a puddle onto his face and bathed his arms. But the respite was only temporary. He could feel the insects settling on his face, and his eyelids were already beginning to puff up with the effect of their bites. He wondered how his companions put up with such an onslaught for they seemed untroubled.

When they reached a place where the path divided, the other Bay Men turned aside, leaving the giant Jezreel to stride forward, his sack of food and drink over his shoulder as if it was empty. Hector trotted behind him, still frantically sweeping aside the insects. A few minutes of hard walking brought them to where the mangroves gave way to more open, marshy scrubland. Here sloughs and ponds of stagnant water were linked by a great network of shallow creeks and channels. Marsh birds – herons, egrets, curlews and plovers – stalked the soggy ground, feeding on insects and small fish. Hector wondered how anyone could live in such watery surroundings, yet Jezreel waded through the obstacles without breaking stride. Soon they came to Jezreel's camp. It was no more than a huddle of simple open-sided huts, their roofs thickly thatched with palm leaves. In every hut were platforms raised on stakes at least three feet above the ground. One of the platforms appeared to be Jezreel's sleeping place, another was his living quarters. A few yards away his cooking place was yet another elevated platform, this time covered with earth.

'The flooding must be very bad,' observed Hector who had quickly understood the reason for this arrangement. Jezreel made no reply but took down a cloth bundle hanging from the thatch and tossed it across to Hector. 'Spread that. It helps against the insects.' Unwrapping the cloth, Hector found it contained a slimy yellow lump of rancid animal fat. Gingerly he began to smear it across his face and neck. The suet smelled and felt foul but seemed to discourage the worst of the insect attacks. Now he appreciated why the logwood cutters seldom removed their broad-brimmed hats. Their headgear prevented the mosquitoes tangling and biting in their hair. 'Make yourself a pavilion over there,' continued the Bay Man indicating one of the shelters. Hector saw that he was to rig up a canopy, using the cloth he had brought from the ship. It would keep away the insects from his bed.

'Know how to shoot?' asked Jezreel. Clearly he was someone who wasted few words.

Hector nodded.

'We'll get in some fresh meat for your captain when he returns.'

The big man reached up and tugged a musket from where it had been stored within the thatch, and handed it to the young man. From a hanging satchel he produced half a dozen charges of gunpowder wrapped in paper, a small powder horn, and a bag of bullets. Checking over the gun, Hector saw that it was an old-fashioned matchlock. To fire it, he would need to load, then add powder to the priming pan and keep the fuse lit until he was ready to pull the trigger. He thought to himself that a flintlock would have been much easier to use in such wet conditions, and could only suppose that Jezreel had been unable to obtain modern weapons.

He followed the giant out of the camp, and was led at the same brisk pace deeper into the swampy savannah. The ground was moist and soggy with a thin layer of rotting leaves covering yellow clay. From time to time they passed scatterings of pale wood chips on the ground. 'Logwood,' explained the big man, and seeing that Hector was puzzled, he added. 'Only the dark heartwood is taken. You must trim away the rest. The sap rind is near white or yellow.'

They walked on in silence.

Eventually they came to the margins of a wide, shallow lagoon. Here and there were low islands covered with grass and small thickets of brushwood. Hauled up on the shore was a small dugout canoe, evidently kept by Jezreel for his hunting trips. The boat was little larger than the one Hector had used in his escape from Port Royal. There were two paddles wedged under the thwarts.

✳

THEY WADED OUT into the shallows, pushing the little craft ahead of them and holding their muskets high. Jezreel gestured for Hector to climb in and take a seat in the bow, then the big man took up his position in the stern and soon they were moving forward across the mere. From where he was sitting, Hector felt the canoe surge forward each time Jezreel took a stroke. By comparison his own efforts felt feeble. Neither of them said a word.

After some fifteen minutes Jezreel abruptly stopped paddling, and Hector followed suit. The canoe glided forward as Hector felt a tap on his shoulder, and the giant's hand appeared in the corner of his vision. Jezreel was pointing away into the distance. On the shore of an island and difficult to see against the background vegetation stood half a dozen wild cattle. They were smaller than the domestic cows that Hector had known at home in Ireland, dark brown in colour, almost black, and armed with long curving horns. Three of them were standing up to their hocks, feeding on lilies. The others were on the shore, grazing.

Behind him there was the sound of flint on steel. A moment later his companion passed him a length of glowing slow match. Hector fixed it in the jaws of his musket's firing lock. Very gently, they stalked the wild cattle, closing the gap without being observed. From time to time one of the animals would raise its head from feeding, and scan for danger.

Hector calculated that they had got within a very long musket shot when, unexpectedly, there came the thump of a distant explosion. For a moment he thought that Gutteridge's sloop had returned and was firing a signal gun. But the sound had come, not from the sea behind them, but somewhere over to his left, from the savannah.

Whatever the source of the detonation, it had stampeded the wild cattle. Tails held high in panic, they abandoned their island and dashed deeper into the lake, then began swimming away. All that was visible was a line of horned heads disappearing in the distance.

Hector was about to turn and speak to Jezreel when the big man's voice said 'Hold still!' and the muzzle of a musket slid past beside his right cheek. The barrel was placed on his shoulder. He froze in position, all thought of paddling gone. Instead he gripped the sides of the canoe, scarcely breathing. He heard Jezreel behind him shifting his stance, and felt the musket barrel on his shoulder move a fraction. There was a whiff of slow match. The next moment there was the flat explosive crack of the weapon firing. The sound was so close to Hector's face that it made his head ring, and left him half deaf. His eyes watered with the cloud of gun smoke, and for a moment his vision was obscured. When the gun smoke blew away, he looked forward to where the cattle had been swimming. To his amazement one of the animals had swerved aside.

The creature was already dropping back, separating from its fellows. Jezreel's marksmanship was far out of the ordinary. To have hit his target from such a distance while seated in an unstable canoe was a remarkable feat. Even Dan, whom Hector considered the best marksman he knew, would have found it difficult to achieve such accuracy.

Already Jezreel was back at work, driving the canoe forward with huge paddle strokes. Hastily Hector joined his effort, for the wild cow was still able to flounder through the water and had turned directly for shore. Moments later it was in the shallows, and with great thrashing leaps was plunging towards safety, blood streaming from its neck and staining the water a frothy red.

The two hunters reached their prey while the animal was still hock deep on the shelving edge of the lake. It was a young bull, wounded and very angry. It turned to face its tormentors, snorting with pain and rage, and lowered its vicious horns.

Hector put down his paddle. The bull was perhaps fifteen yards away, still at a safe distance. The young man poured priming powder into the pan of his musket, blew gently on the burning matchcord to make it glow, raised his musket, and pulled the trigger. At that range it was impossible to miss. The ball struck the bull in the chest and he saw the animal stagger with the impact. But the animal was young and strong, and did not drop. It still stood on the same spot, menacing and dangerous. Hector expected his companion to hold back, until the two men had reloaded, then finish off their prey. Instead Jezreel drove the canoe into the shallows, and leaping out into the water began to wade towards the wild bull. To Hector's alarm he saw that the logwood cutter was empty-handed. There was a long hunting knife in Jezreel's belt but it stayed in its sheath. The young man watched him advance until, at the last moment, the bull lowered its head and charged. The attack could have been mortal. But Jezreel stood his ground, and in one sure movement leaned down and seized the creature's horns before the animal could lift its head and impale him. As Hector watched, the big man twisted and, using his great strength, threw the bull off its feet. In a welter of foam and muddy water, the beast fell on its side, the logwood cutter dropped one knee on the animal's neck, then forced its head under water. For several moments there was a succession of desperate heaves as the trapped animal attempted to escape. Then gradually its struggles eased and, after one last shudder, it ceased to move.

Jezreel held the drowned creature's head submerged a full minute to make sure that it was really dead. Then he rose to his feet and called to Hector. 'Pull the canoe up on land, then come and give me a hand to butcher the beast. We'll take what we can carry, and they can have the rest.'

Following his companion's glance, Hector saw the snouts of two large alligators gliding across the water towards them.

'You'll see plenty of others,' explained his companion. 'Mostly the caymans stay their distance. But if they are hungry or in a bad humour, just occasionally they will run at you and take you down.'

Working quickly, they began to butcher the wild bull into quarters. Here, too, Jezreel was an adept. The blade of his hunting knife sliced through skin and flesh, skilfully working around the bones and severing the sinews, until the slabs of fresh meat had been separated from the carcass. They dropped them into the canoe, and pushed off, heading back towards their camp. Looking over his shoulder, Hector saw the caymans crawling up the slope. As he watched, they began to snap and chew at the bloody carcass, like huge olive brown lizards attacking a lump of raw flesh.

When they arrived at their original departure point, Jezreel secured the canoe. Then he leaned over and picked up a great slab of raw beef from the bilges. With his knife he cut a long slit in its centre. 'Stand closer,' he demanded, 'and take off your hat.' Hector did as he was told, and before he could react, his companion held up the meat, and slipped it over the young man's head so the beef hung like a tabard, front and back, the blood soaking through his shirt. 'Best way to fetch it to camp,' said Jezreel. 'Leaves your hands free so you can carry a musket. If it's too heavy, I'll trim off a portion and lighten the load.' He carved slits in two more of the meaty parcels, and with a double load draped over his own massive shoulders, started walking back along the track.

As they trudged back along the path, Hector asked about the explosion that had scared the cattle. 'At first I thought it was Captain Gutteridge signalling his return. But the sound came from the savannah. It wasn't Spaniards was it?'

Jezreel shook his head. 'If it had been Spaniards, we would have made ourselves scarce. That was one of our companions preparing logwood.'

'But it sounded like a cannon shot.'

'Most of the logwood is small stuff, easy to handle. From time to time you fell a big tree, maybe six feet around, and the wood is so tough that it's impossible to split into smaller pieces. So you blow it apart with a charge of gunpowder, shrewdly placed.'

'The captain asked me to make a list of all the logwood ready to load. Can we do that tomorrow?' asked Hector. But the giant did not reply. He was looking away to the north where a thick bank of cloud had formed. It lay in the lower sky as a heavy black line, its upper edge as clean and sharp as if trimmed with a scythe. It looked motionless, yet unnatural and menacing.

'Tomorrow may prove difficult,' Jezreel said.

*

THE CLOUD BANK was still there at dawn. It had neither dispersed nor come any closer. 'What does it signify?' Hector asked. He and Jezreel were eating a breakfast of fresh beef strips cooked on the barbacoa.

'The sailors call it a North Bank. It could be a sign that the weather is changing.'

Hector looked up at the sky. Apart from the strange black North Bank, there was not a cloud in the sky. There was only the same baking haze that he had seen every day since his arrival on the Campeachy coast. He detected just the faintest breath of a breeze, barely enough to disturb the plume of smoke rising from their cooking fire.

'What makes you say that?' he enquired.

Jezreel pointed with his chin towards dozens of man of war birds that were circling over the area where the hunt had taken place. The fork-tailed sea birds were dipping down in spirals, then rising up, clearly disturbed, and constantly uttering their shrill high-pitched cries. 'They don't come inland unless they know something is going to happen. And these last two days I've noticed something odd about the tides. There's been almost no flood, only ebb. The water has been retreating as if the sea is gathering its strength.' He rose from his seat and added, 'If we are checking on the logwood stocks, we better hurry.'

As it turned out, the logwood cutters still had much work to do. Their caches of timber were widely scattered, and they had yet to carry them to the landing place on the creek. Jezreel was more advanced in this work than his companions because he had the strength of two men. Transporting the billets of wood was as much drudgery as cutting the timber in the first place. The men worked like pack animals, stooped under immense loads which Hector calculated at two hundred pounds a time, and staggering through the swamps. He wondered why the Bay Men did not make rafts of the timber and float them along the many backwaters, but realised the reason when one of the logs slipped from Jezreel's load. The dense timber sank like a rock.

An hour before sunset the wind, which had continued faint all day, moved into the north and began to strengthen. The increase was steady, rather than dramatic, but continued through the night. At first Hector, dozing on his platform, was aware only that the sides of his cloth pavilion were stirring and lifting in the breeze. But within an hour the folds of cloth were flapping and billowing, and he got up and took down the cloth because it was evident that no insects would be flying in such conditions. He enjoyed the respite for a short while, listening to the rushing of the wind as it swept through the mangroves. But soon the wind was plucking at the thatch of his shelter and he found it difficult to get to sleep. He lay there, thinking of Susanna and wondering whether he would be able to see her again after Gutteridge had loaded the logwood and brought him back to Jamaica. Maybe he would have earned enough money from the logwood sale to invest in a commercial enterprise and start to make the fortune that would impress the young woman into accepting him as a formal suitor. Riches, by all accounts, were swiftly gained in the Caribbees.

Eventually he did fall into a deep sleep, only to be woken shortly before daybreak by a rattling noise. The wind was so strong that the fiercer gusts were shaking the entire fabric of his shelter. Unable to rest, Hector swung his legs over the side of his sleeping platform, and stood up. To his shock, he found that he was standing in six inches of water.

As the light rapidly strengthened, he saw that the entire camp site was under water. In places it was submerged to a depth of at least a foot. The flood was flowing inland like a vast river. He dipped a finger into the water and sucked on it. He tasted salt. The sea was invading the land.

Splashing his way out of the hut, he found Jezreel assembling a bundle of his possessions, his guns and powder, a coil of rope, a water bottle, a hatchet, food. 'Here, take these, you may need them later,' he said to Hector, handing him a spare water bottle, a cutlass and a gun. 'What's happening?' enquired Hector. He had to raise his voice for the sound of the wind had now risen to a steady roar. 'It's a North,' shouted the giant. 'December and January is their time and this looks to be a bad one.'

The big man looked round to make sure that he had everything he needed, then led Hector inland towards a swell of rising ground. As they waded through the water, the young man observed that the water level was constantly rising. It was now halfway up the supports of his sleeping platform.

'How much higher will it flood?' he shouted.

Jezreel shrugged. 'No way of telling. Depends how long the gale blows.'

They reached the knoll. Here stood a single enormous tree, fifteen or twenty feet around its base. Lightning must have struck it, for all but a handful of the upper branches were shorn away, and those which survived bore no leaves. Jezreel went to its farther side. There the lightning had left a jagged open gash which extended almost down to the ground. Jezreel swung his hatchet and began to widen the crevice, enough to jam in hand or foot. 'You better climb up first. You are more nimble,' he advised Hector. 'Take the rope and get as high as you can. At least up to the first large branches. Once you're there, lower the rope to me and we'll haul up our gear.'

Half an hour later they were both seated some twenty feet above the ground, each astride a thick branch. 'Might as well make ourselves secure,' said Jezreel, passing him the end of their rope. 'If the wind gets stronger we'll be blown off like rotten plums.'

Fastened in place with a rope around his waist, Hector watched the floodwaters rising. It was an extraordinary sight. A great swirling, rippling brown mass of water was sliding inland, carrying everything before it. Branches, leaves, all sorts of clutter were being swept along. Bushes disappeared. The corpse of a wild pig floated by. What made the scene all the more remarkable was that the sky still remained bright and sunny, except for the ominous bank of cloud which lay heavily on the horizon. 'Will rain come?' Hector asked his companion.

'No, a North is not like a hurricane,' answered Jezreel. 'Everyone knows of the hurricane and the downpours it brings.

But a North stays steady as long as that black cloud is there, and without any rain. But it can be just as fatal if you are on a lee shore.'

By mid afternoon the wind had risen to gale force and was threatening to pluck Hector from his perch. He felt the great dead tree vibrating in the blasts, and wondered if its dead roots would hold. If the tree were toppled, he could not see how they would survive.

'What about the others?' he shouted above the clamour of the wind.

'They'll do the same as us, if they can find a refuge high enough,' Jezreel called back. 'But it's the end of my stay here.'

'What do you mean?' shouted Hector.

'Nothing will remain after this flood,' answered the big man. 'All our stock of logwood is being washed away. Some may stay in place, but the rest will shift and be buried in the mud. It will take weeks to salvage it, and even then it will be almost impossible to bring it to the landing place. A North rarely lasts more than a day or two, but it will be weeks before the flood waters recede far enough for us to begin any recovery. Besides, all our food stores will have been destroyed, and the gunpowder soaked and ruined.'

Glumly Hector looked down at the swirling water. His mind was on Gutteridge and his sloop. Unless the captain had found a truly secure anchorage there was little chance that his vessel would survive.

That evening they ate a meal of cold meat washed down with gulps of water. From time to time they shifted position by a few inches, cautiously easing the discomfort of their perch because the gale still raged. Occasionally a bird flashed past them, swept helplessly downwind.

The gale began to slacken about the time the stars came out and, looking north, Hector saw that the long black cloud had gone. 'That means the North is finished,' Jezreel told him.

They dozed fitfully and at sunrise looked out on a scene of

devastation. The flood water extended as far as the eye could see. Here and there the tops of small trees were still visible, but their branches had been stripped of foliage. The only movement was the small, reluctant swirls and eddies in the brown flood which told that the water had reached its peak and was slowly beginning to recede.

'It'll be some hours yet before we can descend,' Jezreel warned. He leaned his head back against the tree trunk, and there was a companionable silence between them.

'Tell me,' said Hector, 'how did you finish up here of all places?'

Jezreel waited several moments before answering. 'Those scars on my face are the mark of my former profession. Did you ever hear of Nat Hall, the "Sussex Gladiator"?'

When Hector did not reply, he continued. 'You might have done if you had lived in London and visited Clare Market or Hockley in the Hole. It was there I fought trials of skill, gave exhibitions, taught classes too. The singlestick was my favourite, though I was handy enough with the backsword.'

'I've seen prize fights at home,' said Hector. 'But that was with fists, between farmers at the country fairs.'

'You are talking about trials of manhood,' the big man corrected him. He stretched out his hands to show the callused knuckles. 'That's what fistics leave you with, and maybe a flattened nose and mis-shapen ears. Trials of skill are different. They're done with weapons. My nose was shaped by a blow from a singlestick, and the same caused my scars. Had I received a slash from a backsword that would have left no ear at all.'

'It must take courage to follow such a dangerous profession,' commented Hector.

Jezreel shook his head. 'I drifted into it. I was always very big for my age, and strong too. By the time I was fourteen, I was taking wagers on feats of strength – breaking thick ropes, pulling saplings up by their roots, lifting heavy stones, that sort of thing. Eventually I found my way to London where a showman promised me that I would be the new English Samson in his theatre. But I was never quite good enough, and he was a cheat.'

Jezreel leaned over from his branch and spat down into the flood water. He waited for a moment, watching the blob of spittle float on the surface. Slowly it drifted seawards. 'On the ebb,' he commented as he settled back against the tree trunk, and continued with his tale. 'I was always quick, as much as I was strong. Have you ever seen hot work at the singlestick?' he asked.

'Never. Is it some sort of cudgel?'

Jezreel made a grimace of distaste. 'That's what some people call it, but gives the wrong idea. Imagine a short sword, but with a blade of ash, and a basket handle. Two men stand face to face, no more than a yard apart, easy striking distance. They hold their weapons high and make lightning cuts and slashes at one another. Each blocks the other's blow and strikes back in an instant. The target is any part of the body above the waist. The feet must stay on the ground, not moving.'

Jezreel's right hand was above his head now and, with bent wrist, he was whipping an imaginary blade through the air, down and sideways, slashing and parrying. For a moment Hector feared that the big man would lose his balance on the branch and tumble into the flood.

'How is the winner decided?' he asked.

'Whoever first suffers a broken head is the loser. To win you must draw blood with a blow to the head, hence my scars.'

'But that doesn't explain why you are here now.'

The prize fighter waited a long time before he continued. 'Like I told you, singlestick was my favourite, but I was handy with the short sword too. It's the same style and technique but with a sharp metal blade, and when you fight for big money, the crowd wants to see the blood flow freely.'

Hector sensed that the big man was finding it difficult to speak of his past.

'I was matched against a good man, a champion. The purse was very big and I knew that I was outclassed. He need not have cheated. He cut me across the back of my leg, tried to hamstring me, and in my anger and pain I lashed out with a lucky stroke. It split his skull.'

'But it was an accident.'

'He had a patron, a powerful man who lost both his wager and his investment. I was warned that I would be tried for murder, so I fled.' Jezreel gave a bitter smile. 'One thing, though, all that exercise with singlestick or backsword will have its uses.'

'I don't grasp your meaning,' said Hector.

'This cursed flood has put an end to my hopes of making a living out of logwood. I expect my comrades will go back to what they did before – buccaneering. I think I'll join them.'

When eventually Jezreel judged it was safe to descend from their perch, Hector accompanied the prize fighter as they waded waist deep through the retreating flood water. They found their camp was wrecked. The huts still stood, though skewed and made lopsided by the current, but all their contents were either washed away or ruined. There was nothing to salvage. They made their way to the landing place among the mangroves and were relieved that the pirogue was undamaged though they had to extract it from the upper branches of a mangrove thicket where it had lodged. Just when they had succeeded in relaunching the pirogue, the two other Bay Men straggled in. They too had shifted for themselves and managed to climb out of harm's way.

'What do we do now?' asked the man with the scarred face whom Jezreel called Otway.

'Best try to link up with Captain Gutteridge . . . if his ship still floats,' answered Jezreel. The little group stacked their last remaining possessions into the pirogue, then paddled out from among the mangroves, and along the coast in the direction they had last seen the sloop. They had not gone more than five miles when they saw in the distance a sight which confirmed Jezreel's fears. Cast up a hundred yards into the coastal swamp was the dark outline of a ship. It was Gutteridge's sloop. She lay on her side. A shattered stump showed where the mainmast had once stood. The spar itself lay across the deck in a tangled web of rigging. The mainsail was draped over the bow like a winding sheet.

'Poor sods,' breathed Otway. 'She must have driven ashore in the gale. I doubt there were any survivors.'

They paddled their pirogue closer, looking for any signs of life. Jezreel fired his musket as a signal. But there was no response, no answering shot, no call. The big man reloaded and fired again in the air – still there was nothing. The shattered hulk was abandoned, dark, and silent.

SIX

THE NORTH'S baleful effect was detected far to the south. In Dan's homeland on the Miskito coast his people saw the tide recede beyond its normal range, then flood in with unusual strength, and they knew that it signified a great, distant upheaval. The flotsam washed ashore was still being gathered by children from the Miskito villages when Dan came home a fortnight later. He recounted how he and Jacques had been taken by Coxon's buccaneers and sent aboard *L'Arc-de-Ciel* to Petit Guave. The French settlement had been abuzz with preparations for a free-booting raid on the Spanish Main, and the governor, Monsieur de Pouncay, was absent. Rather than wait for his return to decide if their prisoners were guilty of piracy, Captain Coxon's prize crew saw their chance of easy plunder. They volunteered to join the French expedition, freed their prisoners, and recruited Dan to pilot them to the Miskito coast for it was from there that the French proposed to march on the Spanish settlements in the interior. Jacques was happy to join them as he had encountered several former acquaintances from the Paris gaols among the freebooters. But when the French expedition disembarked, Jacques had changed his mind, preferring to stay behind on the beach and watch out for any Spanish patrol ships and wait for Dan to return from a visit to his Miskito family.

'Weren't they happy to see you again?' asked Jacques. He had been surprised to see Dan reappear after less than a week. Dan looked up from where he was kneeling on the sand, about to butcher a turtle for their midday meal.

'Of course. They wanted to hear about all the places I had seen during my travels.'

'And didn't they expect you to stay at home?'

'That's not our custom,' the Miskito replied. 'Our young men are encouraged to join the foreign raiding parties who come to our coast. They get well rewarded as scouts and hunters.'

He turned the turtle on its back and tickled it under the chin with the point of his cutlass. The creature extended its neck, and with a lightning stroke he chopped down with his blade. The head spun away, the beaked jaws still snapping and narrowly missing Jacques who jumped aside.

'How are you going to get into the shell?' the Frenchman asked.

'It's easy. You slip the tip of your cutlass into this slot where the upper and lower shells meet. Then carefully slice sideways, following right around the joint. If you try to cut anywhere else, you'll find it impossible.'

Jacques rubbed the galerien's brand on his cheek as he watched his companion. Within moments the Miskito had prised apart the turtle, opening it like a clam shell.

'Why, the gut's like the intestines of a cow,' the Frenchman noted in surprise.

'I suppose that's because the turtles also feed on grass.'

'But they are sea creatures.'

'If it's calm tomorrow,' answered the Miskito, 'I'll take you out in a canoe to where you can see four fathoms down. You'll see grass growing on the sea floor. That's the turtle's food.'

He turned back to his work and pointed out two discoloured patches of flesh in the body of the turtle, close to the muscles of the front flippers. 'You must cut those out,' he said. 'If you don't, the flesh will have a bad taste when cooked.'

'Just leave the cooking to me,' said Jacques impatiently. He was of the opinion that the Miskito showed a great lack of imagination by only grilling or boiling turtle meat. He had already suggested to Dan that a sauce of lemon juice, pimento and pepper would enhance the flavour.

'As you wish,' said Dan equably. 'For frying the meat, use that yellowish fat on the inside of the lower shell. But please leave me the greenish fat of the upper shell.'

'Is it poisonous?' asked Jacques who felt that perhaps he was too hasty in his culinary plans.

'Not at all. I'll set the shell upright in the sand after we've got all the meat out of it. When the sun has softened the green fat, you can scrape it off and eat it raw. It's delicious.'

A halloo attracted their attention. A hundred yards offshore a dugout canoe was passing down the coast under a small triangular sail. Its occupant was standing up and waving to them. Immediately Dan got to his feet and waved back, beckoning the newcomer to come to land. 'That's Jon, one of my cousins,' the Miskito explained. 'He's been away on a fishing trip.'

Dan hurried down the slope of the beach to greet his relative, and to Jacques's astonishment, as the newcomer stepped out of his canoe Dan fell flat on his face on the sand. For a moment Jacques thought that his friend had tripped. But then the Miskito got to his feet, and his cousin also dropped prone in front of Dan, and lay spreadeagle and face down for the space of a few heartbeats, then stood up again. Next the two men threw their arms around one another and hugged tightly, each with his face pressed against the other's neck. Jacques, who had walked towards them, distinctly heard both men snuffling loudly and with gusto. His puzzlement must have shown, for when Dan introduced the Frenchman, he added, 'Don't look so surprised. That's our way of greeting someone we are fond of and have not seen for a long time. We call it *kia walaia*. It means "to smell, to understand".'

The two Miskito exchanged news and when Dan turned back to Jacques, he was looking thoughtful. 'Jon has been fishing to the north. He heard rumours of a party of white men travelling along the coast in pirogues. Three boatloads of them. They are coming this way, but very slowly, for they are weak and sickly. Also he says that a Spanish patrol ship was seen five days ago.'

Dan asked his cousin a few more questions, then added, 'My guess is that the men in the pirogues are English or French. If so, they should be warned about the Spanish patrol ship. Jon is willing to lend me his canoe if I want to go there to find out more. I could be back inside three days if this wind holds.' Dan seemed eager to make the trip.

Jacques considered for a moment before replying. 'All right then. I'll wait here for you.'

'In the meantime you can try out your turtle recipe on my cousin,' said Dan cheerfully.

*

THE UNIDENTIFIED travellers were much closer than expected. Before noon on the second day Dan glimpsed the three pirogues. They were beached inside a river mouth less than thirty miles from where he had left Jacques. Cautiously Dan steered across the sandbar at the river mouth, keeping close under the bank so that the canoe's sail brushed the overhanging branches of the mangroves which stretched away in an unbroken wall on both sides of the estuary. When he reached the travellers' camp, the first person he saw was Hector. Moments later the two friends were greeting one another with astonished delight.

'How on earth did you get here?' the Miskito exclaimed as Hector helped him haul his canoe up on the muddy bank. 'I thought you were in Jamaica.'

'I managed to get away and join the Bay Men,' Hector explained. 'But we were flooded out by a bad storm, and had to abandon the site. Coming down the coast we met up with these other logwood cutters. They had all suffered the same misfortune. We joined forces, keeping the largest of our boats. But it's been a difficult journey. We've been living on wild fruit and an occasional seabird we shot.'

Dan could see that the survivors were in a bad way. There were about twenty men in the party and they looked emaciated. One man was shivering with fever. 'There's a Spanish cruiser in the area. You know what will happen if they catch the Bay Men,' he warned Hector.

'But they've resolved to go no further until they've filled their bellies. That's why they decided to stop here in the estuary. They intend to go inland and hunt wild cattle or pigs, if they can find them.'

Dan shook his head. 'That's foolish. The Spaniards could be here by then. I'll fetch meat for them.'

'Jezreel!' Hector called out, 'I want you to meet a good friend of mine. This is Dan. He was with me in Barbary.'

The prize fighter's glance took in the Miskito's long black hair and the narrow face with its high cheekbones and dark, sunken eyes like polished pebbles. 'Did I hear you say that you can get food for us?'

Hector glanced into the Miskito's canoe. 'You haven't even brought a musket with you.'

'I won't need one. This is my cousin's canoe and he left his fishing gear in it. But you'll have to help me.'

Mystified, Hector was about to step into the bow of the canoe when Dan stopped him. 'No, your place is in the stern,' he said. 'I'll tell you what to do.'

Under Dan's instructions, Hector hoisted the little sail and together the two men rode the river current out across the bar and to the sea. Instead of heading out to the fishing grounds as Hector had expected, Dan told him to steer close along the shore. 'Stay in the shallows, close to the mangroves,' he instructed.

Occasionally Dan rose to his feet and stood in the bow, silently scanning the surface of the water. Every time he did this, Hector feared that the canoe would capsize through his own lack of skill as steersman. But Dan shifted his weight to counteract any clumsiness and, sensing his friend's uneasiness, would soon sit down again.

'What are we looking for?' Hector asked his friend. He spoke in a whisper for it seemed to him that Dan was listening as well as watching for his mysterious prey.

An hour passed, and then another, and still Dan had not found what he was searching for. Then, suddenly, he held up his hand in warning. His gaze was fixed on something in the water, not fifty yards away and close to the edge of the mangroves. He reached down into the bottom of the canoe, not taking his eyes off what he had seen, and eased out from the bilge a straight staff about eight or nine feet long. With his free hand Dan groped between his feet and produced what appeared to be an oversized weaver's bobbin wrapped around with several fathoms of cord. The free end of the cord was lashed to a barbed metal spike as long as his forearm. Carefully Dan pushed the shank of the spike into a socket in one end of the staff. Then he unwound enough cord until he could slip the bobbin over the butt of the pole. Now he rose to his feet and stood in the canoe, the harpoon in his hand. Using it as a pointer, he showed Hector the direction that he should steer.

Hector squinted against the glare of the late-afternoon sunlight as he tried to make out the target. But there was nothing unusual. The water was green-grey and opaque, cloudy with particles of vegetable matter. He thought he saw a slight ripple, but could not be sure. The canoe slipped forward silently.

Ahead of him Dan had moved into the classic posture of a man about to throw a javelin: his left arm pointed forward, his right arm bent. The hand which held the harpoon shaft at its balance point was close beside his ear. He stood poised, ready.

Hector heard a faint breath, the puffing sound of lungs expelling air. He leaned sideways, trying to see around Dan, hoping to identify the source of the sound. His sudden movement upset the balance of the boat even as Dan threw.

The harpoon soared through the air. But as it left Dan's hand, Hector knew that he had spoiled his friend's aim. He saw Dan twist his body, swivelling to keep the direction of his throw. 'I'm sorry, Dan,' he blurted, apologising for his clumsiness.

His words were lost in the explosive upheaval at the spot where the harpoon had struck the water. The metal spike and the first two feet of shaft plunged out of view. A second later the surface of the sea rose up in a great, roiling mass. A large grey-brown shape surged upwards, water sluicing off a rounded back. Hardly had this shape appeared than it sank downwards almost as quickly, returning into the murky water, and the sea was closing over it in a small whirlpool. The entire length of the harpoon vanished, dragged downward.

The Miskito spun round, plucked the canoe's short mast out of its place and hastily wrapped the sail around the spar. Dropping the untidy bundle on the thwarts he picked up a paddle, knelt in the bottom of the canoe, and began to paddle with all his strength. 'Over there!' he shouted back at Hector who was trying to follow his friend's example. Looking forward, Hector saw that the harpoon's shaft had risen back to the surface, and was floating free a few yards ahead of them. Leaning forward as the canoe came level with the pole, Dan retrieved it. Both the metal spike and the wooden spool were gone. With a clatter Dan flung the shaft into the bottom of the canoe and was already scanning the surface of the water again. He gave a grunt of satisfaction and pointed. A little way ahead floated the wooden spool. It was spinning rapidly in the water, the coils of line unreeling and making the spool bob and twist as if it had a life of its own. The line was being stripped from the reel at a great pace.

'Come on!' urged Dan. 'We must get that too!' He was digging furiously at the water with his paddle. They reached the gyrating spool when only a few turns of the line remained. Dan dropped his paddle and threw himself forward to grab the bobbin. In one swift movement he had hoisted it inboard and jammed the spool under a thwart as he called, 'Hang on, Hector!'

An instant later Hector felt himself flung backward, the thwart striking him painfully in the small of the back as the canoe suddenly shot forward. The line had snapped taut, droplets of water squeezing from the fibres. It had become a tow rope linked to an unseen and powerful underwater force. The canoe swayed from side to side as it tore onward, lurching wildly. The pull of the line was both forward and down, and for a terrifying moment Hector thought that the entire canoe would be dragged underwater as the bow dipped and the water rose to barely an inch below the rim of the dugout.

For three or four minutes the mad, careering rush went on. In the bow Dan anxiously watched the line where it was pulled taut across the edge of the canoe. Hector was sure that the cord was too thin to resist the strain. He wondered what would happen if it snapped suddenly.

Then, without warning, the water ahead of the canoe again burst into swirling turbulence. The grey-brown shape emerged in a welter of foam, and this time Hector distinctly heard the air rushing out of animal lungs. 'Palpa!' shouted Dan in triumph. 'A big one.'

It took a full hour before the harpooned creature was exhausted and by that time the canoe had been dragged far along the coast. Gradually, the intervals between each surfacing of their prey grew shorter as the animal came up for air more frequently. With each appearance Hector could see more of it. At first it reminded him of a small whale, then of one of the seals he had seen when they hauled themselves out on the rocks off his native Ireland. But this animal was much larger than any seal he had known, seven or eight feet long, and far stouter. When it turned its head to look back at the hunters, he saw long pendulous lips, piggy eyes and a sprouting of whiskers.

Finally the creature gave up the struggle. It no longer had the strength to dive. It lay wallowing on the surface, close enough for Dan to pull in on the line and haul the canoe right alongside. From his cousin's fishing gear he produced a second harpoon head, shorter and more stubby this time, and fitted it to the staff. He chose his moment and stabbed down several times. A stain of blood spread in the water. There were a few last convulsive heaves. Then the creature lay still. 'Palpa. Your sailors call it sea cow,' said Dan with evident satisfaction. 'And a good fat one too. There will be enough meat to feed everyone.'

'What does it taste like?' asked Hector looking at the bloated shape. He recalled an old sailor's yarn that claimed such creatures were mermaids because they suckled their young at their breasts. But this animal looked more like an overgrown and bloated seal with a drooping pug face.

'Some say it tastes like young cow. Others that it is like the finest pork.' Dan was lashing the carcass alongside the canoe. 'It'll be a slow journey back to camp. One of us can sleep while the other steers.'

Hector was still conscious that not everything had gone to plan. The hunt had taken far longer than it should. 'I'm sorry that I spoiled your aim, Dan.'

His friend gave a dismissive shrug. 'You did well. It takes years to learn how to strike palpa properly. If my striking iron had been better placed, the palpa would have died more quickly. What matters is that the creature did not escape, and we have the meat we promised.'

※

IT TOOK THE entire night, and more, to sail back to where they had started. The drag of the dead sea cow slowed the canoe to less than walking pace, and the sun was well above the horizon by the time they approached the river mouth. It was promising to be another very humid and hazy day. They were keeping close to the green wall of mangroves along the shoreline to escape the worst effect of the ebbing tide when they heard the distant thud of an explosion.

'What's that!' Hector blurted, sitting up in alarm. He and Dan had changed positions in the canoe, and he had been dozing in the bow as his friend steered the craft.

'It sounded like a cannon shot,' said Dan.

'But the Bay Men have only got muskets.'

Again there came the thump of a distant explosion, followed by another. This time there was no doubt. It was cannon fire.

'Dan, I think we had better leave the sea cow where we can collect it later, and go ahead to see what's happening.'

Dan brought the canoe to the edge of the mangroves. He untied the carcass of the sea cow and fastened it securely to a lattice of roots. 'It should be safe here if the tide does not wash it away,' he said.

Warily the two men edged their little vessel forward until they reached the point where they had a clear view of the river mouth.

A two-masted brigantine was sailing slowly across the estuary, but making no attempt to enter the river. The large ensign flying from her stern was clearly visible, three bands of red, white and gold and in the centre some sort of crest. As they watched, the vessel came within a pistol shot of the far bank and began to turn. A few minutes later she had taken up her new course and was retracing her path across the mouth of the river. Hector was reminded of a terrier that has cornered a rat in a hole and is pacing up and down excitedly, waiting to finish off the prey.

'It's the Spanish patrol ship you were warned about,' he said.

There was a cloud of black smoke and the sound of a single cannon. He could not see where the shot landed, but clearly it was aimed towards the three pirogues still lying beached on the river bank.

'That's to make it clear who has the upper hand,' commented Dan. 'With six cannon a side and maybe forty men aboard, the Spaniards have got it all worked out.' He was backing water, forcing the canoe into the fringe of mangroves.

'What are they waiting for?' Hector asked.

'For the tide to turn. See that line of broken water on the bar at the river entrance. The river current and ebbing tide are too strong for the brigantine to make any headway upriver. Besides, the pilot will be cautious. He's waiting for the flood tide, and when he's sure there's enough water to carry him in over the bar, he'll take the ship upriver and blast the pirogues to pieces.'

Hector examined the Spanish guardship now heading directly towards where he and Dan lay hidden. Doubtless every pair of eyes on board the patrol vessel was looking towards the pirogues in the river. Still, he felt vulnerable and exposed.

He was about to say that a single hit from a cannonball would shatter a pirogue when he felt the canoe tilt underneath him. He grabbed for the rim of the little craft, but it was too late. Water was pouring in over the gunwale. Looking back over his shoulder he saw Dan was leaning sideways, pressing down at an angle, deliberately flooding the canoe. As the water rose within the hull, the canoe began to sink, settling on an even keel until it was awash and almost nothing showed above the surface. Hector slid out into the water. He found that he could stand, though his feet were sinking several inches into silt. By bending his knees slightly, only his head remained above water. 'No point in making ourselves obvious,' explained

Dan calmly. 'Miskito fishermen do likewise whenever they see a strange ship approaching.'

Now the brigantine was nearing the limit of her present course. Hector could see the sailors preparing to haul in on the sheets and braces. Men armed with muskets were clustered along the rail, looking into the river mouth and pointing at the beached pirogues. He heard a shouted command from the sailing master, and again the brigantine began to turn, this time presenting stern and rudder towards him. The guardship was close enough now for him to see that the crest on her ensign was a black eagle, wings spread under a royal crown.

'Is there anything we can do?' he asked Dan.

There was a long silence, and then the Miskito said, 'Hector, do you think you can reach the Bay Men's camp without being seen from that ship? It'll be hard going.'

Hector looked at the distance he would have to cover. It was almost a mile.

'You won't be able to push through the mangroves. They grow together too thickly,' Dan warned. 'You'll have to work your way along the edge of the mangroves, staying in the shallows.'

'I believe I can manage,' Hector answered him.

'Tell the Bay Men to be ready to break out an hour after low water. At that time their pirogues will be able to get over the bar, but the Spaniards will not yet have enough depth to enter the river.'

'And what are you going to do?'

'I'll stay here with the canoe and deal with the guard ship.'

Hector tried to read his friend's expression. 'Is this another of those Miskito skills, like killing sea cows and sinking canoes?'

'Sort of . . . but the Bay Men can make it easier for me. Tell them to gather up all the dead branches and fallen tree trunks and other lumber they can find, and launch them into the river while the tide is still on the ebb. They might even cut down a few trees and float them too.' He gave a thin smile. 'But make sure they are floaters, not sinkers like their logwood.'

'Anything else?'

'You'll have to hurry. There's not more than three hours of ebb left. When I see trees and other trash floating downriver, I'll know that you've managed to reach the camp. As soon as I make my move, you must get the Bay Men to start downriver in the pirogues.'

'How will I know when that is?'

'Find a place from where you can keep an eye on me here. My plan, if it is going to work, will be obvious. Now go.'

Hector turned to leave. The water was pleasantly warm, but rotting vegetation had coloured it a deep brown so it was impossible to see where he was putting his feet. Within a few paces he understood Dan's warning that progress would be difficult. The mangroves spread their roots sideways under-water, and he found himself tripping and stumbling over their new shoots as he half-swam, half waded towards his destination. Soft slime underfoot made it difficult to take a firm step, and often he sank ankle deep into the mud. When he tried to withdraw his foot, the ooze clung to him, holding him back. To keep his balance, he grasped at the mangroves and found that their bark was scaly and ridged. Soon his palms were raw and painful. He tried to stay hidden within the overhang of the mangroves, but there were sections where their matted roots made an impenetrable barrier and he was forced to swim along their outer edge, holding his breath and ducking down to avoid being seen from the Spanish patrol ship. As he floundered on, his breaths came in gasps and he had an unwelcome memory of the final moments of the hunted sea cow.

It was difficult to judge his progress. On his right the wall of mangroves seemed endless, a barrier of fleshy green waxy leaves at head level, their tangle of black and grey roots beside his shoulder. Small crabs scuttled away in fright, disappearing downwards into the water. Black and orange insects crawled upward in rapid jerks. Once he glimpsed the hurried sideways undulations of a snake swimming deeper into shelter. A little farther on he disturbed a colony of egrets and he feared they had betrayed his position as they flapped up into the sky like scraps of white paper.

The biting insects again found him a juicy victim, settling on his face the moment his head appeared above the surface, some delivering a jab as painful as a wasp sting. But his worst torment were the shellfish. Viciously sharp-edged, they clung in great clusters to the roots of the mangroves. Whenever he brushed against them, they lacerated his skin. Soon he was bleeding from dozens of slashes and cuts, and he wondered if blood in the water would attract caymans. He knew that the reptiles lived in the mangroves, and Jezreel had mentioned that he had occasionally encountered pythons in the swamps.

At length he crossed a shallow patch where finally he trod on firm sand instead of ooze, and guessed it was where the sandbar joined the river bank. Then gaps began to appear in the wall of mangroves, and finally he arrived at an opening where he could stagger up the bank and push his way through the undergrowth.

A warning shout stopped him. One of the Bay Men was facing him, musket levelled. It was a logcutter named Johnson who had joined the refugee flotilla as it followed the coast.

'It's me. Hector Lynch. I'm here with Jezreel,' he explained. He was dripping blood, exhausted and covered in slime.

Johnson lowered his gun. 'Didn't expect to see you here again. Where's that Indian friend of yours?'

'He's back beyond the sandbar, waiting. He can help us get clear.'

His statement was met with a look of disbelief. 'That I doubt,' said the Bay Man but he led Hector to where the remainder of the group were gathered in a fold of ground, safe from a stray cannonball. They had abandoned their hunting trip and were discussing what they should do.

'Lynch says that there's a way we can get clear,' said Johnson by way of introduction.

'Let's hear it then.' The speaker was an older man with a mouthful of badly rotted teeth and dressed in a tattered smock. Like his colleagues', his hair hung down to his shoulders in a greasy, matted tangle.

Hector raised his voice. 'Dan – that's my Miskito friend – says that we must be ready to break out an hour after the tide turns.'

'That's nonsense,' someone shouted from the back of the group. 'Our best chance is to wait until dark. Then make a run for it in the boats.'

'Dark will be too late,' Hector answered him. 'Well before sunset the tide will have risen far enough for the Spaniards to sail in. Their cannon will smash our boats to pieces.'

Jezreel came to his support. The big man was standing a little to one side of the gathering. 'If we make a dash for it soon after the tide turns, we do stand a chance because we'll be able to pick our course. Our pirogues will have room to manoeuvre while the Spanish ship is still confined to the deeper water. If we can get around the patrol ship, we can outpace her in the open sea.'

His intervention was met with a murmur of approval from several of the Bay Men and someone called out, 'Better than waiting here to be killed or captured by the Dons. I don't fancy being hauled off to a Havana gaol.'

'There's more!' Hector called out. 'Dan has asked that while we are waiting for the tide to turn, we dump as much trash as possible into the river – dead trees, branches, that sort of thing.'

'Does he think that the Spanish ship will get tangled up in all the driftwood?' This sally brought mocking laughter from the audience.

Again Jezreel came to his rescue. 'All of us know that the Miskito have no love for the Spaniards. I, for one, will do what

Dan asks.' He left the group and began to make his way along the river bank. About a dozen men followed him, and soon they were manhandling fallen trees and dead branches down the river bank and shoving them into the river. Hector watched the flotsam drift away and turn slowly in the current as it was carried seaward.

The other Bay Men showed no interest in helping. Several sat down on the ground and lit their tobacco pipes. Hector walked over to the older man who had been sceptical. 'If you won't help Jezreel and the others, you can at least make sure that everyone is ready to embark the pirogues the moment I give the word. I must go back to where I can keep an eye on the patrol ship, and see what my friend is doing.'

The Bay Man regarded him quizzically for several moments, then nodded. 'All right then. My mates and I will stand by.'

*

HECTOR FOUND a vantage point on the river bank where he could keep watch on the Spanish guard ship and also see where Dan was hidden. The brigantine was still patrolling back and forth, following the same track each time as if there was a furrow in the water. He wondered why the captain did not anchor and wait for the tide to turn, and could only suppose that the Spanish commander wanted to be ready in case the Bay Men made a sudden sally.

He shifted his gaze to where he knew Dan lay concealed with his sunken canoe, but could see nothing except the green border of the mangrove swamp. Dotted about the estuary were the black shapes of the timber that Jezreel and his companions had thrown into the river. A few pieces had grounded in the shallows and lay stranded, but most of them had already been carried out over the bar. Several were already out beyond the Spanish guardship.

He concentrated on the area of broken water where the

river ran out over the sandbar. The wavelets were much smaller than earlier. The tide was definitely on the turn. Soon it would be making up the channel.

Hector looked back in Dan's direction. Still there was nothing to see, only the scatter of flotsam and the Spanish vessel. Each sector of its patrol was taking about twenty minutes. He estimated that when the vessel had turned one more time, the moment would come for the Bay Men to break out from the trap.

He sucked at an open cut on his thumb. The blood was attracting more insects. Then something caught his eye. A chunk of flotsam, a log perhaps, seemed out of place. It lay among the other floating debris, part-way between the Spanish ship and the shore. He looked harder, shading his eyes. Unlike the rest of the flotsam which was nearly stationary, the log was moving slowly. Then Hector realised that it was not a log, but the hull of the upturned hunting canoe. Dan was swimming beside it, quietly pushing it forward. He was headed towards the place where the brigantine was bound to turn.

Hector ran back to where the Bay Men were waiting. 'It's time to go!' he shouted.

They gathered round their pirogues and began to manhandle them into the river. Hector joined Jezreel who was already stepping the mast on their own pirogue. In less than five minutes, the three boats were dropping downriver, their sails filling as they headed towards the sea.

The Spaniards had seen them move. The brigantine opened a ragged fire but the range was too great for accuracy, and the shots splashed harmlessly into the water. Hector counted six guns, all on her port side, and knew that there would be a brief respite while the gunners reloaded.

'Steer for the left-hand edge of the channel,' he said to Otway who was at the pirogue's helm. It was important to lure the brigantine in the direction where Dan lay waiting. A rapid clatter of wavelets slapping against the hull told that the pirogue was now crossing the bar. The water was less than three feet deep, and there was a brief scraping sound as the bottom of the pirogue touched the sand. Hector felt the hull shiver beneath his feet. But the boat's progress was scarcely checked. Now they were in deeper water, and picking up speed as the sail filled in a strengthening breeze.

Two hundred yards ahead the Spanish patrol ship had reached the end of her track and begun to turn. Her port guns had not yet been reloaded. Hector could imagine the gun crews crossing the deck to help their comrades prepare the starboard battery for the killer blow. They would be checking that each gun was properly charged, its shot wadded firmly home, priming powder in place, match burning. All they then had to do was wait until the brigantine came round on her new course and steadied. Then they would make the final adjustment to bring their guns to bear. By that time the pirogues would be within point blank range.

'We're done for,' muttered Johnson, 'but we'll not go without a fight.' He was checking his musket, waiting for the Spanish ship to come within range.

Hector's gaze searched the water beside the patrol ship. He could no longer see the dark shape that was Dan and the upturned canoe. Perhaps the Spanish vessel had run him down.

Then, unexpectedly, the brigantine appeared to falter. Halfway through her turn, she hung in one position, her bow directly downwind, her stern towards the pirogues and unable to bring any of her cannon to bear. There was confusion visible on her deck. Sailors were climbing into the rigging, trying to readjust the sails. Others were scurrying along the deck, apparently without purpose.

'Their helmsman's a right blunderer,' said Otway who was steering the pirogue. 'He's lost control of the ship.'

'Head directly for the brigantine,' yelled Hector. 'There's a man in the water. We have to pick him up.'

Otway hesitated and Jezreel gave him a great shove which

sent him flying. Seizing the tiller the big man set the pirogue's course towards Dan's head which had bobbed to the surface. Hector looked round to see what was happening with the other two pirogues. Both had set extra sails and were increasing speed. They were drawing away. Soon they would be past the Spanish patrol vessel, and out of danger.

There was a ragged volley from the Spaniards, musketry not cannon. Some of the musket balls whizzed overhead, but others puckered the water around the swimmer. The Spaniards had seen Dan. He ducked down, making a more difficult target.

'Now that's a foolish thing to do. Let's see how far he gets,' said Johnson. On the stern of the brigantine half a dozen sailors were clustered at the rail, an officer with them. A rope had been lowered, and one man was climbing over, ready to descend. The Bay Man slid the ramrod back into its place beneath the long barrel of his gun, crouched down in the pirogue, and held steady. There was a second's pause before he pulled the trigger. The noise of the shot was followed immediately by the sight of the sailor losing his hold and tumbling down into the water.

Hector pushed past to where he could look forward, directly down into the sea. He heard a musket ball thump into the woodwork beside him, and more shots from the Bay Men. Less than ten yards away, Dan's head had reappeared, the long black hair sleek and wet. He was grinning. Hector gestured to Jezreel at the helm, pointing out the new course. A moment later, Dan's hand reached up and in one smooth movement the Miskito wriggled aboard.

'What did you use?' asked Hector.

'My cousin's striking iron,' his friend replied. 'I slipped it between the rudder and the stern post when the steering was hard over. It'll have driven in even further when the rudder was centred. They'll not get it free until they have a man down who can hack it out with a chisel. Until then their rudder's jammed.'

Hector was aware that the sound of the Spaniards' musketry

was growing more distant. Jezreel had turned the pirogue so the boat was running directly away from the brigantine, presenting the smallest target. Looking astern, he could see the patrol ship was still crippled, driving helplessly downwind. By the time she was under control again, it would be dark and the three pirogues would have made their escape. Several of the Bay Men were already on their feet, waving their hats at the enemy and jeering. One man turned his back and dropped his pantaloons in derision.

'The Bay Men have agreed to go farther south,' Hector explained to his Miskito friend. 'There are former buccaneers among them who claim to know the hidden places on the coast where their old comrades-in-arms gather. They plan to rejoin them, finding safety in numbers now that there's a Spanish warship on the prowl.'

'Then they'll have to go hungry for a while. We can't go back to collect the sea cow. But it means we can pick up Jacques on our way,' said Dan.

He settled himself more comfortably against a thwart, and Hector found himself contemplating how the unselfish comradeship of men like Dan and Jacques contrasted with the cold-hearted, self-serving avarice of men like Captain Coxon.

SEVEN

Jacques had at last been able to try out his pimento sauce. It was something he had wanted to do ever since he first tasted one of the dark brown berries. The flavour had intrigued him, a peppery mix of clove and nutmeg with a hint of cinnamon. He had bought a handful of pimentos in the spice market at Petit Guave and kept them safe and dry in a cartridge box. Now he crushed his hoard and sprinkled the fragments into the cavity of a large fish Dan had gutted for their supper. Adding coconut milk and salt, the ex-galerien had wrapped the fish in leaves and buried it in a pit of charcoal coals to bake for three hours. Finally, he watched as Hector, Dan and Jezreel sampled the result.

'What do you think of the gravy?' he enquired proudly. He had carefully poured off the juices into an empty coconut shell and was dipping each piece of fish into the sauce before handing out the food.

'I would have added some ginger,' said Jezreel, pursing his lips and adopting a solemn expression.

For an instant the Frenchman took the suggestion seriously. Then he realised that the prize fighter was poking fun at him. 'Being English, you'd put in sugar and oats and make a porridge of it,' he retorted.

'That's if I were Scots, not English. You'll have to learn the difference, Jacques.' The big man licked his fingers. 'But this will do for a start. Some day I will have to show you how to make a decent pudding. Only the English know how to make puddings.'

The banter between the former prize fighter and the ex-galerien had begun within moments of their first meeting when the three pirogues had collected Jacques from the beach where Dan had left him. Then they had continued along the coast to a sheltered inlet which, according to Otway, was a favourite careenage for buccaneer ships. 'It's known as Bennett's Cove,' he had explained. 'If we wait here, there's a good chance that a buccaneer vessel will show up, and we can volunteer for her crew.' Hector thought again of the Coxon's Hole on the chart he'd copied for Snead in Port Royal, but said nothing. His previous encounter with buccaneers had left him wary of joining their company. Anyone associated too closely with them might finish up condemned for piracy and dangling on the end of a hangman's rope.

Fortunately the past two weeks had brought a change in the weather, with day after day of blue skies and brilliant sunshine tempered by a sea breeze which kept off the midges and mosquitoes. So the friends were lounging contentedly on the beach while the rest of their party was some distance away, close to the three pirogues drawn up on the strand.

Jezreel finished eating and lay back on the sand, stretching out his massive frame. 'This is the life. Can you imagine what conditions are like back home? March gales most likely, and rain. Can't say I feel like going back there for a while, even if the logwood cutting didn't work out.'

'Only a dolt would think of making his fortune by chopping wood,' Jacques observed. 'Anyone with brains would let others do the work, then relieve them of their profits.'

'You talk like a thief.'

'I only took what others were too stupid to keep safe,' said Jacques smugly.

Jezreel looked over at Hector, eyebrows raised. 'He was a pickpocket in Paris,' the young man explained. 'Until he got caught and sent to the galleys. That was where we met.'

'Nimble fingers make light work,' announced Jacques lazily. He extended one arm up in the air, and closed his fist. When he opened it, there was a pebble held between forefinger and thumb. Closing his fist, he opened it again, and his hand was empty.

'Saw plenty of tricks like that when I was in the fight game,' grunted Jezreel. 'The booths were full of mountebanks and charlatans. Many pretended they were from foreign lands. You would have done well with that foreign accent of yours.'

'Given an audience, I wouldn't even have needed to speak,' rejoined Jacques.

'No wonder it's called dumb show.'

Jacques shied the pebble at Jezreel who caught it deftly and, in the same movement, threw it back. The stone bounced off the Frenchman's hat, dislodging a small black object which fell to the sand.

'Watch what you're doing! I don't want to smell like a logwood cutter,' said Jacques and was about to tuck the item back into the hatband.

'What have you got there?'

Jacques passed the object across to his new friend who looked at it, puzzled. It was the size and shape of a large black bean, slightly shrivelled.

'Why would you want to wear a dried dog turd in your hat?' Jezreel asked.

'Smell it.'

'You must be joking!'

'No, go on.'

Jezreel held it up to his nose and sniffed. It had a definite musky smell.

'What is it?'

'A cayman's cod. I bought it in the market the same time I

got the pimentos you've just been enjoying.' Jacques took back the object. 'It's a gland. Crocodiles and caymans have them in their crotch and armpit, and they give off a pleasant smell. Better than a reeking blood-soaked smock.'

'Well, thank god you didn't put it in the sauce as well.'

Their exchange was brought to an end by a shout from Otway. He was at the back of the beach where the rise of the dunes gave him a vantage point. 'Ship! Standing in,' he called.

Everyone got hurriedly to their feet and gazed out to sea. The sun was behind them so they could easily make out the pale flash of the sails. To Hector's inexperienced eye the vessel looked very much like the Spanish guard ship, for she had two masts and was a similar size. He felt a twinge of fear that the Bay Men had been caught off guard once again. He doubted that they would be able to escape a second time. But Otway was jubilant.

'That's Captain Harris's ship, I'm sure. I served on her once. We're in luck. Peter Harris is as bold a commander as you could wish.'

He was proved right when the newcomer dropped anchor and sent her boats ashore, towing a string of empty barrels. Captain Harris had called at Bennett's Cove to take on fresh water.

'The ship is headed south to Golden Island,' announced Otway who had found former shipmates among the watering party. 'There's to be a gathering of the companies there. But no one seems to know the full details. It's to be decided by a council.'

'Will Captain Harris take on any new men?' asked Hector.

'That's for the ship's crew to decide.' Seeing Hector's look of incomprehension, Otway added, 'Among buccaneers everything is decided by vote. Even the captain is chosen by election.'

'It makes sense, Hector,' said Jacques. 'No one gets any pay. They work for their share of plunder. The larger the crew, the smaller the share-out.'

Otway had an embarrassed look on his face. 'Of course I've said that we all want to join. But the ship is already over-crowded with more than a hundred men aboard, and they are reluctant to add any more.' He was avoiding looking at the others. 'I am known to them already, so the crew is willing to add me to their number, together with my partner over there.' He nodded towards the one-eyed Bay Man who had worked with him at logwood cutting. '. . . and naturally they'll take Dan aboard if he is willing.'

'Why naturally?' asked Hector. He was not sure whether he wanted to join such suspect company but it rankled that they were being so choosy.

'The buccaneers always need strikers,' Dan explained. 'They are not fishermen and they don't have time to go ashore and hunt. They rely on Miskito strikers to get fish and turtle for them, otherwise they would go hungry.' He turned to Otway. 'Tell your friends that I'll not join unless my three friends here come with me.'

Otway went off to consult with the watering party, and returned with the news that if Dan would bring Jacques, Jezreel and Hector out to the ship, they could make their case to the assembled crew.

✳

WHEN THE LITTLE group came aboard with the last of the full water barrels, they found the crew already gathered in the waist of the ship and looking on with interest. Standing in the front rank was a vigorous-looking clean-shaven man, wearing a cocked hat trimmed with green ribbon. Hector presumed he was Captain Harris, though he took no part in the proceedings. The spokesman for the buccaneer company was a bald seaman with a gravelly voice hoarse from years of shouting.

'That'll be the quartermaster,' muttered Jacques. 'He's as important as the captain. Divides the plunder and looks to the running of the ship. Issues arms and all the rest.'

It was the quartermaster who opened the meeting. Addressing the assembly he announced, 'The Miskito tells me that he will only come with us as a striker if we take on his companions. What do you say?'

'How about the Miskito himself. Is he worth it?' called a voice.

'Judging by the number of turtle shells on the beach, he is,' answered someone who must have been ashore with the watering party.

'That big man looks right for us,' observed another. 'But he could be a clumsy slug with that antique gun of his.'

Jezreel was still carrying his old-fashioned matchlock musket.

The quartermaster turned to Jezreel. 'Your gun might be good enough for hunting cattle, but on this ship we don't use firelocks. By the time you've reloaded and fiddled with the match, your enemy will be on you.'

'Then I would use this,' announced Jezreel sliding the ramrod out from under his musket's barrel. He pointed it at the watching crowd. 'Any of you fellows willing to run at me with your cutlasses? Point or edge, it will not matter.'

The quartermaster beckoned to two crew men who stepped forward and drew their cutlasses. But, aware that their comrades were looking on, their charge was half-hearted. Jezreel merely stepped to one side and dodged them.

'Is that the best you can do?' he asked, goading them.

Now his two attackers were genuinely annoyed. Their resentment showed in the angry slashes they launched at their opponent. One man aimed for the giant's head, the other for his knees. But neither blow landed. The rod in Jezreel's hand darted out, faster than anyone could follow, and both his attackers dropped their weapons, cursing. Each was holding his hand where the ramrod had flicked across their knuckles.

'Stage fighter!' cried someone from the back of the crowd. 'I seen that trick done before.'

'Very likely,' called out Jezreel. 'Would anyone else like to try their luck? I'll face three of you at a time, if you wish.'

There were no takers, and the quartermaster intervened. 'We'll put it to the vote. All who wish to accept this man into our company raise your hands. Any objector speak up.' There was a silent show of hands.

'Who joins with you as your mate?' asked the quartermaster.

'Both my friends,' Jezreel answered placidly, sliding the ramrod back in place.

'Only one companion, that's the custom,' insisted the quartermaster. He was frowning now.

'How about that fellow with a brand on his cheek,' suggested an onlooker. 'He looks as if he can handle trouble.'

'Can either of you read or write?' The unexpected question came from a grey-haired man soberly dressed in a dark suit who was standing next to the captain.

Before Hector could answer, Jacques spoke up. 'Not as well as my friend here. He makes maps and navigates, and speaks Latin and Spanish and talks to me in French.'

'I don't want an interpreter. I require an assistant. Someone who's more adept than just a loblolly boy,' said the grey-haired man. From the way he chose his words it was clear that he was well educated.

'That's settled then,' said the quartermaster. He was anxious to close the meeting. 'We take on the big man and his French friend at full share. The other one, if he shows he's any use, can be signed on as mate to our surgeon. His share can be agreed later.'

As the meeting broke up, the grey-haired surgeon walked over to Hector and, after asking his name, enquired, 'Have you any medical experience?'

'None, I'm afraid.'

'No matter. You will learn as we go along. I am Smeeton, Basil Smeeton, and I had a medical practice in Port Royal before coming along on this adventure. Where did you get your Latin?'

'With the friars in Ireland where I grew up.'

'Good enough to converse in that tongue?'

'I think so.'

'Sometimes when discussing a patient's details,' said Smeeton meaningfully, 'it is better that the patient himself is kept in the dark.'

'I understand. But you mentioned a loblolly boy.'

'Surgeon's helper. Changes dressings and feeds gruel to the bedridden. I'm expecting more than that from you.'

Surgeon Smeeton's urbane manner was at such odds with the rough company aboard a buccaneer ship that Hector wondered why he was there. As if reading his thoughts, Smeeton went on, 'Where we are going – which, incidentally, is a land called Darien on the Main – I expect we will be meeting peoples and races whose practice of medicine is very different from ours. Much may be learned from them, perhaps in surgery but more likely in the use of plants and herbs. It is a subject which interests me greatly. I hope you'll be able to help me with my enquiries.'

'I will do my best,' Hector promised.

'There should be plenty of time for research as we won't be the only medical team with the expedition. Every crew like ours recruits at least one surgeon to sail with them, sometimes two or three. You might say that they enjoy the best medical services that their plunder – or prize as they prefer to call it – can buy.' He gave a wry smile. 'They even take out insurance against injury.'

'How can that be?' asked Hector. He did not think that Captain Harris's crew looked wealthy enough to afford medical care.

'If a man gets permanently disabled during the cruise, he receives a special bonus at the end when the quartermaster divides up the prize – this much for a lost eye, more for a limb that has to be amputated, or a hand blown off, and so on. The rates are all agreed at the start when the crew sign their mutual agreement. Very enlightened.'

By now Jacques had reappeared, a brand new musket in his hands. He was looking pleased with himself. 'How about this! Latest model flint lock issued by the quartermaster. Gave one to Jezreel as well.' He pulled back the cock and squeezed the trigger. A shower of sparks fell from the striking plate. 'No more fiddling around and keeping slow match dry in the rain.' He turned the gun over to show Hector the gunsmith's mark. 'What's more, it's French-made. Look, MAGASIN/ ROYAL. God only knows how it got here from King Louis's armoury.'

Hector took him aside and said in a low voice. 'Are you sure that you want to join up with this crew?'

'Too late. Jezreel and I have already signed articles. We are promised one full share of any loot after the investors have been repaid. You'll be able to put in for your own share as soon as you've proved your worth. Why, you may even get a surgeon's share and a half, and that's as much as the gunner and the carpenter.'

'What about the Bay Men who are being left behind?'

'Oh, they'll be picked up by other ships passing this way,' Jacques said casually.

'But from what the surgeon just told me, we will be away for some time and I had been hoping to get back to Jamaica.'

'But you only recently left there . . .' began Jacques. He paused and gave Hector a shrewd glance. '. . . any special reason?'

When Hector did not reply, the Frenchman rolled his eyes and said, 'Don't tell me! It's a woman.'

Hector felt himself starting to blush.

'Who is she then?' Bourdon asked, smirking.

'Just someone I met.'

'Just met! And you were hardly there any time at all. She must be exceptional.'

'She is.' Hector was increasingly tongue-tied, and fortunately Jacques detected his embarrassment.

'All right then. I won't say any more. But don't be too surprised if she breaks your heart.'

*

THE SURGEON wasted no time introducing Hector to his new duties. As soon as the ship had set sail, he led Hector to where a sailor was sitting in a quiet corner of the deck, with a bandage round his leg.

'Did you ever see a Fiery Serpent?' Smeeton asked.

'No, I don't think so.'

'Then I'll show you one.' Addressing the sailor, he said, 'Now, Arthur. Time to take a pull.'

The sailor carefully unwrapped the bandage and Hector saw that it covered a small stick attached to his leg by a thin brown thread.

'Watch carefully, Hector. I want you to do this job in future.' The surgeon took the stick between finger and thumb and rotated it very, very gently, winding in the thread. Looking closely, Hector saw that he was pulling the thread out of the flesh of the leg. 'That's your living Fiery Serpent. Getting it out hurts like the devil,' announced the surgeon. 'Strain gently, just enough to ease it out, an inch or two at a time, morning and evening. Pull too hard, and the creature will snap, and disappear back inside the flesh. Then you get an infection.' Turning to the sailor, he said. 'You may put back the bandage. Tomorrow my assistant will take a turn or two.'

As they walked away, Hector asked, 'What length will the serpent be?'

'Two feet would be normal,' replied the surgeon. 'Of course it is no serpent at all, but a flesh-eating worm. It causes a burning sensation as it is drawn out, hence the name.'

'And how does the victim acquire such a parasite?'

Smeeton shrugged. 'We have no idea. That is the sort of knowledge we may gain from enquiry among the native peoples. Right now you can put your Latin to use by helping me arrange the contents of my medicine chest. I threw it together in a hurry when leaving Port Royal and it is still in disorder.'

He brought Hector to a small cabin under the foredeck. 'As surgeon,' he said, pulling out a leather chest from where it had been wedged in a corner, 'I have the privilege of a cabin to myself, because it can also be rigged as a sick bay. Everyone else, even our captain and the quartermaster, has no right to any special accommodation. At night everyone lies down and sleeps wherever he wishes on the ship, on the plank as they say.'

He undid a strap and threw back the lid of the medicine chest. Inside was a jumble of phials and jars, small wooden containers, packets wrapped in paper and cloth, and objects which looked like dried plants, as well as an array of metal implements which reminded Hector of a carpenter's tool kit.

'Before we sailed, I was provided with one hundred pieces of eight from the common purse to stock it with what I considered might be needed.'

Smeeton reached in and picked out what looked like a pair of tongs with rounded tips. He snapped the jaws together with a clacking sound. 'The speculum ani,' he announced, 'useful for dilating the fleshy lips of a wound when extracting a bullet. In fact it is designed for dilating the arse gut.' He gave Hector an amused glance. 'You might think that a surgeon's work on such a venture as ours would be concerned mostly with the effects of battle, but it is not.'

He waved the speculum in the air to emphasise the point. 'The chief ailments which afflict the sailor are concerned with his digestion – constipation and the flux. For the former we can administer a syrup of cassia pods or licorice juice at one end or, if there is a stoppage, we may dilate the fundament with this implement and extract the offending blockage at the other end. That will provide comfort and remedy.'

Casually he tossed the speculum back into the medicine chest where it fell with a metallic clatter among the other instruments. 'Over the next few days,' he went on, 'I want you to clean and oil all these instruments, sharpen them as needed, and wrap them in well-greased cloth. They must not be allowed to rust.'

Looking into the chest, Hector noted wicked-looking saws and chisels, clamps and drills, pincers and nippers of different shapes and with strangely shaped jaws, even an ebony mallet.

Smeeton pulled a small cloth-bound notebook from his pocket. 'This is something else you will need. I want you to write a list of all the plasters, unguents, chemical oils, syrups, electuaries, pastilles and simples that you find, together with their quantities. I will advise you what each is suitable for so that you may make your own directory.'

*

HECTOR HAD GOT as far as listing that a plaster of sweet clover would, in Smeeton's words, 'dispel windiness', when their ship reached Golden Island. Six other vessels were already waiting at the rendezvous, a small bay facing directly across to the mainland little more than a mile away. The anchorage was ideal for their clandestine purpose. From seaward it was completely hidden behind the island's rocky peak with its cover of thick scrub and stands of ceiba trees, while a narrow fringe of beach provided level ground for a camp. Numbers of men could be seen moving about under the coconut palms, and a row of cooking tents had been set up on the beach.

'This is almost as large an undertaking as when Morgan sacked Panama. The size of that raid is famous among my people,' commented Dan looking out over the assembled shipping.

'Surely the Spaniards will have taken precautions against another attack,' said Hector. Standing on deck beside the Miskito, he had been thinking about Susanna yet again and wondering if any of the buccaneer ships might later be returning to Jamaica. If so, he would try to persuade his friends to go back there with him.

'The thirst for gold is a great lure,' replied the Miskito. He pointed to a canoe which had just entered the bay and was working its way between the anchored ships, heading towards the beach. 'I'd say those fellows may have something to do with what happens.'

'Do you know who they are?' asked Hector. The dozen or so occupants of the canoe were too dark-skinned to be Europeans. One of them was wearing on his head what looked like a metal bowl.

'They are Kuna, the people who live over there in the mountains.' Dan gestured towards the mainland where ranges of forest-clad hills rose in rank after rank, wreathed with grey wisps of low cloud. On Golden Island the weather was as brilliant and sunny as when they had joined the ship. By contrast the mainland gave the impression of being gloomily drenched in drizzle and mist.

'Hector Lynch,' said a voice behind them. Startled, they turned to find Captain Harris had come on deck. 'Your companion, the Frenchman, said that you speak Spanish.'

'That's true. My mother is Spanish.'

'I need you to accompany me ashore. The captains are holding a council with the Indian chiefs. No one among us speaks the Kuna tongue, but the Indians have lived alongside the Spaniards long enough for them to have a knowledge of their language.'

'I will do my best.'

Harris led the way to a rope ladder, and soon Hector was being ferried ashore with his captain. As he passed through the buccaneer flotilla, Hector could see that Harris's vessel was the largest in the company. The next in size was an eight-gun sloop which seemed vaguely familiar, while the smallest was a pinnace so tiny that it carried no cannon at all. Whatever the buccaneers had in mind, Hector concluded, it depended on their strength in numbers of men, not the firepower of their vessels.

He followed Harris up the beach. Standing in a group beside the path were the Indians who had just arrived by canoe. The Kuna were not as tall as the Miskito, the only natives of the Caribbean he had met so far, but they were well set up and sturdy, with dark brownish-yellow skin and straight black hair. Their faces were dominated by strong noses from which deep furrows extended down to the corners of their mouths, giving them a solemn and severe expression. The leader appeared to be the man who wore the metal bowl on his head which proved to be a vintage Spanish helmet made of polished brass. Like most of his fellows, he was stark naked except for a funnel-shaped penis cover of gold fastened by a string around his waist. From his nose dangled a crescent-shaped plate of gold. Yet the Indian who most attracted Hector's attention was the only Kuna who covered his body. He was wrapped in a blanket from his ankles to his neck. All of his visible skin – his arms and feet, and face – was a ghostly unnatural white and disfigured with red blotches and bites. When he turned to look at Hector, his eyes were half closed, the lids fluttered, and specks of blood were seeping from cracked lips.

Harris politely doffed his hat as he walked past the Kuna, and Hector followed him into the little clearing in the coconut grove where the other buccaneer leaders were already assembled. Hector counted seven captains, together with their aides, and they were standing in small groups, talking together. One of the captains, who was facing away, reached up and scratched the back of his neck. All at once, Hector knew why the eight-gun sloop in the bay had seemed familiar. It was the vessel which had intercepted *L'Arc-de-Ciel*. Even as the realisation dawned, John Coxon turned to greet Peter Harris and his eye fell on Hector. The quick flush of anger which discoloured his features left no doubt that he recognised the young man.

'Captain Harris, it would have been better if you had been with us earlier,' Coxon grated. 'We have been in consultation with the Kuna for these past five days, and are ready to make a decision.'

'I bring the largest company so it was only right that you should wait,' retorted Harris, and Hector detected a simmering rivalry between the two men.

'Let's get down to business,' said another of the captains soothingly. A man of medium height, his round soft face had the down-turned fleshy mouth and protruding lips of a carp. Obviously unwell, he was leaning on a stick and sweating heavily as he looked round the gathering with watery pale blue eyes. Hector thought he detected a whiff of manipulation, of fraudulence.

'That's right, Captain Sharpe. We must not keep our Kuna friends waiting,' agreed Coxon. He crossed to where some benches had been set out under the trees, and beckoned the Kuna to be seated. The pale man in the blanket did not come forward but moved to stand in a patch of deep shade.

As the meeting proceeded, Hector was able to put names to the other buccaneer captains. Two of them, Alleston and Macket, seemed to be lesser figures, for they said little. A third man, Edmund Cook, was a puzzle. For a seagoing man he dressed very fastidiously. He wore a deep, curving lace collar over a loose mauve tunic and had tied a bunch of ribbons to one shoulder. By contrast Captain Sawkins, seated next to him, cared nothing for his appearance. His unshaven cheeks were stubbled and grimy, and he was obviously someone who preferred action to words. He kept glancing impatiently from one speaker to the next, and fiddling with the handle of the dagger in his belt. When Coxon and Harris bickered, as they did constantly, Sawkins tended to side with Harris.

Only two of the Kuna spoke Spanish, and their strong

accents were difficult to follow. With each sentence, their gold nose plates bobbed up and down on their upper lips and distorted the words. Occasionally when no one could understand anything, the speaker would lift up the plate with one hand and address his listeners from under it. Hector was able to gather that the Kuna were confirming an offer of guides and porters to the buccaneers if they would launch a raid against a Spanish mining settlement in the interior. It was clear that the Kuna loathed the Spaniards. According to the Indians, the Spanish miners used gangs of slaves to wash gold dust from the rivers, then brought their production to a town called Santa Maria. Every four months the collected gold was taken on to the city of Panama, and the next shipment was due to be sent out soon.

'Let's not waste any more time.' It was Captain Sawkins who spoke. He looked as though he wanted to spring to his feet and rush into action immediately, sword in hand. 'Every day we spend here increases the chance that the gold will slip through our fingers.'

'What about our ships? Who's to guard them while the men are away?' asked Macket cautiously.

'I suggest that you and Captain Alleston stay here with a detachment,' proposed Coxon. 'The final division of the booty will only be made when we return, and your men will receive full shares.'

A fit of coughing made him look towards Captain Sharpe. 'Do you feel well enough to accompany us?' he asked.

'Of course I do. I'll not miss a chance like this,' answered the ill-looking buccaneer.

'Then it's decided,' concluded Coxon. 'We set out for Santa Maria in, say, three days' time. We march in ships' companies but all under one single commander.'

'And who is that commander to be?' asked Harris ironically. Hector suspected that the decision had already been taken before their arrival.

'Captain Coxon would be the most suited to lead us,' explained Sharpe. 'After all, he was with Morgan at Panama. He is the most experienced.'

Coxon was looking smug. He had slipped his hand inside his shirt front and was scratching contentedly. Hector recognised the gesture.

Then Coxon turned to the Kuna and, deliberately ignoring Hector as the interpreter, he spoke in broken Spanish of their decision. The Kuna looked pleased, and rose to return to their canoe.

'I wonder where they get the gold to make those nose plates of theirs?' muttered a sailor standing next to Hector. The voice was familiar and Hector glanced around to find that the speaker was one of Coxon's men, the sailor with the missing fingers. 'Didn't expect to see you here.' said the sailor recognising him in return. 'Just remember who is in command of this expedition,' and he gave an evil smile.

*

HOWEVER MUCH Hector disliked and mistrusted Coxon, he had to admit that the buccaneer captain knew his business. Before the meeting closed, Coxon gave strict orders that no vessel was to sail from Golden Island for fear that news of the raid might get out. Then the next day every man on the expedition was issued with lead for bullets and twenty pounds of powder from the common stock. In addition, the camp cooks were put to baking buns of unleavened bread, four to a man, as marching rations.

'If this is all we get to eat, we'll soon be asking Hector for those cassia pods he's got in his knapsack,' said Jacques looking dubiously at the food. 'No wonder they're called doughboys.'

He, Jezreel and Hector were on the landing beach in the early dawn of the third day after the conference. Half the expedition had already disembarked, and Dan had gone ahead to scout.

'Don't look so miserable,' he said to Hector who was feeling dispirited that he could not yet return to Jamaica. 'Imagine coming back to your lady with your pockets full of gold dust.'

'As a surgeon's assistant you are not supposed to be involved in any fighting,' Jezreel added. 'Just make sure that the medicine chest stays with the column. A supply of medicines is the next best thing to a keg of rum to keep up the men's morale.'

Dan was coming towards them, accompanied by one of the Kuna guides. 'Hector, can you translate? This man has something to say but I can't follow his Spanish.'

Hector listened to the guide, then explained. 'Everyone is to stay on the footpath. He says the spirits of the forest must be respected. If they are disturbed or angered, they will cause harm.' He shifted the knapsack on his shoulders. It contained a basic medical kit that Smeeton had picked out for him. The surgeon himself had still not landed, and the main medicine chest lay on the ground, awkward and heavy.

'Here, I'll take that,' said Jezreel, lifting the chest on his shoulder. 'That's Harris's green flag up ahead.'

It was another sign of Coxon's competence, Hector thought to himself. The buccaneer captain had given instructions that after landing every man was to muster to his own captain's flag and follow it as the column moved inland. It should mean that the unruly and ill-disciplined buccaneers kept some sort of order on their march and did not degenerate into a chaotic mob. Captain Sawkins and Captain Cook, Hector now saw, had both chosen to display red banners with yellow stripes, but luckily Cook had distinguished his flag by adding the outline of a hand holding a sword.

Captain Sharpe's troop was beginning to move off behind their red flag hung with green and white ribbons. They had been chosen to lead the march and behind them the column slowly got into motion, more than 300 men slipping and stumbling along the shingle beach until they reached a river mouth. Here the Kuna guides turned inland, leading the men through an abandoned plantain grove and then into the forest itself where the trees formed a canopy overhead, blocking out the sunlight. The ground underfoot was soggy with dead leaves and forest mould, the air heavy and damp. The only sounds were the low voices of the men, an occasional burst of laughter, or someone hawking and spitting. The ground sloped upward, the path twisting to avoid places where the trees grew so close together as to be impassable, their trunks wet and glistening. Occasionally the walkers came to a small stream which they splashed across. Those who were already thirsty in the muggy heat, used their hats to scoop up water and drank.

In the early afternoon they halted. The Kuna had already prepared bivouacs for them, small huts with cane walls and thatched roofs built in another abandoned plantain patch. Several buccaneers preferred to go to sleep outside on the open ground, but the Kuna became agitated. The travellers must stay indoors, they insisted. Anyone who slept on the ground risked being bitten by venomous snakes. Hector wondered if this was merely an excuse to prevent the men from straying, but suddenly there was a shout of alarm, followed by some sort of commotion. He saw a cutlass rising and falling. Smeeton, who had joined the column belatedly, hurried off towards the spot, and Hector followed him, curious to see what all the fuss was about. He found a shaken-looking buccaneer holding up the headless corpse of a snake on the tip of his cutlass. The snake was at least four feet long, mottled brown and green. Smeeton found the severed head, picked it up and cautiously prised open the jaws. The poison fangs were unmistakable. 'A true viper, and with a bite almost certainly mortal. Excellent,' the surgeon enthused. He turned over the diamond-shaped head to inspect a yellow patch on the throat, and asked the buccaneer if he could also keep the dead body. Then he stepped behind Hector and the young man felt the flap of his knapsack open. There came the sensation of the dead snake being slid inside. Hector's skin crawled.

'The first reward of our venture,' announced Smeeton from somewhere behind him. 'Cut up into small morsels, it will make an essential ingredient in our Theraci Londini, vulgarly known as London Treacle.'

'What's that for?' asked Hector, uncomfortably aware of the coils of the dead snake pressing against his back. The dead animal was remarkably heavy.

'A sovereign cure for the plague. Snake fragments steeped in a variety of herbs. Perhaps the Kuna will have their own recipe. Fiery Serpent one day, true viper another.' He gave a satisfied chuckle.

*

NEXT MORNING Smeeton was eager to track down a Kuna doctor and begin asking about native medicines. Leaving the expedition to trudge deeper into the cordillera, he and Hector were taken by one of the Kuna guides to a nearby village. Away from the hubbub and disturbance of the column, Hector could hear the sounds of the forest. There were the chattering and cooing of birds, the sudden clatter of wings and sometimes a glimpse of red and vivid green or bright blue and yellow as the birds flew to a safe distance, occasionally settling again on an overhanging branch like an exotic blossom. Close at hand came a succession of bold hooting sounds. Minutes later, a troop of black monkeys came swarming through the treetops. They were foraging for wild fruit and, to Hector's astonishment, deliberately pelted the travellers with the skins and stones left over from their meal. One self-confident male scampered until he was directly over them and purposefully urinated to show his disdain, the liquid pattering down on the forest floor.

The cane-and-thatch houses of the Kuna village were scattered across a spur of high ground, each house approached through its own plantain grove. The centre of the settlement was a longhouse as massive and lofty as the largest barn that Hector had ever seen. Like the other Kuna buildings, it had no upper floor, and its vast roof was held up on immensely thick wooden pillars. In the half-light of the windowless interior the two visitors were introduced to the village doctor. He and half a dozen village elders were waiting for them, reclining in hammocks suspended between the columns.

The village doctor had a lined, intelligent face with dark hooded eyes, and could have been anything between fifty and seventy years old. Luckily, he also spoke Spanish.

'How much time has your friend got?' he asked Hector when the young man explained that Smeeton was a surgeon and hoping to learn from the Kuna doctors.

'We must rejoin our companions later in the day,' said Hector.

The Kuna looked amused. 'For five years I was an assistant to my father. Next I was sent to study with one of my father's friends. I stayed with him for another twelve years. Only then could I begin to look after my patients.'

'My colleague just wants to learn about what plants can heal, and how to employ them. I can take notes and, if it is permitted, take away a few samples.'

The Kuna made a restraining gesture. 'Then he should talk with an ina duled. He is the one who prepares medicines. I am an igar wisid, a knower of chants. Medicine by itself does not cure. True health is to be found through the spirit world.'

Smeeton looked disappointed when Hector translated, and asked, 'Perhaps the knower of chants has some patients at this time that I could see?'

The igar wisid swung down from his hammock. 'Come with me.'

He led his visitors a short distance out of the village to a small hut isolated in a clearing. The building seemed to be on fire, for a haze of smoke was seeping out through the thatch. The Kuna pushed open the low door and ducked inside. Hector stooped to follow him and found himself choking for breath. The interior of the hut was so thick with smoke that his eyes watered and he could scarcely see. A man lay motionless in a hammock strung across the small room. Beneath the hammock stood an array of dolls, dozens of them. Some were no more than six inches high; others three or four times that size. Nearly all were human figures. They were carved from wood, and some appeared to be very ancient for they had lost all shape and were stained black with age. The Kuna doctor crouched down and began rearranging them, crooning to himself. 'Ask what he is doing,' said Smeeton.

'These are nuchunga,' said the knower of chants. 'They represent the hidden spirits which always surround us. They can help restore the patient's soul. The patient is sick because his soul has been attacked. With my song lines I try to summon the assistance of the nuchunga.'

'Let's get out into the fresh air,' coughed the surgeon after some minutes of listening to the Kuna's chanting.

As they made their way back to the village with the igar wisid, Hector asked about the pale-skinned Kuna he had seen at the council meeting on Golden Island. Was he suffering from some sort of sickness?

For several paces, the igar wisid said nothing. When he spoke, he sounded reluctant to talk about the subject.

'He is one of the children of the moon. They are born among us, and never change their colour. Their skins remain white, and their hair stays pale. They are only happy in the darkness. Then they skip and sing. Their eyes can see in the dark, and they shun the light. It is our custom that they only marry among themselves.'

'He had many sores as well as bites from insects. Are you able to help such problems with your chants?' Asking the question, Hector felt a little ashamed. He was thinking not so much of Smeeton's researches, but his own torments from biting insects. He was hoping that the Kuna had something to treat the stings and pain.

'The great Mother and Father created these children of the

moon and they will always be as they are. Chants would have no effect on their condition. Poultices made from forest plants offer a little relief to their suffering.'

They arrived back at the Kuna village and, out of courtesy to the village elders, spent some time in the longhouse, answering their questions. The Kuna wanted to know the number of buccaneers, where they were from, and what they intended. Hector had the impression that the Kuna were pleased to see anyone who would harry the Spaniards but suspicious that the foreigners might wish to stay. It was as Smeeton and Hector were leaving the village to rejoin their colleagues that the igar wisid quietly came up to Hector and placed a small packet in his hand. It was a leaf folded over and tied with a length of plant fibre. 'You asked about the poultices prepared for the children of the moon,' he said. 'I have been able to find this for you. It is some of the ointment used in those poultices and has been given to me by one of the children of the moon. I hope you will find it useful.'

'What does it contain?'

The Kuna gave an apologetic shrug. 'I know only that it contains the seed of a certain fruit whose name has no translation. The seed is hard and black, about the size of a child's fist, and the ina duled grinds it into powder which he then mixes into a paste with other herbs. The paste also cures ulcers and other sores of the skin.'

Hector unslung his knapsack and as he was stowing away the packet, Smeeton asked, 'What's that you've got there?'

'Some sort of skin ointment,' Hector explained.

'Let's hope it's effective. It's not much to show for our enquiries.'

But Hector did not reply. He was noticing that what he had thought was a small dark mound of dirt beside the path had uncoiled itself and was slithering off into the undergrowth.

EIGHT

*

WHITE SPLINTERS of snapped branches, churned-up mud and scrapes where the moss had been knocked off rocks told them when they had rejoined the main trail. Shortly afterwards they met a buccaneer returning back down the path. He was soaked with sweat and in a bad temper. 'Shit-awful country,' he growled, eyeing them morosely. 'I've had enough of clambering through this stinking forest. I'm going back to the boats.'

'How far ahead is the column?' Smeeton asked.

'Over the next crest,' came the surly answer. 'A company of idiots, if you ask me. Some of them are cracking open the rocks and searching for gold. If anything glitters or sparkles they think they've discovered the mother lode.' He gave a derisive snort. 'Fool's gold, more likely.' He took off his hat and wiped the sweat from the browband before heading on towards the sea.

'A very republican rule, as I mentioned,' said Smeeton coolly, 'a buccaneer can abandon a project with the agreement of his fellows, and he will not be treated as a deserter as would be the case if he was a military man. Admittedly, it is unusual to see a single buccaneer turn back. Normally they fall away in groups.'

They reached the buccaneer camp just before dusk and

found the expedition in a sour mood. The exhausted men were lying on the ground or seated in small groups around sputtering camp fires. Everything was already damp, and to make matters worse a brief shower of rain was followed by a fine drizzling mist that soaked through their clothes. In the grey evening light Hector tracked down his friends and found Dan skinning the carcasses of several small animals about the size of hares that he had hunted. Jezreel and Jacques were looking on critically.

'How do you propose cooking them?' Jezreel was asking the Frenchman.

'To my way of thinking they have the head of a rabbit, the ears of a rat, and hair like a pig. So I can broil, fry or bake them depending on your choice,' Jacques replied, a hint of sarcasm in his voice. He sounded weary.

'Just as long as you don't bring out the flavour of rat,' observed Jezreel. Turning to Hector he said, 'The captain was looking for you earlier.'

The young Irishman was surprised. 'Captain Harris?'

'Yes, he wanted you to attend another council with the other captains and a couple of the Kuna chiefs. But I said that you had gone off with our surgeon.'

'Did the council meet?'

'It was a bad-tempered affair with a lot of shouting. I listened on the fringes. Everyone is grumbling and complaining. It seems that no one expected this journey to be such hard going. Coxon was particularly angry. He feels his leadership is being called into question. He and Harris were at one another's throats. Your name came up. Coxon called you a little whoreson – that was the exact phrase he used – and asked Harris why he had brought you along to the last council meeting. Harris replied that it was none of Coxon's business and he did not trust the interpreter that Coxon had provided.'

'Was anything decided?'

'Sawkins is elected to command the forlorn. He's to choose

eighty of our best men to lead the attack when we come into contact with the enemy.'

'Well, at least they got the right man. Sawkins has a reputation as a fire-eater, always ready to lead the charge.'

'Perhaps too much so,' said Jezreel with a slight frown. 'In the ring I learned it's seldom a good idea to rush in. Better to bide your time until you see the right opening. Then strike.'

At that instant there was a shockingly loud explosion very close by. Everyone sprang to their feet and looked in the direction of the noise. A small group of buccaneers had been seated around a camp fire, now one of them was clutching his face and crying out in pain. He seemed unable to get to his feet.

'What in the devil's name was that?' asked Jacques, bewildered. But Hector had grabbed his knapsack of medicines and was already running towards the scene. 'Bring the medicine chest,' he called back over his shoulder, 'and find Smeeton. There are people hurt.'

He arrived at the spot to find the buccaneer was badly burned. His thigh had been torn open by the blast. Hector knelt beside the victim. 'Lie still,' he said. 'A surgeon will be here soon, and we must clean the wound.'

The man was gritting his teeth in pain and staring down at the damaged leg. 'Stupid, stupid, stupid bastard,' he repeated savagely.

Hector gently eased back the shredded clothing. Underneath were patches of charred and blistered skin. 'What happened?'

'It's this rain. Gets into the gunpowder, and makes it useless. Gabriel who has the wits of wooden block was trying to dry out his powder. Spread it on a dish and held it over the fire. Too close, and the whole lot blew up.'

'Hector, I'll take over now.' It was Smeeton. The surgeon had arrived with Jezreel carrying the medicine chest. 'Get someone to fetch a basin of water, and I'd be obliged if you would pass me a pair of small tongs from the chest. Search this man's pack and see if there's anything in it which can be used for bandages.'

For several minutes the surgeon cleaned and probed with his forceps, removing traces of cloth and dead skin. The surface of the thigh was pitted with several irregular wounds, the largest two or three inches across. The skin around them was a dead white or a flaring angry red.

'This is going to take a very long time to heal,' commented Smeeton. With a start Hector realised that the surgeon was speaking to him in Latin.

'Will he lose the leg?' asked Hector, also in Latin. He had a nightmare vision of having to use the saws and clamps he had cleaned and sharpened.

'Only if there is an infection. No bones are broken.'

'What are you two gabbling about!' An angry shout ended their discussion. Coxon was standing over them, his face working with anger. 'God's Bones! Can't you talk in English. What's the matter with this wretch?'

Smeeton rose to his feet, wiping his hands on a cloth. 'He's badly injured in the thigh by an explosion of gunpowder. From now on he'll have to be carried in a litter.'

'I'll not have the column slowed down by invalids,' Coxon snapped. 'If tomorrow morning he cannot get on his feet, we leave him here. He's wasted enough gunpowder as it is.' The buccaneer captain's glance fell on Hector who had remained kneeling beside the injured man. 'You again,' he barked. 'A pity you weren't standing closer to the blast,' and he turned on his heel and strode away across the soggy ground.

'Not much sympathy there,' sighed Smeeton. 'Hector, look in the medicine chest for a jar of basilicon, and add hyperium and aloe if they are readily to hand. You should know where to find them.'

Hector did as he was asked and watched the surgeon spread the salve on the open wounds.

'Best keep your leg covered with a cloth to prevent insects feasting on the sores,' Smeeton told his patient. 'Tomorrow we will decide what is to be done.'

*

NEXT MORNING the injured man could barely hobble, even with a crutch cut for him. So while the column were breakfasting on the last of their doughboys, mildewed and mushy with damp, Smeeton asked Hector to prepare a good quantity of the healing salve. 'We'll leave it with him, and he can attend to his own wound. In a day or so he should be able to begin making his way back to the ships by slow stages. I doubt that he will have the strength to catch up with us.'

That day's march, it turned out, would have been impossible for the invalid. The Kuna guides led the column up the steep side of a mountain. In places the narrow path skirted the edge of ravines and was only wide enough for one man at a time. Here each buccaneer had to hold on to the vegetation to prevent himself slipping over the edge. It was small consolation that the Kuna guides told them that they were now crossing the watershed, and that the next stream they reached flowed towards the South Sea. When they descended the far slope, it was to find that the trail often used the stream bed itself. They had to wade knee-deep in the water, avoiding sink holes and hidden snags.

Eventually, and after another two days of this tortuous progress, the stream grew wide and deep enough for the Kuna to provide a number of small dugout canoes to carry them. But there were only enough boats for half the expedition, and the remainder of the column still had to march along the slippery, overgrown banks. The men who thought themselves lucky to be in the canoes quickly found that their optimism was misplaced. Dozens of fallen trees lay across the stream, and there were so many shallows and rapids that much of each day was spent manhandling the craft over the obstacles. Hector found himself treating numerous sprains and cuts and gashes, and the contents of the medicine chest were rapidly depleted.

Only after a full week of this wearisome marching and canoeing did the Kuna guides finally announce that the buccaneers were close to their target. The town of Santa Maria was less than two miles downriver. That night the tired expedition made camp on a spit of land, and ate cold food for fear that the smoke from their cooking fires would alert the Spanish garrison.

*

HECTOR AWOKE to the sound of a distant musket shot and the staccato beat of a drum. For a moment he lay with his eyes closed. He was aware that he was lying on the ground and that a sharp lump of stone was pressing into his hip but he was hoping to steal a few more moments of sleep. Then he heard the drum again. It was sounding an urgent tattoo. He rolled over and sat up. It was daybreak and he was in a small makeshift shelter made of leafy branches of the sort that the Kuna had taught the buccaneers to construct during their long march over the mountains. Beside him Jacques was still snoring softly, but Jezreel had heard the sounds. The prize fighter was propped up on one elbow and wide awake.

'Last time I heard that noise I was still in the fight game,' observed Jezreel. 'We had a drummer who walked up and down the streets, rattling away and announcing when the next bout would take place. I'd say that this time it means that the good citizens of Santa Maria have learned we are here, and they're getting ready to greet us.'

'Do you know where Dan has got to?' asked Hector. He had not seen the Miskito since the previous evening when Dan had gone off to talk with the other strikers.

'He's probably still with his chums.'

'Get up! On your feet! Time to move!' There were shouts outside, and Hector recognised the hoarse voice of Harris's quartermaster.

He followed Jezreel out of the low doorway to find that the buccaneer camp was stirring. Men were emerging from their shelters, rubbing the sleep from their eyes, and looking around for their comrades or heading off into the bushes to relieve themselves.

'Muster to your companies!' The yelling was insistent.

Captain Sawkins came loping towards them. He was wearing a bright yellow sash that made him look very dashing. 'You and you,' he said briskly, pointing to Jezreel and to Jacques who had just appeared. 'I want both of you in the forlorn. Attend to my flag.' He hurried on, selecting other men for the initial attack.

Left to himself, Hector looked around trying to find Smeeton. A little distance away the surgeon was talking to Harris and the other captains. He went towards them.

'Hector,' said the surgeon catching sight of him. 'Take your knapsack and go forward with Captain Harris and deal with any minor injuries on the battlefield itself. Leave the medicine chest here. I will set up a medical station where the worse injuries can be brought back for treatment. Hurry now.'

Hector found himself following Harris and the other captains through the woodland in the direction of where the drum had sounded. The ground rose steadily and they had to push their way through dense undergrowth, unable to see more than a few yards ahead. Their Kuna guides were nowhere to be seen, and it took nearly half an hour to arrive at a vantage point on a low ridge. From there they had a clear view of their objective, the gold-rich town of Santa Maria they had struggled so hard to reach.

Their first impression came as a shock. They were expecting a substantial colonial town with stone-built ramparts and paved streets, red-tiled roofs and a market square, perhaps even with a fort and cannon to guard its treasures. Instead the scene was of a haphazard scatter of thatched buildings which amounted to little more than an overgrown village built on open land sloping gently down to the river. There was no defensive wall, no gate, not even a watchtower. But for the Spanish flag hanging limp from its pole, the place might even have been mistaken for a large Kuna settlement. In addition the town looked deserted.

'Is that really Santa Maria?' said Harris wonderingly as he stepped back into the fringe of the woodland so as not to be seen from the town.

'Must be. There's a Spaniard scuttling for cover,' observed Captain Sharpe. A figure dressed in an old-fashioned breastplate and helmet had run out from one of the thatched houses and was heading towards a crude stockade built a little way to one side of the settlement.

'That's their only defence,' stated Harris, narrowing his eyes as he gazed down towards the Spanish position. 'The palisade can't be more than twelve feet high, and it's only made of wood posts. That may be enough to defend against a Kuna attack using bows and arrows, but nothing to stop a force of musketeers. The Spanish garrison must be holed up inside, and scared out of their wits.'

'That's no reason for us to be reckless,' said a harsh voice from behind him. Coxon had joined them. He was accompanied by a spear-carrying Kuna. It was the Indian who had been wearing the brass helmet at the original conference on Golden Island, though now he had put aside his shining headgear. 'We will wait for our Kuna allies. They are bringing up two hundred of their warriors in support.'

Coxon was making it clear that he was in command of the attack. 'I have given orders for Captain Sawkins to muster the forlorn in the cane brakes by the river.'

'Surely we should attack at once.' Harris spoke sharply, showing his frustration. 'The Spaniards may have sent for reinforcements. We need to take the place before they get here.'

'No! If we play our cards right, we might be able to get the Spaniards to hand over what we want – the gold and valuables – without a fight.'

'And how would you propose doing that?' Harris demanded. His tone was mocking.

'We pretend that we are a far larger force than is the case, and propose to the Spaniards that they withdraw from Santa Maria unharmed, provided they leave behind the treasury and any gold dust recently brought in.'

'What makes you think that they will accept?'

'It's worth a try,' Coxon answered, and a sly expression passed across his face. 'Besides, if we begin a parley, it will distract the Spaniards from launching a sortie and discovering our true strength.'

Harris looked sceptical. 'There's no sign that the Spaniards are going to leave the shelter of that stockade.' As if to support his words, a ragged volley of musket fire came from the Spanish position. Puffs of smoke burst out from the loopholes cut in the stockade. The defenders must have glimpsed Sawkins' assault party forming up in the cane brakes because the shots were aimed towards the river. There was no sign of the Kuna auxiliaries.

'That makes my point for me,' said Coxon caustically. 'If the Spaniards are concerned for their own skins, they will agree to abandon their position. We will offer them full honours. We have nothing to lose.' He glanced at Hector, a calculating gleam in his eye.

'And, Captain Harris, you have provided exactly the right person to carry our message to the Spaniards. This young man, as you have assured me so often, speaks excellent Spanish. He can take our offer to the stockade under a flag of truce, and we will wait here for the answer. Captain Sawkins will await my signal before he launches the first attack.'

When Harris did not reply, Coxon took his silence as assent. Addressing Hector, the buccaneer said, 'Lynch, you are to approach the stockade carrying a flag of truce. There you will ask to speak to the Spanish commander. Inform him that we are in overwhelming strength – tell him, we are over one thousand muskets. He's no way of knowing our true numbers – and, to avoid unnecessary bloodshed, we are willing to allow him and his garrison to withdraw peacefully. Our only condition is that all valuables are left within the town. If he agrees to these terms, his men will be permitted to retain their weapons and leave with full honours, colours flying and drums beating. Do you understand your instructions?'

'Yes,' replied Hector. He was relieved that Coxon seemed no longer to resent his presence, but a little puzzled by his abrupt change of manner. Coxon now appeared to place his trust in him.

'Good. Put down your knapsack, and use your shirt as a white flag. You'll need some sort of staff.' Coxon glanced at the spear that his Kuna companion was carrying. 'That spear will do. Ask for the loan of it.'

In slow careful Spanish Hector explained to the Kuna what was proposed. The man looked baffled. 'But we have to kill the Spaniards,' he said.

'Get on with it,' snapped Coxon. 'We haven't got all day to stand talking.'

Hector repeated his request, and reluctantly the Kuna handed over his lance. The young man tied his shirt to the shaft and was about to step out into the open when Coxon caught him by the elbow. 'Don't go too fast! Walk slowly. Remember we are also giving Captain Sawkins time for his forlorn to take up position.'

Hector stepped from cover and immediately attracted several musket shots from the palisade. But the range, some four hundred yards, was too great for accurate shooting and he did not even know where the shots went.

Anxiously he held the lance higher and waved it from side to side so that the white cloth could be seen clearly. The musketry ceased.

Hector walked slowly forward. A hard knot of fear formed in his stomach and within a few paces the staff was slippery with sweat from his hands. He took deep slow breaths to calm himself, and concentrated on keeping the white flag visible. After about fifty yards he stole a quick glance to his right, hoping to see where Jezreel and Jacques were with Sawkins' assault group. But a fold of ground obscured his view. He hoisted the white flag still higher and decided that he would keep his gaze fixed unwaveringly on the wooden palisade as if this focus would somehow make them respect his flag of truce.

The ground between the palisade and the edge of the woods where he had emerged was rough pasture dotted with low scrubby bushes. He guessed that the original woodland had been cut back by the Spaniards to give a clear field of fire from the stockade, but over the years this precaution had been neglected. The bushes and long grass had been allowed to grow back so that he was obliged to pick his route carefully, making sure to stay within full view of the stockade. From time to time briars and thorns snagged his breeches, and he wondered what would happen if he put his foot into a hole, tripped, and fell. Would the Spanish musketeers think it was a trick, and shoot? There was no doubt that their marksmen were on edge and that they kept their sights trained on him as he moved closer.

An insect landed on his shirtless shoulder, and a second later he felt the burning pain of a bite. He clenched his teeth and restrained himself from slapping away the insect. He needed both hands to hold the white flag high and steady.

Perhaps three or four minutes had passed since he had left Coxon and the other captains, and still there had been no response from the Spanish stockade. No musket fire, no movement. Everything was quiet. He began to breathe a little more easily. He became conscious of the warmth of the morning sun on his skin, a faint smell of something sweet – rotting fruit on the ground under the bushes perhaps – and a black shape circling in the sky high above the stockade, a bird of prey.

Steadily he paced onward.

He had covered perhaps half the distance to the stockade safely when, without warning, there was a sudden fusillade of shots, followed by a fierce, defiant yell. Shocked, he faltered in his stride, scarcely believing that the Spaniards had ignored his flag of truce. But there was no gun smoke billowing from the palisade, and in the same instant he realised that the gunfire had not come from the Spaniards, but from behind him. It was Sawkins and the forlorn who had begun shooting.

Seconds later came the counter-fire from the stockade, an irregular succession of shots as the defenders responded. This time he clearly heard the hum of musket balls whizzing past him. Some of the Spanish marksmen were taking him as their target where he stood exposed on the open ground. A musket ball slashed through a nearby bush, followed by the noise of the cut twigs pattering to the ground. Another musket ball hummed past his head.

Appalled, he threw away the staff and flag and flung himself to the ground, seeking cover. As he lay there, face down to the earth, he heard another volley of musketry from behind him and then a second cheer.

He lay still, not daring to move. For a moment he considered jumping to his feet and running back towards the woods, but dismissed the idea as suicidal. He was certain to be cut down by the Spanish marksmen.

Another cheer, and this time much closer. There was a tearing and crashing, and the thump of running feet. Cautiously he looked up and to his right. Some forty yards away was Sawkins, instantly identifiable in his bright yellow sash. He was bounding forward through the long grass, whooping and shouting and charging straight at the stockade, musket in one hand and cutlass in the other. Close behind him a score of heavily armed buccaneers was running full pelt towards the Spanish defences. As Hector watched, one of the buccaneers dropped to one knee, took aim with his musket and fired at the palisade. A second later he was back on his feet and careering onward, ready to use his musket as a club.

Within a few moments the first of the forlorn had reached the stockade. Someone must have found a chink between the wooden posts because two or three of the attackers were levering away with some sort of crowbar. A second later a small section of the palisade collapsed, leaving a small gap.

Now the buccaneers were tearing at the opening, making it wider. Later arrivals were thrusting their musket barrels through the loopholes and shooting in at the defenders. In the general mayhem there seemed to be little or no resistance from the Spanish garrison.

Shakily Hector started to get up. 'What the devil are you doing here?' said someone with a French accent. It was Jacques, musket in hand. He was clearly shocked at the sight of Hector rising from the ground.

'I was on my way to parley, carrying a white flag, when you attacked,' blurted Hector. He was still appalled by his narrow escape.

'We didn't see you,' said Jacques. 'You could have got yourself gunned down and that for nothing.'

'But I was on my way to offer the garrison safe conduct if they surrendered the town gold.'

'Christ! What imbecile came up with that idea?'

'Captain Coxon sent me.'

'Coxon? But he must have known that Captain Sawkins' idea of a battle is to charge straight at the enemy. That's why Sawkins was given the forlorn.'

'But Coxon had ordered Sawkins to await his signal before launching an attack.'

'Did he?' Jacques looked incredulous. 'That's the first I've heard of it. Sawkins didn't mention it to myself nor Jezreel or any of the others. He brought us up through cane brakes, and as soon as we had a clear sight of the Spanish position, gave the order to fire and charge.'

'Coxon claimed that the parley would also give the forlorn more time to get into position and prevent the Spaniards from learning our strength.'

Jacques grimaced with disgust. 'Now you may have the truth of it. A white flag can be a ruse. But it was crazy of you to volunteer to carry it.'

'I didn't volunteer,' confessed Hector. 'Coxon ordered me to do it, and I thought it was a genuine parley.'

Jacques gave him a searching look. 'Hector, I would say that Captain Coxon very nearly arranged your death.'

*

BY NOW the fight at the palisade was over, and the Spanish garrison had surrendered. The battle had lasted barely twenty minutes, and the buccaneers had complete mastery of the stockade and the town itself. Hector went forward with Jacques to where the Spanish prisoners were being herded together. They were a sorry-looking lot, men of all ages from teenage lads to greybeards. Some of their weapons were arquebuses so obsolete that they required props on which to support the clumsy barrels.

'No wonder their rate of fire was so dismal,' commented Jacques. 'It must have taken ages to reload. How could anyone ever think that they were capable of defending this place?'

'Perhaps it was not worth defending,' said Hector. He had seen the disappointed expressions on the faces of buccaneers returning from investigating the settlement. They had with them a frightened Spaniard dressed in the clothes of a clerk.

'What a dump!' exclaimed one of the buccaneers. 'Nothing of value. Just miserable houses and wretched people.

'Didn't you find any gold?' asked Jacques hopefully.

The man laughed bitterly. 'There's a town treasury all right. We kicked in the door. But it was empty. This fellow was hiding nearby. He's some sort of a bookkeeper.'

'Perhaps you'll let me question him,' Hector suggested.

'Go ahead. He's in a complete funk. Thinks we'll hand him over to the Kuna.'

The Spaniard was more than eager to answer any question that Hector put to him. The townsfolk of Santa Maria had known for days that the buccaneers were approaching, so the governor had arranged a fleet of boats to evacuate as many of the women and children as possible. The treasury had been emptied out, three hundred weight of gold put aboard a small sloop and sent by river to the capital in Panama. Finally the governor, his deputy, the local dignitaries and the priests had also left. All that remained in Santa Maria were townsfolk who were too poor or insignificant to get away.

'So that's it then,' exclaimed Jacques. 'We've come all this way, done all the marching and wading through rivers and lying on hard ground and eating vile food, only to find that the cupboard is bare.' He gave a snort of disgust.

At this point Captain Sawkins walked up to them. His yellow sash was speckled with flecks of gunpowder, and there was a sword cut in the shoulder of his buff coat. 'What have you managed to find out from this Spaniard?' he asked.

Hector told him about the Spanish withdrawal, and immediately Sawkins was eager to set off in pursuit. 'If we hurry we might catch up with that boat carrying the gold dust. There's a pirogue the Spaniards left behind which we can use.'

He crooked a finger at Hector. 'You come along, and bring that Spaniard with you. He'll be able to identify the boat for us.'

'I am assistant to Surgeon Smeeton. He's waiting for me at the camp,' Hector reminded him. 'I'll need to inform him where I'm going.'

'Then do so, and while you're about it, bring some more medicines with you. We may have some fighting to do.' Sawkins glanced at Jezreel and Jacques. 'You two are still members of the forlorn. You also come with me. Be ready to set off downriver in an hour.'

*

HECTOR RAN back to where he had left his knapsack, stopping to pick up the abandoned spear and put on his shirt. When he got back to the camp, it was to find the bald quartermaster from Harris's ship seated on a log, his head bowed. Smeeton was standing over him and sewing a flap of skin back onto the quartermaster's scalp.

'Hector, there you are,' said the surgeon as casually as if he was in his consulting rooms in Port Royal. 'A minor head wound, and you see the advantages of hair loss. No need to shave the hair away before deploying needle and thread.'

His stitching finished, the surgeon wrapped a bandage around the wound, and the quartermaster got up and walked away.

'Captain Sawkins has asked me to accompany him down-river, in pursuit of the Spanish treasure,' said Hector.

'Then by all means go,' answered Smeeton. 'There's precious little medical work for you here. We lost just two dead in the entire action, and half a dozen wounded, so there's hardly enough work to go around. The other companies have brought along at least a couple of surgeons apiece. In fact we seem to have so many medical men on this expedition that I'm thinking of returning to the ships, accompanying the walking wounded. Now that we've crossed the isthmus I don't expect to add much to my pharmacopoeia.'

'Is it all right if I take some medicines with me?' Hector asked. 'Captain Sawkins requested I do so.'

Smeeton smiled indulgently. 'But of course. It'll be a chance to use those notes you made while sorting through the medicine chest.'

Hector opened the chest and looked inside. The salves and ointments used up during the march across the isthmus had been replaced by Smeeton's collection of items he thought might possess curative powers – dead snakes, odd-shaped roots, dried leaves, strips of bark, seeds, coloured earth, monkey dung, even the skull of a creature like a dwarf elephant that Dan and other Miskito strikers had found feeding beside the river. The animal's flesh had provided fresh meat for three dozen hungry buccaneers. The surgeon had kept the cranium.

Then his eye fell on the packet that the Kuna medicine man had given him. It was the ointment made for the children of the moon as a poultice for their skin sores. He took the packet from the chest, consulted his notes and found a jar labelled 'Cantharides'. Turning his back so Smeeton could not see what he was doing, the young man carefully untied the leaf wrapper of the Kuna medication. Inside was a blob of pale waxy ointment about the size of his fist. Spreading the leaf on the ground, Hector carefully tipped out several spoonfuls of yellowish-brown powder from Smeeton's medicine jar and, using a twig, stirred the powder into the Kuna salve. Then he wrapped up the packet once again, and returned both it and the jar to the chest.

He finished loading his knapsack with medicines, and said goodbye to Smeeton. As he turned to leave, he said casually, 'Have you had a chance to try out the Kuna skin ointment yet?'

'No,' replied the surgeon. 'It would be interesting to do so.'

'Captain Coxon was asking if you had anything to relieve the rash on his skin. The past few days in the jungle have made the itching much worse.'

'So I noticed,' said Smeeton. 'I shall suggest that he tries the ointment. It can do no harm.'

As he headed off to where Jezreel and Jacques would be waiting, Hector was smiling to himself. It was the quartermaster's bald head which had reminded him of Smeeton's store of cantharides powder. Smeeton had cited it as another example – like snake venom – of a poison that could have beneficial properties. Cantharides powder was made from the powdered wings of a beetle and very popular with the buccaneers as an aphrodisiac. More prosaically, Smeeton had said, the powder applied very sparingly to the skin would encourage hair to grow. However, if used in quantity, it brought on violent itching, caused a burning rash, and raised a mass of painful blisters.

NINE

A HUNDRED MILES away in the city of New Panama, the governor, His Excellency Don Alonso Mercado de Villacorta, was shocked by the fall of Santa Maria. The news was brought to the city by stunned refugees who described how the Kuna, given the chance, had massacred the Spanish settlers once they had been disarmed by the buccaneers.

'This has all the potential to turn into a disaster,' he said in his characteristically despondent tone to the emergency meeting he had called in his office. 'A gang of pirates is now on the loose in the South Sea. It is exactly what I and others have been warning the authorities about for years. But no one took a scrap of notice. What are we to do?'

He looked round the conference table. His glance swept past the city councillors and church dignitaries, barely paused on the two colonels who commanded his cavalry and infantry, and came to rest on Don Jacinto de Barahona, the officer in charge of the Pacific naval squadron.

Barahona was thinking to himself that the governor was being unduly negative.

'We go on the offensive,' he said firmly. 'Stamp out the threat immediately. If we don't, other pirates will follow the route they have found over the isthmus. We risk being overwhelmed.'

'But we don't know where to find the pirates, nor their number,' objected the governor. He had a habit of tugging at his right ear lobe when he was worried. 'They could be anywhere. The coast is a maze of islands and inlets. Our forces could search for weeks and not discover them. Meanwhile the city would be left without protection.'

'Could we not ask the Indians to keep a look out on our behalf?' The suggestion came from the bishop. He was newly arrived from Old Spain, and had yet to learn that the Indians were not the devout and loyal Christians he had been led to expect.

'The Indians!' exclaimed the cavalry colonel, his mouth turned down in a grimace. 'It was the Indians who showed the pirates their trail over the mountains.'

'There's no need to go searching for the pirates. They will come to us,' said a quiet, firm voice. The speaker was Capitan del Navio, Francisco de Peralta. His swarthy tan and the maze of lines and wrinkles on his face were the legacy of a lifetime sailing the Pacific Ocean. For thirty years Don Francisco had worn a furrow in the sea between Panama and the southern ports of the viceroyalty of Peru. There was hardly a vessel which he had not commanded, navigated or escorted – galleons with cargoes of bullion, tubby urcas loaded with merchandise, fast pataches carrying official correspondence, even a pasaca-ballo, a flat-bottomed horse ferry, out of which he had once disembarked a troop of cavalry to fight the Aurocanos in Chile. Now, as Capitan del Navio, his ship was a barca longa, an armed brigantine, anchored off Panama City.

'The pirates have succeeded in crossing the mountains, but they find themselves in a quandary,' Peralta went on. 'They must have boats if they are to reach and attack Panama. To march overland along the coast is too slow and too hazardous. The only craft available to them will be small dugout canoes made by the Indians, and perhaps a piragua or two. This makes them vulnerable.'

Barahona had grasped the point Peralta was making. 'We must shut down the sea lanes. None of our vessels are to sail from any port. All those currently at sea will be ordered into harbour,' he said.

'But surely we should send out boats to warn our coastal settlements that the pirates are on the prowl,' protested the bishop. He was feeling piqued that his earlier suggestion had been dismissed out of hand.

'No. The pirates might capture our vessels and turn them against us.'

'What naval forces do we have to defend us if the pirates do get this far?' The governor put the question directly to Barahona though he already knew the answer. It was better that the civilians and the Churchmen were made aware just how acute the danger was.

'There are five merchant ships currently at anchor. One of them, *La Santissima Trinidad*, is a large galleon, but currently she is fitted out as a merchant vessel so has no armament. Then there are the three small warships of the South Sea squadron.' Barahona was careful to describe the colonial navy as an armadilla, a squadron. Its official title might be far grander as an Armada or Fleet, but the merchants of Peru and Panama had been stingy about paying the situados, the special taxes which were meant to fund the colony's defences. So now the royal vessels were few in number, undersize and decrepit. The warships at his disposal were barca longas like Peralta's, a two-masted craft equipped with a dozen cannon.

'Surely that should be sufficient to deal with a handful of pirates in canoes,' sniffed the cavalry colonel.

'Our main problem is not in ships, but in men,' retorted Barahona crisply. As always the land soldiers overlooked the fact that sailors took far longer to train than infantrymen.

'We have enough competent seamen to man just one of the warships. They are mostly Biscayners, so they are prime seamen and excellent at their job. But the other two vessels will be relying on locally raised crews.' Barahona's eyes flicked towards Peralta and the officer seated next to him, Capitan Diego de Carabaxal. The latter was a competent seaman but Barahona was not sure that Carabaxal would have the necessary courage when it came to a fight. 'Both those vessels are short-handed. So I propose stripping the merchant ships of their sailors and redistributing their men to the warships.'

'Is that wise? Without crews they cannot save themselves,' objected one of the councillors. From the note of alarm in the man's voice Peralta suspected that he was part-owner of one of the merchant ships and dismayed at the threat to his investment.

'If any merchant ship is about to fall into the hands of the pirates, it will be scuttled or burned on my orders.' Barahona had the satisfaction of seeing the councillor go pale at the prospect.

'Then it's decided,' announced the governor. 'The armadilla will put itself in a state of readiness to intercept and destroy the pirates while they are still in small boats. The land forces are to concentrate in the city and look to the defences should the pirates succeed in coming ashore.'

The bishop closed the meeting with a prayer for salvation, beseeching the Almighty to thwart the evil designs of the heathen sea robbers, and Francisco de Peralta left the governor's office. He had only a short walk to where his ship's cockboat was waiting. As he crossed the main square of New Panama, he remembered what it had been like the last time the pirates had attacked. Henry Morgan, the great pirate, had marched across the isthmus with 1,200 men. A garrison of four regiments of foot and two squadrons of horse had failed to stop a ragtag force so poorly supplied that the bandits had been obliged to eat their leather satchels during their advance. The entire city, seven thousand households, had panicked. People ran about, frantically hiding their valuables down wells and cisterns or in holes in walls. Then they fled into the countryside, trying to escape before the city was invested.

Peralta had received orders to warp his ship up to the quays. There he had taken on an astonishing variety of refugees and their baggage – nuns and priests, high-born ladies with their children and servants, senior government officials. They had brought the contents of the city treasury, boxes of official deeds and documents, sacks stuffed with church plate, paintings, sacred relics hastily wrapped in altar cloths, chests of privately owned jewellery, gold, pearls, all manner of portable wealth. The value of the cargo rushed aboard his vessel that day had exceeded all that was left behind in the city for the pirates to plunder. In vain he had warned that his vessel was not fit for sea. Its sole defence was seven cannon and a dozen muskets, and her sails had been condemned and taken ashore. No one listened. Everyone begged him to leave port at once and save them and their goods.

What followed had seemed like a miracle. His grossly overloaded vessel had cast off, and his crew had spread a set of topsails, the only canvas they still had on board. It was barely enough to push the vessel through the water. Half-sailing, half drifting on the current, his ship had limped away from the city, and Peralta had spent the next forty-eight hours waiting for the pirates to commandeer local boats, catch up and take their plunder. A score of pirates in a piragua would have been enough. But it never happened. The enemy failed to appear, and for years he had wondered why. Eventually he had learned that the pirates had got drunk. They had wasted so much time on shore, guzzling captured wine, that when they emerged from their stupor Peralta and his precious cargo had drifted away over the horizon.

Don Francisco allowed himself a wry grin at the memory. The ladrones del mar, the sea thieves as he thought of them, were courageous and unpredictable. But they had two weaknesses: a love of strong drink and a tendency to quarrel among themselves. Given enough time, they usually fell into disarray and returned from where they had come.

The Spanish captain reached the little creek where his cockboat was waiting for him. Every member of its crew was a black man because Don Francisco preferred to work with negroes. Most were freed slaves and he found them loyal and less likely to desert in search of better pay in the merchant marine. Now they would have half an hour of steady rowing to bring him to his ship. After Morgan had sacked Panama, the city had been rebuilt in a safer location and the planners of New Panama had been so fearful of an attack from the sea that they had picked an easily defended promontory with shoal water all around it. This meant that the merchant ships and the armadilla were obliged to anchor well away from the shore and had no protection from the city's gun batteries. Don Francisco's earlier moment of cheerfulness subsided into a mood of resignation. Whatever happened in the next few days, he and the two other captains would be on their own. There would be no assistance from the landsmen.

He turned to look back over his shoulder as the cockboat pulled out of the creek. He had a clear view down the coast in the direction from which the pirates would come, and towards the ruins of the city that Morgan had sacked and burned. Most of the buildings had been of fine cedar wood, with beautiful carved balconies. All that had gone up in flames. Only the stone-built structures had survived, and one of them still rose above its neighbours. It was the old cathedral, still in use because its replacement in New Panama had not yet been consecrated. But Morgan's pirates had not got away with everything. Hearing that an attack was imminent, the priests had cleverly camouflaged the cathedral's beautiful altar piece, a soaring masterwork of carved wood smothered in gold leaf. They had painted it black, and the pirates had been duped. They ransacked the cathedral but failed to see the deception. The altar piece remained, and the citizens of New Panama still worshipped before it. As he settled back in his place in the stern of the boat, Don Peralta wondered if he too would be able to use deception to hoodwink the new invaders.

＊

HECTOR WAS thankful that he had been selected for Captain Sawkins' vanguard. It put him well out of reach of Coxon. The buccaneer had tried using the Kuna balm spiked with the Spanish Fly, and the last time Hector had seen him, Coxon's face and neck had been disfigured with a great throbbing rash, a seeping expanse like a grotesque birthmark which was giving Coxon agony. Clearly, Hector felt that it was small retribution for what had happened on the ridge before Santa Maria.

'You were set up,' Jezreel had confirmed when Hector told him what had happened during the attack. 'We could not see you and your flag of truce from the cane brakes where the forlorn assembled. Yet you must have been visible to Coxon up on the ridge. He must have enjoyed watching you walk trustingly towards the Spanish guns.'

'And Coxon himself took care to stay out of harm's way,' the big man added. 'He waited until Santa Maria had fallen before he came down from the ridge. Some are saying that our commander lacks courage.'

Now Coxon was somewhere far behind Sawkins and in the early light of dawn the forlorn was advancing on Panama in boats provided by the Kuna – two large piraguas and five small canoes. Jezreel, Dan and Jacques had been assigned to a piragua while Hector had been provided with a musket and ammunition and put with five other men in one of the little dugouts.

Hector put down his paddle and leaned forward to check the lashings that held his musket to the side of the canoe. Dan had advised him to make sure that the knots were tight, the muzzle stoppered, and the lock well wrapped in waxed cloth so that it stayed dry. Also that his cartridge box was fastened somewhere safe, and well sealed with grease, so he didn't lose the gun or wet the ammunition if there was a capsize.

It had been good advice. The canoe had not tipped over but the four days since leaving Santa Maria had brought frequent cloudbursts, heavy and unpredictable, which had drenched his clothes and knapsack and ruined Hector's last remaining store of food. Only his medical notebook had stayed dry. He had put it inside a watertight tube he had made from the hollow stem of a giant cane, sealing the cut end with a soft wooden plug driven in tight.

Hector picked up his paddle and resumed the stroke. Conversation was limited to talking to the man directly in front or behind. Seated just ahead of him was a weatherbeaten buccaneer by the name of John Watling. His scars and gruff manner of speech with its occasional military jargon marked him as a veteran soldier.

'I'm told that Sawkins can't abide oaths and profanity.' Hector said.

'Doesn't like gaming either. Says it's sinful and I agree with him,' Watling replied over his shoulder. 'If he finds a pack of cards or a set of dice, he throws them in the sea. He makes his people observe the Sabbath too.'

'Yet he doesn't hesitate to plunder fellow Christians.'

'Course not. They're Papists, aren't they? He sees them as fair game and it doesn't matter if we don't have a Jamaica commission.'

The mention of Jamaica made Hector think of Susanna yet again.

'I'm hoping to get back to Jamaica soon. Left a girl there,' he said casually though full of pride. It was an exaggeration but it gave him some small throb of satisfaction to pretend that Susanna was in his life.

'Then you better hope that our venture on Panama turns out to be more profitable than Santa Maria. No one's going to be welcome back in Jamaica without a deal of plunder in his purse.'

'That won't make any difference to my girl,' Hector boasted.

'She'll have no say in it,' said Watling curtly. 'We've left a right bad taste behind us in Port Royal. Our captains told the authorities that they were going to cut logwood in Campeachy. Even got government licences to do so. But the moment they cleared the land, they headed for the Main and began this mischief.'

'I can't see how that will affect me when I get back to Port Royal. I joined up later.'

'It'll make no difference,' grunted Watling. He paused his paddling to take up a wooden scoop lying at his feet and bail out a quantity of bilgewater. 'There's meant to be a truce between England and Spain, and I wouldn't be surprised if we've been disowned.'

'Disowned?'

'Put beyond the law.' Watling made it sound very casual. 'If we come back with our pockets full of treasure, it will all be forgotten. Just like Drake back in the time of Queen Bess. The Spaniards still call him the Great Pirate, but the English think he is a national hero and he was knighted by the Queen.' He half-turned to face back at Hector. 'So if you come home in a ship with sails of silk, then you'll be a hero too. If not . . .' – he made a gesture of rope being placed around his neck, and pulled upward – 'We'll be choked off. All of us that are caught . . .'

Watling's blunt prediction filled Hector with foreboding. It was too late to leave the expedition before it reached Panama, even if he was prepared to abandon Dan and his other friends. No longer did he have the excuse that he was only serving as a medical orderly in the campaign. Captain Sawkins had insisted that he carried the musket if he was to travel with the forlorn. The more he thought about his predicament, the more Hector was undecided whether he preferred the attack on Panama to fail so that the expedition would disband, or for the assault to succeed so that he could return to Jamaica and buy himself out of trouble.

There was a long silence, broken only when Watling commented, 'Nice to think it's St George's Day. A good omen!'

But Hector did not answer. He had counted a total of seventy-six men in Sawkins' tiny flotilla. That seemed far too few to assault a major Spanish stronghold. The rest of the buccaneer expedition was lagging far behind, and he doubted that fire-eating Sawkins would wait for them to catch up. Somewhere over to his left were Dan, Jezreel and Jacques in their piragua, but it was too far away to see which one it was. On his right and visible on the low shoreline against the sunrise was the stump of a tower which one of his companions, a man who had marched with Morgan, said was the Cathedral of Old Panama. The vanguard must be getting very close to its target.

'Three sail and bearing directly down for us!' exclaimed Watling as the sun finally dispelled the last of the dawn haze.

Hector craned to one side to look forward over the seaman's shoulder. About two miles distant were three sailing ships. They were heading straight for the buccaneer canoes which were advancing in no sort of formation.

'Warships by the look of them, barca longas,' said Watling, 'and in a hurry to engage us.'

There was a halloo from the nearest canoe about eighty yards away to their right. It was Sawkins himself. Typically his boat had outstripped the rest, and was several lengths in advance of the company. The captain was standing up in his canoe, waving his hat and gesturing that Watling's canoe should turn directly towards the enemy.

'Not much else we can do,' muttered Watling darkly. 'The Spaniards have the advantage of us. The wind is right behind them, and they can pick their prey.' But he appeared remarkably composed as he bent forward and began to unfasten his musket.

Only when he had checked and loaded the weapon did he look up again. By then it was clear to Hector that the leading Spanish vessel was shaping course to pass through the gap between Sawkins' canoe and the one in which he now sat. It would allow the Spanish vessel to use her gun batteries on both sides.

'Any good with a musket?' Watling asked Hector.

'I haven't had much practice recently.'

'Better if you act as my loader then,' suggested the seaman. 'Get your own gun ready, and hand it to me when I've fired mine. Then take my gun and set it up again. If we're quick about it, I should be able to get off at least three shots, maybe more.'

While Hector prepared his own musket, Watling sat quietly, his gun held across his lap, until the leading Spanish ship was almost within range.

'Stand by to receive cannon fire,' he said softly.

A moment later there was a loud bang and a billow of smoke from the deck of the Spanish vessel. The air was filled with the whistle of flying metal, and the surface of the sea a good thirty yards ahead of the canoe spouted small jets of foam.

'Scrubby shooting at this range,' said Watling dryly.

Again the bang of a cannon. This time the Spanish ship was firing in the opposite direction, towards Sawkins' canoe. Hector could not see where the shot fell.

'They'll do better next time,' said Watling, and he crouched down in the canoe. Hastily Hector followed his example, kneeling in the bilge and bending as low as possible. Nevertheless he felt very vulnerable. Behind him the other men were also ducking down.

Another shot from a cannon, and the sound of metal hurtling through the air. It was much closer this time. There was a sudden drone as something skimmed off the surface of the sea. The Spaniards must have loaded their guns with small shot. Watling let out a grunt as he shifted position. Now he was half-reclining in the bottom of the canoe, the barrel of his musket resting on the gunnel, and taking aim towards the Spanish ship. Hector felt the canoe rock slightly from side to side as the buccaneers behind him also took up their firing positions. 'Steady!' came a warning voice. It was the man farthest in the bow. 'Let me take the first shot.'

There was the sound of a musket firing, the familiar smell of gunpowder, and a slight tremor down the length of the canoe. Hector raised his head and squinted towards the Spanish ship. He could see men on deck and in the lower rigging and the steersman at the helm. Next to him was a man dressed in a long dark coat with slashes of silver braid. He must be the captain. A group of four Spanish sailors were gathered near the rail and, almost too late, Hector realised that they were a gun crew preparing to fire. He ducked down as their cannon spurted a stab of flame, and something smartly rapped the hull of the canoe. From behind him came an oath.

One of Watling's bare feet was pushing against his shoulder as the sailor braced himself and took aim. The crack of his musket was followed by a snort of satisfaction. Then Watling was passing back his musket and beckoning for Hector to hand him his own gun. Another wriggle as the sailor adjusted his firing position, and fired a second shot. Hector had to half-kneel in order to reload the empty gun. His head and body were now well above the level of the canoe's rim. He prised open the waxed lid of his cartouche box and pulled out a charge of powder in its paper wrapping. Tearing off the end of the cartouche with his teeth, he carefully tipped the powder into the musket barrel. Wrapping a strip of paper around a musket ball to make it a tight fit, he tamped it firmly down the barrel with the ramrod. Then, turning the musket on its side, he checked that the pin hole leading to the chamber was clear before he reached for his powder horn and poured a pinch of gunpowder into the firing pan and closed its cover. He was concentrating so closely on his work that he scarcely noticed the sound of the third cannon shot from the Spanish vessel.

Their aim must have been poor for he was only conscious of Watling urging him to hurry. 'Quick! Their helm is exposed.' Hector passed the reloaded musket forward, and this time Watling sat up on his thwart and faced over the stern of the canoe to take his aim. His musket barrel was beside the young man's face as he pulled the trigger. Hector was half-deafened by the explosion. But Watling was grinning with triumph. 'Two out of three,' he exulted, baring his teeth.

The men behind Hector had also been firing, though how many shots they had got off he could not tell. When he next looked towards the Spanish vessel, the barca longa had passed through the gap between the two canoes and was now down-wind. It would take some time for her crew to turn the ship and bring her back into action. For the moment the danger from that direction was over.

A low groan dispelled his sense of relief. The man seated directly behind him in the canoe was holding his shoulder. Blood was staining his shirt. 'Here, let me look at that,' said Hector, and was about to climb back over the thwart with his medical knapsack when he was stopped by a sharp order from Watling. 'Leave that for later,' the sailor snapped. 'Here comes the next one.'

Hector glanced up to see a second Spanish warship steering for the same gap between his own canoe and Sawkins' boat. A broad white, gold and red pennant flying from the warship's masthead indicated that this must be the command vessel in the Spanish squadron.

Watling was speaking to him again, his voice urgent. 'Reload your own musket, and this time use it yourself. We'll not have much support from our captain from now.' A hurried glance towards Sawkins' canoe showed that only three members of its crew were visible in their normal places. Their companions must have been killed or wounded.

There was a nudge in his back. 'Here, take my gun as well!' The buccaneer with the bloody shoulder seated behind him was thrusting forward his musket for Hector to use. 'Aim for the helm, always for the helm,' the man advised, his face screwed up in pain.

This time Hector knew what to expect. Copying Watling's example he lay in the bottom of the canoe and rested the barrel of his gun on the rim of the hull. He drew back the hammer and waited patiently. The oncoming Spanish warship was following exactly same track as its escort. Again the sounds of cannon, the clouds of black smoke, and this time the sharper reports of muskets as the Spaniards on deck opened fire on the small low-lying canoes.

Hector was no longer conscious of where the bullets went. His world narrowed to a single image – the figure of the man steering the Spanish vessel. He focused along the sights of his musket and carefully swivelled the muzzle to follow his target. He was faintly aware of the motion of the canoe on the slight swell, the hull rolling a few inches, just enough to make the target rise and fall in his aim. The motion was regular enough for him to calculate when the moment was right. He took a long slow breath and held it, waited for the uproll and then gently squeezed the trigger.

He ignored the recoil of the butt against his shoulder as he watched, never taking his eye off the figure of the helmsman. The man spun round and dropped.

'Thought you said you were out of practice! My turn now,' crowed Watling who had observed his shot. Within moments another man had appeared at the helm of the Spanish vessel, a replacement steersman, and he was taking control. Watling hunched over his own weapon and took aim. He fired, and there was a brief moment when it seemed that he had missed his mark. The new helmsman was still upright, unharmed. Then, slowly and inexplicably, the warship began to turn sideways, losing speed.

'Christ, what luck!' exclaimed the wounded buccaneer from

behind Hector. The man must have had keen eyesight for he added, 'The main brace is shot through. The mainsail is loose.'

Sure enough, with canvas flapping, the warship was losing all forward motion and veering to one side. The deck guns could no longer be brought to bear on the canoes. The Spanish vessel was crippled.

'There's her commander now!' shouted Watling gleefully. A tall, thin man had climbed up on the rail. He wore a plumed hat and a broad red sash, and there was the glint of gold brocade on the sleeves of his coat. Regardless of his personal safety, he was holding on to the rigging with one hand and with the other frantically waving a white handkerchief over his head. For a moment Hector thought it was a flag of truce and the Spanish officer wanted to parlay or even surrender. But then the young man realised that the Spaniard was not facing the canoes, but looking towards the first barca longa which had led the attack. That vessel was still a quarter of a mile downwind and trying clumsily to work back to return to the fray. The Spanish commander was urgently beckoning to his escort to come to the rescue.

'Too good a chance to miss. Here, give me that spare musket,' gloated Watling. Hector handed him the gun from the wounded sailor, and once again Watling took slow, deliberate aim and fired. The impact of the bullet knocked the Spanish officer backwards off the rail on which he was standing. The white handkerchief fell from his hand and fluttered down into the sea.

'Now we've got 'em!' exulted Watling. 'Come on lads, close the gap.' He picked up his paddle and began to drive the canoe through the water.

The loss of their commander had utterly demoralised the Spanish crew. Dismayed by the accuracy of the buccaneer's musketry, they abandoned their deck cannon, knowing they were dangerously exposed when they stood to load their big guns. Now, instead of standing at the rail or climbing into the rigging to shoot at their attackers, the crew of the warship ducked down and hid out of sight behind the bulwarks, and only occasionally raised their heads to take aim and fire. They had lost the will to fight.

A rousing cheer to his left told Hector that one of the piraguas had at last arrived in support. With sixteen men on board, the piragua rowed straight towards the disabled Spanish warship and, closing to within point blank range, opened up a deadly fusillade of musketry on their victims. One by one the hapless Spanish crewmen were picked off if they showed themselves.

Watling was pointing back towards the first Spanish warship. 'Seems he's seen enough,' he said. That vessel was altering course, withdrawing from the battle and abandoning her consort.

Above the noise of the cheering from the musketeers in the piragua came anxious shouts from the stricken warship. The crew was appealing for quarter. A hand holding a scrap of white cloth appeared above the bulwarks and began to wave the symbol to and fro in surrender. The musket fire from the piragua gradually lessened and finally ceased altogether.

'Sawkins well deserves his victory,' said Hector. He could scarcely believe that a handful of buccaneers had managed to overcome the larger, more powerful vessel so swiftly.

'Our captain's already shifted aboard the other piragua,' Watling told him, nodding towards the south. A quarter of a mile away the second piragua lay alongside the third of the Spanish warships. There was fierce hand-to-hand fighting on deck and, as he watched, Hector saw that the boarding party of buccaneers was being driven back to their own vessel. Only then did he realise that Dan, Jacques and Jezreel must now be fighting alongside Sawkins in his latest suicidal endeavour.

TEN

CAPITAN FRANCISCO de Peralta had willingly followed his squadron commander in setting sail to intercept and engage the enemy's motley flotilla as soon as it was sighted. He watched Diego de Carabaxal's barca longa make for the gap between the two canoes farthest to the left of the pirate's ragged line, and had entirely approved of this bold response to the pirate threat. Carabaxal's cannon should make short work of the lightly built canoes and piraguas. But when Capitan Barahona chose to follow in exactly the same track, Don Francisco hesitated. It was a mistake, he thought, for two warships to deal with a pair of canoes while ignoring the rest of the pirate flotilla. So Peralta had decided to seek out his own target: he would engage the largest of their vessels, a piragua that had fallen behind and, under oars, was struggling to keep up.

The Spanish captain looked up at the cloudless sky. He would have welcomed a change in the weather, but there was no sign of it. The breeze was so gentle that it raised barely a ripple on the indigo-blue sea. The calm conditions would suit the pirate musketeers. They would be firing from a more stable platform than if there was a choppy seaway to contend with. Peralta held a profound respect for the enemy musketry. He recalled the shock of Morgan's raid when its victims discovered that the invaders carried firearms of the very latest model. With their modern guns the pirates had outranged the defenders of Panama, firing two or three shots for every one their opponents had been able to return from their obsolete firelocks and arquebuses. The defenders' superiority in numbers had counted for little.

So now Don Peralta decided to get as close as possible to the piragua and fire into her with light swivel guns loaded with small shot. Once he had decimated her musketeers, he would despatch a boarding party to over-run the survivors.

'Mount our patareros,' he told Estevan Madriga, his negro contremaestre. 'And make sure that the gun crews have all they need. Ammunition and plenty of powder charges close to hand ... and a tub of water for them to slake their thirst. This could prove to be hot work.'

Peralta had total confidence in his contremaestre. Madriga had served with him for more than fifteen years, and there was a bond of mutual trust between them. The Spanish captain only wished that his crew had done more practice with the swivel guns. The penny pinching of the colonial administration meant that any gun drill had been rare. The contadores, the book-keepers, condemned it as a waste of expensive gunpowder.

Peralta chewed his lip in frustration. His ship, *Santa Catalina*, was lagging behind her consorts, easing along at less than walking pace. That too was partly the fault of the bureaucracy. The barca longa's bottom was foul with weeds because the ship had been kept lying at anchor off Panama for more than a month while he waited for permission to take her out of service and careen.

Estevan returned to report that the ship's four patareros had been brought up from the hold. The guns were being checked and loaded and placed on their bronze swivel mounts. With a patarero on each quarter and two in the bows, they gave a field of fire all round the vessel. Unfortunately a shortage of muskets meant that less than half the crew could be issued with firearms. The others would have to make do with pikes and cutlasses. It was all part of the same pattern, thought Don Francisco sourly. He had asked the royal stores for an additional four patareros and, though the guns had been promised, they had never been delivered. Insufficient gunpowder, too few weapons, bad pay – his barca longa was a miniature of the entire viceroyalty of Peru. Brave men were trying to operate a structure that was falling to bits through neglect and parsimony.

He turned to check what was happening with the other vessels in the squadron. Carabaxal had already passed through the pirate line and was manoeuvring his ship to come back upwind. He appeared to have done little damage to the enemy because the two canoes nearest to him were still afloat. Hopefully, Capitan Barahona would be more successful.

A shout from the foredeck brought his attention back to his own plan of attack. A lookout was reporting that the three remaining pirate canoes were altering course. They were converging on his own barca longa. 'Our target remains that big piragua,' Peralta confirmed. 'No one is to open fire until we are in easy range.' He was worried about the patareros. Mounted on the ship's rail the swivel guns looked menacing enough and, if properly handled, were capable of doing great damage. But the patareros had only ever been fired with blank charges to blast out honour salutes for visiting dignitaries or to celebrate the holy days of mother Church. It was typical of the contadores that they had allowed him gunpowder for ceremonials and to flatter grandees, but not for target practice. Outward display came cheaper and pleased the crowds.

Peralta calculated that another ten minutes of *Santa Catalina*'s sluggish advance should bring the enemy within range. He made a tour of his ship, stopping for a brief word of encouragement with as many of his men as possible. He paid special attention to the gunners, two men to a gun. 'I'm counting on you,' he told them quietly. 'Don't believe the old yarn that the foreign pirates are devils from hell. As you can see, they're men, and a scruffy lot at that.'

As Don Francisco returned to his position by the helm, he eyed the gap between his barca longa and the piragua. It was still too far to open fire with any certainty of success. The swivel guns let loose a cruel hail of scatter shot, but their range was limited. The breeze, though very light, was still holding steady from the west.

He came to a decision. 'Contremaestre! We steer to pass to windward of the piragua. I want all four patareros moved to the starboard side.' The guns were light enough to be picked up by their crews and carried across the deck. Alternative mounts were already fixed at several points on the ship's rail. By shifting the swivel guns so that all four of them fired from the starboard rail, he was creating a ready-made broadside.

The last of his gun crews were still heaving their weapon up onto its Y-shaped mount when the first musket shot rang out from the piragua. Don Francisco had expected the pirates to be good marksmen, but the range and accuracy of that first shot startled him. From a distance of 300 paces the musket bullet struck the ship's rail close to the patarero and sent up a shower of splinters. One fragment embedded itself deep in the chest of one of his gunners. The man gave a sudden, surprised cough and fell back on the deck. A comrade immediately took his place, but Peralta noted the looks of fright that passed across the faces of all those who stood nearby.

'Open fire now you have your target,' he called out as if nothing had happened. It was better that the gun crews went into action now, even if the range was long. Gun handling would distract them, and the patareros were simple enough to use. The gunner only had to find his target *por el raso de los metales*, 'by the line of metals', squinting along the crude sights on the barrel and tell his companion when to apply a lighted match to the touch hole.

There was a loud hollow thud like the sound of a slack drum skin hit hard. It was the characteristic noise of a patarero. Don Francisco watched a pattern of small white splashes flower in the sea well short of the piragua. The barca longa was still out of range.

He took a few slow steps along the deck, turned and walked back, careful to keep in full view of the pirates, and of his men. He wanted his crew to see that this was a time to be calm.

Now the musketeers in the piragua were opening up a steady fusillade. They went about their business coolly. Their shots were irregularly spaced so it was clear that they were taking their time to aim accurately. Don Francisco heard several musket balls whizz overhead. A couple of small holes appeared in the courses, the lower sails. Four more of his men were hit by splinters.

At last *Santa Catalina* was in range. A forward patarero fired, and this time the splashes of small shot were all around the piragua. He heard distant cries of pain. The three remaining swivel guns belched their loads of scatter shot. Two of them were poorly aimed, and did little damage. But the fourth gun scored a direct hit, and he saw several of the pirates slump forward.

'Well done!' he shouted as the gunners began to reload. The patareros were of a basic design, loaded by the muzzle, not in the breech. To recharge the weapons, it was safer and easier if they were lifted off their mounts and placed on the deck. There the men sponged out the hot barrel, loaded in a charge of gunpowder and a wad, and finally a canvas bag packed with small shot and broken metal fragments. Minutes later the patarero should be back in place on the rail, and the gunner firing again.

Peralta had to admire the pirates' courage. They did not flinch under the bursts of scatter shot but changed their methods. Only a handful of their men in the bow were still shooting, the rest were straining at the oars, rowing the piragua forwards, roaring and chanting their defiance. They were desperate to close and board.

Let them come, Peralta thought. He had enough men to deal with the onslaught.

A cry from behind him made him spin around. His second mate was running towards the far rail. A hand had appeared at deck level. Someone had climbed up the side of the ship away from the battle. The mate stamped hard on the hand and it withdrew.

Peralta drew a pistol from his belt and hurried to join his officer. Looking over the rail he found himself staring straight down into one of the pirate canoes. It had succeeded in sneaking up, unnoticed, to the stern of the barca longa. There were six men in the canoe, and at least one of them was wounded for he was leaking blood. The faces of the others were turned towards him. Don Francisco thrust his pistol over the rail and fired downwards. It was impossible to miss. The pirate in the centre of the canoe fell back, half in and half out of the canoe.

His second mate was waving a cutlass and screaming curses. Peralta realised that the man had no musket. 'Here, take this,' he shouted, pulling a second pistol from his waistband, and handing it to the man. 'Keep them off.'

He turned and ran back across the deck. He was needed there to direct the patareros. To his dismay he found that the piragua was now far closer than he had expected. Only a gap of a few yards separated the two vessels. A moment later they touched sides and a score of the enemy were clambering on his deck, yelling and whooping like fiends.

Peralta drew his sword, a rapier given him when he first received his commission, and the next instant found himself fending off a haggard, ginger-haired man who rushed at him hefting a boarding axe. Don Francisco felt a heavy jolt as the axe struck his rapier blade. Fortunately it was a glancing blow, otherwise the steel would have shattered. The axe head slid as far as the rapier's hilt and turned aside harmlessly. Peralta took his chance to run his assailant through the shoulder with the point. More and more pirates were climbing aboard, and there was chaos across the entire width of the deck. Buccaneers and his black crew men surged together in hand-to-hand combat. There was an occasional pistol shot, but most of the fight was waged with cutlasses and daggers, cudgels, muskets used as clubs, short pikes and fists. One of his own men was swinging a capstan bar, using it to batter and smash at his opponents. Peralta caught a glimpse of a giant buccaneer who was wreaking havoc with a weapon that the Spanish captain had never encountered before. It was a stubby sword scarcely longer than a cutlass and not as broad in the blade. The giant was wielding it with extraordinary agility, slashing and cutting almost too fast to follow, and he was driving back anyone who challenged him. As the captain watched, the giant cut down two of *Santa Catalina*'s crew.

'Come on! We are more than they are!' he yelled, and flung himself into the thick of the fight. He was conscious of someone at his left shoulder. It was Estevan and he was fighting grimly, protecting his captain's vulnerable side. Peralta shouted again, urging on his crew, and he felt a thrill of pride as they responded with a concerted charge. A score of them began to force the boarders back towards their own vessel. 'Well done! Well done!' he screamed, smashing his sword hilt into a sweating pirate face. His crewmen pressed forward. Now they had the initiative. The pirates were in retreat. Don Francisco was panting with effort. His foot skidded and he almost fell. The deck was slippery with blood. But it did not matter. Already the first of the pirates were jumping back into their piragua; their comrades were fighting a rearguard action. In another few moments the deck of his barca longa would be cleared. Now was the time to smash the enemy into oblivion.

Don Francisco grabbed his contremaestre by the shoulder. 'We must get to the forward patarero, Estevan!' he bellowed in the man's ear. 'Load it with the heaviest shot you can find.

Shoot down into that damned piragua, and send her to the bottom.' Estevan had never failed him in all those years they had served together on the royal ships. He always knew exactly what he was doing. Now he and Don Francisco sprinted forward to the bow, hurdling two badly wounded men sprawled on the deck. As Estevan ran, he was calling out to two of his own men to help him with the patarero.

The four of them reached the swivel gun where it sat on its mounting on the rail. Its muzzle was pointing skyward, left at that angle after the last time it had been fired. Peralta watched Estevan grab the breech and swing the weapon level so that two assistants could take their positions. One man stood at each side of the gun and clasped the barrel. At a command from the contremaestre, all three men heaved the patarero off its mount, then gently laid the weapon on deck ready to reload.

Peralta gave a smile of relief. Now the gun crew was behind the ship's rail, out of sight of the pirates in the piragua. Jeers, confused shouting, and the occasional report of a musket told him that his crew were managing to keep the pirates at bay, preventing them from climbing back aboard the barca longa. In another minute or two, the patarero would be reloaded, hoisted back into position, and then he and Estevan would tilt the gun so that it pointed directly down into the piragua. A single shot at such close range would be devastating. It would rip the bottom out of the pirate's craft, and that would be the end of the fight.

Perhaps it was an ember still smouldering inside the bronze barrel of the patarero which caused the disaster. Or maybe metal struck on metal and produced an unlucky spark, or the inexperienced gun crew bungled their work. Whatever the reason, there was a tremendous explosion on the foredeck. A dozen powder charges ignited simultaneously. Sections of planking flew into the air. Two of the gun crew were blown to pieces, and a blast of heat struck Peralta in the face. He threw up his hands to protect himself from the sheet of flame which followed, and felt a searing pain. Deafened by the clap of sound, he was thrown bodily over the ship's rail and into the sea.

*

HECTOR AND his comrades in their canoe were only fifty paces away when the thunderclap of the explosion occurred. Something terrible had taken place on the barca longa's deck.

'Man in the water!' Hector shouted. He could see the head of someone swimming.

'Let him drown. He's just a Spaniard,' said a voice.

'No! He could be from our boarding party,' Hector insisted, thinking that perhaps it was Jacques or Jezreel who had been in the piragua. He started paddling. Ahead of him, John Watling followed his example. From the Spanish vessel there was no sound at all. Hector supposed that everyone aboard was too shocked and stunned to continue fighting.

When the canoe reached the swimmer, he proved to be an older man with short, nearly white hair. By his dark complexion it was evident that he was a Spaniard. He was supporting the unconscious body of a black man, holding his head above the sea. The negro was horribly wounded. His skin was lacerated and torn, his face a mask of blood.

'Here, grab on and let us help you,' Hector called out in Spanish as he reached down to take hold of the unconscious figure. The swimmer gave a nod of thanks, and the black man was lifted carefully into the canoe. 'You too,' Hector added, holding out his hand. 'Come aboard. You are our prisoner now.'

The stranger clambered into the canoe, and there was something about his manner which indicated that he was an officer.

'My name is Hector Lynch. I'm not a surgeon, but I have a few medicines with me which may help your friend here.'

'I will be grateful for that,' answered the stranger. 'Allow me to introduce myself. I am Capitan Francisco de Peralta, commander of the *Santa Catalina* that you and your colleagues have assaulted. The wounded man is my quartermaster, Estevan.'

'What do we do now? The black man needs proper medical attention,' Hector asked, addressing his colleagues.

'We could bring Peralta to his ship, and get him to call on the crew to surrender,' suggested Watling. He spoke enough Spanish to have followed Hector's conversation with their prisoner.

Cautiously they began to paddle their canoe towards the barca longa. One or two men could be seen moving about on deck of the stricken Spanish warship. There was a thin flicker of flame along the lower edge of the mainsail which had been set alight in the explosion. Someone was attempting to put out the fire, throwing water from a bucket. There was no sign of anyone from the boarding party from the piragua which was still on the opposite side of the Spanish vessel and out of sight.

The canoe had covered less than half the distance when there was a second explosion, even more thunderous than the first. This time it came from the stern of the *Santa Catalina* and was so powerful that it snapped the mainmast and sent it crashing over the side, trailing tattered sails and rigging. A black cloud of smoke rose in the air. Soon afterwards came the sounds of wailing and screams of pain.

Peralta went pale. 'God help my crew. They did not deserve that,' he muttered.

When Hector and the others reached the barca longa, they found carnage everywhere – broad streaks of blood on the deck, broken and shattered gear, scorched planking, the smell of burning. Only about a quarter of the crew seemed still alive, and the survivors were either badly wounded or in a state of shock. Peralta was grim-faced, appalled by the destruction.

Hector and Watling helped the capitan hoist the still unconscious black man aboard and lay him on deck, and Hector knelt
beside the injured contremaestre, trying to remember how
surgeon Smeeton had treated gunpowder burns.

'Any idea who's the senior Spanish survivor?' someone
asked. Hector looked up. It was Sawkins. Miraculously the
hot-headed buccaneer captain was still alive though there was a
bloody bandage round his head, and his buff coat was smudged
with gunpowder. He must have boarded from the piragua.

'This is Captain Francisco Peralta. He's the commander,'
Hector answered.

'Ask him about those other ships. We need to know how
they are manned and armed,' said Sawkins briskly. He was his
usual terrier-like self, eager for action and gazing towards the
four vessels which could be seen at anchor in the roadstead off
Panama. Hector marvelled at the man's unquenchable energy.

The Spanish captain hesitated for a moment before replying.
'You'll find four hundred well-armed men aboard those ships.'

On the deck beside Peralta the black man stirred and opened
his eyes. They were filled with pain. It was clear that he was
mortally wounded.

'There's no one over there. Everyone already volunteered
for this fight,' Estevan wheezed.

Peralta started to contradict him, but Sawkins cut him short.
'I accept the word of a dying man, captain. You have fought
well, and there is no disgrace. What we need now is a hospital
ship.'

The contremaestre had spoken the truth. There was not a
soul on the anchored vessels when the buccaneers reached
them, though someone had attempted to scuttle the largest
of them, the galleon *La Santissima Trinidad*. A fire of rags and
wood shavings had been deliberately set in her forecastle
and several planks punctured with an axe. But the blaze had not
yet taken hold and was quickly extinguished, and a carpenter

was able to seal the leak. Then the wounded, both buccaneers and their enemies, were laid out on the galleon's broad deck to receive attention.

'I doubt that our Captain Harris will live. He was shot through both legs while trying to climb up onto Peralta's ship,' said Jacques. He was watching Hector stitch up a deep gash in the shoulder of a buccaneer.

'Does that mean our company has to elect a new captain?' asked his friend. He had watched surgeon Smeeton use sewing quill and thread to close a wound and was imitating his technique.

'As soon as our wounded are sufficiently recovered, there'll have to be a council of the entire expedition to decide what to do next,' answered the Frenchman. 'Already some of the men are demanding to return to Golden Island. Others are saying that we haven't gained sufficient plunder yet, and they would prefer to continue with the expedition.'

'How will you vote?'

Jacques spread out his hands in a gesture of resignation. 'It doesn't make much difference to me. On the whole I'd vote to go back, but it will depend on who is elected as our new commander.'

Hector turned his attention to the next patient. It was Capitan Peralta, whose burned hands and forehead needed treatment.

'I'm sorry that so many of your crew were killed. They fought very bravely,' he said to the Spaniard. Fewer than one in four of *Santa Catalina*'s crew had survived the carnage.

'Never in my life have I seen such accurate musketry nor met such audacity,' answered the captain coolly. 'I thank God that the people of Panama are safe behind their walls.'

'So you don't think that the city will fall?'

'Last year the city councillors sent the royal exchequer an invoice for the cost of building their new city rampart. They asked to be reimbursed. The response they got from Spain was a question: had they built the wall of gold or silver?' The veteran Spanish commander gave a mirthless smile. 'I assure you it was made of great stone blocks, each weighing several tons.'

Hector reached for a pot of ointment and began to spread salve on the man's wounds.

'How is it that you speak such good Spanish?' Peralta enquired.

'My mother was from Galicia.'

'And what brought you here with this pack of thieves? You don't seem to be naturally one of their kind.'

'I was trying to avoid one of these thieves, as you call them, and yet I now find myself under his command,' answered Hector. He did not want to go into details.

'Then I advise you to get away from them as quickly as you can. When you or any of your colleagues fall into the hands of the authorities here – which will surely happen – you will be executed as pirates. There will be no mercy.'

'I have every intention of leaving this expedition. And I hope I will be able to persuade my friends to go with me,' Hector assured him.

'The quality of his friends often defines a man, though friendship sometimes brings sorrow in its wake,' said the Spaniard, and it was clear that Peralta was thinking of his contremaestre. Estevan had died of his burns.

'What do you think will happen to you now?' Hector asked.

The Spaniard tilted back his head so that Hector could smear the ointment on the forehead where the fire had burned away the hairline, leaving white patches on the skin.

'I expect your colleagues will demand a ransom for me,' he said. 'But whether the authorities will pay is another matter. After all, I no longer have a ship to command.'

'There will be other ships.'

Peralta gave the young man a shrewd look. 'If you are

trying to extract information from me about the strength of the South Sea Fleet, you will not succeed.'

Hector blushed. 'I had not intended to pry. Perhaps your original vessel will be repaired one day.'

The Spanish captain softened his tone. 'It is clear that you are not experienced in the ways of piracy. Your colleagues will not leave a single vessel afloat that they don't need for themselves.'

Seeing that Hector looked puzzled, Peralta continued. 'They fear retribution for their crimes. As soon as your band of thieves moves on, the authorities will commandeer and arm every available vessel and use them to hunt down your gang of sea bandits.'

As if to confirm the Spaniard's prediction, Captain Coxon was heard shouting orders. He was despatching a party of men to the other anchored vessels. They were to return aboard Peralta's fire-damaged barca longa and complete what the explosions had failed to do.

*

IT WAS ANOTHER five days before the wounded were well enough to attend a general council of the expedition. It was held on the deck of *La Santissima Trinidad*, the men massed in the waist of the galleon, their leaders on the quarterdeck. Coxon, Sawkins, Cook and Sharpe were there. Only Harris was missing as he had died of his wounds. Hector, watching from where he stood with his friends beside the rail, could detect a change in Coxon. Now that his rival Harris was gone, the buccaneer captain appeared even more arrogant and self-confident than at Golden Island, and his harsh voice carried clearly over the assembly.

'We have now been three weeks on this Adventure and I have always counselled caution . . .' he began.

'Caution! Some might call it craven,' someone shouted. Coxon coloured with anger. The flush spread unevenly across his face, leaving darker and lighter patches, and Hector was pleased to see that the effect of the spiked ointment had not yet fully worn off.

'At our outset we agreed to take the gold mines at Santa Maria,' Coxon continued.

'And small prize it brought us,' shouted the heckler, but Coxon ignored him this time.

'We have defeated the enemy in open battle, but our position is exposed and difficult. Our supplies are perilously low. We are in unfamiliar territory, and the enemy will regain their strength and may sever our line of retreat.'

'I dislike the man, but he's right,' muttered Jezreel standing beside Hector. 'We are badly overstretched.'

Coxon was speaking again. 'I therefore think it prudent that we return to our ships waiting for us at Golden Island. Once in the Caribbean we can resume our cruising for purchase.'

'What does Captain Sawkins say?' called out a voice. Sawkins' rampaging courage during the battle off Panama had made him immensely popular.

Sawkins stepped up to the low rail which divided the quarterdeck from the waist of the ship and cleared his throat. As usual he spoke bluntly.

'I propose we continue with the Adventure,' he said firmly. 'The walls of Panama are too strong for us, but there are towns all along the coast which do not yet know we are here in the South Sea. If we act boldly, we can take such places by surprise. We might even find their quays heaped with silver bars ready for shipment.'

His words met with a low rumble of enthusiasm from several in his audience though the majority looked towards Coxon again, waiting for his rejoinder.

'A wise man knows when to retreat, taking his spoils with him,' Coxon declared.

'Half a hat full of pesos!' scoffed Sawkins. He was bright-eyed with enthusiasm. 'We can get twenty times as much if we have the courage to stay in the South Sea. I propose that we sail south and plunder as we go until we reach the land's end. There we round the Cape, and sail home, our pockets full.'

Captain Coxon looked openly scornful. 'Anyone who believes that claim is putting his head into a Spanish noose.'

'Do your people always quarrel so openly?' said someone quietly in Spanish at Hector's elbow. It was Captain Peralta who had edged his way into the assembly and was listening to the argument.

'Can you understand what they are saying?' whispered Hector.

'Only a little. But the anger in their voices is evident.'

Hector was about to ask Dan whether he wanted to return to Golden Island when a loud husky voice rang out. It was the bald quartermaster who had served under Captain Harris. 'There's no point in putting this to a vote,' he shouted, and he marched up the companionway to the quarterdeck where he turned to face the crowd. 'Those who want to go back to Golden Island under Captain Coxon's command, make your way to the starboard rail,' he bawled. 'Those who prefer to stay in the South Sea and serve under Captain Sawkins assemble on the port side.'

There was a low murmuring of discussion among the men, and a general movement as the buccaneers began to separate into two groups. Hector noted that the numbers were broadly equal, though perhaps a small majority had elected to travel back with Coxon. He looked enquiringly at Dan. As usual the Miskito had said little and was standing quietly watching what was going on.

'Dan, I'm for going back to the Caribbean. What do you want to do?' Hector said. He had never mentioned Susanna to Dan, and now he was uneasy that he was not telling his friend the true reason for his decision. To his relief, Dan merely shrugged and said, 'I would like to see more of the South Sea.

Few of my people have ever been there. But I will go along with whatever you, Jacques and Jezreel decide.'

There was another shout from the quartermaster. 'Make up your minds and cut the chatter!'

Glancing round, Hector realised that he and his three friends were almost the last people standing in the middle of the deck, still undecided.

'Come on, Jezreel! Come with us!' shouted someone from starboard side where Coxon's volunteers were clustered. During the hand-to-hand fighting on the deck of Peralta's ship, Jezreel's great height and his obvious fighting skill had made him a favourite with the buccaneers.

'Best take your winnings when you're still on your feet, and not try another bout with a fresh opponent. You'll likely finish up with a broken face as well as an empty purse. That's something else I learned in the fight game,' muttered Jezreel. He strolled across to join the group.

'Hey Frenchy! You too! We need someone to show us how to roast monkey so it tastes like beef!' called another of Coxon's group. Jacques, too, was popular with the men. Jacques grinned broadly and set off, following Jezreel.

Hector was overcome with relief. Without special pleading his friends had chosen the course of action that he had wanted for them. He touched Dan on the arm. 'Come on, Dan. Let's join them.' Then he too started across the deck.

He had not gone more than a couple of paces when Coxon's voice rang out. 'I am not having that wretch in my company!'

Hector glanced up. Coxon was standing at the quarterdeck rail and pointing directly at him, his face working with anger. 'He's not to be trusted!' the buccaneer captain announced. 'He's a Spanish-lover.'

A murmur ran through the crowd of onlookers. Hector realised that many of them must have seen him in quiet conversation with Peralta. Others would have known that he was responsible for saving the Spaniard from the sea.

'He would betray us if it suits him,' Coxon continued. His tone had dropped to a low snarl now. Hector was open-mouthed, taken completely by surprise and so stunned by the accusation that he did not know how to respond. The captain pressed home his advantage.

'Someone among us warned the Spaniards at Santa Maria of our coming. That is why we found so little plunder there.' His words dropped into the awkward silence as the general buzz and chatter ceased. 'I have often wondered who it was, and how the garrison was alerted. It was easy enough for someone to send a warning by the hand of his friend the striker.'

Belatedly Hector remembered that in the last day before the assault on Santa Maria, he had seen little of Dan. The Miskito had been away on a hunting trip to obtain fresh food.

Coxon was icily certain of himself. 'I will not include a traitor in my company. He stays here.'

Hector had a quick glimpse of the vindictive expression on the buccaneer's face as the man began to make his way to join the group who had chosen him as their leader.

'If he stays here, then I do too,' said Jezreel. He stepped out of the crowd and began to make his way back towards Hector. His great height made his departure very obvious.

There was another movement among the men who had voted to follow Coxon. This time it was Jacques. He too was abandoning the group.

Hector remained where he was, numbed by the turn of events as his two friends came back across the deck. 'Looks like we're staying in the South Sea,' announced Jezreel loud enough for all to hear. 'Captain Sawkins was always a better bet than Coxon.'

They moved across to the port side where Sawkins' company was assembled and as they did so, Hector became conscious of more movement behind him. Glancing back over his shoulder he saw that at least a dozen men who had previously decided to follow Coxon, had now changed their minds. They too were switching sides. One by one they were deserting Coxon's group in full view of the man they had chosen to follow only minutes earlier.

Suddenly a hand gripped Hector by the shoulder, and he was swung round. He found himself staring into Coxon's livid face. It was contorted with rage. 'No man crosses me twice,' he snarled. The buccaneer captain was shaking with anger. His hand dropped towards his waistband, and a moment later Coxon had pulled out a pistol and had rammed the barrel hard into the young man's stomach. Hector felt the muzzle quivering with the force of Coxon's anger. 'This is what I should have done when I first laid eyes on you,' Coxon hissed.

Hector tensed, already feeling the bullet in his guts, when an arm seemed to come from nowhere, sweeping down towards the pistol and knocking it aside just as Coxon pulled the trigger. The pistol ball buried itself in the wooden deck, and at the same moment someone kicked the buccaneer captain's feet from under him so that he fell heavily to the deck. Looking up, Hector saw that it was Jezreel who had deflected the pistol's aim while Jacques had tripped the buccaneer. Both men were looking grim.

No one made any move to help Coxon though Dan collected the empty pistol which had been dropped, and handed it to Coxon once he was back on his feet.

Aware that the entire company was watching him, the captain brushed himself down without saying a word. Then he stepped up close to Hector, and said in a voice so low that no one else could hear but thick with menace, 'You would be well advised to leave your bones here in the South Seas, Lynch. Should you ever return to a place where I can reach you, I will make sure that you pay for what you have done today.'

ELEVEN

✳

Next morning Captain Coxon and his company were gone. They left before sunrise in one of the captured vessels, eighty men in all. 'Bastards, bastards, utter bastards!' announced one of the surgeons who had decided to stay on. He had just discovered that Coxon's company had taken with them most of the expedition medicines. 'How are we expected to do our job when we lack the remedies. They scamper off, tails between their legs, while we're the ones who can expect to see action.' To show his disgust, he spat over the side of the galleon.

She was now to be their flagship, and at 400 tons made an impressive show with a wealth of gilding to show off her high stern in the typical Spanish style. She lacked cannon, but with luck their victims would not even know that she was in foreign hands until she was within musket range. The men had been debating what to call her. *La Santissima Trinidad* sounded too much like popery. Yet every sailor knew that it was bad luck to change a vessel's name. So at Hector's suggestion they had decided to keep the name but change the language, calling her *Trinity*, and even the most superstitious of their company had been content.

'I've still got a few medicines stowed in my knapsack,' Hector told the disgruntled surgeon. Basil Ringrose was originally from Kent, and Hector had taken an instant liking to him. Ringrose had a friendly manner which matched his open, freckled face topped by a mass of chestnut curls.

'We must put together a common stock of all the medicines that remain.' Ringrose said. 'It's fortunate that I always carry my surgical instruments with me in their own roll of oil cloth.'

It was Ringrose who had amputated one of Captain Harris's legs, trying unsuccessfully to save his life. But the stump had begun to rot, and with gangrene had come death.

'I'm only a surgeon's assistant,' Hector confessed. 'I came to help Surgeon Smeeton of Captain Harris's company, and he's turned back. But I have been keeping notes of how to prepare various medicines using local ingredients.'

'I saw you writing things down and thought that you were helping Dampier over there,' explained Ringrose. He nodded towards a saturnine, lantern-jawed man who was leaning perilously far out over the side of the anchored galleon and staring down into the sea. The man was dropping small chips of wood into the water and watching them float away. Propped against the bulwark was a bamboo tube similar to the one that Hector carried.

'What's he doing?' Hector asked.

'I have no idea. You had better go and ask him for yourself. Dampier seems to take an interest in nearly everything that we come across.'

Hector approached the stranger, who was now writing down something on a scrap of paper.

The man looked up from his quill. Brown melancholy eyes framed a narrow nose above a long upper lip. He looked too scholarly to be a sea thief.

'Tides,' said the man pensively, even before Hector could pose his question. 'I'm trying to work out the source of the tides. You may have noticed that here in the South Sea the tides run much stronger than those we left behind in the Caribbean.'

'I had remarked on that,' said Hector. Dampier shot him a quizzical glance from the sad-looking eyes.

'Then how do you explain it? Surely if the ocean is all one body of water, the tides should be similar everywhere. Some people claim that the fierce tides in the South Sea are made by water rushing through tunnels under the land, flooding here from the Caribbean. But I do not believe it.'

'Then what do you think is the reason?'

Dampier bent his head to blow gently on the wet ink. 'That I have not yet understood. But I believe it is to do with the wind patterns, the shape of the ocean floor, and phases of the moon of course. What is important at this time is to make observations. Interpretation can come later.'

'I was told that you make observations of everything.'

Dampier had a habit of rubbing his finger along his long upper lip. 'Nearly everything. I'm interested in fish and fowl, people and plants, the weather and the seasons. It is my chief reason for travelling.'

'Surgeon Smeeton, for whom I was an assistant, was of a like mind. Though he was mainly interested in the medical practices of native peoples.'

'Surgeon Smeeton, I hear that he has left the expedition. A pity. I knew him in Jamaica.'

Hector felt a quick surge of interest at the mention of Jamaica. 'Do you know Jamaica well?' he asked.

'I was there for a few months, training to be an overseer on a sugar plantation,' Dampier replied. 'But I disagreed with my employer, and the opportunity to go on the account – as these buccaneers call their adventuring – was too tempting. It was a chance to see new places.'

'When you were in Jamaica did you hear anything of the Lynch family?'

'Difficult not to. He was the governor, and his family possess as much, if not more acreage, than any other landowners on the island.'

'What about the son, Robert Lynch, and his sister Susanna? Did you meet them by any chance?'

'Far too grand for me,' said Dampier shaking his head. 'Though I did encounter young Robert briefly. He wanted information about the best conditions for planting indigo. I told him that he was better to consult an established indigo grower.'

'What about his sister Susanna?'

'I never met her in person though I saw her at a distance. A very pretty creature. Destined for a grand marriage, I would say. One day her parents will be taking her to London to find a suitable match.'

Hector felt a stab of disappointment. It was exactly what the surveyor Snead had said. 'So you don't think she would stay on in Jamaica?'

'There's nothing for her there. Why all the questions? Do you know her?'

'I met her just once,' Hector confessed.

Dampier treated him to a shrewd look. 'Sweet on her, are you? Well, that's as strange and curious as anything I've observed in the South Sea, a humble adventurer pining after a grandee's daughter.' He gave a lugubrious sniff, and began to roll up the piece of paper ready to slide it into the bamboo tube with his other notes. Then a thought must have occurred to him, for he looked up and said, 'If Surgeon Smeeton no longer requires your services, perhaps you would lend me a hand in making my observations.'

'I would be pleased to,' Hector assured him, 'though my chief duty must still be to assist the surgeons.'

'Yes, you were talking with Ringrose. You'll discover that he's got clever hands and is as much interested in navigation as he is in medicine. Enjoys making instruments to read the angle of the sun and devising sighting tables, that sort of thing.'

'I had noticed that all morning he's been making a sketch map of the bay and its islands.'

'A very sensible precaution. We have no charts of this area.

We are utterly ignorant of the ports and anchorages, currents, reefs and islands. Such details are known only to the Spaniards. In case we come back here, Ringrose is making notes so that we know just where to anchor, find water and shelter.'

'I worked for a Turkish sea captain once, assisting him with sea charts. But apart from a single ocean crossing, I lack practical experience of navigation.'

'Stick close to Ringrose and you'll learn a lot, though I expect it will be mostly coastal pilotage rather than deep-sea navigation,' Dampier assured him.

*

So IT TURNED OUT. For the next two months *Trinity* stayed near the coast, a hungry predator looking for scraps of plunder. News of her presence had yet to spread to the Spanish settlements and in the first ten days she loitered off Panama she snapped up several unwary prizes, which sailed straight into her jaws and gave up without a fight. One was an advice ship loaded with pay for the Panama garrison, fifty-one thousand pieces of eight, and – equally welcome – fifty great earthen jars of gunpowder which replenished stocks that had run low. Other hapless victims provided rations – flour, beans, cages of live chickens, sacks of chocolate beans which the buccaneers ground to powder and drank mixed with hot water. The captured vessels were small barks and of little value. Anything useful by way of rigging or sails was taken off, then the boarding party smashed holes in their planking and sank them on the spot.

But the weather was against them. Not a day passed without frequent downpours of heavy rain which soaked the men and their clothing. The sails grew great patches of stinking mildew in the muggy tropical heat, and a miasma of damp hung over the sodden vessel. The run-off dripped through cracks in the deck spoiling everything below. Guns and equipment rusted overnight. Bread and biscuits in the cook's stores went mouldy. In search of fresh supplies of food, Sawkins the fire-eater led a

raid ashore. The local inhabitants hastily threw up breastworks
at the entrance to their little town, and Sawkins was tugging at
one of the wooden posts trying to uproot it when he was killed
outright by a Spanish shot. His death only added to the general
sense of disappointment that *Trinity* was wasting too much
time. When the wind failed she was gripped by unknown
currents which one day brought her close to the shore, and
the next night pushed her almost out of sight of land. In June the
rainfall eased, but the sky remained overcast and sullen, leaving
the men frustrated and discontent. They grumbled and bickered,
knowing they needed to progress east and south along the coast
before the alarm was raised. Instead the wind, when it did blow,
was fitful, and almost always from ahead. *Trinity* was obliged
to tack back and forth. The crew found themselves staring at
the same landmarks – a headland, a small island, a rock with a
particular profile – from dawn until dusk, and then again at the
next sunrise. They did not need a chart to tell them that they
were almost standing still.

'What else did your people expect? Did they know nothing
of our equatorial weather?' commented Capitan Peralta to
Hector. The Spaniard was one of the growing number of
prisoners, and the two of them were in the habit of meeting
in the bows of the ship where they could not be overheard.

'Are the rains finally over?' Hector asked.

Peralta shrugged. 'There can be heavy downpours at this
time of year, even into August. I wonder if your comrades will
still want to follow their captain by then?'

Peralta gave Hector a sideways look. The buccaneer council
had elected Bartholomew Sharpe as their new general, the grand
title they now gave to their overall commander.

Hector hesitated before replying, and Peralta was quick to
pick up on the delay. 'There's something a little devious about
him, isn't there? Something not quite right.'

Hector felt it would be disloyal to agree, so said nothing.
But Peralta had a point. There was an unsettling quality about

Sharpe. It was something that Hector had noted at Golden Island. Even then he had thought that Sharpe was a natural mischief maker. Behind the amiable smile on the fleshy, pouting lips was an evasiveness which made one reluctant to trust him entirely. Now that Sharpe had been made general, Hector was even more apprehensive. He sensed the man was self-serving and devious.

'Don't be surprised if some of your colleagues decide to break away on their own when conditions get more difficult,' Peralta continued. 'Your shipmates are easily swayed and can be pitiless.'

To change the subject Hector showed the Spaniard a new backstaff that Ringrose had fashioned.

Peralta watched him slide the vanes of the backstaff along its wooden shaft.

'It seems a more complicated instrument than usual, more movable parts,' observed the Spaniard.

'Ringrose assures me that it will allow us to calculate our latitude position even where the sun is so high in the sky at noon that a normal backstaff is inaccurate. See here . . .' Hector handed Peralta the instrument so he could inspect the extra vanes. 'They allow readings even when the sun is at ninety degrees overhead.'

'Fortunately I don't depend on such a device for finding my position. I know the coast from here to Lima and beyond,' the Spaniard answered dryly. 'And if I am in doubt I turn to the pages in my derotero, my pilot book, and then I know where I am.' He allowed himself a sardonic smile. 'That's your new commander's real dilemma. He doesn't know where he is or what he's up against, and sooner or later his men will realise it too. They are a wolf pack, ready to show their fangs, and their leader may turn out to be equally ruthless.'

❊

HECTOR RECALLED Peralta's warning in the third week of August when *Trinity* overhauled another small coaster. Unusually, her crew put up a fight. They draped waistcloths along the bulwarks in order to conceal their numbers, and men fired old-fashioned arquebuses at the approaching galleon. The battle lasted only half an hour and the outcome was never in doubt. *Trinity* was by far the larger vessel and mustered three or four times as many marksmen. Yet two buccaneers were badly wounded by enemy bullets before the bark dropped her topsail in a sign of surrender and her survivors cried for quarter.

'Search and sink her, and be quick about it!' Sharpe shouted angrily as he watched the canoe which served as *Trinity*'s cockboat being lowered into the water. He was in an evil humour. The enemy's fire had cut up *Trinity*'s newly over-hauled rigging which would have to be spliced and mended, resulting in further delay, and it was three weeks since they had last taken any plunder.

The canoe made a dozen trips between the two vessels to ferry back the captive crew, who would now be held for ransom or obliged to work as forced labour aboard the galleon. On the final trip the buccaneers were crowing with delight and holding up leather bags and glass bottles. The bark was carrying five thousand pieces of eight as well as a generous stock of wine and spirits. *Trinity*'s quartermaster, Samuel Gifford, lost no time in distributing the loot at the foot of the mainmast, and each man came away carrying his share of the coins in his hat. Every fourth man, drawn by lot, also received a bottle.

'Here you!' said Sharpe beckoning to Hector. 'Find out from the prisoners why they resisted when they had no chance against us. '

'Who is your captain?' Hector asked. Only a handful of the captives wore the clothes of working sailors. He guessed they were the bark's sailing crew. The majority – some thirty men –

were too well dressed to be mariners and looked more like minor gentry. There was a priest among them, an elderly red-faced friar who was clutching his gown close around him as though he feared some sort of profane contagion.

A small man in a brown doublet and a stained but costly shirt stepped out of the group.

'My name is Tomas de Argandona. I am the mestre de campo from the town of Guayagil over there.' He gestured vaguely towards the horizon.

'I need a list of everyone's names and where they come from,' explained Hector.

'I assure you that will not be necessary,' said the little man, a touch pompously. 'We are aware that you pirates are accustomed to asking ransom for your prisoners, and we have agreed among ourselves not to participate in that sordid practice.'

'What's he talking about?' demanded Sharpe. There was a nasty edge to his voice.

Argandona was speaking again. 'We were looking for you.'

'Looking for us . . . ?' said Hector, startled.

'The entire coast is aware that you are sailing in these waters aboard the *Santissima Trinidad* which you have stolen. My colleagues and I offered our services to His Excellency the Viceroy of Peru. We intended to seek you out, and then inform his Excellency exactly where you might be found so that he could direct the armadilla to seek and destroy you.'

'But surely you must have known that your vessel was no match for us.'

'We never expected to confront you,' answered Argandona condescendingly. 'Only to observe and report. But once we were challenged, we as gentlemen, ' – and he emphasised the word gentlemen – 'could not decline the battle. Our honour was involved.'

Hector translated this defiant reply to Captain Sharpe who gave a dangerously mirthless laugh. 'Ask the coxcomb if his

honour will allow him to tell us exactly what the Viceroy and
his armadilla are proposing.'

To Hector's increasing amazement, the mestre de campo's
response was utterly frank. 'His Excellency the Viceroy disposes
three great warships in the Armada del Sur but, sadly, all of
them are unfit for sea at this time. So he has ordered an equal
number of merchant ships to be armed with their brass cannon
and placed seven hundred and fifty soldiers aboard them. He
has also sent extra guns to defend the ports. In our town of
Guayagil we have mustered more than eight hundred soldiers
to defend our property and constructed two new forts to guard
the harbour.'

'He's trying to scare us off,' grated Sharpe when Hector
relayed the information to him. 'I don't think so,' said Hector
quietly. 'I think he is being truthful. It's a matter of his honour.'

'We'll see about that,' said Sharpe. Looking round, he saw
Jezreel standing nearby. Taking a pistol from his sash, Sharpe
handed it to the giant. 'Point this at the belly of that sneering
priest over there, and make it look threatening,' he ordered. In
a lower voice he added, 'It's charged with powder but not ball.
I want to scare the pompous little shit.'

Turning back to Hector the buccaneer captain said, 'Now
inform the puffed-up runt that I don't believe him, and I'm
calling his bluff. If he doesn't change his story I'll send his
priest to the hell he deserves.'

The Spaniard was quivering with a combination of fright
and indignation. 'Your captain is a savage. I have already told
him the truth.'

'Pull the trigger,' snarled Sharpe.

A moment later there was a loud explosion and, to Hector's
horror, the friar was thrown backward and fell to the deck. A
great stain of blood spread across his gown. Jezreel, standing
with the smoking pistol in his hand, looked down at the weapon
in disbelief. He was too shocked to speak.

'A genuine mistake,' said Sharpe smoothly. Stepping forward quickly he took back the pistol. 'I thought the weapon was charged but not fully loaded.'

Hector had gone forward to where the priest lay. A dark red rivulet, glinting in the sun, was trickling from under the body and seeping its way to the scuppers. He knelt down and placed his hand on the man's chest. Through the thick brown cloth he could detect a faint heart beat. 'He's still alive!' he called out, looking around frantically for a surgeon. A moment later Ringrose was at his side, his fingers gently probing for the entry wound. 'Gut shot,' he muttered under his breath. 'He'll not live.'

'Get out of my way!' ordered a hoarse voice. Hector was aware of a shadow falling over him. He looked up. It was a crew man by the name of Duill who had always seemed to him to be particularly uncouth and brutish. He had enormously wide shoulders, a short body and a neck that seemed too long to support a small round head. It was as if he had been put together from the body parts of strangers. 'Bugger off!' growled Duill. His speech was slightly slurred, and Hector smelled the reek of brandy on his breath. 'This is what we do to Papists.' He leaned down and, pushing Hector aside, took the priest by the shoulders and began to drag the dying man towards the ship's rail.

'Here, give me a hand,' he called out. A second crew man, obviously one of Duill's cronies, ran forward. He stumbled momentarily, and gave a whooping laugh. The two drunks took the priest by the shoulders and feet and began to swing him back and forth between them like a heavy sack. 'One, two and away,' they chanted, and with a drunken cheer heaved the body over the rail and into the sea. Then they toppled against one another and broke into boozy laughter.

'Savages!' murmured Ringrose. He had risen to his feet and had gone pale.

'The priest was still alive,' groaned Hector. He felt that he was going to vomit.

Ringrose gripped his arm. 'Steady, Lynch. Remember where we are. Look at the men.'

The crew of the *Trinity* were staring at the patch of blood on the deck. Many of them were silent and thoughtful. But at least a score of them were grinning broadly. Suddenly Hector remembered Peralta's warning. They were like a wolf pack gloating over a kill. They had enjoyed the spectacle.

*

'OF COURSE he knew his pistol was loaded,' said Jacques. It was just after sunset on the evening of the murder, and the four friends were gathered by the lee rail to discuss the atrocity. 'In the toughest Paris gangs the leader would select one of his men at random and order him to slit a throat or break an innocent head. If the man refused or delayed, then he was likely to suffer that same fate himself. That was the gang leader's way to gain respect and impose his authority.'

'But I was tricked,' said Jezreel.

'Sharpe's more cunning. He has shown the crew that he's ruthless, and at the same time made sure that he does not have blood on his own hands.'

'So why did he pick on me?' added Jezreel. His face set hard. 'Why was I the one selected to do the job?'

'Because he wants to bind us to him,' said Dan quietly. The others looked at the Miskito in surprise. It was rare for him to make any comment. Immediately, he had their complete attention. 'Remember when Coxon refused to include Hector in his group returning to Golden Island? We stuck together, Coxon was made to look a fool, and several of the other men came over to our side. Sharpe doesn't want that happening to him when he is in charge.'

Hector was beginning to understand the point that Dan was

making. 'So you think Sharpe was making sure we stay on *Trinity*?'

Dan nodded. 'Several men have already approached me to ask if I was satisfied with Sharpe as general. They are plotting to depose him by vote. If that fails, they are planning to leave the expedition.'

'You mean that if we went with them back to the Caribbean, word of the priest's death is sure to get out and Jezreel could finish up on the gallows in Port Royal.'

'Sharpe knows that we stay together as a group, and he needs us,' Dan said, and his unhurried manner of speaking gave his words all the more weight. 'Consider who we are. When it comes to hand-to-hand fighting, no one aboard this vessel is more skilled than Jezreel. The men look up to him. They like him to be on their side when we send out a boarding party. Hector is the best interpreter. Plenty of others can speak some Spanish, but Hector has a knack of getting along well with the Spaniards, men like Peralta. They confide in him.'

'What about Jacques, surely there's nothing special about him?' said Jezreel showing a glimmer of his usual banter.

Dan gave a faint smile. 'Surely you know that on a ship a good cook is more valuable than a good captain.' The smile vanished, to be replaced by a solemn expression. 'As for myself, there are only two Miskito strikers left with the expedition. Without us the company would be even hungrier than they are now. And starving men are discontents.'

That was true enough, thought Hector. Finding enough food to satisfy *Trinity*'s large crew was a constant problem.

'Capitan Peralta said to me as far back as Panama that the expedition would disintegrate,' he said.

'This is worse than when I killed a man in a prize fight,' said Jezreel glumly, looking down at his hands. 'At least that was in a fit of rage. This time I have been made a dupe.'

'The situation is not hopeless,' Hector comforted him. 'Given enough time, the death of the priest will be forgotten or perhaps Sharpe's double-dealing will be exposed. But for the moment our general holds the advantage. However unwilling we may be, he has bound us to him, just as Dan says, and we must wait until matters right themselves.'

TWELVE

HECTOR WATCHED Bartholomew Sharpe throw himself a double four. Passage was a brutally simple game of dice but well suited to the gamblers aboard *Trinity*. They wanted to wager their loot with the least effort and the quickest results. The rules were straightforward: three dice and two players. The first player to get a double using only two of the dice, then threw the third. If the total on all three dice was more than ten, that man won. Ten or under and he lost.

The captain threw again, a five, and reached out to sweep up the coins wagered by his opponent. As he transferred his winnings into a purse, he became aware of Hector standing behind him. 'What do you want?' Sharpe asked brusquely, turning to glare at the young man. Hector detected a moment of unease in his captain's eyes and the briefest flicker of dislike. It was enough to make him wonder if his new captain might become just as much a threat as Captain Coxon, as dangerous but more subtle.

'A word in private, please.'

Sharpe treated his gambling victim to a shrug of false sympathy. 'That's enough for today. I've won back all the money I lent you, and you'll need more plunder before we play again.'

He deliberately left his dice on the capstan head. It was not something he would have risked with more sophisticated gamblers in London or professional players though the three dice were masterpieces of the counterfeiter's art. Two were paired delicately so they tended to come up with doubles. The other, of course, was adjusted so it gave a high number. It was that last dice which had a very slight discolouration of one of the pips, just enough for Captain Sharpe to recognise. Naturally he always took care that he lost several throws before he began to use the three dice in the correct sequence, and now after two months of gambling he judged that he personally held fully ten per cent of all the plunder taken on the cruise.

'Well, what is it?' he asked gruffly as he and Hector moved out of earshot of the gamblers.

'There's a risk of a prisoner uprising,' Hector told him.

'Why so?'

'Because we don't have enough men to supervise the prisoners properly.'

The captain looked hard at Hector. 'Anything else?'

'Yes. It's not just the numbers of prisoners. We've been keeping back those who are wealthy or were officers on the ships we captured.'

'Of course. They were the only ones worth holding.'

'They are the ones most likely to organise an uprising.'

Sharpe made no reply, but looked out across the sea. The sinking sun had coloured the underbellies of the clouds a deep and angry red. It was as though a great fire had been lit beyond the horizon. It reminded Bartholomew Sharpe of the unsatisfactory outcome to the raid on the mainland a fortnight earlier. The Spaniards had already retreated into the hills, taking their valuables with them. He had threatened to burn down their houses and farms unless protection money was paid, but the Spaniards were astute. They dragged out the negotiations until they had gathered enough soldiers to chase the buccaneers back to the beach. In their frustration the raiders torched the farms anyhow.

A few days later forty members of his crew, dissatisfied with the poor progress of the venture, had left *Trinity*. They had sailed away on a captured bark, heading north on the return journey to the Caribbean. Barely a hundred members of the original expedition remained, and that was not enough to deter a revolt among the prisoners.

'What do you propose we do?' he asked Hector.

'Set the prisoners free.'

Sharpe gave Hector a calculating glance. Here was an opportunity to gain the young man's trust. The captain was aware that he and his friends were suspicious and resentful of him. But the trick with the loaded pistol had been a necessity. It had impressed the crew and cowed the Spaniards.

'Are you suggesting this because you are friendly with Captain Peralta?'

'No. I think it would be a prudent action.'

Sharpe thought for a moment. 'Very well. Next time we come to land, you will see that I can be generous, even with my enemies.' In fact he had already decided several days earlier to rid himself of the captives. No one seemed willing to pay a ransom for them, and they had become so many useless mouths to feed.

'Rocks! Rocks! Dead Ahead!' the lookout suddenly bellowed. Sharpe looked up in surprise. The note of alarm in the man's voice indicated that he had been dozing at his post and suddenly seen the danger. 'Reefs! Breaking water! No more than a quarter mile away.'

'Ringrose!' Sharpe shouted. 'What do you make of it?'

'Impossible! We're thirty miles off the coast,' exclaimed Ringrose who had taken a sun sight earlier in the day. He jumped up on the rail and shaded his eyes as he peered forward. 'I wish to God we had a decent chart. This groping about in the unknown is madness. One night we'll run ourselves full tilt onto a reef in the dark and never know what happened.'

'Rocks to starboard as well!' The lookout's voice was shrill with panic. This time his shout caused a surge of activity aboard *Trinity*. There was the noise of running feet as men appeared on the deck and rushed into the bows and gazed forward trying to identify the danger. 'Bear away to port,' Sharpe called out to the helmsman, 'and reduce sail.' The order was unnecessary. Men were already easing out the main sheets and bracing round the yards. Others were standing by the reefing tackles.

'White water to port!' roared a sailor. He was pointing, open-mouthed with alarm. There was a foaming patch on the surface of the sea no more than a hundred paces beside *Trinity*. The galleon had sailed herself into a trap. There were reefs on each side and ahead, and little room to manoeuvre. 'Bring her head to wind!' snapped Sharpe to the steersman.

'Lucky she's so nimble,' said Ringrose beside Hector as *Trinity*'s bow turned into the wind, the sails came aback against the mast in an untidy tangle of ropes and sails, and the galleon came to a halt, gathered sternway and began to fall off on the opposite tack.

'Merde! Look there behind us! We sailed right over those rocks and never saw them.' Jacques had arrived on the quarter-deck and was gazing back towards the expanse of sea which the galleon had just negotiated. That too was boiling up in a white froth.

Beside him, Dan began to chuckle. Jacques looked at him in astonishment. 'What's so funny? We're boxed in by rocks!'

Dan shook his head. He was smiling. 'Not rocks . . . fish!'

Jacques scowled at him and then turned back to stare again at the sea. One of the foaming reefs had disappeared, abruptly sunk beneath the waves. But another had taken its place, fifty paces from the spot. There too the water was boiling upward.

'What do you mean . . . fish?'

Dan held up his hand, finger and thumb no more than three inches apart. 'Fish, small fish. More than you can count.'

Hector was concentrating on a nearby white patch. It was definitely on the move and coming closer to the ship. A moment later he saw that it was formed of myriads of tiny fish, millions upon millions of them, weaving and flashing and churning in a dense mass which occasionally broke the surface of the sea in a white spuming flurry.

'Anchovies!' cried Jacques.

There was relieved laughter from all around *Trinity* as the crew realised their error. 'Resume course!' ordered Sharpe. He, as much as anyone else, had been misled, but he had noted how the crew had taken matters into their hands in the imagined crisis. They had not consulted him, nor waited for orders. It was time that he found something to distract them.

He sent for the gentleman prisoner, Tomas de Argandona. The Spaniard was much less self-assured now that he had witnessed the shooting of the priest, and Sharpe was waiting in his cabin with a pistol lying on his desk. One glance and Argandona told Sharpe what he wanted to know: the nearest town on the mainland was La Serena and wealthy enough to have five churches and two convents. It lay two miles inland and had neither a garrison nor a defensive wall. A watchtower overlooked the closest anchorage but there was an unguarded landing beach some distance away. Small boats could put men ashore there and it was no more than a three-hour march to reach the town.

The general council held on the open deck the following morning went just as smoothly. The men voted overwhelmingly in favour of a raid.

'I propose John Watling to lead the attack,' Sharpe announced after Gifford, the quartermaster, had counted the show of hands. 'He lands with fifty men and takes the town by surprise. I then bring *Trinity* into the main anchorage and we ferry the plunder aboard.'

Looking on, Hector knew that Sharpe was being as wily as ever. Hector had seen little of Watling since the day they had been in the same canoe during the attack on Panama, but he knew Watling was popular with the men. He had sailed with

Morgan and they would follow him without question. He was one of those rigid, grim, old-fashioned Puritans who detested Catholics and observed the Sabbath scrupulously. Also, as Hector had noted, Sharpe had never been able to cheat Watling at dice, because he never gambled.

＊

'LOOKS AS THOUGH we were expected,' Dan said under his breath. He, Jezreel and Hector had come ashore with Watling's raiders as soon as there was enough daylight to approach the landing beach safely. Now they were trudging along the dusty coastal track that would lead them to La Serena. Jacques had been left behind with a dozen men to guard the boats.

Hector followed the Miskito's glance. From a spur of high ground overlooking the track a horseman was watching them. He made no attempt to conceal himself.

'There goes our chance of surprise,' Jezreel commented.

Hector scanned the countryside. The day was promising to be overcast and very humid, and the raiders were advancing across rolling scrubland. Occasionally the path dipped into small gullies washed out by rainstorms. It was ideal terrain for an ambush, and there was a faint whiff of smoke in the air. He wondered if the Spaniards who farmed the area were burning their crops to prevent them falling into the hands of the raiders.

Suddenly there were shouts from the head of the column, and someone came running back, urging everyone to close up and look to their weapons. Hector brought his musket off his shoulder, checked that it was loaded and primed and that the ball had not been dislodged from the barrel, then placed the hammer at half-cock. Holding the gun in both hands he walked cautiously forward, Hector and Dan at his side.

The track had been no more than the width of a cart but now it broadened out as it entered a clearing in the scrub. The bushes had been cut back for a distance of some fifty paces, and at the edge of the clearing were several clumps of low trees.

'Lancers over there, hiding in the woods!' warned someone.

'How many?' called a buccaneer.

'Don't know. At least a couple of dozen. Form up in a square and look lively.'

At that moment came the sound of muskets, no more than a dozen shots. There were puffs of smoke from the bushes farthest from the column and Hector heard bullets flying overhead. But the shots went wide and no one was hurt. He dropped on one knee and aimed his gun towards a bush where he could see the haze of musket smoke still hanging above the leaves. He could not make out the man who had fired, and waited for him to show himself. Away to his right he heard several shots as the buccaneers saw their targets.

Hector's arm was beginning to ache as he tried to keep his gun trained on the suspect bush. The muzzle was wavering, but he was reluctant to waste a shot. It would take a long time to reload, and in that interval the cavalry might show themselves.

Seconds later, the Spanish cavalry burst from the thickets. They crashed out in a wild charge and rode straight for the formation of buccaneers. There must have been about sixty or seventy of the riders mounted on small, light-boned horses. A few riders held pistols which they discharged as they came careering forward, and Hector glimpsed one man brandishing a blunderbuss. But the majority were armed only with twelve-foot lances. Whooping and cheering they galloped forward in a confused mass, hoping to skewer their enemy. Hector swung the muzzle of his gun to aim into the charging body of riders. None of the Spaniards wore uniform or armour. These were not professional troopers, but farmers and cattlemen seeking to protect their property.

He selected his target – a stout, red-faced cavalier astride a dun horse with a white blaze – and pulled the trigger. In the confusion and through the gun smoke he could not see whether his shot went home.

He rose to his feet, placed the butt of his musket on the

ground, and plucked a new powder charge from the cartouche box on his belt. Beside him Jezreel was doing the same. Vaguely Hector sensed that the Spaniards' attack had come to nothing. A scatter of horsemen was galloping back towards the shelter of the woods. One or two bodies had been left lying on the ground, and a riderless horse came tearing past, reins hanging loose, the bucket-shaped saddle empty. Hector charged and primed his gun, selected a musket ball from the bag hanging from his waist and dropped it down the barrel. He was about to tamp the bullet home with his ramrod when, beside him, Jezreel said, 'No time for that!' Hector watched his companion lift his musket a few inches off the ground and slam the butt down sharply so the bullet came up hard against the wadding. 'Saves a few seconds,' grinned Jezreel, as he dropped back on one knee and brought the weapon to his shoulder. 'Now let them come at us again.'

But the skirmish was over. The Spaniards had withdrawn. They had lost four men, while not one of Watling's group had been wounded. 'Honour satisfied, I think,' said Jezreel. 'I feel sorry for them. One of their lancers was carrying nothing more than a sharpened cattle prod.'

The column moved forward, more cautiously now, and two miles farther on arrived at the outskirts of La Serena. It was the first Spanish colonial town that Hector had ever entered, and he was struck by the mathematical precision of the place. Compared to the haphazard jumble of Port Royal with its narrow lanes and dogleg streets, La Serena was a model of careful planning. Broad straight avenues were laid out in an exact grid, every intersection was a precise right angle, each house stood at the same distance from its neighbour, and their frontages matched as if in mirrors. Even the town fountain was located at the geometrical centre of the market square. The two-storey houses were of pale yellow sandstone and most of them had carved wooden balconies, studded double doors and heavy shutters. Occasionally there was a glimpse of a garden or small orchard behind a boundary wall, or the ornate bell tower of a church rising above the red-tiled roofs. Everything was solid, neat and substantial. But what made La Serena seem to be an architect's concept rather than a living township was that the town was empty. There was not a single living creature in its streets.

At first Watling's force hesitated at each crossroads, making sure that a street was safe before they ventured across it, and they kept a watch on the balconies and roofs expecting the sudden appearance of an enemy. But there was no movement, no response, no sound. La Serena was totally abandoned by its people, and gradually the buccaneers became more confident. They divided into small groups and dispersed throughout the town, looking for valuables to carry away.

'Why didn't they lock up behind them when they left?' asked Hector wonderingly as he pushed open the heavy front door of the third house he and Jezreel had decided to investigate.

'Probably thought we would do less damage if we could just walk in,' guessed his friend. He had a trickle of juice running down his chin from a half-eaten peach he had plucked in the garden of the house next door.

'They must have had plenty of warning,' said Hector. 'They've removed everything that could be carried away easily.'

It was the same in every house they entered: a central hallway off which were large, high-ceilinged rooms with thick, whitewashed walls and deeply recessed windows. The floors were invariably of tile, and the furniture dark and heavy, too cumbersome to be moved easily. Halfway down this hallway stood a massive cupboard made from some dark tropical wood. Hector swung open the double doors. As he had expected, the shelves were bare. He wandered into the kitchen at the back of the house. He found a large stove against one wall, a place to wash the dishes, a huge earthenware jar used for keeping water cool, more empty cupboards, a tub for laundry. But there were no pots and pans, no dishes. The place had been stripped bare.

They crossed the entry hall and tried a door on the other side. This time it was locked. 'At last, somewhere we are not meant to be,' said Jezreel. Putting his shoulder to a panel, he barged it open, and went inside with Hector at his heels.

'Now we know what the owners looked like,' commented the big man.

They were standing in a large reception room which the owners of the house had failed to strip entirely. They had left behind a large table, several heavily carved chairs with uncomfortable velvet seats, a massive dresser that must have been fully nine feet wide, and a row of family portraits hanging along one wall. Hector presumed that the paintings in their ornate gilded frames were too big to be carried away.

He walked along the line of pictures. Dignitaries, dressed in old-fashioned doublets and hose, stood or sat gazing solemnly out at him, their serious expressions set off by wide lace collars. The men were uniformly sombre in their dress, and all wore narrow pointed beards except one man who was clean-shaven and had a priest's cape and skull cap. The women were posed even more stiffly and looked self-conscious. They held themselves carefully so as not to disturb the folds of their formal gowns whose fabrics were very costly, silks, brocade and lace. All the women wore jewellery, and Hector wondered how many of the pearl necklaces, diamond pendants and gemstone bracelets were now safely in the hills or buried in secret hiding places.

He reached the end of the row of pictures and came to a dead stop. He was gazing into the grey eyes of a young woman. Only her face and shoulders were shown in the portrait, and she was regarding him with a slightly mischievous expression, her lips parted in the hint of a smile. Compared to the other portraits the young woman's complexion was pale. Her chestnut hair had been carefully arranged in ringlets to show off the delicate sweep of her neck and the creamy skin, and she wore a simple gold locket on blue silk ribbon. Her bare shoulders were covered with a light soft scarf.

Hector felt a rush of dizziness. For an instant he thought he was seeing a portrait of Susanna Lynch. Then the moment passed. It was ridiculous to think of finding Susanna's picture in the home of a prosperous Spaniard living in Peru.

For several minutes he just stood without moving, trying to puzzle out why he had mistaken the portrait. Perhaps it was the smile which had reminded him of Susanna. He looked more closely. Or maybe it was the locket that the young woman in the picture was wearing. He was almost sure that Susanna had a locket just like it. He searched the details of the picture, lingering over them as he sought to identify the likeness between this young woman and Susanna. The more he tried, the less certain he became. He believed he could recall exactly how Susanna walked, the way she held her body, the whiteness of her arms, the slope of her shoulders. But when he tried to visualise the precise details of her face, the picture in front of him kept intruding. He became muddled and anxious. The beauty of the girl in the picture began to overlap and merge with his memory of Susanna. He felt uncomfortable, as if he was somehow betraying her.

His reverie was interrupted by a shout from outside. Someone in the street was calling his name. He was wanted in the plaza mayor.

Leaving Jezreel to continue searching, he found Watling and several buccaneers on the steps of the town hall. To judge by the small pile of silver plate and a few candlesticks on the ground before him, the ransack of La Serena was going very badly. Watling was glowering at a trio of Spaniards.

'They rode into town under a white flag,' Watling said. 'Find out who they are and what they want.'

Quickly Hector established that the Spaniards were an embassy from the citizens and wished to discuss terms.

'Tell them that we want a hundred thousand pesos in coin, or we burn the town to the ground,' growled Watling. He was wearing a greasy and threadbare military coat that must have done service in Cromwell's time.

The leader of the Spanish delegation flinched at the mention of so much money. The man was in his late fifties and had a long, narrow face with bushy eyebrows over deep-set brown eyes. Hector wondered if he was related to the family in the portraits, and the young girl.

'It is a huge sum. More than we can afford,' the man said, exchanging glances with his companions.

'A hundred thousand pesos,' repeated Watling brutally.

The Spaniard spread out his hands in a gesture of helplessness. 'It will take days to raise so much money.'

'You have until tomorrow noon. The money is to be delivered here by midday. Until then my men will stay in possession of your town,' retorted Watling.

'Very well,' answered the Spaniard. 'My companions and I will do what we can.' The delegation remounted and slowly rode their horses away.

Watching them leave, one of the buccaneers beside Watling asked, 'Do you think they will keep their word?'

'I doubt it,' answered Watling bluntly, 'but we need time to search the town thoroughly. I want those churches ransacked down to the gilded statue and side altar, and don't forget to pull up the paving stones. It's under them that the priests usually bury their treasures. Tonight we post double sentries in case the Spaniards try to retake the town in the dark.'

*

FORTY-EIGHT hours later Hector was wondering if he and Dan would be accused of cowardice or desertion. They had slipped quietly out of La Serena without informing Watling and made their way back to the landing beach. There, with Jacques's help, they had persuaded the boat guards to let them use a small canoe to get back aboard *Trinity*. As had been planned, their ship was now moored a few miles down the coast in La Serena's anchorage and waiting to pick up the raiders and their booty.

'Where's Watling?' Sharpe called out to them as the canoe came alongside.

'Still in La Serena,' Hector answered.

'What about plunder?' enquired the captain. He had seen that the canoe was empty.

'Not much, at least by the time we left,' said Hector as he and Dan clambered up the swell of the galleon's tumblehome and onto her main deck.

'But surely Watling and his men took the town?'

'Yes, and with little resistance. The citizens agreed to a ransom of one hundred thousand pesos if our men would leave.'

'Then what are they waiting for?' Sharpe asked.

'Neither side kept the bargain. That same night the quarter-master led out a raiding party of forty men, hoping to catch the Spaniards by surprise and rob them. The following day the citizens of La Serena opened the sluice gates of the town reservoir. We woke to find the streets a foot deep in water.'

Sharpe frowned. 'I suppose they thought it would make it much more difficult to set fire to the town.'

'Watling flew into a rage. When I left, the men were in the churches, scraping off any gold or silver leaf, smashing windows, overturning statues.'

'You should be there with them.'

'It was more important to come to warn you that a trap is closing about them. I tried to tell Watling, but he was too angry to listen.'

'What sort of a trap?'

'Dan went out to scout. He counted at least four hundred militiamen moving into position on either side of the road leading here. They'll wait for our men to come to the anchorage loaded with the plunder. Then they'll cut them to pieces.'

Captain Sharpe stared thoughtfully towards the shore. There was no sign of life. He could make out the flagpole on the tall stone watchtower the Spaniards had built to survey the anchorage. If the tower was manned its occupants would long ago have hoisted signals to alert their forces farther inland. But the flag staff was bare. Nor was there any movement among the cluster of warehouses, or on the broad gravel-and-sand road which led up from the shingle beach and inland towards the town. But anything could be happening out of sight behind the swell of the ground. That is where the Spanish troops could be massing. He took Hector by the arm. 'Let me show you something.' He led the young man to the stern of the ship. 'Look over the rail,' he said. 'What do you see?'

Hector stared down towards the galleon's rudder. There were black scorch marks on the timber and the rudder's fastenings, traces of a fire.

'Someone tried to burn away our steering,' he said.

'If they had succeeded, this ship would have been crippled. Luckily we spotted the fire before it had spread and managed to put it out. Someone came quietly out from shore in the darkness, stuffed pitch and rags between the rudder and the stern, and set it alight.'

Hector thought back to how Dan had disabled the Spanish patrol ship off the Campeachy coast.

'It was a brave thing to do.'

'We found the float the arsonist must have used, an inflated horse hide lying on the beach.'

Sharpe wheeled to face Hector and said fiercely, 'Make no mistake about it. The Spaniards are willing to fight for what is theirs, and fight hard. I want you to return to La Serena. If Watling won't listen to you, persuade the others. Tell them to abandon the place and get back here as fast as possible.'

Hector shook his head. 'Half the men are drunk. They

won't leave the town until they've looted it to their satisfaction, probably by mid afternoon. Then they'll stumble back in no fit condition to fight their way through.'

Sharpe regarded the young man with interest. There was something about his quiet manner which suggested that he had a plan in mind.

'Now is the time to use our prisoners,' said Hector. 'Put them ashore where they will be visible to the Spanish, but keep them under guard. I will go to the Spaniards and tell them that we will release the prisoners unharmed if they allow our men to return safely to the ship.'

Sharpe gave Hector a long, calculating look. 'You're learning this trade,' he said softly. 'One day you could be elected general yourself.'

'I've no wish for that,' said Hector. 'Just let me talk to Captain Peralta and his comrades.'

Sharpe gave a grunt. 'This scheme is your responsibility. If something goes wrong, and I have to leave you on shore, I will do so.'

Hector was about to answer that he expected nothing less, but instead began arrangements with Jacques and the crew of the canoe to ferry Peralta and the prisoners ashore.

❋

'SHARPE IS NOT to be trusted,' was Peralta's immediate response when he and Hector had landed on the beach and the young man told him what was intended. 'The moment your captain sees that his men are safe, he'll decide to take his prisoners back on board and sail away.'

'That is why you – not I – will be the one who goes to find the commander of the Spanish forces and arrange the safe conduct.'

Peralta pursed his lips and looked doubtful. 'Are you telling me that you will stay with the prisoners and personally see that they are released unharmed?'

'Yes.'

'All right then. I am known in these parts and my word will carry weight.' The Spaniard's voice grew very serious. 'But if the sack of La Serena has been barbarous, then I cannot guarantee to hold back its citizens from seeking revenge. My countrymen think of your people as bloodthirsty vermin to be exterminated.'

'I intend to place half a dozen of the prisoners on the top of the watchtower. They'll be standing on the parapet, with a rope around each man's neck. Tell whoever is in charge of the ambush that if there is any treachery, the captives will be hanged in public view.'

Peralta raised his eyebrows. 'You are beginning to think like a pirate.'

'Captain Sharpe said something very similar to me earlier today.'

The Spaniard gave a slow, reluctant nod. 'Let us both hope that your plan works. If there is falsehood on either side, each of us will live in shame for the rest of our lives.' He turned on his heel and began to walk up towards the road leading inland.

The watchtower was some forty feet high and a series of ladders led to its flat roof, passing through small square openings in the building's three floors. With Jacques's help, Hector bound the hands of six of the prisoners, placed nooses around their necks, and ordered them to climb the ladders. They made awkward progress, fumbling their way up the rungs, hampered by their bonds. Hector followed and when he reached the top of the first ladder, he pulled it up after him, and laid it on the floor. The remaining prisoners would be locked into the ground floor of the tower. He did not want them climbing up and interfering. Arriving on the flat roof of the tower, Hector fastened the free ends of the nooses to the base of the flagpole. 'Up on the parapet and face inland,' he told his prisoners. Then he sat down to wait.

*

HECTOR WAITED for half a day. Peralta was nowhere to be seen and there was nothing to do but be patient. The wind gradually eased until it was no more than the slightest whisper of a breeze, and from a cloudless sky the sun beat down on the flat roof of the tower. There was no shade, either for Hector or his prisoners, and after a while he allowed them to be seated. They took it in turns one man at a time to stand on the parapet with a rope around his neck. Hector thought the threat was sufficient.

Twice Jacques sent up one of his captives with a flask of water. No one spoke as the drink was handed round, and then the waiting continued. The parched countryside lay silent and still. There was no sign of any activity apart from a bird of prey riding the air currents and circling over the bush. The only sound was the low incessant rumble of the surf on the beach. Half a mile away *Trinity* rode at anchor on a sparkling sea.

Finally, far into the afternoon, there was movement along the road, tiny figures in the distance, putting up a small cloud of dust. Slowly they came nearer and resolved themselves in an untidy straggle of men. They were Watling's company. Someone had found half a dozen mules and these were laden high with untidy loads of boxes and sacks. But most of the men were their own porters. They were trudging along, hung about with bundles, satchels and bags. One or two had rigged up wicker baskets on their backs to serve as panniers, while a group of four men were pushing a handcart piled with various items they must have looted. Oddest of all was a man with a wheelbarrow. He was wheeling along a companion, who must have been so drunk that he was incapable of walking. At the rear was the unmistakable figure of Jezreel. He and half a dozen other men had muskets on their shoulders and formed a semblance of a rearguard.

Anxiously Hector checked the countryside. Still there was no hint of movement among the scrubland and trees on each side of the road. He could see nothing but tangles of grey-brown bushes, stunted trees, and the open patches where wild grass and reeds grew waist high. Then, suddenly, he saw a glint of light reflected from metal. He concentrated his gaze on the spot, and gradually he was able to make out the figures of soldiers, half a company at least, crouching motionless in one of the washed-out gullies which bordered the road. They were visible from his vantage point high on the tower, but from the road they would have been hidden. Concealed in the broken ground must be the remainder of the Spanish force.

'On your feet! All of you!' he snapped at his prisoners. 'Move to the parapet and show yourselves!'

The Spaniards shuffled forward and stood in line. Several were trembling with fear. One man had wet himself and the flies were settling on the damp patch on his breeches. Another cast a nervous glance behind him, and Hector snarled at him to face the front. He felt demeaned by the whole charade. Hector knew that he lacked the nerve to push any man to his death dangling at the end of a rope, but the barbarity had to continue. Without it, Jezreel and the other raiders would have no chance of reaching the beach alive.

He looked away to his left, along the coast, and to his relief saw two canoes and a ship's launch sailing parallel to the shore, coming closer. They were *Trinity*'s remaining boats. Now it would be possible to evacuate the entire raiding party at one time.

His attention returned to the road. Watling's company were closer now, still straggling along in disorder. To his dismay he saw there were several women in the party. If the buccaneers had kidnapped La Serena's women, then he doubted that the Spaniards would hold back their ambush even at the risk of the public hanging of the prisoners on the parapet. A second glance revealed his mistake. He was seeing not La Serena's womenfolk, but buccaneers who must have found women's clothes in the town, and stolen them. Now they were wearing them as the easiest way to carry them. They made a strange sight, their skirts and shawls worn over smocks and breeches. One man had a mantilla draped over the top of his head to keep off the sun.

Watling's rabble slowly advanced. Occasionally a man would halt and double over, vomiting in the road. Others stumbled and tripped. One fell flat on his face in the dust before he was pulled back to his feet by a comrade. Soon the gaggle of drunken looters were level with the gully where the Spaniards waited in ambush, and for one alarming moment Hector saw a buccaneer break away from the group and run to the side of the road. If he stumbled into the ambush, a massacre would follow. The man was clawing at his breeches as he ran, and he must have been caught short, for before he reached the roadside, he suddenly squatted and defecated in the dust. Gorged on too much fresh fruit from the gardens of La Serena, Hector thought grimly, as the man pulled up his breeches and broke into a weaving run to rejoin the column.

'Canoes ready on the beach,' Jacques called up from the foot of the tower. At last some of Watling's men had noticed the row of figures standing on the parapet. Faces turned up as the returning buccaneers began to wonder what was happening. Others were pointing, and Jezreel and the rearguard could be seen bringing their muskets to the ready. Hector stepped forward, hoping that he would be recognised, and waved at them, urging them to hurry down the final slope to the waiting canoes.

'Don't move!' Hector snapped at his hostages. 'We stay here until everyone is safe back to the ship.'

One of the Spaniards shifted on his feet and asked mockingly, 'And what about you, how will you leave?'

Hector did not answer. Watling's party were sliding and stumbling down the slope towards the beach. He could hear the crunch and clatter of the shingle beneath their feet and, amazingly, a snatch of drunken song. Some of the buccaneers still did not understand the danger they were in. From his vantage point Hector saw Jacques emerge from the base of the tower below him and run forward and speak urgently to Jezreel. Watling was beside him. A sense of urgency finally spread through the entire group. Some of them turned to face inland, reaching for their muskets.

Hector looked towards the ridge at the top of the beach. Now it was lined with dozens of Spanish soldiers. More and more armed men were appearing out of ravines and dips in the ground, or pushing out from the bushes. There must have been at least four companies of soldiers, and they were well disciplined and trained for they took up their positions in orderly formation, looking down on the buccaneers as they splashed out into the shallows and began loading their booty into the canoes. If anything went wrong now, the beach would become a killing ground.

A sudden flurry of movement, and Hector saw Jezreel reach out and wrest a gun away from a drunken buccaneer. He must have been preparing to fire a shot in bravado.

The loaded canoes began leaving the beach, heading towards *Trinity*. Only the smallest one was left, and Jezreel was standing up to his knees in the water holding the bow steady, waiting for him.

From below, a group of men came into view. They were the Spaniards whom Jacques had been holding captive. They were running towards the militiamen at the top of the slope. As they ran they were gesticulating and shouting out that they were Spanish, calling on the soldiers not to shoot. Now the only remaining prisoners were the half dozen men with Hector on the roof of the tower.

He went over the row of hostages, and raised the nooses from their necks. He crossed to the ladder which led down from the roof and began to climb down the rungs. As his head came level with the flat roof, he took out his knife and cut the cords which bound the ladder in place. Reaching the foot of the ladder, he pulled it clear. It would take several minutes for the prisoners to free themselves and still they would be trapped in the tower.

Continuing down the ladders, Hector removed each one as he descended. Reaching the ground, he walked out of the door and onto the beach. He was alone. To his right Jezreel waited with the canoe. To his left, no more than fifty paces away, stood the line of Spanish soldiers. They had advanced down the slope in open formation, muskets ready. Hector remembered how he had gone forward under the white flag of truce to the palisade of Santa Maria. But this time he had no white flag, only his faith in Peralta.

Someone stepped out from the Spanish line. It was Peralta himself. He came down the slope of beach, unarmed, his face sad.

'Your people have gutted La Serena,' he said. 'But I am grateful to you for making sure that my colleagues and I were released unharmed.' Behind him, Hector heard Jacques shouting that *Trinity* was weighing anchor and they must leave now if they were to reach the ship in time. Peralta stared into his eyes and his gaze was unflinching.

'You may tell your captain that the next time he tries to raid us, he and his men will not be so lucky. Now go.'

Hector did not know how to answer. For a moment he stood where he was, conscious of the hostility of the Spanish soldiers fingering their guns and Peralta's flinty tone. Then he turned, walked down the beach and climbed into the waiting canoe.

THIRTEEN

✳

HECTOR HAD grown accustomed to the constant moaning and braying, barking and hissing, bubbling and trumpeting. The clamour had been in the background from the day *Trinity* arrived at the island exactly two weeks after the withdrawal from La Serena. The hubbub came from hundreds upon hundreds of large furry seals which lounged and fought and squabbled on the rocks. There were so many of the creatures and they were so sure of their possession that when the sailors first landed, the men had to force their way through the ranks of fishy-smelling beasts, clubbing them aside. The largest of the bull seals, gross lords and terrors of their harems, had resented the intrusion. They rushed furiously at the strangers, silver manes swollen, long yellow fangs bared, grunting and roaring hoarsely until the seamen fired pistols down their angry pink throats. The dark, almost black seal meat had been welcome at first, but the men soon tired of the taste. Now, if a seal was killed, the carcass was left to rot.

Sharpe had brought *Trinity* to Juan Fernandez at the crew's angry insistence. After the disappointment of La Serena the men had voted to spend Christmas there, far from the constant threat of vengeful Spanish cruisers. Hector wondered how sailors had known about the remote, mountainous island. Juan Fernandez lay 400 miles from the South American coast, and the South Sea was an uncharted mystery to all but the Spaniards. Yet there were men aboard *Trinity* who were aware that this bleak, unfrequented place offered a refuge. He supposed that somehow in the taverns of European ports and Caribbean harbours where sailors gathered, men talked of the island and how they had been able to recruit their strength there, repair their vessels, and relax.

When *Trinity* arrived on a grey, windswept day in early December the island was uninhabited. But it was obvious that people had visited Juan Fernandez because someone had stocked the place with goats. The animals had thrived and wild herds of them roamed the broken scrub-covered uplands. Their flesh was much to be preferred to seal meat, so Dan and the other remaining striker, another Miskito named Will, went off daily with their muskets and came back with goat carcasses draped over their shoulders. However, it was Jacques who had provided the most certain proof that other sailors had used the island as a resting place. Shortly after landing, he had come hurrying back, beaming with pleasure and brandishing a handful of various leaves and plants. 'Herbs and vegetables!' he crowed. 'Someone planted a garden here and left it behind to grow! Look! Turnips, salads, green stuff!'

The crew of *Trinity* had quickly made themselves comfortable. They draped spare sails over the branches of trees to make tents, set up frames on which they barbecued goat meat and fish, filled their water jars at the stream which emptied across a beach of small boulders and into the bay. On Christmas Day itself Jacques had cooked the entire company a great dish of lobsters, broiling them over the fire. He insisted on calling them langoustes, and they crawled in the shallows of the bay in such numbers that one had only to wade out into the chilly water and gather them by hand, dozens at a time. For their vegetable the company had eaten finely sliced strips of tree cabbage cut from the tender head of sprouting palms.

Yet the atmosphere continued to be very sour and unhappy. The crew grumbled about the lack of plunder. The sack of La Serena had yielded barely 500 pounds' weight of silver to be divided between nearly 140 men. They felt this was a paltry sum for all the risks they had taken, and it made matters worse that many of the malcontents had gambled away their booty in the long, dull sea days that followed. By the time they reached Juan Fernandez, a majority of the dice and card players were virtually penniless, and they muttered darkly that they had been swindled. When they did so, they looked towards Captain Sharpe. Unable to prove it, they were sure that he had somehow gulled them.

To leave behind the bickering and the acrimony of the camp, Hector had got into the habit of going for a long walk each day. From the pleasant glen where the sailors had set up their shelters, a narrow goat track climbed steeply inland, leaving behind the groves of sandalwood and stands of pimento trees and passing up through dense thickets of brush. The path doubled back and forth, and after the long weeks spent on board ship he found that his legs were quickly tired by the demands of the steep ascent. Now his leg muscles were aching, and it would take him another hour of hard climbing to reach the crest of the narrow ridge where he liked to spend a few moments looking out over the ocean, quietly contemplating. This morning he needed to hurry because there was to be a general council of the expedition at noon, and he wanted to be back in time to attend. The men were to vote whether Bartholomew Sharpe was to continue as their general and – equally important – what was to happen when *Trinity* left the island.

Hector took deep breaths as he scrambled upward. In places the bushes grew so close together that he had to force his way through, the branches snagging at his clothes. Occasionally he caught the distinctive acrid smell of goat hanging in the air, and once he startled a small herd, three billies and as many she-goats, which ran up the path ahead of him with their odd mincing stride, before plunging aside into the thickets and disappearing. As he ascended, the sounds of the seal colonies grew fainter and fainter from below, and whenever he stopped to turn and look down into the bay, *Trinity* looked increasingly small and insignificant until finally a turn in the path meant that he could no longer see the ship at all. From now on he might as well have been alone in the entire world. To his left rose a mist-shrouded mountain, a gloomy square mass with the shape of a gigantic anvil. On his right the island was a densely forested jumble of ravines and cliffs and spurs and ridges which were impenetrable to anyone except an expert hunter.

Eventually he reached his destination, the narrow saddle of the ridge joining the anvil mountain to the wilderness, and sat down to rest. The crest of the ridge was no more than a yard or two in breadth and the view to either side was magnificent. Ahead of him the ground dropped away in sheer scree and he was looking out over a wave-flecked ocean which spread out to a horizon of cobalt blue. When he turned in the opposite direction, he was facing into the sun and the surface of the sea became an enormous glittering silver sheet across which drifted dark shadows cast by the clouds. Everything seemed far, far away, and the high ridge was exposed to a wind which rushed past, swirling over the crest of land.

He sat in the lee of a great flat rock, clasped his arms around his knees, and gazed out to sea, trying to think of nothing, losing himself in the vastness of the great panorama before him.

He must have been sitting silently for five or ten minutes when he became aware of an occasional small black speck which sped past him, flitting through the air. To begin with, he thought the specks were a trick of his vision, and he blinked, then rubbed his eyes. But the phenomenon continued, momentary glimpses of some tiny flying object which came up from the scree slope behind him, moving so fast that it was impossible to identify, then vanished ahead, dipping down the slope in

front of him. He concentrated his gaze on a clump of bushes a
few paces below where he sat. That's where the flying specks
seemed to disappear. Cautiously he eased himself off the ridge
and, still seated, slid down towards the bush. There was a slight
brushing sensation on his cheek as another of the little specks
flew past, so close that he distinctly felt the wind of its passage.
It vanished so quickly that he still could not identify what it
was. He suspected it was some sort of flying insect, perhaps a
grasshopper or a locust. He came to within an arm's length of
the bush, and waited motionless. Sure enough, there was a
quick darting movement as another of the flying specks came
up from behind him, slowed in mid-air for an instant, then
plunged in among the branches. Now he knew what it was: a
tiny bird, no bigger than his thumb.

Another few moments passed, and then one of the diminu-
tive creatures rose from within the bush. It ascended vertically
and began to hover in the air, its wings moving in a blur.
The bird was no more substantial than a large bumblebee
and astonishingly beautiful. The feathers were green, white and
brilliant blue. A moment later it was joined by a companion
rising from the foliage. This time the plumage was a glossy
dark maroon, the colour of drying blood, which glowed in the
sunshine. A few heartbeats later and the two tiny creatures
began to dance together in the air, circling and dipping,
hovering to face one another for a few moments, then suddenly
diving and turning and making short arcs and loops until they
came together again and stayed hovering. Spellbound, Hector
watched. He was sure that the two birds were male and female
and they were performing a mating dance.

With a sudden pang of memory he recalled the last time he
had seen a hummingbird. It had been just over a year ago with
Susanna when they were travelling towards Port Royal and she
had said he possessed the soul of an artist because he had
compared the whirring sound made by the wings to the noise
of a miniature spinning wheel. Now he listened carefully to the

two birds dancing in the air before him. But he could hear nothing above the sound of the wind sighing over the ridge. An image of Susanna came to mind with painful clarity. He saw her dressed in a long, resplendent gown and attending a grand occasion in London where she had been taken by her father. She was dancing with her partner before a crowd of onlookers, all of them wealthy and sophisticated and of her own social standing. With an effort Hector tried to push the apparition out of his mind. He told himself that he was seated on a mountainside on the far side of the world, and this image of Susanna was entirely make-believe. He scarcely knew her. It did not matter what happened in the next months or years, whether he stayed with *Trinity* and her crew, whether he returned with riches or in poverty. Susanna was always going to be unattainable. His encounter with her would never be more than a chance meeting, however much it had affected him. He should learn from his moment of confusion when he had stood before the portrait of a young lady in La Serena and found himself uncertain of what exactly reminded him of Susanna. As more time passed, he would remember less and less of the true Susanna and what had happened during those few hours he had spent in her company. Instead he would substitute fantasy until everything about Susanna was make-believe. It was an irreversible process and his best course was to free himself of false hope. It was time he acknowledged that he was keeping alive an illusion that had no place in the true circumstances of his own life.

He shivered. A cloud had passed across the sun and the wind brought a momentary chill in the shadow. Robbed of sunlight, the plumage of the two dancing hummingbirds abruptly lost its irridescence and, as if sensing the change in his mood, they darted back into the foliage. Hector got to his feet and began to descend the path back to camp.

✳

HE ARRIVED to find the general council already in session. The entire crew of *Trinity* was gathered in the glade where they had set up their tents. Watling was standing on a makeshift platform of water barrels and planks and haranguing them in his gruff soldierly voice.

'What's going on?' Hector asked quietly as he joined Jezreel and Jacques at the back of the crowd.

'Watling has just been elected our new general by a majority of twenty votes. They've turned Sharpe out and chosen Watling to replace him,' answered the big man. Hector peered over the shoulders of the men. Bartholomew Sharpe was in the front rank of the assembly, over to one side. He appeared relaxed and unconcerned, his head tilted back as he listened to Watling's announcements, his soft round face inscrutable. Hector remembered how he had thought when he had first laid eyes on Sharpe that his fleshy lips reminded him of a fish, a carp, and there was still that same faint air of guile. Seemingly, Sharpe was unaffected by his abrupt dismissal from overall command but Hector wondered what was going on behind that bland exterior.

'We return to the ways of our gallant Captain Sawkins before his death,' Watling was saying loudly. 'Courage and comradeship will be our watchwords!'

There was a murmur of approval from one section of his audience. Among them Hector recognised several of the more brutish members of the crew.

'There will be no more blasphemy!' grated Watling. 'From now on we observe the Sabbath, and unnatural vice will be punished!' His tone had turned harsh and he was staring directly at someone in the crowd. Hector craned his neck to see who it was. Watling had singled out Edmund Cook, the fastidiously dressed leader of one of the companies that set out from Golden Island. Hector had heard a rumour that Cook had been found in bed one day with another man, but had dismissed the tale as mere gossip.

Watling was speaking again, barking out his words.

'Gambling is forbidden. Anyone who plays at cards or dice will have his share of plunder reduced . . .' Watling stopped abruptly, and suddenly his arm shot out as he pointed at Sharpe. 'Hand your dice to the quartermaster,' he ordered.

Hector watched Bartholomew Sharpe reach into his pocket and produce his dice. They were taken from him by Duill, one of the men who had tossed the shot priest overboard while he was still alive.

'What's happened to Samuel Gifford? I thought he was our quartermaster,' Hector asked Jezreel.

'Watling insisted on having a second quartermaster appointed. John Duill is one of his cronies.'

Duill had handed the dice on to Watling who held them up over his head for all to see and called out, 'These are not fit to be aboard a ship.' Then he drew back his arm and flung them far into the bushes. From several onlookers came catcalls and scornful whistles, clearly directed at Sharpe. The demoted captain still showed no emotion.

'Where would you lead us?' yelled someone from the crowd.

Watling paused before answering. His eyes swept across his audience. He looked very sure of himself. When he did finally speak, his voice rang out as though he was a drill sergeant.

'I propose we attack Arica.'

There was a moment's lull, then an excited noisy chatter broke out in the crowd. Hector heard one scarred buccaneer give a subdued snort of approval.

'What's so special about Arica?' he whispered to Jezreel.

'Arica is where the treasure from the Potosi silver mines is brought to be loaded on the galleons for shipment. It's said that bars of bullion are left stacked on the quays.'

'Surely a place like that would be powerfully defended,' said Hector.

Someone in the crowd must have thought the same, for he called out to Watling, 'How can we take such a stronghold?'

'If we attack boldly, we can overrun the town in less than an hour. We'll use grenades in the assault.'

Hector caught sight of Ringrose in the crowd. He was standing beside Dampier, and both men looked unconvinced by Watling's confident assertion. Duill, the new second quartermaster, was already calling for a show of hands to vote on his commander's proposal.

The vote was two-thirds in favour of an assault on Arica, and Watling's supporters cheered loudly, slapping one another on the back and promising their comrades that soon they would all be rich beyond their dreams. The council over, Samuel Gifford was calling for volunteers to help prepare the grenades to be used in the assault.

'Why don't we join the grenade makers,' suggested Jacques. 'I'm growing bored on this island, and it will give us something to do.'

As the three of them walked over to where Gifford was assembling his work crew, Hector found himself agreeing with Jacques. Life on Juan Fernandez had grown wearisome and dull. Five weeks spent on the island was enough. He had no wish to go raiding the Spaniards but he was looking forward to getting to sea again. He wondered if the reason for his restlessness was wanderlust or had more to do with his decision to leave aside his dream about Susanna.

'I need someone to cut up musket bullets in half,' said Gifford. His glance fell on Jezreel. 'That's a job for you.'

He sent Hector to search *Trinity*'s stores for lengths of condemned rope while Jacques was to bring back a large iron cooking pot and a quantity of the pitch normally used to treat the vessel's hull.

When the materials arrived, the quartermaster set Jacques to melting the pitch over a fire while the others unpicked the rope into long strands of cord.

'Now follow closely what I do,' Gifford said as he took a length of the unravelled cord and began to wind it around his fist. 'Make a ball of the twine but do it carefully, from the outside in and leaving the coils loose so they run out freely.'

When he had the ball of twine completed, he showed the loose end of the string which emerged from the centre like the stalk on a large apple.

'Now for the coating,' he announced. He took a sharp straight stick and carefully pushed it through the completed ball. Going across to Jacques's iron pot he dipped the ball into the melted pitch and held it up in the air for the pitch to harden. Then he repeated the process. 'Two or three coatings should be right. Enough to hold a shape.'

He beckoned to Jezreel. 'Hand me some of those half musket balls,' and he began to stick the lead bullets into the soft tar.

'Now comes the tricky part,' Gifford said. Carefully he removed the stick, then felt for the free end of the string. Gently he began to tease the string out of the globe. It reminded Hector of the day that Surgeon Smeeton had showed him how to extract the Fiery Serpent from an invalid's leg.

When all the string had been pulled from the ball of pitch, leaving it hollow, the quartermaster turned it over in his hand.

'I want at least twenty of these,' he said. 'Later we fill them with gunpowder and fit a fuse. When we get to Arica . . .' He hefted the empty grenade in his hand and pretended to lob it towards the enemy, 'Pouf! It'll clear our way to the bullion.'

Watling's promotion had brought a sense of energy to the expedition. In the two days it took for Hector and his companions to prepare the grenades, the buccaneers shifted all *Trinity*'s equipment back onto the vessel, set up her rigging, filled her water casks, replenished the firewood for the cook's galley, struck camp and moved themselves back aboard. All that remained was to take on fresh food. Jacques went ashore on a mission to gather a supply of herbs and greens, and the ship's launch was despatched in the opposite direction with half a dozen armed men. They were to wait at the foot of the cliffs while Dan and Will, the other remaining striker, went inland and drove a herd of wild goats towards them. After shooting as many goats as possible for *Trinity*'s larder, the launch's crew was to collect Dan and Will and return to the ship.

'We'll have to fight our way into Arica so I might as well give you a few tips on hand-to-hand combat while we are waiting for Dan to get back,' Jezreel said to Hector. He handed him a cutlass and stood back, raising his short sword. 'Now strike at me!'

The two of them sparred, Jezreel easily deflecting Hector's blows before making his counterstrokes which usually slipped past his opponent's defence. Occasionally Jezreel stopped and adjusted the position of Hector's sword arm. 'It's all in the wrist action,' Jezreel explained. 'Keep your guard up high, flex the wrist as you parry, then strike back. It must all be one swift movement. Like this.' He knocked aside Hector's weapon and tapped him on the shoulder with the flat of his own blade.

'I don't have your height advantage,' Hector complained.

'Just stick to the basics and stay light on your feet,' the ex-prizefighter advised. 'In battle there's no time for fancy sword play, and you can expect your opponent to fight dirty like so!'

This time he distracted Hector by aiming a high blow at his head, and at the same time moved close enough to pretend to knee him in the groin. 'And always remember that in a close scuffle, the hilt of your sword is more effective than the edge. More men have been clubbed down in a brawl than were ever run through or cut.'

Hector lowered his cutlass to rest his arm. Just then there was the sound of a musket shot, closely followed by two more in quick succession. They came from *Trinity*'s launch which had gone to meet Dan and Will and shoot wild goats. The crew were rowing frantically back to the ship. Clearly something had gone wrong.

'Loose the topsail to show we've heard their signal!' Watling bellowed. Half a dozen men ran to obey his command, and

Hector found himself with the rest of the crew, waiting anxiously at the rail for the launch to come within shouting distance.

'I can see Dan in the boat, but not Will,' muttered Jezreel.

Just then Watling stepped up beside him, cupping his hands around his mouth and using his drill sergeant's voice to call out. 'What's the trouble?'

'Spaniards! Three ships hull-down to the east,' came back a shout. 'They're heading this way.'

'Shit!' Watling swore and turned on his heel, looking out to sea. 'We can't see anything from here. The headland blocks our view.'

He hurried back to the rail and bellowed again at the approaching launch. 'What sort of vessels?'

'They have the look of men of war, but it's difficult to be sure.'

Watling glanced up at the sky, gauging the direction and strength of the wind. 'Quartermasters! Call all hands and pre-pare to raise anchor. We have to get out of this bay. It's a trap if the Spaniards find us here.' He caught a seaman by the shoulder and barked, 'You! Get two of your fellows and bring up all the weapons we have. I want them loaded and ready on deck in case we have to fight our way clear.'

There was a rush of activity as men began to bring the galleon back to life after weeks of idleness. They cleared away the deck clutter, braced round the yards ready to catch the wind, and hoisted a foresail and the mizzen so that *Trinity* hung on her anchor, ready to break free and sail out of the bay at a moment's notice. Quartermaster Gifford himself took the helm and stood waiting.

Watling was back at the rail, bawling at the men in the launch. 'Get a move on! Tie the launch off the stern and lend a hand.'

'What about the men still on shore? We cannot abandon them!' Hector blurted.

Watling swung round, face hard set, his eyes furious. 'They shift for themselves,' he snapped.

'But Jacques is not back yet, and Will was with Dan. He must still be on the island.'

An angry scowl spread across Watling's face. He was about to lose his temper.

'Do you question my orders?'

'Look over there,' said Hector, pointing towards the beach. 'You can see Jacques now. He's standing there, waiting to be picked up by a boat.'

'Let him swim,' snarled Watling. He turned back and shouted at the men to get to the capstan and begin retrieving the anchor.

Hector was about to say that Jacques did not know how to swim when Jezreel, short sword in hand, strode across the deck and stood beside the capstan.

'The first person who slots in a capstan bar loses his fingers,' he announced. Then he casually whipped his sword through the air, the blade making a figure of eight and a low swishing sound as he turned his wrist.

The approaching sailors stopped short. They looked warily at the ex-prizefighter.

'The anchor stays down until Jacques is safely aboard,' Jezreel warned them.

'We'll see about that,' growled one of the sailors. It was Duill, the second quartermaster. He made his way to the quarterdeck. 'General, may I have the loan of one of your pistols so I can put a bullet in that bugger's guts.'

Hector forestalled him. Stepping across to where the ship's armament was being made ready, he picked up a loaded blunderbuss, and pointed it at Duill's stomach. 'This time it's your corpse that will have to go over the side,' he said grimly.

Everyone stood still, waiting to see what would happen. Watling looked as if he was about to spring at Hector. Duill was eyeing the gap between himself and the muzzle of the gun.

Into this tense lull came a languid voice. 'No need for so much fuss. I'll take the launch, if someone will care to accompany me, and collect our French friend. '

It was Bartholomew Sharpe. He sauntered across the deck casually.

'What about Will the Miskito,' Hector asked, his voice harsh with strain.

'I'm sure he'll be able to look after himself,' said Sharpe soothingly. 'He's got a gun and ammunition, and will make himself comfortable until we can get back to collect him or another ship comes along.' He attempted a lighter touch. 'Your friend Jacques is another matter. What would we do without his pimento sauce?'

'Then get on with it,' snapped Watling. Hector could see that the new captain was keen to re-establish his authority and show that he, not Sharpe, was in command. 'The launch picks up the Frenchman, and we waste no more time getting ready for action.'

Twenty minutes later, a relieved Jacques was scrambling aboard clutching a sack of salad leaves, and *Trinity*'s anchor was emerging dripping from the sea as the ship began to gather way.

'Don't fret about Will. A Miskito will be able to look after himself on the island,' Dan quietly reassured Hector. 'There's more to worry about close at hand.'

He nodded towards the foredeck where a sullen-looking Duill was standing by to oversee the catting of the anchor. 'The crew don't like what happened. They think we were prepared to sacrifice them in favour of our friends. From now we'll have to watch our backs.'

FOURTEEN

❋

'EACH GRENADIER will receive a bonus of ten pieces of eight,' declared Watling from the rail of the quarterdeck, his gaze sweeping across the assembled crew. It was a fortnight since *Trinity* had run from Juan Fernandez, easily slipping past the Spanish squadron. Now she lay hove-to off the mainland coast and in sight of the long, dark line of hills which loomed behind Arica.

'If he still has both his hands to count the money,' mocked a voice at the back of the crowd.

Watling ignored the gibe. 'The success of our assault may depend on our grenadiers. Who will volunteer?'

His plea was met with silence. The men were nervous about touching the home-made bombs now they had been filled with gunpowder and fitted with their stubby fuses.

'If you handle grenades properly, they are safe,' Watling insisted. 'I myself will show how it's done.'

'How about giving them out to the bastards who made them,' suggested the same anonymous voice. 'If they get it wrong, they'll know who's to blame.'

The sally caused a ripple of laughter, and Duill was smirking as he stepped forward and beckoned to Hector and his friends. 'You heard what the general said. He'll tell you what to do.'

Hector watched as Watling picked up one of the grenades from a wooden box at his feet. The young man had to admit that Watling, though bull-headed and short-tempered, was prepared to lead by example.

'Each grenadier will carry three of these in a pouch on his right side, and a length of slow match wrapped around his left wrist. When the time comes, he turns his left shoulder towards the enemy, takes up a grenade in his right hand like so, blows on the slow match to make it glow, and brings the lighted match to the fuse.'

Watling mimed the action.

'He then steps forward with his left foot and bends his right knee so he is in a crouching position. After checking that the fuse is burning steadily, he stands up and hurls the grenade, keeping his right arm straight.'

'Let's hope that none of those buggers is left-handed,' shouted the wag, and Watling had to wait until the ensuing guffaws had subsided.

'I propose that *Trinity* stays out of sight over the horizon so as not to alert the defenders to our presence, and under cover of darkness our boats land our force some five leagues to the south of the town. We spend our first day ashore in hiding. At nightfall we leave behind our boats under guard and advance across country to a point close to Arica from which we can launch a dawn assault. We capture the town before the citizens are awake.'

'How many men in the attack?' Jezreel asked.

'Everyone who is fit enough. It must be a forced march if we are to take the town by surprise. Then, as soon as we have seized Arica, we signal to our boats. They come to pick us up and we begin loading our plunder.'

'What happens if the raid runs into trouble? How do we get back to the ship safely?'

'There will be two different signals: a single fire with white smoke tells our boat crews to come halfway to meet us and evacuate the force; two white smokes is the sign that we have captured the town and they enter into harbour to collect us and our plunder.'

Watling gestured towards the distant hills. 'You have all heard the rumour of a mountain which is made of solid silver, and how the Spaniards of Peru keep the native people in chains, toiling away like ants to dig out the bullion. In the next forty eight hours, we will relieve them of their riches.'

✷

'I FEEL LIKE a worker ant myself,' said Jacques at noon the next day. He was burdened down with a musket and cartridge box, a pistol and a cutlass as well as a satchel containing three grenades. He was gasping from the heat. 'This place is a furnace.'

Jezreel had persuaded his friends that they should take on the role of grenadiers. The ex-prizefighter had argued that by volunteering for such dangerous work they might improve their standing with the rest of *Trinity*'s crew. Until there was a chance of breaking away on their own, it was safer if the four of them showed willing to cooperate with their shipmates.

Watling's column had spent an uncomfortable night on the rocky foreshore, shivering in a cold clammy mist that had oozed in from the sea. At daybreak they had set out across country, leaving a handful of men under Basil Ringrose to guard the boats and wait for the signal fires. Within half an hour the sun had sucked up the mist and the day had turned blisteringly hot. The men, ninety-two of them, had marched for hours and had not seen a single house or field or sign of human occupation. The landscape was utterly barren, a sun-blasted expanse of scoured rock and sand with an occasional steep-sided ravine. The only vegetation was a few spiny plants or stunted bushes with dry, brittle branches, and they had not found a single stream or pond where they could refill their water canteens.

Jacques gave a yelp of pain, took a half stride, and sat

down, clutching at his foot. He had stepped on one of the needle-like spines of a desert plant and it had pierced right through the thick leather sole of his boot. 'Surely Arica can't be much farther now,' he said through dry, cracked lips as he began to remove his boot.

'Beyond that next rise of ground, perhaps,' Hector answered. In the distance the low hills shimmered in the heat.

'Why would anyone want to live in such a desperate place,' muttered Jacques as he searched for the broken end of the offending spine.

'To be near the source of so much silver,' said Hector. The weight of his three grenades was pressing uncomfortably on his right hip and he eased the satchel strap across his chest. He had decided against carrying a musket, but wore the cutlass that Jezreel had provided him with.

'I would rather be marooned on a desert island than live in such a hellish place,' Jacques grumbled.

A slight movement on the gravel caught Hector's attention. A scorpion was edging away in the shade of a low shrub whose small white flowers were the only colour in the landscape of drab grey and brown.

'Here comes Dan now,' said Jacques, grimacing as he plucked out the broken spine. 'I wonder what he's found.'

The Miskito had gone forward to scout, leaving his satchel of grenades with Jezreel. Now Dan was returning, musket balanced on his shoulder and loping along as if the blazing heat was nothing. As usual, it was difficult to read anything into his expression.

'Arica's a mile beyond that ridge, and the town is expecting us,' he announced.

Watling came striding up. 'What do you mean, expecting us?' he demanded.

'The Spaniards have built a barricade of timber and earth across the main approach leading into the town. It's manned by soldiers, a lot of them. There's also a fort over to one side, and that seems to have a large garrison on the alert.'

'How many defenders?'

'It's impossible to say. But several hundred.'

Watling took off his broad-brimmed hat, wiped his brow with a large orange handkerchief, and beckoned to Duill, his second in command. 'The Miskito says that Arica is expecting an attack. The place may have been reinforced.'

Duill showed his teeth in a wolfish smile. 'That only goes to prove they have something worth defending.'

Watling brushed the fine desert dust off his sleeve. He turned to Dan. 'Do you think that we've been seen?' he asked.

'Certainly,' the Miskito replied. 'Three horsemen over on our right flank. They have been shadowing us for the past two hours. They know our strength, and purpose.'

'Then that decides it,' said Watling firmly. 'There's no going back. If we are seen in retreat, Arica's garrison will come out in pursuit and things will go badly for us. We stick to the original plan. When we reach the high ground ahead of us, we camp for the night. In the morning we advance on the town and rush the barricade.'

✳

HECTOR WAS surprised that Arica was such an ordinary, rundown place. He lay on the ridge above the town as the sky began to lighten and the streets of Arica emerged from the shadows. They had been laid out in the grid pattern familiar from La Serena. But he saw nothing to match La Serena's fine stone buildings. Arica's houses were unpainted single-storey dwellings made of what looked like humble mud brick. The single church tower was modest in size, and the perimeter wall of the fort that Dan had mentioned was no higher than the flat roofs of the nearby houses which surrounded it. From his vantage point Hector could see down into the parade ground where soldiers were emerging from their barracks and assembling for dawn muster. What held his attention was the makeshift outwork of rubble and earth which blocked the main approach to the town. It was at least fifty paces in length and built to a height so that a defender could rest his musket on it and take steady aim. There were sentinels posted at regular intervals and an officer was walking behind the line, checking that his lookouts were alert. Hector could see no sign of artillery, and for this he breathed a sigh of relief. To attack into the mouths of cannon would have been suicidal.

'On your feet! First rank make ready!' It was Watling, his army training evident. This was to be a disciplined assault, unlike previous campaigns against towns which had often been little more than an unruly rush against the defence. This time the buccaneers were to advance in three waves. The first and second were to alternate, one moving forward as the other gave covering fire, leapfrogging forward until they were close enough to reach the breastwork in a concerted charge. The four grenadiers and a dozen of the older, less active men were being held back in reserve. Under Bartholomew Sharpe they would stay fifty yards in the rear of the attack, ready to be called on wherever the need arose.

'Advance!' Watling was moving forward. Behind him the first wave of buccaneers began to make their way down the slope at a fast walk. Each man had an orange ribbon tied to his left shoulder to identify him in the coming engagement. Hector tried to judge the distance they would have to cover. It was perhaps half a mile. Several outhouses and barns would provide some cover, and there was an occasional fold in the ground where a man could crouch down in safety and reload his musket. Below him the officer in charge of the barricade had already turned towards the town and was gesticulating urgently. He must have seen the movement on the hill. Moments later a squad of armed men came running out from the town and took up their positions at the outwork. Counting them, Hector calculated that there must be at least forty musketeers facing the buccaneer attack. Allowing for the fact that a great many more Spanish soldiers were being held in reserve in the fort, Watling's force was heavily outnumbered. If the buccaneers were to take Arica, they would have to rely on their superior musketry and the professional ferocity of their assault.

The second wave had left its position and was also advancing down the slope. The men spread out in a skirmishing line, wide gaps between them to reduce the target. A scatter of shots came from the barricade, but the range was too great and the firing quickly died away. Hector supposed that a Spanish officer had restrained his men.

'I suppose we should get moving too!' said Sharpe in a relaxed voice. He got casually to his feet as though about to go for a stroll in the country and puffed on a clay pipe. He took the pipe stem from his mouth, blew out a thin plume of smoke, and watched the smoke hang in the air before slowly dissipating. 'Perfect day for a grenadier,' he observed. 'No chance of the match blowing out in the wind.' He glanced up at the cloudless sky and gave a sardonic smile, 'And of course no likelihood of a rain shower to extinguish it.'

Hector held out the length of match cord that had been issued to him. Sharpe sucked vigorously on the pipe, then thrust the end of the cord into the glowing tobacco. 'You've got enough match there for about five hours. Let's hope the battle is over by that time,' he said as he handed it back. Hector blew gently on the glowing end of the cord, wound the extra length around his wrist, then held the burning end between his fingers. He waited for Sharpe to light the match held out by his companions, and they began to make their way cautiously down the hill towards Arica.

The front rank of buccaneers were now within range of the barricade. One by one they paused, took aim and fired towards the defenders behind their earthwork. Hector thought he saw splinters and spurts of dust fly up. There was a scatter of answering musketry from the Spanish defenders, but they were outranged by the buccaneers' better weapons and their response did no damage. The second wave of attackers was passing through the front line of skirmishers, and had taken up their positions. There was no cheering. The only sounds were the flat detonations of their flintlocks, and the shouted insults and defiance from the Spaniards.

Moments later Hector saw the first of the buccaneers fall. The man was on his feet, taking aim, and the next instant he spun round and dropped to the ground. There was a whoop of triumph from the barricade.

Watling shouted an order and waved his orange handkerchief. His signal was followed by a ragged volley and all of a sudden the buccaneers were running forward in a concerted rush. Now they were shouting and hallooing, muskets and cutlasses in hand. A crackle of musketry from the barricade, and this time Hector saw at least three of the assailants knocked down before the first of them reached the earthwork and began to scramble over. There was a glimpse of a single buccaneer – he was almost sure it was Duill – balancing on top of the barricade and swinging his musket by the barrel, using it as a club to strike downward. A dozen of his men had gone wide, intending to get around the end of the barricade, even as their comrades swarmed over the obstacle. For several minutes the outcome of the pitched battle was in the balance. Men were shouting and yelling, hacking and stabbing. There was the clash of metal in the dust and smoke, cries of pain, and several times Hector heard the lighter crack of pistol shots.

The furore began to ease, and Watling was climbing up back on the barricade and beckoning urgently to the reserve. 'Close up, close up,' he was yelling. 'Hold our ground.'

He jumped back down out of sight as Hector and his comrades ran the last few paces to the barricade and clambered over. On the far side was a scene of devastation. Corpses lying in the dust, the ground was torn and tramped and stained with blood. A buccaneer with a terrible gash on the side of his face was stumbling around in a daze, and at least thirty or forty Spaniards were standing or sitting on the ground in a state of shock, their faces black with powder smoke and several of them wounded. 'Guard the prisoners while we move forward,' Watling bawled. There was the sound of more musket fire. From within the town the defenders of Arica were sniping at the attackers.

'Put your hands behind your heads!' Hector screamed in Spanish at the prisoners. They looked at him in disbelief. Hector realised that, without a firearm, he must have looked a harmless figure, with only a cutlass at his waist and the slow match coiled around his wrist. 'Do as he says,' growled Jezreel. He spoke in English but his giant size and fierce scowl made it clear what he wanted. The prisoners hurriedly obeyed.

From within the gateway came the sound of more gunfire, a lot of it. Watling's advance guard was encountering furious resistance. A man came scurrying out from the town, bent low to dodge stray bullets. 'There are more barricades inside,' he gasped. 'The Spaniards have built them at every street corner. Watling says we need grenades to clear them.'

'I'll go,' said Jezreel. He unfastened the flap to his satchel and hurried off behind the messenger. Hector turned back to face the prisoners. 'No one move!' he ordered. Looking around, he saw a musket lying on the ground where it had been dropped by one of the defenders. He picked it up and took a quick glance at the lock. It appeared to be primed and loaded. He pointed it at the captives.

Minutes passed and there was a muffled explosion from inside the town, not far away. Hector presumed the grenade had done its work, for there was a lull in the sounds of fighting. Then almost at once the crackle of musket fire resumed.

'We need reinforcements! Come on ahead!' Duill had

appeared in the entrance to the town. He was dishevelled and streaked with grime. There was a look of urgency in his movements.

'On whose orders?' Sharpe snapped.

'The general! Watling orders the rearguard to enter the town!'

'And what about the prisoners?'

Duill swore at him and for a moment Hector thought that the second quartermaster would strike Sharpe in the face. 'Leave a couple of men in charge of them,' he snarled. 'There's no time to argue.'

Sharpe turned to Hector. 'You and Jacques stay to guard the prisoners,' he ordered. 'Dan, leave your grenades here and go back up the hill. Your task is to keep a lookout for any extra Spanish troop reinforcements arriving. Let us know if you see anything that poses a risk. The rest of you follow me.' At an unhurried walk he set off towards the sound of the musketry.

A groan came from Hector's right. It was the buccaneer with the wounded face. He had slumped against the barricade and, with his forearm, was trying to staunch the flow of blood from his ravaged face. Hector set down his musket and hurried across to him. 'Here, let me bandage that,' he said and reached for his satchel before he realised that it did not contain medicines and bandages, but grenades. The corpse of a Spanish soldier was lying on the ground nearby. The dead man had worn a cotton scarf around his throat. Hector reached down and removed the neck cloth, then began to knot the bandage around the wounded man's head. Behind him, he heard Jacques let out a curse. Hector spun round in time to see at least twenty of the Spanish prisoners running away. 'Halt!' he shouted. 'Halt or I fire.' But he knew it was a bluff. There was no way that he and Jacques could restrain them.

'Not much point in hanging about here,' said Jacques. 'We should see if we can help Jezreel and the others.'

The two of them cautiously made their way into the town.

At the first crossroads they came upon the wreckage of another barricade. It had been made of upturned carts, planks and old furniture. There was a gap where Watling's men must have forced their way through. On the far side lay more dead men, both Spanish and buccaneer. A second crossroads and another barricade, and this time the buccaneers were using it as a breastwork themselves, taking shelter behind it, then standing up and taking shots at the enemy.

Hector spotted Jezreel. He was aiming his flintlock towards a nearby roof top, and a second later he pulled the trigger. A Spanish arquebusier ducked back out of sight. 'Missed him,' grunted Jezreel. He extracted the ramrod from under the barrel, spat on a rag to moisten it and began to clean out the gun. 'We can't keep up this rate of fire. Our weapons are getting fouled.'

Watling was in a doorway, conferring with Duill. The two men beckoned to Sharpe and spoke with him for a few moments before Sharpe came running back, tapped Hector on the shoulder, and shouted to him, 'Collect together the rearguard, and as many men as you can. We must take the fort. Until we secure our flank, we are exposed. The others will deal with the town itself.'

Hector passed the word to Jacques and soon they and some thirty men, including Jezreel, were fighting their way down a narrow street. Ahead of them, Spanish militiamen could be seen falling back, retreating to the safety of the fort. As the last of them passed through the wooden gate, it was heaved shut, and a fusillade from loopholes in the wall forced the attackers to take cover.

Bartholomew Sharpe ducked back into an alleyway and leaned against a mud wall, catching his breath. 'Time for another of our famous grenades,' he said. Hector realised that to this moment he had not fired a single shot but had been swept along in the general confusion. He looked down at his left wrist, and was surprised to see red burn marks on his skin where the lit end of the match had scorched him. In the chaos of battle he had never noticed the pain. He opened the flap of his satchel and took out a grenade. The little bomb looked very ill-made. The covering of hardened pitch had softened in the heat and lost its shape. Several of the half musket bullets had fallen loose. The fuse, a short length of slow match an inch long, was pressed over to one side and stuck into the pitch like the bent wick of a candle. Carefully he prised the fuse straight.

'Try to throw it over the gate! And good luck!' muttered Sharpe as he backed away. Hector brought the glowing end of the slow match across to the fuse and touched the two ends together. He saw the grenade's fuse begin to burn and, forcing himself to stay calm, started to count to ten very slowly. He stepped out from cover and as Watling had instructed, tossed the grenade, keeping his arm straight. The bomb flew through the air and, to his chagrin, thudded against the wall of the fort at least a foot beneath the top, dropped down, and lay on the road.

'Beware bomb!' he shouted and leaped back into shelter, pressing himself into a doorway. Several moments passed and nothing happened. Cautiously he peered out, and saw the grenade lying in the dust. He could not see any smoke rising from it. The device had failed to work. He fumbled in his satchel for a second grenade.

'Don't be in a hurry. Let's use our heads about this,' said Sharpe, who had reappeared beside him. 'You and Jacques follow me.'

He pushed open the door to the house and led the two of them inside. A buccaneer was already in the room, kneeling by the window and aiming his musket towards the fort. Sharpe looked up. The ceiling was made of narrow poles laid horizontally, above them a layer of palm fronds.

'There must be a way onto the roof,' Sharpe said. He crossed the room and pulled open the back door. 'Just as I thought, there's a ladder.' He began to climb its rungs with Hector and Jacques at his heels.

Emerging on the flat roof Hector found that he was level with the top of the wall of the fort just across the street. The roof itself was made of clay and tamped earth. Sharpe gripped his arm, holding him back. 'We don't want to be seen before we are ready, and we've got to get this right,' he said quietly.

Jacques had scrambled up beside them and was already selecting a grenade from his satchel.

'Compare your fuses, and make sure that both are the same length,' Sharpe advised. 'I'll light both the fuses so that the two of you can concentrate on the throw. When I give the word, step across the roof, it's no more than five paces, and hurl the bombs. Don't worry about hitting a precise target, just make sure they fall inside the fort. As soon as you've thrown your grenades, get back here and crouch down.'

Hector unwound the slow match from his wrist, gave it to Sharpe, and then picked out the better of his two remaining grenades. 'Are you ready?' Sharpe asked. Both men nodded, and their commander pressed the slow match to the fuses. They began to burn, the dull red glow steadily eating its way towards the gunpowder. But Sharpe appeared to ignore them. He was gazing out across the roof tops. As the seconds dragged past, Hector found himself sweating with apprehension. He could smell the acrid stench of the burning match.

Finally, and very softly, Sharpe said, 'Now!' With Jacques by his side, Hector started out across the flat roof. For one heart-stopping moment he felt the surface crumble beneath his weight, and thought he would fall through with the lit grenade still in his grasp. Then he was at the edge of the roof, overlooking the street. The top of the fort wall was no more than thirty feet away. Hector swung back his arm and threw the little bomb. It went in an arc over the fort wall, cleared it easily, and dropped out of sight. Out of the corner of his eye he saw Jacques's grenade follow.

There was a musket shot and Hector felt a tug at his sleeve. A defender must have seen them and opened fire. Bending double, the two men scurried back to where Sharpe was waiting. 'Now we wait,' he said.

For what seemed like an age nothing happened. Then abruptly there was the sound of a detonation, followed by shouts of fear, then silence.

They waited another minute, but there was no further explosion. 'One bomb seems to have been enough,' said Sharpe. He cocked his head to one side, listening. 'We've given them something to think about.'

✳

THERE WAS an anxious shout from below. Someone was calling 'Captain Sharpe! Captain Sharpe!' and a worried-looking buccaneer appeared at the rear of the building. He had a bloody rag wrapped around one hand.

'Who are you calling "Captain"? I'm just one of the company now!' exclaimed Sharpe, looking down.

'The general's dead!' cried out the newcomer. 'He was shot at the barricades. We need someone to lead us.'

'Really?' said Sharpe. 'I thought quartermaster Duill was second in command. Let him take over.'

'Duill has disappeared,' answered the man. 'No one can find him, and we're in a bad way in the town.' He was begging now. 'Captain, come back down to assist us.'

Sharpe descended the final rungs slowly and deliberately. 'Do all the men want me back in charge?'

'Yes, yes. The situation is very bad.'

Sharpe turned towards Hector and there was a gleam of satisfaction in his pale blue eyes. 'Hector, tell the men to abandon the attack on the fort and fall back.'

'We are too few,' the exhausted-looking buccaneer was saying. 'Every time we overrun one of their barricades and move forward, the Spaniards come in behind us and reoccupy the position they just lost. We can't spare anyone to look after all our prisoners. Many of them make their escape and rejoin the fight.'

They had reached the main square, and the extent of the raiders' difficulties was all too evident. The main force had fought its way into the heart of the town but the Spaniards had sealed off all the streets leading from the far side of the central square with piles of stone and rubble. They had placed sharpshooters where they could fire on anyone who tried to advance any further, and several buccaneers had been shot down as they tried to cross the open ground. Their bodies lay where they had fallen. Some two dozen of their comrades were now taking shelter in side alleys or crouching in doorways. Occasionally they fired towards the Spanish positions. A group of about twenty Spanish prisoners, clearly terrified, were lying face down on the ground watched over by a couple of wounded buccaneers. It was obvious that the attack had come to a standstill.

'Our wounded are in that church over there,' said their guide, pointing. 'Our surgeons are with them. They broke into an apothecary shop and took some medical supplies. But the longer we stay here, the bolder the Spaniards are becoming. They're moving up closer. It's becoming dangerous even to venture out into the open.'

He ducked as a musket ball struck the wall above his head. Somewhere in the distance a trumpet sounded.

Sharpe took stock of the situation. 'The Spaniards are bringing up reinforcements, and we can expect a sortie from the garrison in the fort when they are in position. Then we'll be caught in a pincer movement, and crushed. We've no choice but to make an orderly retreat while we are still able to do so.'

'What about our wounded in the church? We can't leave them!' said Hector.

Sharpe treated him to a sour smile. 'You're always worried about leaving someone behind, aren't you? As you are so concerned, I suggest you dash off and check on the situation in the church. See if any of the men can be evacuated. Then report back to me. Hurry!'

Hector swallowed hard. His throat was dry and he had a raging thirst. It occurred to him that no one had drunk anything that day. Nor had they eaten. 'Jezreel and Jacques, give me some covering fire!'

He removed his grenade satchel and laid it on the ground. He would have to cross thirty yards of open ground before he reached the portico of the church, and he could be halfway there before the Spanish musketeers realised what he was doing. He took a deep breath and burst out from cover.

As he sprinted across the plaza's flagstones, he expected a musket ball to strike him at any moment. But there was not a single shot and he crashed full tilt into the great wooden door. The heavy black iron handle was in his hand. He tugged the door open and threw himself inside.

After the blinding sunshine of the plaza, the interior of the church was so dark that he had to pause and let his eyes adjust to the gloom. In front of him the nave was a nightmare scene. All the church furniture – benches, carved wooden screens, a confessional, even the lectern – had either been roughly pushed to one side or overturned and smashed. At the far end the altar stood bare, stripped of its cross. Wall hangings had been torn down and were now spread out on the floor to serve as bedding on which lay wounded men. The place smelled of vomit and excrement. From outside still came the crack of musket shots but here in the half-darkness the sounds were moans, coughs and an occasional whimper of pain. Somewhere a man was cursing, softly and steadily, as if to distract himself from his suffering.

Hector looked around, trying to locate the surgeons. Someone was wearing a loose white cloak trimmed with gold and sitting on the step in front of the altar. He seemed to be unhurt. Hector went forward to speak with him. 'Are there any walking wounded?' he asked even as he realised that the seated figure was wrapped in the altar cloth. The man looked up. He was glassy-eyed and his breath stank of alcohol. 'Go look for yourself,' he mumbled. Appalled, Hector seized him by the shoulder and shook him. 'Where are the surgeons!' he shouted. Under his grip, Hector felt the limp and sagging movements of someone who was completely drunk. The man's head flopped back and forward loosely. 'The surgeons! Where are the surgeons?' Hector repeated angrily. The man hiccuped. 'Over there, waiting for a sermon,' he replied. He gave a tipsy laugh and waved vaguely towards the pulpit steps.

Lolling there was another man. He had a bottle in his hand and was clearly as intoxicated as his colleague. Hector recognised one of the surgeons who had worked alongside Smeeton and stayed on with the expedition. He was waving the bottle at Hector. 'Come and join us, young man!' he called out, slurring his words. 'Come and enjoy the finest fruits of the apothecary's skill. The medicine to cure every ailment.' He raised the bottle to his mouth, drained the last of its contents, and tossed it on the floor where it broke with a loud crash. 'That fool Watling is all piss and wind. A hotbrain who led us all into a death trap.' He wiped drool from his mouth with the back of his hand. 'We are the only ones who will get out of this alive,' he announced solemnly. 'We, the honoured gentlemen of the medical profession, are always welcome guests. The Spaniards will look after us. They need our skills. You were Smeeton's assistant, weren't you? So why don't you join us?' His knees gave way, and he sat back heavily on the pulpit steps.

Hector felt nausea rising within him, and a sense of betrayal. 'Won't you at least help the wounded get out of here?' he asked.

'Let them take their chances. Why should we risk our lives?' the surgeon retorted.

Hector made his way among the rows of wounded men.

The injuries inflicted by musket bullets were brutal. Several of the men on the floor appeared to be dead already, others were delirious or lying with their eyes closed.

Sick to his stomach, Hector found his way back to the door of the church. There was nothing he could do to help the wounded, and the longer he delayed, the more dangerous and difficult it would be for Sharpe to extricate the remainder of the buccaneers.

He eased the church door open and peered out through a narrow crack. Little seemed to have changed. His comrades were still pinned down, facing across the barricade, occasionally firing at the Spaniards on the far side of the plaza.

He darted out from the portico and set off at a dead run for the barricade. This time he jinked from side to side to distract the aim of the Spanish marksmen, and once again his luck held. He heard several musket shots, the smack of something which must have been a bullet striking the ground ahead of him. Then he was vaulting onto the barricade, and Jezreel was standing up to grasp him by the arm and drag him into cover.

'There's nothing to be done about the wounded. And the surgeons are too drunk to join us,' Hector blurted.

'Then we delay no longer!' said Sharpe briskly. 'Get the prisoners on their feet and bring them forward to the barricade. We fall back by the same route by which we entered the town. You, you and you . . .' He selected a dozen men. 'Stay here at the barricade. Each of you get behind one of the Spanish prisoners and use him as a shield. Put a gun muzzle to his spine, if necessary. As soon as the rest of us get back to the next barricade, we will give you covering fire. Then it's your turn to retreat, keeping the Spaniard between you and the enemy.'

There was a scramble to abandon the forward position. It was now well past noon, and the day was at its hottest.

As they retreated to the second abandoned barricade, Hector noticed a corpse with an orange handkerchief clenched in its fist. John Watling had been hit in the throat by a Spanish bullet and his shirt front was drenched with his blood. Duill, his second in command, was nowhere to be seen, and Hector presumed that the quartermaster had either also been killed or had fallen into the hands of the Spanish. Sharpe, who seemed to relish his renewed command, set the men to searching the corpses for spare cartridge pouches and bullet bags.

There was no respite from the Spanish counter-attack. As the buccaneers fell back street by street, their opponents kept pressing on, shooting down from the roof tops or suddenly appearing from lanes and passageways to fire and then slip away. The citizens of Arica knew the layout of their town and used that knowledge to their advantage. They paid no heed to their countrymen being used as human shields, and kept up their fire, killing or injuring several of their own people. If Sharpe had not been on hand to steady the buccaneers, their retreat could have become a panic-stricken flight.

Eventually the raiders were at the place where they had started – the barricade where they had first attacked the town in the light of dawn. Here Sharpe took a brief head count. Nearly one-third of the raiding force, some twenty-eight men, were missing. They were either dead or had been captured. Among those who now crouched exhausted in the shelter of the earthwork, eighteen had serious wounds. Everyone was dispirited, drooping with thirst and hunger.

'We'll be shot down like rabbits as we ascend the slope,' said Jacques despondently. 'The moment the Spaniards reoccupy this earthwork, it'll be like target practice for them.'

'Has anyone still got any grenades left?' Jezreel asked. Hector shook his head. He had left his satchel behind after his run to the church.

'I'm afraid I got rid of mine when we began the retreat,' said Jacques.

'What about Dan's grenades? They should be here somewhere,' suggested Hector. He remembered that the Miskito had left his satchel by the breastwork when he went up the hill to act as lookout. After a few moments of searching Hector spotted the bag tucked away in a corner.

He handed the satchel to Jezreel who brought out three grenades, then called out to Sharpe, 'Captain! Get going with the others. My friends and I will cover your retreat.'

Sharpe looked at the grenades and frowned. 'They're unreliable.'

'No matter. They will do the job.'

Sharpe did not need to be asked a second time. 'Come on!' he shouted to his men. 'Turn loose any prisoners. Back up the hill!' He turned to Jezreel. 'Is there nothing we can do?'

'Half a dozen men. Good shots. Place them half way up the slope where they have the range of the Spaniards. That might help.'

The buccaneers began their flight, stumbling wearily up the hill, some using their muskets as crutches, others helped along by comrades.

Jezreel started work on the grenades. He adjusted their fuses until he was satisfied, then buried them in the barricade a few paces apart. Looking over his shoulder to check that Sharpe and the main body of buccaneers were well on their way up the hill, he lit the three fuses and then shouted at his friends to turn and run.

The three friends scrambled back across the rough ground. Behind them came a flurry of shots, and Jacques stumbled and fell. Hector ran across to him while Jacques was struggling to stand up. He seemed dazed and blood was gushing from his head. He clapped a hand to his ear and brought it away. 'The bullet clipped my ear!' he exclaimed with a relieved grin. 'It's nothing.' There was an explosion from the barricade. The first of the grenades had detonated, throwing up a spurt of smoke and dirt. Several Spanish militiamen who had ventured into the gateway, dived back into shelter.

'Two more to go,' said Jezreel with a satisfied grunt.

Holding out a hand, he helped Jacques to stand upright, then put an arm around him and began to assist him up the hill. 'When I was in the fight game, there was a troupe of actors who used our ring as a stage between-times. When they needed to bring on or take off an actor, they had a hidden assistant who set off an explosion with lots of smoke and noise. It worked every time.'

FIFTEEN

✳

'IT WAS A SHAMBLES!' Basil Ringrose was still fuming, his anger fuelled by the fact that he and his comrades had also very nearly fallen victim to the Spaniards. 'Two white smokes! I nearly took the boats right into Arica harbour. We would have been blown out of the water.'

He glared angrily at Sharpe who was standing by the lee rail.

Hector watched the two men bicker. It was two months since the defeat at Arica, yet the panicked desperation of the withdrawal still provoked recriminations. He, Jacques and Jezreel had reached the ridge behind the town to find Sharpe and the others uprooting dry weeds and brushwood to make a signal fire. 'One white smoke,' someone was saying. 'Let's hope that the boat crews are quick about it. We have to get out of here before the Spaniards catch up with us.' The words were scarcely spoken when Dan, who had rejoined them, had said quietly, 'That's not our worry now.' He was looking back towards Arica. From the town were rising two thick columns of white smoke, reaching into the sky on that windless, scorching day and hanging there in false welcome. Dan had gone running to the shore to intercept Ringrose and the small boats before they were lured into the Spanish trap. Sharpe and the rest of the survivors had hobbled and limped behind him, half-dead of thirst and utterly spent. Troops of Spanish horsemen had harassed them all the way, then rolled rocks down the cliffs at them as they scrambled into the boats.

Back aboard *Trinity*, the men had divided into two camps, bitterly opposed: those who blamed Watling for the debacle and those who still detested Sharpe enough to resent serving under him again. After weeks of squabbling, a council had been held to decide the expedition's future. There was to be a simple vote: the majority would get to keep *Trinity* while the minority would receive the ship's launch and the canoes to do with them what they wanted. At the show of hands, seventy had chosen to keep on Sharpe as leader and forty-eight had been against. The losers had taken their share of the accumulated plunder and set out on the hazardous return voyage to Golden Island, intending to make the final leg of their journey back over the isthmus of Panama. Hector was sorry that William Dampier had gone with them, though he himself was in no hurry to return to the Caribbean now that he had given up his hopes of finding Susanna again. The longer he stayed away, the less likely he was to run across Captain Coxon. Hector had no doubt that Coxon remained a dangerous foe and would have his revenge if he ever had the chance.

Ringrose was speaking once more, a frown replacing his normally cheerful expression. 'I say that it was Duill who betrayed our signals to the Spanish. They must have taken him prisoner and tortured him.'

Sharpe shrugged. 'There's no way of knowing. What happened at Arica is in the past. Under my command we'll make no more shore landings against well-defended targets. We stick to what we do best – taking prizes at sea, and we cruise wherever there's the best chance to do so.'

Hector found himself wondering if he and his three friends had been wise to vote for Sharpe. Life aboard *Trinity* had quickly reverted to its former easy-going ways. Dice and cards had reappeared, shipboard discipline had grown slack, the men were irritable and slovenly. Only their care for their ship and their weapons was irreproachable. The men's clothing was falling into rags and they were often short of food, but they kept the tools of their trade – their muskets and blunderbusses – clean and smeared with seal fat against the salt air. Their cutlasses, swords and daggers were regularly sharpened and oiled. Their diligence for the ship was no less impressive. They experimented endlessly with improvements to their galleon's performance by adjusting the rake of the masts or the angle of the spars, and crewmen spent hour after hour seated on deck with needles and thread, working to shape new sails under the direction of the ship's sailmaker, or using marlin spikes and fids to mend and splice and tune the rigging.

Hector felt the deck tilt slightly beneath his bare feet. The warm breeze was strengthening. Beneath an overcast sky *Trinity* was running on a course parallel to the Peruvian coast, which was no more than a faint line on the horizon. As her captain had implied, her hunting ground was the broad strip of sea along which the coasting vessels travelled back and forth between the Peruvian ports. Here, only a week ago, the buccaneers had already taken one ship with 37,000 pieces of eight in chests and bags. Equally encouraging they had captured a government advice boat on its way to Panama with despatches. Hector had translated the official letters and it appeared that the Spanish authorities believed that all the buccaneers had left the South Sea. It meant that the coastal shipping might again be venturing out from their well-defended ports.

He sauntered forward to the bows where Jacques was taking his turn as lookout.

'Has the chase made any move to get away from us?' he asked. Since first light *Trinity* had been tracking a distant sail, and the gap between the two vessels had narrowed to less than a mile. The Spaniard had proved to be a merchant vessel of medium size and, judging from her smart paintwork, a ship that was making money for her owners.

'She's still plodding along. I doubt she suspects anything yet,' replied the Frenchman. He gave one of his sardonic grins. 'Bartholomew Sharpe is a past master in fakery. If we set too much canvas, they would be suspicious.'

Hector glanced up at the spars. *Trinity* was proceeding under plain sail as if she was an ordinary merchant ship going about her business, not a predator closing in on her victim.

'How long before they realise their mistake?'

'Perhaps another hour. *Trinity* has the lines of a locally built ship. That must reassure them more than our Spanish colours.'

'You're beginning to sound like a right sailor.'

'I've grown to appreciate this roving life,' Jacques answered, rubbing his cheek where his ex-galerien brand was now barely visible beneath his deep tan. 'It's better than scrabbling for an existence in the Paris stews.'

'Then it's lucky that our dice fell that way.'

Before the vote in the general council, the four friends had been undecided whether or not to support Bartholomew Sharpe. Jacques had suggested that they leave it to chance by throwing dice. If the number was high, they would vote in Sharpe's favour, a low number and they would side with Dampier and the other malcontents. The dice had shown a six and a four.

'That wasn't luck, as Jezreel and Dan already know,' Jacques confessed.

'What are you trying to say?'

'I didn't waste my time when I was nearly left behind on shore on Juan Fernandez. Do you remember those two dice that Watling flung into the bushes, the ones he took from Sharpe?'

'Were they the dice you used?'

'Yes, I searched for them because I thought they might come in handy one day. I knew they were loaded.'

'I don't remember you gambling against Sharpe.'

Jacques treated Hector to a look which told him that in many ways he was still very naive. 'I didn't. But I watched the pattern of his play. Did you ever wonder why the game the crew is so fond of is called Passage?'

'I think you're going to tell me.'

Jacques allowed himself a crafty smile. 'That's how the English pronounce passe dix – "more than ten", its French name. The game was invented in France and there's little that I don't know about how to cheat at it.'

'So our captain is not the only one who knows all about fakery and deception,' Hector rejoined.

A movement aboard the Spanish vessel caught his eye. The crew were reducing sail in response to the strengthening of the wind. From the quarterdeck behind him came a low command. Sharpe was issuing orders.

'Do as they do, but take your time about it! The slower you are, the more ground we will gain,' he called.

No more than a dozen of *Trinity*'s crew went to obey him. The rest of the buccaneers were hidden, either crouching behind the bulwarks or waiting below deck. A glimpse of so many men would instantly warn their prey that *Trinity* was not an innocent merchant vessel.

'Lynch! Come back here to the quarterdeck,' called Sharpe. 'I'll want you to address the Spaniards when we are within speaking distance. '

Hector made his way back to the helm but his assistance was not needed. Half an hour later when the gap between the two ships was less than three hundred paces, the Spanish ship suddenly veered aside, there was the sound of a cannon shot, and a neat round hole was punched in *Trinity*'s forecourse.

'All hands now!' shouted Sharpe. There was a surge of activity as the full complement of sail handlers sprang into action. Extra sails blossomed along the yards and *Trinity* accelerated forward, showing her true pace. Within moments she was ranging up to windward, rapidly overhauling her prey. Her best marksmen took their positions, some in the rigging, the others along the rail, and they moved unhurriedly, confident in their skill. By contrast there was a panicked flurry of action on the deck of the Spanish vessel. Men were hastily clearing away loose deck clutter and erecting makeshift firing positions. It was evident that *Trinity*'s victim was utterly unused to violent confrontation.

Another bang from the chase's cannon, and again the shot was wasted. It threw up a spout of water as it plunged into the sea well short of its mark. The wind had raised a short rolling sea, making it difficult for the Spanish gun crew to aim their weapon accurately.

'Seems they have only a single cannon aboard,' commented Sharpe calmly, 'and their gunners need some practice.'

Trinity's musketeers had not yet fired a single shot, but were waiting patiently for their target to come within easy range. Samuel Gifford, the quartermaster, had warned them that they were not to waste ammunition. The ship's supply of lead for making bullets had been badly depleted by the raid on Arica.

There was a ragged scatter of firing from the Spanish ship, and a spent musket ball struck *Trinity*'s mainsail, dropped onto the deck, and rolled towards the scuppers. Jezreel reached down and picked it up. The bullet was still warm. 'Here, Jacques, you might return the compliment,' he said, tossing the bullet to his friend.

Bartholomew Sharpe was watching the gap between the two ships carefully, gauging the distance and the speed of the two vessels. 'Hold her just there,' he told the helmsman when *Trinity* was level with the Spanish ship, a hundred yards away and upwind, close enough for the buccaneers to pick their individual targets. The figure of the Spanish captain was clearly visible. He was darting back and forth among his men, obviously encouraging them to stand firm. 'You would have thought they would see sense and surrender,' Sharpe muttered to himself. Hector remembered how Sharpe had tricked Jezreel into shooting an innocent priest, and was surprised by the captain's reluctance to press home the attack. The captain, it seemed, was capable of compassion as well as savagery.

The Spanish had once again reloaded their single cannon and this time the shot struck *Trinity* amidships. Hector felt the hull quiver, but a moment later the carpenter came up on deck to report that no damage had been done. The cannonball had been too light to penetrate the heavy planking.

'Open fire! Clear their decks!' ordered Sharpe after a pause, and the musketry began. Almost immediately the figures on the deck of the Spanish ship began to fall. Their captain was among the first to be hit. He was making his way towards the entrance to his cabin at the break of the poop deck when a musket ball struck him for he suddenly pitched sideways and lay still. Seeing their commander go down, the two steersmen abandoned the helm and ducked into cover. The Spanish vessel, no longer under control, slowly began to turn up into the wind and lose speed.

'Close to fifty paces,' Sharpe told his steersman, and *Trinity* moved into even easier range for her musketeers. *Trinity* possessed the advantage in height, and her marksmen were shooting downwards on their targets now. In a short time not a single Spanish seaman was visible. They had all fled below hatches, leaving only their dead and badly wounded on the deck. Their vessel slowed to a halt, the wind spilling from her sails, the canvas flapping uselessly.

'Call on them to surrender,' Sharpe ordered Hector, handing him a speaking trumpet. 'Say we will do them no harm.'

Hector took the speaking trumpet and had to repeat his shouted instructions three or four times before a small group of sailors emerged warily from the hatches and made their way to the sheets and halyards. Minutes later they had brailed up the sails and the Spanish ship lay rolling on the swell, waiting submissively for her captors to take possession.

'The sea's too rough for us to go alongside. We risk damaging our ship,' observed Ringrose.

'Then lower the pinnace,' Sharpe told him, 'and go across with half a dozen men and see what we've caught. Take Lynch with you as interpreter.' Sharpe was looking satisfied with himself for he had not had a single one of his own men killed or injured, and the Spanish ship appeared to be a juicy prize.

As Hector helped ease the pinnace into the water, Jezreel appeared beside him, carrying his smallsword. 'I think I'll go with you in case it is a trick. The Spaniards gave up all too easily. I'm suspicious that they've merely retreated below deck and are waiting to ambush us.'

Hector murmured his thanks, and the two friends helped to row the boat across to the waiting prize. As he approached the Spanish ship, Hector looked up at its wooden side and, as always, was struck by the fact that the vessel which had seemed so low in the water from a distance, was much higher and more awkward to board when seen from close at hand. Timing his leap, Hector jumped for the rail of the ship, caught hold and swung himself aboard. Jezreel, Ringrose and three of *Trinity*'s men armed with muskets and cutlasses followed him.

The body of the dead Spanish captain was the first sight that met Hector's eyes. It lay where it had fallen, close to the break of the poop deck. The captain had dressed in a faded blue uniform jacket which was now soaked with blood. His hat had rolled off, revealing wisps of grey hair surrounding a bald patch of scalp. One hand was flung out as if still reaching out to open the door to his cabin. Standing beside the corpse was a thin-faced young man, no more than Hector's own age, and he was pale with shock. Hovering in the background half a dozen sailors were casting nervous glances at the boarding party.

'Who is in charge?' asked Hector quietly.

There was a pause before the young man answered shakily, 'I suppose I am. You killed my father.'

Hector glanced down at the corpse. The face was turned to

one side, and the profile was enough for him to see the resemblance.

'I'm very sorry. If you had not opened fire on us, this would not have happened.'

The young man said nothing.

'What is the name of your vessel?' Hector enquired as gently as possible.

'*Santo Rosario*. We sailed from Callao yesterday morning.' The young man's voice was thick with misery.

'With what cargo?'

Again the captain's son did not reply. Hector recognised the symptoms of deep distress and realised that there was little point in asking any more questions. 'There will be no more bloodshed if you and your men cooperate peacefully. We'll search the ship, and after that my captain will decide what is to be done.'

Behind him he heard Jezreel warning the other members of the boarding party to watch out for hidden surprises. Then came the sounds of the men opening up the hatches to the cargo hold.

Searching a captured ship was always a tense time. No one knew what might be found in the darkness of the hold, a desperate sailor lurking with a knife or cudgel, or someone holding a lighted match near the gunpowder store and threatening to blow up the ship unless the boarders withdrew. Ringrose kept a pistol pointing at the crew of *Santo Rosario* while he and Hector waited to learn what the ship had been carrying.

There was disappointment on the faces of the buccaneers as they re-emerged from the hatchways. 'Just some sacks of coconuts and a few bales of cloth which might be useful for sail-making,' one of them exclaimed. 'The ship's in ballast. There are several hundred ingots of lead in the bilges.'

'If it's lead, then that will make the quartermaster happy,' commented Ringrose. 'Bring up a sample so we can take a closer look.'

When the buccaneer returned, he was cradling a misshapen lump of some dull grey metal in his arms. Ringrose took out his knife and scratched the surface of the ingot. 'Not lead, more like unrefined tin,' he announced. 'Gifford will be disappointed. But at a pinch it just might do for making bullets. We'll take one of them back to *Trinity* to try it out.'

Hector turned to the young man. 'My captain will want to see the ship's papers,' he said. 'And any other documents such as bills of lading, letters, maps, charts. Also I need to speak with the pilot.'

The captain's son looked back at him with grief-stricken eyes. 'My father took charge of everything. This was his own ship, held in partnership with friends. He had sailed these waters all his life, he didn't need a pilot or charts. Everything was in his head.'

'Nevertheless I must examine the ship's papers.' said Hector.

The young man seemed to accept the inevitable. 'You'll find them in his cabin.' He turned and walked to the stern rail, where he stood, staring down into the sea, lost in his private wretchedness.

As Hector made his way towards the captain's cabin, Jezreel, who had reappeared on deck, fell in step beside him. 'There's still something not quite right here,' the big man muttered. 'If the ship was sailing empty why did they put up a fight? They had nothing worth defending. And why would such a fine ship as this one be on a purposeless voyage?'

'Perhaps the ship's papers will tell us,' answered Hector. They skirted round the body of the captain and had reached the door to his cabin. Hector attempted to open it. To his surprise the door was locked.

'That's odd,' he said. 'Jezreel, see if you can find a key in the dead man's pocket.'

Jezreel searched the corpse but found nothing. 'We'll have to break it open,' he said and, stepping back, delivered a hefty kick at the woodwork. The door shook in its frame and, just as Jezreel was about to deliver a second blow, Hector heard the sound of the lock clicking back. Suddenly he wished that he was carrying a weapon to defend himself. Fearing that whoever was inside might fire a shot through the wooden panel, he quickly edged to one side, out of the line of fire.

The door swung back, and out stepped a woman.

Hector was so surprised that his mouth fell open in astonishment. The woman was perhaps twenty years old, yet she held herself with the assurance of someone accustomed to being treated with respect, even deference. She was immaculately dressed in a long, dark green travelling mantle trimmed at the shoulders and sleeves with lines of black braid. A broad collar of fine lace emphasised her pale ivory skin. Her hair was so dark as to be almost black and had been dressed in long, loose curls, now partly covered by a light shawl. Her oval face was perfectly symmetrical with a high forehead and large, dark eyes. These now regarded Hector with defiance mingled with disdain.

'I wish to speak with whoever is in charge,' she said calmly. She spoke slowly and clearly as if addressing a dull-witted servant.

Hector stood in stunned silence, feeling foolish. He swallowed nervously and words failed him.

'I am Dona Juana de Costana, wife of the Alcalde of the Real Sala del Crimen of Paita,' she said. 'It would be wise of your captain to make arrangements for my safe return to my family with as little delay as possible. I presume that, as pirates, you are more interested in what you can steal.' She gestured towards the open doorway behind her, and said, 'Please bring out the purse, Maria.' To Hector's increasing amazement a second woman emerged from the cabin. She was of much the same age, but more plainly dressed in a long-sleeved, brown gown with a light collar of white linen. Her head of nut-brown hair was uncovered. She was clearly a companion to Dona Juana. In her hand she carried a small bag of soft leather.

Dona Juana took the bag and held it out to Hector. 'Here, you may have this,' she said with a trace of condescension in her voice. 'It will save you searching the cabin for other valuables. It contains all our jewellery.'

Hector accepted the bag and, through the soft leather, felt the irregular shapes of brooches and the smoother sensation of what he guessed were pearl necklaces. Maria, the companion, had taken up her position half a pace behind her mistress, and was regarding him with similar distaste. She had a darker complexion, lightly freckled, and Hector noticed that her hands which she clasped in front of her in a gesture of exasperation were small and very neat. Neither woman showed the least trace of fear.

He cleared his throat, still struggling to overcome his surprise, and said, 'We wish you no harm, but it is my duty to search the cabin. I need to retrieve the ship's documents.'

'Then do your duty,' said Dona Juana crisply. 'You will find that poor Captain Lopez,' and she cast a glance towards the captain's corpse, 'kept his papers in a chest under the stern window. But I would be obliged if you and your men refrained from touching any of the clothes or personal effects belonging to myself or my companion. You already have all our valuables.'

'I will respect your private possessions,' said Hector finally. 'In the meantime I am sure that my ship's navigator Mr Basil Ringrose would like to make your acquaintance.' Ringrose was standing goggle-eyed at the imperious young lady's beauty. She gave him a glance which clearly sent the young navigator reeling.

'If you'll excuse me,' said Hector and he ducked in through the low door of the cabin to begin his search. Behind him the doorway darkened and glancing back over his shoulder he saw that the companion, Maria, had followed him and was standing, arms folded, watching him. Evidently she was not taking his word that he would not touch the women's possessions. Self-consciously he began to rummage the low-ceilinged cabin. The two women were travelling in some style. A folding dressing table was covered with expensive brushes and toiletries. There was a fine silk shawl draped over a cushioned stool, and two elegant cloaks hung from pegs. A silk rug was spread on the floor of the small, ill lit cabin, and over against a bulkhead stood a large trunk, obviously containing a full wardrobe. He smelled costly perfume.

He lifted the lid of the sea chest that Dona Juana had mentioned. It contained a log book and several scrolls and parchments as well as a thin leather case with several documents inside. They were various letters and bills of lading. Looking through them rapidly, Hector saw that the *Santo Rosario* had been bound for Panama. A letter addressed to the governor from Dona Juana's husband, the Alcalde, recommended Captain Lopez to him in the most civil terms, and there were several notes of credit in favour of the captain and drawn on leading merchants. The notes were for substantial sums of money. It was clear that Captain Lopez had been a wealthy man in his own right and well known throughout the colonial trading community.

He selected the more significant of the documents and tied them together with a length of silk ribbon he picked off the dressing table. He sensed Maria's disapproval behind him. Adding the captain's journal to the bundle, he straightened up and looked around him wondering if there was anything else that he should check. It was common practice for a ship's captain to have a secret hiding place where he kept his most valuable possessions and sensitive papers. 'To save you doing any damage, you will find there's a hidden compartment behind that trunk of clothes,' Maria said. 'It's where Captain Lopez kept the crew's wages and his own money he used in trade.' Her tone was scornful.

Hector pushed the trunk aside and soon found what he was

looking for. The hiding place contained a substantial quantity of coin in bags and a collection of domestic silverware. There were salvers, jugs, silver gilt cups, and four very fine candlesticks. It was evident that Captain Lopez kept an elegant table. There was also a large folder, wrapped in a loose oilskin slip and evidently much handled. Opening it, Hector saw that he was holding a collection of sea charts. The first was a very detailed map of the approaches to Panama, showing rocks and reefs and shoals, and how to bring a ship safely into the anchorage. The remainder of the maps were much less precise. They showed the general outline of the entire South Sea coast, all the way from California to the South Cape.

Summoning one of the buccaneers to help, Hector carried the money and valuables out on deck and put them in a sack, ready to be transported across to *Trinity*. The oilskin folder he kept separately.

Sharpe had already brought his vessel close enough for a shouted conversation across the water, and when Hector explained what he had found, the captain told him to return to *Trinity*, bringing the documents, valuables and the female prisoners.

But when the young man explained these instructions to Dona Juana, he was met with a flat refusal.

'I have not the slightest intention of going aboard your ship,' she announced imperiously. 'If your captain wishes to speak with me, he can come across here.'

Hector wondered for a moment whether he should get Jezreel to pick up the woman and carry her into the cockboat, but Ringrose came to his rescue. Stepping across to the rail he bawled out to Sharpe, 'It would be easier if you would come across with a prize crew.'

To Hector's relief Sharpe agreed to this suggestion and before long the buccaneer captain was standing on the deck of the *Santo Rosario* and Hector was introducing him to the wife of the senior magistrate of the Criminal Court of Paita.

'I am most honoured to make your acquaintance,' Sharpe said, making a bow. His Spanish was slow and clumsy, and from the way he was looking at the young woman, it seemed that he was very much taken with her beauty as Ringrose had been.

'You are the leader of these people?' Juana asked. She managed to put her question as if she and Sharpe were superior to everyone else, should he prove to be in command.

Sharpe preened himself. 'Indeed I am the captain of that ship over there, señora, and at your service,' he confirmed.

'No doubt your own vessel is well appointed but it is hardly likely to offer the same quality of accommodation as this one. My companion and I have managed to make ourselves as comfortable as possible in such trying and cramped conditions. I have informed your assistant here that I have no intention of leaving the *Santo Rosario.* '

Sharpe was positively fawning. 'I would not wish you to be put to any inconvenience, señora. By all means you may stay here. I will instruct my men not to disturb you.' Hector wondered if Bartholomew Sharpe knew what a spectacle he was making of himself.

'Come, Maria, it is time we withdrew,' said Dona Juana and without another word she swept back into her cabin in a swirl of green silk, followed by her companion.

'She should fetch a choice ransom,' observed one of the buccaneers.

Sharpe rounded on him in a fury. 'Keep a civil tongue in your head,' he snapped. 'What happens to the lady will be decided by the council, and in the meantime you have work to do. For a start you can help dispose of the dead bodies, and clean this deck.'

Then Sharpe turned to Hector, who was still holding the bundle of ship's documents, and asked, 'What did you find out?'

'The vessel was bound for Panama. This folder contains a

chart for the final approach. There are also general maps for all the entire coast. Her captain was an important man, a friend of the governor there, and Dona Juana was on her way to stay with him.'

'Lucky fellow,' commented Sharpe.

'There's also a considerable quantity of cash on board, and Ringrose believes that the ship's ballast could be turned into musket bullets.' Hector would have continued but the captain was scarcely listening to him.

'We must show her that we are not barbarians,' was all Sharpe said. 'Confine the ship's officers to the forepeak, and have them give their word that they'll not make trouble, and this evening we will entertain the señora and her companion. On this ship of course. Perhaps your friend the Frenchman can prepare a special meal.'

'What about the captain's son? He's over there.' Hector nodded towards the young man still standing miserably at the stern rail.

'Put him in the forepeak with the last of them.'

'His father possessed some fine tableware; solid silver.'

'Good. We'll use that. Later we can have it broken up and divided among the men.'

* * *

'SHARPE SEEMS utterly smitten,' Hector commented to Jacques in the galley of the *Santo Rosario* that evening. The wind had died away and the two ships lay becalmed on a quiet sea. The Frenchman had been rowed across to the prize, bringing his preferred cooking utensils and dried herbs and a large tuna which he had been marinading in a mixture of sugar and salt. Jacques lifted the lid of a chafing dish, dipped a tasting spoon in the sauce, and said, 'Never underestimate the power of a beautiful woman. Particularly on men who have been so long at sea. Their heads can be set spinning until they are dizzy.'

Jezreel, who was listening in, was sceptical. 'I still think that there's something not quite right about this ship. Maybe her crew put up a fight because they had a brave captain and he did not want to surrender a judge's wife. But there's more to it. I watched how she twisted Sharpe around that elegant little finger of hers. Our captain rolled over on his back and wagged his tail.'

Hector had to agree with him. He was full of admiration for the resolute poise of the two women, but he sensed a hidden reason for the women's attitude, and he was puzzled what it might be. 'If I hadn't read those despatches, I'd have said that Dona Juana was deliberately delaying us because she knows that the Spaniards are assembling a squadron of warships and will soon be here to rescue her,' he said.

Jacques blew on a spoonful of broth to cool it. 'Maybe she didn't know what was in those despatches.'

'Her husband would never have allowed her to set sail if he thought that *Trinity* was still operating in the South Sea.'

'Then you have to ask yourself exactly what Dona Juana wants.' Jacques took a sip from the spoon, then added a pinch of pimento powder to the broth.

'To be allowed to stay on this ship.'

'Anything else?'

'That we weren't to interfere with their private possessions.'

'Then that's where you need to look.'

'But they have been promised that we would do no such thing,' Hector objected.

Jacques shrugged. 'Then make sure that neither they nor Sharpe get to know. Dinner is to be served in the open air, out on the quarterdeck. I suggest while the two ladies and our gallant captain are enjoying my cuisine, someone searches their cabin. Dan climbs like a goat. He can get in through the stern window, examine the cabin and get out again before they finish my dessert – it will be a syllabub of coconut, worth lingering over.'

'I have a better idea,' said Jezreel. 'There's a small hatch in the floor of the stern accommodation. I found it when we were checking the cargo hold. It's normally used by the ship's carpenter when he inspects the tiller trunking. Someone small – either Dan or Hector – should be able to get into the cabin that way.'

In the end it was decided that it would be quicker if both Dan and Hector carried out the search together, and they managed to squeeze their way into the cabin without much difficulty. There they found nothing suspicious except that the large clothing trunk was firmly locked.

'I can't imagine that the ladies feared the crew would steal their dresses,' said Dan. He felt in his pocket and produced the priming wire he used for cleaning the vent of his musket. Slipping the end of the wire into the lock, he gave a twist and a moment later was easing back the lid.

'Jacques would be proud of you. I doubt he was quicker in his time as a Paris burglar,' whispered Hector.

The trunk was stuffed with gowns, skirts, petticoats, mantuas, capes, chemises, gloves and stockings, all so tightly packed together that Hector wondered if it would ever be possible to shut the lid again. He plunged his arms into the mass of taffeta and silk and lace, and began to feel down through the layers. Two-thirds of the way through the excavation his fingers met a solid object. It felt like a large book. Carefully easing it out of the hiding place, he saw that it was another folder, very similar to the one in which Captain Lopez had kept his charts. Hector stepped across to the stern window where the light was better, and turned back the cover. He knew at once that he was holding in his hands the dead captain's private book of navigation. It was filled with his daily drawings and observations. There were diagrams of anchorages marked with their soundings, drafts of harbour approaches, dozens of coastal profiles, sketches of islands, observations of tides and currents. The folder contained a lifetime of Captain Lopez's experience as a navigator. Quickly Hector riffled through the pages. There must have been almost a hundred of them, covered with drawings and notes. Some were many years old. They were sea-stained and frayed, the ink fading, and probably drawn when Lopez first went to sea. Other pages were drafted by a different hand and appeared to have been copied from official books of sailing instructions. 'So it was not all in his head,' Hector muttered to himself as he replaced the folder, burying it deep within the scented garments. Then Dan relocked the trunk, and Hector followed the Miskito down through the little hatchway.

'That's why the captain risked our musket fire. He was trying to get to the cabin to reach the folder,' said Hector when he and Dan got back to the galley and found Jezreel running a large thumb round the salver on which Jacques had served the coconut syllabub. 'He must have known that his ship was likely to be captured and he was determined not to let his navigation notes fall into our hands. He would have dumped the folder into the sea the moment he decided to surrender.'

'But what about those other charts, the ones in the oilskin folder?'

'Those were much less detailed. They provide only the general outline of the coast. To use them properly, Lopez would be relying on his detailed navigation notes.'

'Ringrose is going to be happy. It's going to save him a lot of paper and ink. He's been scribbling away at that sort of stuff ever since we came into the South Sea,' commented Jezreel, licking his thumb.

'Ringrose has been mapping only a small portion of the coast,' Hector corrected him. 'I didn't have time to check just how far Captain Lopez's navigation notes extend, but he was exceptionally well travelled. He may have had precise sailing and pilotage directions all the way from California to the Cape.'

'Is that important?' asked Dan.

'I worked for a land surveyor in Port Royal for a few days, copying maps for him. One day when he was drunk he said to me that really good charts of the South Sea would be priceless. They would be the key to enormous riches. I remember him saying that the Spaniards would murder to prevent such information falling into the wrong hands.'

'Sounds as though they are as dangerous as they are valuable,' joined in Jezreel doubtfully. 'Captain Lopez's charts would be handy for us now, but we've been managing pretty well without them, thanks to you and Ringrose as our navigators. If Dona Juana and her companion are released back to their own people, what happens then? The Spaniards will know we have the folder, and they will redouble their efforts to hunt us down.'

'And anyone they caught would be tortured to learn just how much was known, who else had the same information, and then strangled to silence them.' Jacques added.

Hector thought for a moment before replying. 'Then we'll keep quiet about our discovery . . . At least for now.'

'What about Sharpe? Do we tell him what we've found?' Jezreel asked.

Again, Hector paused before replying. His mistrust of Sharpe made him cautious. 'No. He'll be outraged if he learns that Dona Juana has made a fool of him. We'll do what Jacques did with those dice he retrieved from the bushes. He guessed they would come in useful at some time. These maps could be the same for us when it comes to dealing with Sharpe.'

'And how do we prevent the two women from knowing that we have the charts?'

'We copy them,' said Hector firmly. 'Dan can help me. There was a time when we both drew maps and charts for a Turkish sea captain. Dan's a quick and accurate draughtsman.'

'Even so, it will take time,' Jezreel objected.

'Captain Sharpe seems in no hurry to part company with the beautiful Juana,' said Hector. 'He will be cosying up to her for the next few days. I already have a supply of paper and ink for helping Ringrose. Every time we have the chance, we remove a few sheets from the folder, copy them, and return them. I doubt that Dona Juana or Maria do more than check that the folder is still safe in their trunk. They won't have time to count the pages.'

'How long will all this take?' asked Jezreel.

'Dan and I should be able to complete the job in less than a week. We don't have to make fair copies, only quick sketches and notes. I'll keep the results safe in that bamboo tube I've been carrying so no one will even suspect what we are doing.' He looked at his friends. 'Are we all agreed?'

Dan and Jacques nodded, and Jezreel with a glance at the Frenchman added, 'Jacques, here's your chance to shine. Let's hope you can come up with seven days of dinner dishes and never repeat the same menu.'

In the end it took a full ten days to copy the contents of the folder. Hector had failed to anticipate how often he would be needed to act as interpreter for Sharpe. In his infatuation for the delectable Dona Juana, Sharpe took every excuse to visit the *Santo Rosario*, and Hector had to be on hand to untangle the buccaneer's clumsy gallantry. So it was left to Dan to burgle the cabin while Hector remained outside on deck, deliberately prolonging his captain's flowery compliments to the Alcalde's wife. By the time all the pages had been copied, the crew of *Trinity* were at breaking point with their captain's dalliance. They demanded a general council and insisted that the two women be sent on their way. Reluctantly Sharpe agreed.

'We will sail to Paita, contact Dona Juana's family and arrange an exchange,' he told the crew assembled on *Trinity*'s maindeck.

'What sort of an exchange?' someone had called out.

'The lady in return for a pilot who can guide us in these waters. In addition we'll demand a ransom to be paid in ship's supplies. We are running short of sail cloth and rope.'

'But we can take the sails and rigging from the *Santo Rosario*,' objected one of the older men.

'That is not sufficient for what I have in mind,' said Sharpe. He paused for effect, then called out, 'We need that material if *Trinity* is to make a long voyage. I am proposing that we return back to the Caribbean by sailing around the Cape!'

There was a widespread murmur of approval. Many of the crew were heartily tired of the South Sea. Sharpe looked towards where Hector was standing with his friends.

'I am appointing Lynch as our go-between. Off Paita we will intercept a local fishing boat, and put Lynch aboard so that he can go ashore. He will conduct negotiations on our behalf.'

'What am I to say?' asked Hector. Sharpe was manipulating the situation, and might even be seeking to get rid of him.

'Tell the Spaniards that once we have the pilot safely aboard and received the supplies, we will hand back the *Santo Rosario* and the lady, unharmed. We'll leave the vessel at a suitable rendez-vous which we decide.'

Hector voiced his misgivings. 'Why should the Spaniards believe me? They might just execute me out of hand.'

Sharpe smiled cynically. 'The Spaniards will do anything to speed us on our way, and we still have Dona Juana.'

'And how can they be sure that Dona Juana has not been harmed?'

'Because you will go to Paita with her companion Maria. She will tell them that Dona Juana has been very well treated. Maria will serve as your security.'

Again there was a murmur of approval from the crew clustered around Hector, and before he could raise another objection, Sharpe treated him to one of his sly looks and added in a voice loud enough for all to hear, 'I was very impressed with how you dealt with the Spaniards at La Serena. I'm sure you will do just as well on this occasion.'

SIXTEEN

*

A WEEK LATER, Hector was uncomfortably aware of how thoroughly he had been out-manoeuvred. Sharpe had disembarked him and Maria, Dona Juana's companion, onto a small fishing smack out of Paita, and already *Trinity* had dwindled to a tiny dark shape on the horizon. The galleon, which had been his home for the last fifteen months, would soon be lost from view in the gathering darkness, and Maria was taking pleasure in baiting him.

'Your new shipmates don't seem to like you,' she said mockingly. She was seated facing him on the centre thwart and had noted the surly looks of the smack's crew. They were understandably sullen. *Trinity* had robbed them of their catch of mackerel and anchovies and, to make matters worse, the wind had turned foul. It was going to be a long hard slog for them to sail back into Paita.

'One word from me when we land in Paita and the governor could have you garotted,' Maria added maliciously.

Hector said nothing. A burst of spray struck the back of his neck and he pulled his cloak around him.

'It's no more than you and your companions deserve. They are nothing but arrogant brigands of the sea. Blood-soaked murderers.'

The young woman had a low, musical voice, and the harsh words sounded strange coming from her.

'If the *Santo Rosario* had not opened fire on us, we would not have been obliged to take the vessel by force,' Hector replied.

Maria wrinkled her nose in disbelief. 'You would have pillaged the ship, and not touched us?'

'You call us brigands. So think of us as highwaymen who stop and rob travellers on the road. If the travellers are sensible they offer no resistance and are merely relieved of their valuables and allowed to go on their way. But if there is opposition, and someone fires a pistol, there is bloodshed. The travellers seldom come out best.'

'And why do you choose to make your living by such theft and piracy rather than by honest toil? You don't look or talk like a cut-throat.' Her tone was a little softer, and there was a hint of curiosity in her voice.

'There were special circumstances . . .' Hector began, and was about to explain how he came to be in the South Sea when he thought better of it and instead looked out towards the horizon. *Trinity* was no longer visible. The daylight was almost gone, and the first stars were appearing through rents in the rapidly moving clouds. It was threatening to be a wild night. The little boat was beginning to pitch and lurch on the blackness of the waves. The swirl of bilgewater beneath his feet released the smell of rotten fish. He wondered about Dan and the others.

Maria seemed to read his thoughts for suddenly she asked, 'What about your friends? There's one very big man, I think his name is Jezreel. I saw you often talking with him, and there was the Frenchman who was our cook, and a man who looked like an Indian.'

'They are my comrades, and we have come through many difficult times together.'

'Then why aren't they here with you now?'

Hector decided that the astute young woman deserved an

honest answer. 'All three of them offered to accompany me. But I told them that their presence would only increase the danger. In Paita your people might decide to hold back one or more of them as hostages until your mistress is released, and even then there was no guarantee of their safety.'

'And what about you? Aren't you afraid of being held?'

Hector shook his head. 'No, if your people want the safe return of Dona Juana, they will have to let me go. I am the only one who can arrange her exchange.'

'And what if "my people", as you describe them, decide that it would be easier to torture you?'

Hector tried to meet her eyes, but it was now too dark to see her expression. 'That is a risk I am prepared to take. If you help me and the mission goes well, it means that my friends will be able to return to their homes.'

Maria paused before answering, and Hector detected that her antipathy was waning.

'And what about you? Do you have a family who are expecting you to return?'

'No, my father died some years ago, and I have lost touch with my mother. She is the one from whom I learned to speak Spanish.'

'From Galicia, to judge by your accent. It is surprising that you do not speak Galego.'

'My mother insisted that we learn Castilian. She said it would be of more use.'

'We?'

'My sister and I. But I will never see my sister again.'

He had expected Maria to question him further, but she fell silent, doubtless understanding that he did not wish to talk about his loss.

When she did speak again, it was in a much more friendly tone, almost confiding. 'I understand your feeling of being alone. But not because I have lost my parents. They are still alive as far as I know, small farmers in Andalucia. Life is hard in that part of Spain, and they were enthusiastic when the opportunity came for me to go abroad as Dona Juana's companion. So I was happy to accede to their wishes.'

'And you like the post?'

There was a short pause before Maria replied. 'Yes. I am fortunate. Dona Juana is a kind employer. She treats me as a friend, not as a servant which is what I could be.'

'But you still miss your family?'

'Spain seems so far away. Sometimes I think I will never see my homeland again.'

For a long time they both sat quietly, hearing the run of water along the sides of the little fishing boat as it grew more urgent, and the rising note of the wind in the rigging.

'Tell me about Dona Juana's husband, the Alcalde,' Hector said.

'He's older than her. Perhaps by twenty years, and he has the reputation of being a harsh man. He believes in the stern application of the law.'

'Would he put the law ahead of the well-being of his wife?'

Maria thought for a moment before replying. 'I believe so, but it is always hard to tell with him. He is a man of very strict principle.'

The moan of the wind and the noise of the waves were making their conversation difficult. Occasionally the little boat thrust her bow into the waves, and water came sluicing onboard. Hector had noticed a small cuddy under the foredeck where the fishermen stowed their nets, and he suggested to Maria that she might take shelter there. She stood up from the thwart, reached out to steady herself as the boat lurched, and placed her hand on his shoulder. He was aware of her grip, light but firm, a woman's touch. Then she was clambering past him, her hip brushed his shoulder, and all of a sudden he was swept by the knowledge that she was very attractive. He found himself wishing that she had stayed much closer to him, where he could relish her nearness and learn more about her.

*

NEXT MORNING the last of the gale was still whipping up a lively sea, the waves sending tremors through the hull planking of the little boat as she battled her way towards the watch-tower at the entrance to Paita's harbour. Hector sat on a pile of damp sacking and rope, his back pressed against the mast step. He was bleary-eyed, for he had slept only fitfully, his mind returning again and again to thoughts of the young woman curled up in the dark cave of the cuddy. He rehearsed every word of their conversation, still wondering how Maria had seemed to be able to read his thoughts. From time to time he glanced towards the place where she lay asleep, and waited for her to awake. When Maria did emerge half an hour later and crawled out from the cuddy, Hector had a glimpse of a neat ankle and a small bare foot. Sensibly she had removed her shoes before going to sleep. Maria stood up and turned her face into the wind and her long, loose hair streamed out behind her. In that moment Hector was confronted by a young woman very different from the person he had known aboard the *Santo Rosario*. In the shadow of her mistress Maria had been quietly dutiful and unassuming, easily overlooked, and probably this had been her intention. Now he saw that Maria had the gift of a natural, healthy beauty. As she closed her eyes and took a deep breath, relishing the fresh morning breeze after the stuffy confines of the cuddy, Hector noted the small heart-shaped face with a short straight nose, a soft mouth perhaps a trifle too wide for the delicacy of her features, a skin lightly freckled. Every-thing about Maria was neat and pleasing in a way that was simple and tempting. Then she turned and looked at him and the dark brown eyes under the perfectly arched eyebrows held an almost conspiratorial expression.

'Did you manage to get any rest?' he asked, aware that he felt light-headed, off balance.

She nodded, and all of a sudden Hector was overwhelmed by her presence. She was wearing the fine cloak which he had seen hanging in her cabin, but now it was bedraggled and crumpled, the hem sodden with bilgewater. Awkwardly he started to get to his feet, hoping to find an excuse to extend a hand, to touch her again and help her to climb over the thwart, when, without warning, he was rudely elbowed aside. One of the fishermen pushed passed him. The man was holding a chunk of dry bread and an earthenware flagon of water which he held out to Maria. He offered nothing to Hector. Instead he turned to face towards the land, placed two fingers into his mouth and let out a piercing whistle. In response a watchman appeared on the top of the watchtower. The fisherman waved, making what must have been an agreed code of signals, for the watchman disappeared, and soon a squad of soldiers was running to take position by a gun platform, and a horseman was galloping inland clearly carrying a message to the town.

'What was all that about?' Hector enquired.

The fisherman gave him a black look. 'Ever since you and your rabble attacked Arica we've been asked to keep a special lookout. Told to report any sightings of unknown vessels and report back immediately. Never thought I would be bringing in one of the scum who was responsible. I'll enjoy watching your punishment. I lost a younger brother at Arica.'

The motion of the boat eased as the fishing smack passed into the shelter of the headland protecting Paita's anchorage, and soon the fishermen were changing course to lay their vessel alongside the jetty where a file of Spanish soldiers already stood waiting. Their grey-haired sergeant wore on his tunic the faded red saltire which marked him as a veteran of the European wars.

'Here's one of the pirates! And you're welcome to him,'

called out the fisherman. The boat bumped against the landing place, Hector lost his balance, and he was pushed hard in the back so that he sprawled forward ignominiously onto the weed-covered stone steps. A hand seized him by the collar of his cloak, and he was hauled upright roughly.

'Treat him gently. He's an envoy, not a prisoner!' Maria said sharply. She was being helped out of the boat by one of the fishermen and was glaring angrily at the sergeant. He looked back at her in disbelief. 'He's come here to speak with the Alcalde,' she snapped. 'Escort us to his office at once.'

The sergeant's expression of disgust made his feelings clear as he ordered his men to form up on either side of Hector and march with him into the town. Maria kept pace, walking beside the little group as it made its way past the customs house and harbour offices and the warehouses where the merchants of Paita stored their goods. Looking about him, Hector saw that the town exceeded Arica for prosperity. Besides the usual piles of fishing gear, there were stacks of timber for boatbuilding, ranks of wine barrels awaiting shipment, huge jars which he guessed contained olives for export, and in open-sided sheds he glimpsed wooden crates and bales painted with strange markings. Maria noted his interest and remarked, 'Those have come from China. They arrive in Acapulco with the Manila galleon, and are on their way farther south to customers in Peru. The consulado of Paita arranges the distribution.' She saw his puzzlement and explained, 'The consulado is the guild of merchants. They have the money and the influence if a ransom is demanded for Dona Juana.' But Hector was not thinking of a ransom. Maria's comment had reminded him of the maps and sailing directions he had been copying from Captain Lopez's navigation notes. If the captain had been trading as far north as Mexico to meet the incoming Manila galleon, his knowledge of the northern shores was likely to be very accurate.

By now word had spread that the fishermen were bringing in a pirate. As the little group walked farther into Paita, more and more people appeared on the streets, and they were in an ugly mood. Women as well as men began to shout insults and make threatening gestures. There were cries of 'Hang him but disembowel him first!', 'Hand him over to us. Let us deal with him', and soon the onlookers were throwing lumps of dung and dirt and the occasional stone. Their aim was poor and, as often as not, the missiles hit the escorting soldiers. But occasionally Hector had to duck. He was shocked by the hostility of the crowd. Their hatred was like a physical force.

To her credit, Maria did not falter. She walked beside him, level with the crowd, and did not flinch when she too was hit by mis-thrown projectiles.

Eventually they arrived at the Plaza Mayor. Here a number of sentries were guarding the municipal buildings which stood across from the church, and they joined the escort guards in holding back the angry crowd. Hector, Maria and the sergeant hurried up a flight of steps and into the town hall, the angry jeers of the mob following them. After the gauntlet of their arrival it was a relief to be away from the hysteria of the crowd, waiting in an antechamber while a minor official went to find Dona Juana's husband. He returned to say that the judge was at a meeting with the cabildo, the city council, and could not be disturbed. But the Alcalde was expected to preside over a session of the Criminal Court later that day, and it might be possible for him to interview Hector while the Court was in recess. In the meantime, the official suggested, Maria should go to her lodgings at the Alcalde's house where she might like to rest. The official himself would take responsibility for looking after Hector until the judge was free to speak with him.

The moment that Maria was gone, the sergeant seized Hector roughly by the shoulder and bundled him along a corridor and down a short flight of steps. The official, who had been scurrying along behind making approving noises, produced a key to a heavy iron-bound door, unlocked it, and Hector was flung inside. He found himself in a small stone cell furnished with nothing but mouldy straw and a bench. The only light came through a small window, little more than a slit, high in the opposite wall. Behind him the door slammed shut, and he was left in half-darkness.

He made his way to the bench and sat down, gagging at the stench of urine from the damp straw. Evidently he had been confined in the holding cell for the Criminal Court, and he doubted that anyone would take the trouble to bring him anything to eat or drink. The malice and loathing shown towards him was so intense and venomous that he wondered if Bartholomew Sharpe had made a miscalculation. There would be no exchange of Dona Juana and the *Santo Rosario* because the Alcalde would never negotiate. Instead Hector would be taken out of the cell, tried and executed for piracy. If the mob did not get to him first.

*

HIS INTERVIEW with Dona Juana's husband in mid afternoon got off to a disastrous start. He was led to what appeared to be a private chamber behind the courtroom. There the Alcalde sat waiting behind a massive desk. Clearly he had interrupted his court session for he was wearing his red and gold sash of office over a doublet of charcoal velvet. Hector, dishevelled and unwashed, was made to stand before him while the sergeant who had brought him up from the cell stood so close behind his right shoulder that Hector could hear his breathing. For several moments the Alcalde sat scowling at his visitor and not saying a word. Dona Juana's husband was a hulking, heavy-set man who affected an old-fashioned appearance. His beard was carefully shaped to join thick dark mustaches extending across his cheeks in a downsweep that accentuated the fleshy, peevish mouth and bushy, scowling eyebrows. Hector wondered if such an intimidating appearance was genuine or merely an artificial pose to frighten those who appeared in court before him. But the Alcalde's opening remark left little doubt that his bad temper was real.

'Who do you represent?' he asked rudely. 'Your last captain's head was paraded around Arica on a pole.' Hector supposed that he was referring to Watling whose body they'd had to leave behind.

'I am here on behalf of Captain Bartholomew Sharpe and his company,' Hector began. 'I have been sent to arrange terms for the release of the *Santo Rosario* and Dona Juana who is, I believe, your wife.'

Immediately the Alcalde bridled. 'The identity of the passengers is of no immediate concern. What is evident is that you are guilty of piracy in seizing the vessel.'

'With respect, your excellency. I have come here in good faith to arrange the return of the vessel, her passengers and crew, unharmed.'

'Unharmed!' The Alcalde thrust his head forward angrily. 'I am told that Captain Lopez was shot down, killed in cold blood.'

'He mistook our vessel's approach as aggressive,' said Hector. Maria must have already been interviewed.

'He was callously murdered, and the crime will be punished,' the Alcalde retorted.

'If it pleases your honour,' Hector said carefully, 'I should like to state the message that I was charged to deliver.'

'Then do so!' The Alcalde leaned back in his chair and began to drum thick stubby fingers on the desk.

'Captain Sharpe is willing to deliver up the *Santo Rosario*, her illustrious passenger and crew in exchange for the services of a pilot competent to navigate his vessel southward, and a store of seagoing supplies.'

Hector paused, allowing the Alcalde a moment in which to appreciate that he was being offered a way of ridding himself of the pirate menace.

'If His Excellency agrees to these terms, I have been instructed to guide the pilot to the place where the exchange will take place. Captain Sharpe gives his word that the lady, Dona Juana, will be released unharmed. Afterwards he and his vessel will depart the South Sea.'

The Alcalde looked at Hector with pure scorn. 'What happens to your bandit comrades is not for me to decide. Were that so, I would see to it that Captain Sharpe and all his crew hang from the mastheads of our Armada del Sur. Unfortunately there has to be a due process.' He looked towards the sergeant. 'Take him away, and keep him locked up until further notice.'

The sergeant grasped Hector by the arm and was about to wheel him about. There was just enough time for the young man to add, 'With respect, Your Excellency. Captain Sharpe instructed me to say that if I do not return within a week, he will steer south, without a pilot, and take Señora Juana with him.'

The Alcalde slammed his hand down on the desk. 'Not another word!' he barked.

*

BACK IN his cell, Hector watched the daylight fade through the small window in the wall, and thought of how much he depended on Maria. Only her evidence would persuade the Alcalde and his fellow officials that Dona Juana had not been harmed. Also, they were sure to question her about everything she had seen while a prisoner. They would want to know about *Trinity*, her condition and armament, the morale and number of her crew, and whether Bartholomew Sharpe was capable of carrying out his threat and sailing off if his seven-day deadline was not met, and if he could be trusted to honour an exchange. For a second time in twenty-four hours Hector found himself reassessing Maria's qualities. On the fishing boat she had shown herself to be thoughtful and level-headed, and in the presence of the angry crowd she had kept cool. He told himself that she would not allow herself to be browbeaten by the Alcalde into giving false evidence or understating her case. And knowing her affection for Dona Juana, he was sure that Maria would do everything in her power to convince the Alcalde that he should agree to an exchange.

With that reassuring thought Hector stretched himself out on the narrow bench and closed his eyes. The image that once again floated into his mind just before he fell asleep was of Maria on the fishing boat earlier that morning as she stood up and faced into the wind. She had looked so composed and at ease. He allowed himself a moment's optimism which had nothing to do with his mission to the Alcalde: he speculated that perhaps Maria had been pleased to be starting the day in his company.

A voice speaking English woke him. For a moment he thought he was back on *Trinity*. Then the rancid smell of mouldering straw rather than Stockholm tar reminded him that he was in a cell. 'Well, Lynch, haven't seen you since Arica,' said the voice again. Hector swung his legs off the bench and sat up, conscious that he was very hungry, also that he was sore and stiff from sleeping on the hard surface of the bench.

The door to the cell stood open. Leaning against the jamb was a figure that stirred a hazy, vaguely disagreeable memory. Even seen against the light it was evident that the man in the doorway was well turned out. He was dressed in knee breeches and good stockings and a well-tailored dark blue vest with gilt buttons over a fresh white shirt. He wore expensive-looking buckled shoes and had tied his hair back in a neat queue. Everything about him spoke of prosperity and the contentment of a man of means. It took Hector, still slightly groggy, a moment to identify his visitor. He was one of *Trinity*'s surgeons whom he had last seen blind drunk in the squalor of the desecrated church in Arica. Then the man had scarcely been able to stand, his speech slurred with alcohol, and he had been wearing soiled and sea-stained rags. Now it was as if he had just emerged freshly washed and shaved from a barber shop, ready to take a stroll through a fashionable part of town.

The surgeon's name, Hector now remembered, was James Fawcett.

'I hear that conniving swindler Sharpe is back in command, and that he intends to run for home with his tail between his legs. But I doubt he'll make it with his skin intact,' Fawcett observed. His tone was casual, almost smug.

Hector's mind was in a whirl. He looked searchingly at his visitor. Fawcett was in his late thirties, a lantern-jawed raw-boned man whom Hector remembered from as far back as Golden Island when Fawcett had gone ashore with Cook's company. On the march through the jungle Fawcett had struck up a friendship with Hector's own mentor, Basil Smeeton. The two had often compared medical notes and talked together of the new techniques in surgery. When Smeeton turned back after the disappointment of Santa Maria and its phantom gold mine, Fawcett had borrowed some scalpels from Smeeton and had continued on with the expedition. Later Hector had seen him firing a musket against the Spanish flotilla in the sea battle before Panama. So it was all the more extraordinary that Fawcett should now be loafing about a Spanish courthouse looking like a respectable member of Paita's professional community. It would have been more understandable if he had been half-naked, shackled in chains and awaiting the garotte.

'Don't look so surprised, Lynch. The last time we met I seem to remember telling you that people like ourselves are too valuable to be slaughtered uselessly.'

Hector swallowed. His throat was dry. 'Could you ask someone to bring me some water to drink, and perhaps a little food. I haven't eaten for the past thirty-six hours,' he said.

'Of course.' Fawcett spoke over his shoulder to someone in the corridor behind him. His Spanish was slow but accurate. Then he turned back to face the young man.

'There's no need for you to continue to be cooped up in this disgusting hole. The Alcalde can arrange for you to be transferred to more comfortable accommodation. I've persuaded him that you are halfway to having a full medical qualification. Smeeton always said that you showed great promise, and there's such a shortage of surgeons here that you'll be able to set up your own practice almost anywhere in Peru even without formal credentials.'

Hector was scarcely listening, his attention distracted by his recollection of what had happened in the church at Arica, the charnel house of the makeshift hospital, the wounded men lying groaning on the flagstones of the church floor.

'What about the other surgeon? The other man who was meant to be taking care of the wounded? What's happened to him?'

Fawcett gave a wolfish smile. 'Same as me. He's got a very lucrative medical practice. Not here in Paita but farther along the coast in Callao. Doing very well I'm told. Even found himself a wife, the handsome widow of a peninsular as they call those who were born in Spain. I doubt that he'll ever go back to life at sea.'

'What about the others? The wounded men in the church in Arica? What happened to them?'

Fawcett gave a casual shrug. 'The Spaniards knocked them all on the head. Saved a lot of trouble. Not many of them would have survived their wounds, and those who did would have been tried and executed.'

Hector felt sick to the stomach. Fawcett appeared utterly indifferent to the massacre of the wounded.

'The Alcalde said something about Watling's head being carried around the town on a pole.'

'The worthy citizens of Arica made a real fiesta of the affair. Dancing in the streets, bonfires, self-congratulatory letters to the Viceroy and the Court in Madrid saying how they had vanquished the pirates. Of course they exaggerated the number of the attacking force. Said it was four times more numerous than it really was.'

The mention of bonfires had jogged Hector's memory. 'After we evacuated Arica, the Spaniards sent up two columns of white smoke, the agreed signal to our boats. We thought someone, maybe the quartermaster Duill, was tortured to reveal the signal. It nearly brought our boats into harbour and they would have been annihilated. What really happened?'

There was a slight hesitation before Fawcett replied, and Hector noted that the surgeon did not look at him directly as he gave his answer. 'I don't know how the Spaniards obtained the signal. I have no idea of Duill's fate. I didn't even see his corpse. He simply disappeared.'

At that moment a court usher appeared, carrying a large pitcher of water and some bread, dried fish and olives. Hector gratefully drank, then leaned forward and poured the rest of the flagon over his head, neck and shoulders. He felt better, though he wished he could find a water trough and wash himself properly. He sat up, stared at Fawcett and waited for him to broach the subject which, Hector had already guessed, was the real reason for his visit.

'Lynch, don't be in a hurry to judge me harshly. I came to the South Sea to get rich, to have my share of the wealth of this land. I have not altered that ambition. Instead I've decided to earn it honestly rather than take it at pistol point. I'm using my skills as a healer. I look after people who are ill with fever or have sickly children or need assistance in childbirth. Surely that's something to approve of?'

'So you are proposing that I do the same?'

'Why not? You could settle down here and have a very pleasant life. You speak the language fluently, and in a year or so you too could find a wife and maybe go on to raise a family in ease and comfort.'

For a moment the thought of Maria flashed into Hector's

mind, but he put it to one side. 'And to do this I have to betray Sharpe and the company?' He did not add that he thought this was what Fawcett had done at Arica.

'You owe Sharpe nothing. He would do the same in your position. He always looks after himself, first and last.'

'And the rest of the men on *Trinity*, what about them?'

'I realise you have friends on board. The striker Dan, and Jacques the Frenchman and big Jezreel. It's quite possible that Don Fernando, the Alcalde, will agree to their freedom in exchange for your cooperation.'

'My cooperation in what . . .' Hector prompted him.

'. . . in arranging some sort of ambush where *Trinity* might be lured into a trap and overwhelmed by Spanish cruisers.'

Hector stared down at the floor. Already he had made up his mind. It was the mention of Jezreel which had decided the matter for him. He recalled the day that Sharpe had tricked Jezreel into pistolling the innocent Spanish priest. Spanish prisoners had been exchanged or released from *Trinity* since then, and they would have carried the story of the atrocity back to the authorities. If Jezreel ever appeared before a Spanish tribunal, he would certainly be condemned to a painful death, even if Hector had pleaded on his behalf.

The young man raised his head and looked back at Fawcett still standing in the doorway. 'I prefer to carry out my mission,' he said quietly.

Fawcett looked unsurprised. 'I thought you would say that,' he said. 'I once said to Smeeton that you had the manner of someone who always took his own line even if it meant being out of step with everyone else. I'll tell Don Fernando of your decision. It's up to him and the council to decide what is to be done with you. And I'll ask the guards here to let you have a proper wash. You're beginning to get that prison stink.'

*

THE VETERAN sergeant and two soldiers came to fetch Hector in mid afternoon. Fawcett had kept his word for they took Hector out to a pump at the rear of the courthouse and stood by while he washed himself. Feeling cleaner but still very dishevelled, he was then brought into the same interview room as before. This time the Alcalde, Don Fernando, was not alone. An extra table had been set at right angles to his desk. Seated behind it was a thin-faced man with heavily lidded eyes and an austerely intellectual appearance emphasised by his high forehead and receding hairline. He wore a lawyer's black robes. A few sheets of blank paper and a pen lay on the table before him. Hector, looking around, saw no sign of any secretary or official clerk and this gave him a moment's hope. Whatever was going to be decided at this meeting was to be known to only a few. Even the sergeant and his escort had been told to leave the room.

One other man was present, someone whose weatherbeaten features Hector recognised at once. Seated beside the lawyer was Captain Francisco de Peralta whom he had last seen on the beach at La Serena.

'I believe you already know the Capitan del Navio. He is attending in an expert capacity,' began the Alcalde. His eyes flicked towards the black-robed lawyer. 'Don Ramiro is His Majesty's fiscal. As an attorney, he is here to represent the audiencia, the council.'

The man in the lawyer's robes acknowledged his introduction with the briefest of nods.

Already Hector had detected a subtle change in the Alcalde's manner. Don Fernando was not as openly aggressive as before. His hostility was still there, seething below the surface, but it was being kept in check.

The Alcalde addressed his opening remarks to the fiscal. 'This young man has brought a proposal from the leader of a pirate band operating in this area. You will already be familiar with some of the atrocities they have committed. Recently they captured the merchant ship *Santo Rosario*. The leader of the pirates offers to return the vessel, her passengers and surviving crew in exchange for naval stores and the services of a pilot who can assist the pirates in leaving our waters.'

The Alcalde lifted a sheet of parchment from the desk in front of him. 'This is a deposition made by a passenger on the *Santo Rosario*. It describes an unprovoked attack on the vessel, the butchery of her captain, and the capture and pillaging of the ship. It also states that the survivors of the assault are unhurt.'

'Can we be sure of the accuracy of the deposition?' asked the fiscal.

'I have arranged for the deponent to be available for questioning.' Raising his voice, the Alcalde called, 'Send in Dona Juana's companion.'

The door opened, and Maria stepped into the room. In that moment Hector's eager anticipation of seeing her again turned to disappointment. Maria had reverted to the person he remembered from the *Santo Rosario*. She was wearing a long, plain brown skirt with a matching bodice, and her hair was covered with a simple cotton kerchief. She was deferential and subdued, and she did not even look in his direction. Her face showed no expression as she walked forward and stopped a few paces in front of the Alcalde. The anticlimax was so great that Hector felt as if a chasm had suddenly opened beneath his feet and he had dropped into it.

'Señorita Maria,' the Alcalde began, 'Don Ramiro is an attorney for the audiencia. He wishes to question you about your statement concerning the seizure of the *Santo Rosario*.' He handed the sheet of paper across to the lawyer who took it and began to read aloud. Occasionally he looked up at Maria to make sure that she was paying attention.

Maria listened with her eyes fixed on the floor and her hands demurely clasped in front of her. Hector recalled that this was exactly how she had stood and looked when he saw her on the day he had gone onto the *Santo Rosario* with the boarding party. He even recollected how he had noticed on that day how small and neat her hands were. With a pang, he also remembered exactly how it had felt when she placed her hand on his shoulder and steadied herself as she climbed across the thwart of the little fishing boat.

The attorney continued with his dry, punctilious reading, pausing between the sentences. Despite his inner turmoil, Hector had to admire Maria's memory for detail and the accuracy of her testimony. She described *Trinity*'s slow, innocent-seeming approach in the wake of *Santo Rosario*, and the moment that Captain Lopez had become suspicious. She made no mention of the death of Lopez because, by the time he was shot, she and her mistress had been sent away to the safety of the locked cabin. Her description resumed at the point that she had heard the boarding party attempting to open the door of the cabin and she and Dona Juana had stepped out to confront Hector, Ringrose and the others.

The fiscal reached the end of his narration and looked up at Maria. 'You provided this deposition?' he asked.

'I did,' Maria answered. Her voice so low as to be barely audible.

'Is it accurate?'

'Yes.'

'And no violence was shown to your mistress or yourself, then or at any other time?'

'No.'

'Nothing was stolen or pillaged from you?'

'Dona Juana handed her jewellery and other valuables to the pirates before they made any demands. She wished to forestall any excuse for violence.'

'And that was all that was taken from you and your mistress during this piracy?'

'That is correct.'

The attorney placed the deposition on the table, picked up his pen, and made a note at the foot of the page.

'Señorita,' he said. 'You have heard your statement read out to this gathering and agreed to its authenticity. I would be grateful if you would sign it.'

Maria crossed to the table and, taking the pen held out to her by the fiscal, she signed the deposition. The lawyer set the document neatly on top of the other sheets of paper before him, squaring up the pile with his fingertips. There was something about that little gesture, its air of finality, that alerted Hector. It appeared that the attorney had made up his mind about something significant.

'I have no further questions,' said the lawyer.

'Maria, you may now leave,' said the Alcalde, his voice formal.

Hector watched the young woman walk to the door, and he tried to memorise the moment for he had a premonition that he might never see Maria again. Until she passed from view, he still hoped that Maria might perhaps glance in his direction. But she left the room without a backward glance.

'Capitan, do you have any observations to make?' The Alcalde's truculent voice broke into Hector's thoughts. The judge was looking towards Peralta.

The Spanish captain leaned back in his chair and surveyed Hector for several seconds before he spoke.

'Young man, when we met on the beach at La Serena I gave you a warning. I said that you and your piratical band would not be so lucky next time they came ashore. The events at Arica proved me correct. Only one thing drives your people – insatiable greed. Can you give me any reason why they can be trusted to honour any agreement we might make?'

'Captain Peralta,' Hector answered, standing a little straighter. 'I can give no guarantee. The decisions of our company are made by general vote. But I can say this – and with your seagoing experience you will know that I speak the truth – we have been in the South Sea now for well over a year. Many of the men are looking forward to returning to their homes. I believe that they are in a majority.'

'And what about Dona Juana? We have been told that she is unharmed and that she cooperated in the matter of handing over her valuables. If we agree to the exchange, we expect her to continue to be treated with the respect due to a lady of her quality.'

'Captain Sharpe has already made her welfare a priority,' Hector assured him.

Peralta looked towards the Alcalde, and Hector had the feeling that an unspoken message had passed between them when Peralta continued.

'Your Excellency, I recommend that we agree to an exchange but make sure of Dona Juana's well-being.'

'How can that be done?'

'Send this young man back to his ship. Let him take the pilot with him. That will be the first part of our bargain. The second part will be honoured only after the pirates have brought the *Santo Rosario* within range of our shore cannon. We will send out an inspection party and if they find the lady onboard and unharmed, we will despatch a supply boat with the stores they require.'

'Isn't that taking a risk? Surely the pirates will sail away the moment they have a pilot, and not wait for the stores.'

'Speaking as a seaman, I would say that the intruders' vessel needs a thorough refit. The ship has been operating in hostile waters for so long that her rig will be worn out. There will be an acute shortage of rope and canvas. If her crew are contemplating a voyage out of the South Sea, those stores could mean the difference between foundering and survival.'

'Thank you for your contribution, Capitan,' said the Alcalde, and once again Hector had the feeling that something was left unsaid. 'I would be obliged if you could select a suitable pilot and also draw up a list of appropriate ship's stores. Enough to encourage the pirates to leave our waters, but no more. If the fiscal has no objection, I will make an order for the material to be released from the royal dockyard without delay. I wish to be rid of these bandits, and I am sure that Dona Juana does not want to spend a moment longer in their company.'

*

THE PILOT provided by Captain Peralta turned out to be a small, wiry man whose expression of distaste on meeting Hector made his feelings obvious.

'I hope your ship handles well in bad weather?' he grumbled as he stepped aboard the fishing boat waiting at the quay. It was the same vessel that had brought Hector and Maria ashore.

'*Trinity*'s crew know their business,' Hector replied. He had been half-hoping that Maria would be sent to rejoin her mistress. But the pilot had arrived alone.

'They'll need to,' retorted the little man waspishly. 'Where we're going the weather turns nasty very quickly.'

'You must be very familiar with that part of the coast,' said Hector, anxious to please.

'Enough to know that I wouldn't chose to go there if I had a choice in the matter.'

'I imagine the Alcalde can be persuasive.'

'Someone tipped him off that my last ship had a slimy waterline when we came into harbour.'

'What's a slimy waterline got to do with it?'

'It meant that she was riding higher than when we left our last official port of call. I was accused of stopping on the way to Paita and offloading cargo without paying import duty.'

'And had you?'

The pilot shot Hector a venomous glance. 'What do you think? The captain and the owner were both peninsulares, good Spaniards, so no one is ever going to charge them with smuggling, nor accuse the local consulado who sell on the contraband. On the other hand I am a foreigner. So I am disposable.'

'I thought I detected a foreign accent,' said Hector.

'I'm originally from Greece. In the merchant service hereabouts you'll find Portuguese, Corsicans, Genoese, Venetians, men from all over. Local-born lads prefer to stay ashore and run plantations with Indian labourers. It's an easier life than tramping up and down the coast in merchant tubs.'

'But at least everyone respects a pilot.'

The Greek gave a cynical laugh. 'I'm only half a pilot. The Alcalde and his sort fear that we'll gang up and run for home and take our knowledge with us. So the rules say that I can never serve aboard a ship whose captain is also a foreigner.'

'But now you'll be aboard *Trinity* and that's a foreign ship.'

'Even then my knowledge won't be of much use. I only know the coast south of here, and most of that is a barren, godforsaken land. That's about as much as this addled head can hold at any one time.' The Greek smiled sourly and tapped his brow.

'So you don't have any charts?'

The Greek bared his teeth at Hector in astonishment. 'Charts! If the Alcalde got to learn that I was making charts, or even possessed one, I would prefer to take my punishment as a smuggler. No one except a handful of the most trusted captains are allowed to keep a derotero and they must be Spaniards, like Captain Lopez of the *Santo Rosario*, God rest his soul.'

His remark reminded Hector of the glance that had passed between the Alcalde and Captain Peralta. It dawned on him now that the real reason why they had agreed to an exchange was the need to recover Captain Lopez's folder of navigation notes and sketches. All their talk about Dona Juana's well-being had been a sham. They had insisted that she was treated with respect because then no one would search her belongings and find the derotero.

Hector groaned inwardly. If he had not been so distracted by Maria, he would have worked this out for himself. Then an even more dispiriting thought occurred: the only person who could have told the Alcalde about the hidden derotero was Maria.

Looking back towards Paita's church tower, Hector cursed himself for being a fool. He had allowed himself to be misled. But what made his chagrin even more painful was that he still could not stop thinking about Maria.

SEVENTEEN

'YOU WEREN'T exactly honest with her either,' Dan bluntly pointed out when Hector told him of Maria's deception. 'Neither she nor Dona Juana know that we've made a copy of the derotero. That was done behind their backs.'

It was a breezy afternoon with a scattering of high cloud and *Trinity* was beating out to sea under plain sail. Hector had come back aboard three days earlier and, as arranged with the Alcalde, Dona Juana and the *Santo Rosario* had been left behind at Paita in exchange for the stores from Paita's royal dockyard. The supply of rope, canvas, tallow and tar meant that *Trinity* could be made fit for a long voyage, and as none of the crew relished the prospect of sailing back to Panama and returning through the jungle to the Caribbean, it had been decided to leave the Pacific by sailing south, all the way around the tip of South America.

'Do you think our pilot knows what he's doing? He seems more interested in gambling than in making sure we are heading the right way,' asked Dan dubiously. He was watching the Greek, whose name was Sidias. After telling the helmsman his course, he had produced a tavil board and started a game of backgammon against the quartermaster. Now they were quarrelling as to how the game should be played. Sidias was insisting that they follow the Greek rules, as they were more ancient.

'No harm in following his advice, at least for now,' Hector assured the Miskito. 'He says there's a strong adverse current along the coast and we need to be at least a hundred miles offshore before we turn south. Sidias claims that, by staying well out to sea, we'll trim weeks off our passage.'

'Is he proposing to take us through the Passage or around the Cape?'

'He hasn't said,' Hector answered.

'Not much use as a pilot then,' sniffed Jacques who had walked over to join them. He lowered his voice. 'Will those navigation notes you copied be of any use when we are trying to find the Passage?'

'I can't be sure. We've never put any of them to the test.'

'If Captain Lopez's navigation notes were so precious, I don't understand why Dona Juana did not simply get rid of them overboard. She could have dropped the folder out of the stern window at any time,' said Dan.

'You don't know how those aristocratic women think,' Jacques told him. 'Dona Juana might have known the value of the folder and wanted to make sure it got back into Spanish hands. But more likely she took a delight in believing that she was making fools of a group of slow-witted mariners. It was a game for her, to demonstrate her superiority.'

He fell silent as someone behind them coughed. It was Basil Ringrose who had just appeared on deck, carrying a backstaff and notebook. He looked ill, his skin waxy and pale, eyes bloodshot, and he had difficulty in breathing. Many of the crew believed that he was still suffering from taking shelter under a manzanilla tree on a night he had spent ashore. There had been a shower of rain in the night and he had woken up with his skin covered in red spots from the poisonous drips which had sprinkled on him while he slept. The spots and their burning sensation had long since faded, but Ringrose remained sickly. He suffered from frequent headaches and bouts of near-blindness.

Ringrose reached out and grasped a weather shroud for support as another fit of violent coughing racked him.

Dan spoke up. 'I was just asking Hector if we would be better going around the Cape or through the Passage.'

'The Passage would be my choice,' Ringrose answered huskily. 'Provided we can find the entrance. The coast is likely to be scattered with islands and reefs. We could finish up smashed to pieces.'

'Then why not try for the Cape?'

'Because no English vessel has ever gone that way. That's something our captain failed to mention when he suggested we should sail our way out of the South Sea. The Spaniards and the Dutch have gone round the Cape, but no other nation as far as is known. Even Drake himself preferred the Passage. There are ice islands down there.' He hawked, turned his head and spat a gob of phlegm over the rail. 'Anyway, that's a much longer way. I doubt we'd be back in home waters before Christmas. And who knows what sort of reception we will receive.'

'Couldn't be worse than what the Spaniards will do to us if we stay around here,' said Jacques.

Ringrose treated him to a sardonic smile. 'You forget that we are the rump of an irregular expedition. Captain Sharpe and his friends left Jamaica without so much as by-your-leave to the governor. Not one of our leaders carried a commission to go raiding the Main. That makes us all pirates, if the authorities choose to think so.'

'But Sir Henry Morgan never obtained prior permission when he attacked Panama, and he finished up with a knight-hood,' Hector objected.

'He brought back so much plunder that he was too wealthy to be prosecuted. By contrast, what have we got to show for our efforts? A few hundred pieces of eight for every man? That's not enough to buy our way out of trouble. Besides, we don't have Morgan's connections with the rich and powerful.'

There was a short silence, then Ringrose was speaking again. 'In the time we've been gone from Jamaica, anything can have happened. A new king on the throne, a different governor, wars declared and peace treaties signed. We've no idea of what might have changed, and how that will affect our return. We'll not find out until we get there.' He glanced up at the sky. 'Sun's close to its zenith, Hector.'

Hector walked aft with him to where Sidias was sitting cross-legged on the deck, still absorbed in his game of backgammon. He did not even glance up as their shadows passed over him. Ringrose took the noon sight and wrote down the reading. Hector noticed that his hand was shaking.

'How long do you think it is before we reach the mouth of the Passage?' Ringrose said, speaking loudly so that Sidias could no longer ignore him.

The Greek looked up grudgingly. He wrinkled his brow as if in deep thought before announcing, 'Five or six weeks.' Then he turned his attention back to the tavil board and ostentatiously moved one of the counters, making it clear that he had no interest in further conversation.

*

SIX WEEKS out from Paita, Sidias declared it was time to steer back towards the land and Sharpe followed his advice. As if to endorse the decision, the wind shifted into the ideal quarter, south-west, and with a fresh gale on the beam *Trinity* fairly tore along. The mood on the ship quickly became light-hearted and expectant. For some time past there had been a drop in the temperature of the air, and the men guessed that they were now far enough south to be in the region of the Passage. They acted with a careless exuberance as if to celebrate the final leg of their voyage. Hidden stocks of brandy and rum were broached, and several of the crew were fuddled, staggering and tripping as they made their way about the deck. Hector, however, was increasingly uneasy. He and Ringrose had been using dead reckoning to fix the ship's position. From time to time the two of them had disagreed on progress, the number of miles sailed, and whether or not there had been an ocean current taking them off track. On each occasion Hector had deferred to the more experienced man, partly because Ringrose's illness had made him argumentative and tetchy. Only the readings from the backstaff could be relied on, and they placed the vessel at 50 degrees south. But that was no indication of how close they were to land, and Hector had long ago decided that Sidias was worse than useless. The Greek was a gambler by nature, and would trust to luck that they would make a safe arrival on the coast. Whenever asked how soon they would raise the land, Sidias was evasive. His job, he always answered, was to identify the landfall, then indicate which way the ship should go. The Greek was so aloof that Hector felt obliged to seek him out that evening and ask if he was not concerned about how he would get back to Paita. In reply the Greek gave a dismissive shrug. 'What makes you think I want to leave this ship? There's no reason for me to return to Paita.'

'But you told me that the Alcalde forced you to become our pilot.'

'And he will make my life miserable once again if ever I return there. So I prefer to stay with this company.'

Taken aback by the Greek's self-regard, Hector went to join his friends. It was too chilly at night to sleep on deck, and they had slung hammocks in the aft end of the hold. Groping his way through the semi-darkness, he found Jezreel and Jacques already sound asleep. Only Dan was awake and when Hector told him of his concerns about Sidias' competence, Dan advised him not to fret. Perhaps in the morning they would have a chance to look through the notes copied from Lopez's derotero and see if they would be useful when they eventually made a landfall. In the meantime there was nothing to be done, and Hector should get some rest. But Hector was unable to sleep. He lay in his hammock, listening to the swirl of water along the hull and the creaking and working of the ship as *Trinity* forced her way through the sea.

Hector must have dozed off, for he came sharply awake to the sound of roars of panic. They came from directly above him, from the quarterdeck, and were loud enough to be heard above the sound of the waves crashing against the wooden hull. *Trinity* was heaving and pitching awkwardly, and water was surging back and forth across the bilge. The wind had increased in strength. In the pitch dark Hector rolled out of his hammock and felt for his sea coat. All around him were the noises of men scrambling out of their hammocks, asking questions, wondering what was happening. The shouts came again, more urgent now. He heard the words 'Cliffs! Land ahead!'

Clambering up the companion ladder and onto the quarterdeck, he came upon a scene of confusion. A sliver of moon rode a sky streaked with skeins of high, thin cloud. There was just enough light to show men frantically hauling on ropes, scrambling to reduce sail, and when he looked aft, the figure of Bartholomew Sharpe beside the helm.

'White water close on the port bow!' came a terror-stricken shout from the bows.

'Get the topsails off! Quick now!' bellowed Sharpe. He was half-dressed and must have run out from his cabin. A high-pitched squealing, frenzied and unearthly, set Hector's teeth on edge. For a moment he froze. Then he remembered that among the stores loaded at Paita had been a half-grown sow. The animal was being kept as a Christmas feast. She had sensed the mood of terror on board and was squealing in fright.

Sharpe caught sight of Hector and beckoned him over with furious gestures. 'That cursed numbskull of a pilot!' he shouted above the roar of the wind. 'We're entangled among rocks!'

Looking forward over the bowsprit, Hector caught a glimpse of something which showed white for a brief moment. Perhaps a hundred paces ahead, it was low down and above it loomed what seemed to be a darker shape though he could not be sure. Even with his limited experience he half-recognised waves beating against the foot of a cliff. *Trinity* answered the helm and began to turn away from the danger directly ahead, but almost immediately there was another cry of alarm, this time from his right. A sailor was pointing out into the darkness and there, not more than fifty yards away, was another eruption of white foam. This time he was sure. It was water breaking over a reef.

Sharpe was shouting again, even more angry. 'We've been driven into a skerry. I need sober lookouts, not tosspots. Lynch! Get up there into the foretop and sing out if you see a danger. Take your friend, the striker, with you. He sees things when others can't.'

Hector ran to find Dan and together they scrambled up the shrouds and onto the small platform of the foretop. The wind was strengthening still further, and on their exposed perch they peered forward, trying to see into the darkness. Below their legs the forecourse still bellied out, providing steerage way for the helmsmen. From farther aft came the shouts of men taking in the mainsail, urgently reducing the speed of the ship.

'How much longer until first light?' Hector yelled, trying to keep the alarm out of his voice. He could see almost nothing in the murk, only vague and indistinct shapes, some darker than others. It was impossible to judge how far away they were.

'Maybe an hour,' Dan answered. 'There! A reef or a small island. We're coming too close.'

Hector turned and shouted out the information. Someone down on deck must have heard him for he saw the foreshortened figure of a man running to the helm and relaying the message, then a group of men hastily sheeting in the triangular mizzen sail to assist the action of the rudder in turning the ship. *Trinity* changed direction, clawing up into the wind.

'More rocks, by that patch of foam,' announced Dan. This time he was pointing to starboard.

Hector cried out another warning and, standing up on the platform, wrapped one arm around the foretopmast. With the other arm he pointed which way *Trinity* should go. At that instant a cloud passed across the moon, and there was complete darkness. All of a sudden he was completely disoriented, the ship swayed beneath his feet, the motion magnified by his height above the deck, and he felt dizzy. For one heart-stopping moment his grip on the mast slipped, and he tottered, feeling that he was about to fall. He had a sudden, awful vision of smashing down onto the deck or, worse, landing in the sea unnoticed and being left behind in the wake of the vessel. Hurriedly he clamped his other arm around the mast, clutching it to his chest in a fierce grip, and slithered down to a sitting position. Within a minute the cloud had passed, and there was enough moonlight to see his surroundings. Dan seemed not to have noticed his brief horror, but Hector could feel his clothes clammy with cold sweat.

For an hour or more the two of them conned the ship from the foremast as *Trinity* swerved and sidled her way past one danger and then the next. Gradually the sky began to lighten and, very slowly, the extent of their predicament became clear.

Ahead stretched an iron-bound coast, a vista of grey and black cliffs and headlands which extended in both directions far into the distance. Behind the cliffs rose ridges of bare rock which became the slopes and screes of a coastal mountain range whose jagged crest was lightly dusted with snow. Nowhere was there anything to relieve the impression of monotonous desolation except an occasional clump of dark trees growing in sheltered folds of the austere landscape. Closer to hand were the small offshore islands and reefs which had so nearly destroyed the ship in the darkness and still menaced her. Here the surface of the sea sporadically exploded in warning spouts of spray or heaved and sank in sudden upwellings which warned of submerged rocks and shoals. Even the channels between the islands were forbidding. In them the water moved strangely, sometimes streaked with foam, at other times with the deep, blue-black slickness of a powerful current.

'Hang on!' said Dan. He had seen the telltale white flurry of a squall which had suddenly ripped up the surface of the sea and was now racing towards them. Hector braced himself. *Trinity* abruptly heeled under the force of the wind. From below them came the creaking sound of the foresail spar as it took the strain and then the sudden crack of something breaking. The squall was strong enough to lift a vaporous whirl of fine spray and send it over the ship, darkening her timbers and leaving a slick on the deck. Hector felt the moisture settle on his face and trickle down inside his collar.

A hail from the deck made him look down. Sharpe was beckoning to him, ordering him to return to near the helm. He made his way carefully down the shrouds, gripping tightly in case another squall struck, and reached the poop deck. Sharpe was no longer in a towering rage but seething with subdued anger. Beside him Sidias looked shamefaced, clearly ill at ease.

'Lynch, this idiot seems to have lost his command of English,' snarled Sharpe. 'Tell him that I want some sensible advice, not pretence and falsehood. Ask him in a language he understands what he recommends, which way we go.'

Speaking in Spanish, Hector repeated the question. But he knew already that the pilot had been feigning incomprehension.

'I don't know,' the Greek confessed, avoiding Hector's gaze. 'I have no knowledge of this part of the coast. It is strange to me. I have never been here before.'

'Is there nothing you recognise?'

'Nothing,' Sidias shook his head.

'What about the tides?'

Sidias nodded towards a nearby island. 'Judge for yourself. That line of the weeds indicates a rise and fall of at least ten or twelve feet and that would be normal for the parts of the coast I am familiar with.'

Hector relayed the information to Sharpe who glowered at the pilot. 'What about an anchorage or a harbour? Ask him that.'

Again the pilot could only speculate. He supposed there would be bays or inlets where a ship might find shelter, but anchoring was sure to be difficult. The drop-off from the land was usually so abrupt that an anchor seldom reached to the seabed before its cable ran out.

'We follow along the coast until we find shelter,' Sharpe decided. He had to raise his voice above the moan of the wind. 'God grant that we can scrape through.'

It was a wild, intimidating ride. Every member of *Trinity*'s crew was now up on deck, either spread along the rails or in the shrouds. Even the drunkards had sobered up. They knew the danger, the strain showing on their faces as they watched the reefs slide by. Sometimes their vessel came so close to disaster that her hull brushed fronds of seaweed writhing in the backwash of the swells. Only the skill of the helmsmen, responding to every shift of the current or change in the strength and direction of the wind, kept their ship from being driven into the turmoil of waves which broke and thundered against the cliffs. Finally, after nearly an hour of this unnerving progress, they came level with an entrance to a narrow bay. 'Turn in! And stand by to lower the pinnace,' Sharpe ordered. He had noted the area of calm water behind a low promontory. Here a skilfully handled ship might find shelter and lie at rest. More crucially, a great solitary tree stood on the point of land, only a few paces from the water's edge. *Trinity* sidled in and the crew began to clew up the foresail. As the vessel slowed, the pinnace splashed down in the water, and a dozen men rowed furiously for the land, towing the main cable behind their boat. They scrambled up the beach, made fast the cable around the tree, and *Trinity* gathered sternway. She fell back until the heavy rope came taut, and the ship slowed to a halt, tethered to the land and safe.

A sense of relief spread throughout the ship. Men thumped one another on the back in celebration. Some climbed into the rigging and out along the foremast yard and began to furl the sails. Sharpe was halfway back to his cabin when a last great gust of wind came raging over the promontory and struck the ship. Under the impact *Trinity* reared back like a startled mare against her bridle. The main cable sprang from the surface, water spraying from the strands of rope as they took the strain, and when the full force of the wind drove upon her, there was a loud, rending crack. The great tree holding the ship came toppling down, the ancient roots giving up their hold. *Trinity*, her sails furled, was helpless. The gust drove her backwards across the small bay and, with an impact that shuddered the length of her keel, she struck stern first upon the shingle beach. Above the shriek of the wind, every man aboard heard the sound as her rudder sheered. The vessel was crippled.

*

FOR THREE WEEKS the wounded *Trinity* lay in the bay. A web of ropes fastened to boulders and posts driven into the shingle held her steady against the rise and fall of the tides while the carpenters worked to fashion and fit a new rudder. The great gust had been the gale's final stroke, and the wind was never again so fierce. Instead the weather was continually cold, damp and oppressive. Thick cloud clamped down, obscuring the mountains, so that the leaden sky blended with the slate-grey landscape. Those men who were not working on the repairs reverted to their endless games of cards and dice or prowled the beach and prised mussels off the rocks. They shot penguins to boil and roast. The flesh was quite palatable, being as dark as venison though oily. Dan volunteered to explore inland and came back to report no sign whatever of human life. The interior was too harsh and craggy to support settlement. He claimed to have come across unknown wild plants which might prove useful additions to the near-empty medicine chest, but this was only an excuse so that he and Hector could go ashore. They took with them the bamboo tube containing their copies of Captain Lopez's navigation notes.

Safely out of sight of the ship, they tried to make some sense of their notes, smoothing out the pages and putting them in order.

'I think this sheet shows the coast and the approaches to the Passage,' said Hector. He placed a page on the flat surface of a boulder and weighed the corners down with pebbles. 'But it has very little detail. The mountain range is shown as extending all along the coast, and there are at least two dozen islands marked. But they all look much the same. We could be anywhere.'

Dan ran his finger down the page. 'See here, the entrance to the Passage is clearly shown.'

Hector brightened. 'If our notes are accurate – and Captain Lopez's original is right – I'm confident that I could find the Passage. All we need to know is our latitude.'

Dan rubbed his chin. 'What if there's an overcast sky like these past few days and you cannot take a backstaff reading? I doubt very much that the crew will want to risk this coast again. They've had a bad fright already.'

Hector was about to reassure his friend that even a glimpse of the sun would be enough, when Dan added, 'And if we suddenly announce to the crew that we have these navigation notes, we'll bring further trouble on ourselves. They will want to know why we did not say so before.'

'Then we go around the Cape and not through the Passage, and say not a word to anyone about Captain Lopez's notes,' Hector answered. 'Those more general maps we took out of the *Santo Rosario* are good enough to get us around the Cape if we go to fifty-eight degrees and then turn east. After that, we should come into the Atlantic.'

He rolled up the papers and slid them back into the tube.

'Come on, Dan. No one wants to stay a moment longer in this dreary place.'

*

So it turned out. *Trinity*, with her rudder repaired and rerigged with the cordage from Paita, took advantage of an offshore breeze and threaded her way through the skerries until she reached the open ocean. Shortly after, she turned south and sailed into waters known to her crew only from hearsay. There they came upon sights that confirmed the stories they had heard – immense blocks of blue-white ice, the size of small islands and drifting on the current, whales of monstrous size, and birds who followed the ship day after day, gliding on wings whose span exceeded the width of even Jezreel's outstretched arms. All this time the weather remained kind, and *Trinity* entered the Atlantic without enduring a single storm. Northwards next, the sea miles rolling by, the sun higher each day, and the temperature increasing. With no sight of land or other ship, *Trinity* might have been the only vessel on the ocean. To pass the time, the men reverted yet again to their favourite pastime – gambling. It was as if nothing had changed since the South Sea. Those who gambled lost most of their plunder to Captain Sharpe who, fearful of their resentment, took to sleeping with a loaded pistol beside him. Only Sidias was his rival for winnings. The Greek's cunning at backgammon meant he swept up most of what the captain missed.

Christmas came and Paita's sow was slaughtered and eaten under a clear blue sky while waiting for the fickle doldrum winds. By that time the men were so anxious for the voyage to end that they clustered around Hector and Ringrose as they took each midday sight, demanding to know how much progress had been made. Ringrose's health had improved with the warmer weather, and he had regained his usual cheerful manner. It was he who finally declared that they must make their landfall very soon. The following dawn a low, green island on the horizon was recognisable as Barbados, though the unwelcome sight of an English man-of-war in the offing led to a hastily called general council. It was decided to find a more discreet place in which to dispose their booty, and on the last day of January *Trinity* dropped anchor in a deep and deserted inlet on the rocky coast of Antigua. They had completed eighty days at sea.

'No one is to go ashore until I've had a chance to learn our situation,' warned Sharpe for perhaps the twentieth time. The crew were gazing impatiently at a small stone jetty and a handful of whitewashed houses nestled in the farthest curve of the bay. 'If the governor receives us, there'll be time enough for every man to enjoy his rewards. If he's hostile, then we go elsewhere.' He turned towards Hector. 'Lynch, you come with me. You look more presentable than most.'

Together the two men clambered down into the cockboat and were rowed towards the jetty. Seated beside Sharpe on the after thwart, Hector found himself recalling the last time he had gone ashore with a buccaneer captain so warily. That had been with Captain Coxon more than two years earlier and so much had happened since then: his own flight from Port Royal, the hurricane among the logwood cutters of Campeachy, the steamy march across the isthmus and the near-fatal charge on the stockade at Santa Maria, then the long plundering South Sea cruise that followed. He wondered what had happened to Coxon, whom he had last seen after the frustrated attack on Panama. Perhaps the buccaneer captain had given up seafaring and retired with whatever plunder he had amassed. But Hector rather doubted it. Coxon was the sort of person who would always be seeking to make one last lucrative coup.

The cockboat scraped against the rough stones of the jetty and Hector followed Sharpe up the steps. No one greeted them or paid the least attention. Indeed the few people on hand, a couple of fishermen mending nets and a man who might have been a minor government official, deliberately looked the other way.

'That's encouraging,' grunted Sharpe. 'It seems we don't exist. So no questions asked.'

Without even a nod to the onlookers, he began walking up the unpaved road that led past the little houses and over the brow of a low hill. At the point where the road began to descend they had a fine view over a larger, busier anchorage than the one they had just left. Sharpe paused for a moment to check what vessels lay at anchor.

'No sign of a king's ship,' he observed. Spreading across the slope below them was a modest-sized town of stone-built houses. A single, rather ugly church tower rose above their roofs. To Hector's eye the place looked haphazard and chaotic compared to the orderly Spanish towns he had become used to.

'Are we going to meet someone you know?' he asked.

Sharpe shot him a sideways look, full of cunning. 'Depends who is in charge. Antigua's not as prosperous as Jamaica, or even Barbados for that matter. Only a few plantations as yet, though doubtless they will come. The place is happy to make a bit of money with whoever comes to trade, if the price is right.'

He started down the hill and evidently knew his way for he went briskly along the main street and halted before the front door of a two-storey building more substantial than the others. A black servant answered his knock and when Sharpe asked if Lieutenant Governor Vaughan was at home, the black man at first looked puzzled, then beckoned them inside before retreating down a hallway. A few moments later a loud voice called, 'Who's looking for James Vaughan?' and a stout, red-faced man appeared. He was in undress, had removed his wig to reveal a scalp covered with a crop of short, sparse bristles. Draped around him was a loose dressing gown of patterned calico, and he was sweating heavily.

'My name is Captain Bartholomew Sharpe,' the buccaneer captain said. 'I'm looking for Lieutenant Governor Vaughan.'

The red-faced man took out a large handkerchief and wiped his forehead. 'Jim Vaughan is no longer the lieutenant governor,' he said. 'He's retired to his estate. Cane is the thing now.'

'Then perhaps I can speak with the governor, Sir William Stapleton,' Sharpe suggested.

'Sir William is not on the island. He's visiting Nevis in the course of his official duties.'

All this time the man's shrewd eyes had been sizing up his visitor.

'Captain, I did not see your vessel enter harbour. What did you say is the name of your ship?' he asked.

'We arrived only this morning, and are anchored in the next inlet.' It was clear that Sharpe did not wish to give further details. 'I had hoped to engage in a little discreet commerce during the visit.'

The man in the calico gown needed no further prompting. 'If you would step this way into my study, we can discuss matters in private,' he said.

He led them into a side room which had the bare look and slightly musty smell of a little used administrative office. On the shelves were several ledgers and minute books whose spines were mottled with mildew. The furniture was a plain wooden table and a cupboard, several chairs, and two large chests, one of which was securely padlocked and marked with a government crest.

'My name is Valentine Russell,' said their host, closing the door firmly behind them. 'I have replaced James Vaughan as lieutenant governor.' He crossed to the cupboard and took out three glasses and a squat dark green bottle. 'Perhaps I can offer you some refreshment. My rumbullion is prepared with a dash of lime, some tea and red wine. I find that it relieves the heat.'

The two men both accepted a glass of the liquid which Hector discovered left a metallic aftertaste in his throat. Valentine Russell drank off the contents of his glass in a single gulp and then poured himself a second helping from the bottle.

Sharpe came straight to the point. 'I have some merchandise aboard whose sale could be of mutual benefit.'

'What sort of goods?' enquired the lieutenant governor.

'Some silks, a quantity of plate, curiosities, lace . . .'

Russell held up his hand to stop him. 'Can you supply documents to say where the goods originate?'

'No, I'm afraid not.'

The lieutenant governor took another sip of his drink, his small, covetous eyes watching Sharpe over the rim of his glass. Hector thought that the lieutenant governor had a slight resemblance to *Trinity*'s Christmas pig. Then Russell set down his glass with a rueful sigh.

'I'm afraid, Captain Sharpe, things have changed entirely since the time of my predecessor. More rules, more questions. The authorities in London are very keen to encourage trade with our neighbours, especially those in the Spanish possessions. There have been a number of complaints from Madrid. They refer to hostile acts by foreign ships and their commanders. Much of it is nonsense, of course.'

Sharpe said nothing, but stood gently twirling the stem of his glass between finger and thumb, waiting for the lieutenant governor to continue.

'His majesty's representatives throughout the colonies have been instructed to put a stop to these alleged unfriendly deeds,' said Russell.

'Very laudable,' commented Sharpe dryly.

Russell treated him to a conspiratorial smile which, however, contained an undercurrent of warning. 'The commanders of the king's ships, both here in the Windward Caribees and in Jamaica, have lists of those who are suspected of harrying our new Spanish friends. I myself have not seen such a list, but I understand that they are remarkably accurate. The same commanders have instructions to seize any vessels which may have been implicated in lawless activities, arrest their crews, and hand them over for justice. All goods found on board are to be confiscated.'

'And you say that these strictures apply throughout his majesty's possessions?'

'Indeed.'

'Even in Jamaica?'

As Sharpe put the question, Hector wondered if the buccaneer captain was implying that he would dispose of his plunder in Jamaica if Russell was uncooperative. If so, Russell's response must have come as a shock.

'Above all in Jamaica,' said the lieutenant governor firmly. 'Sir Henry applies the law most strictly. Last month he presided at the trial of two most notorious villains found guilty of taking part in the late raid into Darien. One of the accused saved his life by turning state's evidence. The other, a most bloody and obdurate rogue, was found guilty. Sir Henry ordered that he be hanged from the masthead of a ship in harbour. Later his corpse was transferred to the public gibbet in Port Royal. It dangles there still, so I'm told.'

Hector had rarely seen Sharpe taken aback. But the mention that Morgan was executing his former accomplices made the wily buccaneer pause, though only for a moment. He reached into his pocket and pulled out a double-stranded bracelet of pearls, holding it up just long enough for Russell to appreciate the lustre of the pearls.

'Please give my compliments to James Vaughan when you next meet him,' he said. 'I brought with me this little trinket as a gift for Mrs Vaughan, but as I shall not have the opportunity of seeing them on this visit, perhaps you would be kind enough to hand it on with my respect and compliments.'

He passed the necklace over to the lieutenant governor who admired it for a moment before slipping it into the pocket of his dressing gown. Watching the charade, Hector was sure that the necklace would never reach Mrs Vaughan. Russell gave a small bow and said, 'Captain Sharpe, your generosity is to be commended. I feel that I should await further instructions from my superior before deciding whether or not you may do business on this island. Governor Stapleton is not expected to return to Antigua for another ten days. Should you wish to remain at anchor during that interval, you would be most welcome.'

'You are very kind,' replied Sharpe, 'and as there is much to be done aboard my ship, I wish you good day.' As Hector followed his captain out of the room, the young man was still puzzling where Sharpe had obtained the pearl bracelet which he had used as his bribe. Then he remembered the velvet purse of jewels which Donna Juana had handed over after the capture of the *Santo Rosario*. The jewels were general plunder and should have been distributed equally among the crew. But it seemed that Sharpe had helped himself.

*

'THE ADVENTURE is over and finished!' announced Sharpe on *Trinity*'s main deck in the cool of the same evening. His audience was the general council of the crew, and a long silence greeted his declaration. Looking around, Hector counted less than sixty men. They were all that were left of more than three hundred raiders who had marched inland from Golden Island with such jaunty hopes of winning riches. The survivors were gaunt and shabby, their clothes a mass of patches and mends. Their vessel was equally care-worn, ropes knotted and frayed, sails threadbare, woodwork bleached to a dingy grey by months of sun and scouring spray.

'The lieutenant governor has granted us leave to stay at anchor here for ten days, no more. After that we must depart or face the consequences.'

'Where will we go?' demanded an elderly sailor. Hector

remembered him, a cooper by trade. He had made the barrels that had held their water supply for the long voyage around the Cape, a vital role. Now he was at a loss what to do. For him, like many of his shipmates, *Trinity* had become home.

'It must be each man for himself,' announced Sharpe. 'We go our separate ways. The authorities have lists of some of those who went to the South Seas. Any person on those lists is a wanted man.'

'Who made those lists and who is on them?' The question came from Gifford, the quartermaster. His bald scalp had turned the colour of mahogany, and his skin hung loose on his frame. He looked to have aged by at least ten years in the last few months.

Sharpe shrugged. 'I was not told. But some have already danced the Tyburn jig. Henry Morgan strung up one of our comrades recently.'

Gifford turned to address the entire crew. 'Does anyone wish to elect a new captain and continue with the cruise?'

His question was met with a silence. There was resignation in the expressions of the men. They were weary of voyaging. Those who had kept their plunder were eager to spend it.

'Very well,' announced Gifford. 'As quartermaster my duty is to supervise the final distribution of our prize. As soon as that is done, the company is dissolved.'

There followed an extraordinary ransacking of the ship. Men brought up on deck, piece by piece, all the items that *Trinity* had captured during her cruise and had not as yet been turned into cash – bolts of cloth for sail repairs, kegs of dried fruit, a firkin of wine, some painted church statues looted in La Serena, a spare ship's compass robbed from the *Santo Rosario*, even the lump of lead from her bilge which they had thought to melt down for musket balls. Everything was carried to the capstan and stacked in an untidy heap.

Abruptly, Sidias spoke up. Until now, the Greek had been standing to one side. He was not a member of the company and had no vote in the council. Nor was he entitled to a share in plunder though he had amassed considerable winnings from backgammon.

He walked over and stood by the pile of ship's goods. 'My name does not appear on any of the lists. Therefore I propose that I go ashore and find a broker to purchase these items.'

'How do we know you will not cheat us?' The question came from one of the men who had lost heavily to Sidias.

The Greek threw out his hands in a gesture of resignation. 'I will put down a deposit of fifty pounds in coin for this material. If I sell the stock for more, then I get to keep the profit as reward for my troubles. If I cannot find a buyer, then I would accept the loss. Surely that is fair.'

There was some murmuring among the men, and it was clear that Sidias was not entirely trusted. But when Gifford put the matter to the vote, it was agreed that £50 would cover the value and that the ship's launch would ferry Sidias and his goods to the jetty. After that, he was on his own.

The quartermaster moved on to other matters. 'It will be too dangerous to land as a single group. To do so would draw the attention of the authorities. Instead we go ashore in small groups, over the next few days, no more than ten or twelve at a time and disperse.'

'How do we do that?' asked the cooper.

Sharpe intervened. 'Buy passage on local ships and quietly leave. Your silver will open many doors.'

'And what about those who have no silver?' Hector searched the faces of the crowd, to see who had asked the question. The tone had been bitter. He saw it was one of a dozen or so men who were inveterate gamblers. During the return voyage they had wagered away all their plunder, mostly to Sharpe himself.

There was an awkward silence and for a moment Hector thought that there might be violence. He sensed a wave of sympathy wash through the assembled crew. A couple of the malcontents were armed. They could set upon Sharpe and give him a beating.

Sharpe must have spotted the danger for he turned to Gifford. 'Quartermaster, I propose that *Trinity* is given to all those who have no money. They can use the vessel in whatever manner they wish, though I suggest they sail her to a port where she will not be recognised as a Spanish built. Thus they get away from Antigua and may have a chance to earn some capital.'

There was a murmur of approval from the crew, and the moment of tension passed.

'Neatly done,' murmured Jacques beside Hector. 'Our captain is as slippery as ever. He's got rid of *Trinity* and saved his own skin.'

Gifford was already drawing lots to decide the order of disembarkation. Hector and his friends were among the earliest to be set ashore, and they had barely time to collect their share of plunder which amounted to some three thousand pieces of eight each, mostly in coin but also in broken pieces of plate before they were on their way to the jetty.

As they climbed up the steps they found Sidias already there, seated on a roll of sailcloth and looking very satisfied with himself.

'How will you get all this stuff to the town for sale?' asked Hector.

'I won't bother,' the Greek replied. 'It can stay here and rot.'

'But you just paid fifty English pounds for it,' Hector said.

'And I'll pay your giant friend another five shillings if he carries this into town.' With his foot Sidias nudged the heavy ingot brought up from *Santo Rosario*'s bilge.

'Lead's not that valuable,' said Hector.

'It's not lead,' answered the Greek with a crafty grin. 'Those nincompoops wouldn't recognise raw silver if they shat it out of their posteriors. This "lead" as you call it is a half-smelted silver from the Potosi mines. Fifty per cent pure. On its way for further smelting in Panama. I'd say it's worth seventy or eighty English pounds. Enough to set me up here as a shop-keeper.'

Jacques let out a groan, 'Hector, do you remember how many more of those ingots were in the *Santo Rosario*'s bilge? Seven or eight hundred wasn't it? So many that we thought it was nothing more than ballast and paid no attention. We gave away a fortune. The Spaniards in Paita must still be laughing themselves sick at our stupidity.'

EIGHTEEN

✳

THE SUNNY Caribbean had been left far behind. A small group
of port officials, dressed in long cloaks and broad-brimmed hats,
stood waiting patiently on the wharf for the ship to make fast.
A cold penetrating drizzle was drifting down, soaking everything
it touched. The fronts of the warehouses which lined the dockside
were streaked with rainwater dripping from slate roofs. The air
smelled of damp, fish refuse and wet sacking. This was Dart-
mouth in Devon on a blustery March day, and the four friends
were sheltering under the awning rigged to protect the cargo
hatch of the merchant ship that had brought them from Antigua.
It had been a plodding six weeks' voyage across the Atlantic,
and the ship's agent had insisted on being paid in English coin,
grossly overcharging them. But they had been glad to accept his
price, knowing that every mile would put them at a greater
distance from the South Seas raid. Their only concern had been
to discover that a dozen others of *Trinity*'s former crew, including
Basil Ringrose, were among their fellow passengers.

The mooring ropes were made fast, and the little covey of
officials on the dockside moved forward as a gangplank was
manhandled into place.

Without warning Jacques put out an arm, holding back his
companions.

'What's the matter?' asked Hector.

'I'd recognise a police agent anywhere,' the Frenchman said softly.

'We don't have police in England,' Jezreel corrected him. 'That's only for uncivilised foreigners like you.'

'Call him what you want. But the tall fellow with the satchel is something to do with the law. And those other two close behind are the same. I spent too many months on the run in Paris not to recognise legal jackals when I see them.'

The tall man with the satchel was making his way onto the ship. Behind him, his two assistants took up position on either side of the gangplank, blocking it.

The ship's master, a rotund and genial Welshman with a beerswiller's belly, waddled forward from where he had been standing to supervise the process of docking. Hector was near enough to hear him demand of the stranger, 'From the customs office, are you?'

The tall man did not reply directly but opened his satchel and took out some sort of document which he showed to the captain. Hector watched the captain read through the paper, then glance nervously towards the place where Ringrose and the others from *Trinity* were gathered, waiting to disembark.

'Gentlemen!' he called out. 'Would you be kind enough to step this way? There's something which may require your attention.'

Ringrose and the others sauntered over though Hector could tell from their watchful manner that they were on their guard.

'This is Mr Bradley,' said the captain. 'He comes with a warrant from the High Court of Admiralty and has a watch list of persons whom he has been instructed to escort to London.'

The law officer consulted his hand bill. 'Which one of you is Bartholomew Sharpe?'

When there was no reply, he looked around the little group and read out Samuel Gifford's name. Again he received no acknowledgement, and this time he stared straight at Ringrose and said, 'I presume that you are Mr Ringrose. You fit the description I have here.' He consulted the paper again. 'About thirty years of age though may look younger, average height and well set up, curly chestnut hair and fair complexion.'

Ringrose nodded. 'I am Basil Ringrose.'

'You are to accompany me to London.'

'By whose authority?'

'I am a marshal of the court.'

'This is preposterous.' Ringrose's eyes flicked towards the gangway but he could see that there was no escape in that direction.

'He's taking only those who held some sort of rank on our expedition,' Jacques whispered to Hector.

Bradley folded up his paper and replaced it in the satchel. Turning towards Ringrose he announced, 'We leave for London in an hour's time by coach. Bring only essential personal possessions with you.'

'Am I under arrest?' demanded Ringrose.

'Detained for questioning.'

'And what am I to be questioned about?'

'His Excellency the Spanish ambassador has brought several complaints to the attention of the Court and demands redress. The charges include murder on the high seas, robbery and assault on Spanish possessions in contravention of existing treaties of friendship.'

'His Excellency the ambassador,' mimicked Jacques in the marshal's tight voice, but speaking softly, 'wields a broad brush. Where's that bastard going now? I doubt he's just getting himself out of the rain.' Bradley was following the captain towards his cabin.

'Probably off to inspect the ship's manifest,' said Dan, and was proved right when some minutes later, the captain's steward came over to where Hector was still standing with his friends. 'The marshal's asking for you by name,' the steward said, then added in a lower voice, 'He's a right puritan, that one.'

'I'll be there in just a moment,' Hector assured him, and as soon as the steward was out of earshot he turned to his friends. 'Get off the ship as soon as you can, and disappear! Take my sea chest and my prize money. Anything that may connect me with the *Trinity*.'

'You'll need to keep some money by you if they're taking you to prison, to sweeten the gaolers,' Jacques said.

'I've a few coins in my purse. Enough to see me through. I'll contact you when I know what's happening. Where will I find you?'

'In Clerkenwell,' said Jezreel at once. 'I'll take Dan and Jacques there and find lodgings for us. Ask for "Nat Hall" or the "Sussex Gladiator" in Brewer's Yard behind Hockley in the Hole. That's the name they would know me by from the days when I used to perform the stage fights. It's a rough part of town where few questions are asked. Also it's full of foreign mountebanks who perform in the sideshows when there's bull and bear baiting.'

As Hector turned to go, Jacques clapped him on the shoulder and said, 'Keep your wits about you, Hector, and rejoin us soon. Otherwise Jezreel will have me performing conjuring tricks, and Dan put up on display as a painted Indian.'

Ducking in through the low door to the captain's cabin, Hector came face to face with the marshal.

'Your name is Hector Lynch?' Bradley asked. He had taken off his hat, revealing that he wore his straggly grey hair long and tied back in a queue.

There was no point in denying it. That was the name Hector had used when buying his passage, and it was entered on the ship's passenger roster.

'You speak Spanish?'

The question took Hector by surprise. 'My mother was Spanish. Why do you ask?'

'My instructions are to detain one Hector Lynch, but the name appears on a separate warrant and no physical description is given. Only that he speaks good Spanish. It is important that I make the correct identification.' The marshal had the list of wanted men in his hand. 'His Excellency the Spanish ambassador has particularly requested that you be brought to justice promptly.'

Hector was thunderstruck. 'Why have I been singled out in this way?'

'That I am not at liberty to say,' replied the marshal stiffly. He gave a small, brittle cough. 'Please be ready to leave within the hour.'

*

DURING THE LONG, slow and muddy journey to London in the coach provided for their transport, Hector and Ringrose talked much about the marshal's watch list. When Hector told his companion about the interview with the lieutenant governor of Antigua, Ringrose gave a snort of disgust.

'The greedy swine! He didn't have enough men to seize *Trinity* so he took his bribe. Then the moment we were gone, he informed on us. There was plenty of time for his message to get here ahead of us in that tub of a merchantman, and have the marshal waiting on the quayside.'

'Do you think that Sharpe, Gifford and the others have been picked up as well?' Hector asked.

Ringrose looked thoughtful. 'Probably not Sharpe. He's astute. He told me he was going to Nevis before finding a ship bound for England. He must have suspected that vessels arriving direct from Antigua would be watched.'

The coach gave a sudden jolt on its unsprung axle as a wheel dropped into a rut. Both men had to hold on to their wooden seats or be thrown to the floor.

'Lynch, how is it that marshal's list is so accurate? He even had my physical description.'

'Maybe Henry Morgan had a hand in it. A poacher turned gamekeeper never relents.'

'But I've never met Sir Henry so he could not know what I look like.'

Hector watched the drenched countryside drag by and did not answer. He had his own suspicions of the informer's identity, but he was far more perplexed that the Spanish ambassador should be showing such a special interest in him. He could think of no reason why the ambassador was so anxious to arrange his prosecution.

Finally, after six days of sluggish progress, the coach deposited him and Ringrose at the destination that Mr Bradley had arranged – the Marshalsea Prison in Southwark. Despite brick walls topped by revolving iron spikes and a massive entry gate plated with iron, the Marshalsea proved much more comfortable than *Trinity*'s dank and rat-infested accommodation. They were shown to a set of well-appointed rooms and told that their meals would be brought in from the outside.

'Tomorrow morning, Mr Lynch, you are required to attend a preliminary assessment of your case,' Bradley told him in his punctilious manner. 'Customarily the High Court of Admiralty deals with matters of prizes taken by sea. It decides their legitimacy and value and awards portions. But there are new procedures to adjudicate on matters which might normally be dealt within a criminal court ... that is to say, you will be appearing before a Court of Instance not a Court of Prize. Mr Brice, an attorney to the court, has been appointed to determine how your case should be dealt with.'

*

MR BRICE proved to be a man so unassuming and nondescript that for a moment Hector mistook him to be an under-clerk. The attorney was waiting to interview Hector in the prison governor's office next morning. Of middling height and indeterminate age, Brice's pallid features were so bland that Hector would later have difficulty in recalling exactly what Brice looked like. His clothing gave no clue to his status for he was dressed in a suit of plain drab whose only effect was to make him even less obtrusive. Had it not been for the gleam of penetrating intelligence when he caught Hector's eye, Brice would have seemed a very ordinary person of little consequence.

'My apologies for disturbing you, Lynch,' Brice began in an affable tone. Various legal-looking documents and scrolls were spread on the governor's desk and Brice was leafing through them casually. 'I need to ask you a few more questions in relation to a charge arising from information provided by our lieutenant governor in Jamaica. Namely, that you were an originator of an illegal scheme to despoil the territories of a ruler in treaty and friendship with our king.

'What is the evidence for this charge?'

Brice frowned. 'We will come to that. First, would you be kind enough to write a few words on this sheet of paper for me?'

'What should I write?'

'Some of those exotic Caribee names that we hear from time to time – Campeachy, Panama, Boca del Toro, half a dozen will do.'

Hector, bewildered by the request, wrote down the names and handed the sheet back. Brice sprinkled sand on the wet ink, fastidiously poured the excess sand away, then laid the sheet on the desk. Selecting a large scroll from the pile of documents beside him, he undid the ribbon which held it. Hector had presumed the scroll was some sort of legal document but now he recognised it as a map. His mind leapt back to the days in Port Royal. It was one of the sheets that he had copied for the surveyor Snead in Jamaica.

Brice compared Hector's writing with the names written on the map and gave a small cluck of recognition. 'The same hand,' he announced. 'The deposition placed before the Court states you provided maps and charts, knowing they were to be used in the planning and execution of an expedition contrary to the interests of His Majesty.'

'Who accuses me of this?'

Brice glanced down at his notes. 'The witness has signed his statement and sworn to its truth. He sent this map as his evidence. His name is John Coxon, and he styles himself "Captain". Do you know him?'

'I do.'

'There is also a letter from Sir Henry Morgan, the lieutenant governor in Jamaica. Sir Henry affirms that Captain Coxon's testimony is credible.'

Hector felt a twinge of satisfaction mixed with outrage. He had guessed correctly. It was Coxon who had provided Morgan with the names of those who had been on the South Seas raid. Coxon was the turncoat and informer. He was still seeking to curry favour with Morgan just as he had done when he had tried to hand Hector over, believing him to be related to Governor Lynch.

The attorney was speaking again. 'Did you provide maps to assist the planning and execution of this illegal raid?'

'I was destitute and without employment. I had no idea that the charts would be used in that manner.'

'Can anyone vouch for the truth of this or provide you with character?'

Desperately Hector tried to think of someone who might speak up on his behalf. Snead was far away and would never admit to copying. There was no one else who might speak up for him. Then he remembered the carriage ride from Morgan's plantation in company with Susanna and her brother and the friendship that seemed to blossom between them.

'There is someone,' he said, 'Mr Robert Lynch, the nephew of Governor Lynch, would speak up for me. He was in Jamaica when all this took place.'

Brice looked disappointed. His lips set in a thin line. 'Sir Thomas Lynch is unavailable as he left London only recently to return to his duties as governor. Unfortunately Robert Lynch also cannot be here.'

Hector detected the sombre note in the reply. 'Has something happened to Robert Lynch?'

'Six months ago he died of the flux and, it is said, of chagrin. He had lost a great deal of money in indigo plantation.'

'I'm sorry to hear it. He was kind-hearted and generous.'

'Indeed. Have you no one else to substantiate your story?' Brice was looking at him as if genuinely interested in helping him.

Taking a deep breath, Hector said, 'Perhaps Mr Lynch's sister, Susanna, would be able to give evidence on my behalf in place of her brother.'

The attorney raised his eyebrows in shock. 'Mr Lynch, if I were you I would think carefully before approaching that person. Sir Thomas Exton would not take it kindly that his daughter-in-law is called as a character witness in a criminal case.'

Hector tried to make sense of the reply. 'I'm sorry, I don't know what you mean.'

'Sir Thomas Exton is the Advocate General. He is also the senior member of the Admiralty Court. This means that he will be president of the Court if your case comes to trial. Last month his oldest son John – whom I may say has the reputation as an up-and-coming attorney in his own right – married Miss Susanna Lynch. That is why Sir Thomas delayed his departure for Jamaica. To celebrate the wedding.'

Hector's spirits sagged. The news of Susanna's wedding was not unexpected. He had always imagined that she would one day marry someone of her own background. But the knowledge that she was now the wife of a lawyer somehow made the announcement more hurtful.

'I admit that I copied the maps but I was merely using my experience in cartography in the same way that I assisted Mr Ringrose in making drawings and plans of all the anchorages and places we visited in the South Seas.'

For the first time in the interview Hector sensed that he had said something to assist his case. Brice said softly, 'You made maps in the South Seas? Tell me about them.'

'Mr Ringrose always took sketches of the places where we anchored, and he drew profiles of the coast whenever we were near land. I helped him. Occasionally we took soundings with lead and line. Much as the Spaniards do when they prepared their own deroteros and pilot books.'

'You have seen a pilot book for the Peruvian coast?' Belatedly Hector realised that Brice knew exactly what a derotero was.

'There was one aboard a vessel we captured – the *Santo Rosario*.'

'What happened to it?'

'It was returned to the Spaniards.'

A flicker of disappointment crossed the attorney's face.

'But we made notes and sketches before it was handed back,' Hector hastened to add.

'We?'

'My colleague Dan and I.'

Brice looked at Hector with narrowed eyes.

'If you still have this material, I would like to see a sample.'

'If you allow me to contact my friend, that can be arranged.'

Brice began rolling up the Caribbean chart. 'We will continue our discussion just as soon as you can produce some of those notes. Do you think you could have them available next week, perhaps on Thursday?'

'I'm sure that can be arranged.'

'I'll ask Mr Bradley to bring you to somewhere more congenial than these rather depressing surroundings.' He glanced around the prison governor's austere office as he wound the ribbon neatly around the rolled-up chart, pausing only to say in a quiet, confidential voice, 'Mr Lynch, I would be grateful if you talked to no one about my visit here today.'

'As you wish,' Hector assured him, though he was wondering why a lawyer like Brice knew such a complicated way to tie the ribbon. Either Brice was a fly-fisherman or he had sea-going experience.

*

BY THURSDAY, when Bradley came to collect him, Hector had assembled the material Brice had requested. Dan had brought the bamboo tube containing the notes and sketches, and Ringrose had lent his journals from the South Sea. After Hector introduced Dan to the marshal, the three of them set off on foot into Southwark's tangle of alleyways. An overcast grey sky threatened yet another day of blustery showers as they joined the slow-moving mass of pedestrians, carts and carriages using London Bridge to cross the river. On the far side they turned right into a street lined with tall commercial buildings. After about a quarter mile they came to a shop front over which hung a trade sign showing an outline map of Britain and Ireland. Here Bradley led them down a narrow passageway and then up a flight of outside stairs to a large first-floor room at the rear of the building. Several windows looked out across London Pool and its constant activity of wherries and lighters attending to the needs of the anchored shipping. Beside a broad table littered with drawing instruments, Brice was waiting. With him was a stooped, rather bookish individual wearing a pair of spectacles.

The lawyer came quickly to the point. 'Mr Lynch, please show to Mr Hack your material from the South Sea.'

From his bamboo tube Hector slid the page copied from Captain Lopez's notes which he and Dan had consulted as they tried to decide where *Trinity* had so nearly been wrecked. The paper was creased and stained, and there were scuff marks where they had laid it out on the rock many months ago. Hack walked over to the window to examine their handiwork in the light. Beyond him the surface of the Thames suddenly flecked with white as a gust of wind riffled the water. A moment later came the sound of raindrops spattering against the window glass.

'What do you make of it, Mr Hack?' Brice was asking.

There was a long pause. 'Very interesting. The entrance to the Fretum Magellanicum agrees with Mr Jansson's depiction in his atlas, but here it is in greater detail.'

'Would such information help a navigator attempting the Strait?'

'Most certainly.'

'This provides extra detail,' said Hector holding out Ringrose's journal.

Hack took it from him and began to turn the pages slowly and deliberately until he came to Ringrose's sketch of the anchorage where they had mended *Trinity*'s rudder. Several moments passed before he looked up and said, 'If I had time to correlate the details in this journal with the page of navigation notes, I would be hopeful of providing a chart for this section of the coast.'

Earlier Hector had thought that Hack might be a sea captain. Now he knew that Hack was a professional cartographer.

Brice glanced at the bamboo tube Hector was holding. 'Mr Lynch, you say that you have other pages of navigation notes. Who made them?'

'The captain of the *Santo Rosario*. He was a very experienced mariner, and conscientious. Besides making his own observations, he compiled information from other captains, going back many years. There are details of anchorages and navigation dangers and port facilities.'

Brice picked up a pair of compasses from the mapmaker's table and began fiddling with them, opening and closing them as he considered Hector's statement. 'Mr Lynch, the Spanish ambassador, Señor Ronquillo, is pressing to have your case decided by the Court. He has personally intervened with His

Majesty who has agreed to his demand. I have an offer to make to you.'

'What do you have in mind?' Hector asked.

'If you agree to work with Mr Hack, correlating your notes with the general maps of the South Sea coast, I am willing to represent you in any action brought against you by the ambassador. I will ensure that you receive a fair hearing.'

Hector looked Brice in the eye. He was reassured by that same gleam of penetrating intelligence that he had noted on their first encounter. He decided that he had nothing to lose by trusting the attorney.

'If I'm to work on the maps, I'll need Dan to help me.'

'Of course. That will be easy. There is no mention of him or your other companions on the watch list we received from the Caribbees.'

Brice spoke to the mapmaker. 'Mr Hack, I suggest that Mr Lynch and his colleague Dan spend some time with your staff. Not here at your official premises, but somewhere in the close vicinity.'

Brice gazed out of the window, thinking aloud. 'Of course the Spaniards are aware that we must have acquired some knowledge of the Peruvian coast. But as yet they don't know how much.'

'We also found a folder of more general charts aboard the *Santo Rosario*. They cover the coast all the way from California to the Cape and the Land of Fire,' Hector said.

'And where is this folder now?'

'It was given to Captain Sharpe.'

'Then we will find Captain Sharpe and get it. Our sources tell us that Captain Sharpe has reached London and is staying in lodgings in Stepney,' said Brice. He seemed remarkably well informed. The lawyer looked across at the marshal who had been standing patiently near the door. 'Mr Bradley, do you have with you the watch list?'

Bradley handed him the document, and Brice took a pen and struck out a name.

'It would seem sensible that I remove Mr Ringrose's name from the list of Gaol Delivery.'

'Why's that?' Hector dared to ask.

'Because Mr Ringrose will be your unwitting ally. With his help I'm sure that Mr Hack here can produce a South Sea atlas which will satisfy and distract the king. The basis of that atlas will be the folder of maps now in the possession of Captain Sharpe. The new atlas will be a work of art. It will be beautiful but of little practical use to navigators, and serve the dual purpose of reassuring the Spanish ambassador that we have learned little of real value. Meanwhile the more detailed version – your prime derotero as we may call it – will be lodged with the Admiralty against the time when it might come in useful.'

Brice's expression became very serious. 'Lynch, the Spanish ambassador remains most insistent that you are put on trial for piracy. I gather his people have been working hard to prepare evidence to place before the Court.'

Hector was taken aback. 'But I thought the Court of Admiralty was to oversee the gathering of evidence?'

Brice allowed himself a weary grimace. 'The ambassador has friends in high places, and permission has been granted for his legal counsellor to question you and prepare witness statements.'

'When is this to happen?'

'In three days' time marshal Bradley must bring you to the ambassador's residence where you will be interviewed. I have arranged that I will be present at the meeting and, as promised, I will do my best for you. But please bear in mind that officially we have never met, and that the outcome of the questioning will decide your future.'

*

WILD HOUSE, the Spanish ambassador's mansion near Lincoln's Inn Fields, was a building designed to impress the visitor. Hector was intimidated by the imposing facade, its array of glittering windows separated by tall ornamental pilasters, and set off with a balustraded parapet which ran the full width of the building. Wild House was screened from public view by a tall brick wall and Hector had the sense of entering a secluded, private world as marshal Bradley escorted him across the broad gravel forecourt. A major domo opened the ornate double front doors and escorted the two visitors across a tiled entrance hall under a cupola decorated with scenes from classical mythology. Beyond it a long corridor, hung with tapestries, led to the rear of the house. There, without a word, the major domo indicated that Bradley was to wait in the corridor while he ushered Hector into what was evidently a private library. Most of the wall space was taken up with shelves of books, and the only light came in through a leaded window looking out on a small garden. A log fire was burning in a large grate to keep out the chill.

Involuntarily, Hector was reminded of his examination by the Alcalde of Paita. The furniture had been arranged in much the same manner. At a table, seated with his back to the window, was Brice, now wearing a lawyer's sombre black suit with a white tab collar. He glanced briefly at Hector, as if he had never seen him before, and then looked down and began to arrange the papers on the table before him with the same neat gestures that Hector recognised from the fiscal in Paita. It set him wondering if all lawyers were alike, with identical mannerisms and the same circumspect outward show. Next to Brice a secretary was ready to take notes, and at a separate desk a few paces away sat a man dressed with great elegance in a sleeveless jacket embroidered with silver thread over a white satin shirt. A glimpse of his feet beneath the table revealed that he was wearing fine chamois leather shoes. Hector supposed that he was an embassy counsellor who was to conduct the cross-examination.

'The purpose of this meeting is to establish whether you should face a charge of murder and piracy,' began Brice. 'Señor Adrian,' the counsellor gave a slight inclination of his head, 'is to present the evidence. The proceedings will be conducted in English as far as practicable.'

Hector was not invited to sit so he remained standing, feeling the thick carpet beneath his feet. Brice turned towards the Spaniard. 'Perhaps we may begin?'

The counsellor picked up a paper from his desk, cleared his throat and in strongly accented English began to read aloud. After a few sentences it was clear that he intended to deliver a lengthy preamble to the case. Brice held up his hand to stop him.

'Señor Adrian, from what I have already seen of the documents, the crux of what we have to decide today concerns the capture of the ship named *Santo Rosario* off the coast of Peru. Perhaps we can proceed directly to that event.'

With an exasperated look the counsellor searched through his pile of documents until he found the one he wanted, then once again he began to read aloud. He described the events of that day: the slow approach of *Trinity*, the moment when Captain Lopez had grown suspicious, the firing of the first cannon shot, the musketry that followed. As he listened, Hector slowly became aware that he had heard the contents before. It was, word for word, the same deposition that Hector had heard at Paita, read out to Maria. Grudgingly he had to admire the thoroughness of Spanish bureaucracy. Somehow the colonial officials in Peru had managed to supply the document from half a world away.

Señor Adrian came to the end of his recitation, and Brice turned his attention to Hector.

'Were you present during these events?'

Hector felt trapped. Faced with such a precise and accurate

account of what had happened, he could see no way of saving himself except to tell an outright lie and pit his word against Maria's testimony. Yet he knew that to contradict her sworn statement was a betrayal of what he felt about her, her honesty and her courage. He hesitated before answering, and when the words finally came out, there was a catch in his voice as he uttered the falsehood.

'I know nothing of the events you describe. I was aboard *Trinity* early in her voyage and only for a few weeks.'

The Spanish counsellor looked at him with open disbelief. 'All the accounts we have from Peru speak of a young man, of your age and description, who acted as interpreter and nego-tiator. You – alone of all the pirates – were seen face to face by our officials.'

'You'll have to prove that,' intervened Brice.

'I will, beyond all doubt,' snapped the counsellor. Turning to the secretary he said, 'Summon our first witness.'

The secretary rose from his chair and, crossing the library, left by a far door. He returned a few moments later. Behind him walked Coxon.

Hector suppressed a gasp of surprise. The last time he had seen Coxon had been at Panama on the evening before the buccaneer captain departed to return to the Caribbean. Then Coxon had been carrying plunder looted from the Spanish. Now he was serving them. Hector wondered how the buccaneer had managed to convince the Spaniards of his new allegiance, and at the same time maintain his links as an informant for Morgan. Whatever Coxon had arranged, he was clearly pros-pering. He was expensively dressed in a dark blue coat worn over a fashionably long waistcoat whose sleeves had been turned back to show his ruffled lace shirt-cuffs. Coxon had also put on weight. He was chubbier than before, there was even more grey in his reddish hair, and he was beginning to go bald. Hector enjoyed an instant of satisfaction from observ-ing that Coxon had powdered his face and neck thickly in an unsuccessful attempt to hide the blotches and sores on his skin. Hector hoped that the damage to Coxon's complexion was permanent and owed something to the Kuna salve. Coxon gave him a malicious glance, full of quiet triumph, before turning to face the Spanish counsellor.

'Your name is Captain John Coxon?'

'Yes.'

'And you took part in the assault on His Catholic Majesty's possessions in the Americas two years ago?'

'Only briefly. I had been led to believe that we were campaigning against the heathen savages of the area, and they had been troubling the civilised settlers. As soon as I realised the truth, I withdrew my men.'

Hector was stunned. Involuntarily he thought of the phrase his shipmates used to describe a turncoat. He 'turned cat in the pan'. Hector stole a glance towards Brice. The lawyer's face was expressionless. Hector had a worrying feeling that Coxon's presence had also taken Brice by surprise.

'Do you recognise this person standing here?' asked the embassy counsellor.

Coxon's face was hard-set. He looked Hector up and down as if identifying an item of lost property. Hector was reminded of the pitiless reptilian look he had seen when Coxon seized the *L'Arc-de-Ciel*.

'He was one of the worst on the expedition. A number of your countrymen lost their lives when he promised them safe conduct, knowing that the savages were waiting in ambush to murder them.'

'Where did this happen?'

'At Santa Maria, in the Darien.'

Brice interrupted. 'Señor Adrian, this line of questioning is irrelevant. The charge we are here to substantiate is one of piracy on the high seas. The event your witness has described took place on land and within the overseas territory of Spain, and is therefore outside the jurisdiction of the Court of Admiralty. It will not be admissible.'

The Spaniard looked exasperated. He made a gesture of impatience. 'Captain Coxon, please wait outside. I will need you to give evidence in support of my next witness.'

As Coxon left the room, the smug expression on his face left no doubt that the buccaneer would take pleasure in doing Hector as much harm as possible.

'Please call the second witness,' said the counsellor. He was looking towards the door with an air of triumphant expectation.

Maria walked in.

Hector felt as if all the air had suddenly been emptied from his lungs. Maria was dressed in a plain russet gown with a lace collar, and her head was uncovered. She wore no jewellery and she looked the same as he remembered her, perhaps a little more mature, but just as composed. Hector was reminded of the moment when he had seen her standing in the little fishing boat early on the morning they had landed at Paita. Then, as now, she had seemed so self-contained, so sure of herself, and just as beautiful.

'You are Maria da Silva, and you are companion to Dona Juana, the wife of the Alcalde of Paita?' asked the counsellor.

'That is correct.' Maria's response was strong and clear.

'And you were aboard the *Santo Rosario* when the vessel was attacked by pirates, and witnessed the murder of her captain, Juan Lopez?'

'I did not witness his death but I saw his body later.'

'And you spent the next three weeks aboard the *Santo Rosario*, in company with your mistress, while the vessel was in the hands of the pirates.'

'That too is correct.'

Hector could not take his eyes off Maria. The initial shock of seeing her had given way to an urge to attract her attention, to re-establish contact with her and somehow not let it slip away. But she did not look towards him. Her gaze seemed to be fixed on the papers lying on the counsellor's polished desk.

Her questioner ground on. 'During that time or at any other time, did this man offer you violence or rob your possessions?'

Only then did Maria turn her head and look directly at Hector and their eyes met. He could read nothing in her expression, however hard he tried. To his dismay he saw a disinterest, a blankness as if he was a stranger.

'He did not.'

'As far as you know was he responsible for the death of Captain Lopez?'

'As I said, I did not see Captain Lopez die. I have no knowledge of the matter.'

The counsellor was becoming irritated. Hector detected that he wanted to clinch the matter.

'Maria da Silva, was this man a member of the crew of pirates?'

Maria looked again towards Hector. There was a pause of a few heartbeats and then she said quietly, 'He may have been aboard the other ship, but he never set foot on the *Santo Rosario*.'

Hector thought that he had misheard.

The counsellor was looking utterly taken aback. 'Do you say that he was *not* aboard the *Santo Rosario*?'

'Yes.'

The counsellor picked up the written deposition, and held the paper out for Maria to inspect.

'Do you recognise your signature at the bottom of this document?'

'Of course. That is my signature.'

'And was this statement not prepared in the presence of this young man and the Alcalde of Paita?'

'It was prepared in the office of the Alcalde. But I have never set eyes on the young man before.'

The counsellor took a sharp breath, expressing utter disbelief. 'Maria da Silva, this is a serious matter. You have been brought from Peru to serve as a witness to the piracy of the *Santo Rosario* and the murder of Captain Lopez. Yet you claim not to know one of the gang of brigands who was involved.'

'I repeat, I do not know this man. There has been some mistake.'

Angrily, the counsellor tossed the sheet on the table before him. Maria looked down at the floor and clasped her hands in front of her in a gesture that Hector recognised. It was a sign that Maria was stubborn and unshakeable.

Brice intervened smoothly. 'Señor Adrian, perhaps you have other witnesses?'

The Spanish counsellor was finding it difficult to conceal his exasperation. 'Not now,' he snapped.

'Then we should ask the young lady to withdraw.'

Hector watched Maria leave the room, his mind racing. He wanted desperately to believe that Maria had denied knowing him in order to protect him, but her repudiation of him had been absolute. It appeared that she had no difficulty at all in wiping out any recollection of him. Her rejection had been definitive and credible, and he felt as though a vast, icy space had opened between them. He no longer understood her.

'That will be all, Mr Lynch,' 'Brice was saying. 'You may leave this inquiry.'

Bradley was waiting outside, seated on a bench in the passageway. He got up with a look of concern on his face as Hector emerged from the library, and took him by the arm. 'Are you all right?' he asked anxiously. 'You seem pale. Mr Brice wanted to meet us after the interview, to discuss its outcome. His chambers are not far, in Lincoln's Inn. We should make our way there slowly and wait for him to conclude his business here.'

They had to wait for almost an hour. Brice's offices were what Hector had come to expect of him – two small rooms discreetly tucked away down a side street. Brice's clerk, a taciturn figure with the bony frame and frequent cough of a consumptive, brought them a small tray with two glasses and a bottle of canary wine and then left them alone. By the time Hector had drunk his second glass, he was beginning to feel less numb from the shock of his encounter with Maria. Gathering himself, he forced the recent image of her to the back of his mind, and tried to concentrate on his immediate difficulties: the likelihood of being tried at the Admiralty Court presided over by Susanna's potentially hostile father-in-law and Coxon's perjured claim that he had been involved in the planning for the South Sea Adventure. The future seemed very bleak.

To his surprise Brice, when he arrived, was looking as pleased with himself as his habitual reticence would allow.

'The Spanish ambassador is dropping his complaint against you, Hector,' he said. 'I discussed the matter with his counsellor, Señor Adrian, and we agreed that in the absence of his star witness, that attractive young lady, there is little prospect of his case succeeding.'

Hector took a moment to digest the unexpected news. 'The counsellor seems to have given up very easily.'

'It all goes back to those missing navigation notes. I managed to plant the idea in Señor Adrian's mind that if anyone had possession of them, it would be your captain, Bartholomew Sharpe. Doubtless the Embassy will now concentrate their enquiries in his direction.'

'What about Captain Coxon's accusation that I provided maps and charts for an illegal venture? Will I still have to answer for that?'

Brice allowed himself the glimmer of a smile. 'I am recommending to the Court that Captain Coxon's charge is dropped for lack of evidence. Should he continue to make such allegations, based on the map he sent us, I shall enquire how he acquired it in the first place. I will use the same threat if I hear he is again offering his services to Señor Ronquillo.'

He reached into his pocket and drew out a letter. 'This was

handed to me as I was leaving Wild House after my discussions with Counsellor Adrian.' From his guarded look, Hector guessed Brice had read the contents. He took the page and, unfolding it, read:

Dearest Hector,

Denying you was the hardest thing that I ever had to do in my life. Not until I entered the room did I realise why I had been brought to London and what the consequences might be. I hope you will understand my response. By the time this note reaches you, I expect I will be on my way back to Peru. There I rejoin Dona Juana whose husband has been promoted to the audiencia. I cherish every hour that we spent together. You will always be in my thoughts.

Maria.

Brice had been watching his reaction. 'I would suggest that as soon as your work with Mr Hack is done, it would be prudent if you quietly disappeared. This would avoid any difficult questions which might arise later. If you were thinking of a sea career, a position as a ship's navigator could be arranged for you. Clearly your talents lie in that direction.'

*

HECTOR'S MIND was in a whirl. His circumstances seemed to be changing by the minute. New opportunities were opening up. Yet all he could think of was Maria and what she had been feeling as she stood opposite him in the interview. Above all, that he had mattered to her ever since the days in the South Sea. Belatedly he became aware of Brice waiting for a response.

'What about my friends? Two of them, Jezreel and Jacques, are already lying low. They were with me in the South Sea. They too might be picked up and questioned. And I'll have to ask Dan what his plans are after we've completed our work on the South Sea charts.'

'Berths could also be found for all your friends, if they care to join you,' Brice assured him.

Hector's thoughts were racing ahead. 'If I am to go to sea again, it is on one condition.'

'What is that?'

'That I have a choice of the ship on which we sail.'

Already he was thinking that he would try to persuade his three friends to join a vessel on a westward voyage. That was the direction in which – if he persevered and fortune was with him – he might eventually find his way to Maria again.

HISTORICAL NOTE

On Saturday 10 June 1682 Captain Bartholomew Sharpe and two of *Trinity*'s crew appeared on a charge of piracy and murder before the High Court of Admiralty in Southwark. The advocate general, Sir Thomas Exton, presided. The jury found all three men not guilty, though gave no reason for their decision. The Spanish ambassador to London, who had pressed for their trial, was outraged. Four months later William Hack produced a lavishly illustrated book of Pacific charts, with a dedication to King Charles II from Bartholomew Sharpe. This atlas was of limited practical use to mariners, but other, much more detailed versions of this South Sea atlas entered private circulation.

Basil Ringrose, who had played a major role in navigating the *Trinity*, was never brought before the court. His journal, illustrated with coastal views and harbour plans along the South American coast, was published three years later, also with Hack's cooperation.

Captain John Coxon continued to operate in the Caribbean and turned 'cat in the pan' several more times. Governor Lynch even hired him to hunt down pirates, but Coxon could not resist reverting to his former trade as a buccaneer. He attacked Spanish settlements and looted foreign ships. Several warrants were issued for his arrest. He was never captured.